HUMAN EXPERIENCE

Heather A. Wilson

The Human Experience
Copyright © 2024 by Heather A. Wilson

All rights reserved. No part of this publication may be reproduced, distributed, or transmitted in any form or by any means, including photocopying, recording, or other electronic or mechanical methods, without the prior written permission of the author, except in the case of brief quotations embodied in critical reviews and certain other non-commercial uses permitted by copyright law.

Tellwell Talent
www.tellwell.ca

ISBN
978-1-77941-892-0 (Paperback)
978-1-77941-893-7 (eBook)

For Andrew and Katharine
My Lighthouse and My Sturdy Boat
Your support keeps me sailing in the right direction

I am

    The Far and Distant Light

        Breaking through

            The darkest night.

                To find purchase

                    Upon this earth,

                        To feel renewed,

                            My own rebirth.

                        I am

                          The Far and Distant Light

                    Traveling through

                The Brightest Bright,

        To learn,

      To grow,

     To strive for more,

The Human Experience at its core.

Book One

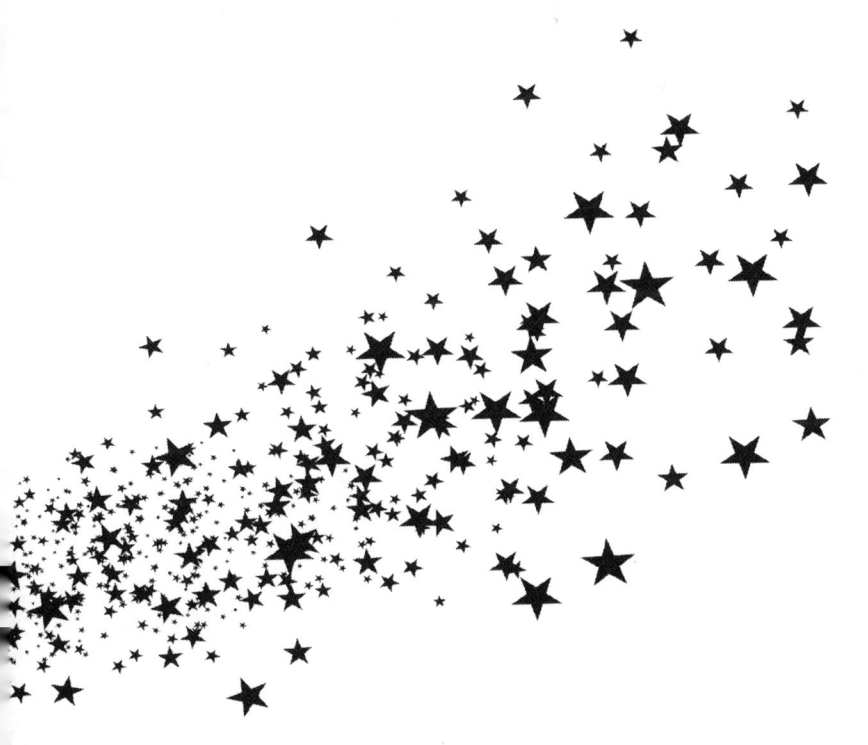

ONE

I open my eyes, but I cannot see anything, except the muted darkness all around me. A consistent thumping somewhere close by seems oddly familiar, yet its source is unknown to me. I attempt to move, but find I have limited mobility, due to the enclosure I seem to find myself in. A sound, muffled and distant, makes me turn my head slightly. I still can't see anything. The muffled sounds grow in intensity. I turn my head again in an attempt to free myself, but find it wedged against something. I attempt to move my arms and legs, when something pushes me sideways. Then another force pushes me back. This pushing repeats again. I begin to feel sore from being pushed and try to let out a cry, but find my mouth does not respond. I sense an invisible force impelling me forward, and then a terrific wrenching on my head makes me feel like it is being pulled right off my body. The pressure mounts as I begin to move, in what feels like a forward motion. Confusion and terror grip me, feeling no control over what is happening to me. The top of my head breaches a barrier, I feel cold air, and within seconds I feel the air on my face. I still can't open my eyes, but I can hear an awful sound I have never heard before. It makes me feel both sad and terrified at the same time. Then my body frees itself completely from its confines, only to feel cold and isolated anew. Although my eyes fail me, I can vaguely discern a brightness surrounding me. I feel myself being gently handled, and wrapped in something warm. Sounds are hard on my ears, and again I feel the need to cry out. This time, my mouth opens, and a wail emerges that reaches far and above the world. It is a wail of terror, but also a cry for recognition. 'I am here! See me, help me!' I am lifted up, still warmly wrapped, and placed onto something warm and oddly familiar. I recognize the smell, and when the sound comes to my ears, I recognize the voice. I blink, and very slowly, a blurry face comes into view. 'I know you, Mother.'

I am born. This in itself would not be considered very remarkable, other than for the new parents and other family members. But this is remarkable, because I remember who I *was* before I came into this form, and *where* I came from, before I entered it.

As a being from the Alternate, we are Light, and reside above the needs of human flesh. Our existence layers that of humans, but is far beyond them in many ways. It is from this perspective we curiously watch and learn. We wonder what it is like to have all of these experiences, and feel all these complex emotions. Some of us have had the experience of human life, some have not; it is by choice, not by fate or decree from some unseen power. Some of us make that choice to transcend into the human realm to have a human life. I am one of those who has made this decision.

Part of the transcendence is to detach yourself from the memory of your "Alternate". It is stored in the collective Light, until the death of the physical form, and then your memories are retrieved. This ensures our ability to have the utmost human life episode. There's just one thing: I still know who I am. I can still remember my Alternate self. Something went wrong. Or maybe it didn't. There is no point in guessing. I am here now, so I will just have to see what happens next.

I open my eyes and indistinctly see a human face smiling at me. I feel warm wrapped in a blanket. I feel. I feel my human flesh. I wiggle a finger, blink my eyes, and open my mouth. I am moving my tiny body and having my first experience as a human. It is uncomfortable, to say the least. I am lifted away from the arms of the human I recognize as my mother, to a set of slightly larger arms, that belong to the person I assume is my father. His large face comes close to mine, and I experience my first kiss. Lightly on my forehead, it feels like a transfer of his love to me. I am overcome with the need to cry. I open my mouth and issue forth an awful wail. I am quickly transferred back to my mother's outstretched arms. I smell her scent, and instinctively know she is my mother. The wailing ceases.

The first two days of my new life have been spent in the hospital room, close by my mother's bed. When I cry, she carefully lifts me to her breast and I take my nourishment, if I want it. Other times she undresses me and changes my diaper. Sometimes she merely holds me close, and gently hums under her breath. It is all good. This is working out very well, so far. From having watched these interactions before, I am fully aware of what is expected of me, as an infant baby. I have observed the way parents interact with their children. I fully expect my experience will be easy to go through, but I could be wrong. It may be complicated, messy and frustrating. I'm already aware of my inability to communicate effectively, other than screaming at the humans: *'No, I don't want to be changed, I want to eat!'*. I don't understand why they can't comprehend what my cries mean. Having an Alternate consciousness in an infant body may not have been a good idea after all.

Eight months have passed by and, finally, I have the humans trained with regards to the implication of each cry and call. My mother is undoubtedly the quicker study, but my father does his best to keep up. I myself have attempted to master several seemingly easy tasks, like holding my head up, and sleeping through the night. I am in training as well.

The dog fascinates me, and vice versa. He is happy to have a human understand him, so he stays by me constantly, especially when my mother lays me on a blanket on the floor. She watches as Fred curls up beside me, or lies on the floor beside my crib as I sleep. When we lie on the floor together, we often have a good talk, before he gets bored, or spies a passerby at the window who needs to be barked at, and leaves me to my own devices. It has never occurred to me to question how I am able communicate with him. It just seems natural, and part of who I am.

My mother has her hands full with a daughter who, from the start, seems to have a definite will of her own. It began when she started introducing solid food into my diet. Little jars with cute infant faces on the labels, indicating this food is meant solely for me. We started with fruit and vegetables being offered on a small spoon. Today she is chirping away in that motherly voice she sometimes uses. "Here we are my little sweetie pie, a new jar today! We are going to start you on some chicken!" Even though I am *technically* about eight months old, I know exactly what a chicken is. It is a living, breathing entity that I will not, under any circumstances, consume. In my mind, chickens, pigs and cows are on the same level as any other living species on this planet. They have a sentient understanding of joy, love, pain, anger and fear. They may not have the same thought processes as humans, but that does not make their existence any less important. Humans have a tendency to believe that, because animals don't *verbally* communicate the same way humans do, they must be stupid, and have no value, other than as a commodity. I am not going to eat any animal as long as I live.

I clamp my little mouth shut as she offers a spoonful. I actually feel like I'm going to be sick as I catch a whiff of the overly processed chicken swill. Next thing you know, I spit up all over my bib. After she removes the dirty bib, she replaces it with a clean one that has some happy bear face on it with the words, *I love you beary much*, in bright red letters under the grinning face. I hold my ground and do not let any animal stew touch my lips. I turn my head from side to side, to avoid the flying helicopter motion of the spoon. After about five minutes my mother sighs, replacing the lid on the jar. "Well maybe if I put some of this chicken in with your sweet potatoes, you'll never know the difference. Or maybe you'd like to see if the jar of beef is more to your liking?" I let out a wail and try to squirm out of my highchair. Her eyebrows shoot up in surprise. I don't think she expected me to respond to her comment in such a specific way, as if I *really* understood what she just said. At this point I don't care one way or the other what she is thinking. All I know is, I will not eat *any* more jars of baby food, period.

The following day I watch as she opens a jar. When she sees me watching, she decides against sneaking any meat into the vegetables. I reluctantly eat the proffered sweet potatoes and apples, but the minute the chicken comes out of the refrigerator, I set in wailing. She finally gives up the fight.

After talking it over with the family doctor she decides to ditch the jars altogether, in favour of homemade vegetables and fruits puréed. The doctor said, almost as a joke, that he thinks she has a little vegetarian on her hands. She looked horrified, but he assured her that there are plenty of things that a vegetarian can eat and still get all the nutrition necessary to be healthy. He gave her some pamphlets and other information to check out on the internet. She hesitantly agreed to try some new recipes to make sure I am getting all I need to grow properly. I think she is sorely disappointed in me, as if I failed a course in Baby 101: eating what your mother gives you and loving it, just like the commercial on television! Then again, I'm not that typical television baby, so she will need to go with the flow.

As spring and then summer arrives, I am delighted to be able to experience the outdoors without being bundled up to my eyeballs in a mummifying snowsuit. Fred barks his joy at being in the yard with his favourite person, other than my father, who is his *absolute* favourite, because he rescued Fred. My mother places me down on the lawn with a few toys scattered around me, while she sits on a garden chair beside me. The new green grass is lush and cool on my bare feet. My tiny hand reaches out to grab fistfuls of grass, and I am surprised to find the roots so fragile, as small clumps pull up in my fingers. I immediately feel horrible for having killed these tiny little green blades of life, and start bawling. My mother mistakes my cry for discomfort and begins to lift me up, but I manage to indicate I want to remain on the grass. She places me back on the ground, where, once again, I take my hand and gently brush the grass with just my fingertips. It tickles, and the grass hums with joy at my touch. I hum back to the tiny lifeforms, feeling connected to the earth through their delicate roots. My mind drifts down to the soil, and I can feel the cool earth, and the myriad of tiny bugs making their life under the roots. I notice each rock and pebble, placed there by Nature to do their job; either in harmony with the other stones, in wearing down the world, so it can rebuild itself, or to shore up the world to keep it firmly where it should be. Rocks are amazing at their job. I stop humming as my tribute to the earth is complete. I look around, and catch sight of my mother, watching me with a curious expression. I doubt she has ever heard anyone hum a song to a lawn before. I turn my attention to the giant Maple tree in the corner of the yard, a silent sentry. Various shrubs and bushes exhibit stages of growth, with tiny buds opening on their stems. Birds in the trees sing various songs of warm weather travels, looking for mates, or finding some bird seed at a nearby feeder. One squirrel, high up in the branches, squawks at us, relaying a message of annoyance about Fred sniffing around his tree.

    The fact that I actually *hear* everything, that all the creatures and plants are communicating, is not lost on me. I feel elation at this discovery, and wonder if it is a bonus of being an Alternate. I know that Fred and I communicate, but I never considered the possibility that it extended to *all* forms of life. I turn my eyes to the squirrel and mentally express, *you are safe little one, Fred will not harm you, will you Fred?* The Beagle wears an expression of disappointment, but agrees to keep the peace. He wags his tail slowly and pretends to sniff at a dead leaf on the ground, all the while, keeping one eye on the squirrel. The squirrel stops chattering and stomps his foot once. Slowly he begins to descend the tree. When he reaches the ground, he glances over at Fred on the far side of the yard, gives one last chirp, and then ignores us as he scrounges for food. I tell Fred what a wonderful dog he is, and the next thing I know, he comes bounding across the yard to give me a lick. I laugh as it tickles my cheek.

My mother watches, with no comprehension of the exchange going on between all the living beings in the yard and me. She is just happy to be outside on a lovely day. I share that happiness. From that point on I want my feet bare every time I am outside, and most times I win the battle, especially when I learned to pull my shoes and socks off by myself. After a while, my parents accept the fact that I am going to have unendingly dirty feet.

My paternal grandmother, whom I happen to be named after, has been a fixture in my life from the start. I connected with her spirit the minute we met. I was only one day old. There is a huge difference in the relationship of a mother and daughter, versus grandmother and granddaughter. Picking up on this immediate connection, I think my poor mother feels a bit outnumbered. Hannah One, as I have come to call her, simply *gets* where I am coming from. She understands my *weird little ways*, even as a toddler, before any words are shared between us. She makes a point of never telling my mother what I need, or what I might be trying to communicate, which is very wise on her part. A new mother, even an experienced mother, doesn't appreciate their mother-in-law advising them on what *they* think is best for their child. It never works out well for anyone.

Hannah One comes over to see me every chance she can. At times I can see the irritation in my mother's eyes, but at other times there is immense relief. Hannah One simply comes to visit because she is drawn to me, naturally, as any grandparent would be. But she also feels the connection. I can sense it.

As I get a little more mobile, she begins to take me to the woods for walks amongst the trees, to hear the birds sing, to feel the breeze fresh and unpolluted by human activity. It is a magical time for both of us. Small Sparrows and Chickadees flit by us, and little forest animals sit and curiously watch us as we pass by. My thoughts reach out and stroke the wildlife, plants and trees, with messages of love. These walks help me stay sane as I wait for my little body to catch up to my adult-sized mind.

My first birthday arrives with all the fanfare that *firsts* usually have. There is the birthday cake with a *number one* candle, lit and melting down one side. My father blows the candle out, but pretends I did it. A few of my parents' friends in attendance of the event, kiss and hug me, although I find the contact a little too familiar for people I don't know. I am quite happy to hear the word "nap" being mentioned, and stretch my arms up to my mother. She carries me off to my room, but not before grabbing my arm and making me *wave goodbye* to all assembled in the living room. A chorus of "aww" is still sounding in my ears when we ascend the stairs. I happily lie down in my crib and close my eyes. My mother touches my face in a tender way, and then leaves the room, closing the door behind her.

I open my eyes and stare at the colourful mobile that hangs over my bed. Cheerful animals sway slightly with the leftover air movement caused by the door closing. As I find sleep evading me, I decide to ponder my situation. So, this is the human experience. If I didn't have my memory, would I be emotionally and mentally developing any differently? Is my awareness of being an Alternate going to influence my emotional growth? Am I going to have an authentic experience? I don't want to over-analyse things, but find myself doing just that. The overthinking, combined with a weariness from all the attention, soon has me drifting off to sleep, as the animals sway above me.

A woman's hand comes to rest on my head. It feels warm, and familiar. I open my eyes, and look at her face. I feel like I should know her, yet I cannot place it. Something about her eyes makes me think she looks a lot like me. She leans over, close to my face, and smiles. "So now you are one. You have so much more ahead of you. I need you to remember to try to go with the flow. You will struggle to fight the current, as your Alternate thinks she knows better. But, in the end, the ride is so much better when you let your boat float, and go with the flow, Hannah." She takes a step back and, still smiling, vanishes.

I wake up bawling, with no memory of what awakened me.

Two

As the months, and then years, turn over each other, I begin to get the hang of being human. Although my body is human, my mind holds a duality of perspective that makes it difficult, at times, to know which way I *should* react to experiences or events that earmark a human life's progression. At the age of eleven, I have a small group of friends whom I like well enough, and who accept me, *warts and all*, as the saying goes. They are easy to read and I comprehend their behaviours, although avoid mimicking them as much as I can. Some of the adults surrounding me are also easy to read. My grade five teacher looks like he'd be happier *anywhere else,* than stuck in this classroom full of rowdy, obnoxious, eleven-year-olds. My parents, who wear an expression of confusion more often than not, try to understand my quirkiness and support me, regardless of how odd they find me at times. My friends are starting to notice boys and have crushes on teenage idols, neither of which occupation holds any appeal to me, as it seems juvenile. Eleven-year-old boys are loud, smelly and usually insufferable. The attractive ones know that they are, and they are so full of themselves it is almost laughable. As much as I want to have an authentic human experience, there are parts I find difficult to navigate through. Being a "tween" is one part I can't wait to be done with.

There are times in life when being a child with a vast understanding of everything has its advantages. You comprehend situations way beyond that of a *normal* eleven-year-old.

Fred, our wonderful elderly Beagle, who loves each of us to the utmost of his doggy heart, is very sick with cancer. It is his time. My dad has been taking him for treatment at the local veterinarian clinic, but now the treatment is no longer helping him cope with his illness. I know Fred is suffering. He simply told me so. *I am old, my body is done with this world, I need to be let go.* Some animals have a stoic sense of duty to their families; they try to hold on, just to be there for their humans. Fred has been holding on, as he senses he needs to, for my dad's sake. He knows his passing will be sad, especially for my dad, as he was the one who rescued him thirteen years ago. He was the one who vowed to give him a good life, free from cages and cruelty. He's been good to his word; no dog could have had a better life, or a more loving human looking out for him. The one final act of kindness a human can do is help their animal companion leave this earth, be released from the pain of their worn-out body. It is one of the most difficult decisions any human can make, to end the life of another. It is a great kindness however, to end suffering.

Fred is suffering now and he needs to be free. I understand that. I also understand that Death is but another stage of existence. His energy will move on, even though his canine form will not. He only needs his energy to be free, to be able to move on to an Alternate existence. My father, looking weary and grief stricken, comes to sit beside me on the floor next to Fred. He reaches out and strokes Fred's soft head. The old dog blinks, closing his eyes, enjoying one last moment of love. "Hannah, Fred is very sick. I know you know this, but it seems like he's not going to get better. The vet thinks he's in pain now, so I need to take him, to be…" he hesitates and swallows hard. I glance at his face and I see his tears. I reach out and gently pat Fred on the head, as I speak softly, "Fred is very tired, Dad. He knows it's his time, and he needs to be free. It's okay, Dad. Fred understands." I put my other hand on my dad's arm and pat it lightly. I feel the need to comfort him, and wish I could reassure him even more, but as an eleven-year-old I am already sounding a bit too wise for my age. He doesn't meet my eyes, but continues to look at Fred. "Will you come with me this afternoon?" He doesn't need to say where he is going, and it doesn't seem inappropriate, at least to me, that a father is asking his eleven-year-old to be witness to such an event. I nod. He stands up and walks out of the room, wiping his eyes with his sleeve.

The car ride to the vet is thankfully short, as Fred is in so much pain that every movement is stressful for him. Sarah, the vet tech, comes out to the car and helps my dad carry him into a quiet room at the back of the clinic. There, a metal exam table, covered with a large soft blanket, dominates the room. There is a small cabinet with two shelves in the corner of the room behind me. I notice a small ceramic dog statue sitting on an upper shelf beside a similar statue of a cat. In between the statues a small plaque is propped up in a frame and reads, *They Leave Paw Prints on our Hearts.*

Sarah helps my dad place Fred on the table. Fred lies there, slowly panting. He is content now that he knows he will soon be free. My dad bends his head and whispers in Fred's ear and kisses his head. I, surprisingly, feel tears come to my eyes. Even understanding the situation, I suddenly realize that I won't be seeing Fred anymore. His bright little face won't be there in the morning to help me greet the day. His warm love won't be nearby to keep me company. I never understood the reason for grief before, but now I truly *feel* it. It's tearing my heart apart. I lean over and kiss his head, mumbling, "I love you, Fred." He blinks and says he loves me too. Dr. Kirkdale, the Veterinarian enters and after briefly examining Fred, explains the procedure to us. Then she proceeds with the injections. Even before the doctor listens for the heartbeat, I am aware of the exact moment Fred leaves his body. I reach out with my senses to touch his heart, no longer beating, and I let out a soft sob I cannot contain. My dad comes around the table to stand beside me and together we hug, sharing our agony for the loss of our friend. Dr. Kirkdale quietly utters, "He is gone." And then she turns and quietly leaves the room.

I look at Fred's body, now an empty shell, and try to think of him, feeling free and at rest for the first time in a while. It helps to picture him this way, and I feel my sobs subside. My father's face is red and slathered with tears. We look at one another for the first time, and I smile weakly. He reaches around me to the cabinet to the box of tissues on the lower shelf. We blow our noses, wipe our faces as best we can, and give one last kiss to Fred, before departing. He is to be cremated and his ashes will reside in a lovely urn. We leave the room and head back to our dog-less house.

One bright spot in my life is getting to spend almost every Saturday with my grandmother, Hannah One. We go exploring in the woods or simply hang around at her house, listening to her extensive record collection, painting, drawing or gluing something to something, which we then present to my parents for them to "ooh" and "aah" over. Ever since I was a young child, Hannah One and I have enjoyed the most interesting conversations. She never questions my ability to communicate so maturely. Now, at the ripe old age of eleven and a half, we discuss all sorts of topics, including her belief that humans, as a species, have potential, but feels that there is so much more out there to be examined and learned. How I sorely want to confirm her belief. I let her speak at length, and simply nod my head, and ask a few questions that I already know the answer to. I am already there; she just doesn't know it.

Today we have decided to take a picnic to the woods. The sun is peeking through several layers of tree branches, and as the limbs of the Maple, Birch and Oak sway gently, the sun splashes the ground with sporadic dancing dots of light. As I express how it resembles a dance, Hannah One suddenly drops the picnic basket and grabs my hand, twirling me around her to some unheard music playing in her head. We both laugh. I reach down and pick up the basket as we continue on.

Small birds follow us along the path, landing on evergreen boughs that whisper gently from the breeze that brushes their pine needle fingers. The tiny birds are very curious of the newcomers. One Chickadee begins to chime, "Chick-a-dee-dee-dee", to which I reply, using a similar rhythmic sing-song whistle. The bird tilts her head and repeats the call. I repeat it back again. Hannah One watches the conversation between human and bird. Another Chickadee lands next to the first one and then another, and soon about half a dozen little black-capped birds are tweeting and whistling up a storm. Hannah One takes the odd sight of her granddaughter singing to the small birds in stride. She is accustomed to my unconventional connection to nature. She simply smiles and waits for the concert to end, before whispering, "That was lovely. I know we have some seeds in our basket if you want to share some with your new friends." Hannah One is an open soul, who finds the *not-so-usual* occurrences that present themselves to her very much like a gift she has been given, and so therefore to be treasured. We find a spot under a very large Sugar Maple that has a rough-edged, smoky-grey bark suit. The canopy above consists of broad green leaves that wave in the breeze. As we lay out our lunch, a few chipmunks and squirrels hover nearby, so we quickly unpack our basket, and share the seeds and nuts we included for such an encounter. It's serene and energizing to sit under the old tree and watch life all around us. The worms, the spiders, the butterflies, the birds, and the squirrels, all of them striving to live a full life, as intended by Nature. The old tree hums as the sun caresses its leaves, and little creatures tend to their homes in its branches, and below its ancient roots. It is also happy to provide shade as we enjoy our picnic.

"I think we should go to the Art Gallery next Saturday. There is a painter whose work I want you to see." In between mouthfuls of a peanut butter sandwich, I agree that we should make a plan.

Hannah One talks about art and her favourite authors, and I talk about some of the books I find interesting, which include some on the subject of anthropology. She never questions why I would be reading something so *grown-up*. She just seems very pleased that I have a thirst for knowledge, like herself, and she loves being able to share her passion with a like-minded soul. I cherish these Saturdays and the freedom of expression it affords me.

I look at the woman standing before me. The face is familiar, and when I look more closely, I realize the woman looks like me, but older, maybe around fifty. It's like looking into a mirror that shows you as an older person. She smiles and sits down beside me, glancing around the woods, then turning her face to the sun. When she speaks, I hear my own voice echoing in hers as she says, 'Hannah, this is a special moment in Time. Cherish it, and cherish her'. She glances over at Hannah One, who has been sitting quietly, watching some Song Sparrows and Juncos flit about in the nearby trees. "Most importantly, try to remember to go with the flow, allow yourself to experience life as the river flows… fight the current and you spend your life in a constant struggle. Allow your boat to float through the storms and you will find it much better downstream… It is important that you take each moment you share with every person you love, as a piece of gold, to hold in your heart and cherish.' She smiles, keeping her eyes on Hannah One as she stands up. She looks back at me, and right before my eyes, she vanishes.

I awake to find myself stretched out on the picnic blanket. I sit up to see where Hannah One is, and find her sitting some distance off, on a flat tree stump, her hand out-stretched, full of seeds. Little Sparrows, Chickadees and Juncos take turns landing and pecking into her palm for a nugget or two, before taking flight towards the branches of an adjacent tree. She turns her head and smiles radiantly, and for some unknown reason, I find myself taking a mental photograph of this image to keep, and to cherish, for later.

An afternoon spent at the city's largest Art Gallery is never a waste of time. The featured artist is truly talented and her paintings are thought provoking. Hannah One and I spend the afternoon talking about the paintings and how they make us feel. We also explore an exhibition of ancient Egyptian artifacts that are displayed in a separate section of the gallery.

We have supper at Hannah One's house and then prepare ourselves to have a quiet evening, playing cards and talking. We both like to get into our nightgowns and then settle down to serious games of crazy eights and rummy. While we get ready, I sit on her bed and watch Hannah One brush out her long hair, which hangs down to the middle of her back, like a silvery brown waterfall. At the age of sixty-one she has a little grey, but she doesn't care about her hair changing colour. She wears it with the same aplomb as the wrinkles that appear when she laughs. During the day she wears her hair pinned up in a bun, as she hates to fuss with it. She can do anything as long as her hair doesn't interfere. She brushes it slowly and methodically. It is almost like a ballet, the movement slow and graceful. I look around the bedroom. It's neat and organized, with some framed photos of the family on her dresser, and one of me on her nightstand. The light is still coming in through the west facing window. The bed has a thin floral-patterned comforter on it. It is a simple room, but one feels cozy and safe here, like a rabbit's burrow. The urge to tell my grandmother the truth about being an Alternate seems to be pushing me towards the cliff edge. There is some voice in my head that wants me to cherish this woman, and cherish our time together, and I can't see how I can continue to have a truly meaningful relationship with her, without being totally honest about who I really am.

I turn to face her, as she comes to sit beside me on the bed, and I ask, "Do you like living here?" It's a silly question because I know she loves her house and garden, and wouldn't move for all the money in the world. I think I'm trying to open up a conversation between us that I know might be difficult to maneuver through. "Yes! I love my little house. It has such personality, and has seen me through so many times, both good and bad. There is peace and security in my home, it almost seems like a living being, taking care of me through all weather, and providing a place for me to keep my memories." I nod, but say nothing. I stand up and cross the room to gaze at a painting she had created years ago. It is a scene of a forest on the edge of a river. It almost feels like a deer is going to emerge suddenly from the trees, and stand at the edge of the water to take a drink. I want to go there; the peace of the painting washes over me like a wave. She is a talented painter.

I turn, and taking a deep breath, continue, "What if you knew you had lived somewhere else, before you lived here? I mean, before you born, you remembered you *lived* somewhere else?" I'm really not doing a good job of explaining myself. Hannah One is quiet for a moment, composing her reply, "Oh, well, I suppose there are people who have the ability to recall their past lives. Sometimes, when someone has a memory of being in a place they have never been before, I think they must have been there in another life." I sit down beside her again. "That's not quite what I mean. What if you *knew* you were from another place, an Alternate place? A place where others exist in harmony and have a curiosity about this dimension, and may even want to come here and be human? What if you *knew* you were from there. Would you tell that to anyone?" I'm still not sure where I'm going to end up with this conversation, but the look on Hannah One's face makes me think I am just confusing the situation the more I talk. She pauses before responding. "Well, my, that is a question. Well, okay, um, let's dissect this statement for a moment. So, you *know* you are from another place, an *alternate* place, and you've come here to be human. Do you have a purpose or mission that has brought you here? Can you go back whenever you want to? Can you communicate with this other place?"

I feel her encouraging questions nudge me along to open up and tell her the truth. "I return to my true form when I die. I cannot communicate with anyone, at least I wouldn't know how to. Besides, I'm not even supposed to *know* I'm here. When we 'cross over,' (I use air quotes to emphasize this silly phrase), our memory of the Alternate is stored in the collective, so we can have a *genuine* human experience, without external influences affecting it. But in my case, I am able to recall where I am from. My purpose is to have the ultimate human life; experience all there is to experience." I look at Hannah One's face. It holds the curious expression of a young child trying to comprehend the answer to, *why is the sky blue*? I know she is trying valiantly to understand all this, without judging or pulling scepticism into the conversation.

"Okay, so, now I know a few more facts. Basically, you are here to have a human life. It would appear obvious that you *are* having a human life, but are you enjoying it? Does this memory of your other existence make it difficult to have a real human experience because it interferes?" I nod, replying, "Yes and yes. I have so much to share with humans, but there is no way to do this, because, for the most part, the human species is too fragile and closed off to the possibility of life in other forms. There are some people who acknowledge the concept, and want to learn about all these alternate existences," I wave my arms around like I'm shooing flies off my head, "but a majority of people would think I'm crazy. Can you imagine having this conversation with my parents?" We both laugh. Hannah One suddenly stands up. "I think you have been given a gift. A treasure that's worth enjoying and using to your utmost. Why not have a human life, but infuse it with your other '*self*'! (It's her turn to use air quotes.) The possibilities are endless when you let yourself go and experience things with both a human perspective, and one from another dimension." She hugs herself and then stretches her arms to the ceiling, exclaiming "Wow! I am so full of questions! But I am so happy that you shared this with me, Hannah!" Once again seating herself, she reaches out and hugs me in a warm embrace that makes me feel accepted and loved for whatever crazy ideas I present. I sigh and lean into her soft frame.

We spend the rest of the evening talking. It's mostly her asking questions and me answering them. It feels good to talk to someone, especially someone who is genuinely willing to learn and understand. She sighs, and looks at me with a warm smile, "You know, your grandfather would have loved you so very much. I wish you could have met him; he was so funny and kind. He never failed to make me laugh every day we were together." She looks reflective as the memories replay in her mind. My grandfather died two years before I was born from a sudden-death heart attack, at the age of fifty-five. One minute he's doing some gardening, the next minute he's not. Hannah One doesn't talk much about him, preferring to keep her memories close to her heart, almost in fear that she might lose one if she opened the box too often. He was the love of her life. She told me that when you've had that kind of love, it's a tough act to follow. She's never looked at another man, ever, even though she was only forty-eight when he died. She said, "life is yours to make of what you will. You should never depend on someone else to make it complete or whole; it is *your* responsibility to be happy and fulfilled on your journey." She is so wise and strong, and her sense of self shines through in her ability to live a full life, without feeling that someone else is needed to make it complete. She glances at the clock and, realizing it's almost midnight, we drag our tired bodies up the stairs, saying a sleepy goodnight to each other as we climb into our beds.

I awake the next morning, wondering if I had been dreaming. Did I actually tell a human being about my Alternate identity? When I descend the stairs and enter the kitchen, Hannah One smiles a knowing smile, and I know it wasn't a dream. However, this morning she only deals out simple questions, like, how many pancakes do I feel like eating? I appreciate the reprieve from all the questions, although I know I'm not out of the woods yet. Hannah One has a curious thirst that is not easily slaked. We eat breakfast and then I ready myself for the trip home. I often have homework for the weekend, but always leave it until Sunday to complete. It's usually something easy, although I make it look like I have to put effort into it. School is more of a social experiment for me, rather than an opportunity to expand my scholastic knowledge. I groan as I get into the car, and Hannah One looks at me "What's wrong? Did you forget something?" I give her an exasperated look, "No, I just remembered that we are learning square dancing in gym this week. That means dancing with sweaty boys." She laughs and starts the engine. "Remember what I said; enjoy the experience! Let yourself be twelve, and feel what it's like to hold a boy's hand for the first time. Or maybe hold a girl's hand. Who knows what you want? Just go with it, stop over-thinking and analysing every move." I try to consider this advice, but part of me still recoils at the thought of having to hold any boy's clammy hand.

Three

The years between eleven and thirteen are filled with firsts for a human female. First time dancing with a boy; first time you realize that you need to ask your mother to buy you a bra; your first period. The years seem to fly by at a pace that doesn't seem consistent with the rest of the world. All of a sudden, I have to think about which classes in high school I want to take. A decision compounded by what stream of education I want to follow. I lean towards an artistic form of education, as I gather the most joy from studying art and reading. My parents want me to have a science-based scholastic career. High school means streaming into a segment that will prepare you to attend university, that will in turn, prepare you for a career. At the age of thirteen, how are you supposed to know what you want to do when you're twenty-five? Even with my understanding of human life, I still struggle to understand my own life. I want to be a writer or maybe teacher, but I also love to paint and draw. As far as my parents are concerned, none of my interests will necessarily set me up in a career. But I am determined to follow my own path.

I stand on a dark, unfamiliar road that is covered with snow, looking untraveled for hours. I feel the cold wind whip at my hair, blurring my vision as I try to see my way forward. A voice echoes in the wind, "It's my life! It's my life..." a young tormented voice wails, but it's not my own. A car whizzes by, sliding precariously along the snow-covered road as the shrill voice of a woman cries out, using her last breath on this plane to exclaim her abject terror. The young voice, belonging to a boy, maybe sixteen, watches from the side of the icy road, as the car careens off into the ether. He sinks to his knees, sobbing.

I awake in a sweat.

High school is a whole new experience for me. I walk the hallways with books clutched to my chest, and marvel at all the ridiculous behaviour that is rampant around me. The blatant sexual overtures, with girls in outfits that hardly cover anything, and boys making remarks and ogling them as they parade by. It's a wonder this species survives to adulthood. I want to be comfortable, so loose-fit jeans and sneakers are my mainstay. I don't care to be ogled. If someone wants to get to know me, they can approach and have a decent conversation with me. The other girls use their cell phones to have conversations and send sexy pictures to potential boyfriends. I feel sorry for girls who feel they have to do this in order to receive the attention of someone else. It shows a lack of respect on both parts, when the decision to become a couple is based on how you look in a photo. This behaviour is not exclusive to teens however, as I learned watching adult friends of my parents on their phones, using apps to pick out potential partners, all based on a photograph. I join in certain activities, as I truly want to be part of the fun, and experience teenage milestones. This is, after all, the point of me being here. School dances are less excruciating now that most boys don't sweat quite as much, although they make up for it with wandering hands. I'm not interested or ready to allow any human personal access to my body.

Today, at the ripe old age of fourteen, my period very unceremoniously arrives. I wake up to find a small circular blood stain on my bed sheet. If I hadn't known what to expect I might have been afraid, or maybe happy, as it signals "the beginning of womanhood". As it is, I am simply annoyed. I have swimming for gym class today. I open my dresser drawer and search for the box my mother very discreetly placed there to be prepared. I gaze at the box with pink flowers and a girl, smiling, on a bicycle. I don't feel like riding a bicycle, that's for sure. I am the last girl in my class to get my period, according to one girl who seems to keep track of these things.

Jamie Beaumont, a tall, athletically built, red haired girl, who possesses a cheeky sense of humour, is a new friend in my very small circle of friends. She confided to me once, that, when she was little, she believed you only got your period *once*. When her older cousin, aged seventeen, mentioned she didn't want to do something because she had her period, Jamie was horrified that it took her *that* long to finally get her period. We both laughed over that misconception. *If only*, we both lamented.

Fifteen is a transitional year. You are too old for some things, like Halloween trick or treating, but too young for other things, like driving a car, or drinking alcohol, although I have heard stories about classmates drinking excessively, and regretting it the next day. Jamie has been invited to a boy's house for a party and the only way she could go was to create a lie to her parents, saying she is going to my house for a sleepover. I don't know how her parents could fall for that. For one thing, I never have sleepovers. But they accept the lie and send her off.

She arrives at my house, and after greeting my parents, who sit comfortably in the living room reading various papers and magazines they subscribe to, we go up to my room to get ready for the party. My parents are dumbstruck when I tell them Jamie will be spending the night. After my younger staunch disapproval of sleepovers, this seems out of character. Nevertheless, they are thrilled I am finally getting with the program. Jamie and I come back downstairs wearing makeup, which Jamie has talked me into trying out. My mother looks up from her paper and her eyebrows go about three inches up to her hairline. She smiles, but says nothing. I suppose seeing your daughter wear makeup for the first time is somewhat of an occasion for some mothers. It makes my eyes itchy. I am looking forward to washing my face when we return home. I tell her we are meeting friends and going to a movie. She nods, still smiling, happy to see her daughter having a social life at last.

The house is on the other side of the neighborhood, so we can easily walk to it. The homes on the street are lit from inside, as people start their evening rituals of television watching and internet surfing. No children play outside now, as it's dark. The air is very cool for late spring. I hug my jacket around me, feeling fingers of cold air trying to sneak in from the bottom. I would have worn a heavy sweater but teenagers don't dress for the weather; they dress to look like they don't care about the weather, or that it doesn't bother them to be freezing or soaking wet. I can't see the logic in it. I'd look over at my friends shivering in their tiny jackets, and shake my head at their stupidity. Tonight, however, I will follow form to fit in. We cross the street and round the corner to our destination. A few stray teenagers are scattered on the front lawn, sitting in the damp grass, or on the steps leading to the open front door. Music can be heard blaring from inside somewhere. As we enter the house I notice several people in the living room, and further back many bodies are milling about in the kitchen, sitting on the counter, and standing everywhere in between. Bottles clink and laughter is heard above the music. I see a few open cases of beer sitting on the kitchen table, and people reaching in to grab a bottle before disappearing into another part of the house. The kitchen leads to the back patio where several teens are sitting in lawn chairs drinking and passing around joints.

This is my first *drinking* party, I quickly surmise. I watch as teens gulp the warm beer, laughing and dancing in the living room. It seems enjoyable enough. Everyone is smiling, talking and telling funny stories to each other. If this is a drinking party, then I can handle this. Jamie reaches into the case and pulls out two beers, handing me one. I watch as she grabs the lid and twists it off, so I mimic her action. I bring the bottle up to my nose and smell it. It smells like socks when you take your shoes off after a long, hot day. I cringe at the off-putting scent and glance over to see Jamie take a drink. She grimaces at the taste, but grins at me encouragingly. I raise the bottle to my lips and take a small sip. It tastes bitter and warm. I'm not sure I can swallow it. I close my eyes and swallow. Yuck. This is going to take me forever to drink, if I can drink it at all. I wish I could secretly pour it out and replace it with water. Jamie takes another swig and shakes her head after she swallows. I believe she is having a tough time with it too, and that makes me feel somewhat better. We take our warm beer and head towards the living room. I recognize a few people, but most are older students that I have only seen passing in the halls at school. Jamie waves to a boy who is standing on the far side of the room. He waves back and makes his way through the dancing bodies to where we stand in the doorway. It's Glen, a grade eleven student who is quite popular. We back-track into the kitchen, where there is a bit more room to stand together. "Hey, you're here!" Glen yells. "Yup!" Jamie yells back. I smile, but remain silent. I'm not sure what the protocol is here. I get the impression that she wants to spend time with Glen, by herself, so maybe I should make myself scarce. I look around for an excuse to leave, when a song comes on that I actually like, so I use that as my cue to exit. "Hey, I'm going to dance!" I yell in their direction as I make my way back into the living room.

    I plop my warm beer onto a table top. I feel the rhythm fill my body; the music envelopes me, and the beat seems to match my heartbeat with the same rhythm. All the muscles in my body move to the pulse of the song. I still marvel at the human body's ability to move, run, and dance. I don't know any popular dance moves; I simply let the music move me. I don't need a partner;

music is my partner. It's such an amazing sensation to actually feel your pulse increase, and pump the blood through your veins to the muscles that raise your arms, move your feet and swing your torso. Humans take it for granted, this wonder of nature, the human body.

I feel myself getting quite warm, and by the end of the song I am sweating. I laugh, flapping my shirt to get a bit of air on my body. Some of the other dancers give me a sidelong look, but I don't care. It's so freeing to be in a human body that moves so easily, and uses all the senses to heighten the experience. I can't help but laugh. I leave my warm beer on the table and go in search of a can of pop.

For the rest of the party, I spend my time keeping one eye on Jamie, while talking with some of the other teens who also decided warm beer isn't their thing. We laugh and talk about the teachers we dislike and the TV shows we are watching. A few drunken bodies flail about us, either making their way to the backyard to throw up, or searching for more alcohol. Either way, the night won't end well for them, or the morning after.

By midnight I decide that it's time to go. I find Jamie, still talking with Glen in a far corner of the living room. "Hi! I hate to bug you, but I think we better go. Remember I told my mom we were at the movies. She might ask questions if we're out too late." In all honesty, I'm exhausted. My face feels clammy and my eyes are stinging from the makeup and the smoke in the room. Jamie looks disappointed, but nods in agreement. She stands up and Glen follows us out onto the front porch. They lean in together for a long kiss, to which I turn and look off in the other direction. "Can I walk you home?" Glen asks. Jamie looks hopeful, but I shake my head. I think it's best if we head home minus any male company. We leave Glen standing on the porch, watching as we fade into the night.

Four

I watch myself continue to grow and develop, as time wings onward, like a bird soaring past the window. I strive to maintain a balance between my human nature and that of my Alternate. I'm beginning to allow myself more opportunities to experience life, without stopping to analyse or question the reasons why. I simply do it. Now, at the age of sixteen, my emotions and reactions to situations are becoming *more* human.

The forthcoming end of the school year provides another excuse for teenagers to have a party. I am once again invited to tag along with Jamie. The party is at Joanne's house this time, a girl we befriended just after she transferred in mid-term in January. Joanne is a lively girl with little inhibitions, and became popular quite quickly. It appears that her parents are in the military, and are going away for a three-day weekend on an assignment, so she decided to coordinate this with a blowout party to celebrate the year's end.

The house is loud and full of teenagers doing the usual teenage things. Drinking is number one on the list. At the age of sixteen I have no taste for alcohol, unlike everyone around me. Everyone is drinking, and doing shots, laughing, taking lots of selfies with drunken friends and talking very loudly to be heard over the music. I'm not sure why, but the music, the noise, the lights and the energy are intoxicating to me. There is a freeness of spirit in evidence here; youthful freedom from consequence or concern for what the morning may bring. Part of me wishes for the freedom from always over-thinking my life. Jamie hands me a can of something she retrieved from the refrigerator. I pop the tab and take a drink. It's actually very cold, which helps. It's sweeter too, so I glance at the label. It's some sort of vodka mixed with raspberry juice. Not bad, sort of pop-like in its carbonation, with a bite. I take a few more sips, and it tastes even better than the first sip. My tongue feels tingly from the tart-sweet raspberry juice, and my head starts to feel a bit light. I take another swig and another one. Soon the can is empty and I find myself looking for another one. I open the refrigerator and see that the whole thing is stuffed with cans and bottles. I laugh, reaching in to grab another can.

After my third can, I feel the room sway and my eyes become unfocused, but I also notice how awesome the music sounds now, and how I have a desire to dance. I enter the living room where the music is loudest, and begin to sway to the beat. It holds me up and moves my feet; I feel like I can fly up and touch the night sky. My human brain is having a ball, but somewhere there is a voice inside me exclaiming, *this isn't a good thing, stop it*. I find myself yelling, "For crying out loud, shut up and live!" Everyone around me stops, looks at me, then bursts out laughing. "Yaa, Hannah! Go for it!" All I hear are voices cheering and laughing. I feel a pair of hands come to rest on my shoulders. I turn around to see Jim, a boy from my English Lit class, smiling at me. "Hey Hannah, how the hell are ya'?" He slurs his words, weaving back and forth somewhat unsteadily on his feet. "Hey Jim, it's fucking awesome!" Okay, another first, as I have never used a swear word before. It feels great. It feels fucking great! "This is my favourite music. I *love* music. We don't have music in the Alternate, we don't make it, or have it, or play it, or anything! The Alternate sucks! I'm so happy to be *here*!" He smiles, replying, "Ya, whatever. That sucks, but, like, hey, ya, we're here, so let's just party!" He leans in to grab my arm in an attempt to spin me around. We both end up on the floor in a heap. Laughing, we try to get up, but we are both so drunk we can't find where *up* is. "Hey, let's go have a party *upstairs*." Jim is pointing to the ceiling, and I laugh "Ya, I think I can fly up there, just wait!" I close my eyes to focus and feel the room spin. "First I need another thing of booze; this room is spinning too much. Raspberry fizzy helps!" I claw my way over his prone body to grab the side of the couch in an effort to get to my feet. The kitchen is just as crowded and noisy as before, but I hear nothing of it. I pin my eyes on the fridge door and make a bee-line for it. I swing it open and grab a can, not bothering to read the label. I pop the tab up and take a sip. It tastes sour like grapefruit, not like raspberries at all, but by now my tongue is numb, and I don't care. I turn to see Jim in the frame of the doorway, leaning on it as if it's the only thing keeping him upright. His long brown hair is unkempt and his shirt is undone, but his smile is very enticing. He points to the ceiling again, and I laugh. I wonder what kind of party is better than the one on the main floor, but I guess it wouldn't hurt to check it out. I make my way over to him and he reaches out to grab my hand. He leads the way through throngs of people in the narrow hallway. We get to the stairs and I stop a moment to take another long drink of the bitter booze. He starts to ascend the stairs, towing me behind him like a kid pulling a wagon. I roll along, surprised to find my feet only stumbling once going up the carpeted stairs.

    The air is stuffy in the dark hallway, and the sound of music seems muffled and distant, as we make our way past a couple of closed doors. Jim stops at an open door that appears to lead into a guest room. A sudden burst of laughter from downstairs makes me conscious of the distance between the party goers and the two of us. It doesn't yet occur to me to wonder why no one else is upstairs dancing, or talking in groups. Jim, still holding my hand, leads the way into the dark room, steering us towards the bed. My head feels cloudy, and I find myself unable to focus, either with my eyes or my mind. It's all swimming around me. It feels like the world is one large snow globe and some giant is shaking it to see the snow fly. As we reach the bed I'm grateful to sit down, as all of a sudden I feel like I'm going to pass out. Jim sits beside me and leans in to kiss my cheek. I laugh at the thought of this being my first kiss. Another first to put in the book. All I want to do is lie down, close my eyes and let the world stop snow-globing. Jim kisses my neck. He moves his hand away from mine and places it on my leg. I feel a strange sensation in the pit of my stomach. It's not nausea, as it holds a sense of excitement. I turn my head as Jim comes close with his lips and kiss him on the mouth. It is one thing to study and try to understand the human sexual response, but another to be in the middle of it. It feels both arousing and frightening at the same time. I feel Jim's hand run up my body to my breast and the sudden urgency with which he starts groping around is alarming. I freeze, pulling away. "Oh, um, no." I utter. He doesn't look at me, but speaks into my neck, "Come on, it'll be fun. You'll enjoy it with me," he mumbles. And then he kisses me again and pushes me flat onto the mattress.

My head is so foggy I can't think my way out, but part of me is also excited, so I allow him to move me and touch me. He starts undoing the buttons on my blouse, while he constantly moves my hand to grasp his crotch. All I can feel is worn denim over something hard. I let him continue undoing my blouse. Another loud noise from somewhere in the house makes me stop, and suddenly I hear my inner voice for the first time since I started drinking, yelling at me, *Hannah! Get out of this situation, it's not safe!* My head is swimming and I feel like I might throw up. I drop my hands away from him, and attempt to raise my body into a sitting position, but Jim has me pinned down. His hand goes to the zipper on my jeans. I reach out to grab his hand, but he pins my hands up over my head with only one hand and somehow he's able to pull at my clothes until I'm exposed. By this time, I stop struggling, for it only hurts my arms the more I attempt to move, but I keep repeating, "No, no no..." It falls on deaf ears.

He has stopped seeing me as a human being, if he ever saw *me* at all to begin with. Now my body is simply a means to an end. A gratifying end for him, but not for me. It seems like it's over in the blink of an eye, and yet it also feels like an eternity. The muscles in my groin have constricted so tightly it is a wonder he is able to penetrate at all, but he does, and now the pain of those rigid muscles being violently breached sears through me like a hot iron. I lie like a dead fish, caught by the large net that is his overheated body lying on top of me. After he's done, he collapses on me, breathing heavily. He manages to say, "See, told ya you'd like it." I push him off me, roll over and throw up on the floor. He scrambles to the far side of the bed, "Oh geez man, gross." This is the last thing he says to me before standing, zipping up his pants and leaving the room. I lie on the bed, my clothes still asunder, my head pounding, and my eyes so full of hot tears I'm certain I will drown in them.

Soon, I regain my composure enough to get dressed, although I still feel like the world is all out of focus and off kilter. I stumble out of the bedroom, feeling very ashamed. I feel ashamed for throwing up, but mainly for putting myself in the situation I found myself in. I asked for it. I led him on, and so I got what I should get. All of my logic and reasoning can see no other conclusion to this scenario.

My entire groin area hurts and my head hurts almost as much, so I decide to sneak out and go home before I see anyone. I specifically do not want to see Jim. He is right and I am wrong, and I don't want to see him, full of arrogance and self righteousness. I actually don't want to see anyone, because I'm sure they all know what happened and will judge me, and not well. I make my way down the stairs, the noise of the party now harsh and overwhelming to my ears. I find the front door and without anyone paying any heed to me, I simply step out into the night.

The room is dark, but I can see a light glow emanating from someone standing beside my bed. She doesn't have a lamp or a candle, it is she herself who glows. I blink, rubbing my eyes, and struggle to sit up, still feeling the effects of the night I had. She stands there, smiling, and as my eyes focus more clearly, I can make out her face. She has brown wavy hair that comes to her shoulders, and green eyes, but it's the expression on her face that makes me recognize her. It is me, only it's an older version of me. Somewhere in my mind I know I have seen her before, in another vision. I close my eyes, and lay back down, still believing it's an alcohol-induced dream, but then she speaks. "Hannah, you are stronger than you believe. You are more powerful than you know, and over time you will discover this, and own it. Always remember that, whatever trauma happens in your life, you are strong and will find your way through it to the other side; and then you can let it go, and continue to move forward. Do not make harbour in your sadness or fear. Let it go…" The light fades, and I fall into a deep dreamless sleep, from which I will awaken, not being able to recall the vision, except for the words, "You are strong. Let it go…"

The following morning, I feel as if I'd swallowed an entire desert. My throat is dry, my head is throbbing, and my eyes are swollen from crying. I look like Death when I finally emerge from my room to come down to the kitchen for coffee and a litre or two of water. On Sunday mornings, we usually have a pancake breakfast together, but there is no way on earth I am facing food with this massive hangover. My mother glances at me, her eyebrows rising, but remains silent. My father is already out cutting the front lawn. After getting myself a large glass of water, I plunk myself down on the couch and reach for the television remote. I feel no desire to talk or be talked at, so I want to put the television on as a wall to keep out the conversation beast. It doesn't work. My mother enters the living room and clearing her throat, she comments, "I hope you had fun with your friends last night." It's a trick of course; she can see I'd had too much fun, so it isn't really a casual statement so much, but a way of pointing out that I'm not fooling anyone. She does not say another word about it; I think she knows her disapproving tone is enough to set me on the straight and narrow. It isn't her tone, or her disappointment in me, that makes me feel bad. I have enough guilt and shame to cover that without her help. I noticed a blood stain in my underwear this morning, just another reminder of my horrible behaviour. How am I going to face everyone at school? I can't even wrap my head around it. Being a teenager is hard enough, now I have added fuel to the immature, adolescent fire of gossip, innuendo and teasing.

As I finish my glass of water and stand up to retrieve a cup of coffee, I glance at my phone to see that Jamie is calling. She asks if I want to go for a bike ride. No way, I utter. She seems miffed about my response, but doesn't push me. I can't tell her what happened. Trying to put a *mental* handle on my embarrassment and shame is one thing, but to actually *talk about* my humiliation is out of the question, even to my best friend.

Monday morning brings rain which suits my mood: Grey and overcast. Although my head is now clear and my stomach settled, I am emotionally in a dark, rainy place. I drag myself out of bed and prepare for school. I know I can't evade the inevitable, so I decide to rip the band-aid off in one go, and face the school hordes and the consequences of my actions. For some reason I believe that every single person in my school, even people I don't know, now know exactly what happened.

I walk down the street toward school as if I'm walking to a funeral. I see Jamie huddled under an umbrella, waiting for me at the corner. "So, hey... are you feeling better today? I figured you were too hung over yesterday, so that's why no bikes." She laughs and looks at me to see if I understand her ribbing. I don't smile or laugh. I nod my head, as that is all I can manage. "So, like what happened to you? I tried to find you at Joanne's later, but someone said you'd already left. I had an awesome time, but I won't be seeing Glen anytime soon, the jerk." She looks sideways at me, hoping I'd ask why. "Why?" I say mundanely, out of politeness. I honestly couldn't care less; the way I'm feeling, I'd be content to see all males of the human species drop off the planet. "He started making out with Melissa at the party. I'm like, well, fine, dick, I wasn't into you anyway." She sounds hurt nonetheless. I nod, but make no remark. She stops and turns to face me. "Well, what the hell is wrong with you? You usually have like, good words for me, make me realize I'm better off or something, and today it's like you're some kind of zombie." She says angrily. I stop, looking down at my feet, and the rain bouncing off my running shoes. *Just tell her*, the voice in my head whispers. *She will understand.* I feel the tears in my eyes spilling over and mingling with the rain drops as they plummet to the sidewalk. "Well, I guess something happened at the party." I stammer. How do you share the most shameful moment of your life? There is no way to convey the way it makes you feel, like you're less than deserving of anything good, since you were so stupid and reckless.

Jamie grabs my arm and says, "Oh my god, Hannah, tell me. What happened?" I look at her hand grasping my arm and feel as if it's a life-line being tossed to a drowning swimmer. I look up to see concern all over her face. I take a breath and begin. "I had a lot to drink. Way too much. I felt awesome and invincible. Jim was there, and, well, we decided to party upstairs. I let him do things..." I choke on the words as they stick in my throat. Jamie's grip tightens, as she asks, "What do you mean by '*you let him do things*?'" I take a small breath, trying to steady myself. "Well, at first it felt good. I liked kissing. Then he kinda' pushed me down and grabbed at my clothes. I said no, but I guess he didn't hear me or something..." I feel like I stopped breathing all of a sudden, and gasp as if I'm being suffocated by the words I'm uttering. "You mean you said *no*, and he wouldn't listen." She said it like a statement, not a question. I look at her face and see the frown creasing her forehead. "I mean," she continues, her voice louder,

"You said *no*, you said *no*, and he wouldn't stop?" This time I nod my head and say, "I tried to stop him, but, but, he said I'd enjoy it. He pinned my hands down. He tore two buttons on my blouse." I sob openly now, as if the wound is fresh cut, and then begin to hyperventilate. Jamie drops her umbrella; it spills carelessly onto the wet sidewalk. She wraps her arms around me as if I would blow away in the next gust of rainy wind. I cry on her shoulder, wrapping my arms around her in a tight embrace.

Eventually, the sobbing subsides enough for me to break the embrace, and bring my soggy sleeve up to my eyes to try to clear them. Jamie drops her arms and stands looking at me. "Did you tell your mom?" she asks, although she already knows the answer to that. "No way! I'm not telling anyone. Ever." The finality in my voice sounds certain, but the look on Jamie's face indicates this isn't a good idea. "Hannah, you have to go the doctor. You need to be checked out. What if you're pregnant or get an STI from him? You can't ignore this." I know she is right, but the thought of telling anyone else is so overwhelming, I don't think I can do it. "Doctors understand these things, they help. It'll be a good thing." Again, I know, rationally, that this would be the right option to keep my body physically in the best condition to continue my human experience. It is simply the mental anguish that I have a hard time facing. "I'll go with you, if you like. Then we can go shopping or grab a bite to eat." Jamie always has a way of sneaking a shopping trip in with whatever plans we make. I smile despite myself. "Okay, I will call the doctor. My Mom can't know about this, so it will have to be after school." Jamie takes my hand and squeezes it.

I have my life-preserver in my best friend beside me, helping me stay afloat through the rest of my horrible day at school. That day is filled up by some general gossip about me making out with Jim at the party, and someone told me it was Jim himself who started the rumour. My lack of popularity however, is a blessing in disguise, because most people don't really know who he is talking about, so the interest wanes fairly quickly. I see Jim in class, but he doesn't acknowledge I am in the same room. I am okay with that, and because I am so embarrassed and ashamed, I don't want to make eye contact with him in case it all shows on my face, like a bad rash.

FIVE

The day for my appointment has finally arrived. One week has felt like a lifetime, as I struggle to come to terms with the whole thing. As promised, Jamie comes along for moral support. The office is almost empty, as I have one of the last appointments of the day. Our family doctor is male, which I haven't been concerned about, up until now. Today I feel the pit of my stomach clench as I sit in the waiting room. The receptionist calls my name and then hands me a paper gown as I enter the tiny exam room, blandly telling me to undress completely from the waist down, with the exception of my socks, and that the doctor will be in shortly. Dr. Emmanuel is a man in his mid-forties, with greying temples crowned by jet black hair. He wears half glasses for reading but never takes them off, so he is always tilting his head down to peer at you over the rims. He closes the door and takes three steps to sit down on his swivel chair beside the small table where he takes notes.

"So, Hannah, what brings you here today?". I wonder how many times a day he utters that question. I clear my throat and begin the speech I have practiced in my head. I want to stay calm and not get upset, as this won't help either of us. I launch into my story. He sits looking at me over his glasses, until I'm finished explaining my situation, and then he simply blinks. "So, you had intercourse with no protection and now you are worried about the consequences." I look at him for a sign of compassion or understanding. I only see annoyance, and judgement. "I didn't know I'd have intercourse, so, um, I wasn't thinking." I feel like I'd been sent to the principal because I didn't have my homework done. He blinks again, standing up. "Okay, well, hop up on the exam table and swing your legs up. Scoot your rear end down and put your feet in the stirrups. Let's see what's up there." His insensitive remark is cutting, and I am less than impressed by his manner. I feel the dryness of the paper-covering on the table against my skin as I lie on my back, staring up at the white cork board ceiling. I feel his hands, in sterilized gloves, brush against my knees. "You need to relax your legs." He says impatiently.

I have never had an internal exam before, so I don't know what he is doing. All I know is, I am very uncomfortable. Suddenly I feel fingers press against my vagina. The muscles automatically contract, like a door slamming shut. "You need to relax. Think happy thoughts." Is he kidding me? Happy thoughts while a strange man is delving into my most personal of areas? I try to think of something nice, so I concentrate on the image of the tree in my backyard. I think of the various wildlife friends who live in the tree. I can almost feel my heart rate lowering as I take myself to that place. A voice from deep within sings out, *let it go, remember you are strong...* I hold onto these words like my life depends on them. Then I feel a cold, hard metal object scraping inside of me, as I picture an ice cream scooper in a barrel of ice cream. I start to say something, but then it's abruptly removed. The doctor stands up, turns away, and pulls off his sterile gloves, tossing them in the waste bin. Without looking at me, he remarks, "You can sit up now. All done." He begins typing notes into the electronic file, but never says a word. I swallow hard, believing the worst. I must be pregnant with a baby who has an STI. That's the only reason he won't look at me. He can't bring himself to tell me the truth. He completes his notes, stands up again and hands me a paper that the printer just coughed out. As he is reaching for the doorknob he utters, "You'll be fine. Here's a lab request for pregnancy blood work. My receptionist has information on contraception, just ask *her* for it. If you decide you want to go on the pill, make another appointment. The swab will come back from the lab soon. We will call if there are any issues." And that is it. He opens the door and closes it quickly before I can blink. I sit frozen on the edge of the exam table, the paper gown drooping off of one shoulder.

Jamie sits looking at her phone as I come out to the reception area. There is no way I want information about contraception, and furthermore, to have to ask for it when there are listening ears in the waiting room area is not something I would ever subject myself to. Jamie stands up and looks at my expression. I smile weakly at her, and head for the exit as fast as I possibly can without running.

"So, what did he say?" Jamie wants a full report. I tell her every detail from start to finish. She shakes her head after my monologue. "Man, what a dick! He didn't explain what he was doing down there? What an asshole!" She touches my shoulder. "It's going to be okay. We'll just have to wait for the results of the tests, and then you can forget it." I stop and look at her. "Forget it? How can I forget this? I am so ashamed of myself! I'm so embarrassed! I brought this on myself. I'll never forget how stupid I was." I take a sharp breath to stop myself from crying. Jamie stops in the middle of the sidewalk and grabs me by the shoulders. "What? What? What do mean *you* brought this on yourself? Oh man, you are so wrong... no means no! Haven't you heard that? You shouldn't be ashamed, *he* should be! That prick should have respected you enough to stop, but he didn't. You should not be embarrassed, *he* should be!" Her voice is getting high pitched and louder the angrier she gets. "No means no, Hannah! He had no right to force himself on you, regardless of the situation. *That* doctor is a dick; he didn't even bother to tell you it's not your fault!" She turns and pokes her middle finger at the doctor's office sign. "Men are dicks!" She stretches her arms above her head and yells loudly, "Men are dicks!" Various passersby stop and glare at her. One woman nods her head in agreement as she passes us on the sidewalk. I laugh for the first time in days.

Saturday is my day with Hannah One, but I am not in the right frame of mind to spend the day exploring art galleries, or some other equally artistic pursuit. I was able to make an excuse last Saturday, but a week later I find myself unable to continue lying to her. I know she will worry about me if I cancel two weeks in a row, so I decide to chin up and pretend all is well.

We sit in her living room after sharing a delicious lunch, and try to decide what to do with our afternoon. I make some noncommittal replies to her questions. She notices my lack of enthusiasm, and comes to sit beside me on the couch. "Hannah, I know it's none of my business really, but are you okay? If you have something you need to talk about, you know I am all ears and no mouth. It goes no further than this room." She looks at me with concern on her face. I feel the tears behind my eyes as I fight with myself, tell her or don't tell her? Will she be disappointed in me? Will she be angry? I really want to talk about it, so I decide to let her in on my misery. As I speak of the incident I can see her face creasing with a frown, and her lips are pursed in a hard line, but no other emotion shows. Once I have told her everything, including the horrible experience with the doctor, I look down at my hands and realize I have been clutching the hem of my shirt. I loosen my grip, but keep my eyes downcast. Hannah One clears her throat and says, "You have been violated. Your body has been violated. You had no control, no power, no say. I ask you now, what do *you* want to do about this? You can take your power back by choosing how much you allow this person to influence your journey. *You* be the driver of your own car, you decide what direction you go, what path you want to follow now. You need to know *you* have the power, you have the say, and you have the control. No man, or for that matter, no person should ever have power over you or your body, regardless of the situation." She takes my hands from my lap and holds them in hers. They are warm and soft. I feel age in her skin, as dryness replaces the moisture of youth, but they are beautiful hands, full of creative energy and love.

I look at her face and she is smiling, even though there are tears in her eyes. As the tears flow down my own cheeks, I swallow, feeling my throat dry and constricted. "I'm not sure which way to go. I'm still very confused about how I feel. I really want to forget it. I want to get on with my life and just pretend it never happened." Hannah One nods, "Yes, that is one way to go. This is your path and I cannot say whether it is right or not. I just know that when we try to deny that a bad experience has happened to us, the memory has a way of returning to us, to remind us that we need to resolve it. You might need to carry this in your "forget-about-it" bag for a while, but eventually you'll need to unpack that bag and look at what you're carrying." Her words make sense to the part of me that can see the bigger picture. But the human part of me still aches for division from facing that truth, that image that replays itself on a horrendous loop in my mind, and sees no end, no resolution. I sit still for a few minutes, not uttering a word, deep in thought. *I am the driver and I decide which way my car will go.* At one point I think I would have driven it off a cliff, but now I think simply driving in unending circles will work for me. I stand up, turning to Hannah One, and announce, "Let's see what movies are playing this week. I'm in the mood for popcorn." She nods, but makes no other comment, knowing she has to let me find my way ahead.

Six

One week rolls into the next, like a never-ending somersault, until it is finally the last week of school. Exams and final assignments fill my days and nights and leave little room for other thoughts. Word has spread of another big end-of-year blow out party, but I'm not going, no matter what. Jamie understands my decision, and although I know she is disappointed, I can't be convinced to change my mind. I have had enough of that teen experience, and not interested in revisiting painful memories. I had waited for what seemed like forever for the results of the STI and pregnancy tests, only to have no word at all from the doctor's office. I finally called and inquired, only to get a very nonchalant, "everything's negative" from the receptionist. I suppose their viewpoint is *no news is good news* and not worth informing the patient about. I decided to change physicians to Jamie's family doctor. Jamie explained my situation to her doctor. She was very kind, and reluctantly allowed me to switch over to her. Doctors are hard pressed to take on new patients, so I feel lucky to be taken on by her. When I saw the new doctor, she was reassuring, and asked if I wanted counselling, to which I replied, "No thanks, I want to put it behind me and get on with my life." As I said this, Hannah One's words rang in my ears, 'You can carry your "forget-about-it" bag for only so long.' I am still carrying the bag, and intend to do so for a while longer.

After my last exam I have to prepare for my first summer job, which will take me away from home for the entire summer. I applied to be a Camp Counsellor. My mother had heard that a local church-run children's camp was looking for responsible, mature teens, and she mentioned it to me. At sixteen, I'm not sure how I fit the "mature" category, but I suppose, during my interview, I came across that I am *mature enough*. While answering their questions, with regards to my camping experience, I fudged my responses slightly. I mentioned having gone on family trips, and canoeing through school programs, whereas the fact is, I've never been in a tent or set foot in a canoe. I suppose I impressed them with my demeanor, because they hired me right there on the spot. They were looking to fill the position of girls' counsellor, who could double as a nature counsellor. The pay is minimal, but the experience itself is what caught my interest. I have one more week before I head north to spend eight weeks at Birchlake Camp. My mother shows little emotion about my leaving, although she did go shopping with me to buy a new bathing suit and other essentials I'll need, including writing paper and stamps. I guess that is her way of indicating that I'm supposed to write to her throughout the summer. My dad keeps quizzing me on *"what-to-do"* scenarios. *What do you do if you meet a bear? What happens if you fall into hive of bees? How long should you wait after eating, before going for a swim?* He also made up my own personal first aid kit, to keep with me in my cabin. The camp has a registered nurse on staff, available twenty-four seven, but he assures me this kit will be better to have on hand, just in case. I pack it with my other gear, knowing it will ease his worry. Jamie is mad that I am leaving for the whole summer. She has a job at the local Walmart, which is paying her more than she'd make as a counsellor. The camp covers the cost of meals, so my expenditures will be next to nothing, which means most of my pay will go right into my bank account. I am looking forward to this experience. Canoeing, camping under the stars, and making meals over a campfire are all things I have seen on television and movies, but have never actually experienced. I spend a few weeks collecting sheets of information on nature programs for kids, and was surprised one evening when my dad suggested a trip to Bentley's, the local bookstore downtown, to stock up on nature reference books for me to use. I love the thought of having nature guides and identification books to refer to. My dad talks about the initial drive we will take in a few days to deliver me to the camp. He likes planning the logistics of what route to take, and what our departure time will be. He loves having all his ducks in a row, well ahead of duck time. I am happy to let him organize this aspect of things. It honestly makes little difference to me, as long as I get there.

The day arrives, bringing sun and clear skies. The family van is packed with several suitcases and boxes containing my life for the next eight weeks. I had met a few fellow counsellors who advised me to bring extra clothes, and funny items that can be utilized for skit night, and other theme days that run throughout the summer. I had no funny clothes but packed some of my dad's old clothes that are stored in the basement for the day he'll "lose the weight" and fit into them again. So, in other words, old clothes he'll never wear again. I have all my books and papers packed, along with two magnifying glasses Jamie gave me. I think she stole them from her young cousin, Kenny, who likes using them to burn bugs. I am happy to be her partner in crime, simply to save the bugs.

The drive is about two and a half hours long, in which time my parents have one big argument and several curt discussions about the direction of travel, and the schedule for bathroom breaks. I'm so thankful to have headphones to tune out the noise as I sit in the middle section of seats in the spacious van. I have noticed over the past year this growing rift between them. It seems like every subject is contentious, even small things. I want to say something like, *'hey you guys, don't sweat the small stuff'* but that sounds rather glib and insensitive. I know, from studying human interactions, that this is merely one phase of a downward spiral in the disintegration of a marriage. I'm not upset at the notion of them divorcing, but I do feel sad. They must have loved each other at some point, and believed they could build a life together.

The camp is nestled in a large wooded area that borders on a pristine lake. It is very serene, from what I see through the trees. The parking lot is lined with about ten cars, all with trunk lids open and car doors opening and slamming shut. A tall, handsome young man stands at the far end of the parking lot, near to what I assume is the dining hall, a clipboard in his hand. He wears a large straw hat that has what can only be described as a large chomp-mark sized hole in the brim. He wears a camp sweater that bears the name 'Birchlake' in large yellow letters across the chest, and smaller letters stitched over his heart spelling out the word 'Director'. We climb out of the van and stretch our cramped legs. My dad starts to open the back doors and sort through things, when my mother tells him to hold his horses until we know where my cabin is located. I dread the thought of that long drive home for them. Thankfully they can put the radio on to lessen the uncomfortable silence.

As I approach the Camp Director, he recognizes me and grins broadly. He waves as he glances down at his clipboard. His name is Dave, but everyone calls him *Stork*. I don't ask why. Jamie told me I'd probably come home with a new name, but I didn't understand what she meant by that. Now I assume that she meant I'd get a nickname. "Hey, Hannah! Welcome to Birchlake Camp! It's great to have you here! I'll give you your cabin assignment so you can get settled in. There's coffee, cold drinks and sandwiches in the dining hall for you and your parents to enjoy. We'll have a staff meeting at four o'clock, once everyone has arrived and all the parents have vamoosed!" Every sentence he speaks is delivered with a level of enthusiasm I almost find exhausting. I will soon learn that *Stork's* gusto is the gas in the fuel tank that keeps the camp lively and fun.

We find my cabin and are pleasantly surprised to see it has a beautiful view of the lake. It is a long rectangular-shaped building, divided into three connecting cabins. The door on the far-right leads into the ten-to twelve-year-old girls' cabin; the door on the far-left is entry for the thirteen-to fifteen-year-old girls' cabin. The middle door leads into the counsellors' quarters. The floors are grey painted plywood, the walls are bare studs, with many years of graffiti, including names of former campers and staff, written all over the aging wood. Six sets of bunk beds line the walls of each of the camper cabins, each with its own lumpy mattress sitting atop ancient bedsprings. One large window in each cabin allows for light and a view of the lake. I appear to be the first arrival, so I have my pick of beds in the counsellor cabin. The best view is from the bed on the far wall, so I claim that as my own. My parents help me carry all my gear to the cabin, then quickly, but subtly, I direct us to the dining hall for coffee and sandwiches. I am keen to send them on their way and not prolong our goodbyes.

The thought of being a counsellor to girls who are only about two or three years younger than me is almost laughable. But that is what I've been assigned, so I have to brace myself for early-teen girls, with all the drama that comes along with them. Within two hours, the other three counsellors arrive, unpacking and talking non-stop about what the summer will hold. Two of the girls were counsellors here last summer, so they are the most excited when discussing the male staff members. Who is returning? Who do they like this year? Who broke up with whom since last summer? The talk is endless, and frankly, a bit tiresome. The other newcomer, Janice, seems equally bored. I exit the cabin to stand on the rocky outcrop about fifteen feet away, so I can get a bit of a break. As I'm taking a long look at the beautiful lake stretching out before me, I hear the screen door creak open and Janice emerges to come stand beside me. We smile at each other and then turn to look out at the water. Janice lets out a big sigh, "This is beautiful. It'll be nice to canoe out there. I looked at the canoes and they are in pretty good shape, but the row boat has a leak I'll have to fix." She is the Canoe Instructor and seems to have a pretty extensive knowledge of boats in general, or at least it appears that way to someone who's never been in a boat. I turn to look at her, and notice her athletic build and general sense of confidence in the way she stands, erect and sure of herself. I suddenly wonder if I will be able to keep up with this adventure, physically, as well as mentally. "Oh, that's good. Maybe you could take me out in the canoe tomorrow, if there's time. I have to admit, I've never been in one." Janice's eyebrows shoot up. "What? Holy geez, well, sure, I think you'll need to get in a boat before the kids arrive. You don't want them to know you're a newbie canoe-be!" She laughs and I smile, feeling like I'd made a nice connection already. I turn back to look at the lake again before changing the subject. "After the staff meeting I have to set up my nature hut with my supplies. I hope the kids like my program. I've never been around too many kids, so this should be interesting." Another surprised expression crosses Janice's face, but she simply laughs again. "Man, who did you blow to get this job?" and she laughs as I start to object, saying, "They must've seen some potential in you, and hey, you'll probably figure it out as you go. That's how it is sometimes." She shakes her head, "Just don't let your kids know how green you are or they will eat you alive!" She giggles. "How hard can it be to do the camp counsellor thing?" I mumble. Janice shakes her head again, and says, "Hannah, you have no idea!".

Seven

The day of the campers' arrival is upon me, and a feeling of unease sits on my shoulders. Am I really going to try this? I see other counsellors preparing and know that it's too late to turn back, and worrying won't change anything. I stand in the parking lot as the buses arrive. Children of all sizes come pouring out of the open doors. Some of them are so excited, as their loud, shrill squeals echo off the trees. I sense the nearby wildlife draw a collective sigh of resignation as the noisy summer commences again. Many of the counsellors are equally excited as returning campers make their way into their outstretched arms. I stand off to the side, my clipboard tucked into the crook of my arm. I'm looking for older girls, and as I spy them I try to get their attention, without success. They are gathering like moths to a flame around a very handsome male counsellor named Dominic. As the buses empty, I know I have to get my campers organized, so I take a deep breath and plunge into the fray. "Raccoons! Raccoons! I'm here for the Raccoons!" What a ridiculous thing I just hollered, but the actual name of my cabin is *Raccoon*. The youngest camper cabins are labeled *Chipmunk, Mouse,* and *Salamander*. The ten-to-twelve-year-old campers have to contend with names like *Squirrel, Weasel* and *Rabbit* and the oldest are *Raccoon* and *Otter*. Thankfully there is no Skunk cabin; labeling a cabin as *Skunk* would certainly open the door for some bad body odour-type ribbing and bullying.

The next sound I hear is the booming bass tone of Stork, issuing a one-word command; "Campers!" Everyone stops and notices his right hand shoot up above his head, his large frame a big presence in the parking lot. I quickly learned the expression, *when the hand goes up the mouth goes shut*. Stork stands quietly as one or two young campers still voice their dislike for mosquitoes while their counsellors nudge them into silence. Stork slowly lowers his hand, a big smile across his broad face. "Welcome! Welcome, one and all! Okay, campers you need to get to your counsellors, so, in case you don't know, I'll tell you who they are! Okay, Chipmunks go with Yvonne!" Yvonne waves to all the little bodies that start to gather around her. Stork lists off the cabin names from the youngest to the oldest. He finally comes to the Raccoons. "Okay, Raccoons go with Hannah!" I put my hand up trying to look cool and wave nonchalantly. None of which comes off as cool; it looks more like the *Queen's royal wave*. Oh well. Ten girls start picking up their suitcases and sleeping bags and gather around me. I smile and some of them smile back, although a few girls look rather sullenly at me, as if to say, *"Oh no, are we stuck with you?"*. I ignore their expressions and ask if anyone needs help carrying their bags. Ten hands shoot up. I sigh. It's going to be a long day.

The first night of camp is a disaster. These young teenaged girls are bound and determined to make noise throughout the night, sneak out if possible, and just make it impossible for me to get any sleep, for fear of what they'd try to do next. I enter their cabin with an attitude of my-way-or-the-highway, and it falls on deaf ears. My strict routine isn't going to fly, and when I think about it, I would probably react the same way, if I were a typical teen. A new battle strategy would need to be formulated if I am going to survive these girls. I really do want them to have a good time, and from the look of things, I think that is pretty well written in the book anyway.

I talk with Janice a lot because she seems to have good advice when it comes to dealing with the campers. Experience taught her that having a friendly guiding hand is more likely to be successful for girls who, let's face it, chronologically, are only two years younger than us. So, I vow to be friends and be a lighthouse in the storm of female teenage angst that inevitably happens, especially when boys are involved.

Camp life settles into daily routines, activities, sunburns, scrapes, poison ivy rashes, and bug bites. Nights are filled with camp songs, getting smoke in your eyes, tripping on the trails in the dark with a faulty flashlight as your only guide, all the while avoiding the resident Porcupine who told me he likes to chew on wooden outhouse doors and floorboards because they are salty and taste good.

It's Pirate Day, so I am partnered with Mark Greene, a male counsellor I don't know very well. He seems to look like a bookworm type; tall, thin, with dirty blonde hair and silver rimmed glasses. He is shy, but pleasant enough, and has a wicked sense of humour, which makes itself known as we cheer on our team throughout the treasure hunt and other activities. I never realized these types of silly games, that have no real purpose other than simple amusement, could be so enjoyable. My human brain is pointing an accusatory finger at my Alternate, as if saying, "See, I told you it's fun!" Mark is the counsellor for the oldest boys' cabin, the Otters, so we end up being paired together a lot through the summer, helping us form a unique friendship, which is an unexpected bonus.

The last night of first camp is very emotional for everyone, myself included. I have come to like my girls, and the routine is going so well I don't want any change to come and make waves. But every two weeks it will be the same farewells and change of personalities in the camper cabins, so I have to get used to it. The final evening includes a traditional camp dance. The girls are going crazy, applying makeup and fussing with dresses they have carefully packed especially for this night. I don't really have a *nice* outfit, as no one told me I'd need a dress, but I find a clean blouse that I like, as the colour reminds me of the sky, and I have a white pair of chinos I have never worn because the colour is very impractical for day-to-day work. My mother had packed them, saying, "You never know, you might need them." Guess she was right, and I make a mental note to thank her when next I see her. The other counsellors don various outfits ranging from dresses to skorts, so I don't feel totally under-dressed. I slip on my sandals and gather the girls.

The kitchen staff have cleared away all the tables in the dining hall after supper, but left the benches along the walls for sitting on if you didn't want to dance. Every single light in the hall is ablaze, no low light mood setting allowed here. Stork is in one corner by a small table that houses two very large speakers and a CD player. He has his head down looking through stacks of CDs, choosing appropriate songs and piling them up to the side. Some of the campers mill about him, making requests. The CD collection the camp has is very old, so he is disappointing many of these young music lovers. If you were a camper from 1975 though, you would love this collection.

After the dance is over, I herd the girls back to the cabin where they tell stories about their encounters, laughing and crying about this boy or that. I sit on a bed and watch the interactions with interest. This is what it's like to be a teenage girl. They want to be strong, independent, and take no prisoners. Yet there is a side of them that still wishes for the fairy tale romance boy to come and simply hold their hand and love them, in the most pristine way. I shudder, a brief recollection seeping into my thoughts. I close my eyes briefly and wish them all well; to be able to achieve the self confidence and belief in themselves that they will need to plow through some of life's challenges they will inevitably face. I secretly wish that for myself as well.

Once the girls get settled in, I'm able to leave the cabin along with one of the other counsellors, leaving Janice and Emily in charge. We head back to the dining hall. Stork allows the staff to have a bit of time off in the evening, taken in shifts, so we can socialize and relax. The music still plays quietly, a few counsellors looking through the old CDs for something recognizable. One of them chuckles as he picks up a particular disc, and quickly places it in the player. Next thing I hear is this simple guitar riff, soft and gentle. Everyone lets out a groan, but many jump up and take the person next to them for a dance. I look around and suddenly find my hand being grabbed by Mark. He pulls me up and starts to sway. He smiles at me and says, "Love this old tune, what a classic." I hate to say I don't know it, but I can't recall ever hearing it. "Um, what is this?" I ask. Mark chortles, "Oh geez! Are you from the moon? Haven't you heard *Stairway to Heaven*, ever? Classic Zeppelin". He shakes his head and attempts to pull me closer in a slow dance. I immediately stiffen up. I am not yet prepared for being close to any male again. I need more time to think or reason it through, at least that is what I keep telling myself. But this reflex is instinctual, not rational.

Mark notices my apprehension but keeps dancing slowly, keeping enough distance between us so we can continue to talk facing each other as we dance. I find myself relaxing as my personal space becomes my own again. Mark seems quite comfortable to have a chasm of space between us as we dance. He says, "You'll like this song, it has so many variations of tempo... it's really about a woman who gets a lot of money, only to find out her life sucks anyway, and that she won't get to heaven because of it. It's really weird, but it's also really awesome." Once the faster tempo portion of the song is done, the song finishes on a sad simple phrase, *"and she's buying a stairway... to heaven..."* Everyone in the room laughs, breaking apart from each other and starting to head back to the benches. I stop and look at Mark. He smiles and holds my hand for a brief moment, then drops it, and returns to sit with some of the others. A simple encounter that makes me feel human again. He saw me, he recognized me and he respected me. He saw me as a person, he recognized my discomfort, and he respected me enough to back off. This is the first step of many on the path to rebuilding my trust in men.

The white door in front of me has a silver handle. I reach out and turn it, and the door swings inward. I enter. I see a long white hallway in front of me. It tunnels off into eternity. A door on my left beckons me to open it. I grasp the handle and try to turn it. The door will not open. Then I notice the lock. I have no key. I press my eye to the keyhole, and find myself being drawn through it, to the other side. There, I stand on a ledge, overlooking a vast array of stars in the night sky. I see the stars, bright and dim, sparking and dying, and rebirthing in new form. Nova and super nova. Black hole and milky way. Immeasurably dark and unyielding, yet it calls upon me to look at the wonder, and weep for those who will not look. It is there for all to see, yet blind are those who will not look. I implore the sky to let me join with the vastness, to become nova; to flare brilliantly, and then diminish to nothing. The uncompromising nature of the Universe ignores my plea, simply continuing to shine, and wax and wane as the moon presents its slivered face. I beseech the unknown to let me return, let me back in, let me come home. I miss the Light and its infinite freedom. The sky moves on as the earth revolves, and I stand alone, as the path I have chosen to travel awaits my human feet to journey onward.

A shiver wakes me. I find my bare feet engulfed by the cold night sand of the beach, right by the water's edge, my arms still outstretched above me in a pleading posture. I look up at the night sky, seeing dim points of light, laid out in patterns that astronomers of old have named: Cassiopeia, Ursa Major, Orion, and so many others. I shiver again, for I am wearing only my thin nightgown. The cold dead of night shocks my consciousness into the *Now*. I turn, and carefully make my way back along the dark trail to my cabin.

The cool morning light arrives early, or so it seems. As I sit up and hug my sleeping bag around me, I feel coarse dry sand scraping my legs inside the bag. How did sand get into my sleeping bag? I unzip it and pull my legs out, only to discover very dirty bare feet. A vision walks through my mind, but it is veiled and indistinct. The morning bell sounds, and all thoughts, except getting the campers out of bed, leave my mind.

It is very sad to see the last camper shuffle onto the bus, on this, the last day of camp. As that big yellow school bus pulls out of the parking lot, I sense a chapter in my life ending. I'm not sure if I'll come back next year. I need to make a lot of money for university, and the salary of a camp counsellor does not come close to covering it all.

Then it is time to say goodbye, with many hugs, to all the staff members, as we promise to get together in the city during the autumn sometime. I doubt it will happen. Except for Mark and Janice, I have made no strong connection to anyone else. I am happy to have gained two wonderful people in my circle and will make an effort to keep in touch with them. I actually feel teary as I say goodbye to Mark. He has restored my faith in the male species. I know that regardless of whether or not any get-togethers with other staff occur, we will always stay connected, one way or another. We hug and he says, through unabashed tears, "I wanna see you a lot, so make sure you don't forget me!" We hug again, and then part ways to greet our respective rides home. My Dad has come alone to pick me up, mumbling that my mother wasn't available, with no further excuses offered. I am actually relieved, because the thought of another two-and-a-half-hour drive with the pair of them squabbling, was something I have been dreading. We pack my bags and gear into the van and I turn for one last look at the lake, the trees, and even the dining hall, and thank them all for a wonderful summer experience.

Eight

The Light is pure, concentrated and joyful. I see it for its true self, and I too, am joyful. It is one, like myself, traveling this plane, to learn and expand the understanding of All within itself. It plays with the beam of Light I stretch out, and we intertwine as One, yet remain separate, as our physical humanness anchors us in the Here. The Light plays upon my senses, and I feel the familiar sense of peace, calm and balance I carry when existing as an Alternate. The Light coalesces into the form of a man, with a tall build, looking to be around my father's age. His mischievous expression leads me to believe he has a sense of humour that isn't always appreciated by those around him. His outward compassion and love for me is evident, as mine is for him. We embrace like old friends. He extends his thoughts to me, and I hear the echo of his voice say, "I can't wait until we meet on the human plane, I have so much to share with you."

The autumn coolly slips into winter, with little fanfare, other than frost on the grass and the need for a heavier jacket when I leave for school in the morning. Autumn can make me melancholy, as it signals the onset of the numbingly cold winter, which I always find challenging. I understand the need for seasons, as Earth requires them to refuel, rebirth, lay to rest the old and dying, and soar with the new. When I was little, I marveled at the artistry of the snowflakes as they danced down from above. That feeling quickly wore off, especially when it became my job to shovel the front walk.

School is a series of stress-filled days now. It's a full throttle, high pressure time to make every assignment count towards the best grades. We have decisions to make, applications to fill out, scholarships to strive for, and little time for anything else. I have decided to pursue a Bachelor of Humanities degree. I feel a sense of irony when I utter the title, as I believe I am already studying humanity. But the more I read about the courses, the more intrigued I become. Getting to read influential books and discuss ideas or viewpoints that are presented in literature, philosophy and other art forms, sounds like my kind of studying. Writing a great work is like painting a masterpiece that is cherished. This fascinates me. Alternates have no spoken or written word. Our thoughts transcend All. In some ways it makes things easier, but there is no music to it, no visual reward of seeing the colours mix and create imagery on a canvas, no reading to the last word to find out the ending. It is in the creative that humans find their communal humanity.

I am focusing on achieving the best marks during Christmas exams, so when January rolls around I can confidently write applications to universities. It all seems to be flying past me and my friends. I see Jamie in a few classes and we try to have lunch together, but otherwise we hardly see one another. Mark has dropped off the planet, but I assume he is neck deep in it too. Today, summer never looked so good as when I slipped and fell in an icy puddle and my study notes got soaked.

A feeling of despair washes over me. No one will understand, and no one will care. I sit on the edge of my bed and look at the bottle in my hand. A prescription for my mother, diazepam, to help her with "her moods". It is now the remedy to my own shadow of a life. I look out the window, and see March bringing more snow. I am glad I won't have to walk through that anymore. I will just be sleeping, forever.

Opening the bottle, I pour out what looks like twenty pills, and then reach over for the glass of water I left on the nightstand. Stuffing as many as I can into my mouth, I take a large gulp of water and try to swallow, but end up choking. I spit some pills out on the bedspread and carefully pick them up and slowly put two in my mouth and swallow, and then another two.... A knock on the bedroom door startles me. I hear my mother's voice, asking if she can come in, let's talk. I don't answer her, I simply stare at the bottle and wish for it to be over. She opens the door and, seeing the bottle in my hand, yells out to my father to call nine-one-one. She rushes over and grabs the bottle as I feel the room sway around me. Good, I'm going to sleep now. I close my eyes, but I can still hear my mother calling out, "Mark! Mark! Oh my god!"

I sit up in my dark bedroom, sweat pouring down my back. A dream, that is only partially visible, lingers in a corner of my mind, but I cannot look directly at it, as it shifts and fades through a cloudy veil. I feel terribly sad, but panicked at the same time, although I can't reason why.

Commencement or graduation can be a major point in human life. It signifies the end of teenage-hood and the commencement of adulthood. For some, it truly is the commencement of a new life, a new adventure and a huge step away from all that's familiar and secure. For some students it's merely another step in what will seem like an endless flight of educational stairs.

Jamie is accepted at a university in Thunder Bay for a Physical Education degree. She wants to be a Physical Education teacher so badly, she joined every sports team she possibly could, and volunteer-coached a girls' minor league volleyball team as well. Her resumé looks pretty impressive.

The evening of graduation finally arrives with as much hoopla as I expected. My family, including Hannah One, gather for a celebratory dinner before the ceremony. It's a very nice restaurant, with white tablecloths and red cloth napkins. Everyone raises a glass in a toast to me, which I find embarrassing. We get through the rest of the dinner amicably enough, even though I know my parents are barely speaking to one another now. Hannah One and I hold up the conversation for the most part, and that is fine with them.

Arriving at school and getting into the gown and cap, we begin filing into the auditorium to the horrendous sound of the junior band playing, "Pomp and Circumstance". The band finally, and mercifully, stops playing. The principal rises from his seat on the stage and makes a small speech addressing the graduates. Then it is time for Jamie, the valedictorian, to make her speech. It's funny and to the point, which is Jamie to a tee. No bullshit about achieving dreams or striving for perfection. She ends her speech by proclaiming, *if we can all make it out of this place alive there is hope, but only a bit*. It is hilarious to the students who love every word, but the faculty wear the expression of people who expected one thing, and got another. It turns out the speech Jamie submitted to the teachers for approval is not the speech she just delivered to the graduates. Who would stop her once she began? What would they do to her, expel her? It is the perfect topping on the cake of high school we have been consuming for four years.

Walking across the stage when I hear the principal call, "Hannah Rose Casey", is strangely satisfying to me. I hadn't really thought I was all that excited about this ceremony, but truthfully, I am happy to receive my diploma with Honours. I have worked hard this past year. The academics were fairly straightforward, it was balancing all the other pieces on the board that had me sweating sometimes. Academics is one thing, but being a member of the choir, the art forum and the school newspaper had me bouncing around like a kernel of corn in a hot pot.

After the event I meet everyone in the foyer outside the auditorium. I get hugged soundly by Hannah One, and lightly, yet warmly, by my parents. They say how wonderful I looked as I walked across the stage. They look at the diploma that sits inside a thick black paper folder. The gold seal seems to glimmer at me as I glance at it. I let my mother take the diploma home to keep it safe. They wave goodbye and head for the exit, along with several other parents and relatives who had come to witness this rite of passage. The students are offered refreshments in the cafeteria, and then a dance is to start in the gym in about half an hour. I'm not really keen on the dance, but I realize how I might regret missing out on this experience when I look back on my high school years. So, I square my shoulders and ready myself for dancing.

NINE

Before the summer is fully launched I am able to spend time with Mark, as he prepares for another summer at Birchlake. He's the Assistant Director this year alongside Stork. That will mean a much better paycheque for him. He texted, asking if he can come over to see me before he leaves. We have been staying in touch through the year, although there was a period of about six weeks, around March, when I didn't hear from him. I assumed he was busy with stuff, so I didn't worry. There is some thought or image tugging at me from somewhere, like trying to remember something, but the thread of that memory is lost, and sometimes may only be found when one stops *trying* to remember. When he finally got in touch he seemed a little down, but I'm not the best reader of emotion, so once again, I attributed his mood to trying to cope with a hectic school year, and did not look any deeper.

He pulls into my driveway in an old Toyota he had bought last year. He has nicknamed it *The Toy*. I can't understand the desire humans have to name inanimate objects, or to have such emotional attachment to them. This human attachment to material objects seems odd to me, although the human part of me understands the desire to hold on to a certain object, as it seems to help connect you to your past, or to a person. My mother once asked me, as she was helping me clean out my closet, what toys did I want to keep, and what should we donate? I said nothing needed to be kept, but for some reason she kept several items, stating that *someday* I might be happy to have kept them.

Mark jumps out of the car and comes to sit beside me on the porch step. We aren't the type of friends who like to hug, so we simply nod in greeting, as he says, "Well, I'm ready for camp. I'm going to miss you so much! I wish you were coming back." I already explained about the need for money to jump start my university career, so there is no need to reiterate the reasons. I simply shake my head. "You're going to have such a great time, swimming and everything, while I slog away at Wally-world." He looks down at his shoes, and clears his throat. "Well, I'm really excited to get away for a while. This has been a rough year for me, but I'm doing better now. Um, I need to, no, I want to tell you..." he trails off. I turn to face him, seeing how seriously he is struggling to say what is on his mind. I say nothing, allowing him time to gather his thoughts.

He swallows a few times before he continues, "Last March, I was going through some bad shit. I was really depressed, and almost well, oh, crap this is hard to say, but, I was going to kill myself." I sit there, first stunned by his confession, and then shocked to think that my friend, whom I have shared so much laughter and good times with is, in truth, suffering. "I thought I'd be happier to be done with it all. I couldn't see my way ahead. Hannah, it's just been so crap, but now I've decided to try to be *myself*, so I want you to know something. I'm gay." Tears roll down his cheeks, and my heart breaks to see my friend in so much pain. I take both his hands in mine and squeeze them, "Mark, you must have been really struggling with this. It can't have been easy." I feel tears well up behind my eyes, suddenly relating to his inner battle to have to keep his true self living under a bushel. "I'm so glad you feel comfortable enough to share this with me. You know it makes absolutely no difference to me who you love. *True* human love recognizes no barriers, it will happen, regardless." He smiles, and a bit of the old Mark twinkles in his eye. "In March, when

I got so depressed, my mom found me trying to inhale her pills. Well, that freaked her and my dad out so much!" A vision of a pill bottle flashes across my mind, and then the face of a woman in distress. I try to ignore the images, and refocus, as Mark continues; "But they were really good, and got me counselling through the doctor I saw in the emergency room. They knew I needed a lot of support. I was actually thankful for their interference, after I gave up being mad at them for stopping me. They've been great since I came out to them, and with my therapist's help, I'm seeing things more clearly." He squeezes my hands one last time and then drops them as he stands up. "I just really wanted *you* to know. I'm sorry, I wasn't ready to tell you sooner." He shrugs. I look up at him and smile, "Please don't apologize. This is your story, and you tell it the way *you* want to. I'm just happy to know you're feeling better now. You know, this human emotion stuff really is worth all the hassle. It's kinda interesting to actually, well, uh, *live*." Mark looks at me quizzically, but just shakes head and murmurs, "You are so weird..."

We decide to head to the mall for ice cream and spend the day together, before we'd be apart for the next two months. There is a slight change in Mark's demeanor as we walk around the mall, licking our cones and window shopping. He seems more at ease with himself, almost more fluid in his movements. He turns to me, as if reading my thoughts. "You know how great it is to finally be myself? Not to hide how I feel, how I truly think about things. I don't have to pretend to be something I'm not." I know that feeling of hiding your true self very well. He continues, "I can really be myself around you; but then, I'm always comfortable with you, almost like, well, like I sensed you are a kindred spirit." He grabs my hand and laughs. It feels very natural to hold his hand, and actually very pleasant. I'd never held hands with anyone, other than my mother when I was very young, so this is new to me. I squeeze his hand as we continue walking. I want desperately to share my secret with him, but this is his moment today, and it would be totally blown away if I reveal my own truth. Another time perhaps, if at all, I can let him in.

We walk around a while longer before coming to sit by the mall fountain. The water splashes lightly as the spray of the fountain shoots upwards. Mark turns to me and says, "Do you remember the night we danced to Stairway to Heaven?" I nod, as he continues. "Well, I have to confess I was so relieved when you pulled away from me as we were dancing. I kinda felt like I was supposed to do that thing where you dance extra close to a girl, but I was not really into it, like the other boys were. I was so relieved when you sorta kept a little distance between us. It made me feel like, well, like I'd been let off the hook." He laughs, and I smile, remembering the dance and how it made me feel.

"That was a special dance for me too. It restored my trust in humans as a species, when you were so respectful towards me." I turn to face him, "I had a really horrible experience with a guy, and it left me feeling like I was to blame. It shattered my trust in men completely." I look down at the water, and then continue, "You helped me regain some of that trust and understanding that there really are decent men in this world." Mark looks concerned, but asks no questions, and I'm glad not to have to explain myself further. He reaches out and gives me a hug. He whispers in my ear, "The fates really did have a plan by bringing us together. Remind me to send them a fruit basket, will you?" We laugh, standing up, and, after each of us tosses a nickel into the fountain, we make our way back to *The Toy*.

With the end of summer comes the new excitement, and anxiety, of starting university. I am really excited to begin this new chapter in my life. From what I had seen on the summer tour, the campus is mid-sized. It's an off-shoot of the larger campus, which has thousands of students in attendance. This campus, known as *Glenmont*, supports around five hundred students who are studying various degrees. It has lovely grounds, rich with green lawns and old trees that line the walkways and grow beside the old ivy-covered buildings. It is a different atmosphere here, compared to high school. While still young and lively, it holds a slightly more mature atmosphere, apart from some of the silly activities that take place during *Welcome Week*. I avoid those, as they seem to involve a lot of drinking. I don't worry about making friends. I'm able to keep in touch with Jamie, although she is living six hours north of me now. Mark is attending another university in the city, but we promised to keep tabs on each other. I do, however, find as the weeks go by, that having acquaintances in every class is helpful. The workload is tremendously different from high school and even though I can keep up, it's nice to bounce questions or ideas off fellow classmates. The students formed study groups or partners, depending on the size of the class. My Canadian English Lit Prof suggested partners. I look around the room, as people turn to each other to pair up, and I see him, smiling at me. I smile back. He is sitting two rows over, so he picks up his books and makes his way to the empty seat in front of me. He turns his body so he can face me. "Hi, I guess we could be partners, if that's okay. I'm Julian." He smiles. "Yes, sure, of course. I'm Hannah." I smile back. We both hold onto our copies of Margaret Atwood's *Lady Oracle*, the book we'll be dissecting first. We have our assignment, so we set about discussing the topic, drawing our comparisons, and finding the hidden meaning behind all the complicated symbolism this book offers. As we talk, I find myself looking at his face more closely. I'm not immune to men's physical charms, but I am wary of them, still. He is tall and broad shouldered, but compact in frame, which indicates he has a fit body under his crew neck sweater. He has large brown eyes; a crop of wavy brown hair that falls down to the nape of his neck; when he speaks, it is thoughtful. I feel that he is probably the kind of person who speaks his mind, but chooses his words to carefully reflect his viewpoint. He has hands that show creative labour, as there is evidence of oil or acrylic paint around his fingernails. He notices me looking at his fingers, and he sighs. "Yes, well, the problem with painting before a class, is leaving enough time to clean up before you have to rush off to some lecture or something. Today my hands only got a minor scrub down." He laughs and folds his hands together, rubbing his fingers. I swallow, somewhat embarrassed that he discovered me taking a survey of him, "I think that's great to do painting. I mean, to be a painter." I can't believe I am stumbling over my words so much. *Hannah, get a hold of yourself. Don't be ridiculous.* "I love painting, but, well, I'm not great at it." He looks at me a moment, eyes narrowing, before he asks, "What would *you* love to paint? I think greatness comes from pouring love into the subject you paint. If you don't *love* your subject, it shows in your work." I consider what he is saying and I agree. "Well, I had to paint still life in high school. We had models from time to time, fully clothed, of course." Not sure why I added that last part. I continue, "I like landscapes. Earth and sky, water, trees. That sort of thing. I usually end up painting a scene from a picture in my head." He nods. "Yes, but I bet if you took your paints and canvas outside, you'd marvel at what work you could do. I love landscapes too; I find capturing a place at one moment in time onto a canvas is kinda cool, but very challenging, unlike someone with a camera who can simply point and shoot. They capture the scene, but not always the *true essence* of the scene. Does that make any sense?" Before I can reply, he continues, "Painters have to transfer the energy of the scene through their brush onto the canvas. It's a blank page that needs to be filled with energy and life." He takes a breath and adds, "Okay, guess I've said way too much, and now you think I'm some kinda crazy painter-guy." He shrugs, looking down at the paperback on the desk in front of him, almost appearing embarrassed for sharing so much information with a stranger. I realize he may be needing some assurance that I don't think he's crazy, so I utter, "No, no, not at all. It just sounds like you really have a thing against photographers." He glances up at me, and, seeing me grin, he chuckles.

As the weeks progress, I spend more and more time every day with Julian. At first it was because we wanted to get our English Lit assignments done, but with each day, we found other excuses to hang out together. Finally, today, Julian has asked me out. It's actually a painting date. He suggests that we go to a local park for a painting session. He has all the art supplies we need, so I offer to bring a picnic lunch, so "we can keep our strength up after all that rigorous painting we'll do". It's such a silly joke, and I immediately feel silly for saying it. But Julian laughs, and says that maybe he'll need to take extra vitamins, too. He has a way of making my stupid comments not sound so stupid.

He offers to swing by my house to pick me up and, as we load the picnic into his car, my dad makes a brief appearance in the driveway, just to *say hello* to this new friend I've made. Thankfully, it's a brief encounter, in which Julian makes my dad laugh. As we part, he shakes my dad's hand. Good first impression, I say to myself. I just hope I won't get the third degree about him when I return home. The first time Mark came over to my house, my mother asked twenty questions, to which I gave little or no response. Nosy parents, even with good intentions, can be so annoying.

With autumn's season in full swing, I love seeing the trees with vibrant colours aflame. I already feel inspired to paint just by looking at them, as we stand in the parking lot arranging our gear. We unload the art supplies, but leave the picnic in the trunk for later. Julian carries two folding chairs and a small folding table, while I carry the art supplies housed in two rectangular cases with handles. Another small backpack Julian carries holds flasks of water for us to drink, and for cleaning brushes. We make our way along the trail until we come to a clearing which leads to the most wonderful view of a pond and a small glade. Puffy brown cattails sit atop thin dying stems, and other marsh grasses line the sides of the pond, tan and brown from Autumn's cool hand touching them. The glade has numerous autumn wildflowers, like Asters and Hawkweed, adding colourful bursts of purple, white and yellow amongst the jade and auburn greenery. The red-stemmed Dogwood bushes lend a contrasting colour to the scene as well.

I often come here with Hannah One to have picnics, so I know this spot very well. It is my favourite place in the world, but I never mentioned it to Julian. "I love this place, so I thought we should paint here." He says as he gently drops the chairs, and starts unfolding the small table. I stand for a moment and enjoy the scene. It's absolutely perfect, simply because I love this place, and I love that Julian shares the same feeling about it, too. We set up our paint trays and other supplies, and sit down to draw. Sketching feels light and free as I let the pencil move across the paper. Julian concentrates on his own work, but occasionally asks me something or makes a suggestion. We work in silence as the small birds chirp quietly in the surrounding trees, almost as if they don't want to distract us from our creations.

We spend more than an hour painting with little or no conversation. Finally, Julian puts his brush down and says, "You know, I'm getting hungry. Why don't I run back to the car and grab the picnic?" He leaps out of his chair and dashes off down the trail before I can so much as blink.

Ten minutes later he returns with the basket and a blanket. He places the basket on his chair as he unfolds the blanket and lays it on the flattest bit of ground he can find, under a nearby Maple tree. He takes the basket over and kneels down as he examines the contents. As he unpacks two sandwiches he makes yummy noises, to which I roll my eyes. "Really? Getting excited over peanut butter sandwiches? I think you need to get a life!" I laugh as I rise and join him on the blanket. Fresh fruit and cookies are in other containers as well. The ice packs in the bag have kept everything nice and cool so the MacIntosh apples will have a crispy crunch when you bite into them. My stomach growls, and I realize, I am fairly hungry too.

We sit quietly as we eat, while looking out at the pond. Julian breaks the silence by commenting, "Good picnic." He smiles, taking another bite of his sandwich. I nod in agreement. "I'm an expert peanut-butter sandwich maker from way back." He laughs and suddenly leans over and kisses me. It isn't on my lips, which is good, because my mouth is full of sandwich. It's on the cheek, and merely a brief kiss. It seems almost more intimate than a kiss on the lips. There is a familiarity to it, a casualness to the motion that makes it seem like we are some old couple, married for forty years and have been through this so many times. It almost doesn't take me by surprise, and *that* fact takes me by surprise. I blink, but simply continue eating my sandwich.

After we have filled our stomachs, we pack up the lunch leftovers, and turn our focus back to painting. The light has changed somewhat but the essence of the scene remains, so we continue on into the afternoon, until we both decide we are happy with our paintings and will call it a day. He looks at my painting, and exclaims; "Now that's a painting! I love it!" I have to admit, I poured a lot of energy into its creation, and I am very satisfied at the outcome. The brush feels like a natural extension of my hand and I simply guided it across the canvas to create a scene I love.

We sit for a few minutes allowing the paint to dry somewhat before packing up the gear and making our way back to the car. I carry our canvases outstretched like two trays. After placing everything in the trunk, Julian turns to me and takes my hand, kissing my open palm. "See, I told you. If you love your subject it will show in your art. I loved your work today; it has a life and energy all its own. This was a good day." He drops my hand slowly. I smile, but say nothing. Julian had made this a good day, and as we get into his car I hope to have more days like this.

Ten

For the next few weeks Julian and I spend as much time together as we can. Our conversations are always stimulating, because the topics, like art and music, are subjective, not logical or rational; it's based solely on our emotional reaction to what we view or listen to. We have many discussions that revolve around what Julian is studying: Linguistic Anthropology. He studies how the use of language influences human social behaviour. The fascination I have for the human emotional and verbal response to situations makes this a topic I can delve into for hours. It's a learning expedition for me. He seems very pleased that I am so interested in his studies. We are both busy with academic studies as well, and as the school year progresses, we find it more and more challenging to get together, but by November the pace I've been traveling at becomes more manageable, or I become more adept at handling it. Either way, I'm able to manage my classes and have a social life as well. I don't think I would have been so busy if it weren't for Julian. He has numerous friends in a variety of circles, so we are always off to a music event or party. In some ways I miss my quieter life before all this socializing, but then I look at what I am experiencing, and remind myself that this is why I came here. The experiences are more than I imagined they could be. The only time I feel apprehensive is when Julian hangs out with certain friends who like to party. He drinks too much, or smokes something, and then he is not the man I know. After one particular party he went overboard and threw up in his car as I was driving him back to his place. I told him I would not go out to these parties any longer, if he's going to continue to act this way. His drunken frame, leaning on me with the weight of a dead man, swore up and down that he will stop.

My mother announces that we have to go out for a celebration on November twenty-third, which is my birthday. She says that it's a big occasion to turn twenty, so she wants to mark the turning point with a family dinner. She casually asks, "Why don't you bring that young man, um, Julian, along. Your dad says he's very nice." I suddenly realize that, although we've been dating for a few months, I have never had him meet my mother. She continues, "I guess you've been spending a lot of time with him, so I'd like to meet him, too." I blanche at the thought of dragging Julian along to a family dinner, but then again, his presence might be one of the only redeeming parts of the evening. "Well, he's really busy with school, but I'll ask him." She seems happy enough with my response, so she let it be.

The evening of my birthday dinner arrives, bringing with it the first snow of the season. It is light, and dances on the wind before settling down in nooks and crannies around the outside of the house. I have left the choice of restaurant up to my mother, as it makes little difference to me. I call Hannah One to make sure she is coming. Another bright spot in the evening, and to be honest, I want *her* to meet Julian. I have spoken so much about him to her, I think it's time they meet.

Julian shows up wearing a clean pair of dark dress slacks and a jacket, with a dress shirt that is undone at the neck. He looks relaxed, comfortable and very handsome, even with his wave of brown hair somewhat disheveled. I'm nervous about this evening. Up to this point we haven't really talked about our relationship. We haven't *done* anything, other than kiss and hold hands. It isn't that Julian doesn't try to do more, but I say that I'm not ready for *that* yet. He tries to understand, but I know he is disappointed.

My mother enters the living room and offers her hand to Julian. "It's so nice to meet you, Julian. I hear you have been very busy with your studies, just like Hannah. What are you studying?" He shakes her hand and launches into a small description of what his academic stream consists of, to which my mother asks appropriate questions and makes interested noises. I can't tell what she is thinking. My dad walks in the front door, after wiping a stray bit of snow off the van, and announces that we should get ready to leave, as we have to swing by to pick up Hannah One on the way to the restaurant. Julian looks at me quizzically, "Hannah One?" Oops, I forgot to mention her name. I usually refer to her as *my grandmother*, so this is the first he's heard her name. "Yes, my grandmother, she's Hannah One, so I guess I'm Hannah Two." He laughs, smiling at my parents. "Well, if Hannah One is anything like Hannah Two, I'll be her number one fan!" My father chuckles, but my mother wears a skeptical look, like she knows she is being fed a line, and surprisingly, I have the same expression on my face.

The restaurant is one of a chain. The type where you can go to any location anywhere on the planet, and find the identical décor and menu. We are seated at a table that has been reserved, and our waiter presents us with dinner specials and all the usual rigmarole that waiters do. I locate some vegetarian options on the menu by the cheerful green leaf they so kindly placed beside the description of the entrée. My mother always checks before making a reservation, to make sure that the menu includes vegetarian dishes, and I appreciate her effort to support me.

Dinner goes smoothly, aside from the noticeable tension between my parents. It seems that any little thing pushes them over the edge from civility to a passive-aggressive tone in a blink. The rest of us ignore it the best we can. Hannah One engages Julian in the most animated conversation about the Group of Seven, which I thoroughly enjoy being a spectator to. Creative minds need other like-minded energies around to feed them, or they starve to death from the mundane. I smile, as they obviously feed off each other's creative energies. My mother has offered me a chance to have a glass of wine. I am legally allowed to have one, but I decline. I feel that alcohol is not a substance my body will ever take kindly to, so I decide avoidance is the best course of action. She merely shrugs and orders herself a glass of wine. Julian decides to have a glass as well, to *keep my mother company*, he whispers to me. I say nothing, but hope he doesn't overindulge.

After dinner is over we all climb into the van. Julian and I sit in the middle row on the bench-style-seat, with Hannah One nearest the door. She wants to continue her conversation with Julian, so has refused the front seat my mother proffered. I sit in the middle with Julian on my left. He reaches out and takes my hand. Then, strangely enough, Hannah One reaches out and takes my other hand. Julian looks down and laughs, quietly saying, "So, I have competition?" She chortles and squeezes my hand, as if conveying the message, "Oh, I like this one!". I smile, and feel very contented.

We drop Hannah One off at her house. I watch as she walks up the steps and enters the front door, then uses the traditional porch light flash as a signal that all is well here. As she opens the door to wave at us, the light from within spills out and pours down the steps, like a lighthouse beam. It looks warm and inviting, and something inside me wants to be there, with her, in that light.

The remainder of the drive is quiet, so I simply look out the window and watch as the world passes by. It was a nice evening in some ways. I loved seeing Julian conversing with Hannah One. It reminds me of the way he and I talk together. Our conversations are animated, and chock full of things to chew on, intellectually. I think part of my attraction to him is this constant repartee. He reminds me of Hannah One, in that we can spar in our discussions and yet find common ground on so many points. It makes my mind breathe and expand from exertion. It feels invigorating.

We pull into the driveway and I ask Julian if he wants to come in for a while. My parents ignore our conversation, simply mumbling their good nights and exiting the van without looking back. He sighs and says, "It's been a nice evening. I like your grandmother, Hannah One. Wild, you guys are like the same person, only a generation apart. I'd like to see her again, she's really great." He turns his head to look out the window. We sit there, feeling the van's heat dissipate. I shudder, as I'm wearing a thinner coat than I really needed for this cold night. It is a full minute before he speaks again. "I think I will probably hit the road. I have that essay due, and I need to study for exams." He sighs again and reaches over to put his arm around me, and pull me closer. He leans in and kisses me. It is a long lingering kiss. There are a lot of words in this kiss that he leaves unexpressed. An unspoken passion, an unspoken feeling of connection and need for continuity of this bond. I respond, but instinctively withdraw after a minute. I know it can't lead anywhere tonight. He takes a breath and looks at me, uttering, "Yes, I definitely need to study if I'm going to pass that Canadian History exam in a week. And this," indicating our kiss, "isn't helping. Happy Birthday Hannah!" He dislodges himself from me and reaches out to open the door. I take his hand and smile, saying "I'm a really good study buddy, in case you ever need one!" He laughs and pulls the van door open. I feel the cold night air attack my body, so I quickly exit the van to stand in the driveway, and watch as he crosses the slippery drive to get into his car. I wave good bye as he backs out and speeds away. As I watch the tail lights disappear up the street, I suddenly realize how conflicted I feel about Julian. He has a beautiful sensitive nature that I love, but there is some small corner of him that holds his darkness, and it is not somewhere I want to go. Do I want to count on the hope that he will not venture to the darkness and pull me there with him? Do I want to try to help him with whatever internal struggle he may be waging with himself? Do I care enough to travel this road with him, or am I denying the truth, that he may not be right for me? Too many questions, with no easy answers. A sudden shudder makes me realize just how cold I am, standing there in the driveway as the snow filters down, light and feathery. I turn and dash towards the warm house, dragging my thoughts with me.

No birthday is complete without a celebratory "date" with Mark. Every year on our respective birthdays we go out and have a nice dinner and talk the night away. Ever since we began university it's becoming more difficult to find time to get together, so I'm really looking forward to our night out.

Mark meets me at the restaurant. We order our food, and Mark orders some wine. The waiter asks for identification from both of us. It's the first time I have had to show my card to prove I am over nineteen, and even though I said I have no intention of having any wine, the waiter brings two glasses with the carafe, anyway.

Mark begins the conversation with an excited tone. He loves his new life at university. It gives him the chance to begin fresh, not having to hide his true self. Now he feels free to shed his mask and join in the world on his terms, as much as possible, and it makes him shine. He tells me, in great detail, about a group of friends he made on campus. They get together as often as university life allows, and go out dancing, or simply hang out to drink and party. Mark said the first time he danced with another man it was like coming home. He almost cried. He's so happy, happier than I have ever seen him. I smile to see the light in his face return. I ask if he has met anyone special, and he laughs. "Hannah, there's no way I'm tying myself down right now! I'm having way too much fun!" I caution him to be careful, both emotionally, and physically. He assures me he's alright and knows how to take care of himself. His sense of freedom is something I almost envy, because I struggle daily to balance the duality of my own existence with the world. My question is, if I continue to allow my Alternate a voice in my daily life, will it not influence or even diminish my own human emotional reactions? My Alternate viewpoint often hinders me, and it's frustrating. And yet, even if I told people about being an Alternate, it doesn't change the fact that I am the one who needs to find the balance between my human mind and my Alternate's perspective on things. Mark's new outlook on life is something to celebrate, and so, I rejoice in his new found sense of self.

Mark, after his animated description of his life now, looks at me directly and asks, "Well? Tell me all about *him*!" I make a blank face like I don't know the *him* he is referring to, but he lets out an exasperated huff. I grin and begin my own diatribe. "Well, Julian is pretty great. He has a way of seeing things that mirrors my own, so we get along really well. Hannah One loves him!" Mark rolls his eyes like this news is a surprise. Mark loves my grandmother, and she him. She has a wonderful way of seeing the light in every person she meets, and when Mark told her his news, she simply hugged him and said, "Love knows no skin colour, no age, and certainly no genitals. It's all good, when it's love!" and the two of them laughed. Mark said he was so happy to have the love and support from *both* of the Hannahs in his life.

I look down at the table for a moment before continuing, for I'm not sure what to tell Mark about Julian. So many wonderful images cross my mind, but the dark clouds also make themselves known. "Hannah, come on, tell me something juicy! What's he like in bed?" He laughs because my expression is one of abject horror. "Mark! Lower your voice, please. That's not something I'd ever talk about, even with you. Let's change the subject." He looks upset that his joke has misfired. "Oh, sorry Hannah, I was only joking. It isn't something I'd *ever* want to picture anyway, it's like thinking of your sister having sex. Oh, dear god, get out of my head!" He grimaces as he bangs his head with his hand. I can't help myself and chuckle a little. He leans forward and whispers, "*Miss Priss* has *not* left the building, so watch your remarks young man!" *Miss Priss* was the character I'd bring out at camp when he and the boy campers would get a little too lewd around my female campers. Sounding awfully similar to my own mother at times, I would change my voice to sound older and admonish the campers for being vulgar. It made them laugh, but it would also diffuse the sexual tension occurring between the two groups of bored teenagers. Miss Priss came in handy quite often.

Our food arrives, which gives me a slight reprieve from discussing Julian any further. Mark pours out the last of the wine into his glass, but not before offering me some, for the umpteenth time. I shake my head. He jokingly says he is disappointed that I won't drink wine at all, because he bought me a bottle of really expensive select wine as my birthday present, and obviously it was a waste of money. I laugh, knowing full well he didn't buy anything for my birthday. We have a pact about gifts; we don't exchange them, not on birthdays or Christmas. Neither of us ever has money, so we decided what money we do have we'd spend on a good meal and a gab. At the mention of a gift, I recall that I did actually want to ask Mark his opinion on what to get Julian for Christmas. The holiday is fast approaching in about four weeks, and I still have no idea what I should buy. This is another first to cross off the list in my "Firsts Book"; having a boyfriend at Christmas (or at any time of the year, for that matter). I need the gift to be just right, not too serious, but not a joke either. I have no clue what will fit the bill.

I dab my mouth with my napkin and place it back in my lap before posing my question, "Um, so, I need to buy Julian a Christmas present. Any suggestions? And keep it clean," I add for good measure. He had just raised a forkful of food to his mouth, so he ponders my question while chewing. After he swallows, he takes another sip of wine before answering. "Well, let's see. He likes art, music, books... the same as you, pretty much. What would you want to buy yourself for Christmas? Just reverse that idea and give it to him." I look at him sceptically, but then consider it for a moment. "That's not half bad. We do have similar tastes in all those things, so what would *I* like to receive?" It's my turn to pop a forkful in my mouth, and consider the possibilities. Mark continues to eat, but has one eye on me as I give it some thought. "Well, oh yes! I know the perfect book. I haven't mentioned it to him, but I think it's an amazing book, about the life of Tom Thomson, who happens to be one of my favourite painters from the Group of Seven. Julian loves his work too, so we both drool over the paintings at the Art Gallery. This book has all his works in it, including his Algonquin drawings. It also talks about the rest of the group and its history. It's a fascinating book! I'm actually surprised he and I haven't talked about it together..." I trail off as I glance at Mark, who seems more interested in the dessert menu than my idea of a Christmas present. "Oh yes, that sounds, snore... I mean that sounds good. Guess I was thinking more along the line of edible panties or black lingerie!" I lightly whack his forearm and he scowls, but I know it doesn't hurt. "Miss Priss is back in the building!", I announce, and he grins.

Eleven

December brings a noticeable change in my sleeping habits. I'm not sleeping well due to these vivid dreams I'm experiencing; it feels like I'm in a continually wakeful state, with people in the room carrying on conversations around me. I am so deeply involved in these visions, yet upon waking I can't recall any of the details of the conversations. Sometimes I see colours. Other times I'm in the body of an animal scurrying along the forest floor, or a bird soaring in the clouds. But more often than not, I simply hear disconnected voices, like eavesdropping on a conversation in the next room. Sometimes the voices seem to be attempting to communicate with me directly. At other times, there are so many voices I wake myself up yelling for them to be quiet. The first time I yelled out, I heard my dad call out from his bedroom, "You okay, Hannah?" I was disoriented, but not frightened, so I merely replied with a reassuring, "Yup".

The following morning my mother asks me if I had eaten anything unusual the day before, because she had read that eating unusual food, especially late in the day, can cause bad dreams. I skeptically dismiss her claim. After a few of these nightly outbursts, no one pays me any attention. I am however, becoming more and more irritable, as the lack of sleep is wearing me out. With winter exams and other final assignments due before the Christmas break, I feel a lot of pressure. I have always tried to keep myself healthy and well rested, but somewhere in my mind I know

I have experienced flashes of dreamlike memories throughout my life, like some stranger visiting me, or being in a place I know I've never been before. These interactions are really beginning to take a toll on me.

Julian notices, of course. I snapped at him today, and that was enough for him to see I'm not myself. Real arguing is not a bridge we have come to, yet, although I did lay down the law once about his drinking. This overtiredness is making our relationship a bit tense. He asks if I'm feeling alright; do I feel a cold coming on, or something? I'm so tired I simply utter, "I'm hearing too many voices when I sleep, that's all. They won't let up, and I'm so tired of being talked *at*." He nods, but says nothing. When I think about it, what would you say to someone who basically just pulled a *Joan of Arc* on you? *Hearing voices? Oh, that's too bad, hope they shut up soon.* It surprises me when Julian, after a reflective moment, replies, "I heard about this holistic healing centre from a friend who is into all sorts of alternative therapeutics. I think he said it was on Greenland Street. Do you remember meeting Jackson?" I shake my head. Julian has so many friends, I have trouble keeping track of them all. "You should call that place to see if they can do something like, oh, I don't know, clear your chakras or something equally crazy!" He laughs at the apparent absurdity of it all, but it makes me think. I mentally make a note to call The Healing Centre when I have a minute to myself.

My appointment is set for ten in the morning, and I arrive a few minutes early to get my bearings. I walk through the front door of the Centre, and immediately feel a sense of *energy*. Two women sit in big arm chairs in an alcove off the main area, looking at books and talking quietly to each other. They look up and smile when I enter, but go back to their conversation. A woman appears through an open doorway to the right of the main entrance. She is wearing jeans and a t-shirt that reads, "You are here" with a large image of the Earth under the letters. She has long black hair that is streaked with purple highlights. She has sandals on her feet. You couldn't find a more stereotypical-looking hippie image than what stands before me, but she has a sense about her, and I feel an instant spiritual connection to her. She smiles, extending her hand, "Hi, I'm Grace Chaplin. You're Hannah, right?" I take her hand; it's warm, and I feel a small vibration of energy go through me. "Hi Grace. Yes, that's me. The one with the voices in her head." She laughs and motions for me to follow her into a treatment room. It's dimly lit, has a long, cloth covered cushioned massage table in the centre of the room, with two small chairs lining one wall. A small table in a corner holds a cd player, various gongs, tuning forks, chimes and crystals. She indicates I can sit on the massage table or the chair, so I choose the chair. She seats herself in the other chair and, still smiling, waits for me to talk. I start telling her about my lack of sleep because of these dreams and the voices I hear talking *at* me. She nods, but doesn't interrupt me. I continue on, with more details about my dreams, and what colours I see behind my eyes at times. When I finally feel like I have shared all the information I can, I glance at her long enough to catch an expression of awe. It is only there momentarily, and then her normal smiling face sets itself up again. She reaches out and takes my hands and, still remaining silent, closes her eyes. She seems to be somewhere far away. Then I feel tingling in my hands, and it spread up my arms, making my muscles twitch. She breathes deeply and opens her eyes, releasing my hands. The twitching stops. "I think your energy centres are blocked. I sense a great conflict inside you, and this blockage is hindering you from resolving it. I can help shift this blockage, and then we can work on the other issues." She stands up and points towards the table. A little hesitantly, I ask, "What will this session involve? "

She describes *Reiki* as the art of moving energy, and says to think of this energy as water; she is a faucet, and I am the basin into which the energy flows. I am not unfamiliar with the movement of energy and the term "Reiki" coined by humans. I am amused by her simplistic metaphor, but it is certainly an effective image that could help humans understand the concept more clearly. I just wonder how deep she will travel inwards, and if she might unearth my Alternate while exploring my energy connections. She has me lie down on the soft quilted fabric that covers the table. The pillow is also soft, yet I hardly notice it cushioning my head. She pulls another warm sheet up over my body. She takes a few steps over to the small table and pushes the start button on the player. The tolling of soft gongs and low chimes echoes in the room, and far-off wind chimes resonate quietly. It creates a peaceful slate of noise that seems to be sound, music and energy in one, but without intruding on conscious thought.

    I lie there and close my eyes. I need no further direction, as I immediately relax, and Grace senses that. She takes a few deep breaths with her hands poised about four inches above my feet, and then slowly begins to gently guide her hands up my covered legs. She continues further up my body, taking shallow cleansing breaths as she works. The motion is not unlike wiping the floor with a cloth, only the cloth never touches the floor. She works her way from my feet up to the top of my head. She never utters a word; the only sound is the rhythmic chime of a light gong, and her breathing in and out, as she moves the energy through me. I can feel myself lighten up, almost like I am leaving my physical form.

I see the forest floor, like in my dream, only this time it is my own body that lies on the ground. I feel the tender shoots of grass beneath me. I feel the roots of the grass reaching down to drink from the soil and get fed. I feel my own roots dig deep to also drink from the soil, while feeling the sun shine on my face. Another deep breath from Grace, and I am flying over the Earth about ten feet high, as a dragonfly, wings of gossamer, whispering to myself as the breeze carries me; "Trust in the Power of Light". I feel the light breeze carry me higher, as I become the wind itself, and I am above the trees, fluctuating with the pulls of energy from the earth, the sun and the stars. Waves of colour fill my eyes. Yellows and greens dance like licks of fire, and melding together, slowly becoming a rich shade of blue, that is like the night sky. I feel myself blend with the colours, the sky, the stars, the earth. I see myself call out to the stars, as I did in my dream on the beach, only to have them blink back at me, signaling that home is but one breath away. The blue veil begins to descend and I feel myself come to rest on nothing but air. The energy swirls and embraces me, like a familiar friend, and I feel love.

I don't know how long I have been lying on the table, but I begin to sense it is time to return, so I slowly come back to the *Now*, and open my eyes. Grace takes one last breath, her hands coming to rest at her sides. "How are you?" she asks. I have no words. I have no way to express my experience, so I simply nod my head and attempt to sit up. "Take your time. You've had a good session; cleared a lot of shit, that's for sure." She comes around to the far side of the room and sits down in the small comfy-looking chair. I sit up and swing my feet over the side of the table, but don't try to stand. I still feel disconnected from my body, so I don't quite yet trust my legs and feet.

Grace sits quietly with her eyes closed, as I sit regaining my senses. She takes another deep breath and exhales. She opens her eyes, stands up and smiles at me. "Well, that was a good session. Do you want to try another one next week?" I blink at her as if I'm seeing her for the first time. I laugh for some reason. The emotions running through me are vast and differing. An absolute joy and sense of freedom glows inside me. *Of course, I want to do this again, are you kidding?* I swallow and say, "Yes, I think that would be good. But I'm still wondering what am I supposed to do about the voices at night, keeping me awake?" Before Grace walks out of the room, she simply turns her head, and over her shoulder comments, "Oh, those. Just tell them to be quiet and go away! That usually works for me!" She laughs, and goes in search of her appointment book.

Twelve

Christmas is fast approaching, and I'm happy to have Julian's gift organized. I'm knee deep in exams, and due dates for final papers loom over me, so there is little time for thinking about much else. My last day of classes is December fourteenth. Julian mentioned that his mother has invited us for dinner on the fifteenth. His tone, when telling me this, was less than enthusiastic. He never really talks about them, so I have no idea what to expect. We decide that we will exchange our gifts that evening, as well.

His parents' house is located in an upscale community, just north of the central hub of the city. The streets are long and winding, lined with ancient trees, bare of leaves now; tall pillars marking the way. Trees sleep in winter, just as humans sleep at night. I look up at these tall gentle giants as we pass, and wish them a good rest. As we drive along, Julian notices me looking out at the trees and says, "The houses on this particular street are over one hundred and thirty years old. These trees were planted at the time the houses were built. There is character to this neighborhood that you won't find in other suburban communities, especially ones that are owned by developers. They plow everything down and build as many houses or condos on site as possible, and screw the landscape. I hate those places; I'll never live in a place with no mature trees." My thoughts exactly. I turn my head and reply, "Yes, I find it hard to comprehend why some humans have to assault the

Earth so harshly and irrevocably just to gain wealth. In the end it makes no difference, rich or poor, we all move on, and you don't take it with you. There are plenty of ways to make a living without killing trees and soil in the process." I see Julian nod in agreement, but I also see a slight hesitancy, and wonder if I have touched a sore spot. By the look of it, his parents must have money to live in this neighbourhood, so it's possible I just inadvertently insulted them.

We reach the house and now I see why he was hesitant to agree. The driveway is long and loops around to the front of the house. The garden in front is big enough to be its own park. Even in winter, I can tell it is well manicured and luxuriously rich of foliage. The house is not overly huge, but obviously what some call *manor-like*. The two-storey brown brick home is covered with dried ivy vines that snake around white trimmed windows, and the cobblestone walk that leads to the bevelled cut glass inserts by the front door simply reeks of times past. The house must be very handsome looking in the summer. Several windows are lit from within; some have Christmas lights, twinkling in the dark of night. The large white painted front door hosts a huge evergreen wreath that is decorated with red and gold ribbons and holly berries. I can faintly pick up the smell of the drying boughs as we get nearer.

Julian takes my hand as we make our way up the steps to the front door. Just before he knocks (yes, he knocks), he squeezes my hand gently, almost as if he himself needs reassurance. The door is opened by an older woman, who exclaims, opening her arms, "Julian!" She is dressed in a gold-coloured angora sweater, with cream-coloured slacks. Her jewelry clangs around like chimes as she hugs her son. Large gold bracelets and hoop earrings are in danger of catching on Julian's wool scarf. The woman disengages herself, and sets her sights on me. Her hazel eyes are tepid in warmth, and the skin around them appears somewhat drawn, in concern. She has a large mane of blond hair that she wears short and puffy on her head, not unlike gold candy floss. "You must be

Hannah. It's so nice to meet you." She extends a ring covered hand to me. I pull my wool mitten off my cold hand and gently shake it. Her skin feels dry and somewhat sandy, with age, but her hand is much warmer than mine and she pulls away quickly as she reacts to my cold fingers touching her. Her face is well made up, which makes me feel a bit under-done. I don't wear makeup because it hurts my eyes and I don't like it. I am who I am, like me if you want; I don't need to paint myself up.

"It's nice to meet you too, Mrs. Halliday." She motions for us to come inside. "Oh dear, please, call me Maude." She replies as she shoos the man, who had been standing behind her, back into the foyer. He is tall, in his early fifties, with dark black hair streaked with bits of grey that run from his temples to the back of his head. He has a large frame, and broad shoulders, indicating a football player past. He steps around Maude and comes up to me, extending a meaty fist for me to shake. "Hey there. I'm Gerry. Gerry Halliday. Welcome!" He sweeps his arm wide to indicate his home is open to visitors. I take a second to glance around and notice the high ceiling, and the staircase that wraps around the back of the room. The centre of the foyer is filled with a large white artificial Christmas tree, ornately decorated in red ornaments. No other colour on the tree, only red. It looks like something you'd see in a home decor magazine, or possibly a horror movie. It has no personalized feel to it. In my house the tree has ornaments and lights of all shapes and colours. Some ornaments are cherished pieces from Hannah One, or my other set of grandparents, who had both passed on before I was born. Some ornaments are clay or popsicle stick creations I made during my first years in school. Other ornaments hold small pictures, like the one of Fred, our beloved Beagle. The lights are the typical Christmas colours, red, green and blue.

I feel Maude's eyes on me, so I turn and say, "What a lovely tree." She smiles and waves at the tree, replying, "Oh yes, it's the foyer tree. We love to decorate for the season." She turns and walks through a doorway on the left side of the entrance. I feel hands on my shoulders as Julian helps me remove my winter coat. I pull my feet out of my winter boots, and, with dismay, realize I have forgotten to bring shoes with me to change into. Julian notices my unease and smiles, as he takes his boots off as well. Together we make do with our stocking feet. He gently takes my hand again as we follow Maude into the living room. It is lavishly decorated with antique furniture pieces that are older than time itself. I would love to spend a day simply looking at each piece and learning its story. The carpet is lush and thick underfoot. Another artificial Christmas tree looms large in a corner of the room. This one is the traditional evergreen colour, and equally as stylish. It is covered in small white lights, but all the ornaments seem to be coordinated, and match each other. Again, there are no personal touches added to the tree. Somehow, it makes me sad. The thought that Julian doesn't have Popsicle stick ornaments and pictures of dead pets on a tree makes me feel like he is missing something. It is a beautifully crafted tree, no doubt, but about as personal as a form letter.

The dinner, as it progresses becomes a nightmare, one from which I cannot wake up. I am presented with a shrimp cocktail to start. This is followed by Cornish rock hen. Julian remarks to his mother that he had specifically mentioned that no *meat* is to be served to me. She dismisses the accusation with the simple, and often-used excuse, "Dear, shrimp isn't *meat*." And she emphasizes her point using air quotes around the word meat. "And chicken, well, who doesn't eat chicken? It's not *meat*." Her exaggerated expression is typical of people who don't understand the vegetarian or vegan choice. I sigh, but say nothing. I eat my salad and the vegetables on the side of my dinner plate, but leave the food with a face alone. I send a prayer of appreciation to the hen for her sacrifice. Julian looks mortified, but I get his attention and smile. "Besides," Maude continues, "You know you should have spoken to Miranda about this. I can't be expected to remember everything." She takes a sip of wine from an elegant goblet, and turns her eyes to fix on me. "Miranda is our chef. She is a wonderful cook, especially at preparing prime rib!" Gerry finally decides to join the conversation; "Oh yes! It's my favourite! It's too bad the doctor told me to cut down on the ol' red meat, or I'd eat it all the time!" He laughs and ham fists his wine glass. I am surprised the delicate stem doesn't snap in his big mitt. Julian glances at me and sees my discomfort with the direction of this conversation. He clears his throat, quickly launching into a new topic of discussion. "I may have a line on a summer placement. I'll be working in a research lab at the university. They're looking for students to examine specific areas of historic linguistics that may have had an influence on certain historical events over the last century. It should be fascinating, and will help me with my thesis next year." He smiles broadly. He is always happy when talking about linguistic anthropology. It is his passion, and it shows in every word he speaks. His mother looks a little displeased, uttering, "What? I thought we'd be doing the lake again this year! You love the lake! We will all have a chance to be together and meet up with the Simcoe crowd. This year we are hosting the opening weekend fête! You can't miss that!" As she speaks, her voice climbs higher and higher in pitch, until the last word she utters is barely audible, unless you are a dog. Julian thumps the table with his fist, a scowl suddenly appearing across his face, the like of which I've never witnessed before. "Mom, the debate is over! I am going to *work*. I want to do this; I need the money for next year." He unclenches his fist and lets it drop off the table. Gerry stares at his son with a hard expression. "Julian, you know we'll pay for whatever you need for school. I wish you'd stop this stupid *independence* thing." It is obvious that they have had this argument before, and Julian has stood his ground, but with the harsh expression Gerry wears, I could see how it may cause someone less determined to rethink their point. I would not want to be on the receiving end of his wrath.

Julian looks like a kettle about to boil, but he lowers his voice in an attempt to quell his anger. "Dad, I appreciate your offer, but like I said before, I want to do *this* on my own. I need to stand on my own feet for once, and feel like my own man." I am beginning to gain a different perspective of Julian. I believe his intention is admirable, as he wants to find his own way. But I feel uneasy, seeing his anger emerge so suddenly, and that he has evidently inherited this quick fuse from his father. Not being familiar with his relationship with his parents, I can only surmise that his utter frustration and anger is due to an ongoing struggle for his independence from his parents. By the look of it, they don't see the point in his desire to "be his own man". A little red flag raises itself somewhere in my mind, but I dismiss it as quickly as I see it waving.

The meal ends with a trifle heaped high with whipped cream, which I decline, indicating that I am full. Julian also says no thank you, partly because he wants to support me, but I also think he's lost his appetite. We sit and dutifully listen to his parents chat inanely about Christmas gatherings at various friends' homes, or the trip to Spain they have planned for March.

Finally, after the last after-dinner liqueur is served, the conversation grinds to a halt. I don't attempt to strike up any more discussions, and frankly I'm exhausted from the entire event. Julian focuses on the small liqueur glass in his hand, and makes no eye contact with anyone, a sullen look on his face. His mother takes a dainty spoonful of trifle, and continues to drink wine. Gerry, who seems oblivious to the tension in the room, makes "yummy" sounds as he finishes his trifle quickly, and then indicates he is in the mood for a cigar. Maude reminds him of her rule of no smoking stinky cigars around her, so he excuses himself to enjoy his cigar alone in the *smoking room*. I briefly wonder just how many rooms there are in this cavernous house, and if each one is designated a sole purpose. Later Julian explained that his mother had named many of the rooms based on what activity was to be done in each: the smoking room, the reading room, the breakfast room and so on.

I know Julian and I have a plan to exchange our gifts after dinner, but it seems impolite to leave his mother alone at the table. We sit and wait for her to finish her dessert. Julian takes another glass of wine, and focuses on drinking that, to the exclusion of all else. He has been carefully indulging in wine throughout the meal, and now I know I will be the designated driver later on. Maude puts the spoon down on the edge of the crystal plate, and dabs her mouth daintily with a Christmas-themed cloth napkin. She looks at Julian and says, "I think I'll leave you two now. I have some correspondence I'd like to finish in the study. Feel free to *hang out* as you kids say!" She giggles, clearly feeling the effects of the wine and liqueurs she has inhaled all evening. She rises and gently places her napkin on the table. Then she reaches out and gracefully hooks her newly refilled wine glass. Turning away from the table, she heads for the doorway. Before leaving the room, she turns, and with one well manicured hand delicately gripping the frame, she says; "It was so wonderful to meet you, Hannah. I hope you have a pleasant holiday season." Her parting words sound like something you'd read in a Christmas card from your insurance agent.

A middle-aged woman enters the room, carrying a large empty tray, and begins clearing the dishes. Julian rises and I follow suit, happy to be done with this ridiculous meal. Julian comes around the large table and takes my hand. He nods to the woman and says, "Thank you for all your help, Miranda." She smiles weakly, but does not look up from her task. I secretly hope that whatever money she is paid it is more than enough to cover the daily challenges I imagine she faces with such employers as Maude and Gerry.

Julian starts directing me out of the room while commenting under his breath, "I can't begin to say how sorry I am for tonight." He waits until we reach the foyer before continuing. "I should have warned you, but I didn't want to scare you off. My parents are who they are. I learned a while ago that I cannot change them. I can barely tolerate them, but as far as making them become persons I'd be proud of, well, that seems like a lost cause." He guides me across the wide foyer to a smaller room off to the right. It is once again tastefully decorated with yet another Christmas tree gracing a corner of the room. This one is silver in colour, with blue ornaments on it. I laugh and without thinking, comment, "Is there a room in this house that doesn't have a Christmas tree in it?" I expected Julian to laugh, but he frowns. "Maybe the downstairs bathroom." Then he laughs and hugs me. "My mother loves to decorate for the holidays. She doesn't actually *do* any of the decorating, but she is good at delegating it to Miranda, and the cleaning lady." I look at the tree and envision Miranda, that poor woman, having to cope with decorating numerous trees perfectly so each will please Maude.

We decide to stay at his parents' house to open our gifts. A little voice in my head said it would give Julian time to cool off before I make the uncomfortable suggestion of me driving us home. With Julian's quick temper, I am a little unsure how he might react to me wanting to drive, but I will endure his anger if it means we don't get into an accident. I stand, looking at the tree, as Julian retraces his steps to the foyer to retrieve the bags that hold our presents.

I pull my gift out of the bag while Julian does the same. We take steps towards each other, both of us grinning like silly kids, and extend our gift-bearing hands. We move over to sit down on a large burgundy and gold tapestry couch and face each other. "Who opens first?" I ask, almost giddy with pleasure. I just have the feeling Julian is going to love this book. I want to see his expression as he turns the pages and marvels at the artwork contained therein. "Why don't you go first? After all, "ladies first"." I frown, disliking that old expression. When I glance at him I see he is teasing, so I smile. "Okay, okay." I lift the beautifully wrapped gift from my lap, and silently note the similarity in size and weight to my gift. I carefully pull the ribbon and tear the paper off one end. I can tell it is a book. I tear the last of the paper off to reveal the exact same book that I have bought him. How in the world did this happen? We have never discussed this book, nor have I ever indicated that I wanted this book, yet here we are. Julian looks at my face and frowns, "You don't like it?" He sounds hurt. "Oh, no, no, no. I *love* this book! I just can't believe *you'd* get it for *me*. Thank you so much." Julian smiles, turning his focus to his gift. I am about to say something but he tears open the wrapping like a lion ripping into its prey. He blinks as he looks at the book. Confusion crosses his face at first, and then he smiles and begins to laugh. His laughter breaks the tension of the evening into tiny fragments that I see dissolving into thin air. I too, laugh, as we look at the matching books. Neither of us can say anything, so we simply sit on the couch, and smile at each other.

I finally clear my throat and say, "I'm so sorry about this. I can return it and get you something else." Julian clutches the book and shakes his head, "No way! I *love* this book! I *want* this book!" I laugh because he sounds like a greedy child wanting his toy. "Okay, that's fine." I smile, looking down at the shiny colourful cover and run my fingers over the artwork on the paper jacket. Julian notices the way I caress the book and says, "Well, let's get you a different book then. How about Harris or Macdonald? I know you like their work too." It's my turn to clutch the precious book to my chest. "No way! I want *my* book too!" And again, we start laughing. We sit on the couch side by side, poring over the pages, every so often making a remark about a painting or drawing we come across. It is one of the best Christmas gifts I've ever received. The rest of the world fades away while we sit in that small living room; the lights of the silver Christmas tree lending a shiny bluish-glow to all objects nearby, and reflecting off the gold tapestry couch, while the antique furniture hums with old memories, and seems to absorb the wonderful love that emanates from the two humans now nestled in the centre of it all.

Thirteen

To have a date on New Year's Eve is another first to add to my list. Other years have been celebrated either with a few friends or, simply staying in with my parents. This year it seems that everyone is doing the *date thing*. Mark has a boyfriend now, and Jamie is home from university with Neville, her new beau-in-tow, so it's been decided that we will go out for dinner, and then a night of dancing at a new club. How any of us can afford it is anyone's guess. I have been frugal with my earnings from the summer, so I'm able to pay my own way. Julian starts to object, then mentally calculates how expensive the evening will be, and decides to accept my offer. Regardless of his parents' wealth, he is still determined to be independent of their financial support. We picked a moderately priced restaurant that isn't too far from the club we will go to afterward, to ring in the New Year. It's also been decided that I will be the designated driver, since everyone knows I won't drink alcohol. I'm not happy about the prospect of driving a bunch of drunken people home, but since it's the cheapest and safest way to go, I agree. I ask my dad to borrow the van, and after the initial shocked look on his face fades, he reluctantly says yes.

The night is cold, the kind that goes right to the bone. But it's clear and dry. Julian leaves his car at my house, parking it in the driveway. My parents had said he could sleep on the *couch*. The emphasis on the word *couch* almost makes me laugh out loud. Of course, that's where he'll sleep. I'm not about to have sex with my boyfriend, for a myriad of reasons. Not the least is, just how unromantic would it be to have your parents possibly lurking in the vicinity.

Once Julian, Jamie, Mark and his new boyfriend Laurence arrive at the house, we all pile in to the van. The space of the vehicle is such that each couple has their own row. Mark and Laurence climb into the very back, Jamie sits in the middle, and has a seat open next to her for Neville. The passenger seat in the front is, of course, for Julian. It takes about ten minutes to drive to Neville's house. It's funny, Neville went to the same high school as Jamie and me, but the two of them had never connected there. He is a tall, handsome, muscular black man, with a smile that would melt icebergs. There is an indisputable warmth about him, and his laugh fills the room. It's no wonder Jamie is head over heels. He is studying environmental science at the same university that Jamie attends, and although they have no classes together, they, nonetheless, manage to sneak in moments throughout the day to keep connected.

Mark's date, Laurence, is extremely shy, with a big shock of beautiful blond hair. He is very tall, well over six feet tall, with piercing blue eyes. He is studying art at O.C.A. They had met at a mutual friend's birthday party, about three weeks before Christmas. His reserve makes me wonder what drew these two together, as Mark is the polar opposite of an introvert. I just wonder how long the attraction will last. Mark is smiling and laughing at Jamie, all the while holding Laurence's hand. It is sweet and wonderful to see him happy, so I dismiss my doubt with a shrug.

We have a noisy meal at the restaurant. The waiter is wearing streamers and a party hat, and tries to hide his disappointment at having to serve a bunch of university students. No big tippers here, is his consensus. We decide we will leave the guy a decent amount; after all, it could be a miserable night to be a server. I've heard acquaintances, who work as servers, say that it can be dismal, or it can be very lucrative, depending on the customers. After dinner we spill out onto the sidewalk and head for the dance club. I'm happy to walk a few blocks over to the club to get the cold night air into my lungs. Mark stumbles along, looking like he's already "feeling no pain" as they say, with Laurence holding his hand and keeping him upright. Jamie and Neville are about a half a block behind us, laughing loudly at some private joke. Julian attempts to keep pace with me, as but as he had kept up with Mark's alcohol intake, his movements are also a bit unstable. As we approach the club, the base is so loud, you can almost feel the beat of the music in your chest. Bright neon lights flash on a marquee reading, "The Place". This is a new dance club that opened in early October. I have never been to a club like this, so this is another first for me. Although not a fan of loud music that makes your heart cower in your chest from the reverberation, the atmosphere is electric and contagious. Jamie grabs my hand and laughs. "Shit, are we going to dance or what?!" She yells as if I can't hear her. Mark starts gyrating in the middle of the sidewalk, and all I can do is laugh. The man is going to scare Laurence away with his insane behaviour. Laurence reminds me of a Deer. You coax it slowly and calmly, and sure enough it will eat from your hand. From the look on his face, this Deer is looking for ways to flee back to the woods.

 I take hold of Julian's hand and guide him, and the rest of the motley crew, to the front door. A heavy windowless metal door swings outward, and the sound is deafening. The smell of old beer and body sweat wafts over us like a wave. The walls of the entrance hallway are black, with glow-in-the-dark graffiti painted all over them, like a city tunnel or train boxcar. The lights are dim, except on the huge dance floor where there is a large disco ball rotating slowly, with several spotlights aimed at it from various angles, making shafts of light bounce off each miniscule mirror. Speckles of coloured light whirl round the room like frenetic fairies. It is a place filled with the absurd. The bar area is lit by long blue neon lights attached to the wall near the ceiling, that stretch its entire length. Below the lights, behind the bar, the wall is a series of dart boards lined up in pairs, like some massive dart shooting range. I quickly count twenty boards. I glance up and see the DJ playing the heart-thumping music, housed in a cage-like booth overhead, which appears to be only accessible via a metal catwalk. I see a human holding a headphone to his ear and bouncing around as the music encases every single body in the place. There are no tables or chairs, only old wooden church pews that line the walls from one side of the room to the other. People are dancing and holding their drinks at the same time. Needless to say, the floor is very wet. The painted murals in the main room consist of scenes with people and city landmarks, including an old Red Rocket streetcar. It's bright red and yellow neon paint glows from the lights bouncing off the mirror ball. One wall has a painting of a man with a big black moustache, wearing a large white chef's hat, holding a tray over his head. The words "The Place" sit upright on the tray like he is about to serve the name, along with the pizza he just made, to some customers. Humans enjoy the absurd, and this decor is certainly an eye-full.

We make our way to the bar and everyone eventually orders their drinks. I'm drinking sparkling water. Once we have our drinks, we find a pew on the far side of the huge room and sit for a few minutes, taking it all in. By now, it's after ten, so it's getting packed. People are milling around in clumps, or dancing their souls off on the dance floor. The music continues to be eyeball-splittingly-loud, so conversation is impossible. We sit and watch the crowds of people, until Mark hears a song he loves and screams, jumping up, spilling most of his drink all over his hand. He laughs, lifting the remainder of it to his mouth and downing it in a few gulps. He throws his plastic cup on the floor and seizes Laurence's hand, dragging the tall blond onto the dance floor. Jamie and Neville place their cups gently on the floor under the pew, with hopes they don't get knocked over, and take off to the dance floor as well. Julian looks at me with a questioning expression, but I shake my head. I think somewhere in my brain I have decided I'm going to be the babysitter for the night, so I have to watch my charges, including their drinks. Julian shakes his head, as if reading my thoughts, and gently takes my plastic cup from my hand, placing it on the floor near the other drinks, and pulls me up to join the others. I'm not much of a dancer, but then looking around, I feel like I'm not alone in that category. Bodies everywhere are simply flinging arms and legs and hair this way and that, as the music carries them along. I find the beat and begin to allow my body to move along with it as well. Pretty soon I'm laughing and enjoying the loud crazy night along with my friends. Julian goes with Jamie to get another round of drinks, weaving their way through the throngs on the dance floor. Neville takes my hand and begins dancing with me, his long tall body lithe and expression-filled. I feel like a mannequin next to him. He notices my awkward expression, so he gently holds both my hands and helps me find the rhythm, just by swaying back and forth. I'm mesmerized by the motion. Dance is one human expression that conveys so much emotion; it's simply marvelous to watch. Dance can express happiness, sadness, grief or joy; it is used to connect spirit to the earth, and in return, there is a fusion of the dancer's energy to the Universe. Even a clumsy dancer connects to the energy. It is all in the intention.

As the midnight countdown approaches, I feel tired of the noises and the stuffy stale air inside the club, which makes my eyes dry and itchy. Everyone, including Julian, is very drunk, and having a great time, so I'm not going to be a wet blanket and suggest we leave. I know the drive home will be challenging enough with a vehicle full of rowdy drunk friends; I don't want to deal with *mad*, rowdy, drunk friends. We continue dancing, and when the DJ finally announces the start of the count down, we all stand in a clump and shout the numbers together. At the stroke of midnight everyone yells, "Happy New Year!" hugging each other and kissing, as tradition would have it.

Julian kisses me long and hard, his mouth tasting of stale alcohol. I am not thrilled by this exchange of saliva, but at the same time, his kiss causes a reaction to bloom in my gut, so I return his kiss with more enthusiasm than I might normally. He continues for another minute, before breaking the lip lock and nuzzling my neck. His hands are wound around me like a snake around a tree. He leans into me, partly because he's so drunk, but mainly to get closer. I allow him the lean, because I don't want him to fall over. I find his ear and yell into it, "Why don't we sit down?" He nods and drapes his arm around my shoulders as I lead the way to an empty pew in the corner. We sit down, but Julian keeps his arm around me, and brings his other arm to encircle me in a bear hug. "This is awesome, I love this!" He leans over and kisses me again. His hand drops down to rest on my thigh. I try to keep this kiss short, but he is on a roll now, and wants more. His hand starts sliding up from my thigh to my blouse. He cups my breast and lets out a moan that, even with the loud music blaring around us, I can hear. I freeze. This is not going to happen again. I'm not about to let a drunken man take advantage of me. It doesn't matter that I am in love with him, it just isn't right.

I take his hand and place it back on his own thigh, but like a rubber ball it bounces back to my chest. I break the kiss and yell, "No!" He looks at me with unfocused eyes, and says, "Come on Hannah, I've waited, like what, almost four months, it's gotta be soon, you know, gotta be..." he lets his head sag on my shoulder as he tries to paw me yet again. As I move his hand away, he grips my wrist in a very tight hold. I feel a sharp wrenching pain and yank my hand away as his grip loosens. A sudden flashback to having my hands pinned over my head makes me feel nauseous. His voice is loud in my ear, his breath hot and stinking of alcohol, "You owe me! Jesus, I've been, like so good, waiting and waiting, Christ, Hannah..." I stand up, making Julian topple over onto the floor. "What the hell Hannah! Don't be such a bitch!" He yells. He is looking up from where he lies sprawled on the floor, wearing the same angry, frustrated look he wore that night at his parents' house. The red flag waves so hard in my mind's eye, I can't ignore it this time. "No! Enough!" I yell again, my body rigid with anger and fear. I can't bring myself to look at him any longer, so I turn and make my way through the crowd to find Jamie. Yelling over the music, I tell her it's time to go. She sees that I'm upset, so she doesn't question it. I pull Neville's arm and yell into his ear, "Julian is over there," and I point across the room. "Can you help him, he's too drunk to walk by himself." Neville grins like the Cheshire Cat and lets out a huge laugh. He doesn't say anything, but makes his way across the room to retrieve his drunken comrade. I wave at Laurence, who is standing nearby fending off Mark's attempts to kiss him, and he nods in agreement. It is time to go.

 I reach the heavy metal door and open it to find myself washed in frigid cold air. It feels like coming up to the surface after being underwater too long. I gulp in a lungful of fresh winter air and begin to feel slightly better, but my throat hurts from yelling all night and my head feels heavy and sore. I make my way from the entrance, out of the path of exiting patrons, to stand on the far side of the walkway, and wait for everyone. Neville comes out first, his arm around Julian, holding him upright. Julian looks like he's been hit by a truck. He staggers as he walks, while attempting to carry on some sort of conversation with Neville, who simply agrees with whatever garble Julian utters, focusing on keeping him upright. He makes Julian lean up against the outer wall of the club as we wait for the others. Soon enough, Jamie comes bursting out of the door laughing loudly as she and Laurence drag Mark by the hands. Mark is also laughing, but Laurence looks fairly miserable. I get the feeling this will be the last time I'll be seeing Laurence. They spy the three of us and, laughingly, make their way over. I start walking towards the van, without so much as a comment or command to the group that they follow me. They fall in behind and loudly make their way the few blocks to the vehicle. Once there, I turn and say to Jamie, "I want Julian in the middle row with you, by a window, so if he throws up it's not on me or the inside of the van." She looks at me and giggles again. She wheels around and yells to the gang, "Okay, let's get our asses in the van before she leaves us behind!" Everyone laughs and begins piling in.

The drive home is awful. Jamie keeps trying to reach over from the middle row to play with the radio on the dashboard. "I need tunes! Shit, I can't reach the radio!" Suddenly music comes blaring out of Mark's cell phone. It's too loud and the distortion is horrible. He and Jamie sing along as the others simply sit, either with their eyes closed, or, in Laurence's case, looking for the emergency exit. As we make our way across the city, I finally hear him speak up from the back, "Hannah, my street is coming up on the right, you can drop me here, that's okay." Mark's face goes dark as he turns to Laurence, "You've gotta come back to Han's", he slurs. I pull the van over and come around to the passenger side to help Laurence climb over bodies to get to his freedom. I really can't blame him. I'd have abandoned ship too, if I could. He straightens up as he leaves the van and mumbles, "Thanks for driving us, night." He turns to walk away as quickly as he can. He disappears around the corner before anyone can say another word.

In the back of the van by himself, Mark starts to cry. I feel sorry for him, but part of me feels angry too. Laurence and I had both felt the need to defend our personal space tonight. I just know my sympathy lies, in this case, with Laurence, more so than with my friend. "He was gonna come back..." Mark wails away. "This was his first time... he wanted me to be his first..." again the wailing. It begins to make more sense to me as I hear this. Poor Laurence. I can't imagine a less sensitive way for someone to experience their "first time" than by being drunkenly pawed at. I swallow down the image that passes before me, remembering it like it was yesterday.

A few minutes later we pull into the driveway. Neville helps Julian out of the van, who is, at this point, very quiet and sullen. He is ready to crash and sleep it off, which I am more than happy with. Mark sits in the back, until Jamie reaches over the seat to try to coax him out. I am more than done with this evening, so I want everyone out of the vehicle and in the rec room without any more dramatics. I simply state, "Mark! Get out or you can sleep in the van tonight. Either way, I don't care." He makes his way out, still sniffing and takes hold of Jamie's hand, giving me a dirty look. I pretend not to notice. My throat hurts, my eyes hurts, my brain hurts. My heart hurts. I want my bed and the solitude of my room. As I get the front door unlocked, I turn and quietly say, "My parents are sleeping, so shut the hell up and go down to the rec room right away." Jamie giggles, but when she sees my stern expression she stifles her laugh. The lights have been left on so no one trips over anything in the front hallway. I know my parents are aware that I'd bring everyone back here to sleep it off, and sure enough the rec room is made up with two air mattresses on the floor, as well as the pull-out couch all ready for drunken bodies. Neville drops Julian on one air mattress, Mark curls up, still sniffing, on the loveseat in the corner, while Neville turns and grabs Jamie, landing in a heap on the pull-out. I return upstairs, lock the front door and turn out the lights. I can hear some murmurs from the rec room and then Jamie laughs. After that, it is quiet. I make my way upstairs, and finally close my bedroom door behind me. Flopping on my own bed, I feel the desperate need to shower, but I'm so tired I simply lie there until sleep takes me away.

Fourteen

I pry my eyes open to see the numbers nine zero nine beaming relentlessly at me from the cold impersonal digital face of my clock. I can't recall the time I hit the pillow, but I believe it was around two a.m. My mouth is dry, like I have eaten sand. I feel like I have a hangover without having consumed alcohol the night before. I begin to imagine how my friends in the basement must feel this morning. I have no sympathy. I stretch slowly and realize I'm still in my clothes from the night before. I roll to the edge of the bed and prop myself up. I slowly stand up and go to the window to look out at the backyard. The big tree stands quietly in the corner of the yard, waiting for spring. The sun shines down brightly, as if it has something to prove this morning. I squint from the blinding glare, turning back to face my silent room. I strip my clothes off and don some flannel pajamas. Comfort and relaxation are top priority today. I will have a shower later, after I have seen the basement occupants on their way. I venture out in the hallway and notice the other bedroom doors are still closed. It has been about a year since my dad moved into the guestroom, saying my mother was having some sort of sleeping issues, and preferred to sleep alone now. Quietly, I creep past the doors and down the stairs to the kitchen to make a pot of coffee.

As I watch the coffee maker take forever and a day to fill the large pot, my dad enters the kitchen, wearing a bathrobe over his pajamas, and the large warm-looking slippers I bought him for

Christmas. He smiles as he sees me. "Happy New Year, Hannah. Did you have fun last night?" Before he sees me scowl, I turn and reach into the cupboard for two coffee mugs. I quickly fix a small smile on my face before turning back to him and answering, "Yes, it was fun. Sorry about the mass casualties in the basement. I'll get them out of here soon." Dad laughs and says, "No hurry, I'm sure they will be feeling the pain this morning, so be gentle with them." I shrug and reply, "Well, it's their fault for over-doing it. I'm just glad no one threw up." Again, my dad laughs.

A few minutes later, he disappears up the stairs to his room, carrying a mug of hot coffee and a small plate holding a bran muffin he had heated up and slathered with butter and jam. Yesterday's paper is tucked under his arm. I fill my mug and head to the top of the basement stairs, and hesitate. Am I in such a hurry to wake them up, or can I just enjoy this first cup of coffee in peace? I turn back towards the living room and take a seat by the bay window. I look out onto the new world; made new by human standards of time, otherwise it is the same world as it was yesterday. I sit quietly with my coffee and turn my thoughts inward. How is this day going to play out? I'm still feeling angry and hurt by Julian's actions. I notice the skin around my wrist is a dark red colour. I rub it and it's sore, a soreness that reaches my heart and makes it ache. I feel my trust in him slip away like the mist at dawn as the sun's rays touch it. Drunken behaviour is like the Pandora's Box fable. Once the lid is opened by a human's unbridled drunken mind, many buried behaviours make themselves known. Things get said that cannot be taken back. Actions lead to situations that cannot be undone. Some might think that an "innocent" assault by a drunken boyfriend is not worth ending a relationship over, but I won't rule out this course of action. Doubts about his motives creep in and replace trust with questions. My belief that he respected me enough to let our relationship grow at a pace I am comfortable with, has been replaced by insecurity and suspicion. The possibility that I'll have to compromise my sense of self, just to be the type of person *he* wants, is something I am not prepared to do.

My head hurts as I try to reason with my feelings about Julian. I begin traveling down the road of excuses for his behaviour; *he was drunk, he didn't mean it, I know he cares, he just wants me to be more affectionate, I'm overreacting to his anger...* but my mind slaps me as best it can, saying, *there's no excuse.* You say no, it means no. His anger manifesting itself in such a way is not a behaviour I can condone.

I take a sip of coffee and look out the window again. A Crow sits in the tree branch, surveying the ground for any bit of food to peck at. His shiny black wings seem to absorb the sun and reflect it outward, as he shimmers. I want to be that bird this morning. His only concern is basic survival; food, water and warmth. Human relationships are so convoluted; the baffling complexity of it all scares me. There is no absolute here, it is all so connective, but so tangled. Love can be attached to hurt, anger with disappointment, and forgiveness with distrust. I finish my coffee and stand up. I want everyone to go home. Hannah One is coming over later, and I want to shower and then have some time to relax. If everyone sleeps until noon and then hangs around, I'll never be rid of them. I take my cup back into the kitchen, and check to see how much coffee is left in the pot. I am going to need more java to arouse four hung-over friends. I decide to serve what is left and then make a fresh pot. I venture down the stairs, uncertain of what I'll see in the rec room. Hopefully everyone is decent and no one has been sick. To my relief I see that the bodies, in various states of repose, are pretty much the way they were when they crashed the night before. Mark is lying on the loveseat, his long legs sticking uncomfortably out at one end. Jamie and Neville, still on the pull-out, look like some romantic movie couple with their legs and arms entwined as they sleep together. It almost makes me smile. Julian is curled up in the fetal position, a small bundle of blanket-covered misery on the air mattress. I can't look at his face.

I clear my throat and announce loud enough to wake the dead bodies, "Hey guys. Morning. I have coffee on the go upstairs in the kitchen. Get up now, get up. Time to go..." A few groans emanate from various corpses, but no one really makes an effort to rise. "Guys, you gotta get up. I got stuff to do, I want you to go..." no point in being subtle when talking to hung-over, brain-dead young people. Jamie opens her eyes and lifts her hand to wave to me; "Hi Hannah, shut up and go away." She snuggles her face into Neville's chest. As my not-so-subtle request seems to fall on deaf ears, I reach over to the table and pick up the TV remote, pushing the *on* button. A loud voice booms out from the television as a news anchor discusses ways to cure a hangover. How appropriate, I muse. This time it's Neville who groans, stretches, and rolls over onto his back. He opens his eyes and smiles at me. This man is full of smiles, full of joy that seeps out of his pores. He sits up and pokes Jamie. She grumbles and curls into a ball clutching all the blankets. He laughs and tickles her, making her shriek.

Mark is the next one to attempt to sit up. He must have slept crookedly, because he moves like an arthritic old man. He hunches over as he stands up. Slowly he stretches his arms up to the ceiling, unfurling his spine. He is the first one to speak, "Dibs on the can..." and he makes his way to the stairs and disappears up. I turn to see Julian moving slowly, stretching out his limbs as he rolls onto his back. He begins to sit up, and that is enough for me. As long as people are vertical I know it won't be long before the desire for coffee will drive them to the kitchen. I turn and leave the rec room without another word, leaving the television on.

Within about ten minutes everyone is up, and have a hot mug in their hands. They all sit around the living room sipping their coffees with little or no conversation occurring. I stay in the kitchen and make another pot. I can't even look at Julian this morning; I just want him to leave. Thankfully he seems somewhat embarrassed himself, and keeps quiet. He comes in the kitchen with his empty mug, placing it on the counter. He merely mumbles he is going to leave and that he'll call me later. I nod, but make no response. He hesitates before turning, as if he wants to say something more, but then decides not to, as he turns back to the living room to say goodbye to the others. He offers Mark a ride home, which he accepts. The two of them gather their shoes and coats and head out the door. A blast of frigid air pushes past them into the house. It is definitely a day for me to stay warm inside, and fume.

Jamie enters the kitchen with two mugs in her hand and begins to wash them, but I shake my head. I touch her arm and say, "Just leave them; I'll wash them up later. You guys can get going, that's okay." She frowns, asking, "Are you okay? I'm really fuzzy about last night, but I kinda remember something wasn't right. Do you want me to send Neville home so we can talk?" I pick up my mug and pour myself another cup as I reply, "No, that's okay. Something I just want to chew on by myself. Maybe later I'll call you. Hannah One is coming over too, so I just want to relax for a bit, maybe take a shower before she gets here." Jamie nods, but I can tell from her body language she is reluctant to leave. I ignore her hesitancy, taking my cup and walking out of the kitchen before she can ask any more questions. She turns and makes her way to the front door where Neville is waiting with two coats in hand. He smiles and says, "Thank you, Hannah, for letting us use your basement as a drop zone last night. I wish you and your parents a very Happy New Year." He grins, and I can't help but smile back. I wish them both a happy New Year before they open the door and another blast of arctic air blows in. Once the door shuts, I feel utter solitude creep over me. I carry up my coffee cup up the stairs and head back to my room.

I feel the day drift by as I lounge on my bed. I sleep for a while, but then decide to wash the cares of last night off my body in a hot shower. I get dressed and wait in my bedroom for Hannah One to arrive around three, for our usual New Year's Day supper with the family. I sit in my gloom, trying to pull myself together so I can have a pleasant meal with everyone. I have already decided to end things with Julian. The reality of actually saying the words to him is something I dread, but also something I long to get done. Finalizing it means I can move forward, and not look back.

As the face of the clock reads three, I hear the front door open, and voices in the front hall indicating the arrival of my cherished grandmother. I venture down the stairs and stand in the living room to welcome her. I see she is wearing her heavy-duty winter boots and a jacket that reaches down to her knees. A wise choice on a day as cold as this one. Once she has shed her layers, she turns to see me standing in the living room. As she is about to wish me a Happy New Year, she sees my face, and it sticks in her throat. Her eyes widen slightly, but she gives no other indicator that she can tell I am not myself. My mother is busy hanging up her coat, and my father has disappeared into the kitchen to put the kettle on. She gives me a hug, and whispers, "I can see you are feeling a bit off, can I help?" I pull back to look at her face and try to keep myself from tearing up. I look up at the ceiling and swallow. Hannah One takes my hand and announces, to no one in particular, that she wants to see my latest drawings, so we will just dash up to the bedroom and be right back. She spins me around and drags me up the stairs before I can blink an eye. My parents ignore us, as they are so accustomed to the two of us putting our heads together and plotting things, that this sudden move has little impact on them. As we enter my room she closes the door and leads me over to the edge of the bed. I feel such relief to be in my room with Hannah One, I never want to leave it. Hannah One sits beside me and takes my hand, but says nothing. I clear my throat, which is still sore from the shouting last night. "So, we all went out last night to a club. You know I was the designated driver, because, as usual, I wasn't drinking, but the others were, including Julian." I pause, wondering if I should just skip the details, or tell it like I remember and see her reaction. I glance at her, but she has a calm, non-committal expression on her face. I continue, "They all drank a lot, especially Julian. He got so bad he had trouble standing." It almost sounds like I am setting up the justification for his behaviour, by explaining just how drunk he was. I stop myself from this train of thought. "He made a move on me, actually he really hurt my wrist." I pull my sweater sleeve up to show the red bruising marks. "And then he called me a bitch because I wouldn't let him grope me in public, and because I'm not willing to have sex with him yet. It was horrible." I feel the tears on my face now, as I continue on. "He said that he'd been good waiting for me, so why wouldn't I put out now? He was so angry! Calling me a bitch! He really hurt my wrist!" The pitch of my voice gets higher as the scene replays itself in my head, and I feel my throat constrict. Hannah One's hand tightens on mine slightly, and I look at her face again. This time I see anger in her eyes. She speaks quietly, "How awful for you, my dear sweet girl. This must have been so traumatic." She wraps her arm around me and I collapse into her. I feel the world of hurt harbouring inside me slowly ebb away with each sob.

After a few minutes, I wipe my face with the edge of my comforter, making Hannah One grimace as she pulls a clean hanky out of her pocket. She hands it to me and asks, "What would you like to do now?" I swallow. "I am done. I have nothing but mistrust now. His anger seems to be right there, just under the surface, and it frightens me to think how easy it could emerge, especially when he's been drinking. No, I'm done." I look down at my hands, hands that he had kissed and held, and then my eye catches a glimpse of the book he had given as a Christmas present. I choke up, trying to ignore the knife that is slowly ripping down the centre of my heart, leaving it shredded and aching. I am drained of tears, leaving nothing but a dull throbbing ache behind my eyes. Hannah One sits patiently beside me, still keeping her arm around me like a shield. With her free hand she takes hold of my hand and gently clasps it before saying; "You are a strong, independent young woman. *You* make your life what it is. You are not defined by the relationships you have; *you* define yourself. I know how much this must devastate you, believe me, I know. And there is nothing I can say that will lessen the pain, so I won't even bother. All I ask is that you remember this; what *you* make of this human life is defined by the choices you make, and these choices can help you learn. Learning from everything, both good and bad, is one of a human's most precious gifts. When we learn, we grow, and that makes the journey more enriching." Her remarks are not lost on me. When I can, I will don my cap of reason and be able to see her point. Right now, that damn cap is getting blown off by the human emotional wind that blows everything around.

Hannah One stands up and heads for the bedroom door. She looks back at me and smiles sympathetically, saying, "What a mess you are my dear. If you'd like to avoid parental snooping, I can make an excuse for you to skip dinner. These menstrual headaches do come on very quickly." She winks as she leaves, closing the door quietly. I sigh heavily and flop back down on my bed. I am so glad for the respite from the parental inquisition I would have received if I came to dinner with swollen puffy eyes and a snotty nose. I close my eyes, feeling relief from the light.

My restless napping is interrupted by my stomach growling. I look at the clock, and realize it's almost eight o'clock. I didn't hear Hannah One leave. It's very quiet, which leads me to believe that my parents are in the basement rec room, watching television or reading. I take the opportunity to sneak down to the kitchen. I get a plate out of the cupboard and pile some leftovers on it before placing it in the microwave to reheat. When the microwave beeps in completion, I carefully take out the hot plate of grilled veggies and vegetarian meatloaf and sit down at the dinner table. With each bite I ponder my situation. The conclusion that I keep coming to is that it will be better to end things with Julian right away, on the phone, as I'm too nervous to do it face to face. With the inconsistency of his temper, I want to be safe. That way, the worst thing that might happen will be that he hangs up on me. I can live with that. I just hope he understands that I can't build a relationship that has mistrust and coercion at the heart of it. Now, having a full stomach, it gives me the courage to call him. I know that if I put it off it will eat away at me until I might be tempted to cave in and forgive him. I have to hold onto my resolve and remember that this relationship doesn't define who I am, or how I feel about my life and my choices.

It takes about four rings before he picks up. His voice sounds far away, as if he doesn't have the phone to his ear. It also sounds like he is half asleep. "Hey..." is all he can muster for a greeting. I swallow, and keep a picture in my head of him sprawled on the dance floor, looking at me with an angry expression. "Hi, it's me." As if he isn't already aware of that. "We need to talk. I'm sorry to say this, but I think that, after last night, I have decided that it would be better if we stop seeing each other. I just don't want a relationship where I don't feel safe and respected." There is a long pause on the line before he speaks. "Hannah, I know I was an asshole last night. But you gotta understand, that's not *me*! I've been under a lot of pressure, from my parents, from the profs, and then it feels like we aren't getting anywhere...." He trails off, and I realize he isn't really apologizing for the behaviour, but excusing it. He is trying to play the victim card, and I can't stomach what I am hearing. Before I can say anything, he continues on, "I am sorry that you feel like I don't respect you. But really? Haven't I been nice, and patient, and hey, I got you that book. That must mean something!" His voice is becoming harder, and I know that no matter what I say next, unless my words condone his behaviour and his excuses, he will not hear me. I try to stay calm, but I can feel my blood pressure rising. "So, you think calling me a bitch and crushing my wrist so hard it bruised, is the best way to show you care and respect me? Julian, you need to look at what is driving you down this destructive path. Own your behaviour and take charge of steering yourself to a better path." His laugh is full of disdain as he replies, "Well, Miss High and Mighty, get the fuck off your high horse with your stupid metaphors. I like to drink, it helps me relax, so what the fuck!? I won't have *anyone* tell me what to do, not you or my parents! Have a good life and hope the next guy you meet is a eunuch!" And then the line goes dead.

I hold the phone away from my face and look at it, as if I have never seen this piece of electronics in my life, and immediately drop it on the bed. No one has ever told me to fuck off before, and it stuns me for a moment. My shock is quickly replaced by anger. It begins as a slow burn in my feet and makes its way up, until I feel my fingers tingle and my chest burn and my face flush, and finally the top of my head feels like a volcano erupting. I want to scream, but I have to swallow it for fear I'll scare my parents to death. I pick up a random pillow and chuck it across the room. Throwing it is not even a bit satisfying. I grab the knob of my bedroom door and swing it open. I stomp down the stairs and head to the front door. I don't even notice my dad in the kitchen, until he says something. "Hey kiddo, hope you're feeling better. Where are you going?" He asks as he watches me angrily thrusting my feet into my boots and hastily zipping up my winter coat. "Need some air. Back soon." It's all I can say as I hold the volcano in check. I open the front door and march out into the frigid night.

Feeling the cold January air on my face is immediately soothing, and I stop in the driveway to take a big breath. I realize I have hardly taken a breath since dropping my phone on the bed. I take another deep breath and feel a bit light-headed, but the cold air in my lungs feels sharp and gives me a sense of clarity. I start to walk with no particular goal in mind. I just need to move. I see the odd person pass by, clutching their coat to them, bracing themselves against the cold. I don't experience the cold, or notice the darkness around me, with only the street lights to guide me along. I concentrate on breathing and walking. I leave my mind blank as I walk, too afraid to touch the anger or the furious thoughts that fuel it. Eventually I come to the park and start walking along the shovelled path. The street lights are fewer and dimmer here, and I take a moment to stop and look up at the night sky. Through the haze of city lights, I can see a few stars attempting to shine, but they seem resigned to the fact that city dwellers are not interested in viewing them, so their effort to shine is minimal. I take another deep breath. This time I feel something in my throat and before I know it I let out a huge scream. It isn't the kind of scream you hear women perform in silly horror movies; this scream is full of anger, frustration and even sadness.

Having purged myself with the ferocious scream, I turn and start walking back towards my home. There, standing about ten feet away, is a woman. She wears a light yellow-coloured dress that sways in some unfelt breeze, and her feet are bare. My initial surprise at seeing her standing there is instantly replaced with concern, as I view her bare feet. She must be lost, or homeless or something. I look closer, and then she smiles at me. I know that face. It is me.

I am so stunned I cannot move, or speak. She takes a few steps closer, and as the dim street light casts a glow upon her, I notice the streaks of grey in her hair and a few laugh lines around her eyes. She looks up at the night sky.

I always wonder why no one ever looks up at the stars anymore. Humans take them for granted, like they are something so commonplace, so banal, that they hold little reverence for them. It is sad, but then again, that is human nature. Humans often don't realize the value of something until it has passed, and is no more. Julian will, someday, come to understand that his ways damaged many of the possibilities he could have had for happiness. He was his own saboteur. You, Hannah, are strong, and growing in the Light. You need only remember to keep believing in yourself. Let this go, Hannah. There is more on the horizon, and you need only allow your boat to sail on to new experiences. Just remember to go with the flow.

The image begins to pale, but I call out, and she turns to me. "How am I seeing myself like this? I don't understand? How are you *here?*" She laughs gently, and whispers, as her image fades, *you will just have to keep flowing onward to find out!*

I stand alone in the park, with her words reverberating in my head. Suddenly feeling the cold on my face, I realize my toes and fingers are becoming numb. Avoiding my thoughts, as they are too jumbled and confused to figure out, I concentrate once again on moving my feet and breathing evenly through the wool scarf I have pulled up around my face. As I round the corner and see my house, I quicken my pace until the light of the front hallway beams at me through the door's window. I open the door and heave a heavy sigh, as if I have trekked a great distance hauling a horse on my shoulders. I sink down to the floor, still in my boots and coat, and finally notice the tears that are running down my cheeks.

The following five months of school with limited socializing brings me to the end of my first year at university. I heard, through a friend of a friend, that Julian suddenly switched majors in the new semester in January, and is now focusing on a business degree. I was surprised to hear that, as he has been so passionate about what he had been studying. This same friend mentioned that he was offered a lucrative position in his father's construction business, if he changed his stream. Julian had always said he didn't want to build houses where once there were farmers' fields. I never saw him, thanks to the fact that he had to change campuses when he changed his major. A classmate of mine also mentioned she saw him at a pub crawl one night in the early spring. He was very drunk and making a fool of himself over some girl he wanted to dance with. The memory of New Year's Eve flashed in my mind, and I nodded, knowing full well how that must have looked. I secretly wished him well, as I know he will face many disheartening challenges through his life. I decide to turn my focus onto myself, and what my future journey can be, knowing it is completely by *my* choice, and not by anyone else.

Fifteen

There are spans of time in one's life that appear unproblematic, without the huge waves in the water that often make you change course or veer from the projected target. You float along with your paddle in the water, moving it gently, according to which way the soft current pushes your boat. It is only when you look up from your paddle, that it may actually surprise you to see that the shoreline is close at hand.

I spent four years with my paddle in the water and my eye fixed upon the bow of my boat, not interested in looking around to admire the scenery, or even look into the water. My attention was wholly on academics, because that's where I felt safe and sure of what I was looking at, what I was delving into. Human relationships were, unless already grandfathered into my realm, off the books. I had no interest in making close friends of my classmates, and although I was congenial enough, I never went to parties or the other events that are a mainstay of university life. Romantic relationships definitely held no appeal.

At the age of twenty-four, I have now reached certain academic marker points, but in that quest I abandoned many others, including the development of any close personal relationships with those I spent my days with. I still keep in touch with Mark and Jamie, but our lives are leading us so far apart it is a challenge to keep the connection.

My university graduation is tiresome, but necessary. It is a replay of high school, with my parents and Hannah One in attendance. We have had a nice meal, and now make our way to the auditorium where the ceremony is to be held. Hannah One takes me aside for a moment before the ceremony begins and whispers to me, "I could not be prouder of you." She smiles and squeezes my arm. A simple statement, but it means the world to me.

Today I begin full time hours where I have been working at part-time throughout university. The first summer after I began university, I was given the opportunity, thanks to Grace, to work in a locally owned bookstore. Grace had made friends with a couple through her meditation group. They mentioned that they needed help running the store. Grace arranged to introduce me to Gwen Bentley, a woman in her late forties, with short greying hair, bright intelligent blue eyes and a passion for reading that led her to opening her own bookstore. Evelyn Gary, her partner, a smart beautiful black woman, has a face any painter would love to put to canvas, and a twinkle in her eyes that suggests she has found her inner happy place. They have owned and operated *Bentley's Books* for fifteen years. Gwen and Evelyn love the bookstore, but also wish to travel, and focus more on their life together as they grow older. Owning and operating your own business is tough, let alone taking time off to have a personal life. Soon enough, I was knee deep in the daily operation of the business, learning all there is about running a bookstore. Other than Hannah One's house, it's the one place I love to be at the most, and I am thankful for this entering my life when it did.

Bentley's Books is a small store nestled in a section of the city known as "the old part" of downtown. Each building attaches itself to the next in a long row of two-story red brick, flat roofed structures. Where one long row ends there is an alley between it and the next row. The bookstore is next to a shop that sells natural health products and eco-friendly merchandise. The store on the other side has been vacant for some time, and shows no promise of occupancy any time soon. Two stores opposite Bentley's see a fair amount of traffic due to their popularity in the community. A second-hand clothing store aptly named, "Gently Loved", features used clothing that is really funky, or vintage. The other one, a coffee shop, "The Sit N Sip" always has the most wonderful aromatic smells of coffee beans and sweet treats. The treats are locally made and brought in daily. The tarts, cookies, squares and cake slices have that wonderful flavour that only comes from real ingredients and home baking. The coffee shop was renovated to restore the original wood flooring, which creaks when you walk on it. The exposed red brick walls are the original walls, and the general decor is like entering someone's living room, complete with large overstuffed chairs, tiny side tables and small floor lamps that light the area in a warm glow. Two walls are devoted to shelves of books that are free to borrow and read. People often leave books on the shelves for other avid readers to enjoy. The owners, Jon and Cristina, never rush you out. It's like a long pause in your day, meant for you to refill your body and mind. Refilling with coffee might not be the best thing for your body, but I always think the focus is on the pause itself. Quite often Bentley's Books donates items to the shelves, without any fuss, but Jon made a sign that reads, "Books generously donated by Bentley's Books across the street... please shop and support another local business that supports us!" Our community is like a family; propping each other up, and rooting for each store to be successful.

    The bookstore itself is a warm and inviting space. When you enter you see that every wall is covered with shelves, from the floor to about seven feet up. The middle of the store is dissected by two long two-sided shelving islands. Another rack to the left of the front door houses a variety of newspapers. The lighting is bright, but not harsh, and well positioned for optimal viewing of the products. The hardwood floor, also the original like the coffee shop, is soft, and creaks in certain spots. Towards the back end of the shop is a set of wide stairs leading to the basement. When Gwen opened the shop she envisioned a children's section downstairs, complete with areas to sit and read and for kids to play if they got bored while Mom or Dad shopped. She soon realized that strollers and stairs were not a good fit, so now the basement houses second hand and discounted books only. The back of the shop is devoted to children's literature, and although the space is limited, there are two comfy chairs big enough for two to curl up in for a read. A very tiny office, with a bathroom off to the left, lies nestled in the rear of the shop. When taking a quick break, this is the only spot to retreat to, but I always feel claustrophobic crammed into the small chair by the desk. I am thankful to have the coffee shop across the street to escape to for my lunch hour.

I'm not the only part-time person working in the bookstore. A young woman named Janice, who, coincidentally worked as a counsellor at Birchlake with me, fills in the hours I'm not there. I log the most hours, and soon it's evident that I have an aptitude for business. Although I have been well versed in the logistics of running the bookstore, I have a tendency to fall short in the customer relations department. Gwen has decided to teach me more about the interpersonal skills one needs when dealing with customers. She has the patience of a saint and a smile that wins over even the most aggrieved customer.

Sixteen

The Universe is made up of units of energy. These units materialize themselves differently, according to their intention. Some energy massively coalesces into planets, stars or other bodies in the cosmos. Other energy focuses on the minuscule, like the tiny earth worms, whose purpose is to recycle the earth's soil. The energy is the same in either form, just the purpose or intention is different. All forms of energy are needed to sustain everything; no one unit of energy is more or less important than another. Humans often put themselves above this basic principle, and believe they are the top of some imaginary ecosystem pyramid. It is not a pyramid; it is an interconnected web.

As I continue my journey with Grace, who administers a variety of energy healing practices, I'm now able to crack open the door I had shut to the Alternate plane. I didn't realize I had shut it, but I must have. Somewhere in my human mind, I subconsciously closed that avenue to the energy within me. As I release some of my baggage, those past hurts and doubts that pull at the hem of my confidence, I sense the energy surge through me. I find a new freedom of self. As Hannah One had said, the control in how I direct my life's journey is in *my* hands.

Grace's Centre is not far from the bookstore, so today I have time to have a session before heading into work for the afternoon. I stop to peruse the front door. Grace always posts information about upcoming events at the Centre on the door and adjacent window. Three small posters are front and centre and catch my eye. A women's meditation group; a special workshop all about crystals with Grace; and a man named Arthur Monaghan is offering *journey sessions*. These are but a portion of the events and groups available once you walk through the front door. I step inside to find the usual serene interior setting, as some sort of chime-like music whispers quietly in the background. I remove my shoes and coat and turn to head towards the room I assume Grace will be in. I spy an older man, probably in his mid fifties, with short cut greying hair, sitting quietly in one of the big comfy chairs in the alcove off the main area. I smile at him, but don't strike up a conversation. I always wait to see if people want to strike up a conversation with me. I hardly ever initiate it. This man sits with his hands folded in his lap, and appears to be in a meditative state, although he does smile back at me. Something inside me makes me want to sit down opposite him, and wait for Grace, instead of going to the healing room, so I do.

As I presume the man is meditating, I hope I won't disturb him as I quietly prepare myself for the session. I begin clearing my mind and breathing slowly. I have only taken one or two deep breaths before the man unfolds his hands and stands up. He stretches up to his full height of over six feet, as if he's just awakened from a nap, and is rising from his bed. He sits back down and looks directly at me. "Hello Hannah, I'm Arthur." I blink for a second, somewhat taken aback as to how this stranger knows who I am. Before I can ask, he continues, "Grace mentioned you were coming in for a session today. I wanted to introduce myself, and offer to help you on your journey." I look at Arthur and wonder what Grace had told him about me. I have no idea what to say to Arthur, so I simply stare at him. He does not seem discouraged by my lack of response. He merely smiles and leans back in the chair before continuing the conversation. "Let me tell you about myself. I am a Spiritual Journey Facilitator. I help those who are on the path to their higher self. I think you are on this journey, am

I correct?" I simply nod. There is an energy surrounding this man that is both peaceful and electric, simultaneously. I feel as if I want to hop in a car with him and journey to the far reaches, but only if the car is afloat on a cloud. He smiles again and says, "Yes, you are on the right path. I can tell. You have a lot of hesitancy, however. If you're interested, I can travel with you for a session. You can see where you have been, so you will understand more fully, where you are headed." At this point I laugh out loud, and it makes his eyebrows rise. I did not mean to laugh, but the thought of him guiding me along to see where I have come from seems ironic, and funny. Since I already know from whence I came, it seems a bit redundant, but I can't explain that to him. "Sorry about that. I didn't mean to be rude. I'm just uh, nervous, that's all." I try to shrug my shoulders and seem nervous, but he ignores the posture and replies, "I know many people who think this is horse shit. Once you start the journey however, it all comes together. Grace seems to think you might benefit from some guidance, but of course it is completely your choice. I can see a very unique energy flow in you that differs from most people I have encountered, so I myself am intrigued to explore further." He stands up and bends over to pick up a notebook and his coat. "Feel free to get in touch with me. Just ask Grace, she knows how to reach me." He smiles again, leans towards me and extends his hand. I shake it and experience a small jolt of energy exchange between us. It is my turn to raise my eyebrows, but he just chuckles, and walks out the front door.

I sit back in my comfy chair and close my eyes. Arthur intrigued me with his comments. I haven't really given any thought to *past* lives. It's possible Arthur has some answers, or new insight that I may be missing. I'm so deep in thought, I don't hear Grace come into the alcove and speak my name. It's only when she touches my shoulder that I jump, startled out of my mind-filling speculations. She laughs and says, "Yes, Arthur has that effect on people". I stand up and follow her into the healing room and find myself stretching out on the table, all much without awareness of motion. Grace suggests a few deep cleansing breaths, as she can see I am distracted. I pull my focus back to my body and the systems that make it run. I listen to my heart beating; the rise and fall of my chest as my lungs expand and contract; I feel the muscles in my jaw slacken, without realizing I have been clenching it. My spine slowly loosens and the small of my back compresses onto the table. I focus solely on the physical, and once again marvel at the structure I am housed in. My eyes close and my shoulders relax as my breathing becomes shallower and slower. My stomach muscles relax and then my pelvis unwinds. I didn't realize I was straining so many parts of my structure, and I silently promise to pay better attention to the stresses I put on my body.

As I enter a meditative state, I find myself floating up and away. The external sounds of the room, like Grace's breathing as she moves the energy through me, and the soft gong-like music that plays softly in the room, are replaced by silence. The silence isn't absolute, as the energy flow itself creates a subtle white noise that you only hear if you truly listen with all your senses. Using my inner eye, I view the space I am now entering. I see only light. I am accustomed to this because in the Alternate that is all there is. We are Light and exist only in the beams of light. We have no physical form. I feel at home, for lack of a better phrase. It is a scene I have played out many times before, and suspect that I am going to replay it over again, but this time it feels different. There seems to be an intensity of purpose for me, as if I am looking for some message or meaning.

Then I see the flower. A Daisy planted in soil; its face turned up to the light. I have been in this scene before, with Grace's healing hands guiding me, so it is comforting and familiar, but there could be a reason why the energy is showing me this vision yet again. Is it to help me look for a deeper meaning that may aid in my quest for understanding? I stop questioning and simply let myself *Be*.

I become the flower and feel my face warm with the light. My feet dig into the dirt, for my roots go deep and solidly into the earth. My petals are caressed by a breeze, and I sway with the current of air. I look once more and I am the dragonfly, hovering over the flower, my wings fragile, like stain glass prisms reflecting the light, yet sturdy and strong. I lift my body up with the soft wind and float along, feeling the sunlight touch my wings and face, and see the Earth below smile to view such beauty in the sky. I find a small branch of a tree and land, only to find myself lying in human form on the forest floor. My back warms with the Earth's heat; I feel the roots and shoots below me growing into me and through me. I become the soil and grow the flowers, the plants and grasses of the forest floor, and stretch my roots down to drink from waters well below the surface. The waters travel the course through the soil to the pond. I become the pond, and I see myself looking into its depths. My blue-green-yellow eyes watch as the image blurs by the slight motion of Water Skeeters and Damselflies skating across the surface of the pond, using the water tension to keep from sinking below the surface. Turtles and Muskrats swim in the depths, along with other aquatic beings. The water whispers to me, "I am Light", and I hear the echo of the trees, flowers and grasses singing back; "We are Light". Finally, the air itself sounds all around me, ALL is Light. I become One with the energy and allow myself the grace to see that I too, am Light.

Energy is not sedentary and fixed, but flows like water and moves like wind and adjusts itself like the bending branches of the trees as they are touched by that wind. How one energy form moves may affect other energies around it, but this is to be expected and part of the way the Light works to keep Life in motion. Without movement and change, Life has no drive. It becomes stagnant like a pond covered in weeds. What I did in choosing *this* life may have caused the rearrangement of energies, but there was a reason for it, and by understanding that I'm where I am supposed to be, at this point in Time, all other questions and worries are not important.

I smile, and suddenly feel tears on my face. This is the message I was meant to receive.

Slowly, I return to my conscious form, yet clinging to the beauty and peace of the energy that still vibrates within me. I know that I can visit anytime; I simply need to be quiet, and still my inner monologue long enough to open the door. I become aware of Grace's hands moving the last remnant of energy across my body. I blink, knowing I need to rouse my physical self soon.

Within a few minutes, I open my eyes and look around. Grace is seated in a comfortable chair in a corner of the room with her eyes closed. As I slowly sit up she opens her eyes and smiles. "That was something, wasn't it?" I nod, unable to speak. "I really hope you decide to sit down with Arthur. I think he would be a good guide for you along the path. He may have answers, or at least he can help you find the answers you are looking for." She stands and opens the door to the room and soft cool air enters. My face is flushed, so the cool air feels refreshing. I stand up and as I'm leaving the room, I glance back to the table, and smile, feeling the Light within me burning bright.

Seventeen

As the Christmas season arrives with all the bustle of shoppers in the bookstore, I find I have little time to think about much, other than book inventory and completing my own gift shopping in time. Tonight's plan, however, takes me away from the inventories and shopping. I am excited to have dinner with Jamie and Mark, so we can catch up. I don't have a lot to add to the conversation, feeling that life is a little mundane and predictable, compared to my previous years being a busy university student. Jamie has landed a job as a Physical Education teacher at a school in North Bay. She is home for the Christmas break, and then heads back just before New Year's Eve. Mark works at the mall in one of the trendier men's fashion stores. He never really did anything with his degree. He loves his job though, apart from the poor hourly wage. He tries to convince men to dress for success, or fun, depending on the customer, and he appears to be a natural at choosing just the right look for each person.

"Please tell me you are going to get yourself a life! We have gotta find you something or someone to get you out of that bookstore!", Jamie exclaims over after-dinner liqueurs that Mark ordered for the two of them. Mark laughs, agreeing, "Geez, Hannah, how can you just do the same shit day after day? I know my life isn't all glamour and excitement, but I'm having fun, and meeting all kinds of people!" He begins describing the three different men he had had dates with over the past month or so. Jamie sips at her drink smiling, but then looks somewhat reflective. She and Neville have parted ways. It happened about a month after they graduated. He was heading off to parts of Europe on a student exchange excursion, while Jamie planted her feet firmly in North Bay to begin life as a teacher. It was a sad parting, but they both felt it best, since long distance relationships are hard to maintain, even with the best intentions. I know she misses him terribly, but is trying to turn her attention to the future and what that might bring. The restaurant is noisy, with many tables full of Christmas partiers in full swing. It prevents any sort of heart-to-heart talks, and that might be just as well. Jamie has begun to accept the ending of the relationship, and now focuses on her career. Mark seems oblivious to Jamie's angst, and continues to talk about various young men he is seeing or wants to see. Jamie takes Mark by the arm and says, "Hey, I love you, but we need to help Hannah with *her* love life. Your pursuit of love is great, but let's focus on *this* poor girl, here." And she points her finger in my direction. I dislike this topic of conversation and want to change the subject as quickly as I can, "I am fine thanks. Please, leave it alone. If the time comes I will know it. In the meantime, I am content and busy." Jamie's eyebrows shoot up, "*If* the time comes? I hope you mean *when*. I know you're contented, but there's a difference between being content and being happy." She smiles, and I know she means well. Mark leans across the table and mutters, "What about our waiter? He is adorable, and I'm certain he's straight!" He laughs and I feign a slap to his face to push him away. We all giggle, and I sit back in my chair for a moment, appreciating how lucky I am to have such good friends.

Christmas day brings snow that covers everything in a blanket of white about three inches deep. The wind has died down, and leaves a sense of calm over the world that feels graceful and serene, like a swan floating on a pond. I look out my bedroom window to see my lovely old tree standing alone in the backyard, with one little squirrel sitting hunched up in the crook of a limb, his long black tail draped over his back like a fur cape. It is a quiet and easy day, as my parents prefer to keep it simple. Hannah One will arrive around ten-thirty and, as usual, we will exchange gifts and then sit around drinking coffee and munching on sweet rolls.

After a morning of eating sweets, Hannah One and I agree the time is right to head out. We don our warm winter wear and venture out on our traditional walk in the woods. We climb into the van and I drive to our favourite conservation park, which is about fifteen minutes from the house. The roads are clear of snow and only slightly wet. The parking lot is also clear, and I can't help but think of the person who had to rise early, leave their family on Christmas morning, climb into their cold truck and plow the roads so other people can get around to visit relatives and friends. I am thankful to whoever plowed out the parking lot, because that means we can have our walk in the woods.

The trees are heavy with layers of snow and bend their branches down to adjust to the load. The trail has been cleared by the conservation group that manages the forest upkeep, although it is slightly deeper from the previous night's downfall. The sun begins to shine as the clouds part and quickly drift away. It's as if the sun saw us and decided we should be shined upon as we walk. It becomes very bright, like it has been saving up its light for a week and has to be extra brilliant on this particular day. We both put on sunglasses, for the glare off the snow is blinding. The air is crisp and makes my nose hairs sting. This type of weather makes you so aware of your body; how the cold makes you wake up and take notice, like when you drink a cold glass of water on a hot day. You can actually feel the coolness trickle down your throat and into your body. I feel the chill, but also the warmth of my woolly socks around my feet, my thermal mitts keeping my fingers from numbing up, and my hat encapsulating the heat rising from my body, keeping my ears from feeling the wintry temperature.

We walk the snowy trail in silence for a while. We emerge from the wooded area to a meadow that many decades before held a homestead and barn. The decayed remnants of a small barn can still be seen poking up through snow banks, the large cobblestones piled in some sort of shrine to times past. I like to imagine what life must have been like for the humans living here. It most certainly was challenging, as it was so secluded from the nearby town, that would one day become a large city. The deep stream that winds its way through the old park would have been the water source, and there must have been a large garden for vegetables, as a cleared plot around what is left of the barn, would suggest. The garden has long been overgrown by weeds, but the rocks piled up on the hem of the plot seem to indicate the area was used for growing something. A simple time, filled with the demands of survival, not like the modern stress of building what is considered a successful life which, for some, appears to be based on the attainment of material possessions.

As we plod through the snow, a brownish lump far across the meadow catches my eye. At first it appears to be a small, dried-up bush, but as we walk it moves slightly, and I stop to look more closely. There is no wind to cause the foliage to move, so I wonder, what am I actually looking at? Then the voice enters my head. It is not so much words being uttered, as emotions. I sense fear, anger, sadness. I step off the trail and begin walking towards the object. Hannah One stops when she realizes I'm veering off the path. At first she just watches me, and then when she sees where I'm headed, she follows, stepping into the footprints that I leave in the deep snow.

As I approach, the brownish lump begins to take shape, and I realize what I am looking at. A Red-tailed Hawk sits in a heap on the cold snowy ground. When I'm about six feet away, he turns his head to me, and I see the emotions in his eyes. Fear springs to the forefront as he begins to struggle to escape, only to end up flailing about. Obviously he is caught on something. I clear my mind before attempting to communicate. Hannah One has stopped about ten feet behind me. She knows better than to speak, as she understands how that would frighten the bird. Once I have cleared my thoughts, I gently reach out to touch the mind of the Hawk. I convey reassurance, letting him know I will not hurt him, and I am no threat to him. He blinks, and remains still and wary of me. I convey a sense of concern for him. *Let me help you.* He blinks once again, his sharp keen eyes leveling me in one fierce look. It takes a moment before he responds, but I can see his body relax minutely enough that I know he will accept my help. *My talon is caught, I cannot fly.* He turns to look down at the ground. *I saw a mouse and dove in to get it, and now I am the prey. I am caught.* A cawing sound from somewhere off to my left pulls my eyes up to see two large black Crows sitting in a tree that rims the meadow. Neither move or caw again; they simply perch there, as if waiting for something. Then one final sharp *CAW* erupts from one of them, rupturing the membrane of silence that has enveloped the woods. *They wait. I am easy prey once I am dead. They wait for that.* I know Crows are the "cleaners" of the world, as are Turkey Vultures, and I don't abhor their roles, as they are part of the cycle, but the thought of them pecking away at this beautiful creature, who met such a tragic, avoidable end, does not seem right. I return my attention to the Hawk. *May I come closer to help you?* The Hawk sits perfectly still; acceptance underlined with wariness in his mind. I take that to be my approval, or at least as much as I will get, so I slowly make my way over to him. Hannah One stays where she is, either being sensible of the situation, or maybe a bit wary herself of the large bird with the pointed beak. I assume it is the former.

    I kneel down beside the Hawk and begin to remove the snow from around him. He squirms slightly, not used to being so close to a human. He is still fearful, regardless of the pledge of safety I made to him. I dig down until I can see an ancient piece of wired fence line, probably used to corral the pig or other livestock in the pasture beside the barn. I take off my mitten and dig around carefully until I feel a gnarly talon wedged into a loop formed by the tangled wire. I slowly manipulate the talon until I feel it move out of the loop and become free. The Hawk immediately pulls his leg up to his body. He sits still for a moment, turning his amber eyes on me. I look into those eyes and feel the earth drop below me, as I soar into the sky and feel the cold air current carry me aloft, higher and higher.

I look down to the snow-covered mantle of earth, and feel it radiate its own joy at seeing the beautiful bird flying free. I turn my eyes to see two human forms in the snow, still and small compared to the vast world I see around me. I look over to see the sun, pale in winter's grip, but still shining brightly for all to marvel in its glory. To my right I see the Crows take flight and head farther north, no meal for them at the ready; they decide to hunt elsewhere, their black silhouettes stark against the blinding white snow. I sense my own hunger in the recesses of my body, and know I must hunt if I am to survive this grip of winter's hand on the earth. Slowly I circle around, descending back down to the meadow, to hover gracefully above the ground, only my wing tips creating a pattern in the light snow. I look over to view two humans, one of them being me.

I blink my eyes in time to see the Hawk flap his mighty wings to pull his weight up and up towards the sky. Suddenly I am aware of my surroundings, on the ground, feeling the snow in my boot, my hand numb from exposure, and my backside sore from crouching down so long. The Hawk has given me a gift, the only one he could that holds such significance; his perspective of the Earth and all its majestic loveliness, from high above the ground, where Hawks and other winged ones live their true best: Catching a current and surfing the atmosphere.

I sink back in the snow until my back is lying on the ground, my eyes seeing nothing but sky. I try to etch every detail of the experience in my memory, as I sense this will be one of those moments that I will look back upon and wish to relive, as age claims my body and I'm unable to venture into the woods.

Then I notice Hannah One standing over me to the side, partially blocking my view. She looks down with both concern, and amusement, on her face. "Well, that was fun!" She laughs, her voice echoing over the meadow. A few Chickadees in a nearby Blackberry bush whistle back their own glee. I look back to the sky and I spy the shape of the Hawk, very high up, coasting with a current of air, and then circling around, as if watching me. I smile, and send my own gratitude to the Hawk for sharing his vision with me, and wish him safe flight. He turns with a slight tip of one wing and his circling begins to widen, until I can see him no more.

Arriving home, we share a hot meal with my parents and then make our way to my bedroom, to talk over what happened on our walk. Hannah One questions me about what happened when I *spaced out* on her, after the Hawk had taken flight. She says that when the Hawk took off, it appeared as if I sat frozen in time, staring straight ahead, with no ability to respond to her. I tell her every detail of my linking with the Hawk, and our shared vision in the sky. She's not surprised by my account. She merely sits beside me, wearing a reflective smile, while holding a distant look in her eyes, as if she herself is taking flight.

We sit on my bed, enjoying a shared special secret. Hannah One turns and cups my hands in hers, "How lucky you are to have these amazing experiences! And, oh, to be able to communicate with all that Nature has set upon this Earth, I can only imagine!" She squeezes my hands as she continues, "And how lucky am I that you share all these astounding adventures with *me*!" She drops my hands to embrace me in a warm, loving hug.

Book Two

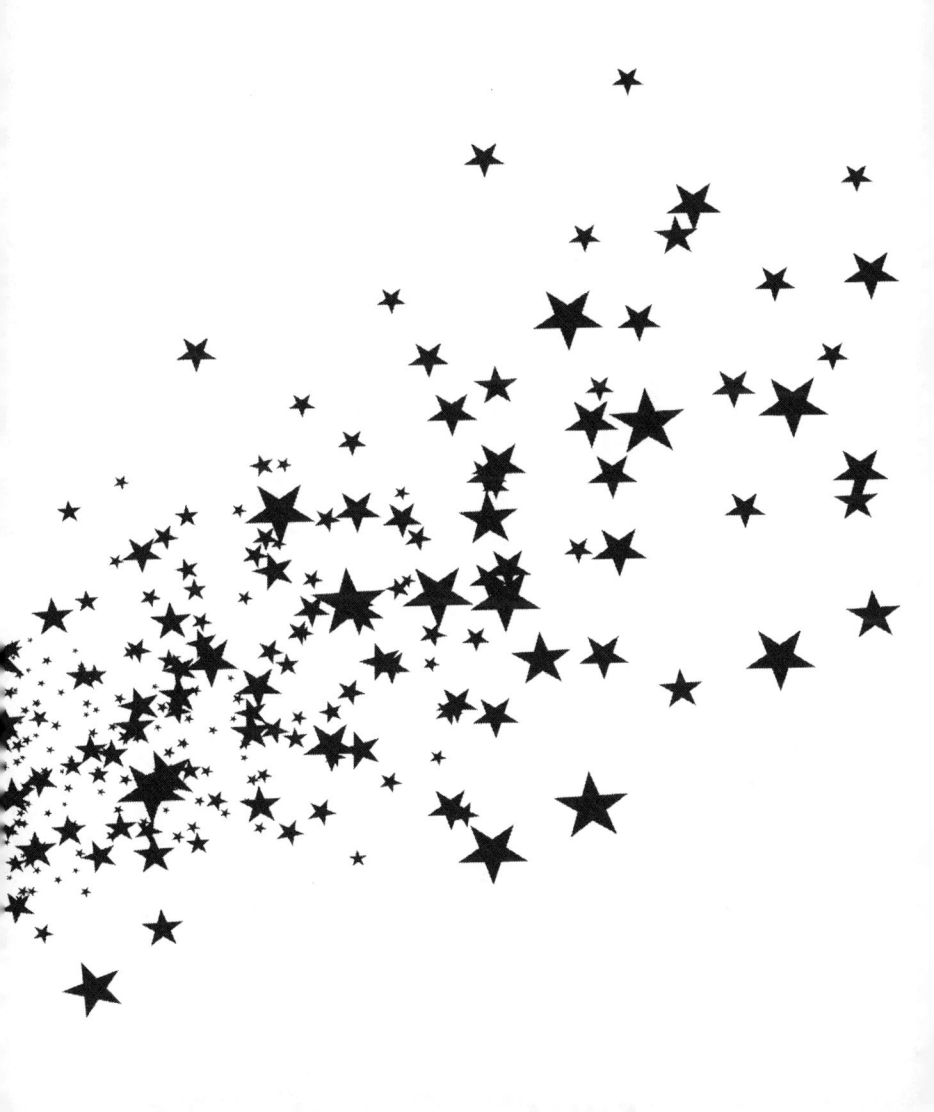

ONE

The sound of a duck quacking forces me to open my eyes, and drag my foggy brain out from within its sleepy cocoon. I was having such a good dream; full of interesting things to view, and people who seemed familiar to interact with, yet in my waking life I know I've never met them. The overall emotion of the dream, as it fades with every quack, was one of love and acceptance. I blink a few times, realizing that the insistent quacking is in fact my cell phone ringing. My very best friend, Jamie Beaumont, has programmed my ring tone to quack like a duck when she is calling me. Being as technologically challenged as I am, I haven't figured out how to change it. Now it quacks mercilessly, like an irate fowl telling off an intruder who has entered the farmyard. I reach out to my nightstand and pick up the phone. "What?" I hoarsely croak. I know who it is so I dispense with politeness. I glance over at my clock which reads eight fifteen. "You are never gonna guess what!" Jamie's enthusiasm seems over the top for a Saturday morning, especially before my first coffee. Without stopping to hear any reply, she continues, "The Board of Ed in Toronto has asked me to join the staff at Chester Avenue Public School this fall!" She practically screams, which makes me hold the phone away from my ear. She continues, "That means goodbye North Bay! Hello roommate!" I blink at the phone, as I'm still holding it away from my ear. It's too early to play twenty questions, so I simply ask,

"What?" She groans, and repeats her news and then adds, "I'm back, and I need a roommate. And you, my friend, are it!"

At the age of twenty-eight I have no real ambition to move out. I am very happy paying a moderate rent to remain at home while I pay off my student loans. I have my job at the bookstore and relatively little other expenses, so my debt load is shrinking very fast. I have only one credit card that is religiously paid off every month, if it carries a balance at all. I see Jamie and my other best friend, Mark, struggling to pay their loans and feel sympathy for them. Mark has moved in with Brian Janson, a young man who works as a nurse. They had met through mutual friends and found an instant attraction, both physically and emotionally. Brian is creative and has a wonderful sense of humour. Most importantly, he gets Mark. He understands his moods and his insecurities. Mark also recognizes Brian's foibles and is equally accepting of them. They make a good pair. They moved in together about a year after they started dating. They found a small one-bedroom apartment in the west end.

I swing my legs over the side of the bed so I can sit up and properly pay attention to what Jamie is proposing. "Move in with you?" I ask. She squeals with delight; "Yes! It'll be so great! I've already started looking at rental ads on-line. I have given notice here at my place and they were so awesome they let me off with thirty days instead of sixty." She continues to talk about the ads she's read and their locations in relation to the school and the bookstore. I'm still stuck on page one with, *it's time you move out*. I realize Jamie has stopped talking, and is expecting a response from me. I look around my room. It's home, and I'm quite comfortable here. I could probably afford to move out, so the money isn't an issue. It's the change in my path that gives me pause. I have been plodding along rather routinely for the past three years, and seem to have found a rhythm to my days that I find acceptable, if a little boring. I know what to expect and I have control over things in general. But do I want to live my life this way, lots of control, but no adventure? I hear Jamie ask, "Hey, Hannah, are you still there? Did you hang up or something?" I pull my attention back to the conversation and say, "Um, well. Let me think about it. It's a big thing; I want to make sure I can do it, you know, with money and stuff." It sounds lame, and even I know it's the sound of someone copping out. Jamie sighs, "Hannah, this will be good, I promise. When I get back to the city next week we can go look at places, and you'll see. I'll be the best roommate you've ever had!" She laughs and hangs up on me.

Summer days can make you feel like the world is alive and growing with possibilities. The early summer sun lends warmth to the beginning of days, making everything it touches bright and concentrated. Colours are deeper, smells are richer, and sounds are absorbed by the fluttering leaves on the trees. Sometimes it feels like the world is taking a break, and heaving a deep sigh of contentment. Summer often lends a lazy feel to afternoons and early evenings.

I sit in the backyard, pondering the possibilities of my decision. I lean my back against the ancient trunk of the tree that I call *friend*. It stands silently, ever the vanguard of the world. A tree is rooted in one place its entire life, viewing the world daily, from one perspective. That view changes so very slowly as it grows that the tree hardly notices, until it towers over the Earth, and feels its top boughs brush the floor of the sky. My tree is content enough to stand here, not moving, only bending with the weather. I am not a tree, however much I'd enjoy that idea. I feel the hard bark dig into my shoulder blades as I lean back and look up into its boughs. A few squirrels slowly climb through branches looking for fresh green leaf shoots to nibble on. I feel the late day sun caress the side of my face. I turn my head and close my eyes to absorb a few of the last rays of the day. Such contentment I cannot find anywhere else, aside from the woods I walk. I feel privileged to be a part of this day, with these creatures, and the tree. I will hate to leave my backyard behind if I move. But I am not a tree. It's not natural for humans to stay still in one place, frozen in Time and Space, waiting for the elements to wear them down. If I am to have the ultimate human experience, I will need to move.

As I soak up the last of the day's warmth from the fading sun, my mother emerges from the house, a glass of wine in her hand. She looks tired, but I get the sense that she has had a good day. She grabs the back of an old lawn chair and hauls it over to where I sit in the grass, still leaning up against the tree. "Mind if I join you?" she asks lightly. "Sure, pull up a tree", I smile. She glances up into the branches of the tree, and, seeing the squirrels, a slight frown crosses her face, but only briefly. She takes a sip from her glass. Glancing over to gauge her mood, I decide she may be receptive to the conversation about my impending move. "So, I got a call from Jamie this morning. Seems she got a job offer to teach at a public school, here in the city. She's moving back from North Bay in a few weeks." My mother's eyebrows rise slightly; "Really? That's good. I thought she wasn't suited to that isolated small-town life. She will be happy to be back here, in civilization." I look to see if she is joking, but she seems quite unaware of her small-town biased remark. I look down at the grass, pretending to play with a blade as I reply; "Well, actually, she really loved North Bay. There was a lot of stuff going on, and she felt like she was part of a community there. It really is quite civilized, I'm sure." Before she can respond, I continue, "She is looking at apartments for rent, and wondered if I might want to be her roommate." My mother's expression doesn't change, but she looks back towards the house and sighs. "I knew this day would come, and here we are." She turns her head to face me and smiles. "I think that's a great idea. You will love having a place of your own to decorate, and have friends over. Yes, I think that's a great idea!" Her voice carries a slightly high pitched, *really I'm fine but I'm not,* tone. She takes another sip of wine. She sounds happy and excited, but at the same time her body language and facial expression convey a feeling of anxiety, and sadness. I try to think of something that will ease her concerns. "I'm not even sure that I want to move, but I feel like it's time to start a new chapter in my life. I'm going to need help with this, so I hope you are available to help me with the logistics of the move, and maybe even decorate the place, once we move in. You know I have no taste!" She looks at me as if to say, don't patronize me, but then she blinks and replies, "Yes, I'm always here for you. Any help you need, just ask. And you do have taste; it's all your own, as it should be. Just because it's not mine doesn't mean it isn't good." She takes a final sip, draining the glass. She lowers the goblet to perch on her thigh as she takes a deep breath and exhales. We sit looking around the garden, watching the sun dip lower in the west, and simply enjoy each other's company in silence, until dusk descends and we decide to return to the house to see what's for supper.

Two

As the weeks turn into months, it has become old hat to live where I do, and the homesickness I first experienced has faded. I still go home every week to visit, have a meal with my parents, and sit in the backyard, whenever time allows. I also spend as much time as I can with Hannah One. She often comes over to the apartment and hangs out with us, which Jamie loves because she never knew either of her grandmothers, both having died when she was very young.

Heading into her late seventies, Hannah One is getting a little frailer, but retains her inner glow and vitality. I see her hands becoming stiffer, and quite often her knees give her trouble. She still does her daily walks and keeps her interests front and centre, which gives focus and direction to her days. She loves living in her own home and vows to stay as self-sufficient as she can for as long as she can. I don't blame her; I would fiercely guard my independence above all else at her age. Her outlook is, if she can manage, then why not stay. About once a month, Hannah One comes to the bookstore to purchase a new book. Then we venture across the street to the coffee shop to drink coffee and discuss all manner of things.

I watch from the front counter as she browses the section on archaeology. She is curious about everything, so no section of the store is left unexplored by her. I'm busy with a customer, but notice when she starts up a conversation with a young man standing nearby. The man smiles and points to a book on the shelf, which he then pulls down and passes to her. They appear quite involved in their conversation. It makes me smile. This is so typical of Hannah One. She is always talking to strangers, engaging them in conversations that often end up being a little more personal than they expected. I look at the man and gauge him to be around six feet tall, as he stands tilting his head down slightly to talk with my nosy grandmother. And although I don't put stock in my age-guessing prowess, I figure him to be around my age, or possibly a few years older. He has a full head of sandy-brown hair, and when he smiles at her, the smile is genuine, warm, but full of mischief. I shake my head, knowing full well this man will have a story to tell his friends later about the old broad who flirted with him in the bookstore. Hannah One isn't actually flirting, that's just her style. She can be very mischievous, but in a curious, good-natured way.

As the clock chimes eleven, Janice arrives to relieve me from my duties, so I can go for coffee with Hannah One, who is still fully engrossed in the conversation with the stranger. After gathering my coat, I slowly make my way over to her, hoping she will sense my approach and end her socializing session with this poor man. No such luck. As I get near, Hannah One turns her head, smiles, and waves me closer. She takes her other hand and places it on the man's forearm. Many people might find this an invasion of their space, but he simply smiles and looks at me. His eyes are almost clear blue, like crystal clear water. I have never seen such a striking colour.

"Hannah, are we going for coffee now? Good! Owen is joining us!" She smiles, grasping the man's arm even more firmly, as if he might try to escape. "Oh? Um," I mutter, but before I can say anything, she continues, "We've been having the most interesting chat, and I would hate for it to end. So, coffee here we come! Owen, you'll love the tarts they have there, they are so good..." she carries on, almost without taking a breath, "Hannah, I know you will find him as interesting as I do, so let's go!" And with that, she drops his arm and heads towards the door. Owen simply shrugs and smiles, following after her. I put on my coat and make it to the door as they go out. I hear Hannah One describe exactly what sweet she is going to have with her coffee, and Owen laughs as he agrees on her choice. We make our way across the road, Owen taking my grandmother's arm to steer her, although she is the last person who needs steering. She clucks on about the coffee and how often she comes to visit me, and then, as if remembering me, they both turn to make sure I am still in tow.

The coffee house is fairly empty, so we easily find a table with four chairs. Hannah One takes her large handbag and places it on one of the chairs, and quickly pulls out the chair beside it, leaving me no choice but to sit beside Owen. I am beginning to feel like a mouse in a maze. I know there's a way to get out of this, but I just can't see it. Owen unzips his jacket and places it on the back of his chair. "Hannah?" he asks. "Yes" both of us reply. "Oh, of course, sorry, I mean Hannah *One*. Can I get you your coffee and butter tart? Of course, I mean can I get you both coffee and a tart?" He looks at me and smiles, yet I sense a bit of nervousness on his part, and it makes me feel a little better to think I'm not the only one more than a little uncomfortable about this obvious set-up. I nod, replying, "That is so kind of you. Let me help you carry the food back from the counter after we've ordered."

As we stand in front of the glass display case, looking at the tempting array of sweets, Owen turns to me. "I should really introduce myself properly, I'm Owen, Owen Ross. I just want to say that I'm sorry to intrude on your coffee date with your grandmother. She was quite persistent with her request, and I didn't want to be disrespectful. It is totally weird though, as I don't know either of you, and you don't know me. But I will tell you upfront, I am not a serial killer, so rest easy!" He winks and lets out a small chuckle, as he sees my expression go from *what the hell?* to, *oh he's joking around*. I try to laugh, but it comes out a bit gargled, like it sticks in my throat. I turn my attention back to the display of sweets, pretending to be interested in picking out a tart, as the server asks for my choice.

I silently agree with him about the situation being weird, but knowing my grandmother, I should not be surprised. She, almost on a daily basis, attempts to get me to make more friends and expand my inner circle. I try to say I am happy with the two, maybe three friends I have, but then when I hear myself say that, I know she's right. I realize he is waiting for me to comment on his remark, so I reply, "Yes, it is weird, but quite in character for Hannah One. She is always doing stuff like this. You don't have to stay if you're uncomfortable. I can tell her you forgot about an appointment or something. She just likes interesting people, so obviously she found you interesting." Owen nods, "I like weird. It makes life more interesting. Besides, I hear from a very reliable source," and he jerks his head in Hannah One's direction, "that the butter tarts here are the best in town, so I can't miss the opportunity to see for myself." He turns back to the counter and pays for the entire order. I mumble my thanks once more as I take one of the two trays holding our food. He slips a ten-dollar bill in the tip jar, and heads back to the table.

The conversation never lags as Owen and Hannah One carry on, touching on a variety of subjects. It turns out that Owen is a freelance writer, with an environmental science background, so this opened up many avenues of discussion. It also explains why he has time enough in his day to sit around with strangers, chatting and drinking coffee. He writes a lot of articles for various internet news outlets and magazines, and also contributes to one or more of the city papers on a regular basis. His articles centre on environmental issues, and with his education and work with a variety of organizations, including Greenpeace, he seems highly qualified to write in this field.

Every so often, Owen tries to pull me into the conversation by asking me my opinion or ideas about the topic of discussion. I venture my opinion, and they both nod in agreement, before diving back into the thick of it. I sit there holding my hot mug between my cool hands, and for the first time I really look at this stranger who has so entranced my grandmother. His face is slightly weather-beaten; it's a face that has been *one* with the elements, often, and enjoys it. His eyes are sharp, but kind. His hands are soft looking, but also sturdy, like they are accustomed to hard work. His frame is average, not too athletic, but healthy and slightly muscular. I suddenly imagine what he might look like with his shirt off, and find myself absorbed in the thought. So much so, that when he catches me looking at him, I don't turn away, but hold his gaze. His eyes are like magnets and I am metal, being pulled into them without resistance. He smiles, returning his attention back to Hannah One.

Soon enough our coffee cups are drained, the butter tarts are no more than a few crumbs on the plates, and it looks like this meeting is over. I sigh inwardly, for although I have enjoyed sitting here, I still feel uneasy about the whole situation. I hold my breath as my grandmother rises from her chair and reaches for her coat. Owen helps her put it on and she accepts the help with a smile and another touch on his arm. I wait to see if she will attempt to throw us together again, by suggesting another coffee date, but she says nothing, except how much she has enjoyed herself and hopes we can do it again sometime. Owen smiles and reaches over to help me on with my coat. I look at him as if to say *I'm perfectly capable of putting on my coat,* but a look from Hannah One makes me accept the kind gesture without protest. He holds the door open for the two of us, and we step out into the cold day. Owen zips up his winter jacket and then stuffs his hands in the pockets. He turns to us and says, "Well, it's been a lot of fun. I hope you both have an excellent day. See you around sometime!" And without waiting for a response, he turns on his heel and heads off down the street. I look at Hannah One, expecting to see disappointment written on her face for the failure to secure a second meeting, but all she does is smile. She grabs my arm and guides me back across the street towards the bookstore, saying nothing more about our coffee date.

The forest is warm and still, without any breeze. The dried pine needles are brittle and spiky under my bare feet. A lone dragonfly hovers over my head and then lands on a nearby branch. Bees buzz industriously over a patch of yellow and orange Hawkweed. The birds and animals take respite from the warm midday sun, in shady corners of the forest, under leafy boughs, or in burrows dug into the cool earth. I wander down the worn path to the edge of the pond. I stick my feet in and feel the cold water tickle my toes. I look down at my body, and notice how green my skin is. I look at my hands, turning them this way and that, and watch how the light twinkles off their emerald hue. I am surprised to see the elfin features of my eyes and elongated pointy ears, as I glance at my reflection in the still water. My head is crowned in leaves of varying shades of green. A gleeful laugh erupts from inside me. My laughter chimes and echoes across the water, making the birds chirp and butterflies flap their wings. Although I cannot see clearly, I know my eyes are crystal blue, as the sky on a clear day, and tendrils of sandy-brown hair cascade down through my leafy crown. I don't recognize myself, but at the same, I do. I twirl around and lose my footing, landing in the water, creating ripples that fan out, wider and wider. I laugh again, and this time I hear Hawk echo back my laugh. I stand up, wading out of the water and back up the path. All of a sudden, I stop and gaze around me. Now I understand my role. I am a Guardian of Nature's Creations, and must do all that I can to protect these treasures. With a swell of love, I open my arms and let it all become me, as I become It.

I open my eyes, feeling the soft cushions of the couch under my body. Still feeling disoriented, I realize I'd fallen asleep while reading a book about the history of Greenpeace. Owen's face flashes briefly before my unfocused eyes, and then disappears.

THREE

Working for a living is a necessity for most adult humans to progress along the timeline, but some have a harder time of it than others. I am fortunate in that I love my job, or at least most of it. I am trying to learn more effective ways of dealing with difficult customers, but all in all, I have a handle on most of what it takes to run the bookstore. Gwen and Evelyn have been able to take more time off, and enjoy traveling, experiencing all the fascinating places in the world that time and budget allow. They have just arrived home after a trip to Ireland, so they have decided to host another house party. Their parties usually attract interesting and off-beat people, and I enjoy meeting these unique souls, often wondering if an Alternate resides within them.

This party seems to be heading in the same direction, until I see *him*. There he is, leaning against the kitchen door frame, holding a beer and smiling. My inside eye sees his face in my dreams, and I blink and there he is, still there. He turns his head, and smiles directly at me. He's in conversation with Janice, and continues on. I am frozen, unable to move from the spot where I stand. Should I approach? Should I ignore him? As Gwen passes by me, she notices me looking at Owen and she says, "Oh, let me introduce you to Owen. He has such interesting stories to tell, I know you'll love him!" She takes my arm and pulls me across the room to stop in front of him. No turning back now. Gwen introduces us; Owen pretends that this is our first meeting. Gwen explains that she and Owen became friends when the "Save the Library" protests were being staged at City Hall. Some politician thought it would be a great cost-cutting measure to close some of the libraries throughout the city, but he was wrong. The outcry from the public was swift and loud. The policy never made it off his desk. Gwen's story ends as she gets distracted by Evelyn waving at her to come into the dining room. She smiles as she turns away without another word, leaving us standing there. Owen leans in slightly and whispers, "Thought it would be easier to play dumb, than trying to explain how we already know each other." I smile and whisper back, "it will be our secret." He winks, and produces a dazzling grin. All of a sudden, my world is clearer, warmer, and focused. I don't know what happened, but I feel like I've arrived home. I grin back.

The following week Owen stops by the store every day, to buy a newspaper, or browse books. It has almost become my obsession to look up every time the door opens, to see if it's Owen entering. I don't mind these daily visits, and I get the feeling he doesn't either. Our conversations are effortless, as we talk about what articles he's writing, or new books I have found I that can't put down.

Finally, three weeks after Gwen's party, Time appears to deem it the right moment for Owen to ask me out on a proper date. The only problem is that I almost miss the invitation, hidden in a comment he is making about a new restaurant he wants to try, with me. He asks in such an off-hand way, I don't see it as an invitation, I only hear him commenting about a new place he's interested in. He blinks when I don't respond right away. It takes my brain a second to piece together the invitation that lies hidden in his comment. Then I swallow and look back at him. He's smiling at me, almost like he can see the wheels turning in my head. Then he laughs. His laugh is deep, like a baritone. I smile, and want to say something witty, but all I can do is nod and mumble; "I'd love to try that place. I hear it's really good." He pulls out his phone and scrolls his calendar app while suggesting a date. "How about

Friday? Oh, but I may be out of luck; you're probably busy, since that's only three days away…" his voice trails off and this time it's me who chuckles. Busy? I haven't been busy on Friday nights since university, I think sarcastically. I don't bother to mention my dull weekly schedule, so I merely utter, "Oh, um, no, I'm as free as a bird!" Owen smiles, tucking his phone back into his pocket as he heads for the door. "Great! I'll meet you here at six on Friday, and we can walk to the restaurant together. It's only about five blocks away." I nod in agreement as he pulls open the door and disappears into the world. Friday at six can't come soon enough.

That dinner has led to more meals shared, and spending time walking the woods, discussing our mutual love for the natural world and concerns for it's future. I stopped comparing Owen to Julian a minute into our first conversation, as the similarities end with the two of them being human males. Owen possesses an energy and light I have never felt with anyone else. His love for nature touches my core. We often spend time at my apartment, with Jamie making an appearance now and then. Her job keeps her at school very long hours, so we really only connect on the weekends. She has reunited with Neville, so between the two of us, we are ships passing in the night. We talk about the four of us going out together sometime, but it never seems to happen. Mark is also busy, as now he's the manager of the men's clothing store he works at. He has his sights set on fashion design, but is reluctant to go back to school to study the subject, as he feels he's getting a better education learning on the job. Mark is still with Brian, and the two of them seem content with their lives, which makes me remember how much turmoil he went through to arrive at this happy point. Trying to balance my work, hanging out with Jamie, Owen, my parents, and Hannah One, is beginning to wear on me. Owen can see my struggle and is very understanding. He offers to spend time with Hannah One to alleviate some of my stress, which makes me like him even more. During one of our walks in the woods, Owen had briefly mentioned that his parents had died in a car accident years ago. Since he did not elaborate on the sad topic, it didn't feel right asking questions, and so I let it drop. He is also without grandparents, so he is pretty much *orphaned*. Hannah One, upon hearing this, decided that she would be Owen's adopted grandma. We all laughed, but I could see a gleam in his eye that meant he was very moved by this. So, it was no surprise to me when I arrived one Saturday to visit Hannah One, that Owen was there, helping her dig some holes in the garden for the new plants she bought. He was very happy to help, and I can tell he has come to love Hannah One almost as much as I do.

Sitting in the middle of a field filled with colourful wildflowers and long green grasses that tickle my legs, I turn my face to the sun to feel its touch warm my skin. The grasses begin to sway and separate, to present a large brown Groundhog. He blinks, and proceeds to come forward until he sits about four feet away. He also turns his face to the sun, and smiles a big toothy smile. I am not startled by his presence, only curious. He turns his head to look at me. He says, "I am Death without dying. I am the dream-like sleeper, who walks between the worlds during my hibernation. It is within our death-like dream phase that we are most powerful, as we connect with Spirit. You are one who knows that Death is but a step onto the plane of Alternate existence. You know of what I speak. Humans are odd, because some fear Death above all else, yet paradoxically some fear Living, more so than Death. It is All, and then it is Nothing. Leave your physical body as Spirit travels onward. Body becomes Earth, becomes new Life, becomes Death. It is All, and then it is Nothing." He pauses, closing his eyes. As he begins to speak again, clouds shift in front of the sun, making me shiver. "Death visits you; one will be holding the hand of Death, not to awaken, only to move onto the Alternate plane."

I awake with a start and feel cold clammy sweat all over my body. I pull the blanket closer as I roll over to see the clock showing four a.m. I have an intense need to call Hannah One, but can't remember why. Knowing it's too early to disturb her, I close my eyes and promise to call her when I get up in three hours.

As with any dream, one tends to forget, or only recall certain aspects of it, once it is released into the Dream realm. I wake to the beep of my alarm clock, vaguely recalling having been awakened a few hours earlier, but can't remember the reason why. The only thing I see in my mind is a field. As I often have dreams that involve the natural world, my recollection doesn't overly concern me. I promise myself that I will try to remember more later, but in the meantime, I have to get ready for work.

As I sit on the bus, a thought keeps pinching my brain, right behind my eyes. It is annoying me so much I wonder if I'm having an aneurism or something. A brown furry shape crosses my inner eye, and I begin to recall my vision. A Groundhog, the sun, flowers, Death. I reach up and push the stop bell-button, even though I'm blocks away from my actual stop. I step off the bus and pull out my cell. I quickly dial Hannah One's number and then wait anxiously as it rings. Without realizing it, I'm holding my breath. Only when she answers do I gasp for air. Her voice on the other end is like a symphony to my ears. The relief washes over me in waves, and I lean against the building for support. "Hello?" she repeats. I clear my throat and say cheerily, "Just me! Checking in…" I didn't know if telling her I thought she was dead is a great way to start a conversation. "Hannah? Are you okay? You sound funny. You don't usually call me when you're outside. I can't hear you very well." I quickly decide not to tell her about my dream. I can do that later, when I have more time. "Sorry, you just popped into my head, so I thought I'd just double check that we are still on for Saturday?" We have made plans for a trip to the Art Gallery, likely with Owen in tow. "Oh, yes of course!" Her voice is enthusiastic. "I'm looking forward to it! I hear Owen is taking us out for lunch first." This is news to me, but then the two of them always seem to make plans without my knowledge. Suddenly a car horn blares close by, breaking my reverie. "Ok, I think I'd better go now, or I might get run over!" We end the call with the usual sentiments of love and "see you soon". I stuff my phone back in my pocket and turn to walk the remainder of the distance towards the bookstore.

With each step I take along the sidewalk, I find my thoughts wandering to the field, and the cryptic message of the Groundhog. Holding the hand of Death. Who was he talking about? Should I call my parents? I dismiss that thought, as I'm certain one of them would have called immediately had there been an emergency, regardless of the time. I walk the remainder of the way with my eyes unfocused, and almost pass by the store before I realize I have reached my destination. I push the front door, but it doesn't open. I suddenly notice that the CLOSED sign is still showing. Funny, I thought Gwen was opening this morning. I look inside to see if I can see a light coming from the back room, but it's dark. Well, we must have gotten our wires crossed with the schedule, which happens now and then, even with a small staff. I pull out my set of keys and unlock the door. I'm greeted by the alarm buzzing and quickly step over to the unit and press the alarm-off code. Then all is silent. I switch on the lights and the store becomes the warm charming little nook I know and love. I shake my head to jiggle loose the random thoughts of Groundhogs and Death, and proceed to get the store ready for customers. I have just hung up my coat when my phone rings. It's Evelyn. I am about to cajole her about Gwen's misstep in opening, when I hear her sob. Gwen Bentley, a woman in her mid fifties, with no outward signs of illness, died last night of a heart attack.

She had mentioned over the past two days that she felt a little *off*, slightly nauseous, with heartburn as well. She was dismissive of her ailment, tacking it on to the idea that she ate something that didn't agree with her. Right after dinner last night, however, she began to feel worse, so Evelyn insisted they go to the hospital.

After waiting for hours in the emergency room, she was sent home with anti-nausea medication, and told to rest. As I hear this news, I recall reading an article about the fact that more women die from heart attacks every year as their symptoms are often mis-diagnosed. It was only after midnight when she awoke with a searing pain in her jaw, that they realized something was terribly wrong. The ambulance arrived and whisked her back to the hospital, but by the time she was admitted, it was too late. She died at four a.m.

I hold the phone in my hand and cannot speak. I see the Groundhog, his face tilted toward the sun, smiling a toothy grin. Holding the hand of Death. Gwen is not sleeping the dream-like sleep of Death *without* dying, from which she can walk the ethereal plane and return when awakened. She has left her body; It is All, then it is Nothing. Another sob from Evelyn brings me back, and I realize I have to say something. "Oh my god, Evelyn. I can't believe this. Would you like me to come over to be with you? Or I could just keep things running at this end? Whatever you need." Evelyn mentions she has her sister and another friend with her, so she suggests I keep an eye on the store, and until further notice, I will be in charge of everything. I try to comfort her again by saying that things will be fine here, and that if she needs any additional help, I am only a call away. She hangs up, and I stand in the middle of the store, staring at the phone in my hand.

Even though I understand the role of Death in human existence, I'm still shocked. Gwen was in good health, or so it appeared. It makes no sense, but then it never does. I look around at the books on the shelves, the pieces of artwork that adorn any bare space on the wall not covered by shelving. She had insisted we only display artwork done by local artists. Her hand is everywhere in this store. Her soul, her innermost energy is sewn into the fabric of this place. I can't think of it without her being here. I place the phone back in my pocket, and sink to the floor, my legs feeling like jelly. I feel a sob in my throat; I open my mouth to let it out and it is so mournful, it shakes me to my core.

Four

As word quietly spreads, the store becomes the centre where friends meet to share their grief. It's not uncommon to have five or six people congregate at the back of the store, just to share their collective sorrow. I don't have the heart to ask them to meet elsewhere, as they feel the same about the bookstore as I do. It is full of Gwen's love and life, and those who know her want to relish every last moment before this energy is forever lost. So many flower arrangements have arrived that I am running out of room to display them all. Evelyn has not been to the store, but has received many tributes at their home, so she is well aware of the magnitude of affection being shown in the community. She is planning a party, a "Celebration of Life", since Gwen had specifically said she never wanted a funeral. The house will be open to all who know and love her, and want to share in this commemoration. Several businesses up and down the street offer to supply food, drinks and anything else needed to make it easier on Evelyn. It's slated for Saturday, starting just after one o'clock. Gwen had always enjoyed a good party, so Evelyn is determined to make it everything she would have loved. My heart aches for her, but I know planning this event helps her get a sense of closure, and gives a focus to her days. She shows no interest in the store, relying on me to keep things running.

I decided to hire an extra staff person to help fill in the gap left by Gwen and Evelyn's absence. Cristina, the woman who owns the coffee shop across the street, had given me the name of a friend, Mila Savic, who has experience in retail, and has studied library science at university, so she knows her stuff. She is more than happy to help out. Mila will cover the Saturday shift so Janice and I can be at the house helping Evelyn with the party. I want to have a discussion with Evelyn about the possibility of keeping her permanently, but I'll wait for the right time, as she really doesn't need to concern herself about the logistics of the store right now.

Saturday morning showers threatened to put a damper on the day's celebration, but now, as noon marks the face of the clock, the sun appears and begins to dry up the puddles. I line the front veranda with all the bouquets from the store, creating a beautiful sea of floral colours. Evelyn merely glances at the flowers, showing no interest in who sent them. I close my eyes for a minute to see if I can sense Gwen's presence or energy in the house, but nothing comes to me. I am not surprised, as human energy, once it leaves the body, needs time to acclimate to a new existence. They can transcend quickly to a new plane, or they can be stuck between planes, feeling unresolved. Often there is a guide to help them move along, but if they are reluctant, it can make for a difficult transition. Although I can't be certain, I like to imagine Gwen being only too eager to explore a new dimension, yet very aware of leaving behind her beloved Evelyn. She would hope they will be together again some time, if that's what their energies desire.

The kitchen counter is full of borrowed dishes, cups and cutlery, enough for an army. A hug coffee urn sits on the far end of the counter, brewing quietly. The kitchen table is covered with an array of sweets and sandwiches. The fridge has a good selection of beer, wine, and juice stuffed onto every shelf. Nothing has been forgotten, as Cristina and Jon, from the *Sit N Sip*, have made sure of that. Quiet music plays somewhere in the house. People start arriving just after one, entering very quietly, as if into a library. It's so different from the usual party vibe, with laughter and conversations emanating from all the rooms; the air feeling a-buzz with *Gwen energy*. Now it's like a funeral parlour, without the casket. Evelyn sits in the living room, wine glass in hand, and smiles as people begin to pour into the house and greet her. She is wearing a bright yellow sweater with a beautiful blue-green silk scarf tied around her shoulders. Despite the bright colours, all of which are Gwen's favourites, Evelyn looks frail and tired. She stands up and meanders around from room to room, almost as if trying to find something to do. People group together and talk quietly, avoiding her, as if she is too delicate to include in their sombre discussions.

Suddenly Evelyn clears her throat and announces to the room in general. "I know everyone thinks it's respectful to be quiet, and whisper their condolences, but I'd much rather the music is turned up and we dance, and share stories about my marvelous *G*! Please! This is supposed to be a party! Gwen would be so mad to see such sadness in her home." With that, she raises her wine glass in a toast. "To my marvelous G!". Everyone lifts a glass and repeats the toast. There is a sudden shift in the mood of the house. People relax and start telling stories about Gwen's various adventures, and laughter spills out and around everyone, like a balm. It brings me to tears. I don't know why, but it feels like I am witnessing the end of an era; there will never be another *Gwen party*. I leave the kitchen and make my way out to the backyard. A giant Chestnut tree greets me, and its shade brings a bit of cool relief. Before I can take another step, I feel someone touch my elbow. I turn to see Owen. He had entered the house just as Evelyn spoke up. He hadn't seen me until I was heading out the backdoor. He looks at my face, and seeing the grief registering in my expression, takes me in his arms for a gentle hug. I let the tears fall for a few minutes, feeling drained. The whole week has taken its toll on me. Owen doesn't say anything. He too feels the weight of loss, as he and Gwen were good friends, too. We hold each other, supporting our shared grief, while sounds of music and laughter fill our ears. Gwen would have loved this party.

I watch the Spider weave her web. "All things are connected", she whispers. "All energy, all bodies, all molecules, All. If one line breaks or falls away, the web's essence is altered. Tear it down, rebuild it, move it, lose it, it can Be again, in another form, as Life adjusts to the change. Life is full of webs being attuned and rebuilt. Look at your web. It is tenuous, you need to tear it down and rebuild." Hannah… Hannah…

I blink, realizing Jamie is speaking to me. I look over at the spider in the corner of the ceiling, but she says no more. "Hannah, Hannah! Earth to Hannah! Geez, I know I talk *too much* about stuff, but really, you could *pretend* to listen." She stands up and stomps out of the room. I blink again, the spider's message of change resonating in my mind, leaving me to wonder how I'm supposed to rebuild my web. A minute later Jamie comes back in the room, a weak smile on her face. "Sorry for snapping at you. Just feeling a bit stressed about the wedding." Jamie is getting married to Neville. She tore down her web, and is rebuilding it to include Neville. Interesting.

Five

Now, two months after the last Gwen party, the world seems to have settled into a new rhythm. At least my world has. Work comprises most of my waking hours, with Owen and my family filling whatever is left over of each day. Evelyn tried to return to the store, but I could see her heart wasn't in it. She agreed to have Mila stay on permanently, as she has no desire to return to the floor to work. Owen comes by regularly with coffee and sweets, and words of encouragement. He knows I need to concentrate on keeping things running smoothly, and with the holiday season fast approaching, there is plenty to get organized. He never complains about how little time I spend with him. He himself has been traveling for work, and is in the middle of compiling research for a book he wants to write someday, so his plate is also full. It makes our time together all the more special, as we both know we need to make the most of it. We decide to make Friday night a special date night, something we both desperately need. I have been longing for time alone with Owen, to be close to him.

 Tonight, we are driving to the other side of the city, to an out-of-the-way antiquated Inn that has a marvelous restaurant. It is very rustic, and very romantic. There is a kinetic energy brewing inside me, drawing me closer to Owen, day by day. It feels organic, natural, and my trust in this feeling helps me to let go of my hesitation.

With dinner completed, I quietly suggest that we check to see if there might be a room available. Owen's eyes widen at my scandalous proposal, but he quickly recovers and makes his way to the front desk. I stand in the foyer, looking around at the exquisite, lovingly preserved architecture, dating back to the early twentieth century. The feel of thick carpets underfoot, and the charm of the furnishings, makes me believe I could be visiting someone's home.

Owen returns, holding up a key fob. He looks questioningly at me, but I merely smile. I take his free hand and we make our way to the room on the second floor. As we approach the door, I pull Owen into my body and kiss him. It's a long, slow kiss, that leaves no misinterpretation. He quickly opens the door and we slide into the room, still locked in each other's embrace. Neither of us reach for the light switch, concentrating on finding the bed, while still holding each other. I feel an overwhelming desire, like nothing I have experienced before. I reach up to Owen's shirt and begin to unbutton it. He does not attempt to unfasten my dress, almost as if he is letting me choreograph this dance. With control in my corner, I am able to set myself free. I gasp for air as the fire inside consumes me. We tumble over onto the floor, and laugh for a moment, then continue to kiss. Owen sits up and leads me back to the bed, but not before I strip off my dress and underwear. He tears off the remainder of his clothes, and we fall onto the bed in a hot mess. My hands caress his body, taut and smooth, his skin hot and tantalizing as I slide my tongue over his chest. He moves his hands over me like a sculptor modeling supple clay, soft yet firm. There is passion in his touch, but also a sense of indulgence, like running his fingers over silk, enjoying the sensation it brings. I shiver as the craving sweeps over me. I cannot have him close enough. All my inhibitions vanish. The ultimate human expression is mine now, free of self doubt, pain and humiliation. Owen enters me and the world becomes mine.

We finally relax in each other's arms, sweating, naked, and full of the Universe and its wonders. Then we slept; cradled together like two pieces of a puzzle, unwilling to break apart and lose the image of what we have created together. As I fall into sleep, I hear a voice in my mind whisper, *you are home.*

My phone rings and I see that it's Evelyn calling. After a few minutes of polite conversation, she asks if I would be able to come over to her house to discuss the bookstore. It has been three months since Gwen's death, and she has hardly set foot in the store since then. The first time she visited, she broke into tears, exclaiming that she saw Gwen everywhere she looked in the store, and it was too hard for her. I sense that this meeting will answer my question about whether or not the store will remain open.

I walk up the front path to their house, recalling that the last time I had passed these doors was the day of Gwen's Celebration of Life. No more colourful flowers on the verandah, only folded up lawn chairs, and a few stray dead leaves trapped in the corner by the wall. Evelyn looks only slightly brighter than when I had seen her a few weeks ago. I take a seat on the couch and Evelyn makes herself comfortable in the small easy chair opposite me. She clears her throat and begins. She talks about how heart-sick she is at the thought of closing the store, but she has no energy or desire to keep it going. It was Gwen's passion, not hers. Then she looks at me directly and asks, without pause, if I would like to buy her out. That thought hadn't even crossed my mind. I was just beginning to imagine my life without the bookstore, and the image made my stomach ache. It's an idea that could be possible, but do I want to take on the responsibility? At the age of twenty-nine, am I ready to handle this massive challenge? Would I be eligible for financing to cover the cost of buying her out? I sit still, feeling a whirl of questions and possibilities tumble around in my head. Evelyn sits patiently staring at me. I tell her to give me time to think it over, and I will give her my answer as soon as possible. She wears a small smile, but sadness still frames her face.

After I get home, I call my dear dad. He is by no means a financial *whiz*, but he is the only person I know who has had experience with mortgages and other financial dealings with banks. I explain the situation, and after asking a few questions, I hear the excited tone in his voice growing. Not only is he over-the-moon happy that I have come to him for advice, but he says he has a few notions already brewing. We make plans to meet at the *Sit N Sip* to discuss these ideas.

The cafe feels warm, and smells of coffee beans and sugar. A lone reader sits in a big chair in a corner, nose inside a book, sipping a large mug of something hot. I smile as I glance around, feeling great affection for this place. I remember my first meeting with Owen, skillfully choregraphed by Hannah One; I remember Gwen and me sitting here, having a coffee, as she interviewed me for the job in the bookstore. A bittersweet tinge of sadness touches my heart at that thought. And here I am now, about to sit down with my father to contemplate the purchase of the same bookstore where I had so desperately wanted to be employed, all those years ago.

After we get our coffees and two oatmeal cookies, we find a quiet table. Sitting down, he places a red folder on the table just out of range of his coffee. He reaches over and opens it, rummaging through the papers, until he pulls out a single page and places it in front of me. "Here is what we have to do." After I glance at it, he picks up the paper and begins to read aloud. "*The seven steps you need to do when buying a business.* Number one," I touch his arm to interrupt him. "Um, I haven't made up my mind about buying or not. I just want your opinion." An expression of disappointment flashes briefly across his face, before he smiles and says, "I guess, by the look of this folder, you are getting my opinion. Hannah, I think this is *your* opportunity, *your* time to reach out and take what you truly love, and that is *this* bookstore. I have seen you, over the years, pour your soul into it. And now, well, I think it seems like it's in your blood. My opinion is, buy it."

Buying an existing business is complicated, even when you know the business and its owner. Evelyn and I decide to keep it as simple as possible, which means doing our own evaluation of the business, drawing up our own letter of intent, and completing the due diligence that comes with researching the process. My father is a huge help, acting as interpreter when legal jargon gets confusing, and, when a witness signature is needed, he provides one, along with Janice. The most troublesome area is going to be financing. From my reading, I surmise that the potential buyer needs equity, or a down payment, to bring to the table, when applying for a small business loan. This is where my father has stepped in, yet again. I have some savings, but certainly not enough to cover it, so my dad has offered to fill in the gap. He considers it an investment in the business, and in me. If the time comes to sell it, he will simply recoup his investment. At first, I refuse to accept an interest-free loan. This is risky, and I hate the thought of him losing money, but my father keeps assuring me that this is something he can afford to do. My mother knows about the plan to buy the store, and she is very supportive, and doesn't question any aspect of the loan.

Finally, all the pieces are in place. The business licence is transferred to my name, the money exchanges hands, figuratively speaking, and Evelyn says her goodbyes for the last time, standing in the middle of the store. She promises to visit now and again, but we both know the pain may still be too much for her, even after time passes.

At the end of my first day as sole proprietor, I take a moment before I lock the front door, to look around the store. I see possibilities, I see traditions that should be kept. I see Gwen's dream staring at me, willing me to adopt it as my own and carry on. What I see now belongs to me, and this thought alone makes me glow.

Six

I awake to the sound of giggling, and a male voice mumbling something like, "enough already." Neville has moved into our apartment, so he and Jamie can save more money for their wedding. How much money will it take to get married at City Hall, and host a party at a local restaurant after the ceremony? I believe they just want to be together, and I can't blame them. I feel a heavy arm draped across my torso, and carefully try to extract myself. Owen himself is spending more time here, and it feels good, albeit still unfamiliar, to wake up next to him. We haven't talked about moving in together, but the thought has crossed my mind, as I am certain it has crossed his too. I pull on my robe and make my way to the kitchen to start a pot of coffee. It's Sunday, which means I don't have to work. I have been at the store six days a week for the past three months, as the Christmas season came and went, and then year-end inventory was tackled. Now, six weeks into the new year, I'm able to take a bit of time off and reconfigure how the store is to be managed. Janice and Mila are great at multi-tasking, but Janice has really come through as a makeshift co-manager all these months. I think it's time to make her role more official. This type of commitment deserves to be recognized, both by promotion, and by salary.

The coffee pot gurgles reluctantly to life, probably feeling over-used and abused, and in need of retirement. Maybe Jamie will get a coffee maker as a wedding present, then we can donate this old one somewhere else. Out of the corner of my eye, I see a naked man walk along the hallway to the bathroom. Neville has no qualms about his body, letting the world see him for all his beauty. And he is a beautiful man. Both inside and out. I have gotten used to the naked parade, so it hardly phases me anymore. It's only when my parents, or Hannah One, are visiting, that it can be a little uncomfortable. Not so much for Hannah One, who expresses her appreciation directly to Neville for sharing his beauty with her, and making her body shiver with delight. They laugh, and I cringe.

I see Owen emerge from my room, in boxer shorts and a tee shirt. He sleeps naked, but is aware of social constructs enough to know he would not be welcome if he sits on the furniture with his bare ass. He catches me, pulls me in for a kiss, entwining his arms around me, almost cutting off my air. I struggle, giggling a bit, until he finally relents, loosening his hold, but keeping a hand on my back. He leans forward to stare at the coffee pot, willing it to brew faster. I step back and return to the living room. Clothing and books adorn the couch and chair, and two dirty plates, cups and various papers cover our only table. I scan the room for an empty place to sit down, then I shove a pile of clothes onto the floor to make room for two on the couch. Owen enters a few moments later, handing me a hot cup and sitting down beside me on the couch. I hear Jamie call out from her bedroom, "Coffee ready?" I reply, trying not to yell too loudly, "Yup!" The sound of the bed frame squeaking is all I hear, as she pulls herself off her mattress. Wearing an oversized tee shirt with her university name emblazoned across the chest, Jamie traipses into the kitchen for some much-needed java.

It's going to be a typical Sunday in our apartment. Then my phone rings.

The name "Mom" appears on the screen. Since it's unusual for her to call so early on a Sunday, my reaction is immediate concern.

I answer before the third ring. "Mom? Hi, what's up?" I try to keep the concern from my voice, to no avail. "Hannah, don't panic, but it's your grandmother. There's been an accident." Images of a car crash, or an airplane flying into her house, flash across my inner eye. "Accident? What do you mean? What happened?" She quickly relays the story of how Hannah One was attempting to get a large bowl down from a high cupboard and she slipped off the step stool. She has broken her hip. My mother continues, as I envision Hannah One sprawled on the floor; "She has one of those emergency call buttons on a necklace, so she pressed it and the ambulance got there very quickly. The response company called your father. He's at the hospital now. I just thought you'd want to keep your dad company while he waits for news." Her comments are laced with regret, a regret that she herself feels no compunction to go there, and support her husband. I doubt he would really want her there anyway; it's become obvious they don't like each other much, anymore. I quickly thank her for calling, and tell her I'll let her know how Hannah One is doing, later in the day. She thanks me and says she appreciates getting an update whenever possible. No matter that she and my dad don't like each other, I know she cares about Hannah One.

I quickly fill Owen in on the situation, as I get dressed. He immediately starts putting on his jeans and sweater. "You don't have to come. I can call you later to let you know how she's doing." He looks at me without smiling, and replies, "She is *my* grandmother too." And with that, we both grab our phones and head out the door.

After Owen drops me off at the front entrance, I quickly find my father, sitting in a waiting room that's situated on the first floor, near the emergency area. He sits still, looking white, his pepper greying hair making his face look paler and aged. He glances up as I approach and then stands up, opening his arms to hug me. He had sent a text with an update, so by the time I actually arrived, I was fully aware of her current status. We take our seats, and wait. Ten minutes later I see Owen coming down the long corridor, having found somewhere to park. He steps up to my dad, who remains seated, and rubs his shoulder in an attempt to comfort him. The two of them have a very amiable relationship.

Today we are fairly fortunate, as Hannah One was whisked through a very empty emergency room to get admitted, and is quickly being prepped for surgery. It will be a long wait until we hear anything, but none of us is willing to leave. My father adores his mother, as we all do. She is a beacon of light and the anchor in the storm we all so much need.

Half an hour passes before Owen stands up, stretching out his long frame to knock out the kink in his back. "How about I find us some coffee? I think I saw a coffee shop in the lobby as I came in." He hardly waits for a response before heading off. I assume both of us nodded to him, but my head is so unfocused, I can't be sure.

Another ten minutes pass, and finally a nurse enters the waiting room, with Owen following in behind her, carrying a cardboard tray of coffees. He stands there, a look of uncertainty on his face. The nurse smiles as she approaches, "Mr. Casey? Oh good, you're still here. Just an update on Mrs. Casey." It sounds odd to hear Hannah One being referred to by her surname. To everyone around her, she is always Hannah One. "The surgery went smoothly, as expected. She is in recovery and will be for some time, until we move her to a room. She won't be seeing anyone today, but you're welcome to return tomorrow, during visiting hours." She begins to turn away, having relayed all the message she intends to, and not waiting for questions. I speak up before she can disappear. "Will she be okay? How long will she be in the hospital? Will she be able to walk unassisted ever again?" The nurse keeps the placid smile on her face, but I notice the impatience in her stance, indicating that she doesn't have the answers I'm looking for, and needs to get on with the one-million others tasks still waiting to be completed. She takes a breath and turns to my dad, "Mr. Casey, your mother will be here until we think she is well enough to be discharged. That could be a week, maybe even two. She'll have medication for pain, and be registered for rehab, as well. That's all I can say at this point." And without further discussion she turns and walks away.

Owen takes a seat next to my dad and pulls a cup out of the tray and hands it to him, and a second one to me. We sit in silence, sipping the strong, somewhat bitter tasting coffee. No one suggests leaving, as if a collective unspoken reluctance to depart holds us in place.

As I open my eyes, the sight of bright Daisy-patterned wallpaper greets them. A slight disorientation makes me uneasy, until I recall the fact that I'm in the guestroom at Hannah One's house. It's a warm, cheerful room, with the morning sun peeking through the curtains. Several paintings adorn the walls, all created by my grandmother's hand. I run my hand over the quilt draped over me, a creation of my great-grandmother, whose name momentarily escapes my morning brain. Yesterday, at the hospital, it was decided that I would check on Hannah One's house, to make sure no faucets were running, or element on the stove left on. Both my father and I have a tremendous attachment to this house, and want to make sure it's safe and sound while its primary resident recuperates in hospital. I arrived midafternoon, finding the house in a tranquil mood, just awaiting the return of Hannah One. There was something about the silence, the lack of her energy bouncing off the walls that made me feel sad for the house itself. It was then that I decided to stay overnight, to keep it company. If I'm being truly honest, it was a comfort I myself needed, to be near her things, her energy, as it drifts ethereally around the rooms, even without her being here. Owen offered to stay with me, but there was something about the solitude of the house I desired, to help process the situation. This accident could mean many changes to her life, as well as my own. She will need someone to be with her when she leaves the hospital, possibly for months or more. At the age of seventy-eight she is still living independently and without mobility issues, but this will definitely be hampered by a new hip, at least for a while.

I pull myself out of bed and make my way to the kitchen to find some coffee. I make a small pot, sitting down at the kitchen table to await the brew. Sitting at her table, I envision all the meals shared together; the craft projects and jigsaw puzzles completed; most importantly, all the lively discussions we had. This table has witnessed a lifetime of talks about *everything*. Now, as I look around, I realize how much this house means to me. It is the eye of the storm, a harbour in a dark night, a warm blanket on a cold winter day. Somehow the house itself seems to have these invisible arms that have taken me in, cradling me and giving me the comfort that is missing by Hannah One's absence.

An image of me moving into the extra bedroom upstairs, making this my home alongside the person who means the most to me, my grandmother, makes my gut flutter with excitement. It feels totally right to do this. The more I think about it, the more ideal it all seems to be. The timing is perfect, as Jamie and Neville are getting married, and, as it turns out Neville's sister, Kaleisha, is immigrating from Jamaica soon, and will need somewhere to stay. She can take my bedroom in the apartment, so I won't be leaving Jamie out of pocket for the rent.

I smile, feeling a warm glow in the pit of my stomach, knowing this is the right move, for Hannah One and for me.

SEVEN

The move to Hannah One's house went very smoothly. I have everything settled before Hannah One is released from the hospital, so I can focus on her when she comes home. I decided to leave all the furniture in my apartment bedroom, which includes a bed with a new mattress (thanks to Owen complaining about lumps in the old one), a dresser and a nightstand. All these things, aside from the mattress, were bought at a thrift shop, so they hold no sentimental value. I think of Kaleisha arriving and needing a decent place to sleep, so I am happy the furniture will be of use. Kaleisha's visit seems very fortuitous, but I soon learned the reason for her arrival in May. Jamie is pregnant. Being as unobservant as I tend to be, I haven't noticed the slight weight gain, and the change to looser fitting clothing. She has been dying to tell me, but wanted to get through the first three months before telling anyone. There is a history of miscarriages in her family, so Jamie is a little nervous about the pregnancy. That's why Kaleisha is arriving early, to get settled in before the baby's arrival in early July. She is Neville's older sister, and has helped in the rearing of most of the LaTour children, so she will be a great help. Jamie exclaimed she knows nothing about being a mom, and with her own mother unwell, Jamie can't count on her for help, so having Kaleisha there will certainly set her mind at ease. Jamie wants to work for the rest of the school year, but that is cutting it close. Her dedication to her children in her class makes me certain she will be a wonderful mother.

The most difficult task in the move is Hannah One. She is dead set against me "giving up my life to tend to her", but I assure her it is anything but that. I told her Jamie is having a baby, and with Kaleisha moving in, I'd need to move out anyway. My father decided to take a leave of absence from the accounting firm, so he can help her manage day to day things, like rehab appointments. I will simply be there in the evenings and mornings to help her, if need be. She reluctantly agrees to have me move in, but wants to make it clear that she'll be up and at it in no time.

I walk along the familiar path in the woods, as I always do, whenever I have enough free time to go there. I slow my pace as I come to the field where, what seems like eons ago, I rescued a Hawk who was caught in some old fence wire. I look over to the spot where I knelt to free his talon from the wire, and try to envision my flight once more, as Hawk and I became one. Only this time, I remain anchored to the ground, as if being held by an invisible thread.

Then I see her. She sits upon a tree stump, facing away from me. Her long grey hair pulled into a braid which runs down her back. There is something so familiar about her, I believe I am seeing Hannah One. How did she get out to the woods with her bad hip? I call out to her, but she ignores me. I make my way through the colourful wildflowers and long blades of grass to stand about ten feet away. Looking more closely, I now see it's not Hannah One. "Oh, I'm sorry. I thought I knew you. I didn't mean to interrupt your peace." I turn to move away, but she rises from the stump and turns to look at me. Her motions are stiff, as if she has been sitting for a while. When she turns I can see her weathered face. Once again I am struck by a sense of familiarity. She smiles. "Hannah, I'm glad you're here. I was beginning to think you wouldn't come." She does not move, but lifts her face to the sun. "I have always loved it here. I love the feel of Sun on my old body. I love to hear Nature's song, and join in the harmony when I can." I say nothing, only because I am still trying to place her. A customer at the store? A friend of Hannah One? She turns her face back to me and says, "I just wanted to say this to you. As you travel through this life, let go of the past, all your pasts, and embrace the Now. Now will not be here Forever. Forever will come soon enough, as all humans discover. Time has given you a gift. Embrace Time, don't waste it. It's all the things old people regret, and can never re-do. Don't waste your time on analysing each moment. Allow yourself to go through it all, the good and the bad, as this is what makes the human experience so complete." I blink in confusion. As I'm about to ask her who she is, I hear a knocking noise. I turn to see where it is coming from…

The knock at the front door of Hannah One's house wakes me up. I sit up and swing my legs off the couch. It's Owen at the door.

He arrives with bags of groceries. We are getting the house set for Hannah One's homecoming tomorrow. I gave him a detailed list of all her favourite foods he was to pick up. He plunks the colourful cloth bags down on the counter and begins unpacking fresh vegetables, fruit, her favourite bread and muffins from the bakery, along with other items I know she will eat. It's important to keep her healthy. Normally, she eats like a Sparrow, and if left to her own devices, she would only eat nuts, fruit and crackers all day.

After the last bag is emptied, Owen turns and pulls me in for a long, lingering kiss. He has really enjoyed staying here with me, playing house. He has even made himself useful by repairing some things that, although not crucial to the running of the home, are annoying when they don't work very well, like the leaky shower head. I snuggle into his arms and close my eyes. I can still see the old woman. Her words fresh in my mind. *Embrace the Now.* Of course, this seems to be obvious. Hannah One always says, *if I only knew then what I know now.* But hell, then there wouldn't be much point in the journey, would there? The strangely familiar woman also mentioned letting go of *all* my pasts. Let go of being an Alternate? Or let go of the constraints that this knowledge has placed on me? Analysing every step seems to be part of my daily routine, but maybe it's time to let that go. Maybe it's time to experience life without the parameters or conditions I use to buffer me from some situations I believe may cause me grief. So many questions, and no way to get answers. I keep my eyes closed and snuggle in closer.

The house visibly brightens the minute Hannah One steps through the front door. Owen is in the lead, holding the door open with one hand and her small overnight bag in the other. She insists on walking, without the walker, into the house, but not without leaning on me. The only way the doctor would sign off on her release was that she promised to use the walker until she is stronger. Now, it sits obediently at the foot of the front steps, awaiting its next use.

Hannah One looks around the living room, as if she has been gone for a year, and not only ten days. "It's funny, I have gone traveling for stretches of time and returned home refreshed and exhilarated by my adventures. This time I am just damn relieved to see this old house again. It's like missing an old friend." She gets herself to the couch and gingerly sits down, running her hands along the cushion, almost like stroking a favourite pet. Owen takes her bag into the bedroom we set up in the back sunroom so she can avoid the stairs, and then exits the front door to retrieve the walker. He isn't staying long. He and I discussed the fact that Hannah One will need a quiet day or two to transition back to being at home, but with the added change of me being here *all* the time. Owen wheels the walker in to the hallway before entering the living room to sit down for a moment. "There's lots of food in the fridge, but if there's something you're hankering for, just call me!" Owen grins, obviously happy to have his adopted grandmother back where she belongs. She smiles at him, but her face is drawn and tired. The physical effort of simply getting home has worn her out. Owen notices it and looks at me. I nod, without saying anything. He rises from the chair and crosses the room to give Hannah One a kiss on the cheek. "I'm very happy to see you home, and I'm sure you're happy too. I'll take off! You girls will have things to do. Don't talk about me too much while I'm gone!" He winks as Hannah One lets out a chuckle. He gives me a quick hug and kiss before disappearing out the front door.

I watch him pull out of the driveway, and even though he can't see, I wave goodbye. I turn to see Hannah One struggling to get up. I rush over, but she attempts to wave me away. I ignore her and take her elbow to help her stand. "Enough already!" She barks. I know she is tired, as it's unlike her to snap at anyone when she knows they're only trying to help. She looks at me with a mixed expression. I can't read it well, so I simply wait for her to say something. She looks away towards the sunroom door. "I think I should lie down; I am not feeling myself." She turns and eyes the walker in the hallway. She makes her way over and places her hands on the handles and pushes. Slowly she drives herself through the kitchen to the makeshift bedroom in the back sunroom. I have it filled with colourful plants, and one of her cherished paintings. The pullout couch, moved so she can view the garden from her bed, is made up with her favourite quilt and many pillows. Books lie stacked up beside the bed, along with her old brass cowbell, to be rung if she needs a hand and I'm out of earshot. She smiles as she enters the room, seeing the sun beaming in through the curtains. "Oh, my, you have gone to a lot of trouble! It's lovely." She gets herself to the bed and sits on the edge. I kneel down and take off her shoes. She lies back and closes her eyes. She seems to fall asleep as soon as her head hits the pillow. I quietly leave her to rest and convalesce.

I never really noticed how the months began to blend together. My father went back to work after the first month, and now

Hannah One is mobile and much the same as before the accident. She has put on weight, but the doctor says it's a healthy weight, as she was a bit too thin, before the fall. I have begun to cook more interesting meals, since I now have an audience to cook for. We laugh and struggle to make our way through some of the failed dishes, and rave at my successes. Owen has literally made himself quite at home, much to Hannah One's delight. She is happy to have him live with us part-time, although he still has his own apartment, for the time being. Her initial reluctance at having me move in seems to have vanished. The look I saw on her face the first day she arrived home, was a mixture of relief and fear. After she felt better, she confessed her fearful thoughts to me. She worried that her independence and her spirit would be forever diminished by the effects of this accident. Her age never bothered her before, but now she feels it. She is still, at times, sad, but tries to be grateful for the mobility she still has, and continues to pursue greater flexibility as she dutifully performs her daily exercises.

    I feel like I've found my true home. Growing up in and with this house, it feels natural to return and stay; like it was meant to be. I am starting to find the balance in my life, with my business, my family and with Owen. It is a hectic, sometimes lop-sided type of balance, but I seem to have discovered a way to juggle it all. The words still echo in the corner of my mind, *Embrace the time, let yourself go through it, all of it, the good and the bad.*

    The evenings are still warm and light enough that we can enjoy sitting in the garden after supper. Owen is on a trip to a writers' workshop he is facilitating, so it's just Hannah One and me enjoying the peaceful green, quietly soaking in the last of the day's energy through the streaks of fading sun that peek around the trees. The Crickets sing to find their mates, the last Mourning Dove sits perched on the fence, cooing quietly, and a lone Toad makes the odd *churr-up* sound near the small pond Owen has landscaped into the garden over the summer.

I look at my grandmother. I study her hands, resting in her lap. I glance up to see she has her head tilted, looking up at the leaves as they catch the fingers of the setting sun that tickles them. She has a contented look on her face, and it makes me smile. She catches me looking at her and gently laughs; "Either I have something on my face, or you have something to tell me." It hadn't occurred to me, but in fact I do. I have had a longing to tell her about my dream, or vision, or whatever it was, when the old woman came to me with that message. I need to get another perspective, and I want it to be *her* perspective.

"Well, yes, I have something I need your opinion on." I proceed to tell her my tale, trying not to leave out any detail. Hannah One's forehead creases, as if she is concentrating very hard on what I'm telling her. Then she closes her eyes. I finish my story and wait for her response. A few minutes later I wonder if she has drifted off to sleep, but she opens her eyes and smiles. "How lucky you are!", she exclaims. "You have all these wonderful insights given to you, possibly by some guide, or spirit, or who knows what! This *person* has deemed it important enough to visit you, and tell you to smarten up! That is something many humans would either love to hear, or would ignore completely, happy to continue on in their dreary lives. My opinion is, you have been given a chance to shift your mind-set to one that will make your human experience so much fuller. I don't know what I would have done had some old lady in a dream given me a message like that when I was thirty. I was busy raising your dad and keeping my husband happy, so I would not likely have felt the *need* to change, even though it might have opened more experiences for me. You have the chance *now*, to make sure you are living it *all*. I think you are an amazing woman, Hannah; I am so proud of all you have accomplished, and all that you have become. I think this is a sign that you need to continue to allow yourself to be happy, to go after what gives you bliss; live it *all*. Let go of that doubt, just live it *all*." She turns to look out over her beautiful garden, and continues, "Don't wake up one day, at the ripe old age of seventy-nine and wish you had more time, wish you had been smarter with your youthful years. Don't carry regrets through life, as they will only keep you weighed down in the mire of the *what-ifs*."

I wait to see if she has more to add, but instead she grasps the arms of her sturdy lawn chair and rises up, stretching her arms up over her head and waving them back and forth. "I am a tree in the breeze! I will drop my grey hair leaves all over the lawn so you'll need a comb to gather them up!" She giggles at my confused expression. I am not sure where that odd comment came from, but I laugh at the silliness of her remark, after such an eloquent speech.

Eight

On June twenty-ninth, at four o'clock in the morning, the world welcomed Aidan Damerae LaTour. The name Damerae means "a boy of joy". And joy is what he brings to Jamie and Neville. All babies have a special glow about them, fresh into creation, like a small blossom yet to bloom.

I got the call from Neville around nine a.m. that morning. He sounded happy, but exhausted. Jamie was asleep, after several hours of difficult labour. They would be in the hospital until tomorrow, then back to the apartment. I knew Jamie wouldn't want extra visitors in her hospital room, as I assumed her parents would crowd in to see their first grandchild. I told Neville I'd text first, to make sure it was alright to visit, once everyone was settled in at home. I was aching to see the baby, and Jamie, but wanted to be considerate. I thanked Neville for taking the time to call me and told him to go to bed. He laughed, and said he was on his way, which led me to envision him sitting naked on the couch, a beer in one hand and the phone in the other. It was my turn to laugh.

The bookstore bustles with business as the summer months and the nice weather encourage more foot traffic along our old street. We have undergone a few renovations, thanks to some brilliant ideas from our newest staff member, Nouri Vasile. An engineering student whose family immigrated from Iran five years ago, he has a fresh perspective and a keen eye for design. The store hasn't expanded the space, just utilized it more efficiently. The changes have received many positive comments from regular customers, who, although they loved Gwen's vision of her dream, also love the idea of the store evolving and updating itself. Between Nouri's vision, Janice's skill at organizing, and Mila's smooth manner with the customers, this is a winning team. Today, as the hot July sun melts the afternoon away, Grace has arrived to pick up some books she had ordered. Arthur Monahan, her Spiritual Advisor friend I had met one time, a few years ago, is in tow. He is still full of light and energy, and when I look in his eyes I feel as if the Universe is looking back. He is a little intimidating, but also someone I am very drawn to, and I wonder why I never took the time to get together with him; I remember deciding that I didn't need his help, I already knew whatever it was I needed to know about my journey, past and present.

Janice retrieves Grace's order from the backroom, while I stand and talk with these two balls of cosmic energy. Fortunately, the store is empty right now, so we have the ability to talk without being interrupted. Grace smiles, saying, "Arthur is doing individual energy sessions. You should sign up!" I see Arthur smile, but hold his hand up, "Now Grace, don't go pushing me on Hannah. She knows I am here, and when it is right, she will find me." I notice he uses the word, *when*, and not *if*. He continues, "She knows when to *embrace* what feels right, don't you Hannah?" He turns and winks, so only I can see it. It seems a little creepy to me, but at the same time I am wholly intrigued. Using that word *embrace*, makes me think of the old woman. Did he sense I have a guide, who is telling me to embrace the *Now*? Grace breaks into my thoughts as she replies to Arthur's comments; "Arthur, sometimes we need a hand to see what is in front of us. We are so busy looking ahead that we overlook over an opportunity right before our feet, and then we miss it." I look around the store, suddenly unsure of what to say next. Without giving it more analysis, I open my mouth and say, "Sure, sign me up! Sounds interesting. Maybe I'll learn something about myself." Without my analytical brain picking it apart, my gut just went ahead and jumped feet first into the unknown abyss. Embrace the *Now*. Well, okay, here we go!

I arrive at the Healing Centre about half an hour earlier than my appointment time with Arthur. I had a long day at work, and I need time to decompress before tackling this *exploration*. I can't imagine what I hoped to gain by doing this, as I already know what and when and where I came from. The voice inside repeats, *let it go! Explore and have fun! Maybe Arthur will learn something new today, too!* I take several deep cleansing breaths as I sit in the quiet nook off the main entrance. Grace emerges from a hallway to my left and silently waves and points to her office. She has just finished a session of Reiki and energy work on a client, and is heading to her office, I assume, to set the client's next appointment. The peace of the room envelopes me as I try to erase the day from my mind.

Arthur enters the lounge about ten minutes later, after gently ushering a young woman to the front door as she clutches a handful of tissues, eyes puffy from crying. Human reaction to an exploration of self can often bring about tears – tears produced by the release of a blockage, or happy tears from the elation felt when the energy imbues itself in their system. I stand up, thinking I should follow Arthur into the room, but he says, "Just give me a few minutes. I need to clear myself, and the room." He smiles and turns away. I sit back down as Grace enters the lounge and takes a seat next to me. She whispers, "I wish I could journey with you; I think it will be so interesting." She smiles and squeezes my hand. I wish I held her outlook, but I still have my doubts. "Yes, it will be interesting, I just hope Arthur isn't bored." Grace laughs quietly, "Arthur is never bored doing these sessions. He will often come along with whoever is doing the exploring, so he gets a front row seat to whatever the person is experiencing." When she sees my shocked expression, she quickly adds, "Oh no, I mean, he only accompanies you if you give him permission. There are so many people who are afraid to explore on their own, as if they will get lost, or they are frightened of what they will find, so he offers to keep them company." She pats my hand, attempting to reassure me. My shocked expression comes from the thought of Arthur discovering my secret, of being an Alternate. I am not afraid to explore, in fact it will be, as humans call it, like a trip down memory lane. Just as Grace is about to continue, Arthur appears in the doorway. "Ok Hannah, let's begin." He turns as I stand up to follow him to the room at the end of the hall. I glance back to see Grace, a mischievous grin on her face, waving at me.

The room is dimly lit and warm, but not stuffy. The same type of comfortable massage-style table that Grace uses is in the centre in the room, taking up much of the space. I notice a small chair in the corner, but gently take a seat on the edge of the table, letting my legs dangle. Arthur walks around and seats himself in the small chair. He looks so big and tall in it I sense it's not a great fit for him, but he makes no comment about it. He takes a few deep breaths and then looks at me, quietly saying, "Now, as with all who come to explore, I need to explain how we can make this a *successful* trip. A calm mind helps, an open mind is even better. I will merely be a guide from the outside. If you need my help I am here; if you need a friend to tag along, then I am your man, but otherwise I simply help you open the door." He takes another deep breath. "Get yourself comfortable on the table. Cover yourself, if you'd prefer. There is a light blanket there at your feet." I lie down, leaving the banket untouched. "Perfect. Now a few deep cleansing breaths; make sure to close your eyes. Let your mind free itself, and open up to the Universe." A moment of silence, and I feel the tension leaving my body, my energy being called upon to open my mind and spirit to all that is. Arthur continues quietly, "Yes, envision yourself floating, free of care, free of your body, the only thing you are is Light. When you are free, tell me, so we can continue." I love to float, and could do that for an hour, but

I know that isn't the point of being here, so I mumble, "I'm free now." The room starts to fall away, there is only Light. Arthur's voice comes from somewhere far away. "Good. Now I want you to imagine a door. It can be any type of door, any design you want to imagine. When you see your door, say, I see my door." I easily see a door, painted white, with a glass door knob. "I see my door."

"Good. Would you like to open it and see what's on the other side? If you do, simply open it." I look at the beautiful bevelled-glass knob and reach out to it. The glass edges feel firm against my hand as I grasp it and turn. The door slowly swings open, revealing a long hallway in front of me. "Can you see the hallway?" Arthur asks. I look through the doorway and respond, "Yes, and I see many doors." I take a single step into the hall. "Good. Each door is a life lived. Each with its own unique qualities, all with some quality that connects every door to each other. It is up to you to open a door, or leave it closed. It's up to you." I slowly walk along and stop in front of the third door. It has no markings on it, yet I am drawn to it. I grasp the handle; it's made of brass. It opens and there is nothing but light; Bright yellow light. As I step through the doorway, the light encircles me, swallowing me and lifting me up. I am home. I hear Arthur's voice, but this time it's so near it's like it's inside my head. A streak of yellow waves and speaks to me; "Hi Hannah. It's Arthur. Welcome home!" The elation I first felt at being once again with the energy source of my creation is immediately discarded, as I try to look directly at the wavering yellow beam and understand what is going on. "Sorry for the surprise. I just thought this might be the best way to let you know, you're not alone as an Alternate human. I am here, as are many others on Earth. We are all awake to our Alternate selves. It's not just you."

Suddenly the light around me spreads out, morphing into an immense web. Crystal threads string out across the Universe, with tiny beads of light running along, like dew dripping off a spider's web in the morning. I am a bead of light, clinging to a strand. All the other beads twinkle and bounce, as other droplets move along the filaments. I marvel at the beauty of the structure, its delicate and highly intricate design stretching to infinity. I feel infinite myself, as if I am not just a single bead, but I am all beads, and I am the threads upon which the beads sit and move. I sense an immense feeling of connectedness, and yet I can feel my human body react as tears flow down my cheeks. The web grows brighter and brighter until once again I stand in the doorway, my hand still on the brass handle. I step back into the hallway and close the door. As I turn, I notice the door from which I had originally entered the hallway. It is now closed. I look at the back of it and see that about half of it is lined with rows of images, like small photographs on a wall. I walk up and look closely. I see pictures of me. They remind me of old polaroid square photos. The first picture is of me on the day I was born. As I scan along the horizontal rows, each picture represents a moment, an emotion, or an event of my current life. I see a picture of me with Fred, our old Beagle. It makes me smile. I see pictures of Julian and me painting in the woods. I see pictures of every horrible moment, and every joyful moment, of this life. My eyes come to rest on the last row of pictures, just above the door handle. The row is filled with images of Owen, and Hannah One. The row consists of all the moments that make up my life as it is, now.

    I turn to see Arthur standing in the hallway, not far away. He smiles and I smile back at him. With so much to process, I had almost forgotten what he has just revealed to me. He is an Alternate too. He walks up to the door and starts looking at the pictures. "Wow, you've been having a lot of experiences this time around. Oh, I love this one!" and he points to the picture of me with Fred. I have never seen a door like this before, so I have to ask, without taking my eyes off the pictures in front of me, "What is *this* door?"

    "It's not actually *anything*, and yet it's *everything*. It is a collective database of your memories or pinpoints in Time that hold significance to your journey, that you have been subconsciously storing *here*, over your lifetime. That is why it ends here." He points to the last picture in the row, which is picture of Arthur and me standing in a white hallway, looking at photos on a door. "As you go through life, the door will hold more and more, until it is full." I look at Arthur and say, "You mean, until I die. Then the door is no more." Arthur shakes his head, "The door is merely a representation of your cache of memories. The pictures are not actually mounted on there, to sit here, then disappear when you physically die. They are planted in your spirit; they are planted in the spirits of those who shared the experiences with you. It is like the web. It is all connected, and therefore it will be woven into *you* throughout time." I nod, and reach for the glass handle of the door and open it, so I can, once again, float up. With so many thoughts weighing me down now, I cannot float, so I gently sink to the ground, feeling the Earth below me, which then becomes the table I'm laying on. Slowly I sit up, and turn to face Arthur. He stands up and comes towards me. Silently we share the embrace of long-lost friends.

We exit the room, and see Grace sitting quietly in the lounge, reading one of the books she had recently bought at the store. She looks up and smiles as we approach. "Well? Hope it was a fascinating exploration." She stands up, closing her book and tucking it under her arm. Arthur and I look at each other and giggle. Grace continues, "Say no more! If the Universe wants me to know, it will tell me, but I am dying of curiosity, nonetheless!" She laughs, and walks off to her office. "Bye Grace!" We both say simultaneously. And then we chuckle again. She waves over her shoulder, but does not reply.

We decide to find a quiet place to sit and talk. Hopping into Arthur's car, we head to a nearby park. I was about to suggest sitting on a park bench, but I really don't want our conversation overheard, so we stay in the car. I turn so I can face Arthur, and ask; "Why didn't you just tell me, the first time we met? I've been struggling all these years; it would have been nice to know this information a while ago." He shrugs, replying, "You know as well as I, the Universe sets things up to happen the way they should. You were meant to go through the experiences you had, to make you the human you are today. I think if I told you the truth earlier, I might have changed your course, altered your experiences, so your journey might not be as it should." He pauses long enough for me to ask, "Then, why now? Why tell me now, or at all, for that matter?" Arthur sits still for a moment, thoughtful. "Well, to be honest, it's my own need that drove me to reveal myself to you. I myself have been feeling isolated, and although I thought this is part of my journey, the Alternate aspect of me longed for like-minded companionship. Sure, there are friends like Grace, who have the ability to connect with other realms of *being*, but she doesn't have the actual awake Alternate duality that you and I have. I identified her as an Alternate, but she does not know it herself. I don't want to wake her up and spoil her journey. When I saw your Light, it was too tempting not to explore."

This is a lot to digest. I feel as if a huge hole in my life is slowly filling itself up. We both sit silently for a few minutes, Arthur very cognizant that I need time to process. I close my eyes and return to the door. Suddenly I have another question, "Why use doors? It seems like a very simple metaphor for something that is so vast and complex." Arthur grins. "Well, I just started you out the way I start out any human who decides to explore. The human mind is complex, yet delicate, and prefers imagery that can be easily comprehended. Showing them a straight hallway, with options of doors to choose from, is easier for their minds to envision and explore. If I show them that, in fact, existence is not a straight line backwards or forwards from them, but a web of interconnecting threads and avenues, in all directions, it would be too vast for their senses to process. Many would simply shut down, feeling too overwhelmed by it all."

We sit for another hour, talking about our experiences, our isolation, our longing to return to the Alternate when the complexities of human emotions seem to overwhelm us. Arthur talks about his work; He explains that by continuing to help humans explore other dimensions, he is hoping to support them as they open up to the Universe, and all it has to offer them. He was very despondent when he first saw how closed off most humans can be. When he met Grace, he felt as if he had been given a platform from which he could work with those who are, at the very least, open to changing their perspective on their human existence.

"So how did you know I am an Alternate? I have always wondered if I am meeting other Alternates, but unable to see it for myself. How did *you* know?" Arthur smiles and looks out at the park, seeing the green of the grass, the perfectly manicured gardens, and the trees maintained to provide just the right amount of shade, without cutting out the sun completely. "Funny how humans like to be so neat and tidy with their natural surroundings. Sorry, off on a thought there... yes, well, it was easy because I recognized your Light. It is one of two Talents I have. We, meaning all humans, and Alternates, we all have a Talent, possibly more than one, which comes from Spirit. It just needs to be recognized in oneself. Some can paint, some can draw, play an instrument and other creative Talents, while others possess Talents that lean more towards the cosmic connection of All; psychics, clairvoyants, healers like Grace, that sort of thing. With your connection to your Alternate consciousness, your Talent is heightened, so you can easily use your mind empathically with lifeforms on this planet. For instance, you communicate with animals and plants, walk in the dream realm, and transfer to the mind of another, when you will it. You may not have developed your Talents to the utmost yet, but you will. My Talent is seeing the formation of Light in *All*, and Time. Or more precisely, the ability to move through spaces in Time. For those who seek their truth, I can escort them to a time in the past, whether it be in this life or another. I can help them understand the concept of Time as a web, and not the linear passage that humans ascribe to. Humans that are open to the idea of alternate realities most often have Alternate energy in them. They just don't know it." He hesitates before continuing, "My Talent has one other aspect I am reluctant to tell, but I know you will respect my wishes, and not ask me to *use it* under *any* circumstances with you." I am intrigued. What Talent could be so bad he would not want to share it with me? "As I said, my Talent is manifestation of Time frames. That means I can see a person's past, their present life, and, well, their future." I am stunned by this revelation. "Arthur! What an immense thing to cope with, as you must know what's going on with everyone around you!" He frowns. "It doesn't work quite like that. I would need to study the patterns of Light in a life, and then I can see what lies ahead. It's like a blueprint, only it's drawn in pencil. As a human makes changes on their journey, the blueprint erases and draws new lines. It's fluid, not clear-cut. I can see the structure, but the details are limited to what the pencil sketches. And besides, I don't like telling anyone their future, because by doing that, I am in fact influencing it." I nod, understanding the effect that, for instance, knowing you are going to die in an airplane crash. You would never travel on an airplane after learning this, and this change makes other factors in your life change, and then it becomes like dominoes. Foreknowledge can knock down the entire life you were *meant* to have.

    I sit still, silently digesting all that's been said. My mind races back to one stream of information Arthur shared about my Talent. "What do you mean when you said I can transfer my mind into another? I know I can share thoughts with other Alternates when we are together, as we are one in Spirit, but to actually *transfer* to another human being?" He looks out the window again, replying, "Think of the Hawk you rescued. Did you not say you took flight in his mind when you freed him? That was a transference. You just didn't know it. It is simply hitchhiking, not taking over. It can be a wonderful thing, as you can see the world through a variety of perspectives. But I advise using caution when you enter into the mind of another human. You may see things you don't want to see." I quickly realize he is warning me against abusing this Talent I am developing, and I agree that I'd never want to see into the mind of those I love. It just seems sneaky and disrespectful. He continues, "You can work on developing your Talent, so that, over time, you will be able to move around in your mind, visit your past memories, dream-walk in a controlled way, so you know where you are going, and *when* you are. Remember the Dream World has no Time, it has no constraints on where you go, and when you go. You can just go! It's actually a pretty cool Talent you have!" He laughs.

I suddenly feel a pang in my stomach and realize it's almost seven. Owen and Hannah One will be wondering where I am, so I tell Arthur I have to get home. He offers to drive me, and I gladly accept, as it gives us more time to talk while we navigate the city streets in his old car.

NINE

One tradition I am sorely missing is the Christmas party that Gwen and Evelyn hosted each year. After Gwen died, Evelyn stopped giving parties, and eventually sold their lovely old house, as it was too much for her alone. When I bought the bookstore, I was still living in a small two-bedroom apartment with Jamie. It was not conducive to a Christmas party, at least not a "Gwen-style" party.

Today, with Hannah One's approval, we are hosting *our* first annual Bentley's Books Christmas Party at the house. There will be food, drinks, friends, and maybe even caroling. Janice is bringing her new girlfriend Amelia; Mila decided to invite her roommate George, who works at the library. Nouri is bringing his grandmother, Nasrin, which will be wonderful, as she can meet Hannah One, and hopefully they will become friends. I invited Jamie, Neville, his sister Kaleisha and the baby. I haven't seen much of Jamie; She has returned to teach, taking only two months off after giving birth to Aidan, as she fears she will lose her teacher-standing with the board. With cutbacks occurring all the time, it's tough getting a foot in the door, let alone keeping it there. She misses her baby, but Kaleisha is an excellent fill-in mom, so Jamie is able to have her career, and enjoy her family without the guilt many new mothers experience when they return to their jobs. Grace and Arthur are also on the guest list. Mark is in Paris for fashion week, so he can't attend, which is disappointing. It seems like our boats are drifting farther and farther apart, and it's with great effort we keep paddling back to each other. I sense that one day we will reconnect, but for now we both have to see where our boats take us. Hannah One had the option of inviting some of her friends, but she declined. She said she is thrilled to spend time with the people Owen and I invited, as she doesn't get to see them often enough. I extended an invitation to my parents as well, but they both declined, finding one reason or another to avoid attending a social event together. They both expressed feigned enthusiasm over our family Christmas breakfast I will host, although I'm not looking forward to the tension they might bring along with them that day. Owen suggests I change my perspective on this issue, stating; "One day you'll look back, and you'll have only fond memories of these breakfasts, and wonder why you disliked them. So, make the most of them while you still can." He is very sensitive when it comes to family relationships, even challenging ones, which I assume is due to his parents' deaths years ago, and missing out on making more memories with them.

The Sit N Sip coffee shop owners, Jon and Cristina, are also stopping by and fortunately for us all, bringing a tray full of treats for dessert. To me, pot lucks are the best kind of party to host, as you don't have to cook much, only what you volunteer to bring, and you get to try new and interesting dishes. The dining room table is full to bursting with good food. The traditional Casey Christmas tablecloth peeks out around the dishes laid out on it. It's a white cotton fabric with a simple pattern of holly and red and green garlands running along the edges. A large colourful wreath takes up the centre of the cloth. Hannah One bought it at a charity bazaar about fifty years ago, and surprisingly, through one messy boy and a spill-prone husband, it has remained clean and relatively stain-free decades later. Hannah One said the secret was she only used it when her in-laws were visiting, and *her boys,* meaning my father and grandfather, were then told to be on their best behaviour and not spill anything. Now, she couldn't care less what happens to it; if a spill occurs, then it will just get cleaned up. She was actually thinking of giving it away, as she's tired of it, but for some reason, I told her to keep it. It's part of our family tradition now, so it holds meaning to me. I think that Owen's words regarding "fond memories" still resonate in my head.

The tree is gaily decorated, and sits twinkling in the corner of the living room. Strings of lights are strung up the stairway banister and frame the windows. Christmas tunes, on records no less, play quietly on the old stereo Hannah One uses regularly. She's always loved collecting records, and she has amassed quite an eclectic collection over the years. She has everything from classical operas to Stompin' Tom. She says all music has merit, as it is produced by the Creative Spirit within.

People who don't know each other begin introducing themselves, with a lot of attention being paid to Aidan. He is a beautiful boy. With almond coloured skin, dark eyes and hair, he is glowing with an energy I know Arthur will recognize. His expressions remind me of Jamie, his mother. Neville is a wonderful father, so loving and attentive, to both his son and his wife. I almost envy the piece of happiness they have carved out for themselves. Then I see Owen smile and wink at me from across the room. I smile back. I have no reason to be envious.

After the last guest bids a fond farewell, and the last of the plates are stacked and ready for washing, Hannah One sits down in the living room and sighs. This has been both exhilarating and exhausting for her. "You know, twenty years ago I would be geared up to wash dishes and clean up, but now, I am done-in." I sit down beside her. I take her hand in mine, and reply, "You were the life of the party, I mean, besides Aidan! It's no wonder you're pooped." I smile, knowing just how much fun she must have had today. "Go on to bed. I will put Owen to work. He needs to work off all those desserts I saw him scarf down!" From the kitchen I hear a muffled rebuke, but ignore him. Hannah One slowly stands up and begins to make her way out of the living room, turning to glance around the room. "This house loves all the young energy you've brought in. When you moved in, I was so reluctant to give up living an independent life, alone, thinking the independence kept me young and moving. But I was wrong, it is *you*. You keep me young and moving. I love you so much Hannah, you are the light of my life." I hold back tears as she turns and heads towards the stairs. I call out, as I hear her slowly ascending, "I love you too, so very much." No, I definitely have no reason to be envious of Jamie.

The snowfall descending on the woods lies thick on the branches, and piles up on the top of our toques. Owen and I walk through the quiet forest, absorbing the silence like a sponge. After a busy Christmas season at the store, I am looking forward to getting through our last year-end sale, and then starting anew in January. After so many years, I am now quite capable of handling irate customers, even Christmas crowds that can be extra taxing. I inhale the cold fresh air, feeling a snow flake enter my nostril. I rub my nose as it melts inside.

Owen has been offered a job with one of the major newspapers in the city, reporting on big issues of climate change and other environmental topics. He will write articles, and have his own weekly column. He is tired of traveling so much to do lecture tours, so he is happy to set his roots down and have more regular hours. It gives us a different structure in our relationship too. There is a constancy now that I enjoy.

We continue on the trail until we come to the old wooden bridge that crosses a small creek that, in the spring time, will once again hum with movement and life. Now it sleeps through the winter, its surface frigid and still. The snow catches in the crevices of the frozen creek, producing beautiful designs. I love to see Nature's creative artwork display itself like this.

Owen stops to look out over the far landscape, taking a deep breath. He loves this forest as much as I do. It's one of the joys of our relationship, to share our love for the natural environment.

He turns to me, smiling. He takes a step closer, but doesn't reach out to touch me. Instead, he tugs off his glove and reaches into his pocket. He pulls out a small black box. I don't have time to react to seeing what sits in his palm. He clears his throat and quietly says; "I couldn't think of a better place to ask you this. Uh, um, for someone who writes for a living, I don't seem to be able to express just how much I love you. But I will try, today and everyday. If you will have me." He opens the box and there sits a beautiful yellow topaz gold ring. The band is made up of intricate interwoven scrollwork that leads around to four very tiny gold leaf-shaped prongs, that hold the most beautiful square yellow topaz. "Will you marry me?" He looks at me, his blue eyes alight with loving energy. There is no need to analyse, or doubt my answer. "Yes, I'd be so happy to marry you, Owen!"

He takes the ring out of the box and, after I slip my mitten off, he places it on my finger. Perfect fit, of course. We hug a long time, and then Owen pulls back to give me a slow, gentle kiss. It is a kiss that spans time, and stops the world from turning on its axis. The snow holds its place in the sky. All that is holds its breath in this moment. When we finally pull apart, I see the world afresh. The snow is brighter, the air crisper, the woods reverberating from the energy we cast out.

We decide to head back home and make hot chocolate, and tell Hannah One the good news.

Ten

A suitcase lies open on the bed. Three carboard boxes sit on the floor by the closet. I pull open the top drawer of the dresser I stand in front of, and view several pairs of neatly folded boxer shorts and pairs of socks, folded in on themselves to be kept from straying. I scoop up the entire contents of the drawer and unceremoniously drop all of it into the suitcase. Opening the second drawer, I begin pulling out pairs of shorts and track pants, and sort them into two piles. Keep and donate. The keepers get tossed into the suitcase, the donate land in one of the boxes on the floor. As I sort through the pants, a folded sheet of paper falls out onto the bed. I reach down and pick it up. It is a hand-made card. The front of the card bears a drawing, a little girl and a man. They are holding hands, both eating ice cream. I open the card, and read the colour-pencil lettering inside. "Happy Father's Day Dad! You are my Favourite Dad!" I feel my throat catch. I place the card carefully into a sleeve of the suitcase so it won't get bent or lost. As I move towards the next drawer to be emptied, an image in the mirror above the dresser catches my eye. A man, late fifties, greying hair, glances at me. I know that man, it is my father.

I awake from the restless sleep, not sure of just what happened. Why am I dreaming about my father? It doesn't feel like a dream, it feels more like I was there with him, going through his things, helping him pack up his belongings. Arthur had mentioned that I have the gift of transference, but I am still uncertain how it works, or how to control it. Was I there beside him, or was I *there inside him*? I hope I have not inadvertently dropped into a personal moment that my father experienced. It seems intrusive, yet for some reason, I feel like I needed to be there. His pain was reaching out to me, and I connected to it. I had no way to help, or let him know I was there for him. It's frustrating, but maybe this is something I can learn to control, as my Talent opens itself to me.

I reach over to the nightstand and pick up my phone. I know it's early, but I have a strong desire to speak to my dad. The phone rings, but the call ends up in voicemail. I leave a brief message, asking if he'd like to get a coffee one day this week. Hanging up, I immediately dial Arthur's number. He picks up on the second ring, knowing from his screen that it's me. "Hannah, I knew you'd call. It's about time we begin fine tuning you. I'm not sure what happened, but I have been feeling a shift in your Light, so I know you were up to something!" He laughs, but continues before I can say a word; "I'll meet you at the Centre Tuesday night. Grace has given me a key and my own studio for sessions, so I am all set up for us." We settle on a time, and hang up. I glance over to see Owen sound asleep; the calls didn't disturb his deep slumber.

The usual fanfare occurs as more friends find out Owen and I are getting married. I have had a few remarks on the unusual choice of stone for an engagement ring, as diamonds seem to be customary, but as anyone who knows me can see, this is the perfect ring for me. Jamie gushed with excitement when she heard the news. She herself wanted a small quiet affair, but, she exclaimed, her best friend needs to be fussed over. It's causing me to panic, but Hannah One reminded me that this is part of the adventure. She wants me to enjoy this special day, and not worry about having the spotlight on me. They both know I would like something very simple. The thought of eloping had even crossed my mind. Hannah One pulled a guilt trip on me by saying, "Oh well, if you want to deny me the pleasure of seeing my one and only granddaughter get married, that's okay." Then she placed a hand on her forehead, feigning weakness. I wasn't buying it, but at the same time, part of me was buying it. So, I relented, and allowed some fussing to occur. Owen is happy with whatever plans are being set, as long as it is done with care for the environment, which means no balloons, and birdseed is to be tossed, instead of rice, if that silly tradition must be abided at all. He would have eloped as well, but he bought Hannah One's comment hook, line, and sinker. He truly loves his adopted grandmother, which means keeping her happy.

Owen had suggested the whole family go out for lunch to celebrate. I knew, instinctively, this was not a good idea. I had a feeling, after my vision of my father, that things are not alright between my parents. My father had returned my call later that same morning I had reached out to him. He suggested we meet for coffee *soon*, but he'd have to let me know *where* we'd meet in a few days. Our customary spot was the Sit N Sip, but for some reason that wasn't in his game plan. I tried to press him further, but he cut the conversation short, saying that he'd call soon. I finally told Owen that something was *up* with my parents, and although I didn't know exactly what it was, I knew it wasn't good. I suggested that it might be better if I go visit my mother on my own, to share the news and see how it goes with her. He agreed, as Owen is not one who likes being involved in other people's personal dramas.

Walking up the driveway, I am struck by how small the house appears to me now. As a child, it seemed like a big house, with a large front garden. Now it appears diminished, as if the house has shrunk as I grew. It's still a pleasant house, with a nice, neat garden in front. I recall many days of sitting on the grass in that garden, watching the world pass by, enjoying the sun with my mother by my side. I smile, as the memory gives me a warm glow inside.

I open the door and enter into the tastefully furnished living room, where I find my mother sitting on the couch, cup of coffee in one hand, the remote in the other. It seems a bit unusual to find her watching television in the middle of a Saturday afternoon, but who am I to judge. She looks surprised as I enter, and then I remember I had forgotten to call ahead. She doesn't like anyone dropping by, so I always call to let her know I'd be coming for a visit.

"Oh no, sorry Mom. I forgot to call. I hope you don't mind me dropping in." By the looks of it, I doubted she was in the middle of something really important. She clicks the tv off and stands up slowly. "No, no, it's fine. I was just being lazy. Everyone keeps telling me about this new show I should be watching, so I thought I'd give it a try." She comes over to me, cup still in her hand, and gives me a one-armed hug. She turns and takes a few steps over to sit in her favourite chair, placing her cup on the small table beside her.

I make myself a cup of tea and come back into the living room to sit on the couch. I notice a few things missing, like the old clock that always sat on the sideboard. There are two blank spots on the walls where some paintings once hung, and the old recliner chair my dad lived in is also gone. I make no comment. "Have you talked to your dad in the past couple of days?" I shake my head, issuing a silent no. "I figured as much. Well, there is no easy way to tell you, so I will just say it. Your dad and I are getting a divorce." No surprise registers on my face, which gives my mother pause, but she continues, "I suppose you might have seen it coming. You are very astute." I only nod in response. "He has rented an apartment over on Concourse Street." She sighs, looking around the living room. "To be honest, I've been sitting here watching television to avoid what is coming next. The house is going to be sold." This time I can't help but register my surprise. My eyebrows rise and my mouth opens, but I can't figure out what to say. She continues without waiting for a response. "I have to sort through and pack up all this stuff, and then move as well. Part of me is so very sad to leave this house, but part of me will be glad to get somewhere new." She stops talking, and I look at her face to see the tears streaming down her cheeks. I am still uncertain that any words I can find will help her feel better about the situation. I cannot process the idea that this house, full of my childhood memories, and the garden with the old tree I love so dearly, will soon belong to someone else.

We both sit for a few minutes in silence. I find it hard to look around the room, so I stare at my tea cup, composing my response to this news. Finally, after what seems an eternity, I say, "I'm here to help you, whatever you need. You don't have to go through this alone." She looks at me with an expression of relief and appreciation. "I appreciate that. Yes, I think that between the two of us, we can get this place ready for buyers. I hate having to do this 'staging' thing, but the realtor says it will sell faster." She uses air quotes to emphasize the word *staging*, before continuing, "It means I have to pack up all my knickknacks and pictures, so it has a more generic look." She loves her knickknacks. I stand up and walk around the room. "Okay, well, we can start there. You can store your treasures at Hannah One's house in the basement, so when you want them back, they are not far away." At the mention of Hannah One, my mother's face clouds over. "Oh, I don't think so. I doubt she will want me to do that. It's her son, after all. She will likely be glad to see me leave." I am shocked by this statement. I have never heard Hannah One utter one mean word about my mother, or I believe, would she even think it. She is a firm believer in allowing people the privacy to have their own journey, even her own son. If they were having marital trouble, which I know she knows they are, it's not her place to take sides, or disavow one over the other. She just doesn't think that way.

"Oh Mom. You're wrong. Hannah One will be sad about this change in your relationship, but she will never take sides. Has she ever given you reason to doubt her love for you? She will support you, and Dad, through this." My mother lowers her head and nods. "Yes, sorry. You're right, she's always been a great mother-in-law. I just didn't want to admit it. She helped me a lot, and I resented her for needing that help. Here I am again, needing her help, and I guess I am still resenting it." I smile and try to lighten the mood by saying, "Now who is being astute!" She looks at me, and, realizing I am poking fun, she chuckles a little, while wiping her face with the sleeve of her sweater.

It's not until I get home that I realize I forgot to tell my mother about the engagement. I suppose, after all, it would not have been the most appropriate time to tell her about love and marriage. We merely discussed the logistics of organizing boxes, possibly having a garage sale, and other tasks necessary to clear the house out for the move. We work best together when emotion is not in the equation. Deep inside I know we both feel very emotional about this, but it won't help us with what lies ahead. Hopefully it will not take long for the house to sell, so my mother can focus on building a new life for herself.

Eleven

Planning a wedding is not something I ever thought I would be enthusiastic about. Truth be told, I never actually gave the notion of marriage much thought. I've never had expectations of marrying Owen; I was quite content with the status quo. Watching my parents go through a break up after thirty-three years leads me to believe that it's a good thing I have taken my time to reach this particular milestone in my life. This morning I'm venturing out to visit my dad at his new apartment, for the first time. He called and told me his new address, and that he's looking forward to seeing me. He left out any detail about how he is coping with this change. I try not to worry about him, but the thought of him being alone, much like my mother, makes me sad. But staying together for the sake of convenience is not the solution either. It will take both of them time to acclimatize to their new lives, but in the long run, I know they will be better off than if they stayed together.

    I arrive at the old four-story brown brick building and enter the front door. A buzzer system on the lobby wall lists names and corresponding numbers to press to connect to the apartment. I scan the list until I see Casey, and then press 324. The speaker makes a crackling sound, and I hear my dad's cheerful voice say, "Come on up!". Cooking smells greet my nose as I walk the third-floor hallway. Muffled television sounds and a few voices can be heard as I pass each apartment. As I approach 324, the door swings open, and my dad takes a large step out into the hallway. He has a smile on his face as he waves at me. We hug in the doorway, and then I proceed into the apartment first, through the narrow entranceway.

The living room is furnished with a wooden table and two chairs, a small loveseat, and his old recliner in the corner. A small television sits on top of a bookshelf that presses up against the wall, and a secretary desk sits nestled in another corner of the room. I turn to take in a nook that passes for a kitchen. It seems comfortable enough for him, and after he proudly shows me the bedroom, complete with a double-sized bed that fills the room, I realize he actually likes his tiny apartment.

He has a pot of coffee already brewed, and he pours out two cups. He opens a box of cookies, neatly arranging about half a dozen on a small plate, which he then places on a pretty place-mat on the table. He moves over and sits in his recliner as I sit down on the loveseat. There is no coffee table so I just hold onto my cup. The cookies remain untouched on the table.

"Well, here we are." He smiles again. I nod. I'm not sure which way the conversation might go, but before I have a chance to wonder, he continues, "Yup, here we are. I hope your mom is doing okay with the house. She didn't want my help with packing it up. I took what I wanted, but most of what I packed is in storage for now. I'm, um, in transition right now, so I didn't want to unpack a lot of stuff." My brain zeroes in on the word, *transition*, so I ask, "Transition? What do you mean?" He clears his throat and looks at his coffee cup. He takes a small sip before looking up. "Well, there is something I maybe could, or should have told you before now, but I didn't know how you'd feel about it. Now that your mom and I are officially separated, I really want to tell you." He takes another sip of coffee and presses on; "Your mom and I have not been happy for a long time now. She could not afford to buy-out my half of the house and carry the household bills alone, or move out on her own, so we continued living together, like sullen roommates. I don't resent that, it's just the way the cards were dealt. I was finding it really tough; I was very lonely. One night, after we had had another disagreement about something, she actually said I should just find someone else to *cozy up to...*" he trails off, wearing a frown as he appears to be reliving the argument in his mind. "Well, it hurt me that she was so dismissive of my feelings. And then I wondered if she was *really* giving me permission to see other women? It seemed disrespectful to her, but honestly, it was an enticing idea. Now, with her retirement fund kicking in, she has decided not to buy me out, as it's too much for her to worry about on her own. So, we have agreed to sell it." His frown deepens. He pauses again, and takes another large gulp of coffee. I feel as if he is avoiding the main thread of the discussion, about this *transition*, but I know he will get to it, sooner or later. "Well, so, I, um, started dating again, even when I was still living at the house. I kept it discreet, and I never told your mother. I was so lonely, and it felt so nice to have the companionship I used to have with Caroline," he glances at me, "I mean your mom. We got married so young, we hardly knew how to be *ourselves*, let alone how to be someone's wife or husband. We did the best we could, but in the end, we just had nothing in common. What was common to us as twenty-somethings, was not anything we could relate to as we turned fifty, and so on." He rises out of his chair and reaches over to pick up the plate of cookies and offers it to me. I shake my head, and he nods silently as he puts the plate back on the table and retrieves two cookies before sitting down again. He takes a big bite of one and as he's chewing, I try to fill the void in the conversation with some platitude about his relationship. "Dad, it's not uncommon for a couple to grow apart. It happens. Now you and Mom can start over, like a blank page, and write your story from today onward." I have read too many soapy platitudes about relationships on social media. I can hardly swallow that line myself, and now to dish it up to him seems almost glib. He nods and swallows the last bite of cookie before he continues; "Well Hannah, I suppose that blank page appeared nearly two years ago. That's when I met Shelagh." He looks at me for a response. I feel my eyebrows raise slightly, but I remain as non-judgemental as I can.

The Alternate inside me wonders why he had been so reluctant to tell me this news, but my human side understands the implication. He is worried about the repercussion of such an affair on his relationships, both personal and professional. When I say nothing, he continues, "We met at a single's social club. It wasn't a dating club, it was for single people who just wanted to meet other single people and strike up friendships, and do things as a group, like outings to the theatre, or ball games, you know, that sort of thing." He waves his hand around and drops of coffee fly out of his cup onto the floor. He stops waving, but continues, "I've made some great new friends, but it was tough, I didn't want them to know I was still married, so I had to be careful about what I said, and could never invite anyone over. It was hard, and I felt guilty. So, I finally confessed to Shelagh, as she was one of the friends I felt I could trust for some honest feedback." He chuckles, "Well, I did get an earful from her. She is Scottish, so she has a no-holds-barred kind of attitude. But in the end, she remained my friend. She suggested I leave the group until I wasn't deceiving anyone any longer. I told her I'd miss everyone, but her most of all. And that's when she suggested that she and I keep in touch. And we did." I cannot remember the last time I had seen my father smile the way he is now, when he mentions Shelagh. It makes me glad to see him so content. He has never been so open about his feelings before, yet he doesn't seem self-conscious or uncomfortable sharing such personal details with his daughter, and I feel like we have entered a new phase of our relationship.

He stands up and again reaches for another cookie, but then decides against it, and sits back down. "One more thing, since I'm spilling my guts here. I haven't really unpacked things because, well, Shelagh and I have decided to move in together. Maybe even buy a house!" He grins widely, but with a hint of hesitation in his expression, as he waits for my response. It takes no time for me to relieve him of any guilty feelings he has, by saying, "Dad, I'm really glad that you have found someone. Wow! Two years is a long time to keep that under wraps. I understand though. It's good to see you so happy." The expression on his face turns to a combination of relief and pleasure. "Hannah, I was worried you would hate this. I know you and your mom have challenges with your relationship, but she is still your mom, so I would understand if you disapproved of this." I sit for a moment in thought. There comes a time in every child's life that they finally see their parents as real people, not just as an icon of mother or father. They view the cracks, the weaknesses, the insecurities, and the true strength of character. It is how the child reacts to this new perspective that shapes their future relationships.

I stand up and place my cup on the table before coming to stand in front of my father. He looks up and smiles as I lean over to place my hand on his arm. "Dad, I think it's important you know that my approval or disapproval should never move you away from what brings your life joy. I know we all think we need the approval or acceptance of those around us to pursue a dream, but in the end, it is your life and you should find your happiness based on your own Light, not that of others. As long as you are happy and feel your life is full, then that's all that matters." He rises up to hug me, spilling more coffee on the floor as his arms embrace me. He pulls away, pacing over to the kitchen to get a towel to wipe up the spills, and exclaims over his shoulder, "Now, I have to ask you if it's okay to bring Shelagh to the wedding!"

Darkness surrounds me. A cold biting wind whips at my body and pushes at me. I lose my balance and fall onto a cold surface. My hands become numb as they touch the hard snowy ground. I climb to my feet, peering around me. It is darkness everywhere I look. The howling of the wind is relentless in my ears. I feel the sting of driving snow hit my eyes, and I squint from the pain.

Suddenly, a lone figure stumbles into view. A teenage boy bends his frame against the brutal wind and snow. He is wearing a thin winter coat, no gloves or hat, yet appears oblivious to the cold. As he staggers along the icy road he is yelling at some invisible adversary. "I hate you! I won't let you ruin my life. It's my life! It's my life". Then he begins to cry, gently rubbing the dark bruise forming around his left eye. I am about to approach him and ask if he needs help, when a car comes over the crest of the icy snow-covered road. It careens towards the boy, making him jump out of the way to avoid being hit. It enters a curve up ahead, that is barely visible, even with the high beams on. The speeding car swerves off the road, and slides down a steep embankment. The boy screams. He tries to run towards the fallen car, but the snow and ice make him slip and fall, knocking his head on the icy road. He lies there, unconscious. I run over to the edge of the embankment and peer into the gloom, but all I see is a set of red tail lights far below in the ravine. They blink like a malevolent set of eyes, before disappearing completely, leaving me staring into a dark abyss. I glance around as the scene begins to fade. The wind stops howling. The snowfall ceases. The darkness closes in around me.

The last thing I hear before I wake up is a woman's voice, echoing in my mind, "Truth that can be found, will set him free. He carries his sorrow far too long. Set him free. Owen, Owen, Owen..."

I lie naked in bed, shivering, feeling like I had just been standing unprotected in a blizzard. My hands feel damp, but it's from sweat, not from snow. I listen, but all I can hear is the steady breathing of the sleeping figure next to me. Owen has not moved or been disturbed by my sudden awakening. I remain still, as my mind races back to the vision. Was the teenage boy I saw really Owen? Who was in the car? *Why* am I seeing this dream or vision? How am *I* supposed to set him free?

I shiver again, so I roll onto my side and curl up in a ball. Then I feel movement from the other side of the bed, as Owen's arm comes to rest across my rounded body. He moans and stretches, briefly raising his arm to the ceiling before bringing it to rest across me once again. He mumbles something about really needing coffee to him wake up, as he has been having weird dreams all night.

Arthur enters the bookstore and waves at Janice, who stands on a step stool, arranging books on a top shelf in a corner of the store. Her hands are full of books so all she can do is smile and nod her head. Arthur is a regular at the store now, so all the staff recognize him. He comes in about once a week, buys a magazine or a book, and then the two of us head across the street for coffee. I am anxious to talk to Arthur about my vision of Owen in the snowstorm. I haven't spoken of it to anyone, especially not Owen. If this is some dark secret from his past, how am I supposed to bring it up in a casual conversation? *How are you doing? Oh, by the way, was that your parents I saw tumbling over a cliff to their death?* Sure, that would go over well.

I relate my vision to Arthur, who sits leaning forward in his chair, his elbows on the table and his eyes closed. He appears to be wholly focused on listening to every word I utter. When I stop talking, he slowly opens his eyes and says; "Well, our knight in shining armour does have a dent or two in his breastplate. I was beginning to worry about him. *Too good to be true*, you know the saying..." he trails off as he sees I am not amused. "Okay, well, this certainly is very tricky. How are you going to talk to him about this, without telling him *who* you are?" I sigh. "I was hoping you'd have the answer to that question. Should I say anything at all? I mean, he has never talked about his parents, and certainly never said anything about their death, other than it was in a car accident. When he told me, I didn't want to press for details, as he had such a pained expression on his face." Arthur nods, "Yes, human brains can shut down when tragedy affects them. They live in denial, or they simply re-write the story until the new story becomes their truth. It is easier to live with a false narrative than face the pain and suffering of looking at the naked truth. Maybe Owen rewrote his story, maybe he's in denial. I think you are missing the point here, Hannah. The woman told you to *free* him. 'The truth will free him' or something like that. Somehow you are supposed to help him face this truth, and possibly get him through to the other side of it." Arthur sits back in his chair and rubs his chin. "And yet, I don't know how you'll do that."

I look at the half empty mug in front of me. To make Owen face a truth that he may have hidden from everyone all these years could be devastating to him, and possibly to our relationship. And yet the voice haunts me, pleading with me to set him free. I know I will have to come up with a plan to help him, but at the same time, not give away my secret. I leave Arthur chatting with Cristina in the coffee shop and I return to the bookstore. The remainder of the day I am distracted and unable to get anything accomplished, so I decide to head home early. Nouri is in charge of closing up the shop at six, and since he has been well trained in end-of-day closing procedures, I leave it all in his capable hands.

I find the house empty when I get home. Hannah One has been invited to join my father and Shelagh at a live theatre event, so they are having dinner before heading to the show. It makes for perfect timing, as I want to talk with Owen, and having the house to ourselves, uninterrupted, will help.

I begin pulling a few vegetables and other items out of the fridge to prepare for dinner, when I hear the front door open and Owen's voice calling out. "You home?", he calls as he dumps his bag on the floor, and takes his shoes off. I leave the kitchen to meet him in the hallway. He smiles when he sees me, and part of me is so happy to see him, yet part of me dreads what is about to occur. I have figured out a way to bring a discussion around to the topic of parents, and hope that it will be disguised enough to allow him an opportunity to open up about what happened.

He crosses the hall in a few steps, reaching out to give me a hug and a kiss. I hug him back a bit mechanically, my mind on what

I am going to say next. He takes no notice of it, releasing me and heading to the kitchen to take a beer out of the fridge. He makes his way into the living room and sits down with a loud sigh. "Long day?" I ask. He takes a swig from the bottle and replies; "God, I love to write, but I hate all the office politics that goes on around me. I'm starting to miss my days of freelancing on the road."

As I make no reply, he continues, "Not that I would go back to that now. I'm too soft, and like coming home to you at the end of each day." He smiles and holds out his hand for me to come sit beside him. I sit down, but don't lean back into him as I might have at other times. "I'm glad to come home to you too." And then I hesitate. "Um, I guess we are lucky to have each other. When I look at my parents, I don't think they ever had the sort of connection that we have. I *do* love you so very much." Owen has a curious look on his face, as he knows I'm not one to talk so emotionally about relationships.

I plow on before he can interject. "I wish I had been able to know *your* parents. They must have been wonderful people to have raised such a thoughtful, brilliant son." I smile, as this is the truth; it isn't just a line that is a means to an end. Owen frowns, but says nothing for a moment. I wait, in case he wants to say something, but when he remains silent, I add, "You know, it must have been awful to lose them so young. If you ever want to talk about how that made you feel, I am here to listen." Owen stands up quickly and crosses the room to sit in the large comfy chair that Hannah One loves to sit in. "I wasn't *that* young, I told you, but it was years ago. It's no big deal. I was sad, now I'm getting on with my life." I hear the echo of his voice from the vision, *My life, my life, my life...* I look at him and ask, "Weren't you fairly young when they died? I seem to recall you said you were about sixteen?" I lie, as he never said that, but hope he doesn't notice. "I just mean that it must have been so difficult, when it happened so suddenly, with no warning. And you never got a chance to tell them you loved them, or anything like that..." I trail off, thinking this is going very badly. It is. "What are you talking about?" Owen stands up again, and paces the room. "I don't want to talk about my parents. They died. Case closed. I might have been young, but it doesn't change the fact that they are gone, and there is nothing I can do about that. You need to drop this, Hannah." His final words are not a threat, but a warning about treading on thin ice. I ignore the warning, as I am too far from shore now.

"I mean, I mean, if they had this accident, it must have been awful to see. I mean, to know, that you can't take back anything you might have said, or done… I mean, if that was what you were feeling." A hole the size of a stadium opens and I am dropping myself into it. This conversation has gone off the rails quicker than I can blink. "What are you talking about? Why are you going on about this? I don't want to talk about it, nothing will change by talking, so drop it." He walks out of the room to stand in the kitchen. He picks up an acorn squash, and I wonder if he is going to throw it at me as I follow him into the kitchen. "Owen, I'm sorry. I didn't mean to upset you. I just need you to know that whatever happened, it wasn't your fault. You don't have to feel guilty about their death. It was an awful storm, it was icy, the road was dark. It was not your fault." I know I have put all the cards on the table, and this is going to be a make-or-break moment.

Owen turns and looks at me with a frown creasing his forehead, "How do you know what happened? Who have you talked to? What did they say? I don't know where you are getting your story from, I just wish you hadn't been so nosy and pried into my past. It's none of your business." His voice stays level, as he is trying to keep from letting the anger he is feeling erupt. "You need to drop this, and if you ask me again about this, I will walk out that door." He steps away as I try to approach and take his hand. "Owen, I am sorry. You just need to know that they forgive you, they don't want you carrying this guilt with you, it's not good for you. It's not good for them either." Well, that is the icing on the cake. He bangs his beer bottle on the counter, walks down the hall, shoves his feet into his shoes and, grabbing his coat, storms out the door.

I wait up until Hannah One comes home from the theatre. The moment she sees me, she knows something terrible has happened. I'm curled up on the couch wrapped in a knitted throw blanket, feeling a desperate chill running through me. Hannah One sits down beside me and puts her hand on my arm. I burst into tears. There is so much emotion overwhelming me, I have no way to control it, or channel it rationally. Hannah One slowly rubs my arm as I sob for a few minutes, trying to purge myself of the pain. Finally, feeling drained, I sit upright, and wipe my face on the blanket. I look at Hannah One and whisper, "I think Owen is gone. I don't know what to do." Hannah One frowns, saying nothing. What can she say? I continue, "I pushed too far. I was trying to help, but I couldn't figure out how. I made him face it before he wanted to. He was very angry…" Hannah One shakes her head, replying, "I'm so sorry. I am a little confused about this. Do you feel comfortable telling me what happened? I don't want to pry, but if I know the story, maybe I can help." I realize I haven't told her anything about my vision. I clear my throat and begin to tell her what I saw. "I really shouldn't be telling you this, it is, after all, Owen's private memory. Please don't tell him I told you." She nods in agreement, so I continue to tell her what I saw in my dream-walk, and the ensuing argument I caused by trying to confront Owen about his tragic past.

Hannah One listens until I've told her everything, and then she sighs. "Oh, my dear, that is so sad. How horrible for Owen. I know you were just trying to help his parents by delivering the message, but I wonder if there wasn't another way to do it. Some humans don't do well examining a past trauma when they aren't ready to face it. It's a difficult situation you're in." She pauses, looking around the room, deep in thought, "He must wonder how you know the details; does he think you're having him checked out or something? It would explain how defensive he was. If I thought my fiancée was having me checked out, I would certainly question the lack of trust there." This aspect of his reaction hadn't occurred to me. "He must have felt terribly violated. Like I had his background looked into..." I swallow. How can I explain my detailed knowledge of the accident, without telling him about being an Alternate? Hannah One must have had the same thought as she states, "Hannah, I think you are going to have to tell him the truth. Otherwise, he'll never trust you. He will always have doubts about you. All trust will be gone."

She stands up and begins to head to the stairway. "Go to bed. Try to sleep. Tomorrow will be here whether you stay awake or sleep, so you might as well try to rest. It will all be clearer in the morning, I suppose." She shrugs her shoulders and turns, grasping the banister as she makes her way up to her room. I clutch the blanket around me hoping against hope that things *will* be clearer in the morning.

The morning sun brings no clarity with it. Spending a restless night in a half sleep, I drag my weary body out of bed. As I stand by the bedroom door, I look back to the untouched side of the bed, and briefly wonder where Owen found a place to rest.

After a brisk shower, I dress and go down to the kitchen. I find Hannah One busily making a pot of coffee. She smiles as I sit down at the old wooden table, but doesn't ask how I slept. It must be obvious, from the dark circles under my eyes that no brisk shower can erase, that I have not slept well. Once the pot is brewed, she pours a cup and places it in front of me before filling her own cup and sitting down opposite me. We sip our coffee in silence for a few minutes, until a ping on my cell phone indicates I have an email. Reluctantly I pick up my phone. I open my mail browser to find an email from Owen. I swallow and put the phone down. Hannah One sees the blood drain from my face, but remains silent. It is a massive sinkhole that hasn't dragged me all the way under, yet, but it has me up to my chin, and it's winning. I take another sip of coffee before putting my mug down, and once again pick up my phone. I notice there is no title in the subject line. No indication of what I will find in this email. I begin to read.

> Hannah,
> I don't know how to express myself very well right now, but since I don't want to talk to you directly, I think an email will have to suffice. I am angry and hurt by your obvious 'investigation' into my past. I don't know how you got the details about my parents' accident, unless you had someone actually explore my background. Maybe you have located my Aunt Regina, someone I have never mentioned to you, and got her version of events. Either way, I am devastated by this invasion of my privacy. How could you do this to me, to us? I have a past that needs to be in the past. It has nothing to do with the person I am today. Why did you feel the need to look into it anyway? Have I ever given you reason to doubt my love or commitment?
> I am staying with Colin for now. He said he would stop by this morning to get some of my things, until I decide what I want to do. I don't know how to get past this. Trust is something easily broken, but not easily mended.

I reread the email twice before placing my phone on the table. I look at Hannah One, who has been sitting quietly with an expectant look on her face. I quietly utter, "You were right, he thinks I hired someone to look into his past, or check him out. He has lost his trust in me. I ruined it." I begin to cry. Why was it so vital to unearth the truth? Couldn't I have ignored it, and been happy with the way things were going? Deep down I know it would eat away at me, wondering if Owen has some secret pain I could lessen for him. I know I had no choice but to pursue this to the bitter end. And what a bitter end it appears to be.

Hannah One rises, coming around the table to put her hand on my shoulder. "Dear, I'm sorry, but I think the only way to mend fences is to be honest with him. If you tell him and he rebuffs your explanation, well, you aren't any worse off than you are now." She rubs my shoulder, as if trying to infuse her love into my body. I look up at her and nod in agreement, as words stick in my throat, unable to be voiced.

At two o'clock I hear a knock at the door and Hannah One opening it to welcome Colin inside. He exchanges quiet pleasantries with my grandmother, and then proceeds to gather some clothes and Owen's laptop. He says nothing to me, other than hello. Colin is Owen's best friend, and is slated to be best man at our wedding. I can't blame him for the cold shoulder. Five minutes later, he leaves with all the items he was tasked at retrieving.

I sit quietly in the living room, watching the afternoon sun catch the glass prism ball Hannah One had Owen hang in the window. It sends shards of colour across the ceiling, like tiny dancing fairies. Any other time I would smile and marvel at the colours and the whimsy, but today all I see is the memory of Owen, with Hannah One directing him, strategically locating just the right spot to hang it, and then him hammering a small hook into the ceiling and looping the string through it. They both admired the hanging glass form, and then laughed when the sun did its job by catching the light and splitting it into rainbows that splashed across the room.

I had texted Janice earlier to say that I was not feeling well, and asked if she could cover my shift at the bookstore. Even though it's her day off, she went into work, without hesitation. I could not leave Mila alone to run things, so I was relieved that Janice was so gracious to do this for me.

Sitting in the chair seems to be the only thing I can do. I am stuck in limbo, in a quagmire that keeps me from moving one way or another. It isn't until Arthur walks through the front door and I unfurl my legs from under me to stand up, that I realize how stiff I am. It appears that Hannah One had called him and asked him to come over. Although she doesn't know that Arthur is also an Alternate, she has her suspicions. I never told her, because it isn't my secret to tell. If Arthur wants to share it with her, then that is for him to decide.

He walks straight into the kitchen, and plugs in the kettle for tea. He smiles as Hannah One enters from the back sunroom. "Hi, HO…" Arthur has nicknamed my grandmother HO, short for Hannah One, and all other connotations aside, she laughs every time he says it. "It's time for tea, and I brought butter tarts from Sit N Sip." He gently places a small pink cardboard box on the table. Arthur is quite at home here, and right now I find it comforting that I don't have to play host to him. Hannah One smiles at him, "Lovely, dear. I'm just sitting out in the sunroom, knee deep in my detective novel, so would you be kind enough bring my tea and tart, when it is ready?" Normally Hannah One would never ask anyone to *serve* her, particularly in her own home, so I sense she is trying to give Arthur and me the opportunity to talk, without her present. I smile at how much she takes care of me, every day, in whatever way she can.

After the tea and tarts are distributed, Arthur and I sit in the living room. I tell Arthur what I have done, ending with the exchange between Owen and me that led to his departure. Then I read him the email. Reading it out loud is like a dagger poking my heart with each word spoken.

Arthur scrunches his lips together, like he has just tasted a lemon. Then he says, "Oh Hannah, what a mess. You really blew this one up, didn't you?" If he is here to make me feel better he is doing an awful job at it. "What was I do to Arthur? The vision was clear that Owen is in pain. I had to try…" I trail off as he closes his eyes. One of Arthur's Talents is connecting people with their past selves, and sometimes their present *true* self that they are denying. He helps them understand the potential connection of energy that is within each human, if given the chance to be awakened. "It is clear he doesn't know the whole story about that night. His version gives him a suitcase full of guilt to carry throughout his life. The truth of the situation may not eliminate the suitcase, but may shrink it to a more manageable bag he can carry. But for us to help him, it will mean we will have to tell him the truth about us, *both of us*." He emphasizes the last three words. "It will take a collective energy to help him see the truth, but only if he agrees to do it in the first place. Do you think you could convince him to do a session?" I have my doubts, and say as much. "Fine. I know he and I aren't that close, but maybe I could talk him into trying it, as a way to save his relationship, if he still wants to…" Arthur looks at me, and a sad smile crosses his face. "Hannah, this may work, or it may send him running away in the opposite direction. There is no clear answer." I nod my head and state, "As HO says, I can't make it any worse by trying." Arthur nods. "Okay, well then, let's get started."

Once again the snowy darkness surrounds me. This time however, I feel another presence close by. It's Arthur. We have been experimenting with the union of our Talents, to be able to gain access to this vision. He can take me back there because I have "lived" the experience through Owen's mind. Now it has become a recollection incorporated into my memory bank. Since I still don't know exactly how my Talent of dream-walking works, I have no control over where, or even if, I would see this vision again. Arthur is the bridge that allows us both to revisit the vision. Once we are able to establish this connection, we know that if we can bring Owen into it, Arthur can expand the viewpoints, and I will keep all three of us anchored in this memory. Arthur is able to adjust the view, to see Owen's parents, in a cabin, as they argue. It's in the past, Owen's past, even the parts he did not see, but all images are connected to the same memory thread that Arthur can walk along to view. It all seems to be there. We just need Owen, to complete the picture.

Giving Owen a few days to cool off is Arthur's idea. Left solely up to me, I would not have waited. Then again, I rushed this whole thing to begin with, so I decide that Arthur is the better judge of timing in this situation. We wait it out for two days, then I sit and watch as Arthur calls Owen. It has been two of the longest days I have ever lived. I miss his voice and his energy surrounding me, lifting me up when I need it. I can only hope that he misses me, too.

Arthur asks him if he would meet to talk about the situation. Owen rejects the invitation, stating that he isn't interested in hearing whatever *he* has to say. Arthur calmly replies; "Owen, I know it's a time you want to forget, but if we could talk, I think I can shed new light on things you don't know." He pauses and then continues, "I know how you got your black eye." Owen is silent on the other end of the phone. He told police he got it when he fell on the ice. He coughs, and then firmly states; "Arthur, I don't know what game you're playing. I'm sick of you and Hannah sticking your noses in. Enough already. I fell on the ice, end of story." He's about to hang up, when Arthur quickly adds, "A father's approval can be hard won, and when it isn't, it stings the soul, like a black eye."

Arthur waits to see if the phone will go dead, or maybe he has *hit his mark*, as they say. Owen's voice comes across deep and sad, "Fine. We can meet. Just the two of us. I can't see Hannah right now. I just can't." Arthur, feeling pleased at winning this small victory in the long battle, replies, "That's fine Owen. I just have one other favour to ask. If we could meet at Grace's Healing Centre, I'd really like to show you something. It will be worth your while, I promise."

At five o'clock the next day, Arthur waits in the small lounge area near the main entrance of the Centre. I disappear into another room so Owen won't know I am nearby. My close proximity to Arthur while we attempt this union isn't crucial, but I want to be close at hand, to ease my own worry. I leave the door open slightly, and stand behind it, peering through the crack, so I can view him entering the Centre. Suddenly the door opens and Owen walks in, cautiously glancing around, like an animal entering a cage. Arthur stands up and walks over to welcome him. Owen shakes the proffered hand, and then looks around again. He is looking for me, and when he doesn't see me, part of his face shows relief, but his eyes show disappointment. Arthur leads him to the softly lit room where he holds his sessions. Owen looks through the doorway into the dark room, and hesitates. Arthur reassuringly says, "I promise there's nothing to be worried about or afraid of in here." Owen bristles at the suggestion of being frightened. "I'm not afraid. Just not sure what the hell is going on." He steps inside the room and Arthur quietly closes the door. He motions for Owen to sit on the cushioned table, but he wants to remain standing. Arthur makes his way over to his small chair in the corner and seats himself. He takes a deep breath and quietly begins; "Owen, I don't know how much Hannah has ever told you about what I do here." Owen shrugs. "Well, I'll take that shrug to mean *very little*. Okay, I'll explain." Owen looks at him impatiently, but Arthur continues, unfazed. "Some humans are curious about their life and their journeys, both present and past. Part of what I do is help them explore who they are, and who they were, and how it all connects with the *Now*. You must sometimes wonder why you have such a deep passion for the environment. Where would this passion have come from? Was it something you were taught about as a child, or does it feel more organic, like it's just part of who you are? Some of these passions, behaviours, abilities or Talents are actually things we have carried with us, as we travel from life to life." Owen leans against the table and folds his arms together. His body language shows a limited receptiveness to this line of discussion. Arthur, recognizing the walls beginning to build around Owen's mind, decides to be blunt. "I have a Talent for connecting people with their pasts, and help them through past traumas that have re-shaped them into someone other than the person they are *truly* meant to be. It holds you back, it makes you second guess your value as a person. Abuse can do that." Owen's eyes widen. "How do you know about that?" he asks quietly. Arthur smiles and says, "My boy, I have seen it first hand, no pun intended." He frowns, but continues, "You have carried this story with you all these years, but it is not the whole story, merely a segment you have adopted to be your truth. It's not the whole truth. I want to show you the entire story."

He rises out of his chair and takes a few steps to stand in front of Owen, who still leans against the table. "Please let me help you. Do it for yourself, for your life. As you said that night, you don't want *him* to ruin your life."

The last statement makes Owen grasp the edge of table, and Arthur guides him, as he attempts to sit on it, looking stunned. He gently helps him to lie down, his head coming to rest on the pillow, his arms once again crossing in front of his chest, almost like a shield to protect himself. Arthur puts a hand on his arm, and Owen begins to loosen his grip, until his arms slowly come to rest at his sides. "I'm so confused. How does Hannah know this, if you are the one who can see into people's pasts? Did you tell her, or something?" Arthur sits down again in his chair and takes a deep breath. "My boy, it will all become clear, very, very soon. I hope you will trust me enough to guide you along now, to revisit a time, a painful time, but one that needs to be seen, for the truth to be set free." Owen lies silently staring up at the ceiling. Arthur takes his silence for acquiescence, and so he closes his eyes to begin. "Owen, close your eyes, take a few deep breaths to relax. Let your mind drift to open space, and your thoughts turn off completely, as hard as that might be right now. At some point you may see a door in front of you. When you see it, just tell me you see it." Owen breathes deeply a few times, trying to still his inner conflict. A few minutes pass, then he whispers; "I see it." Arthur takes another deep breath, exhaling calmly. "Good, look closely at the door, what is it made of? What colour is it? What does the handle look like? You don't have to tell me; I can see it too. I love old wooden doors, so much character." Owen almost speaks, but Arthur continues. "Now, if you're ready, go ahead and open the door. Good, see the hallway in front of you? Can you see all the doors that stretch out before you? These doors are lives past. You can choose to go to one, and open the door to visit, or you can simply step into the hall and close the door you just opened."

Owen sees a long white hallway, with white doors that run down either side, as far as he can see. There is something about stepping too far forward that makes him uncomfortable, so he just takes a few steps in so he can close the door behind him. He turns around to face the door. "Good. This door we just passed through represents your current life. Look at the back of the door. Do you see the pictures?" Owen spies dozens and dozens of images, in row upon row, across the door. He scans the top photos, but as his eyes move along the rows, the images become dark and threatening, with pictures of pain and anguish at the hand of his father. He looks down, unable to bear it. Then his eyes catch sight of an image of Hannah. It is in the coffee shop, the day they met. She is eating a butter tart, with a single crumb stuck to her lip. He almost laughs at the memory. He wasn't sure if he should tell her she had a big crumb on her lip, so instead he simply watched her, until she obviously felt the intrusion on her skin, and quickly licked it away. The pictures that follow are bright, glowing and full of Hannah. They all beam a bright yellow glow, but there is also a tinge of darkness underneath, that seems to penetrate and slightly discolour the images. Except the last one, which is rimmed in darkness. It shows his angry face, leaning over the kitchen counter, telling her to mind her own business. He lowers his eyes, pain seeping into his chest.

Arthur stands behind him now, quietly allowing him time to acclimatize himself to his door. Owen turns, looking surprised when he sees him standing there. "What is this place? How can *you* be here?" Arthur smiles, replying, "I'm not *really* here. But then neither are you!" He laughs as Owen frowns. "Sorry. I know it's confusing, and probably overwhelming. Let's just take this one step at a time. This door represents your present life moments, the good, and the bad. We will be looking at one moment, one image in time that has influenced all other moments that have come after it." Owen turns back to the door and points to a picture. He knows exactly which moment Arthur is referring to. He feels the tears sting his eyes. "I don't know how to face this again. I killed my parents; they are dead because of me. There is no changing what happened." Arthur says gently, "We do not change that which has passed by in Time. But we can look at the truth and see it for what it is. And you will see, when that happens, it will reshape your life to be where it is meant to be." Owen concentrates on the image of a boy, screaming in a snowstorm.

I am linked with Arthur through this whole exchange, and know the moment he looks into the image that I have to connect with Owen. I reach out with my mind and gently attach it to him, and then to Arthur.

The three of us stand in the dark cold night as the snow pelts us unmercifully. Owen turns and sees me standing there. "Hannah, what the hell? How..?" his question is cut short as the young teenage Owen stumbles into view. Arthur takes Owen's hand and says, "We will walk back a bit. There is something you need to see."

The darkness melts into a scene with only dull bare light bulbs showing the very basic interior of a hunting cabin. A middle-aged man sits in a chair by the fireplace, poking it incessantly with a fire iron in one hand, a glass full of dark liquid in the other. An open bottle of whisky sits on the table beside him. "Fucking fire won't stay hot. Fuck this, Owen! Get in here!", the man bellows, and then belches. A woman, dressed in a winter coat and hat, sits in the far corner, trying to blend in with the dull walls. She keeps her eyes lowered, looking at her brown wool mittens, afraid to look at the man.

A young teen, Owen, appears from another room at the back of cabin. He wears a thin winter coat, but has no gloves, or hat on his head. When he exhales, he sees his breath in the air. He stands in the doorway, not attempting to approach the angry man to see what he wants. "Get the fuck over here! This fuckin' fire isn't hot. Get more wood, and get it going … shit!" he exclaims as he attempts to stand, only to spill the whisky on his jacket. He stumbles across to the woman who cowers in the corner, "Why the fuck didn't you tell me there was going to be a snowstorm? Didn't you look at the weather before we left? I don't know why I brought you two morons anyway, you can't hunt…" he teeters around, and then stumbles back to his chair, mumbling about hunting in November, and the fucking weather. Owen has not moved from the doorway. He looks over at his mother. She continues to stare at her mittens. A slow fuse of anger, one that has been smouldering for years, begins to burn its way up his spine. He can't take any more abuse at the hands of this man. He has stayed quiet for fear his father would take it out on his mother, but his anger cannot be contained any longer, and he can't stop himself.

"Why the hell didn't *you* check the weather before we left? You are perfectly capable of doing that yourself! Don't blame Mom for this!" Owen waves his arms around, indicating the storm outside. The man stops poking the fire and stares at Owen, raising the iron rod to point towards the young boy. "What the fuck did you just say to me, boy?" He stands up and lurches forward, dropping the heavy iron and his whisky glass as he tries to right himself. Seeing the broken glass on the floor, the man becomes enraged. "Now look what you made me do! You son of a bitch!" He suddenly lurches forward, his closed fist nailing Owen in the eye before he can move out of the way. His mother jumps up and yells. "Please! Sean, please! It was my fault! I should've checked the weather! I'm just so stupid!" She begins clutching the man's coat, and pleading with him. Owen steps back, sickened by his mother's need to throw herself in front of the angry man, ready to take the brunt of abuse that is directed his way. The man reels away from the woman's grasp, trying to aim for Owen again, but the boy quickly turns and runs out of the cabin. He knew his father wouldn't follow him out into the cold night. He stands there and takes a few breaths, trying to calm himself. *Should I go back in and get my mother out of there? I don't know what to do! I hate him so much; he has ruined my life.* The young Owen takes a step off the old ragged porch into the deepening snow, and begins walking along the road. As he disappears into the night, the scene fades, to slowly revolve back into the cabin, where Owen's parents remain.

The woman sits back in her chair and glances frantically at the door. She wants to have her son back with her, but she also hopes he will flee, and never look back. The wind howls and rattles the windows. The drunk man slouches in the chair, still cursing the cold and his miserable lot, being stuck with two useless humans in his life. He grabs the bottle and begins drinking directly from it, ignoring the broken glass all around his boots.

After a few minutes, Owen's mother starts to worry about her son, out in the storm, alone, with only his thin coat to protect him from the elements. She gives a fleeting look at the man slumped over by the fire that is no longer lit, and decides she should go out to look for Owen. She imagines him lying frozen in a ditch, and she can't live the rest of her life without her son. She always believed misery loves company. She needs Owen in her misery, to be miserable with her. She stands up and heads for the door. As it creaks open, the man in the chair looks up, and yells at her. "Where the fuck are you going? Hope it's not after that son of a bitch... he can't even get a fire going! Freeze bastard, you little shit!" He gets to his feet as she continues to leave the cabin. "Oh! So that's what you want... want to play in the snow with your snotty nosed brat? Let's go find him then, and you can sit in the snow together and freeze!" He grabs her by the arm and drags her out of the cabin. He flings open the car door and pushes her into the passenger seat. She is afraid of being in the car, but more afraid of what he would do to her if she tried to run, so she just sits there. Part of her still wishes Owen would just appear before them, and so she wouldn't be alone with this man, who, she wants to believe once loved her, but now finds life with her too unbearable to face without a gut full of booze. She recalls buying him bottles upon bottles to keep him 'happy', so he would leave them alone. When it made him abusive she would cling to Owen, in hopes that her young boy would someday figure out a way to end this torment.

She sits numbly in the passenger seat as the man stumbles through the snow to the driver's side. She knows he's too drunk to drive, but she simply doesn't care anymore. *Maybe we will die in a crash, then I can be free of him.* It is one of her last thoughts.

The car starts with a rumble, and the wiper blades struggle to push mounds of snow off the windshield. The man puts the car in gear and jams on the gas petal, sliding all over the icy road. The woman looks at the man behind the wheel, *maybe if we die…* she keeps seeing it in her mind. The peace of letting go, she can just rest, and not live another day feeling guilty for placing the burden of her salvation on her son.

The car speeds up over a snowy incline and the headlights catch the image of Owen by the right side of the road. The man laughs, and then yells, "Let's play chicken!" He turns the wheel so the car begins heading towards the teenager. Owen attempts to move, but the surface is so slippery he can't get far enough off the road. Suddenly the car veers back to the left and heads off down the road. It weaves from one side to the other, as his mother struggles to take control of the steering wheel away from her drunken husband. He tries to push her away, but she finds the strength she never had all those years that he abused her. She holds onto the wheel, until the car mounts the side of the road, and, seeing the barrier sign, aims right for it. She starts to scream as the car falls, but with the realization that this may be the *actual* end, she simply shuts her mouth, and closes her eyes, picturing her son, free at last.

The three of them stand once again by the image door. Owen is pale and trembling. Arthur puts his hand on his shoulder. "Now you see, Owen. Your mother was done with this life. She chose to take your father too, as a way for both of you to escape his abuse. In the end, it was *her choice* to kill them. It wasn't *your* fault. She needed to escape this life that she was so unhappy in. She used you throughout her life as a crutch, in hopes *you* would, one day, free her from your father's grasp. But, in the final moment, she understood that for her life to change, it was up to her and no one else. Unfortunately, she chose death as her way out of it. She was unable to see a bigger picture, wherein the two of you leave the abuse behind, and begin a new life. She could not imagine a life without the abuse. She only saw death as the answer to this tragic life of hers. She set herself free, with her last thought being of you and the freedom she had brought to the both of you. Owen, I hope you can see now, that *you* are not to blame."

Owen, with tears streaming down his face, looks at Arthur, and then at me. I have not said a word throughout the session, fearing I might say the wrong thing. "I still don't understand any of this…how did you know about this, if Arthur didn't tell you? How can *you* be here?". He blinks away the tears, and then rubs his face with his hands. Arthur smiles. "I think we can continue this conversation once we have completed your session today. Owen, would you like to open your door?" Owen turns and sees that the images on the back of the door have changed somewhat. The darkness that had discoloured the photos after the accident has lessened. There still remains a dark hue behind many of images, but there also appears to be Light trying to make itself seen. I feel a touch of optimism as I look at them. Owen reaches out and touches one photo, of the two of us, smiling, and it feels warm to his touch. He wears a faint smile as he moves his hand over to turn the door knob.

I enter the room that the two men are in, and see Owen lying quite still, his eyes closed. As I close the door behind me, Owen's eyes slowly open, and he squints. He sits up and he reaches out his hand to me. I take the steps separating us, and grasp it. He holds it as if it's a life line, keeping him from slipping over a precipice. Arthur stands and quietly leaves the room, smiling, as usual. I see the expression of confusion and pain on Owen's face, and hope I can explain what just happened. He pulls me closer and wraps his arms around me. I feel him quietly sob into my shoulder, and I hug him tighter. The pain seeps out from every pore of his body. It floats in the air, almost ghostlike in appearance. Then, like a morning mist, it dissipates. I am so focused on comforting Owen, that I fail to sense a new Light that now resides deep within him. He raises his head to look into my face. I smile. I stay silent so he can lead the conversation, ask questions if he wants to, and begin to comprehend as best he can.

"What just happened to me? How can I have seen that? Why were you there?" Questions flow out of him and I know it will be a long conversation we have ahead. "I want to answer all your questions. I have so much to tell you. I hope it will all make some sort of sense, at some point." I look at the door. "I think, if you're willing, we should talk at home. I'm sure Arthur wants to close the Centre now, and go home. Please Owen, just come home with me." I hold his hand as he slides off the table. He pauses long enough to glance at the spot where, moments ago, he lay his head. Did he think some evidence of what happened would show itself on the pillow? He slowly turns his eyes to focus on my face. He nods in agreement, still clutching my hand. I open the door, and lead him out of the room. Hand in hand, we say good bye to Arthur, and make our way to Owen's car.

We arrive home and immediately go into the living room to sit on the couch, facing each other. The house is empty, as Hannah One is at a friend's, playing cards. I take a few deep breaths to steady myself. Owen sits staring intently at me. I take his hand in mine and begin; "I want you to try to be open-minded about what I'm going to tell you. I know it will be difficult for you to believe, but sometimes you have to take a leap into the unreal, just to learn that it's *actually* real." Owen's frown indicates I am wasting time, and need to start answering his questions. "Okay, well. There are many more planes of existence than just this one. The myriad of forms that are created by energy, or what I call *Light*, live in between the layers of this human existence, and other realms. We are all energy; it is simply a matter of how we coalesce into being that makes us different. Human energy, or Light, is housed in our bodies, much like a battery casing holds the energy. Where I am from, we don't have *bodies*. We *are* energy, we *are* Light. We don't need a structural form to *be,* we just *are*. In my world, sometimes there are those who are curious to explore existence in a different form, even that of a human. So, we are able to transcend and join with the energy of an unborn human baby, allowing us to experience an entire life as a human. Usually, we don't retain our memory of being an Alternate, as that hinders the experience." At this point Owen holds up his hand. "Wait, please. I keep hearing you say 'we'. I'm confused. Are you trying to tell me you're one of those things?". He looks perplexed, and maybe even slightly repelled. "Owen, what I am saying is this. I am human, in body and in mind, just like you, just like everyone around us. But I am more than human. I am an Alternate, as well."

Owen's frown creases his forehead so deeply I think he's going to get a headache. "So, you came into a baby's body, and now you are a human who remembers she is from somewhere else." He stands up and paces across the room. "Hannah, you are asking me to believe something, well, crazy! It's so far-fetched; I don't even know how to think." He returns to his seat. "You asked me to keep an open mind, so I will try." I look around the room, wishing Arthur was here. He has a much better way of explaining these things than I ever could.

"Usually, if an Alternate wishes to have the human experience, they cast aside their memories of their Alternate selves, so they can have a human life that is authentic. When, like me, you still have your memories, it complicates things because of the influence that part of my mind can have on my perspective. But I have worked hard to balance the duality of my mind. Now, as my Talents reveal themselves, and begin to evolve, I am faced with a whole new set of challenges." Flashes of dream-walks, and communicating with living beings, other than humans, crosses my eyes.

Owen tilts his head curiously. "So, you have your old memories, plus you are getting a *talent*? Like super powers or something?" He laughs at the absurdity of what he is asking. I chuckle as I reply, "Not like Wonder Woman or the Hulk. That might actually be fun. No, my Talent is dream-walking. Right now, it occurs when people I know are experiencing, or have experienced, a trauma. I seem to be able to connect with the actual scene that causes the pain, but I don't have any ability to change it, or interact with anyone within the scene. I am merely witness to the event, and if I am given a message, it is up to me to follow through with delivering the message." I take a breath, and stand to stretch my arms out, feeling the tension in my body. "I need some water; would you like a drink or something?" Owen looks out the window, lost in thought. "I was having a nightmare about the accident that night, and then the next day you were asking me about my parents. Did you dream-walk in my nightmare?"

I sit back down, forgetting the need for water. "Yes, although it was not intentional. I still don't seem to be able to control where, or when I walk. I saw the scene of you on the road, and the car plunging over the embankment. But the message from your mother," and, with the mention of her, I take his hands in mine, "Owen, she wants you to know it was her choice to go over that cliff. She sees you struggling with the guilt, and she needed *me* to tell you, it was not your fault. She wants to be free, but your pain keeps her tethered here. Free yourself, so you can free her." He looks down at our hands clasped together. Tears begin to slide down his cheeks, and he heaves a sigh. "I've been carrying this heavy secret with me all these years. I always thought I was supposed to do more, but I was just a kid. I really *want* to stop carrying this, I just want to let it go..." he stops talking, shaking his head. There is nothing more I can say or do to walk him through the process of releasing the pain and guilt he has felt for so long. I sigh deeply, feeling a burden lifted. Message received, and I feel the Universe smile.

TWELVE

I enter the kitchen to the sound of Hannah One singing, her voice clear and melodic, filling the room with joyous musical notes. She loves to make up her own songs. She simply hears a melody in her head, and sends it out to the Universe, until she senses its completion. I pause in the doorway, letting her voice wash over me, drinking in every note, knowing one day this image will be one I see on my door. She turns toward the stove where a pot of something is stewing, and, seeing me standing there, continues to sing, and takes hold of my hand, twirling me around, just like when I was a little girl and we danced in the woods. After a few twirls, I start to laugh and she can sing no more, as she is full of laughter, too. The joyous atmosphere has been prevalent in the house, now that Owen has returned. Hannah One never inquired about the process by which I was able to make this move happen, and I did not tell her. It's Owen's story to tell, or to leave on the page, as he turns to a new page. All she knows is he is now aware of me being an Alternate. The deluge of questions keeps coming on a daily basis, from both of them, now that it is out in the open, and I do my best to answer every query.

The wedding is only nine days away now. I'm glad to have Jamie paddling this boat, as I had all but given up trying to figure out venues, food, and other trivial things that seem to be important for such an occasion. Owen's friend Naveen, who works at the university studying Entomology, offered the use of the Butterfly Conservatory on the university grounds, for our wedding ceremony. Naveen is a true romantic, as he told Owen he would love to get married with butterflies floating all around him and his intended. We have kept the list of people invited to the ceremony to a select few, so the space can accommodate them, without crowding.

Jamie arrives, toting my wedding dress over her arm. It's wrapped in a cloth dress bag, so Owen cannot see it. Again, I wonder what the big deal is about this aspect of things. Something being good luck or bad luck has nothing to do with the way a situation plays itself out. Things are because they are, good or bad. I have cleared out a spot in the guest bedroom closet to hang my dress until the big day. As I hang it up, I can't help but unzip the bag to view the dress again. I look at the champagne-coloured A-line cocktail dress, with small embroidered roses on the tulle. It has a full, tea-length skirt whose hem comes halfway between the knee and ankle, a boat neck and short sleeves. An invisible zipper runs down the back. I was not interested in white, or full length, and certainly nothing with bling or frills. This dress is perfect. It has an ethereal quality to it, like wearing the morning mist. I bought open-toed silver high heel shoes that complement the dress nicely. Hannah One is lending me a bracelet she wore when she married my grandfather. It is sterling silver, with mother-of pearl stones embedded in the silver. The simple design, and sparkle of iridescent colour, adds just the right touch.

We are fortunate to have so many friends to help us with our special day. Naveen has offered the Conscrvatory, while Mila's cousin Joseph, who owns a banquet hall, offered the use of one of the smaller rooms for a reception, for a fraction of what it should have cost. We want a small number of people at the ceremony itself, but also want to share the day with all our friends, so the party will include them.

My mother wanted to help me pick out the flowers for my bouquet. She loves flowers, and gardening, so spending time at a florist is the perfect assignment for her. She never pushed her preferences on me, only made suggestions of additions, or alternatives to, something we were being shown. I really thought this was a lot of fuss over something so insignificant as a bouquet. Later, I said as much to my grandmother, but Hannah One stated; "The point is not the act of picking out flowers. It is the act of including your mother in your life. She is experiencing a new stage in *her* life, as she sees her only daughter getting married. This event is not without impact on her, so it's important that you not be dismissive of these small interactions with her. They aren't small to her." She patted my hand. I replied, feeling like once again, I missed the lesson being presented to me, "I wonder if I'll ever get the hang of these complicated human emotions." Hannah One laughed and said, "I'm eighty, and I'm still learning! Good luck kid!"

Owen arrives home after a visit with Grace. Arthur suggested that he try to get some energy clearing, as that might help restore balance to his spirit. He is on a waiting list for a PTSD therapist his family doctor referred him to, but that could take a while. In the meantime, Owen appears open to what Grace's skilled hands can accomplish. He looks happy, yet tired. He sits down at the kitchen table and watches as I shell peas I've just bought at the local farmers' market. I never ask him about his sessions with Grace, as what you face while having energy work administered can be highly emotional. I assume that if he wants to share his experience with me, he will. In between shelling, I point to the kettle. "Tea? Or maybe coffee?" He chooses tea. After I plug the kettle in, I sit down and continue shelling, while we enjoy a quiet moment together. Owen looks at his hands as he speaks; "I think I'm going to call my Aunt Regina. I owe her an explanation for abandoning her, after my parents died. I always believed she blamed me for the accident. She was so devasted at losing her sister." He shifts in his chair, somewhat uncomfortable. I remain silent. My opinion should not count here. I hear his words as merely a statement of intention. I am relieved that he is heading in the right direction, and decide to say as much. "I'm glad you're open to the idea of a reconciliation." I smile, as he stands up and prepares two cups of tea at the kitchen counter. He places a steaming cup in front of me, and holds the other cup as he sits down again, blowing on the mug's contents to cool it slightly. It seems like he is expecting me to say something more, so I choose my words carefully before speaking. "I am so happy to see you working through this, and doing all you can, to find your way back to the life you deserve. I love you, and will support whatever you decide is right for *you*." He smiles, as if my affirmation of his intention is the icing on the cake. He sips his tea, deep in thought. Suddenly, he laughs, which startles me. "I might even invite her to the wedding! She is a bit of an acquired taste however, so it might cause a few feathers to be ruffled." He chuckles as I reply, "I'm sure she's not *that* bad. After all, you are her nephew, and you're pretty damn good." I toss a loose pea at him. He smiles, picking it up off the table, and throwing it back at me. "Hannah, you have no idea!"

It's now five days before our wedding, and I feel very sick to my stomach. Hannah One assumes it's nerves, and Jamie has arrived with all sorts of antacids, ginger tea, and some other weird homemade remedies that I am to rub on my chest, or ingest. Nothing seems to help. I text Grace and make an appointment for one o'clock.

I enter the Centre and note a slight aroma of incense, which proceeds to make me queasy. I have never had a reaction to scents before, but now my olfactory system is working overtime. Grace brings me into her room, and I lie down on the comfortable table, ready to relax. Grace is also of the mind that my nausea is likely due to stress, and last-minute worries before the big day. She assures me I'll feel a bit better after letting it go. She smiles, saying, "Hannah, everything is in order, and with Jamie in charge, all you have to do is *go with the flow.*" Somewhere deep in my mind an echo of those words resounds. I close my eyes, and Grace begins her session.

Standing in a field of flowers, I glance around. Yes, my escape is always to a place of nature and wild things. I can just stay here, and then it will be easy to go with the flow. The tiny bees make their rounds on colourful flower tops, birds sing lazily in distant Poplar trees, the sun casts a warm glow over my body, and I feel lost in this world. The Earth under my feet welcomes my roots, as they start to grow deeply down into the soil. My arms stretch out like petals of a flower, opening for the first time to the Light. My eyes catch the glimmer of a tiny speck floating in front of me. It's not a Bee, or an insect. It is a tiny dapple of energy. It glows green, yellow and blue. It floats closer to me. I cannot see any distinct shape, like a fairy or sprite. I sense that it is full of love as it draws nearer, and then suddenly passes into me, like water into a sponge. I feel it inside, aglow. It comes to rest, deep within me. I cry. I recognise a new energy within me, a new life, a new human.

I lie still as Grace completes the session. I want to throw my arms up in joy, but I know this secret has to stay mine, until I can tell Owen. A baby, our baby. I leave Grace shortly after the session, walking home in a daze.

Thirteen

As much as I long to tell Owen about being pregnant, part of me still wants to keep it a secret for a while. I know it won't be difficult at the wedding, as I already avoid alcohol, so no one will think it unusual. Once all the stress and chaos of the wedding is over with, and we are safely ensconced in our secluded honeymoon cabin on Shadow Lake, four hours north of the city, I will share the news with him. My nauseousness seems to have greatly diminished after Grace's treatment, which I am very thankful for. To everyone's best guess, it was simply nerves.

Two nights ago, Owen's Aunt Regina arrived at the airport from Calgary. Owen asked if I wouldn't mind staying home while he went to pick her up. He felt it better to have their first face-to-face meeting without anyone else there. I was relieved I didn't have to make the trip, as I was tired from a full day of activities that were all focused on me.

After she checks into her motel room, Owen brings his aunt directly to the house to meet me and my family. My father has joined us, but left Shelagh out of it, as my mother is present. It's a bit awkward to have to cope with the obvious tension when my mother, father and Shelagh are in the same room together. On the outside, they are very polite and cordial to each other, but I sense all three of them will be very glad when they can part ways, and leave family gatherings to a minimum.

Aunt Regina is everything Owen said she would be, and more. She booked herself into the cheapest motel she could find, after insisting she won't stay at the house and *be in the way*, but then proceeds to tell us all, repeatedly, how horrible her motel room is. She is so happy to meet me, and yet I get the impression the jury is still out on whether she will *truly* like me or not. I do not ingratiate myself on her - either she likes me or she doesn't. I can't worry about her regard for me, even though she is Owen's only living relative. She has an opinion on everything, and shares it, whether or not she is asked to. She hopes she isn't seated near any plants during the ceremony, as she is allergic to anything green. She mentions her gluten sensitivity, and hopes we have made arrangements for her dinner to be gluten-free. I leave the living room to join Hannah One in the kitchen, who appears to be taking an awful long time getting herself a glass of water. She grins and winks at me when I enter the kitchen. No words are necessary between us; we both know what the other is thinking. Then we giggle. I hug her, grateful I don't have an Aunt Regina to cope with on a daily basis.

The morning light creeps through the blinds and pokes at my eyelids. I spent a dreamless night lying next to the man who will, today, become my husband. My hand instinctively lies across my belly, and I softly stroke it, as if to soothe us both. I can hardly wait to have this day over with, just so I can tell Owen, and share the joy I've had bottled up inside me for the past week. A slight movement from Owen makes me turn my head. His body is warm and heavy next to me. I reach out a hand to touch his hair, and trace the line of his spine down his back. I love his skin, his eyes; the way he tilts his head when concentrating very hard; his smile, his passion and commitment to things that are important to him, like me, and Hannah One. I love every inch of him, and I ache to be with him always. He slowly rolls over and opens his eyes. We smile, looking at each other, caught in time, without needing words to share the understanding that we are about to start a wonderful new chapter in our life together.

The best man arrived and whisked Owen out of the house to prepare for the ceremony, slated for three o'clock. Jamie arrives at the same time and flaps her wings until all the roosters have left the hen house. Then she settles in to focus on me.

My bouquet, which arrived yesterday, sits perched in a vase on the kitchen counter. I chose wildflowers - Daisies, Sweet Peas, Violets and Zinnias, tied together with a champagne-coloured ribbon that matches my dress colour. The dress hangs from the shower rod in the bathroom, and my shoes and other accessories are laid out in the bedroom.

Jamie begins to fuss with my hair. Although I would prefer it be left loose and hanging down, she shakes her head in disagreement as she rummages through her huge makeup bag to produce a small box. She pulls out a small ceramic butterfly hair clip and pins up one side of my hair. I admire the pretty clip, and must admit it looks beautiful. Jamie nods her head, as if to say, told you so! She applies a bare touch of makeup, which I feel uncomfortable wearing. Once again, when I see the finished product, my face carries a glow that makes me smile. I issue my thanks for her persistence, regardless of the reluctance I voiced during the whole process. This day is as much for her, and for Hannah One and my parents, as it is for Owen and me. The last step is getting into my dress without ruining her hair and makeup artistry.

The moment finally arrives when, dressed and properly coiffured, I descend the stairs to my awaiting parents and Hannah One. They all gasp as they see me. My mother has tears in her eyes, and Hannah One beams with joy. My dad, reaching out his hand to help me down the last step of the stairs, whispers, "Oh my god, Hannah! You're so beautiful! You are perfect." His voice catches in his throat. I glance at him, to see tears in his eyes.

Neville waits outside by the sedan he had rented to drive us to the Conservatory. Jamie will drive Hannah One, but both my parents and I will go in the sedan. My father takes the front passenger seat, giving my mother some time to sit in the back with me, and hold my hand. She hasn't stopped crying the whole time. She smiles at me as I squeeze her hand reassuringly. Her smile carries joy, not sadness. She is so elated it is spilling out of her. She doesn't need to say anything, I know how much she loves me, and wants me to be happy. And I am; so very happy.

Grace had made the arrangements for the officiant of the ceremony. She suggested her friend, Louisa Hutchinson, a Unitarian Universalist Minister. We met with her and she kindly agreed to join us in wedlock. Today it's Grace's task to get Louisa and Arthur to the conservatory on time.

The Conservatory is a beautiful, gigantic solarium, filled with dozens of tropical flowers and enormous shrubs, a small pond that a few Koi call home, and masses of butterflies fluttering from one plant to another. There is an area by the main door that fits the chairs we needed, which are arranged into two groups, leaving a short aisle running up the middle between them. The air is fragrant, warm, but not stuffy. I peer through the glass doors to see the people we invited to the ceremony, many of them seated and quietly chatting with each other. A few butterflies float over their heads, like miniature colourful clouds, passing high in the sky. It's so delightful, I laugh. Neville escorts my mother and Hannah One inside, and helps them find their seats. Shelagh has taken a chair in the middle of the cluster, not wanting to intrude on the *family* row of chairs. Her sensitivity towards my mother's feelings is much appreciated, by both my father and me.

Louisa stands at the front of the grouped chairs, leaning down slightly to talk with Grace, who is seated. The minister wears a long, cotton robe that has every colour of the rainbow on it, with patterns of animals, flowers, and the sun and moon adorning the front and back. There are hand-sewn beads all along the hem and sleeve cuffs that sparkle as they catch the light. It's a beautiful robe, and seems to embody my own spirit, with all its colours and points of light.

The bookstore is closed today, so all my employees, who are friends now, can attend. I see that Janice has brought her girlfriend Amelia; Mila sits with Nouri, who has included his grandmother Nasrin as his plus one. In front of them sit Arthur and Grace. Owen's Aunt Regina sits up front, taking a chair next to my mother. I close my eyes for a moment, and send my mother the patience to bear the abrasive woman's attitude for the time they must be together. Jamie and Neville sit alongside Mark and his husband Brian. They have been together for a few years now, and decided to make it official a year ago. The two of them are holding hands, while looking up and talking about the butterflies. I feel a warm sensation in the pit of my stomach to see Mark finding his love and happiness, just as I have found mine.

Suddenly I hear Fred Astaire's voice singing, *The Way you Look Tonight,* as the two glass doors are opened by two Conservatory employees. My father takes me by the arm. He winks at me and smiles at my confused expression. No one said I'd be walking down the aisle to music; let alone a song I have always found so charming.

Yes, you're lovely, with your smile so warm, and your cheeks so soft, there is nothing for me but to love you, and the way your look tonight.

I can see Owen's face clearly; his beaming smile and amusement at "pulling one" over on me. My dad leads me slowly down the aisle, savouring each step we take. I glance around to see everyone smiling, while some whispers are shared, of which I catch a word or two, like *dress* and *beautiful*. I focus my attention on the man waiting at the head of the aisle, standing next to Louisa.

Owen wears a suit of navy blue, which highlights his fair hair. A small yellow Daisy boutonniere sits cheerily on his lapel. The bright yellow face of the flower makes me smile even more. His tie is sky-blue coloured, and his crisp white shirt flashes cleanly under his dark suit jacket. I have never seen him look so handsome, and I feel a desire to touch him and have that beautiful body close to me. *Later*, Hannah, *later*, I say silently to myself. The walk seems long, and yet in a blink, I am standing before him with Astaire's final words; *Lovely, never, never change, keep that breathless charm, won't you please arrange it 'cause I love you, just the way you look tonight...*

We look a each other and grin. I think we are both surprised that we look so nice when we get dressed up! Taking each other's hand, we turn to face Louisa. She begins the ceremony by greeting everyone and asking them to add their love to this day, so the happy couple will have a strong foundation on which their marriage can grow and thrive. Just as she gets to the part where we say our vows, I hear the sound of whispers from the seated guests. Some are pointing above our heads. Out of the corner of my eye I see my father smiling, and pointing a finger at my head. I look up. There, circling above me, are dozens of butterflies. The flashes of brilliant colours, from yellows, oranges, iridescent dark blues to glistening blacks, is mesmerizing to watch. The swirl of butterflies slowly descends and I can feel some of them land in my hair, some on my bouquet, while others dance around me. I can hear tiny gleeful voices in my mind. It's a collective *love-in* of butterflies, all ecstatic about my presence, and the glow of energy I must be emitting. Their collective voice rings in my ear, and when one butterfly lands on my hand, there is new joy over the discovery of the baby's energy, nestled deep inside me. I try to contain my laughter, but when others in the assembled group begin to giggle, I can't help it. A joyful giggle erupts from me, and it spreads over the group like a wave of electricity. Soon everyone is laughing, and the butterflies, jolted by the sudden noise, begin flapping over to the seated guests and land on their heads, while some ascend to perch on the greenery around us.

Louisa, as she wipes laughter tears from her eyes, announces to the group, "Well, now that we have the butterflies' blessing, shall we continue?" Everyone settles down, but the smiles never leave their faces for the remainder of the ceremony. When Owen places a beautiful white-gold band on my finger, and I slide an unpretentious gold band upon his, we are married.

Entering the small banquet room after the ceremony I am struck by the loving energy that emanates around the room. There are thirty-five guests milling about, holding their drinks and chatting in small groups. I notice Aunt Regina has cornered Shelagh at a table, and by the look on the Shelagh's face, I get the feeling she wishes she could find the emergency exit, fast.

My mother looks gorgeous in a satin-like Prussian-blue dress adorned with small gold threads running through it that shimmer when she moves. I watch as she helps Hannah One get seated at the family table. She graciously takes the seat on the other side of Aunt Regina, although my grandmother would have no difficulty interacting with Owen's aunt. Hannah One has the patience of a saint. My father sits next to Shelagh, and Louisa takes her seat on the other side of Hannah One. The other tables are a *free for all* as far as seating arrangements go. I didn't want to have a whole lot of structure to this party; I just want everyone to have fun.

The meal is very good, though I only eat a mouthful. I watch my friends and my family as they laugh and enjoy themselves. Owen notices my lack of appetite, but doesn't persuade me to eat. I glance over at him sitting next to me, and notice his eyes on me. We smile, and then he leans in for a kiss, forgetting we are in a roomful of people. The clanging and cheering that erupts as we kiss makes me pull away, and mock-bashfully duck behind my cloth napkin.

After dinner there is plenty of time for dancing and more socializing. The music begins and people start to crowd the dance floor. I look over at Owen, wondering when it would be polite to make our exit. I am riding high on energy, but I can see the end of the ride, as it slowly ebbs. Owen doesn't notice, but leaves the room momentarily. When he returns he is holding a large, flat square paper bag, from which he pulls out a record album. He hands it over to the DJ, leaning over the table to talk to him. My attention gets diverted as I watch Hannah One make her way to the dance floor with Mark. She moves and jiggles her old bits to the rhythm, and giggles as Mark tries to find the beat. They laugh and cajole for a few minutes, until she takes his hand and motions for him to please help her to her seat. I know she loves to dance, but between her hip and her age, the body just doesn't want to move like it once did. But by the smile on her face, I know she enjoyed the dance. Mark leans over to kiss her on the cheek before he returns to Brian, seated at the next table.

The song ends and the DJ turns on a microphone and announces; "Let's hear it for the happy couple!" and everyone applauds, some letting loose a cheer or two. "Okay folks, this one is just for Hannah and Owen." The lights suddenly dim, and a tune I know very well begins to play. It's Ella Fitzgerald singing, "Night and Day". Owen makes his way over to me and extends a hand. I reluctantly accept it. Feeling very self conscious, I am only too aware that all eyes are on us. The song begins with its heavy brass beat and then its plucking violins mimicking the sound of a ticking clock, with Ella's silky-smooth voice slowly gliding through the first verse to the chorus;

Night and day, you are the one... only you beneath the moon and under the sun... Whether near to me or far, it's no matter darling where you are, I think of you... Night and day...

Owen holds me in his arms and moves me around the room. I close my eyes, and we are in the living room at home, dancing to our favourite song, alone. My body relaxes and we sway as the words fall over us like a waterfall...

Night and day... I think of you... under the hide of me, there's an oh, such a hungry yearning burning inside of me... and its torment won't be through, 'til I spend my life making love to you... day and night, night and day...

The final notes from the saxophones, and then the big brass ending make me open my eyes, and bring myself back to *Now*. Owen still holds me tightly, and I never want him to let go.

After a few hours, we leave the party in full swing, with my father and Shelagh trying to teach people how to dance the Gay Gordon. My mother and Hannah One left an hour before we did, getting into the sedan with Neville's help, who was kind enough to leave the party and drive them home. Hannah One is staying with my mother for the night, to give the newlyweds *the run of the house*, as she so blatantly put it. I objected at first, but Hannah One refused, and insisted on giving us as much privacy as she can tonight. As the two of us bid farewell to everyone, the last thing I do is toss the bouquet, per Jamie's instruction. Nouri's grandmother, Nasrin, accidently catches it. It's one of the funniest moments of the evening.

By the time we return to the house, exhaustion overcomes me. I have never felt so tired in my life. I keep having to remind myself that my body is growing another human inside of it, so I'm bound to feel challenged in the energy department. Owen insists on carrying me through the front door. He places me gently on my feet when we reach the foot of the stairs. "Well, Mrs. Ross, how about we take this upstairs?" He kisses me, a long passionate kiss. I respond, and slowly we make our way up the stairs, my exhaustion forgotten.

The morning arrives, and brings with it a long drive north to the cabin we have rented. I am aching to walk in the woods, forget the world, and just live in Owen's arms. I can't believe how much I sound like a romance novel these days. I want to blame the hormones, but the truth is, I am so very happy.

The car inches its way along the gravel sideroad that runs parallel to the shore of the lake. Through the trees I can see the lake; small whitecaps curl the surface as the breeze pushes the water. I am silently wondering how much farther it is, when the car turns in to a long dirt laneway. We creep up the well-treed drive, watching for potholes, for about a third of a mile. As we round a bend in the lane, a small cabin comes into view. Owen parks the car and we both step out into the fresh air.

All of my senses are immediately rewarded as the breeze coming off the lake greets me; the sound of birds singing high up in the trees tickle my ears; and the aroma of the pine needles that cover the forest floor touches my nose. We walk around to the front of the cabin that faces the lake, and look out at the water. A short wooden dock, that gently sways with each wave that touches it, juts out about fifteen feet from the stony shoreline. A canoe rests, upside down, on wooden planks about twenty feet away from the dock. The deep navy-blue water beckons me, but I know that, since it's only the second of May, the water would chill me to the bone. I won't be brave enough to go for a polar bear swim, but I believe Owen will be. I gaze across the huge expanse of water to the hilly tree-line along the distant shore. The condensed greenness of the far-off tree tops resembles a gigantic crown of broccoli. I follow the shoreline with my eyes, until I turn and look at the cabin. It's a bungalow-style wooden cabin, with a wrap-around porch, large bay windows that overlook the lake, and surrounded on three sides by pine trees. It's not fancy, but it's also not the basic shell either. The perfect amount of roughing it, without really roughing it.

We unpack the car and begin locating where things are stored in the kitchen, like a pot to boil water, and cups for tea. The refrigerator is cold and ready to take our food. The person who rented the cabin to us explained that all the amenities are available, including electricity, but no internet. I am glad to see a flush toilet and a shower, as I'm not in the mood for *totally rustic*. The single bedroom houses a serviceable double bed, one white painted dresser and two old nightstands, with a small table lamp on each. We brought our own pillows and bedding. My father insisted we pack his extra large down-filled sleeping bag, which could be unzipped and used as a comforter. Now I am glad we took his advice, as I suspect this cabin may get pretty chilly during the spring nights.

After we eat some sandwiches and have a cup of tea, we walk along the trail that runs next to the shoreline. I'm too tired to canoe, and just want to commune with the trees and wildlife. Owen asks if I want to be alone on the walk, but I tell him he won't interfere with my connection to the natural world around us. He frowns, so I add the comment that I will fill him in if the gossipy squirrels tell me anything worth repeating. He smiles and squeezes my hand as we continue our walk.

The evening brings the colder air, so I am glad to have a small woodstove to light and take the chill off. Owen found a box with five slightly used pillar candles, and set them on the table, along with the Corning Ware dishes we found in the cupboard, plus two bright orange placemats. Our salad and pasta dinner never looked so beautiful.

Once the dishes are done, we retire to the small living room, and after Owen stokes the woodstove, we curl up on the couch together, soaking up the silence. Owen is a man who likes to *be doing*, so I realize how much effort it takes for him to simply sit and enjoy the peace surrounding us. I reach my hand up and turn his face towards me to kiss him. "You are wonderful. This has been the best day for me. I love it here so much. Can we stay forever?" He laughs, "Well, I could probably work from here if we could get internet, but running a bookstore from afar? Might be tricky?", he chuckles as I poke him. "Besides you'd never want to leave Hannah One out of this adventure, so where would she sleep? We'd have to get bunkbeds or something!" I laugh at the image of Owen and I crammed onto the top bunk, while Hannah One takes the lower bunk. Then another figure pops into the image: a baby, sitting on the floor, wondering where it will sleep. I sit up. Owen begins to move, thinking we are done with the compulsory peace and quiet time, and now we can go have sex. I remain seated however, deep in thought. He sits back down and takes my hand. "I love you, Hannah. I want to spend my life learning what it is to be you. I would do that here, or anywhere you want to go." I lean against him, feeling the muscles under his sweater twitch as he moves his arm around me. "Owen, I have something to tell you. I don't really know how to, except just to say it. I'm pregnant." I feel his body stiffen slightly, but then he suddenly jumps up off the couch, grabbing my hand to pull me up. He hugs me fiercely, and I fear I will stop breathing. "Oh my god, Hannah, oh my god…" he exclaims, his voice muffled against my shoulder. He pulls away to look at my face. "This is, oh, this is wonderful! I mean, I can't believe it…" he suddenly stops and frowns, "Are *you* happy about this?" I smile and nod, tears welling up in my eyes. I blink them away, but new tears merely take their place. Owen takes my hand again, and we sit down on the old couch. "How did this happen? I thought we had *that,*" and he points to my crotch area, "covered as far as birth control goes?" I shake my head. "I don't know the physiology of it, but, the package does indicate that the pill is *only* between ninety-one and ninety-five percent effective. I don't know Owen, but it wasn't on purpose. I want you to know that." Owen looks shocked and immediately replies, "I never even considered that! Hannah, I know that we would have talked about a family, when the time was right for *you*, especially with the business and Hannah One to care for." He places his hand on my stomach. "Did you get a test done or see the doctor? Do you know the due date?" He is smiling, with tears still evident on his cheeks.

"Well, to be honest I haven't done a test, or been to the doctor. But I know, I just know. She came to me in a vision." Owen looks at me, a mixture of surprise and scepticism crossing his face. "It's a girl? She *came* in a vision? What did you see?" He tries to keep his voice calm. I close my eyes and see the field again, a scene I have replayed in my mind every night since I first saw it. "It's kind of hard to explain, but she came to me as a little ball of light and life, and then I felt her inside me. I don't know how I know it's a girl, I just do. You will have to trust me." Owen's eyebrow twitches at the use of the word *trust*. He sits there, keeping his hand, and his eyes, on my belly. "Hannah, there's one thing I have learned recently; it's that I will always trust your visions. I *really do* trust you."

We sit for a few more minutes, letting the moment settle into the frame of our lives. Not only are we newly married, now we can add *expectant parents* to this joyful scenario. I close my eyes and sink into the bliss, while cradled in my husband's arms.

Leaving the cabin after seven wonderful days is very difficult, yet I feel the pull of the world tugging at me to return to it. We discussed that I should see a doctor to get more details, like a due date, before telling anyone. I love having a secret with Owen.

I turn to view the water one final time, and, on cue, tiny whitecaps appear on the surface of the lake, waving its farewell to me. I raise my hand and wave goodbye, and thank the lake for lending me its peaceful rhythm throughout our stay. The breeze carries through the pine trees, whispering its own parting message, filling my mind with serenity. I could cry, because I want so desperately to stay and commune longer, but I know I cannot. I promise to return, and slowly, reluctantly, turn and head towards the car.

Fourteen

Having the doctor's information in hand, Owen and I begin to tell our family and a few friends about the baby. The estimated due date is December twenty-first. The first person we tell, of course, is our housemate, Hannah One. She cries and hugs us both, proudly proclaiming, "Holy shit! I'm gonna be a *great* grandmother!" I have hardly ever heard Hannah One swear, which makes her proclamation all the funnier. She makes me sit down and immediately starts to fuss over me. Owen steps in and argues that, if anyone is going to fuss, it will be *him*. He continues, "You better save your strength for when our daughter arrives, as I bet she'll be a handful!" One thing Owen and I agreed upon was to keep the gender a secret, at least for a while. I gently remind him, but he simply shrugs his shoulders and laughs. "I can't help it. I want to shout it to the world!" He cups his hands around his mouth like a megaphone, "Hey world! Guess what? It's a girl!" Hannah One laughs and the two of them launch into a long conversation about changing the spare room into a nursery, and buying a crib, along with all the other paraphernalia babies require. Owen picks up a large pad of note paper and a pen off the dining room table and begins drawing layouts, and making lists. I sit there, contentedly tired, watching them talk, until I drift off.

Hannah One and I decided to invite my mother over for coffee to tell her the good news. Owen is going to be busy with an article deadline, so it will just be "the girls," as my father would say. I greet her at the front door, and usher her into the kitchen where Hannah One sits at the old table, folding a few newly-washed cloth napkins. When my mother enters the room, Hannah One rises from her chair and hugs her as tightly as her old arms can manage. "Caroline! I'm so happy to see you. I've made some squares, so I won't hear anything about dieting today!" She releases my mother and goes over to the counter to pick up a large plate of date and lemon squares. My mother smiles, "I'm sure I can find room for one, maybe two." She chuckles, and it's nice to see her smile, which happens more often these days.

When the coffee is perked, we decide to sit in the living room. My mother doesn't notice that I'm drinking ginger tea, instead of my usual coffee. I read about the effects of caffeine on the baby, so I immediately cut my intake down to one cup per day, in the morning. I still need that cup to get my engine started. Ginger tea is for the slight nausea that nudges at my body every so often.

Once we are seated with squares dotting our small China plates, and hot cups in hand, I smile and clear my throat. "Mom, I have some good news. It seems that you are about to be a grandmother." I grin, hoping she will be as happy as I am. She blinks, needing a moment for the news to sink in. Then she places her cup on the table beside her squares, and stands up. She comes over to me and takes my hand, pulling me up. She hugs me. My mother is not one to display physical affection, unlike my father. Whenever she hugged me, I felt like it was extra special, and worth relishing. Today, her hug conveys a thousand words she cannot say. She finally pulls away and returns to her seat. She has still not spoken a word. She reaches over and pulls a tissue out of the box sitting on the small side table. She wipes her eyes and looks at Hannah One. "Oh my god! What is that going to make *you*!" and we all laugh. The remainder of the afternoon is spent making plans for shopping trips to stock up on maternity clothes and baby things. I am definitely up for some clothes shopping, as things aren't exactly loose-fitting anymore.

Today Owen and I have luncheon plans with my dad and Shelagh. As they are in the process of moving in together, Shelagh invited us over to her apartment so we can get to know each other better. I think she believes she still has to win me over, but, truthfully, I like her because she makes my dad happy. That's all that matters.

Shelagh has a tidy, very homey-looking place. A few hand-sewn quilts, placemats, pillow shams, and curtains, are in evidence throughout the one-bedroom abode. My father had mentioned that hand-stitching is one of her hobbies. As she seats us on her couch, she indicates that my dad should take the small recliner opposite us. She herself does not sit down, but goes over to the sideboard and produces a large rectangular white box, with a beautiful silver and gold bow resting on the lid. "I'm so sorry, my dears, this was supposed to be ready for your wedding day, but my brain was overloaded by packing my own and your father's kit. I'm so boxed up I sometimes see cartons in my sleep!" She laughs at her own joke. Her brogue is not so thick that you can't understand her, but enough of a lilt that makes it charming to listen to, regardless of what she is saying. She hands the package to me. It's a good size, and a bit heavy, so I need both hands to grasp it. Owen reaches out to add his hand to it.

We place the box on the couch between us and I pull off the lid. Lifting the layers of tissue away, I spy a white cloth. I see colourful stitching, but folded up I cannot make out the pattern. I stand up, pulling the cloth out of the box, letting its length drape down in front of me. I find the corners and spread my arms wide to view as much of the pattern as I can. Shelagh takes a step forward and helps me unfurl the cloth so we can all see its full design. "It's a bonny tablecloth!" Shelagh exclaims. I begin to look at the hand-sewn images along the edges of the large cloth, as they cover the entire hem, as well as each corner and the centre. So much detail, so much care and attention sewn into this fabric. The images are of wildflowers and animals. "Your Da told me how much you love nature, so I thought to myself, Shelagh, she would like a cloth where she can have the wee beasties and her flowers to look at, whenever it suits her." She laughs again and this time I laugh too. It is beautiful; the flowers are colourful and intricately woven all along the hem, and as I look more closely, I see rabbits, squirrels, raccoons and birds, playfully residing in all four corners. In the centre of the cloth, she has sewn three oval ringlets of Daisies, which are my favourite flower. It is a piece of art made with care and love. I am extremely moved by her effort. I gently refold the cloth and place it back in the box, before reaching out to give Shelagh a hug. "I love it! It's perfect! We will cherish it, and only use it for special occasions!" Shelagh's eyes widen, "No, no my dear! It's not to be kept for good. Use it, and love it, that's what it's for, not waiting for a special day. I don't believe in keeping things you think special hidden away, only to see a few days a year." She steps back and excuses herself while she checks on the soup that is simmering away in the kitchen. "She does make good soup!" my dad chimes in as he watches her leave the room. She can be heard, from the kitchen, squawking and laughing at something she found funny. My father smiles.

Lunch not only consisted of cock-a-leekie soup, but the best homemade biscuits I have ever eaten, complete with butter, cheese, and jams; followed by vegetarian scotch pies. Instead of the traditional meat filling, she devised her own recipe, using tofu. The pie is surprisingly good, and I compliment her on making the effort to work with tofu, which can be a bit tasteless if not cooked the right way. She chuckles, saying she discovered that the secret to making it more palatable is to marinate the tofu in whiskey for four days. I blanche, and discreetly eat around the alcohol-soaked tofu. Owen raises an eyebrow at me, and when Shelagh leaves the table he quietly takes his fork and picks the tofu chunks off my plate and into his mouth. After he swallows, we giggle at each other. My dad glances at us, but most likely assumes we are having a "newlywed moment", so he doesn't ask questions.

After everyone has coffee and dessert, except me, which Shelagh tries not to take offence to, we return to our designated seats in the living room. Shelagh has pulled a dining room chair into the living room and perches on that. My father tries to give her his comfortable seat, but she won't hear of it. She says, "besides that, I'll be popping back into the kitchen to soak a pot or two, in a minute." Owen and I look at each other and smile. He nods and I take a breath in preparation for my announcement. "Dad, Shelagh, we've got news. We are having a baby." Shelagh claps her hands and utters her congratulations, but it's my father's face that draws my attention, to the exclusion of all else. There is an expression that carries both astonishment and elation. Tears fill his eyes. He stands up and comes over to me. I stand up and we hug. A daughter and father sharing that special moment when she becomes a mother, and he a grandfather. I feel the tears clinging to my eyes and spilling down my cheeks. He pulls away to look at me and grin. He shakes his head, but no words come to him. His joy is complete. Then I whisper in his ear, "Don't tell anyone, but your *granddaughter* can't wait to meet you." His eyes widen, and his mouth opens, but I make a *shh* sound which stops him short of sharing this secret news. He hugs me again and whispers into my ear, "And I can't wait to meet her!"

The bookstore continues to be profitable, and I am very thankful, in part, to Janice's management, for its success. As I enter the door, I get a flashback to my first time coming into the shop, seeing books floor to ceiling, artwork dotted throughout, and a wonderful portly woman smiling, ready to help me find the perfect read. Gwen would be proud of how we've managed to keep Bentley's Books alive and thriving. Mila has been offered a job at the library and is leaving us. She studied library science at university, so it's her dream job, and we are very happy for her. It does leave us short staffed, as Mila took a lot of shifts. Janice mentions that she has been screening applicants and found two she likes. I suggest that she hire both, because soon I won't be able to fill in when needed. Janice looks quizzically at me and, as I point to my slightly protruding belly, she erupts in a delighted squeal. "Holy crap! That's wonderful!" she bellows. Fortunately, there are no customers in the store, only Nouri, who's head shoots up from the book he's reading, when he hears Janice exclaim. "Hannah, this is great! I bet Owen is over the moon happy!" I nod, recalling the beautiful smile on his face when I had told him.

"So, Janice, I think that if you like these two potential hires, I will leave it to your discretion as to the hiring of one, or both. We have the budget to take on both, so you have my blessing. But do as you see fit." This is not the first time I've given Janice the lead, and I have every confidence in her managing it all without trouble. "Great! I'd like to show you the applications anyway, just so you're up to date." She pulls out file folders and hands me the top one. "This young woman, Cindy Sakamoto, is one who caught my eye. She reminded me of myself, a bit. Full of organizational ideas, plus she has had experience working at Pages Bookstore, the one in the mall, so she is familiar with book retail." Pages is a big box store, our main rival. It will be interesting to pick Cindy's brain for ideas, and to see what differences she finds working for an independently owned bookstore, versus a large chain store. "I like her!" I announce, without reading her resume any further. "The other girl is a bit different. There is something about her, I don't know, maybe it's a *quality*, or something. It's hard to describe, but I just liked her." She hands me the second folder, and I open it to see a resumé that features a colour photograph of the applicant alongside her name, Angela Barry. She has long dark hair, a pretty smile, and almond shaped eyes peeking through tortoise-shell glasses. I read through her brief work history, which is short and unrelated to working in a bookstore. She included babysitting jobs, a telemarketing job that, if I did the math correctly, only lasted thirteen days, and a camp counsellor job, at Birchlake Camp. I smile. "Janice, you did read her resumé, right? She worked at Birchlake!" Janice nods. Janice and I met at Birchlake Camp, and worked alongside each other as counsellors. That time seems like eons ago. "Are you sure you're not letting your fond memories of camp colour your judgement here? I mean, she doesn't have a lot of experience doing, well, anything really…" I trail off, suddenly remembering what my resumé looked like when I applied to Bentley's Books over ten years ago. Suddenly I feel a little guilty for being dismissive of Janice's choice. "I think that if you have seen some quality in her, then she must be worth hiring. Good choices, Janice." I hand the folders back to her.

I feel my stomach constrict, and I know the nausea monster is announcing itself for the usual afternoon session. I stand up, and say that I have an appointment with the doctor, so it's time to head out. Janice smiles, both for the news of the baby, but more so, I believe, because I have placed my trust in her to keep the boat afloat, which she knows she can accomplish.

Standing on the edge of a long wooden dock, I feel the slow, rhythmic undulation of the pier as the waves move under and around it. The waves increase, and the dock begins to rock slightly. The entire lake is slate grey, almost black in places, while white-crested waves cruise to the shoreline, pushed along by the increasing gale. The only sound is of a long howling wind, that chills the soul when you hear it. The sky is flat and unyielding in its blankness. I look out and spy the far shore. It's but a thin black line on the horizon, with no distinguishing features. The vista before me is bleak and isolating, and despair blossoms in my heart. Trepidation seeps into my body, as the rocking of the dock increases, and I cannot keep my balance. I bend my knees and sway, in an attempt to stay upright, until I lose my balance, and suddenly find myself falling. I hit the water, but I don't get wet. Any sound of a splash is silenced by the water encasing me in its frigid grip. I sink down in the depths, but I am not gasping for air, I am not drowning. Oddly enough, I can actually smell fresh cut grass as I sink deeper and darkness surrounds me, as the water closes in. It wraps itself around me like a heavy, cold blanket. I cannot see anymore, not even the darkness. I find my eyes closing, and I drift away, until there is nothing.

Lying in bed, Owen is grasping my shoulders, trying to wake me up. I am screaming and thrashing my arms, as if fighting for my life. He holds onto me until I begin to come around. I lie there panting, a film of sweat coating my body. Disoriented, I glance around to see the afternoon sunlight beaming through the window, and the clock, which reads four-thirty. Owen's hands still hold me tightly, an anxious look on his face. He tries to get me to sit up, but I feel too weak. I feel such a tightness in my chest, and in my throat, that I can only manage to whisper; "Something bad has happened."

Five minutes pass. I sip the glass of water Owen insists I drink, but recoil as my phone begins to ring. He reaches out and picks it up, answering it on the third ring. "Hello?" Owen recognizes the caller, but cannot keep the uncertainty from his voice. "Shelagh? Wait, what? What? Hold on…" he passes the phone to me without a word, and I look at his outstretched hand holding the device like he's offering me a vial of poison he wants me to consume. I swallow, taking the receiver from him and weakly say, "Hello, Shelagh?" I hear her sobbing as she exclaims; "Oh dear, Hannah you must come! It's your Da!"

Fifteen

My father never wanted a funeral. He did, however, request in his will that his ashes be interred, with those of his father, in the family plot. Hannah One agrees. She has barely said anything since that horrible day.

Sudden-death heart attack, just like his father before him. His father had been fifty-five when he died; my father was fifty-eight. One moment he was standing there, the next he looked dizzy and fell over. Shelagh was with him; they were standing in the freshly mowed front yard of the house they wanted to buy. The realtor called nine-one-one, but he was gone by the time he hit the ground.

I find myself unable to pull my body out of bed when morning finally makes an appearance. Nothing can bring me out of this deep, black hole I am buried in. My Alternate mind reels from the extreme pain my human side is experiencing. *Such sorrow, deep, aching, never ceasing, overwhelming grief that drowns the Light. You are drowning.*

I find no joy in my pregnancy. There is only the painful fact that my dad will never meet my daughter. I cannot see my way past this grief. Owen holds Hannah One and me afloat as best he can. A daughter losing her father, and a mother losing her son. It is a tremendous task, but he loves us both so much. He would move mountains if he thought it would help.

Owen and I, along with my frail grandmother, meet my mother and Shelagh at the cemetery. There is a small, square hole dug into the ground, with a green cloth draped around the four edges of the hole. A headstone about five feet away carries the name, James William Casey, along with the inscription, *Always Loved and Remembered*. There will be a new stone carved to include my father's name.

Since there is no minister to say, "everyone please pray", or a choir to sing *Amazing Grace*, we merely stand gathered together and let our collective sorrow take centre stage. Shelagh pours a shot of whisky into the grave. Hannah One does not cry. I fear she is dried out from crying for the past two weeks. She leans against Owen for support and strength. My mother holds herself stoically, glancing off to the nearby trees, or up to the sky, every time she feels tears pricking her eyes. Regardless of the fact that their marriage was over, she had spent the better part of thirty-five years with this person, through the birth of their child, and all the other ups and downs of life. I know she is devastated.

There is nothing I can say to lessen any of their grief, not when my own is so crushing. From somewhere deep inside, I can feel a sorrowful voice crying out. It echoes through the deepest part of my sadness, searching for a way to get out and be heard. Finally, this muted voice begins to move through my body, like water rushing towards the wall of a dam. It hits the wall and spreads out, searching for a crack or hole from which to escape. This grief-filled voice can no longer be contained, as it breaches the wall. I hear myself sob, as the wall crumbles. It bursts forth. My pitiful wail reaches the sky, shoots to the moon, and beyond, until my mother wraps her arms around me, hugging me closely.

Two weeks after we put my father's ashes in the ground, I must say good bye to the house I grew up in. It feels like I'm losing all the landmarks that have made my life what it is now. My dad was the captain of the boat that kept me on course, and the house was the treasure chest on the boat, that held all my childhood life experiences safe and untarnished. A part of me knows that it is just a house, and that the memories are part of *me*, to take along throughout my life, but the physical nature of the house itself now evokes such strong emotion, I can't rationalize it away.

    I enter the front door and see my mother leaning over a box perched on a folding chair. She looks up and smiles as she sees me. "Hannah, hi. Just packing up last minute stuff from the kitchen. Can you take a look in the upstairs closets to make sure I didn't miss anything?" I nod. Crossing through the living room, I see me, lying on the floor, on a sweet knitted baby blanket, with Fred sleeping by my side. I turn, and see me coming down the stairs, in a dress, ready for the first dance at school. I feel a lump in my throat. I glance into the dining room, and even though it's empty, I see the table, set for Christmas lunch. My father sets out tiny gag gifts by each place setting, my mother leaning in from the kitchen, asking if he'd check to see if the front walk needs another shoveling. I turn away, and walk up the stairs. I check the bathroom first, and find every cupboard bare. Next, I enter my parents' room, and there I see me, lying on the bed, while my father folds laundry. We are just talking about inane things that were important at that particular point in time, like school work, or his new office computer. What I wouldn't give to have just one more conversation with him. I quickly check the closets and find them empty. Wiping away my tears, I finally enter my room. I see my bed, the posters on the walls, my rainbow-coloured curtains, but, all of it, only a memory now. I have already cleaned out every inch of this room, but check the closet one last time. I do not want to imagine who will be using this closet next. I do not want to think about who will walk into this house and make it their own.

    As my mother continues to fuss over another box, I quietly slide out the back door, to have one more moment in the backyard. I walk over and place my hand on the old tree. I reach out and tickle the tree with my mind. Its slow, sullen response leads me to believe it is unhappy. *You are here.* It responds slowly. *Yes, I have come to say goodbye. We are moving away. I hope the new family finds joy under your boughs.* Again, I feel a swelling in my chest, as if saying goodbye to a very dear old friend. I hear the echo of the tree's voice in my mind as it says, *Humans will come, and go, but I wait for no one. I will either continue on my path of growth, or I will die and become earth again. As brief as you have been in my realm of life, your presence in my existence has made a difference. Thank you.* The tree inwardly sighs, and stops communicating. I smile, turning to glance up one last time into the tree's lofty boughs and healthy green leaves that sway gently in the breeze. *I wish you well, dear friend.* I turn and head back towards the house.

My mother stands looking out over the yard from the door, a sad wistful look on her face. I know she is having a difficult time with this move, particularly now. As I approach the door, she steps towards me and hugs me. I feel her shoulders move slightly, as she cries quietly. I tighten my hug on her as I too can no longer contain the sadness I feel, and there, in the doorway, clinging to each other, we silently share our joint heartache.

There is a knocking at the front door. The thumping is non-stop, and increases in volume, like a drumming sound. I get out of bed and make my way down the stairs. I stand before the door. I can hear my father calling to me, 'Hannah! Hannah! Why can't I get in?' My hand freezes on the door knob. Am I supposed to open it? Why is he locked out? If I had known he was coming, I would have unlocked the door for him. 'Hannah, where is everyone? Why can't I come in? Please..." The pleading in his voice breaks me and I sob, reaching for the door knob.

Owen gently takes my hand off the front door knob and tries to lead me back upstairs. "Hannah, honey, come along to bed. I don't know where you are going, but it's nighttime, not time for a walk." Am I awake? I feel so dazed, I cannot differentiate between the awake and the dream, still hearing my dad's voice crying out.

Owen settles me back into our bed, and once my head touches the pillow, I hear nothing more.

Five nights of door knocking and sleep-walking are enough for Owen. On the morning after the fifth night, he calls Arthur. He explains what is going on, and wonders if Arthur can help. I sit sullenly in the kitchen chair. I have no memory of these episodes, only a vague recollection of dreaming about my dad. I think Owen is overreacting, until I see the distress in his eyes. He is afraid for me. He so much as admits his fear, saying, "Hannah, this must be a dream-walk. But you keep having it over and over again. I think it's repeating itself until you figure it out. You are going to get sick from not sleeping. I'm worried about you, and the baby."

Arthur arrives about three hours after Owen called. I am napping on the couch while Owen reads in the big armchair, with one eye cocked on me. Even asleep, I feel him watching me. My hope is that Arthur will reassure Owen that this is nothing to be worried about, lots of pregnant women have vivid dreams, and even sleep-walk.

Arthur walks into the living room, peering around to the kitchen before asking, "Where is my darling HO?" Owen takes a seat again in the large armchair in the corner of the room, as he replies; "She's at her exercise class this afternoon, and then having an early dinner with Caroline." Arthur looks disappointed that he won't see his *favourite old lady*. The first time he called her that, Hannah One called him saucy, but beamed nonetheless. He paces over and takes a seat next to me on the couch. I begin to recount as much as I can remember about the sleep-walking episodes, and Owen adds one or two details as well. Arthur sits quite still and thinks for a few minutes, closing his eyes and rubbing his forehead with his fingers. Suddenly he opens his eyes and looks directly at me, stating, "This is not a dream-walk, and it's not a memory of past events. This is something different. Can't quite put my finger on it." He closes his eyes again and continues to rub his forehead, like he's getting a headache. Owen and I sit quietly, waiting to see if he arrives at any definitive answer.

Finally, after a few minutes, Arthur says, "The only way I can figure this out is to look at your past images. You know, your door. Now that you have had this happen it could appear as an image on your door. The event is certainly significant enough to warrant an image being placed there. We can enter the image and see what actually occurred in the sleep-walk, as the *entire* scene will be linked into that image, just like it was with Owen's parents." At the mention of that traumatic memory the three of us explored, I look over to see Owen's jawline tighten slightly, but he remains silent. I need more clarity on this, so I ask, "So, you're saying that by finding the image on my door, we can see what I was dreaming, and figure out why I keep dreaming it?" Arthur nods. Owen stands up and paces to the window. He turns slowly and says, "Okay, then. What do we need to get started?"

We all agreed I'd be more comfortable if I can stretch out on my bed. Arthur sits in the chair in the corner of the room and Owen sits on the bed beside me. I close my eyes, and, although not necessary, Arthur talks me into a meditative state. Drifting down, all the colours of the world disappear, and nothing is present except white light. It is peaceful and calm. I hear Arthur's voice somewhere around me, guiding me to look at my door. I see before me a white door, with an ocean-blue coloured doorknob, suspended in the middle of the frame. The door has no hinges. I reach for the knob but it evaporates, like mist. No, this is not *my* door, it belongs to someone else and I am not supposed to see it, yet. I gently touch my belly.

Turning again, I spy a glass door, with a brass handle. Although it's made of glass I cannot see through it. I reach for the knob and it turns in my hand. I step through the doorway and turn to look at the back of the beveled glass door, expecting to look through the glass to the other side, but the surface is opaque. A massive array of images, row upon row, run horizontally from the top to just above the middle section of the door. Arthur stands near me, waiting for me to find the image.

I glance over the pictures, and try to avert my eyes as I view images of the day my father died, and his funeral. These pictures have a dull dark glow around the edges. The next image is of me, standing at the front door, with Owen, looking worried, standing behind me. I point to the picture, and Arthur leans in. I touch the image with the tip of my finger.

I am in my bed, trying to sleep. A voice calling out to me makes me sit up and leave the bedroom. My father calls to me from the front door. I stand in front of the door and hear his plaintive cries. Part of me aches for him to come through the door, but another part senses there is something wrong with that. He should not be here. Arthur stands behind me and says, "Go ahead, open the door for him." I lean forward and turn the handle.

There is a burst of light, and then I see my dad standing in the doorway. He still looks like my father; his face holds that smile, and his eyes shine with love. He opens his arms to hug me, but I hesitate. He frowns. "Hannah, I am glad you let me in. It's so confusing here. I just want to come home." He steps into the front hall. I step back. He ignores me as he looks around. "I want to smell the cooking in the kitchen, hear my mother singing, watch you and Owen planting flowers in the garden, and I want to see my granddaughter."

A cold hand circles my heart. It is reality taking hold and squeezing. I can't decide if I will just let him be here, stuck in-between, to exist vicariously through the lives of those he holds dear, but never to be a part of any of it. Every molecule in me aches to keep him with me. He is my father, and I cannot let him go. He stands there, waiting for me to let him venture farther in, to ingratiate himself into the shadows of my life, only to be an observer, not to be observed, or acknowledged. I step forward and take his hands. Oddly, they feel warm. He squeezes my hands. "Dad, I am so happy to see you. I love you so much, I, I..."

and words begin to fail me. The pain of losing him wells up into my chest, and I feel like I will suffocate in this torment. "Dad," I choke out, "Dad, you need to listen to me." He turns his eyes on me, and for the first time I see that the energy of life is missing. He is still my dad, but his spark, his human Light is no longer aflame. It is not gone, just suspended in limbo, unwilling to move onward. "Dad, this is not the place for you, now. There are others who can help you find where you should be, where your Light will thrive and move on. You will be unhappy being stuck here." I continue to hold his hands and burn the memory of his touch into my soul. "I know you want to be here, to see your granddaughter, watch her grow and create a life for herself. I wish that with all my heart. But it can't be. Dad, you died. You are Light now; what you see is but a reflection of who you were, and cannot let go of." His grip loosens on my hands, but I keep hold. "Dad, what lies ahead is so much more than this", and I wave my head around, indicating the house, and me. "You will see and understand so much more by allowing yourself to step into the All. Don't sit here by the door and never leave. I could not bear that." A look of distress crosses his face as he utters, "Hannah I would never want to hurt you. It just seemed like I was supposed to be here. It feels like something is keeping me here. And now that I see you, I believe I am meant to stay here."

Suddenly I realize that part of the reason he can't leave is because I have, unknowingly, been keeping him here. My sorrow has reached out to the Universe and caused his energy to shift into neutral, so he is stuck here. I have to let him go. "Dad, I'm sorry I kept you here. Now, it's time for me to let you go." I reach out and hug him. I hear a familiar dog barking as Fred appears at his feet. "I'm glad you've come to understand why your dad has been knocking at your door. I've been waiting for this whole thing to be resolved, so I can help him move on." I smile at Fred and give his head a loving rub. Fred turns and says to my dad, "You have but to follow, as I will lead you on. Your next adventure awaits." My father turns his eyes to me, a look of hesitation on his face. "I'm not sure about this. How can I leave *you? What if there's nothing ahead for me?". I try to keep my voice from cracking, as I whisper, "Dad, you will be okay. Trust in Fred, he won't lead you astray. I'll be okay too. You have been a wonderful dad, and I will always love you. But it's okay for you to go." My heart aches as I say these words, but I know I have to let go of this sorrow so he can be free. He steps back, looking around one last time, and smiles. "This was a pretty good life. The best part of it was you, my daughter. Hannah, I am so proud of who you are, and how you live your life. Please remember me, but try to let go of the sorrow and the pain, so you can let the good stuff be all you remember of me." He turns and walks out the door, following the wagging tail of his best friend, Fred.*

Owen holds me as I sob in his arms. The rupturing pain I feel throughout my body is simply the sorrow being ripped from me, letting go of the devastating misery that has held me prisoner all these months. As I take a breath, I feel my daughter kick for the very first time.

Sixteen

The summer has stretched as far as it can into September. The warm days, now less frequent, mix with the turning of the leaves to autumn shades. It's pleasant today, as I sit in the garden with a cup of something hot, and Hannah One for company. We sit silently in our comfortable lounge chairs and soak in the warm air, the smell of leaves and soil, and listen as a few Chickadees sing in the branches of a nearby tree. Hannah One whispers, so as not to interrupt the concert, "I always wonder what they are going on about? Do birds gossip the same as humans?" She chuckles. I smile, extending my mind out to listen in on the birds' chatter. After a minute or two I turn to her and report. "It would appear that the conversation is about where to winter this year. The general consensus is to stick around *here*, since the bird feeder always seems to be full." Hannah One nods, grinning at the information shared. "Yes, we will keep a hefty supply for these little ones, and anyone else who happens by." I suddenly feel a kick, and instinctively place my hand on my belly. "Ooh, ouch!" I exclaim as the kick lands its mark inside my abdomen. Hannah One looks over. "Is she kicking you again?" I nod. We decided to tell Hannah One and my mother about the baby's sex. My mother was happy to start shopping with a girl in mind.

Well into my twenty-eighth week of pregnancy, my body has settled into a rhythm, albeit a bulkier, less comfortable one. The nausea of early months has vanished, and now the cravings are making themselves known. I have a hankering for bananas. It is one food item Owen can't keep enough of in the house. In the middle of the night, it's not uncommon to find me in the kitchen, peeling two bananas and eating them, while leaning against the counter. In the morning, Hannah One or Owen often finds evidence of peels on the counter. I remember eating the bananas, just not actually waking up to do so.

Life has settled into a routine now, and I am comfortable with its pace and predictability. Owen, on the other hand, seems restless and discontented, and while I sit in the garden, soaking in my environment, he is out in the world, trying to save it. Yesterday he traveled to Ottawa to report on the climate change protests that are continuing to occur outside the Parliament buildings. He tries to keep an objective view when reporting for the paper, but confesses it is becoming harder to keep his own opinions out of the news he reports.

He has been seeing a therapist for months now and appears to be working through some issues, but is reluctant to talk about his sessions, and I don't push it. He simply states that his therapist wants him to work on becoming his *true self*. I hesitate to worry about him. He is very independent, and prefers to works things out on his own, rather than ask me, or anyone else, for help. I wonder if this is typical for married people to grow together, but at the same time, grow apart. I saw my own parents attempting unity, mainly to provide me with a sense of stability. But I saw through their façade of a happy home life, and always wished they had been more honest with each other, earlier, in their marriage.

I glance over at Hannah One and ponder what her married life had been like. "Did you, and uh, Grandpa, ever find your marriage was getting a little mundane?" Hannah One laughs, and looks at me with a quizzical expression on her face. "Of course! What is life without the mundanity? Quite a bit of it was very routine and banal, except the part where he died before his time." She frowns. "I still wonder what my life would have looked like if he were still here with me." She looks down at her old hands. "Life gives you a mixture of highs, lows, and in-betweens. It's the in-betweens that make you appreciate the highs when they occur, and it's the lows that make you wish for more of the in-betweens, just so you can catch your breath and regroup. Does that make sense to you?" She winks. I nod in response. "Owen and I seem to be *in-between* right now. He seems discontented." I take a sip of my herbal tea. Hannah One sighs. "Hannah, I hear it is very typical for a man to feel a bit out of sorts when his wife is having a baby. With all eyes on *you*, he may feel left out." I contemplate this notion, but then disagree with the idea that Owen feels that way. "No, I doubt that. He seems to be happy and excited, and with the *two of you* organizing the nursery and all its gear, I think I should be the one to feel left out!" I chuckle, and she smiles. "Yes, it's been so much fun! When I was having Daniel, your dad, it was a different time. Your mother would help you with making some baby clothes, and then you would check with your husband to see how much could be spent on a crib. We were fortunate that James, your grandpa, had a good steady job at the advertising agency, so I could buy a *new* crib." She smiles softly, as her eyes lose focus and she squints slightly to look at the memory, but finds it hard to see clearly. "I thought it would be a good investment, as we would use it for all the children we had." She frowns, "But, it turns out Daniel was to be our only child. You have to go with what life gives you…" she trails off. I see from her expression that she is getting a little tired, and I'm about to suggest we both take an afternoon nap, when I hear my phone chiming inside the sunroom.

By the time I manage to get myself out of the lounger, the phone ceases its ringing, and a little beep indicates there is a message. I look at the screen to see who called. It was Owen, likely checking in to see how we are getting along here. I push the voicemail button, and listen for the message he left me. Owen's voice sounds hurried and short, "Hannah, damn, I didn't want to leave this on voicemail, wish you'd picked up! Need to tell you,

I've had a bit of trouble here, actually, I think I'm being arrested, but maybe not. I'm being detained here at the police station. It might be on the news so I wanted you to know before that…" he sounds out of breath and the background noise keeps drowning him out, as someone shouts, and a loud speaker blares a muffled announcement. "I can't talk long; They might take my phone or something! Who knows! I'll call you later when I know more. Love you!" and the message ends. I sink down onto the soft sofa bed that Hannah One often uses for her afternoon naps in the sunroom. I redial my voicemail to listen again, as I'm sure I misheard the message. How could Owen get arrested? Hannah One enters the sunroom from the back door and, seeing the concern on my face, stands beside me as I silently push the button one more time. I put the phone on speaker so she can hear the message. After the call ends I push the button to save the message, and then place the phone into my pocket.

Hannah One sits down beside me. "Well now, that's a shit storm." She isn't trying to be funny. I nod, still too confused about the situation to make any reply. Hannah One shakes her head. "It must be a mistake, or a misunderstanding" she continues, "Owen was a reporter on the scene, at the protest, why would they arrest him? Maybe he just got caught up in the crowd and placed in with the protesters, or something…" she trails off, as she herself tries to piece it all together.

I know I won't be able to nap now, as my mind races and I feel my blood pressure rising. Hannah One stands up and mumbles something about having a rest in her room, but if Owen calls I am to come wake her. I agree, and watch her slowly glide through the doorway and make her way through the kitchen. I take the phone out of my pocket and stare at it, willing it to ring again. Wanting nothing more than to hear Owen call back and say it was a mistake.

Looking at the clock in the kitchen I suddenly grasp the fact that I've been sitting here for over an hour waiting for my phone to ring. I stand up and stretch, feeling the tension in my body coil like a spring. I shove the phone into my pocket. I spy a few dishes in the kitchen sink, and a pile of clean laundry that needs folding, so I busy myself with these tasks, while I wait for my phone to ring. The exhaustion runs through my veins, and after a few minutes I need to find a place to perch, and wait. I sit on the couch and pick up a magazine.

Three hours later, the phone rings. I open my eyes to the realization I had dozed off. It's Owen. He sounds exhausted and irritated. "They finally released me. Guess having reporter credentials helped, as they don't want any bad publicity for a false arrest. I'm leaving the city now, I should be home in a few hours, we can talk then." I have a million questions, but his tone indicates he isn't interested in answering any questions over the phone, so I will need to be patient.

Hannah One had long gone to bed by the time he pulls into the driveway. As he enters the house I walk to the front door and lean in to hug him. He looks tired, and his response to me is perfunctory, at best. He drops his travel bag on the floor and takes off his jacket. I ask if he wants a drink, and he nods. I return with a beer to find him stretched out on the couch, looking like he'll drift off any second. I can't let another minute go by without learning the whole story. I make a coughing sound to jolt him awake, as I place the beer on the coffee table in front of him. He sits up, stretching out to grip the bottle, and takes a long drink. I sit down in the large armchair across the room, waiting expectantly.

Owen sighs after a swallow of beer, "Shit, what a day. I never thought it would swing that way." He takes another lengthy drink. I say nothing, trying to keep my facial expression neutral. I don't want him to know how worried, angry and scared I have been all day. He puts the empty bottle back on the table and raises his arms up over his head in a long stretch. "Well, I guess I should fill you in…" his flippant remark misses the mark, and I don't smile when he glances my way. "Okay, well, the CEN were staging another protest outside Parliament, once again calling for clean water rights on the First Nations land." Before his trip he had filled me in on who the protesters were and what they were protesting about. The CEN is an acronym for *Clean Earth Now*, an activist group that focuses on calling out various levels of government for their lack of commitment to greener strategies. In this particular case, their protest aims to bring awareness about the total neglect of these communities who need access to clean drinking water. Owen looks at the empty bottle, a look of indecision on his face. I make no offer to get another beer for him. He leans back and rubs his eyes. "You know Hannah, sometimes I feel like all I do is write about what is wrong with this world. I never *do* anything about it." He shakes his head, distracted and losing the thread of the conversation. "Oh ya, okay; so, they were doing their usual peaceful sit-in, when this one over-zealous cop decided to manhandle one of the protestors. I was pretty close to the whole thing, so I could see that she hadn't provoked him or anything. It was just a cop who was tired of putting up with people exercising their right to peacefully protest. Well, you know, I started shouting at this cop to let her go, and the next thing you know I'm in the middle of about ten people, trying to free this woman from the cop. Then about six cops swooped in and started grabbing *all* of us, and oh shit! It was chaos!" His voice is getting louder, and I place my finger to my lips to indicate that he shouldn't wake up Hannah One. He cringes and mouths the word, *sorry*. He stands up and strides into the kitchen for another beer. I sit and wait patiently for his return.

He ungracefully flops back on the couch and the beer sloshes a bit out of the top of the bottle. "Oops, geez, I can't win today." He puts the bottle up to his lips and slurps up the drips that run down the side. "Okay, so, we are all getting pushed and shoved to the ground now, and the cops start cuffing us. I tried to sit up and tell them I'm with the press, but they ignore me, and next thing I know I'm cuffed and in the back of this large van. They take us to the police station, and then we sat there for almost five hours. Then they just let us go. No Charges, but also, no apologies or anything." He really looks at me for the first time since he got home, and seeing my pained expression, realizes I have been sitting here, worried to pieces, waiting for him. "I am so sorry you were worried. I thought you might not worry too much, but I can see you've had a tough time wondering what happened to me." He lifts the bottle to his lips for another long swig. He continues, "You know though, this day got me thinking. I have been trying to *tell* everyone how to make this world better so our kids," and he points at my belly, "can have a safe clean Earth to live on. I feel like I need to *act* on what I say. I can't keep playing environmentalist without actually making a difference somewhere. It's kinda hypocritical." He sits quietly for a minute. His inwardly focused dialogue leads me to believe he is trying to come to some conclusion regarding his role in the world. "My therapist and I have been working out why I'm so restless, and I've started to see why, especially after today. Hannah, I know this will sound crazy, but hear me out. I wasn't even going to consider this, but now, I'm starting to see what I need to do…what is going to help me…" He seems to be having an epiphany as he plops the second empty beer bottle onto the table. He stands up and starts pacing the room, as he continues. "I was talking to Colin last week, and he was telling me about this program he's working with now, in Africa. He's headed back in two weeks, around October ninth I think, and, well, he wants me to join him." I look at him with an expression of shock and confusion. He continues, ignoring my expression. "It'd only be for about ten weeks, but Hannah, oh my god! I'd be working with school kids! I'd be teaching them about environmental issues; we'd be doing a seed and propagation program, working with local farmers to show them more effective ways to grow crops. And then there's the cultural exchange Colin has been working on, linking a school *here* with one near Nairobi. It's an amazing program!" He pauses to take a breath but then forges ahead, as if spilling all the information at once will be less shocking to me. "I mentioned the program to Peter, my boss at the paper. You remember meeting him at the wedding, right?" I nod; fully aware he has not even looked at me the whole time he talks. "Well, he thinks I should go, so I can create a series of articles, week by week, on what is happening there. This is a win-win, as I still get paid for doing my regular job, while doing this amazing thing!". He finally stops and looks at me, to see if I am showing the same amount of enthusiasm for his idea as he is. I am not. He hesitates as he reads my expression; "I didn't tell Peter I'd do it, I just wanted to see how it might fit into things here…" his arms wave around the room, indicating *I* am part of the "here" he refers to. "Hannah, I need this trip. Like I said, my therapist believes that *I* need to be *involved* in my life, and not just skate through it. I feel, lately, like my life has become, well, like I am living, but not *really* living. What I mean is that, I need to feed my passion for the environment and keeping it safe and clean. I have back-shelved this passion, because *we* have a life that fills up so much and," he stumbles when he sees the hurt expression developing on my face, "Oh no, I mean, I love *us*. I love you, so, so much. It's just that, there is something inside me that feels like I'm ignoring my calling. I *need* to make a mark in this world, even if it's just talking to some children in Nairobi about taking better care of their piece of the Earth. It's something." He finishes his speech and looks hopefully at me.

What am I going to say? No, you can't go off to Africa and leave your very pregnant wife, just so you can fulfill your calling? I sit still, trying to construct a sentence that will convey just how badly timed his new found desire to *make his mark* is. "Ten weeks? That will be cutting it close to the due date." Owen pauses, almost as if he's forgotten about the arrival of his daughter in approximately twelve weeks. "Oh, don't worry, I'll be back in plenty of time, at least two weeks before she gets here." I wonder what crystal ball he has looked into, to be so precise in his statement of the imminent arrival date. "Well, the doctor said there is a window on either side of the date she gave us. You would hate to miss the birth of your daughter, I would think." He looks at his hands as he quietly utters, "Hannah I need this. If I don't do this *now*, I'll never have the opportunity again. How would it look if I took off and left you with a new baby? That just wouldn't be right." I silently ask him if leaving his very pregnant wife is any less wrong? He kneels down in front of me, as I sit rigidly in the chair. He takes my hands, "I will be here for you, and our daughter, through thick and thin, but if I don't take this opportunity now, I will regret it forever." Forever is a long time, I think to myself.

I suddenly feel more than exhausted. I feel drained of emotion, drained of life, drained of reason. Letting go of Owen's hands, I rise up out of the chair, an ache making me place my hand in the small of my back. I want to sleep, and not think anymore about anything, for as long as I can. "Fine, I don't want to stop you from going. I know this is important to you, so I will support you. But if she comes early, well then, that's just something *you* will have to reconcile with *yourself*." I turn, not waiting for a response, and head up the stairs.

October ninth rears its ugly head, no matter how hard I wished for Time to stop. Owen has spent the better part of two weeks packing, getting various paperwork completed, a quick doctor's exam and a few precautionary vaccinations. His gear, piled up by the front door, is a daily reminder that he is leaving me. I feel no anger, or sadness. I only hope that this trip allows him the opportunity to shift his perspective on how he views his life.

His flight to Nairobi will be over fifteen hours in length, and with the time difference, he will lose seven hours. The plane leaves Toronto and lands in Jomo Kenyatta International Airport at approximately six in the evening, their time. He and Colin will spend the first night in Nairobi, before heading out to Limuru, a rural town in Kenya's highlands. I myself would have loved to travel to Africa, if I weren't so busy being extremely pregnant. Part of me is envious of Owen being able to *up and leave* at a moment's notice, and wonder why he didn't think of doing this a year ago, before I was a baby-making machine. I dismiss that thought immediately. I can't imagine Owen would *intentionally* leave me out of his adventure.

The alarm beeps at six a.m. startling me out of a deep sleep. I feel heavy, both physically and emotionally. Owen, on the other hand, bounces out of bed like a kid on Christmas morning. He quickly showers, and then heads to the kitchen to make coffee. Hannah One, being an early riser, is already busy making some toast and pulling out jars of jam from the fridge. She has been reservedly excited about his trip. I know that somewhere inside she is concerned about the timing of this trip, in relation to the birth of our baby, but she never voiced her opinion. She merely engages Owen in conversations about what he will experience on this passion-filled trip. He has printed out a stack of pages on the program and how he will be involved, as well as information about the Maaasai Mara Reserve, which he specifically wants to visit while there. She was thrilled to get all the information and asked many questions, finally coming to the conclusion that, after reading all about it, it is a wonderful opportunity. She glanced at me when she said this, but I remain unchanged in my opinion about this trip. I will support him, but I don't have the heart to be his head cheerleader.

Now, as the clock reads eight-thirty, I hear the taxi pull into the driveway. Hannah One already said her goodbye earlier, as she left the house for her morning walk around the neighbourhood. I stand in the hallway as Owen takes his bags out to the awaiting cab. He returns after he shuts the car trunk, and asks the driver to wait for another minute. He doesn't care, the meter is already running. Owen bounds back up the front steps into the house.

I look at him, and smile unconvincingly. He takes me into his arms and kisses me. A long slow kiss that is meant to hold both of us over the next ten weeks. I embed that kiss in my memory, so I can look at it, and remember how much he really does love me, even though he's thousands of miles away. A sad realization that I will be alone now to finish out my pregnancy, makes me hold him as close as I can, and whisper into his shoulder, "I love you". He takes my face in his hands and kisses me again, slower but shorter, and then glances toward the cab. "I love you too. I will try to call tonight. And I will email you as often as I can. If anything happens…" his voice trails off, like he doesn't want to speak about the pregnancy, out of guilt for leaving me now. I shake my head, "Go, I'll be fine. I don't plan on having any trouble, and if something comes up I have Mom, and Jamie and Arthur, and even Hannah One is around to keep me upright." He smiles, giving me one last hug and, without another word, he disappears into the morning light.

I did not wait by the phone for his call, and it was a good thing, because the call never came. I received an email the next morning that simply stated that he had arrived, and he and Colin had crashed at the hotel, exhausted from jet lag. By the time he woke up, with the time difference, it would not have been a good time to call. He promises to call as soon as he can.

Seventeen

One week becomes two, as I am slowly getting used to sleeping in an empty bed. I have finally stopped looking for him to come through the door at the end of the day. I trained myself to make smaller pots of coffee, and make smaller meals for Hannah One and me. The emails are more frequent now, full of interesting tales of the people, wildlife, and what Kenyan cuisine he is now hooked on. I read them to Hannah One, who sits with her eyes closed, as if picturing the scene in her mind. She misses traveling, so I know she is living vicariously through Owen's vivid descriptions of his adventure.

I am more uncomfortable as each week rolls into the next. My mother has offered to help with grocery shopping and attending prenatal class with me. She laughs at how much parenting has evolved since she was a young mother, thirty years ago. Her support through all of this has been the island in the stormy sea for me. She never openly criticizes Owen for leaving, but anytime his name arises, she has a frown on her face. I know she wants to say something, but is trying hard not to.

Eventually, October's colours fade into November's dull leafless days, which slowly drag all of us into December. An early snowfall makes everything look clean and white, but when it melted away, the dull greyness returns, which matches my mood.

As my due date approaches my belly has grown to the point where I have a hard time doing mundane things, like putting on my shoes, or bending over to pick up something I dropped. Forget about trying to sleep: My dreams are vivid and wild, full of colours and movement, but nothing of substance. It's like I'm standing in the eye of a tornado, while all these colours and shapes blur around me, so I can't discern anything in particular. I wake up feeling tired and overworked.

The bookstore is a well-oiled machine, thanks to Janice. I try to drop by every other day to check in, but my fatigue is pulling me back home to lie down as often as I can. I have complete faith in Janice and Nouri. Being kept in the loop about the day-to-day operations through emails and texts, I have little worry, as I know things are running smoothly. My focus is just getting through the day, one hour at a time.

I keep my eye on December eleventh, as that is the day I get my husband back. I am anxious to see him, but more anxious about how he will feel about coming home. I hope he won't be full of regret that he could not stay longer in Africa; my wish is that he returns with a suitcase full of tales to tell, and a renewed sense of self that helps him move forward and be happy with his life, here, with us.

The morning of the eleventh arrives with a gift, in the form of a slight increase in my energy levels. I decide to do a little light housework, and make some oatmeal cookies, which I have a craving for. I have not felt this good in weeks, and I attribute it to Owen's imminent return later this evening.

My mother arrives mid-afternoon, carrying groceries and a large box of newborn diapers that were on sale. She has been filling in for Owen's absence with great gusto, and I appreciate it. She gently sets the bags on the counter and begins unpacking the contents as I enter the kitchen. The smell of the fresh baked cookies wafts over me, and suddenly I feel dizzy. I grab the doorframe to keep me from falling. My mother turns and, seeing me clutching the wall, rushes over to grab my arm. I stand unsteadily for a minute, leaning on my mother's arm, before I feel something wet between my legs. *Don't tell me I've peed myself,* I think, in shock. But then a drop of blood lands on the floor between my feet. My mother looks down at it, and immediately takes my hands, leading me to the kitchen chair. "Sit there. Don't move, I'm calling an ambulance." I think she is overacting, maybe a pinch of blood is normal, a sign of impending labour, perhaps. I try to stand, but feel slightly nauseous, so I just remain seated, and close my eyes. She returns to me, still on the phone with the dispatch. "Yes, nine months, yes. Due date isn't for another week or so, around the sixteenth. Blood, yes, no," then she looks at me and asks, "Do you feel nauseous?" I nod. She continues to answer the questions from the operator, and then finally hangs up. She bolts out of the kitchen and up the stairs to retrieve the delivery bag we had packed two days ago in anticipation. When she comes back down the stairs, she places it by the front door. "They want to send an ambulance, to be on the safe side. No need to worry, I will…" I don't hear the rest of her sentence as a massive pain strikes my gut and I cry out. It feels like some giant is squeezing my insides to make fresh juice. I try to remember the breathing technique I was shown in prenatal class, but I simply start gasping. My mother puts her hands on my shoulders and says, "Breathe, slowly. There, that's it. Try to focus on your breathing, don't gulp for breaths, slow down…" The pain begins to subside. I feel more blood pooling between my legs as I sit on the kitchen chair. Part of my brain is thankful I wasn't sitting on the couch.

    Hannah One enters the front door, after completing her walk, to find us huddled together in the kitchen. She looks worried, but she just crosses the kitchen to sit in the chair opposite me, and calmly begins to talk to me about things, to keep me distracted, while we wait for the ambulance. It's when she mentions Owen that I begin to panic. "He won't be here! I knew it! He will be on an airplane while I give birth!" Frustrated tears stream down my face. Then another contraction hits. My mother continues to coach me through it gently, murmuring *breathe...breathe...* Hannah One goes to the door to watch for the ambulance, and within five minutes it arrives.

Two young women, with a variety of gear strapped to belts around their waists, wheel a gurney up to the front step, leaving it there until they assess the situation. They quickly come through to the kitchen. After a brief examination, they determine that, with assistance, I can walk out to the gurney. My maternity dress clings to my backside, covered in blood. My mother drapes my winter coat around me as best she can. She turns to Hannah One, and the two of them quickly discuss how best to reach Owen. I pay little attention to anything, other than placing one foot in front of the other. The strong women have a hold of me on either side as we descend the front steps, and then help me onto the awaiting gurney. My mother says, as they lift me into the ambulance, that she will meet me at the hospital with my bag. She looks frightened, Hannah One holding her arm, looking white and frail. I smile and wave. I try to reassure them both by saying, "Guess it's baby time! If you see my husband, tell him where to find me!" Their forced smiles are the last thing I see as the ambulance doors close.

The contractions are coming regularly now, but it is the pain I am experiencing between them that has the doctor concerned. My heart rate is elevated as well. They check the baby's heart rate and find that, it too, is rapid. I can't be certain what time I arrived at the hospital; I just know I've been in this labour room for hours. Now a decision has been made that a cesarian section is going to be necessary, as they suspect complications. It will be safer for the baby, and for me, to do the C-section. At this point, I am so overcome by pain, distraught about Owen's absence, and concerned for my baby's well-being, I would have let them do a tonsillectomy, if they thought it would help.

My mother sits in a chair in the corner of the labour room, reading a book, but every so often she stands up and comes over to me. I tell her she doesn't have to stay, there are lots of nurses here to help me, but she insists on keeping me company. As soon as the nurses begin preparing me for surgery, they ask her to go to the waiting room. She takes hold of my hand and squeezes it, as she leans over to kiss my forehead. Before straightening up, she whispers, "I'll be here, if you need me." Then she reluctantly lets go of my hand and leaves the room.

Wheeling me down the hall, I can't help but cry. Owen isn't here, and this birth is not what I imagined it would be, in the slightest. I feel so alone as I lie on the gurney in this cool, sterile room, with glaring lights, and no one talking *to* me. A sudden pain makes me yell out. It's worse than a contraction pain. It feels like my insides are being shredded. The doctor works quickly, and without much fanfare, she announces that I will need a general anaesthetic. The nurse leans in close to my face and says, "Just think, when you wake up you can say hello to your baby!" I want to punch her for making such a flippant comment. I want to be *awake* when she enters the world, be able to hold her, and see her face, and have her see mine right away. My tears soak the table under my head. Another spasm of pain erupts inside, then a mask covers my mouth, and I hear someone saying, "now, just breathe slowly". Then I feel nothing, everything is gone.

I see the doctor make a cut across my lower abdomen, and then avert my eyes, as the scene feels brutal and harsh. I cannot however, look away for long as I need to witness my baby's entrance into this world. I see her face, covered in muck, eyes closed. She looks like a doll, but she glows from within, a bright yellow light. They lift her over to a nearby station to clean her up and assess her health status. Then I hear the doctor say something about the uterus being damaged, too much blood loss… I lose interest in her words, choosing to focus solely on my baby. A bright shining light, that only I can see, emanates from her chest. Her life energy, a powerful little force, is hard at work. They clean her face, her nose and eyes. They wrap her in a warm blanket and place her in the portable basinet. I ache to reach out and touch her, hold her, smell her, but my body will not move, my legs feel bound, my arms, wrapped in invisible ropes, will not lift free. Then I cannot see, smell or hear anymore. I fall back into the dark.

Streams of purple light dance across my closed eyelids. The streaks move and sway gently as blossoms of navy blue erupt and merge with the purple, undulating to some unheard rhythm. I want to reach out with my mind and explore the Alternate energy that has come to me, but a sudden glaring white light erases any trace of colour and movement, and the sound of a human voice invades my conscious mind, forcing me to claw my way back from this heavy slumber.

I open my eyes to see a nurse leaning over and checking on something attached to the top of my hand and it pinches when she lifts it. I frown from the discomfort, and she notices I am awake. "Nice to have you with us again. You will be a bit groggy for a while longer, so don't try to move or anything. Just relax, and let us look after you." Her voice is calm and pleasant. I can't get my mind to focus. The room, with its bright overhead fluorescent lights, is swaying slightly and I feel dizzy. I close my eyes and try to go back to sleep, but a face appears before me. My daughter.

With my eyes still closed, I attempt to speak, feeling my hoarse, dry throat protest against use. I sense that the nurse has come back to stand beside my bed, asking, "You okay? Would you like some ice chips?" I nod, and attempt to pull myself up into a sitting position. My body does not respond, feeling like a one-hundred-pound bag of wet sand. The nurse places her hand on my arm and pats it gently, "I don't want you to move. Let me help you. You've had major surgery, so everything is going to be a bit wonky for you right now." Surgery? I try to recall what happened. I remember the faces of my mother and Hannah One, standing at the front door looking worried as I was lifted into the ambulance; I remember blood, and I remember the doctor saying something about my uterus. The nurse returns with a small plastic cup containing ice chips. She presses a button on a control by the bed, and the head of the bed rises slightly. She brings the cup to my lips. "Now just take one or two at a time. Try to suck on them, don't bite. Yes, that's good." Her soothing tone reminds me of my mother, attempting to help me breathe while I was having contractions. After two pieces of ice, I am able to cough slightly, and clear my throat enough to say, "My daughter?" The nurse smiles and fusses with the sheet on the bed, "Oh yes, she's a lovely little thing. She came through the birth like a champ. Her Apgar was eight, which is very good, all things considered." I want to ask what she means, but I focus on asking the most important question, "Can I see her?" The nurse, whose name tag reads, Belinda, turns and checks some other device attached to me before responding, "You are still in recovery, dear. Once you are back in your room we can bring her to you. Won't be long, just rest now, and I'll move you along when I think you're ready." And before I can ask anything else, she crosses over to the door, lifts her hand to the light switch and flicks off the horrible overhead lights, leaving only one small fluorescent light on, over the counter by a small sink in the corner of the room. I close my eyes and try to picture *her* face, but the hands of sleep pull me off my mindful platform, to the dark dreamless slumber that awaits.

It seems like only a few minutes pass before the lights come back on as Belinda enters the room to check on me. She hums under her breath as she works. I feel slightly more coherent now, as the effects of the anaesthesia slowly leave my system. I still can't move, so I just accept the fact that my body is not ready yet. I resign myself to quietly lying still, and waiting. Belinda's face hovers over me, an automatic smile painted on her face, as her eyes and hands concentrate on checking my status. I want to ask more questions, but I somehow think she would rather focus on getting me moved out of the recovery area. "Good, I think we are ready for the wheel down the hall." She goes to the large door and swings it wide open and, with her foot, she flips the door stop down to keep it open. She sticks her head out into the hall and waves at someone. Another nurse appears, and the two of them approach the bed on either side. A few clanging noises as the brakes are released on the wheels of the bed, and then they guide me out into the hallway. I now lie flat, watching the ceiling tiles that pass by overhead. The lights are very bright, and I squint as we move along the corridor, finally turning my head to the side and closing my eyes again. Around a corner, through another wide door and my bed comes to a stop. I open my eyes to see a large window, with the morning sun peaking through the drawn blind. My bed appears to be in its final position with the wheels locked into place, as one of the nurses pushes the button to raise the head of my bed a few degrees, so I can sit up slightly. I immediately feel better in this position, although it is not fully raised. Belinda paces over to the window and pulls the drawstring to open the blind. The sun, through a tinted window, shines into the room and splays across the far wall. I am happy to see natural light, and realize how lucky I am to have a decent room, with a pleasant window view. Belinda checks on a few devices, and mentions the catheter that will come out tomorrow. She rearranges my pillows and moves the rollaway table closer to my bed. She scans the room, to make sure she hasn't forgotten anything. "My daughter?" I ask again. "Oh yes, of course. I believe she is on her way. You won't be able to lift her out of the basinet, or stand up to change her, or any other movements that could upset your stitches. The other nurses will go over all the details." She smiles at me one last time before turning and heading out the door.

As I wait to meet my baby, I carefully run my hand across my torso over my hospital gown. I feel stiches across my lower abdomen. The skin feels hot, and aches. The door opens wide and a nurse appears, backing into the room, pulling a basinet along with her. She smiles slightly. She is young, and I wonder if this is her first year as a nurse. She wheels the basinet over and locks the wheels as it comes to rest beside my bed. My eyes immediately go to the bundle wrapped up, lying inside. The nurse reaches in and lifts her out.

I open my arms as the nurse brings her to me. I look into the face of my daughter. It is the most beautiful thing I have *ever* seen. She opens her eyes, frowning slightly at the light. Her eyes are blue, like Owen's. She has brown wispy tufts of hair, same colour as mine. I stare at her, and the rest of the world fades into nothing. Her tiny fingers reach up and I take hold of her hand. It is so tiny. She opens her mouth and issues a small cry. Then it occurs to me that she must be hungry. I don't know how long I was in recovery, so what did they do with her all that time? I look at the young nurse and ask, "Has she eaten anything? How am I supposed to feed her? I don't know how to breast feed!" A slight panic starts to hit me. She glances at the door, as if hoping a more experienced nurse might suddenly swoop in to help. "I think she got a bottle in the nursey, but I'm not sure. I can find out, if you'd like…" I know asking her any more questions is not going to allay my panic, so I simply say, "maybe there is a nurse around that could help me with this feeding thing," and I point to my breast. The young woman nods, and quickly leaves the room.

The baby continues to cry so I place my finger to her lips and she takes hold of the tip and begins to suck. It is a strange sensation, but it appears to bring her comfort, so I keep it there. Ten minutes later a stout, older woman in a pink uniform enters the room. Her smile is tepid as she strides over to the bed, a bottle in her hand. She frowns as she glances at the infant, "Yup, she is hungry. After a C-section it takes about five days before the milk comes in. Here is a bottle to get you started. If you decide you want to breastfeed, we can show you the ropes in a day or so." And with no other advice or remarks, she turns and walks out.

Caw! Caw! CAW! A large luminous Raven flies by overhead, a black smudge in the blank sky. In his beak he carries a Robin's egg. The shell still unbroken, its beautiful blue-green colour peeking out through the dark maw carrying it. A Robin flies behind the thief, desperate to save her egg. Her frenzied chirping falls on deaf ears. A voice echoes in my head, 'the Robin chases what is already lost to her. She needs but retrace her flight to her nest, as there is still one fragile new life awaiting her. One precious treasure that needs her love and protection. Focus on that singular, special pearl within your nest, and you will find your joy complete.' The vision fades, as the Raven flies away, becoming a small black dot on the horizon.

The afternoon brings my first visitor. It's Owen. He sheepishly opens the door and enters, holding a big bouquet of wildflowers in front of him. I smile at him as he approaches the bed, placing the flowers on the small table. He leans in to kiss me, long, but gently. For a moment the whole world falls away, and it's just the two of us, in the cabin, watching the sunrise over the lake. I missed him more than I can admit, and I am devastated that he wasn't able to witness our daughter being born. His eyes stray from mine, and search out the basinet. His breath catches as he reaches in and lifts his daughter to his chest. He gently moves the blanket to see her face more clearly. The tears stream down his cheeks. He looks over at me, a radiant smile across his suntanned face. "She is beautiful, Hannah. She looks just like you...." I chuckle slightly, "Wait until she opens her eyes, you'll find she has you in there, too." He continues to hold her as he comes back to the side of the bed. I can see regret laced into his blissful expression. "I am so sorry I wasn't here. By the time my flight got in, and I turned my phone back on, it was around ten. I came right to the hospital, but they wouldn't let me be with you. I guess there was some sort of complication?" He sounds unsure, and I assume the doctor did not tell him much. I glance at the bundle in his arms, sleeping soundly. "They haven't told me exactly what happened, yet. The nurse wants the doctor to go over the details with me, whenever she gets here. I know there was a lot of blood. I had to be put under, and now I have a bunch of odd-looking stitches down there." And I point to my lower gut. Owen frowns. Just then the baby makes a cooing sound, waking up from her sleep. "Owen, can you ask a nurse to fetch a bottle? I guess I don't have milk yet, and she will be hungry." He leans over the bed, placing the baby in my arms, and goes in search of a nurse.

Five minutes later he returns, looking concerned. "Finally able to talk to a nurse and ask for the bottle. Boy, are they overworked out there! I think there's only about six nurses for this whole ward. Must be a tough job." He shakes his head. I am getting tired, so I motion for Owen to take her out of my arms. "The nurse says I'm not supposed to lift her, change her, or do anything that might tear the stitches, so I guess you're on diaper duty, Dad!" He smiles, replying, "My pleasure!" He places her on a nearby change table and, with an expertise that surprises me, he changes her diaper without pause. "I know your mom and Hannah One are dying to visit, but they offered to wait until tomorrow so we can have today together." I imagine the two of them, so eager to meet their grand and great granddaughter. I am anxious to see them as well. I need to see their faces, and let them see mine, especially after the scare we had.

The door opens and a doctor walks in. She looks familiar. She introduces herself as the doctor on call last night who performed the surgery. "Good afternoon, Hannah. Oh, you must be the dad!" She looks at Owen, who simply nods. "Well Hannah, we have some things to go over. Is it okay for your husband to remain, or would you prefer we talk alone?" I state that Owen should stay, so she continues, "Well, it looks like *baby Ross* is doing just fine, which is great to see." She looks at my chart with a slight frown creasing her forehead. "Now, we should go over what happened, as I'm sure you don't remember it clearly." I nod. A cloudy image of an operating room, and my insides open to the world, passes through my mind, and I grimace. "We had a complication, as you may remember. All the signs were leading to a uterine rupture, which I must say is uncommon. Unfortunately, it did occur, and we had to take steps to stop the bleeding. I'm sorry, Hannah, but the rupture was so severe, causing so much blood loss, that we could only do one thing, and that was to remove the uterus." She stops talking, to let her words sink in. Owen's face goes white. I blink, confused. "What does that mean, exactly?", I ask hesitantly, part of me knowing what it means, but needing to hear it from the doctor, to make it a reality. "Hannah, I'm sorry. We had to remove your uterus, which means you can't get pregnant again. I am so very sorry for this outcome. If we had any other option we would have gone that route, but this was the only course of treatment open to us." She looks down at the chart, trying to figure out a good way to conclude this horrendous conversation. "I will leave notes about after-care for you to take home, which will be in about three days. It will be about six to eight weeks before you should try any *heavy* lifting. There will be other information that you will find helpful, but if you have any questions, please feel free to call my office and we can set up an appointment." She reaches over and pats my arm. "Congratulations on your new baby." She says without fanfare.

I look at Owen, but he has turned his attention to the baby in his arms. No more children? A cold fist clenches my stomach, and I feel sick. A vision of the Raven enters my mind. *Focus on what you have, not on what you have lost.* I feel the tears brim my lashes, but suck in my breath to calm myself, and turn to focus on the bundle my husband cradles. She is the one precious pearl that needs my love and protection.

The following morning, Owen proudly accompanies my mother and Hannah One to the hospital, to show off his lovely new daughter. Always hating to arrive empty handed, Hannah One brings me a small stuffed toy, a Rabbit, which I immediately fall in love with. It reminds me of our walks in the woods. My mother, being a more practical soul, brings an extra maternity nightgown, and my phone charger, both of which I need. The baby is asleep in her basinet, so both *Grands* can only lean over the edge of the bassinet to peer at her sweet little face, hoping not to disturb her. I appreciate that they are sensitive enough to let sleeping babies lie. She and I had been awake through parts of the night, with a nurse coming in to help, so I am happy to see her sleep for a little while.

Owen stands on the far side of my bed, holding my hand, an eager expression on his face. "Time to tell them?" He is excited to share our secret. I nod; my excitement is tinged with sadness, but I try to keep it from registering on my face. Owen, noticing my expression, suggests, "I think *you* should tell them." I gently smile at him, and whisper, "sure." I look at the expectant expressions on my mother and Hannah One's faces, and feel the rush of happy news overtake the sad undercurrent that touches my Light. "Well, after not much debate, we decided that your granddaughter, and great granddaughter," I nod at Hannah One, "Will thus be named, Claire Daniella Ross." My mother smiles, not a note of disappointment registering on her face that her grandchild will not carry any name from her side of the family. Hannah One begins to cry, reaching for the chair behind her, as Owen rushes around to help her sit down. Hannah One's middle name is Claire, and of course, her only son, and my father, was named Daniel.

Hannah One reaches into her purse and takes out a handkerchief. She wipes her eyes, and then slowly stands up, taking a few steps over and leaning into the basinet, whispers, "I'm so very happy to meet you, Claire Daniella Ross."

Eighteen

I cannot wait to sleep in my own bed again. The drive home from the hospital seems to take forever. Owen securely fastened Claire in the baby carrier in the back, and I sit gingerly in the seat beside her. "I feel like your chauffeur!" Owen jokes, as he looks at me through the rear-view mirror. I smile, but can't think of any funny reply, so I just turn my attention to Claire. She sleeps peacefully in the car seat, swaddled up to her eyeballs, as the chilly December weather nips at every inch of exposed skin.

As we pull into the driveway, the front door opens and Hannah One steps out onto the front porch as Owen shuts off the engine. She has an annoyed look on her face, which is unusual, but then I see Arthur emerge from the house, and I understand her irritation. I am exhausted from lack of sleep and just want to lie down while I have the opportunity, and Arthur's unannounced arrival means I will have to stay up and visit.

He waves as he catches my eye, and I frown at him. He merely chuckles and retreats into the warmth of the house. As I carefully make my way up the front steps, Hannah One is already talking to me from the porch. "I'm so sorry Hannah, I told him now is not a good time to visit, but he says he simply has to see you, and that he won't stay long. What could I do?" She is so distraught; I worry it isn't good for her. "It's fine, really. Arthur can stay for a few minutes and then I can be rude and tell him to go. He will be okay with that." I make my way through the front door, and then argue with my dear old grandmother as she insists on helping me off with my winter coat. Owen stomps through the door, trailing snow on his boots. In his arms he carries our daughter, still in the car seat, with two bags hooked over his forearms. "Why didn't you just go back for the bags?", I utter irritably. He grins, ignoring my prickliness, and replies, "I didn't want to miss seeing you toss Arthur out!" I don't laugh. Still wearing his boots, he enters the living room and places the baby carrier down by the large armchair, Claire continuing to sleep soundly. Hannah One makes her way into the kitchen and begins to prepare a large pot of tea. Arthur, sensing his uninvited intrusion, quietly enters the kitchen and sheepishly helps her arrange cups on a tray. I eye the stairs and wonder if I can make a quick get-away up to my bedroom, before being cornered by Arthur, but I'm not fast enough. Seeing me standing in the hall, he leaves the kitchen and walks up to give me a hug. I cringe at the strength of his embrace, still feeling tender throughout my entire body. He releases me, looking into my eyes, he whispers, "I want to talk to you, but we need to be alone. Wanna' go to bed together?" and he giggles so loudly, it makes Claire start. Owen, gently taking Claire out of the car seat to place her in the bassinet in the corner, looks over at Arthur and narrows his eyes, indicating he is not impressed by his uninvited and disturbing presence.

My mother had bought this basinet to keep in the living room, so I don't have to be attempting the stairs a hundred times a day. I can rest on the couch and have Claire nearby, or I can be upstairs and she can be in her crib, in her room. My mother was happy to help out by buying things she never had when she was a young mother. The sale of the house has given her more financial security, even after buying a smaller, more affordable condo nearby. I inherited the residue of the house sale proceeds that was to be my father's portion. He had not changed his will to include Shelagh, so any and all assets came to me, including the investment he made in the bookstore. I feel sorry for Shelagh, as she lost her love, and her chance for a happy life in a new home.

I look at Arthur, and know that whatever he has to say, he can say it in front of my family. "Arthur, whatever it is, just tell me. I don't care who knows. I'm too tired to care about anything much right now." Arthur shrugs and returns to the kitchen. I cross the living room to cautiously sit down on the soft couch. I sink into the cushion, feeling like I'd love to close my eyes and sleep right then and there, were it not for the room full of people fussing around me. Arthur appears from the kitchen carrying a large tray of cups, full of hot steaming herbal tea, and carefully places it on the coffee table. Hannah One follows him with a large plate of brownies. These days, she only bakes when she is feeling worried. I imagine the freezer full of sweets, after the events of the past four days.

Owen hands me a cup and gently sits down next me, placing his arm around me, as if protecting me from whatever it is Arthur has to tell me. Hannah One takes her tea and a tiny plate with half a brownie on it, to sit at the dining room table. Arthur picks up his cup and helps himself to two brownies, then finds a comfortable spot in the large armchair opposite me. He smiles the entire time he scarfs down the brownies. "HO! These brownies are the most amazing brownies I've ever had! You are such a great baker!" She smiles at him, and answers, "Thank you. Old family recipe, and I hope that old family never want it back!" She grins. Arthur laughs while crumbs of brownie fly out of his mouth. Owen looks like he is about to throttle him, so I interject, "Arthur, as happy as I am to see you, I am damn exhausted, and want to go to bed. Please, for the love of whatever! What is it you need to tell me?" Arthur takes another sip of tea and then places the cup and the empty plate back on the coffee table. He leans forward in his seat and looks only at me as he speaks, "I had a vision. It was not a past life, but a present life vision for *you*, Hannah. It happened at twelve-eleven on December twelfth." I note that he is stating the birthdate and time my daughter entered this world.

He raises his eyebrows as he continues, "I saw a glowing brightness, and then purple and blue Light, and we all know what that means!". Owen is about to say something, but Arthur continues quickly, "Yes! It means that the Alternate energy was welcoming a *new* energy into the earthly world. Hannah, surely you must have seen it when she was born. A special glow?" I think back to my vision of her birth, as I saw it from outside my body. The doctor gently pulling her out through the incision, and seeing her face, and the glow, the bright yellow glow. How had I not recognized that? I look at Arthur, but cannot speak. He smiles, "Hannah, this is amazing! How wonderful!" Owen, who can't take another moment of being in the dark, speaks up, "Can someone please tell me what is so wonderful? What are you talking about?" Arthur grins, and announces, "Claire is an Alternate! Just like her dear momma!"

I lie in bed, trying to find a comfortable position. There has not been any discussion since Arthur made his announcement. He had usurped the conversation, until I could not take another minute, so I simply proclaimed that, "any and all visitors are to disembark at this station, as the Hannah train is no longer in service." Then I stood up and walked up the stairs.

Lying on my back, my head reels. Does she know she's an Alternate? Do I tell her? Do I keep it a secret, and hope she never knows? If her Alternate is awake, should I reach and connect with it? My eyes hurt, and I feel the salty tears running down and pooling on my pillow. I hear the door open quietly, and Hannah One enters the room. She looks pensive, which is unlike her. "I'm sorry sweetie, I was just checking to make sure you are okay. Do you need anything? Would you like Owen here?" I move slightly to make room for her to come sit beside me on the bed. "Please come here, sit with me for a few minutes." She comes over and as she perches on the side of the bed, she takes both my hands in hers. She glances around the room. When she looks at me, there are tears in her eyes. "You know I always wanted a house full of children. I couldn't seem to make that happen, as I had two miscarriages after your father came along. It does my heart good to see new life in this old house. I just wish your dad could be here to see Claire." She bites her lip. "Oh, my dear, I'm sorry, I don't want to upset you. We have had such a time, and now *this* news! As amazing as it is, whatever will we do about it?" It is a rhetorical question, as she knows there really is nothing that can be done. *Just go with the flow...*

I hesitate before telling her the news that eats me from within, but take a small breath and begin. "You know I had trouble with the birth. Um, it wasn't *just* a C-section, it was a hysterectomy..." I cannot say another word, as each syllable sticks in my throat. I am reluctant to tell anyone else, but not her. I know she will understand my sorrow. Hannah One looks away, and I know she is crying. I squeeze her hands, and she squeezes mine in return. "Oh, my dear, I am so sorry. You must be feeling so conflicted right now." I carefully sit up, so I can hug her. In between my quiet sobs, I utter, "Most of my heart is filled with joy to have Claire, but a corner of it grieves for all the children I can never have." We cry quietly together, until we can cry no longer. She pulls a hanky out of her pocket and wipes her eyes, and then reaches into her other pocket and pulls out another hanky and hands it me, "It's my spare, and it's clean." She smiles gently. I take her hanky, and brush at my tears.

"I won't try to advise you on how to grieve for this loss. All I know is, Claire is such a blessing in our lives, we must cherish her, and love her, and if she knows she is an Alternate, then we can help her along with that, too." I tear up again, remembering the day when I was ten years old, we sat in this very house, on her bed, and I told her my truth. She was as compassionate and wonderful then, as she is now. "I am so lucky to have the best grandmother in the whole Universe."

Book Three

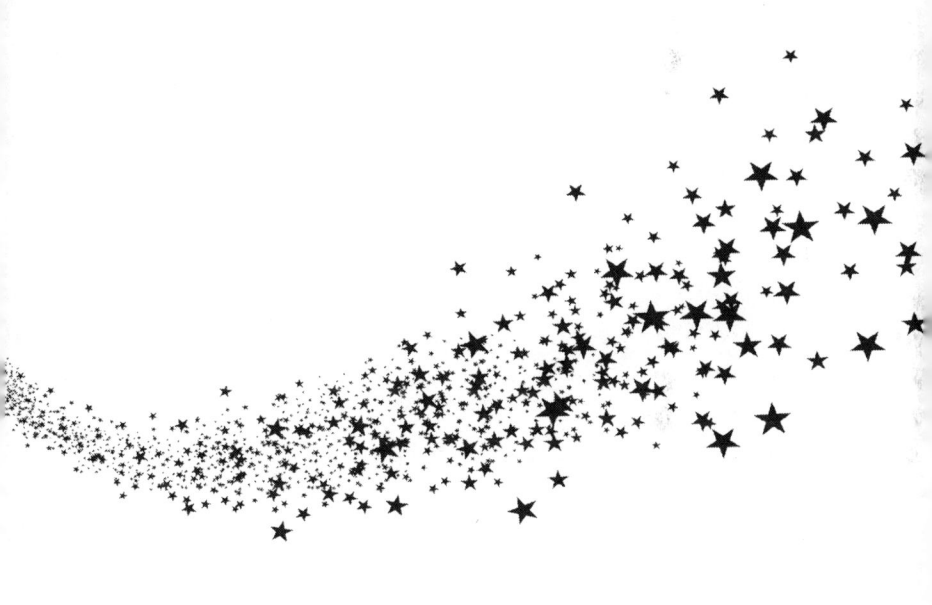

ONE

I enter the darkened bedroom. Glancing around, I notice the colourful animal posters on the walls, the small side table, strewn with cardboard picture books and stuffed teddy bears. The air smells of talcum powder. I spy the white crib in the corner, and slowly approach, my footfalls silent on the carpet. The baby lies on her back, her little hands in fists above her head, like she's doing a sleepy cheer. She is wearing a bright pink onesie, adorned with a smiling giraffe and elephant spread across the front. I reach out to touch her little tufts of curly brown hair, and stroke her face. Her head is warm, and her skin feels soft, and new. As she stirs, I slowly remove my hand. She looks at me with questioning eyes, green eyes that see the world differently than other one-year old babies. I lean over and whisper to her, "You are one today. You have so much more ahead of you. I need you to remember to always try to go with the flow. You will fight the current, as your Alternate will think she knows better. But, in the end, the ride is so much better when you let your boat float, and go with flow, Hannah." I turn, giving my infant self one last smile, then vanish.

    Claire's first birthday arrives along with the first snow. A small family party had been planned to celebrate the milestone, but that is in jeopardy, as the weather has plans of its own. My mother, who lives about five minutes away, suggested she could walk over to the house, but I quickly dissuaded her. She's been having issues with her knees lately, most likely the onset of arthritis, and I didn't think trudging through the snow would help at all. Jamie and Neville are also stuck at home with Aidan, their two-and-a-half-year-old son. They finally moved out of the apartment and into a condo, which they are renting. It has a nice little backyard with a small patch of grass, and a large gnarly Oak tree. Jamie is happy, although she has little interest in having any more children, at this point. Her teaching career is so rewarding and challenging, that, between her class and Aidan, she cannot see stretching herself any thinner. Neville was disappointed, as he comes from a large family. A woman has such a hard time with this societal pressure to *Be All*; wife, mother, carry a career on her shoulders, and pursue interests of her own. I can't blame her for wanting to keep the load bearable. Yet a small part of me actually resents the fact that she has a choice. I have no choice, and although my love for Claire fills every molecule of my being, there is a dim shadow of sadness that lingers, where there might have been more children.

Hannah One sits in the sunroom, eating a pear I had cut up for her, as she watches Claire and I play in the newly fallen snow. With only her face exposed to the elements, Claire giggles each time a snowflake lands on her nose. Her bright blue eyes blink, like little camera shutters, capturing the moment in her memory. She is a very happy baby, who rarely cries, appearing to have such a sunny outlook on the world. There is a sense of energy that radiates out of her, and one who is nearby always benefits from it. Each time I hold her, my heart feels full, and my head less troubled. When Owen holds her, he says he feels very relaxed, and not as stressed out. Hannah One mentioned that when she sits with her, she feels like her old body is relieved of age, and she can dance a jig! I laughed, and said that I would pay money to see that! I understand that we are not the most objective when it comes to our sweet girl, but others have mentioned her calming effect as well. I know that Claire must have a Talent, and begin to wonder if it has something to do with healing.

Arthur is a regular visitor now, ever since his announcement that day when we brought Claire home from the hospital. He is watching over her, to see if she becomes aware of her Alternate energy. He gently explored her mind, and found that she is not *awake*. The unusual energy lies dormant, but Arthur senses its willingness to be connected to her human self. We just want Claire be a toddler before exploring what lies waiting inside. I remember, all too clearly, as does Arthur, the frustration of being an *awake* Alternate in the body of an infant. It's not fun, only frustrating. We decided to let her have time to develop, and simply enjoy the pleasure of being a baby.

I look at Claire, and can't believe her first birthday is already upon us. It seems like only yesterday she was a newborn, and we both struggled to figure out our roles as mother and daughter. Now, as she crawls over and places a snowy mittened hand in mine, we seem to fit together, like two parts of a whole. Our connection is intense, and, at times, leaves Owen feeling a bit distant from the bond. He works on creating his own relationship with her that is strong and unbreakable, yet ever since Arthur announced that his daughter is an Alternate, he struggles to comprehend that her *status* will not compromise their relationship in any way.

Owen decided to take another trip to Africa, and is due to leave in about three weeks. He feels like he has left a lot of work uncompleted, and wants to return to see two particular projects through to fruition. As I sit on the ground playing snow angels with Claire, my thoughts drift back to that day when Owen finally laid his truth out for me to see. It was a difficult conversation, but in the long run, it was a necessity for the survival of our marriage. I recall the pained expression on Owen's face when Arthur announced that Claire is an Alternate. He appeared downcast, as if everyone had been given a present, except him. I was in such a state of shock, I walked out of the room and decided to talk to him about it in a day or so, hoping he would have a better perspective on the situation by then.

When I finally asked Owen for his opinion on how to handle Claire's *new found state of being*, he shrugged, and sullenly answered that *he wouldn't have a clue, and besides, why ask him, when Arthur would be the one to consult.* I fumed at his immature remark. "Well, Owen, *you* are Claire's father, not Arthur. I should think you'd want to be part of the decision process." He responded angrily, "Well, if I *were* part of the decision, then I'd decide that she should NOT have an Alternate in her! She's just a baby! Can't they" and he waved his hands around, indicating some invisible beings that he assumed were floating around him, "just leave her alone? I don't understand, *why her?*" His expression was dejected, and I was tired of seeing it.

"Owen, you have to stop feeling like you are being left out, just because you don't carry an Alternate. It just doesn't work that way! It has nothing to do with who you *are*." Owen didn't look at me, but stared out the window. I continued, hoping I could convince him to change his viewpoint. "Once an Alternate decides to become human, they are drawn to the energy that creates the form. Like-energy attracts like-energy. It's sort of random, but not totally arbitrary. Think of it like, uh, like a big tray of apples. Your eye goes over the display, and rests upon one you are drawn to. It may be that it's really shiny, or you like the colour of its skin, or it has some other attribute that pulls you to pick up *that* particular apple. It's not that the other apples aren't good, they just don't have the same vibration of energy that the Alternate has, and therefore, there's no attraction. It's not that you are a bad apple, it's merely that the timing wasn't right." I wasn't sure my analogy was apt, as I wasn't certain how *I* would feel about being compared to an apple, but it was the only thing I could think of off the top of my head. "Owen," I tried to take his hand, but he stood up and crossed the room, "Owen, please try to understand. There are millions upon millions of humans who never have an Alternate inhabitance. And those that do, for the most part, never know it. It doesn't lessen the person you are, standing here today, nor does it lessen my love for you. Honestly, I wish I weren't *awake*, it would make things so much easier." He turned, and for the first time, I saw slight relief in his eyes. "Are you just saying that to placate me? I don't need to be coddled. I know I'm acting like a spoiled kid, but, it's just so difficult to understand…" he trailed off.

He came back to sit beside me on the couch. As he spoke, he kept his body turned away from me, not yet ready to let go of his pent-up frustration. "I've always had a poor image of myself. I know it has to do with the abuse from my father. Always hearing you're not good enough tends to make you believe it's true." He coughed, attempting to hide the crack in his voice. He continued, "I always thought that whatever life gave me, I should consider myself lucky, as I don't deserve much." I was about to interject, but he held his hand up to stop me, "That was *before* I met you, and, well, before I started therapy. I just couldn't see any redeeming quality about myself. I just took up space. Then I started reading about these groups that are trying to make a difference, saving the world, that sort of thing. I figured, hell, why not join in, at least I could try to make a difference, even though I had my doubts." He looked down at his hands, and sighed. "I had a goal to make something of myself, and prove my father wrong. It fueled me, for a while, but then I started to lose momentum, as the fight seemed endless. I felt like I'd let myself down, failed to make any difference, so maybe I wasn't going to earn the *quality of self* I needed so badly. Then I met you." He turned, briefly smiling at me, as he took my hand. I resisted the urge to speak up. I felt that this was something he needed to purge himself of, and any comment I make would only be an interruption. He looked down at my hand, the beautiful topaz ring faintly glimmering on my finger.

"I thought I had finally found that quality I was looking for; I found it with you. Or, well, to be honest, so I thought. I believed I had a new purpose, or some sort of re-imagined goal, of a happy life with you. I was so wrapped up in *us*, nothing else seemed to matter. Then, when you and Arthur revealed yourselves," a frown crossed his face, "it felt like, once again I seemed to be lacking in the *worthy* department. It's just *plain old me*, hitching my wagon to a star, literally." He tried to smile. "I began to realize that I had assumed *you* could provide me with a sense of worthiness. It's not fair to place the onus of propping up my self-esteem at your feet, but that was the subconscious choice I had made. When I heard you talk about being an Alternate, I felt like a battery-operated flashlight next to the sun. I wanted to shine like the sun, too. But that meant I still needed to find that elusive *thing*, my purpose, to make me believe that I have the quality of self, the worthiness that I had been searching for, all those years before I met you."

He let go of my hand, and stood up, stretching, releasing the tension in his body that must have been choking up his insides for a long time. He kept his back to me as he continued; "Africa is my quality. I *can* make a difference there, and it fills me with pride, no, joy! Joy to see the faces of the people I help, as we bring clean water systems to them; and yes, pride too, in seeing the children yearning to learn, *from me,* about how to be good custodians of the Earth." He turned, and I could see that the smile in his words was not evident on his face, "Han, as much as I love you and Claire, I know that part of me isn't done with Africa. I still need to see it through; to feel that sense of accomplishment, and feel proud of my contribution to making their lives a little better. I hope you can understand this." He took a few steps towards the kitchen door and turned, "But, as far as Claire's *situation* goes, I want her happy, I want her safe, and I want her loved. Whatever *you* want to do, as long as she is those three things, I don't care about the rest." He turned and walked out of the room.

A whimper from Claire, indicating she is getting tired or cold, brings me back from my recollection. I stand up, and reach down to pick up the little bundle of snowsuit that sits on the snowy ground, looking up at me expectantly. "Okay, Claire, let's go inside and see what Hannah One is up to!" She giggles as I pick her up, and we head back into the warm house.

Spring is my favourite time of year. The freshness of each day, and the greening up of the world makes life seem more optimistic. Even when the weather remains cold, or even snows, you know it's not the start of a bleak time, but the last whimpers of winter, gasping its final icy breath before Nature sends it on its way, and ushers in the New.

Claire, now almost a year and a half, is full of energy, inquisitiveness, and glee. She brightens each room she is in. She fills my heart with such joy, that, even when I get frustrated with her for not going to sleep when I want her to, or turning her nose up at some new type food I offer, there is this understanding between us that, this is how it is supposed to go. Owen adores his daughter, and once he let go of his uncertainty about her *situation*, he has adapted to the role of *Dad* like a second skin. He spends every moment he can with her. I think a small part of him still carries guilt over leaving me when I was very pregnant, and then again when Claire was about thirteen months old. At the time, I believe he was torn between his aspiration of finding self-worth, and his responsibility to be a good father and husband. When he departed for Africa for the second time, I understood why. I see his time in Africa as part of his journey that will hopefully help reframe his view of himself. My wish is that Owen will be able to let go of the image of himself as insignificant; a self-portrait he has carried for so many years that still holds influence over who he is now. Owen had no one in his corner as a young man; now he has a whole raft of people who love and support him, and I think he finally *believes* that. My heart aches when I envision that teenager on the cold road, alone and desolate in so many ways.

Owen returned from his second trip to Africa in mid-April, with a better outlook on his life. He was given the chance to complete two projects that meant a lot to him. The experience gave him a better perspective of his life. It helped him realize how important his family is to him, and how lucky he is to have so many other blessings, like a great job, a home, clean water, and healthcare. He was finally able to see that he can make a difference to his self-worth simply by being kinder to himself, trusting in his ability to be a good father and husband, and a productive member of his community. He doesn't have to change the world to find meaning in his life; he simply needs to recognize that the change must come from within. I was so happy to hear that he came to this conclusion, and relieved to see the brighter light in his eyes.

As I stand outside the front door, Owen sees me watching him with Claire, as he kneels over, planting new annuals in the front garden. I smile, and he grins as he points to Claire, sitting beside him, wearing blue overalls and a short-sleeved yellow tee-shirt. She is holding a miniature trowel in her tiny hand. She looks up at me, and I see a large brown smudge of dirt running down her face, from the bridge of her nose to the bottom of her chin. She raises the trowel up to her mouth and licks it. She spits out the dirt and giggles. I place my hands on my hips, ready to chastise Owen for not watching her more carefully. He is laughing, and Claire is giggling, so I find I cannot ruin the moment by being cross. His gleeful reaction to his daughter's playful mischief makes me smile. I step off the front porch and come over to the pair, kneeling down to wipe her face with the sleeve of my sweater. She squirms as I attempt to clean her off, almost as if she enjoys having dirt caked all over her face. I stop attempting to clean her up, but with my hand still on her chin, I say firmly, "So, you'll eat dirt, but you won't eat squash! You're such a connoisseur!" I laugh, and she giggles at seeing her mother's cheerful expression. Owen stands up, wiping his hands on his jeans, and pulls me up to stand beside him. He hugs me. Then he kisses me. With the tension our relationship has been experiencing lately, this simple act seems to be the salve we both need. I kiss him back, slowly, lovingly. No matter how challenging our life together has become,

I still love him with every fibre of my being. Claire whines, and reaches her little hands up to us. Owen bends down, still keeping one arm around me, and scoops her up, making us a triangular love sandwich. We put our heads together and smile, as Claire's healing energy washes over us, blanketing our huddle in loving, healing light.

Two

I survey the ground from high above the tree line. Soaring along on a current of air, my sleek black wings slice through the ether with ease, like a hot knife through butter. My Raven eyes spy each blade of slender emerald-green grass, sparkling with morning dew; every flower, with their various colourful petals and leaves, turning their faces to catch the sun as it slowly slides across the sky; I see tiny insects crawling along the surface of the planet, and burrowing into the rich, nourishing earth. My Raven ears perceive the sound of another Raven, unhappily cawing somewhere within the trees, not too far in the distance. I turn my wings and my body adjusts to change my direction. My peripheral vision takes in the wide expanse of my enormous wings, black iridescent feathers shimmering in the sun like black gold. I glide towards the sound in the woods. Another despondent CAW sounds, allowing me to zero in on the location of the Raven. Soon I descend, until I come to rest on a dead, yet substantial, Elm branch that juts up into the sky, like a bony finger of Death. Looking towards a twisted old Hawthorn tree, I glimpse the black shape of a bird, gripping a branch, not too far below me. The Raven is small, and hunched up, reminding me of a cold child huddling, with its arms wrapped around its legs. I swoop down to land on a nearby branch, and look at the young Raven. I caw in dismay as the bird turns her head to look at me. I see her bright blue eyes, full of fear and uncertainty. "Mommy, what is happening to me?"

I blink, as a small hand takes hold of mine. I stand staring into the blank sky, where moments before I had observed a Raven passing by us. I glance down to see Claire tugging at my hand. "Mommy, come on. You are too slow!" She pulls me along a few feet, then releases my hand to run ahead to where Owen stands, about twenty feet away. His face carries a frown, looking at me with concern, but drops the expression quickly, as Claire runs over to him. "Daddy, tell Mommy to hurry up! I want to look for dragonflies at the pond!" Her voice is full of enthusiasm, her young body eager to run, and her mind hungry to discover her world. I scan the sky one last time, and finding it empty, quickly walk along the trail to catch up to the two intrepid explorers.

Claire, having passed the age of five, is full of questions, curious about everything around her - the perfect age, between being too young to comprehend some things, but not old enough to know the world's troubles. I watch, as she and Owen balance their bodies on some large flat rocks that sit firmly by the pond's edge, wedged between the dry shoreline and the stream. They lean over carefully as they search the water for nymphs. Owen is telling her all about damselflies and dragonflies beginning their lives in one form, living in the water as nymphs, only to emerge as another form, with beautiful wings to fly their lives away. That reminds me of Claire and the possibility of how her life will go; beginning as a human, only knowing the world through one set of eyes, but to eventually emerge as an Alternate, with a whole new perspective. The vision of the two Ravens seems to point to the inevitability of her *waking up*. I can only hope it isn't too soon.

After we tuck Claire in bed with her favourite teddy bear, Owen and I sit down in the living room to talk about what happened in the woods earlier in the day. "You were frozen there, just standing like a statue. Claire was calling you, but you had your eyes closed. I knew something was going on." Owen's voice rings with concern. It's becoming more often that I have visions while awake, but not usually while walking with my family. I tell him what I saw, and he frowns. "I don't know, I don't like this scenario. Can't *you* stop it from happening?" The accusatory tone in his voice indicates the blame for this whole predicament falls at my feet. I shake my head and respond, "*I* have no control over this Owen! It just doesn't work that way." He stands up and begins sorting papers on the table. He is teaching Journalism at the local community college, and since it's mid-terms, papers are a regular sight covering the table. "Well, I guess you should contact Arthur and figure something out. You two always seem to know what's best for our daughter," he mumbles distractedly. I know he means I should text or call Arthur, but his bad-tempered tone jabs me, making me reply sarcastically, "I will send him a message right now... hello, Arthur? Come in, Arthur?" as I mimic a mind reader, placing fingers on both sides of my temple. Owen is not amused, ignores me, and continues shuffling papers. I go into the kitchen to text Arthur, leaving Owen to stew in his mid-terms.

Arthur's response comes through quickly. He advises a *wait and see* approach. He is not panicking, and he says neither should I. I am tempted to ask him if he might look into Claire's future, to get a better idea of if or *when* she may awaken, but remembering his stern warning that I should never ask him to do that, I think better of it. I decide to try to heed his advice and *let it go*, but my nervous stomach tells me I might be wrong.

It's two weeks into the school year, and Claire's class has an excursion planned. They are going to our favourite conservation area, where we always walk. She is full of excitement at the prospect of showing her new friends her most cherished place in the world. She hasn't stopped talking about all the things she has learned from her father, that she wants to share with her classmates.

Friday morning, with the sun shining, and the promise of a beautiful day to be in the woods, Owen drops Claire off at school on his way to the college. She waves energetically as he turns and walks back down the sidewalk to his car. She literally bounces into her classroom, full of anticipation.

My thoughts drift to her about four hours later while I'm rearranging shelves at the bookstore with Cindy. I feel my phone vibrate in my pocket. It's the school calling. They request I come immediately to pick up Claire, and take her home. Panic lacing my voice, I ask if she has been injured. They will only say that she is upset about an incident and cannot be consoled, so they feel it best that she goes home. I drop everything and race to the school to retrieve my daughter.

I arrive at the Principal's Office to find Claire sitting in a chair in the corner of the room. Her face is swollen from crying; red puffy eyes and flushed cheeks the likes I have never seen on her. Her tee shirt is rumpled and her pants have mud stains all over the thighs. What could have happened to make her so miserable? The principal is standing behind the counter, but upon my entrance, comes around to stand next to Claire. When Claire sees me, she slides off the chair and rushes over, clinging to my legs. "Mommy!" A huge wail erupts from the little body. I look at the man with a questioning expression. He shifts slightly on his feet, and then proceeds to tell me what happened. "The class was doing a lesson on aquatic life in the pond, and several children had small butterfly nets to catch frogs, and other *things*," he shivers, as if even the mention of bugs makes his skin crawl. "Claire did not like the children catching *things*, and began to try to stop them from using their nets. It seems that one child found a large frog and was showing it to the other children, when Claire grabbed a net and cast it over his head. It made the boy fall and he scraped his leg."

He looks down at Claire, and with a low snipped voice, says, "That's not how we solve our problems is it, Claire? Violence never solves anything." He straightens up and looks at me, as Claire's grip on my legs tightens. I pause for a moment, trying to understand the situation more clearly. "That doesn't sound like Claire. Are you sure you have the whole story? Is it possible the boy was harming the frog, or scaring the other children with it, and Claire stepped in to stop him?" This seems the likeliest scenario, as Claire would never hurt anyone intentionally. "Where was the teacher when this was going on? Why were the children allowed to *catch* the wildlife in the first place? What does that teach them? It harms, or even kills the poor creatures, and serves no learning experience, other than illustrating that humans are big, and can take whatever living thing they like, whenever they like? Where is the stewardship lesson? Where is the attention to responsible excursions into the woods, where you harm nothing and take only photos?" I realize that, as my diatribe escalates, I am drawing attention from other staff who are standing nearby. Since I do not care who hears me, I continue. "This barbaric practice should not even be in the curriculum! There are plenty of other options for observing aquatic life and other living things in the woods." I stop talking, noticing that the principal has a deep frown on his face. He ignores my outburst, evenly replying, "Nevertheless, Claire has injured a classmate. Zero tolerance towards bullying, that is our policy. Claire will need to apologize to the boy. Then we can get on with having a very successful school year, right Claire?" With her arms still wrapped around my legs, she merely turns her head to the man, and defiantly says, "Only if *he* apologizes to Ol' Toad." I had to bite my lip to keep from laughing. That's my girl! Standing her ground, and not giving up the fight she so strongly believes in. I decide to echo her sentiment. "Yes, Mr. Davies, that is a good idea. Once the boy apologizes to the toad, Claire will come back to school, and make amends. Until then, she will be with me." And with that, I reach down and take my daughter's hand and leave the office.

As we reach the car, I decide that I need to address this issue with Claire right away, rather than wait until we get home. As she climbs into her car seat and begins working the clips to fasten her seatbelt, I come around to the other side of the car, and slide into the back seat beside her. "Aren't we going home, Mommy?" Claire's eyes are still red, and she sniffs again. Unlike Hannah One, I have no hanky up my sleeve to give her. "Claire, I just want to have a chat about today, before we head home." Her expression clouds over, but I persevere. "Can you tell me what happened? Why did you hit the boy with the net? That isn't like you, I just want to know your side of it, as I don't think your teacher got the whole story right." As I say this, indicating that I am on her side no matter what she tells me, her face softens.

"Well, um… I guess it started when Mrs. Callaghan began handing out the nets. I asked her why we were using nets, and she just told me that we were going to have some fun. So, I thought I'd see if this was fun that you and me and Daddy could do too. But then…" her voice starts to rise, "then, the kids started to wave them around, trying to get my dragonflies, and my butterflies, and, and…" she stops to take a breath. I don't interrupt, but let her continue at her own pace; "then Justin started putting the net in the water, by the edge, you know, right where we saw the tadpoles that day…" she frowns. "Justin caught our lovely big Ol' Toad," she begins to cry. Ol' Toad is a beautiful large toad we sometimes see sitting by the water's edge, large unblinking eyes watching, as we enjoy the scenery around his pond home. It breaks my heart to see her so upset and I find myself choking up. "Oh Claire, that must have been horrible, poor Ol' Toad!" I take her hand in an attempt to soothe her. She lifts her other hand to wipe her eyes. "Mommy, you and Daddy told me how important it is to respect nature, and when we go to the woods we're going to Nature's house, and we shouldn't wreck anything, or harm any animal. Well, it was so bad. The kids were walking on all the flowers and pulling them up, and throwing stones in the pond, and then Justin…" she cries again. I have to try to get her past this point, so she can get it off her chest. "Did Justin hurt Ol' Toad?" She nods. "He grabbed him out of his net and squeezed him. Then he started chasing other kids with poor Ol' Toad in his hands. Oh Mommy, it was bad, I feel so bad…" she bursts into a loud sob. I sit, holding her hand, and try to think of something to say to calm her down, and take this immense hurt away from her heart. It pains me to think her sensitive nature has been violated by this ignorant and harmful act. What can I do to help her? Then I have an idea.

"What about you and me taking a walk in the woods, right now? We can see if Ol' Toad is there, and check to make sure he's alright? We will go now, just to make sure everything's okay? What do you think?" Claire nods, unable to speak. She starts to wipe her snot-covered face with her sleeve, when I spy a small towel on the seat that I hand to her, "It's not Hannah One's hanky, but it's better than your sleeve!" She manages a weak smile, as I get out of the back seat and get into the driver's seat to start the car.

The autumn has begun to touch the trees, mostly affecting the Sugar Maples, turning some of the leaves into flames of red and yellow. Autumn has a somewhat melancholy air about it, as the end of the season of growth is at hand. We walk quietly along the trail; Claire almost meditative in her gait. Normally, she would be looking all around her, soaking in the energy of the trees and the animals. Now she seems almost forlorn, like she has hurt her best friend's feelings. I take her hand and we stop. "Sweetie, I want you to know that you did everything right. Well, maybe not *netting* that boy, but everything else. You tried to protect our woods here, and I am very proud that you stood up for it! It isn't your fault that your teacher didn't see what was going on. Sometimes it's hard to watch so many children at once." I don't want to find fault with the teacher, but I still find it impossible to comprehend the methodology used for teaching this "nature lesson". The curriculum is certainly behind the times when it comes to teaching children about ecology and respect for the environment.

Claire looks up at me, her father's eyes staring at me, but full of pain and hurt. "I don't know why people are so mean. Why can't they be nice, like us?" It is a question I know no answer to. I shake my head. "Claire, I'm sorry. I really don't know why. I think that part of it is that they haven't been taught to respect the environment. Years ago, humans really didn't think it was bad to do bad things to the water, or the air, or our woods. Now, it's getting a bit better, with new rules, and more people learning how doing bad things makes it bad for *all* of us. But really, I don't understand how humans can be so cruel to nature." I wish I had some magic answer to alleviate her worry, but I cannot lie to her.

We reach the pond, and I can see where the children have trampled some Asters, and several fall Daisies have been pulled up and tossed. The grasses and brush near the pond edge are flattened, as if several pairs of feet stamped it all down. It is a mess, but not irreparable. "Sweetie, look at the grass by the edge of the pond. It's dried and ready to die, so, thankfully the damage wasn't done to growing grass. It's still such a mess. I agree with you, we shouldn't be wrecking Nature's house." Claire carefully picks her way through the brush to stand on her favourite rock and look into the pond. I keep my fingers crossed that Ol' Toad is nearby. I stretch out with my mind, feeling for the life energy of the large amphibian. I feel a few small frogs and fish, deep in the water, and turtles that are burrowing into the mud at the bottom of the pond. Then I feel *him*. He is in the water, on the far side, away from where any human can reach him.

Ol' Toad, there you are. Claire and I are here to make sure you are alright.

A single *burr-up* sound from his enormous gut lets Claire know he is nearby. She turns and smiles, her face alight with glee. "Mommy! Did you hear that! Ol' Toad just called out to me! Hello Ol' Toad! I hope you're okay! I'm sorry about Justin, he is so stupid and mean! I hope you're okay!" The plea in her voice makes my throat constrict. I touch the toad's mind one last time,

I am sorry humans are so cruel, and I hope you are not injured. I hear a distant echo in my head, an ancient sounding voice resonating deep within. *Ol' Toad will do what I do, until it's my time not to do. I know the little one heals all, and I feel her healing me now, and I thank her for her care.*

I stand near Claire and feel her healing energy as well. It radiates out of her like the sun. I close my eyes, turning the palms of my hands outward as I slowly exhale. I too, feel healing energy flow through me from the Universe to the damaged area around us. Our combined loving energy coats the pond, the trees, and the animals, in a flood of healing Light. I hear a Chickadee chime, the crackle of dried grass as it gasps out its final sleepy breath, the water ripple over stones as it moves gently along, and a squirrel chitter in a nearby Poplar tree. Claire has no idea that she is emitting this energy, and I don't know how I am channeling it myself, never having done this before, but there is a collective *sigh* throughout the woods as the Light touches every leaf, and every flower. Claire stands entranced with her eyes closed, her face aglow, no longer swollen or red.

Finally, after one long inhale and exhale, I lower my hands. Claire opens her eyes, and looks out across the pond. "You know what, Mommy? I feel a lot better now." She reaches up and takes my hand. I look at her beautiful face and reply, "Me too. Now, how about we go to the bookstore, and see Janice?"

Three

The dilemma about Claire's future at her school has been resolved with a bit of fortuitous timing. As Claire accompanied me to the bookstore today, she got to see Cindy, who, as luck would have it, works part-time as a teacher's assistant at an "alternative" school. (I smile at the reference.) Elizabeth Street Public School has a program, aptly named *The Voyager Class*, wherein the curriculum is structured in a more open-concept format. The children are integrated into a variety of learning modules, depending on their abilities. For instance, the class Cindy works with consists of children from the traditional grade one-to-three range. The students are encouraged to work at whatever level best suits their confidence and aptitude. Claire would be working at a higher level, and thrive in an environment that is more progressive and socially conscientious.

I am intrigued and I pepper Cindy with questions. I feel that this might be a much better fit for Claire. As it is only the early part of September, the class is still settling in, and some students, at this point, decide that they prefer the main-stream structure of a traditional classroom. So that means there is space for Claire to join the class.

A few days later, Claire settles into her new class like Cinderella in her glass slippers. She loves the teacher, and the students are lively, creative and eager to learn. There are times when the older kids help the younger ones with certain tasks, or learning modules, and then times they all learn about a subject together. The process is fascinating to observe, as the younger children seem to thrive with challenge and the older students advance with more self-confidence as they learn and share. It is a communal effort to support and nurture a compassionate learning environment. Claire simply glows, as she thrives in her new class.

As November bowls over October, Owen announces that, for my birthday, he is taking me away for a night at our favourite old Inn. This particular Inn holds a lot of sentimental value to us both. I object to this extravagant event, using Claire as an excuse to tone the celebration down to a dinner out, but Owen has already set all the pieces in motion. Claire is going to stay with Jamie and Neville, and my mother is going to have dinner with Hannah One and stay for the evening. My lovely old grandmother is becoming frailer now, and needs a bit of help with things like meal preparation. I would not enjoy my night away if I worried about Hannah One the whole time, so I appreciate my mother's help. Jamie is happy to have Claire stay with her. Aidan likes Claire; she seems to have a good influence on him. Jamie said he always behaves so much better when Claire is around. At seven and a half years old, Aidan is much like his father; a free spirit, with little regard for authority or social standards. It's challenging for Jamie, but with her teacher's hat on, she is usually able to help steer his attitude into something more agreeable to the situation.

I pack a small overnight bag, secretly stowing away a piece of new lingerie that I bought as a surprise for my thoughtful husband. We drop Claire off, and I watch as she and Jamie cheerily wave goodbye from the porch, as we pull away from the curb.

The Inn has not changed in the years since we last visited. We check in, go to our room to leave our bags, and then go down to the restaurant for dinner. Owen made a reservation for one particular table; the same one we had been seated at years ago. It's nestled in the far corner in a small alcove. I take in the ambiance of the place, feeling the tension of late ebbing out of my system. It is hectic at the bookstore, as the Christmas shopping season is underway; Claire's class is busy and needs more parental volunteers, so I have stepped up more often, and Hannah One has been needing more care of late. I feel stretched thin.

The candles on our intimate table flicker and sway with the air movement, almost hypnotic in their dance. I hear live music quietly playing somewhere off in another room. The sweet jazz sound of the piano, stand-up bass and drums, coalesces with the warm air and candlelight dance, to create the perfect storm for my senses to open and relax. It's actually hard for me to keep from mentally fading out. I find myself being pulled off to dream-walk, as an image of Claire flashes across my mind. Suddenly I find myself trying to stand up, to break out of the trance. Owen, with a startled expression, drops his napkin on the table and stands up as well, grasping my forearm, to prevent me from falling. I lean slightly forward and take a small breath, and, looking over at him, I try to smile. "Sorry, just felt a bit, well, weird, you know." He does not smile back, but comes over to pull out my chair and help me sit down again. "Are you okay? Should we leave?" The concern in his voice touches me. "No, no, I'm fine. Just a bit *unplugged* for a second there. It's all good now." Owen relaxes minutely as he comes around to take his seat again, keeping his eyes on my face, unsure if he can believe me. "Was it, you know, ah, um, a vision or something?", he whispers. I can't be certain it wasn't a message trying to come through, but fearing it might ruin this special evening, I merely smile and suggest that we give Jamie a quick text to check in with her. Owen pulls his phone out of his pocket and sends a text, with a quick reply from Jamie, stating, *'all's well stop bugging us and go have sex already!'* I laugh, knowing Jamie's crude sense of humour. Owen frowns as he places the phone back in his pocket. "Did you see Claire in a vision? Is that why you wanted me to text?" He is determined to get an answer from me, but I persist in keeping it light, by answering, "Not at all, I think I just haven't eaten much today, so I'm probably light-headed, that's all." Owen nods, his tension easing somewhat by my explanation. He picks up the menu, and leans over to whisper, "Well, okay, lets order some decadent appetizers to get us started. I can't have you passing out on me before the night has even begun!"

I feel Owen's hands on my shoulders as I stand by the edge of the bed opening my bag. I quickly pull my new outfit out of the bag, and then wiggle out of his grip to change in the bathroom, so I can make "an entrance". I'm really not one to wear silly frilly things, but after all this time together, and after all the drama over the past few years, I feel like I want to lighten things up, and bring a fresh surprise to our intimate life. For months after Claire was born, Owen had treated me like a porcelain doll, frightened I would break if mis-handled. I knew my body had been through a trauma, but once the doctor gave me the all-clear, I assumed we would pick up where we left off. Owen seemed to think he would hurt or damage me if we made love. I loved him for being so considerate, but after a few months I had to convince him it was safe, and that I really wanted to be intimate again. He felt like he was to blame for the difficult birth, saying that maybe if he'd been here, it would not have gone that way. I told him that under no circumstances would his presence have made a difference to my uterus rupturing; it was going to happen regardless. He carried a lot of guilt right after the birth, but it was months before we addressed it. I was too focused on Claire to notice. Tonight, I want to open a new door, let go of past hurts and frustrations. Now, turning thirty-six, I want to break with routine, and find new avenues to explore in our relationship. Hence, the lingerie.

I emerge from the bathroom, seeing Owen propped up on the left side of the bed, his long legs stretched out in front of him. He is naked, which, for some reason, causes me to laugh. How is it men don't *need* to wear anything special as a turn-on for their partner; they just let it all hang out? Owen grins as I pose by the door, a little uncertain of myself. It's out of character for me to do something like this, but that is what the whole night is for, breaking out of character. I saunter over to the bed and stand beside him. His hand comes up and strokes my thigh, running up to the black lace trimming my hip. It is a wonderful sensation to feel the fabric and his touch. I lean over and kiss him, making him shift slightly, until I straddle on top of him. Kissing him is like attaching myself to the Light; there is an energy coalescing between us, creating a power surge that drives the desire. My hands run along his chest as I kiss him, and his hands find my breasts and caress them. The feeling of passion mixed with power is intoxicating as I straddle him. It feels like we have been apart for years, only now finding our way back to the yearning we felt when we first found each other. Soon enough, the teddy is tossed over to the floor and our bare skin melds into one sweaty, fiery layer of desire. He rolls on top and enters me as I arch my back. The world is another place, far away, all the cares and worries of life fade into nothing. There is only the Now, and the Here.

As I feel my body climb to the point where it will explode in a sensational orgasm, I suddenly blank out. I see nothing, hear nothing, and feel nothing. I sense an energy stream close by, but cannot see it. I panic, wanting desperately to return to Owen, and immerse myself in him, but I can't find my way. Then, a bright light beams into my eyes, and as I blink, I can just make out a small figure standing in front of me. It is Claire. I scream her name as I try to reach for her, but she is falling away into the abyss of dark behind her. She stretches out her hand to grasp mine, but we are already too far apart. I keep screaming out her name, hoping she will hear me, and know I am going to save her. The blackness envelops me as Claire's little form soaks into the ether. *Why am I Here? Why?* Her gentle voice rings in my ears, to the exclusion of all else.

I open my eyes to find Owen embracing me, trying to get me to stop screaming. My naked body feels cold and exposed, and I try to reach for the bedsheet. Owen grabs the edge of the blanket and pulls it up to cover me. He says not a word, his expression says a thousand. I have been screaming our daughter's name, and he knows that means trouble.

Within two minutes my phone rings. It's Jamie's number on the screen. I answer, already knowing that we have to go to Claire immediately. Jamie sounds terribly apologetic, saying that Claire had a nightmare, and seems inconsolable. She says that Claire has been screaming, but now she is simply crying and repeating, *why am I here?* I know Jamie would take that statement literally, thinking that Claire is disoriented waking up at *her* house, but the reality is, it means something else. She is *awake*.

As we pack up our few pieces of clothing to get ready to leave, there is a knock at the door. Management is *just checking*, as there had been a complaint about a woman screaming. Owen apologizes and states that I had had a nightmare. I come to the door to reassure the man I am not being murdered, or whatever else might have crossed his mind. Seeing me standing in front of him, he seems satisfied, but as a parting remark he says, "Please try to refrain from any more *nightmares*, it's disturbing the other guests." Owen replies, "that won't be an issue, we are checking out. Please have the bill ready for us in five minutes." The man's eyebrows rise, but he says nothing. He merely turns and disappears down the hall.

On the drive to Jamie's house, I text Arthur. It's no surprise he responds right away, as he would surely have felt the shift in energy. His suggestion is to take Claire home and then assess the situation. If needed, he would come over, but he has faith that I can help Claire through this transition.

There is something about her words that make me feel uncomfortable. *Why am I here?* If an Alternate wakes up, surely they would be aware of the *why*. They might, at first, be disoriented by their containment within a human structure, but I assume they would adjust fairly quickly to the new form they inhabit, as I did when I was born. Unless this is something completely different.

We pull up in front of Jamie's condo and see the front porch light shining. By this time, it's after midnight. Owen gets out and runs up to the door. Jamie meets him as he mounts the steps two at a time. Claire is bundled in Neville's strong arms, still in her nightgown, with her winter coat wrapped around her, her little legs dangling, with her winter boots bumping each other as she is carried. Owen opens his arms and cradles his daughter as he descends the steps carefully. I jump out to open the back door and help him get her secured in her seat. Jamie waves from the porch and mouths the word, *sorry*, to which I merely nod my head and mime that I will text her. To her, and Neville, this is merely a child who is homesick. I know the truth, and the panic I feel inside is mine to carry, alone. Maybe not completely alone, as I know Owen is rattled, but he keeps it hidden as best he can.

Still half asleep, Claire doesn't say anything, but I can see her face is swollen from crying. She buries her head in her coat, like a cocoon. I take Arthur's advice and don't try to engage her in conversation while we're in the car. I wait, frantically formulating what I will say, as we drive the last fifteen minutes home. I take a big gulp of air as the house comes into view. Owen pulls into the driveway, turns off the car and jumps out of the driver seat in a matter of seconds. He opens the back door and gently unfastens Claire's seatbelt. She has fallen asleep. My heart aches to see her limp little body fold itself into his arms as he lifts her out of the car. I race ahead to open the front door and turn on the hall light. I wonder, briefly, if I should awaken Hannah One. If she hears thumping around the house, she might get frightened. But I can't bring myself to leave my daughter's side, so I opt to take the chance that she will hear our voices, and know it isn't someone breaking in.

Owen carries Claire into the living room and gently lowers her on to the couch. She still has her coat wrapped around her, and as she clutches at it in a sleepy doze, I gently remove her boots. I bite my lip, seeing Claire lying there, so vulnerable looking. I just want to catch her up in my arms and never let her go. Then she slowly opens her eyes and looks at me.

"Mommy? What... where is Jamie?" She blinks and looks around the room, confusion registering on her face. She sits up, still holding her coat around her. Owen stands beside me, looking down at Claire with a kind, but intense expression, his blue eyes like laser beams scanning her face, looking for trouble. I take Claire's hands. They are cold. I rub them gently between mine. "Oh my, your hands are cold from the drive home. Let me warm you up, sweetie." Claire blinks, and glances down at her hands in mine. "What happened? How come I'm home? Didn't Jamie want me to sleep over?" I swallow. Her voice, filled with childlike concern, rips at my emotions. "Oh no, sweetie, it's just... well... you had a nightmare, and um, well, Jamie thought you might be happier if you were at home, with us." She shivers, and I gather her into my arms, as Owen pulls the blanket off the back of the couch and drapes it over her. I wonder if her body is in shock, even though I believe her mind shields her from the event. Owen sits down beside her and wraps his strong arms around her little body. He looks across to me, each of us speaking volumes with our eyes.

After a few minutes, Claire's body goes limp, and I assume she has fallen back to sleep. I whisper to him, "Looks like she's asleep again. I want her in our bed tonight, with us, so can you carry her upstairs to our room? I just want to write a note to Hannah One." My grandmother, being an early riser, often makes her way to the kitchen hours before anyone else in the house wakes up. When she sees the closed bedroom door, and our bags in the front hallway, she will worry that something is wrong. A note, briefly explaining the situation, will quell her concern. Owen carefully lifts Claire and easily carries her up the stairs. I quietly enter the kitchen to write the note, pausing long enough to wonder if I should text Arthur once more. Claire's mind closing up again is a concern, but part of me wants it to remain closed. The shock her Alternate felt at being awake seemed more than her human side could handle. Arthur may be able to gently explore the memory, and make sure she is okay. I decide against contacting him until morning. Exhaustion suddenly washes over me, and all I want to do is go to bed. I leave the note on the counter by the coffee maker, and silently make my way up the stairs.

As drained of energy as I am, I find sleep eluding me. I lie awake, listening to the sound of Claire's slow rhythmic breathing as she sleeps dreamlessly beside me. Owen's light snoring sound reminds me of waves smoothly lapping a shoreline, and I find myself start to float, like a piece of driftwood gently carried by the water's movement. I become fluid, without body or form, merely buoyant in my Light. I hover above the water, seeing no reflection, only Light. To be Light is not to carry these human burdens of daily struggles, where finding the right path seems insurmountable at times. Wafting up, my Light becomes one with All, and I feel joy and peace. I see other Light beings around me, harmonious in connection. One Light that beams brightly makes me think of Claire, and her Light. Her innocent Light is made up of energy that contains a pure, powerful joy, a *new* bliss that, for some reason, makes me imagine a super nova, exploding and creating new Light to coalesce into Being.

Wrapped in luminosity, I look down upon my world, and realize how much I love being part of it. As difficult and heartbreaking as it has been at times, I see it is part of my journey, and made for me to experience. I know that I have the strength to deal with whatever challenges come my way, and feel such gratitude for having this strength, especially right now.

Morning light sneaks around the edges of the blinds, and I squint, feeling like I've only just closed my eyes. I glance at the clock, which reads seven thirty. I hear muffled sounds coming from the kitchen, no doubt Hannah One making herself a cup of coffee. I turn my head to see two sleeping forms next to me. Our daughter lies between Owen and me, her face soft as she sleeps. He has his back to us both. His breathing slow and steady indicates he is still soundly asleep.

I gingerly sit up and peel back the covers, careful not to disturb either of them. I swing my legs over the side of the bed and stand up, reaching for my bathrobe. Quietly leaving the room, I shut the door and make my way downstairs.

Hannah One is attempting to make a *full* pot of coffee, and as she is raising a carafe full of water to the top of the coffee maker, I see her fumble with the heavy glass carafe. She carefully lowers the pot to the counter and frowns. Something as easy as making coffee has become a chore for her. I assume she is trying to make a huge pot in anticipation of everyone waking soon. She reaches over to the drawer and pulls out a small measuring cup and begins to scoop the water from the carafe into the coffee maker. "What are you doing?" I ask, as I enter the kitchen and stand beside her. She smiles, replying, "Making coffee." She continues to transfer small amounts from the pot into the machine. "Can I help you with that?" Hannah One stops and looks at me, a small grin on her face "Where's there's a will, there's a way!" She finally decides the carafe is a weight she can lift and takes hold of the handle to carefully pour the remaining amount of water into the top of the coffee maker. She flips the lid down, and pushes the button to begin the brewing process. She smiles in satisfaction and turns to me, "So, do you want to tell me what happened last night?" She moves over and takes a chair at the kitchen table. I step over to the cupboard and pull out two mugs, and retrieve the container of oat milk out of the refrigerator, leaving the carton on the counter by the machine.

I take the chair opposite her at the old table. I heave a heavy sigh. Where to begin? "Well, it's hard to explain the events, as *I'm* not even sure what happened…" I pause, closing my eyes. I remember the wonderful dinner, and the feeling of total abandon as Owen and I found each other on that bed in our room. I blink, trying to skip past that part. Hannah One continues to sit and look at me, unaware that I feel a bit red cheeked. "Well, I guess the short version is that Claire had an, *episode*, for lack of a better word. She seemed to become *awake* while she was sleeping at Jamie's house." I know she comprehends what that means, so I don't need to explain. "Jamie called to say that Claire was pretty upset from a nightmare, and maybe she'd be better off with us. Through the evening I had been sensing something, so when Jamie called, I knew right away." I glance over to see if the coffee has brewed yet, but it is still chugging away, dripping slowly into the carafe. Hannah One frowns. "Does this mean she is aware of, of, being, you know, an Alternate?" As open as she is to the knowledge of Alternates, Hannah One is still a bit overwhelmed by the fact that her granddaughter, and great granddaughter, are housing Alternate beings. "No, actually, now I don't think she is fully awake. I think she may have had a brief connection, but the experience was so frightening that her mind shut it down. When she woke up, here at home, she didn't seem to have any memory of it." Hannah One visibly relaxes. She too, is reluctant to have Claire's world disrupted by the change that being awake could bring. She clearly remembers the struggle I went through as a young girl to balance the duality of thought and behaviour.

A little voice from behind me whispers, "Mommy? Can I have some cereal?" Claire stands in the kitchen doorway, her brown hair tussled from sleep, her feet bare. She is clutching her favourite stuffed bear, one we named *Reddy*, as his fur is reddish brown in colour. I stand up, coming over to pick her up. She is almost six, and getting too heavy for lifting, but I feel a sudden desire to scoop her up in my arms and hug her, forever. I hug her tightly as I take a few steps back over to my chair. Sitting down, I place Claire in my lap. She leans into my frame, still holding her bear. "Claire bear why aren't you wearing slippers? Your feet will get cold!" She blinks, looking up at me with sleepy blue eyes, "My slippers are in my bag, and I don't know where it is." I had discarded her bag in the front hallway when we got home. "Oh no, I forgot. Your bag is in the hall, by the door. What kind of cereal would you like this morning? Do you want oatmeal?" She nods, and then wiggles off my lap and makes her way to the hallway. I can hear her rummaging through her bag. I open the cupboard and begin pulling out oatmeal and other ingredients that Claire likes in her cereal, like raisins and cinnamon. Hannah One checks to see if the coffee is brewed and, seeing the ready light blinking on the machine, she begins pulling the mugs closer to the heavy carafe. This time I step in, suggesting I pour the coffee while she measures out the oatmeal for Claire. She hesitates, but not being totally unreasonable, she relents and focuses on measuring out the ingredients in the bowl. "She seems like herself." She remarks quietly. I nod and look over to the doorway. "I just don't know what to do. I suppose I could call Arthur later, and have a talk with him, see what he thinks."

Claire re-enters the kitchen, her feet covered in bright rainbow-coloured slippers. She places Reddy on the table as she climbs into the kitchen chair, waiting for her warm breakfast to be served. "Mommy?" I turn my attention to her. "Yes, sweetie?" Claire blinks, remaining silent for a moment, almost like she is listening to something, then she nods. "Mommy, *we* would like to have some blueberries in our oatmeal this morning, please." I pause while pouring the second mug of coffee, and, fully turning to face her, I reply, "I'm sorry Claire, what did you say?" Thinking she is still sleepy and merely misspoke. She pulls Reddy close to her chest for a hug as she says, "I asked if we could have blueberries?" I put the carafe on the counter and come to kneel in front of Claire. "What do you mean, *we*? Do you mean you and Reddy Bear?" Claire shakes her head, and then pauses once again, tilting her head, listening. "I mean me, and my new friend, the one inside my head."

Arthur and I stand in his healing room at Grace's Centre. I look around, confused. Arthur says, "This is the first memory for this Alternate, who lives in Claire. This is where it began." I turn to see Owen on the table, sitting up, his face streaked with tears. I reach out to touch him, but I make no contact. Then I realize that Arthur and I are but shadows, leaning into the Light, to view the scene. I look over and see Arthur sitting in the small chair in the corner, his usual smile on his face. The door opens, and I walk in. I go directly over and wrap my arms around Owen. The embrace, infused with my empathic Talent, cracks the shield Owen had held up around him for all those years. Then I see it. The Light gently drifting in, through Owen's groin.

I watch silently as Arthur reaches out with his Light to converse with this new energy.

Hello?

Yes, I am here.

Are you an Alternate?

I don't know what that is.

Are you from the Light?

Yes, as we all are. I am from the Nova. We were one, then we were many. I found myself drawn to a fractured energy that needed healing, but the human was completely closed off. This human body was a fortress, where torment and guilt erected walls around his Light that were rigid and impermeable. But there was one weak spot, and I discovered it in the sacral chakra, in the human genitals. It appeared to be the only spot open to the Light, as this male and female human related to each other. I infused myself in this chakra and began healing. Once I felt the Light open more fully in this body, I was pulled into another energy source, as Claire was created. I sensed I could reside in her Light. When her mind suddenly opened a new channel, I was able to travel this path directly into Claire's thoughts and emotions, one which I had never explored before. The complexity of these feelings confused and disoriented me, and I became lost in it all.

Do you understand your situation now?

I am learning; as the child learns, I learn. She leads; I will follow. I am adrift without Her Light guiding me. She is my Gaia, and I, her Fae.

Fae, that's a pretty name, isn't it? Can we call you Fae?

Yes, if that makes it easier for you, but I am also Claire, I am Light, I am Healer, I am Nova, so my name is of little consequence to me. I am All with One, as you are.

Arthur opens his eyes and smiles at me, as I come back to us sitting in the living room. Claire sleeps on the couch by his side, curled up under a blanket, clutching Reddy. He looks at me and raises his eyebrows. "What an absolutely amazing exchange with Fae! Super Nova amazing! Her energy is so brand new, as in, super nova kinda new – it's just amazing!" He beams. Owen sits in the chair across the room, a frown creasing his face. "Well? What's going on?" His voice is edged with worry and impatience. I sit for a moment and think about what Fae said. She had merged with a fractured energy, belonging to Owen. Before I can say anything, Arthur chuckles, "Owen, it's all *your* doing! You're the reason Claire has this Alternate in her!"

Owen's face is white as he leaps out of his chair. "What? How... what?" he is stunned. I wish Arthur had not been so flippant with this revelation. I know Owen will need to be guided through this discovery slowly, so he will understand its significance. He looks at me, his eyes pleading for an explanation. "Arthur, would you mind taking Hannah One out to the kitchen to make a pot of coffee?" Arthur nods, looking at my grandmother, who has been surprisingly quiet through this whole thing. "Come on HO, we know when we're not wanted!" and he chuckles, following Hannah One through the kitchen doorway. I can hear the two of them start to natter at each other immediately, like two old chickens after the farmer leaves the henhouse. "Owen, I know this must be confusing, and such a shock. I'm sorry Arthur wasn't more tactful. I'll walk you through what I learned, so we can both look at this and figure out the situation, together." I take his hands, and feel the tension in his grip.

I relay the entire scene for him, step by step. He still looks confused as I conclude, so I add, "Sometimes we build up protective walls around us to avoid being hurt. We don't want to be vulnerable, and yet part of us still yearns for human connection, human interaction. We allow our *physical* nature to provide that contact, avoiding the need to tap into our emotional side. So, Fae found a way in through the only place that still remained open to the Light." Owen grimaces, as if the infiltration had been painful. He whispers, not wanting anyone to hear his question, "So, it, she, Fae, went into me through my *penis*?" He swallows. I smile, thinking of the male ego, and the huge significance they place on their *manhood*. I don't attempt to make a joke or be glib, as it isn't appropriate. I simply reply, "Well, not really. We have energy centres throughout our body, and the sacral area happens to be one of them. It was open so she just kinda used that as an entrance. It wasn't like she *actually went* into your penis." His face blanches, but I continue, "You were in need of healing, and she found a way in. Once she felt you were able to move forward, she found herself a new home, so to speak." He glances over to Claire, who stirs slightly as she rolls on to her back. "Is she going to be alright?" The tenderness in his voice makes me swallow. He loves Claire so much, he must feel like he is to blame, as his go-to behaviour is based on his past abuse. I touch his face to make him meet my eyes, "All I know is that Fae conforms to Claire's human aspect. She is going to be fine. You are not to blame for this. There is no blame on anyone. It is just the way the Universe works. She is going to be wonderful, especially with such an amazing dad loving her." He smiles weakly, and I know he wants to believe me, but is still grappling with this whole thing. There is nothing more I can do to alleviate his apprehension, so I simply reach over and hug him.

Four

One of the milestones of human growth and development is reaching one's tenth birthday. There is such emphasis placed on numerology of tens. It is a divine number, which, if you follow numerology, means a return to unity. And that is what our house seems to be mirroring, as Claire turns ten years old. The symbolism of *ten* has been ringing throughout this particular year, as Owen and I celebrate our tenth wedding anniversary in May, Hannah One celebrates nine decades on Earth, and I see my fortieth birthday arrive with a flourish of snow. Time is marching on, regardless of all else, as it will.

    Claire is now fully integrated with Fae. It's like raising twins, but with only one body to buy clothes for. It has become so common in our everyday conversations to refer to Claire as *they* or *them*, that one time I let it slip while in Claire's classroom, and the teacher took me aside to quietly ask me if the class should be using that pronoun form to address Claire. I appreciated her sensitivity to the issue, but it was awkward to attempt to explain that my daughter does not identify as *they* or *them*. I causally remarked that it was just a simple slip of the tongue. "I'm so exhausted from all this running around, I don't even know my own name some days!" The teacher nodded, a bit confused by my response, but let it go.

    Every summer, from the time Claire was almost three, we booked a two-week holiday at the cabin we spent our honeymoon nestled away at. It's a much-needed escape from the world. Life seems to dish up so much at once, it's become increasingly hard to keep up with all of it.

As Hannah One ages, I don't like leaving her alone for any length of time. In the past, I asked my mother to check in on her, but now, even though she is only in her in her mid-sixties, my mother has a lot less of the energy and focus needed to take care of a ninety-year-old. My mom, who prided herself on a sharp mind and work ethic, seems to have lost her edge. I attribute it to retirement and aging, but it does worry me at times, especially when she begins to repeat herself.

Hannah One loves going to the cabin. We pack her favourite comfortable lawn chair and she is happy to sit and watch us as we swim, or do some sort of nature craft. She is glad to be included. Since the cabin only has one bedroom, Owen and Claire camp out in a spacious tent we bought. I wanted Hannah One to have the bedroom to herself, but she insisted we share the double bed. It seems very natural to climb into bed beside her. She is still my rock in the storm. As much as I want Owen to be my rock, my grandmother is so deeply rooted in my life, she is my true harbor.

The sun glimmers across the water as we sit together, watching Owen and Claire canoe along the shoreline just to the east of the cabin. The water is calm, with an aqua green colour that reflects the white clouds that drift by high above the landscape.

Hannah One sits in her chair with a cup of coffee in hand; Those hands, now carrying many wrinkles of time well spent on Earth. Her face still glows with a youthful curiosity, and I know Fae has helped her to keep her Light shining through these past years. She glances over at me as I sit next to her, my own coffee mug sitting on the small table between us. "Don't forget your cup there. Nothing worse than cold coffee." She smiles. If I looked in a mirror to see my future self, I can only hope to be like her. Even in the face of losing her husband at the age of forty-eight, having to undergo hip replacement surgery, and losing her only son, she retains a bright glow of life. I look at her face again, lines of life carved into it, like a sculptor creating a work of art. "Are you happy with the way your life turned out?" I'm not sure why I asked that, but I feel a need to make sure she is content with the way her journey has gone. She sighs. "I don't know if happy is the right word to describe it. There are moments I wish I never had to live through." She looks at me as I nod in agreement, knowing some of the points in time she refers to. "But, if you don't have these terrible times, I suppose one would have a happy, bland kind of life. I think I have been blessed, for the most part. I can't believe I have such an amazing granddaughter, who has opened my eyes to worlds beyond. My beautiful grandson-in-law who fills the void a mother feels when she loses her only son. He is the most loving son-in-law I could have asked for. And now Claire; such a treasure. Yes, I suppose I can say I am happy that my path took me through such wonderful adventures, and so much love. So much love." She places her cup on the table, and reaches into her pocket for a hanky. I reach across the table and touch her arm. "I'm sorry. I didn't mean to upset you." She turns to look at me, her eyes full of tears. "These are not upset tears; these are gratitude tears." And she smiles, wiping her face.

The cell phone rings. I crack open my eyes to find the bedroom pitch black, except that the screen makes a bright rectangular light on the ceiling. It keeps ringing. I pick up the device and see that it's my mother calling. "Mom? What's going on?" It's three o'clock in the morning. Hannah One stirs beside me, slowly sitting up and reaching over to turn on the nightstand lamp.

"Mom? Hello?" At first there is only breathing on the other end. Then her voice comes through, sounding panicked. "Hannah? Where are you? I went to the house, but everyone is gone!" I blink, not sure I am awake. "Mom? Mom! We are here, at the cabin. We've been here for a week now. Mom..." there is more breathing and then she replies, "Oh, yes, of course. Silly me, I thought you were home now. Sorry to bother you." And then the phone goes dead. She hung up, as if she had dialed a wrong number. I jump out of bed and before I can explain to Hannah One, I race outside to the tent in the backyard. It is so dark, with only the kitchen light streaming through the window to illuminate the landscape, I have to be careful not to trip over anything. I approach the tent and take hold of the zipper. I bend down to enter the tent, carefully stepping over what appears to be Claire, curled up in her sleeping bag. Owen groans as I touch his shoulder. He opens his eyes and smiles, thinking I have come out to have a midnight cuddle. I whisper, "Get up and come in the cabin. I need you." I gingerly make my way back out of the tent, leaving the zipper door open.

Hannah One is sitting on the couch in the small living room, wearing a warm housecoat and slippers. She has a concerned expression, but does not ask questions. She knows that once Owen arrives, I will tell them both what happened. Owen quietly opens the door and stands in the living room, not sure what he should be doing. I take a breath, feeling the panic that's been gripping me loosen slightly as I speak. "Mom just called me. She had gone to the house and freaked out because we weren't home. I had told her the date of our return; I even circled the dates on her calendar. I think something is wrong!" The alarm in my voice makes Owen come over and take my arm. "Hannah, I'm sure it's okay. She just got confused, maybe she heard you incorrectly." But Owen isn't even convincing himself with that statement. Hannah One rises up from the couch and says, "We cannot drive home at three o'clock in the morning, it just isn't a good idea. Why don't we begin to pack up, and leave at the first light?" Her sane suggestion is met with nods from both of us. She turns and walks into the bedroom. I look to Owen, feeling like a wall is crumbling inside me. I want to cry from worry, from disappointment at cutting our holiday short, from frustration at not knowing what's going on at home. Owen takes me in his arms, and for a brief second, I feel safe and sheltered from the world again. His voice echoes in his chest as I lay my ear against it, "We will get home, and figure out what is going on. You know your mom, she has been a bit absent-minded lately, but that can happen as people get older. If things are okay, we can always return here for the rest of the week." As much as I want to trust in his words, some part of me knows we will not be back.

The four-hour trip, which began at six in the morning, seemed to take a millennium to complete. I keep calling my mother, but it goes to voicemail. We pull into the driveway, half expecting to see our house on fire. It is quiet. I help Hannah One out of the car, and, after taking her and Claire into the house, Owen and I jump back in the car to drive over to my mother's condo. The streets are fairly empty, being Sunday. We pull around the corner, half expecting to see *her* house on fire, but it too, is quiet. I pull out my house key and run up the steps to the door, Owen at my heels. We enter the condo and immediately begin to call out. "Mom! Are you here, Mom?" Owen checks the kitchen, "Caroline? It's me Owen here, just checking in!" I race up the stairs to her bedroom. She is asleep in her bed. I come over to the bedside and lean over to place my hand on her shoulder. I gently nudge her awake, "Mom, Mom. Wake up." She blinks and looks at me, confused. "Hannah? What's wrong? Why are you here? You're supposed to be at the cabin…" she sits up, just as Owen walks through the bedroom door. Her eyes fly open at the sight of the anxious expression on his face. "Has something happened? Is it your grandmother?" I straighten up, my own confusion swirling in my head. "Mom, you called me at three a.m., don't you remember? You were looking for me." She struggles to free herself from her bedsheets. I help her to swing her legs out so she can sit on the edge of the bed. I reach over to pick up her housecoat that lies draped on the end of the bed. I hand it to her and she stands up to put it on. Owen gently says, "How about I put on some coffee?" He quickly backs out of the room.

"Mom, do you remember calling me?" She looks at me as bewilderment registers across her face. "I don't think so. I was sleeping, I was sleeping..." her voice trails off as she tries to jog her memory.

Owen comes back to the bedroom as my mother heads to the bathroom. He indicates that I should come to the kitchen. "Mom, you just freshen up and I'll be right back." I leave the room, feeling annoyed that Owen doesn't seem to be able to handle the simple task of making coffee. I am about to say something, when he points to the fridge. "Open it." His expression is blank, so I have no idea what I am about to discover. I pull open the door and look inside. There is her jewelry box, her purse, a small sculpture, a porcelain vase and some vinyl records, all crammed in between containers of food and drinks. The incongruity of the scene leaves me speechless. It's Owen who utters quietly, "Storing her valuables in the fridge? Not even sure how to ask her about this one..." he rubs his chin. I shut the door and sit down at the kitchen table, suddenly feeling the lack of sleep mix with my anxiety, and it drains me of reason. My mother walks into the kitchen, smiling. She goes about getting cups out of the cupboard. She acts as if this is a normal visit, nothing out of the ordinary. Owen continues to make coffee, while I sit, stunned into silence.

"So, Caroline. I noticed a few things in the fridge. That's an interesting place to keep them." My mother frowns, opening the refrigerator door. "Yes, that's because no one looks in there. Robbers won't take my things if they are hidden in a good place." Owen doesn't miss a beat, as if this is the most logical, normal conversation he's had all day. "Good idea. I certainly wouldn't think of looking in there." She smiles, obviously happy to receive the approval from her son-in-law. I stand up, feeling a bit nauseous, and go to the front door to step outside. The warm morning air does not lessen the panic I feel in the pit of my stomach. I just need to think straight, and I can't do that sitting there in the kitchen. It's obvious my mother has either developed dementia or has had some other issue which is changing her sense of reality. Either way, she needs to be looked after.

After a few deep breaths I turn slowly and make my way back into the house where I find Owen and my mother sitting, each with a cup of coffee, in the living room. Owen is talking about the cabin and what Claire was doing, just like any other visit. My mother appears to be listening, but every so often she does not respond to a question Owen asks of her.

It is time I take things in hand. "Mom, I forgot to tell you that we have a doctor's appointment today, shortly. So, we should get dressed and go." My mother looks a bit puzzled, as if somewhere in her mind it is saying, *this is Sunday, how can you have an appointment on Sunday*? But she merely shrugs and stands up. She begins to head for the stairs and I follow, afraid to leave her alone. She takes no notice of me following her. Just before I leave the living room, I turn to Owen and whisper, "hospital."

Five

Residing in a human body is much like driving a car. All the elements of the engine, like the human body, need to work together to allow the car itself to function. If one part does not work, other parts may step in and compensate for the malfunction, up to a point. The compensation will eventually lead to a compromise of integrity of the other parts that are attempting to carry the load, and then the whole system fails to work. No matter how much the driver, which is Spirit or Light, wishes that the car would work, it's impossible without the body parts working in union to produce the desired motion, or process of thought.

And so it is for my mother. A mini stroke caused a chain reaction of vascular dementia, which has led to the weakening of her cognitive abilities. I sense her struggling to comprehend what is happening, while at the same time, her mind escapes the confusion by producing an alternate reality. The concern over possible future strokes makes it imperative that she have some sort of continuous support. I cannot fully commit to her care, as I am already handling day to day life with Hannah One, now approaching ninety-two, and Claire, not to mention running my business and having a husband to maintain a relationship with. After further discussion with the doctor, we agreed that having a live-in caretaker would best suit the situation, until she can be moved to a long-term care facility. The wait list for a good residence is at least one to two years.

As Fate would have it, I found the right person to care for my mother, right under my nose. Angela Barry, who was an employee at the bookstore, until she decided to return to school to become a home healthcare provider, has recently graduated and is looking for a job. I feel immense relief at being able to hire someone I already know, and trust. Angela has a true caring quality about her, and for someone so young, she has a very mature outlook. It's only a matter of convincing my mother to work with her. During one of her lucid moments, I was able to have a conversation with her about the situation. She agreed, after hearing my statement that hiring Angela would take the burden off of me to care for her on a daily basis.

Angela moved in and has found a routine that best suits my mother. She still has days of complete competency, in which she talks about current events, shows an interest in her family, and eats well. She likes walking, so the pair of them have a daily walk through the neighborhood, and sometimes, when the weather is cold or rainy, they walk at a mall. Physical activities are one important factor in staving off future strokes. Then there are the days when she is not herself. The world is out to get her; she needs to hide her valuables; she will not eat, or she simply talks about her life as a child, living in her childhood memories. Angela feels a little overwhelmed at times, and at those times she calls me. Between the two of us, these days are handled as best they can be. I count the days until I can move her into a good residence, as I worry that Angela might decide this is not a good fit, and quit, and then where will we be?

The cold October wind brings the last of the autumn leaves to the ground. My cell chimes as I busily ring through a customer at the bookstore. It's Arthur. He's been thinking about my situation and has come up with an idea he wants to discuss with me. I invite him for dinner, after I leave the store at six. Owen has become a great cook, which is immensely helpful as I often get delayed at the store and don't get home until after seven. And, besides which, whoever said that it is up to the woman to cook all the time! Owen usually gets home around four thirty, after picking Claire up from after-school care. Hannah One manages well on her own, as I make her a lunch in the morning before I leave, and she can still manage her way around making a cup of tea. She reads a lot, or sits in the garden, and tries her hand at sketching. Her hands are arthritic, but she can hold the pencil and move it around, and often creates lovely roughed-out sketches of flowers or a landscape. Her paintings, created when she was younger, still adorn the walls around the house, and are considered true treasures to all who view them.

I arrive home around six-fifteen to find Arthur with Claire, in the living room. He is addressing Fae about her experience as part of a super nova. He never seems to grow tired of exploring that, and Fae patiently answers all his questions. Arthur, now in his seventies, has a habit of repeating himself at times. When I remind him that he's already told that story, he simply says, "Good! So you won't forget it, in case I do!" And then laughs.

After Owen's delicious supper, I begin clearing dishes, with Claire's help. Owen comes up behind me and takes my hand, saying, "Why don't you and Arthur go have a chat? Claire and I can do up the dishes, eh, Claire bear?" The expression on Claire's face is cloudy, but she doesn't argue. It's Friday night, and she wants to do the things that all eleven-year-old kids do; talk to or text their friends about all manner of pre-teen topics.

Arthur and I go into the living room, Hannah One following along. She loves Arthur. Well, the feeling is mutual, as Arthur adores Hannah One. The two of them sit down side by side on the couch, while Arthur takes one of her gnarled old hands in his. "If only I were older, then we'd make a perfect pair! I just don't want your friends calling you a cougar, going after a *much younger* man!" Hannah One laughs, and slaps his hand. His gentle teasing makes her smile, and I appreciate his love for her, as it brightens her world. Arthur, still holding her hand, turns to me and says, "Okay. Here it is. Your mom, bless her, is having a terrible time of it, no question. I just wondered if there is something we, and I mean, you, me, *and* Fae, can do collectively, to help ease her mind somewhat. What do you think about showing her our side of things, maybe taking her to her door, letting her see her life again? I know it doesn't help her mental state as it is now, but her Spirit, her Light, is fracturing under the erosion of her body, and I hate to see this happening."

I look over at Hannah One, but she offers no opinion. She obviously wants to see where my thoughts are before stating her view. I look at my hands, trying to visualize how this would help her, instead of confuse her all the more. I am on the fence about his idea. I'm not sure I want Claire involved, although Fae's Talent for healing would be a bonus. I look at Arthur, his face expectant, "I'm not sure. Don't you think it will just confuse her? She might not be able to distinguish this realm from the other. It may just send her too far over." I am leaning towards the *no* side, when Arthur responds, "that's why Fae would be present. Her Talent for healing could mend the fracture, help Caroline find her path, or at least help her to feel less disconnected from her life. It may give her peace. I can guide her, you can support her, Fae can heal her. It might help… but I doubt it will make things worse." he concludes with a gentle smile. Hannah One finally ventures her opinion; "I think that, if it were me, and I couldn't think straight, I would appreciate any form of comfort that helps my troubled mind. Claire is old enough now to know the situation, and Fae can also help her to understand the nuances of it. I think Caroline must be having such a horrible time. My heart breaks for her." Her chin trembles, and her eyes well up. I know Hannah One must feel so blessed to have reached her age with all her faculties, and reasonably good mobility. I look at her and picture this happening to her, and the answer becomes clear to me. I would not hesitate to help her if I thought she was struggling, or in pain, so why wouldn't I help my mother?

As a family we decide to set aside the following Sunday to try this experiment. Each and every one of us has an important role to play in this event. Since we can't reasonably ask my mother to cooperate, we have to wait until she wants to nap, thus creating an open passage in her mind for us to enter. Owen will be watching her as she sleeps, just to make sure that if she wakes up suddenly, she will not be alarmed. Hannah One is also there to act as an anchor, a person who she can mentally hold on to, as my mother often knows who *she* is, regardless of her state of mind. Arthur will be the guide, Fae will provide the calm healing presence required to approach the fractured Spirit, and I will act as her anchor once we are in her mind. She will not recognize Fae, and never seems to recall who Arthur is, but she will know my face. I am counting on her Spirit to recognize me.

I pick up my mom at her condo, telling Angela that we decided to have a family day, and that she can have a much-deserved afternoon off. Since she lives with my mother, I know we can't do this session in the condo as we need uninterrupted time, with no curious onlookers. Angela is happy to have some time to herself.

Caroline enters our house and asks, "Is Daniel here? I haven't seen him today, so maybe he's with his mother?" Her confusion, and the mention of my father, makes me bite my lip. I'm not about to tell her that my father passed away years ago, as that would upset and confuse her more. I simply take her hand and lead her to the couch in the living room, saying, "Mom, he's busy right now with work, but he might try to come for a visit later." She nods, seemingly fine with the explanation.

Arthur is in the kitchen with Hannah One, and Owen is upstairs at his makeshift desk in our bedroom, grading papers. Claire is in her room, reading. I didn't want everyone around when she first arrived, as I thought it would be a bit overwhelming. As soon as she sits down, Hannah One walks in from the kitchen, holding a cup of tea. She comes over to my mother and leans in to pat her arm. "Caroline, my dear, how are you today?" The sweet, almost condescending tone would have made my mother livid, under *normal* circumstances, but today, she merely looks at the elderly woman standing there and replies, "I'm fine. I had a good breakfast." Hannah One nods, replying, "Well, that is very important. I'm glad you ate well. Would you like a cup of tea?" My mother glances at the mug, and frowns, "I don't think so." Hannah One smiles, "How about a cup of coffee? I know how much you like coffee." There is a pause, and then my mother smiles, "Yes, I do. I like coffee, could I have a cup?" Hannah One pats her arm again. "Of course my dear, I have a pot all ready. I will ask my friend Arthur to bring you a cup." She turns, leaving us sitting on the couch together. There is a vacancy of expression on my mother's face that makes me think she doesn't quite remember where she is at this moment. I don't want to rock the boat, so I just sit with her and wait for the coffee. Soon enough, Arthur comes out of the kitchen with a large tray. It holds four cups, filled with coffee that are already milked and sugared, and a plate of cookies. He places the tray on the dining room table and picks up a cup. He approaches my mother, who looks up at Arthur and frowns, uttering, "Hello. We haven't met, I'm Rose." Arthur holds out the cup to her, which she takes with both hands. "Hello Rose, I'm Arthur. It's so nice to meet you." Rose is my mother's middle name. This is not the first time she has met Arthur. I stand up and cross over to the table and pick up a mug and take a sip. It has sugar in it, and makes me scowl. "Who put sugar in *my* coffee?" I ask irritably. Arthur points at the cup and chuckles, "I put sugar in *my* coffee, sweetie, and that's *my* coffee!" I put the mug back on the tray and pick up a second one, "Are we sugar-free in *this* one?" Hannah One frowns at my rudeness, but says nothing. My irritability is fueled by the tension I feel about this whole crazy expedition. I need to stop and breathe. I turn to the room in general and say, "Sorry, I didn't mean to be rude." Arthur smiles, and Hannah One nods, happy I am apologizing. Everyone is a bit anxious, so it's unfair of me to claim sole sovereignty over that emotion today.

I hear footsteps on the stairs, and turn to see Owen enter the living room. My mother looks up and smiles at him, "Daniel?" Owen frowns and looks at me for help. "No Mom, he is still at work. He might come by later. This is Owen, do you remember Owen?" She blankly nods, turning her eyes to the mug in her hand. Owen finds a chair in the corner and sinks down, looking worried. Hannah One sees his expression and says, "Owen, dear, there is coffee ready, if you'd like me to get you a cup." Owen smiles at his adoptive grandmother, rising up out of his chair as he responds, "Thank you, I think I'll just grab a cup myself, and maybe an extra cookie while I'm there!" He winks at her and smiles. I am grateful that she has such a calming influence over him. He respects and values her enough to listen to her reasonable tone, which isn't always the case with me.

I hear Claire call down from the top of the stairs, "Mom? Is it okay? Can we come down?" I walk over to the foot of the stairs to avoid shouting from the living room and upsetting the tone of the room. "Yes, Claire, come down. There's juice and cookies in the kitchen." She quietly comes down the stairs, her feet barely touching each step. She is extremely sensitive to the environment, and I know she is feeling the need for discretion right now. This is part of Claire's Talent. Fae has mentioned many times that her counterpart has a sensitive Light, and is much the Empath, like her mother. Their combined Talents make Fae and Claire a beautiful force of nature.

After about an hour, I can tell my mother is tiring, so I suggest that she lie down on the couch for a nap. She agrees and I help her get comfortable with a pillow and blanket. It's important to keep her in a familiar room, where she is already feeling relaxed. Hannah One remains seated at the dining room table, but Arthur,

Owen and Claire leave the room, to sit in the kitchen. I sit in the arm chair across from my mother, pretending to read, all the while watching, as her body becomes more relaxed and sleep overcomes her. When I believe she is truly asleep, I go into the kitchen to sit with Arthur. Owen quietly makes his way back into the living room to sit where I had been, his frame filling the chair. Arthur, Claire and I sit at the kitchen table and, jointly, begin to descend. With our eyes closed, we feel the world slip away from us. Claire, who decided to hold my hand at the last moment, seems a bit nervous, but Fae reaches out to soothe her. We land in a field of flowers and long-stemmed grasses. Fae stands before us; her green skin shimmers in the sun with an iridescent glow. Her features are true Fae, with slightly pointed ears and eyes, long slender arms and legs, and her body virtually growing leaves and mosses in lieu of clothing. I have seen her true form before, but it never ceases to amaze me. Her sharp, yellow-green eyes, with flecks of blue that sparkle, are bright and playful. Beside her stands Arthur, stretching his arms up and embracing the sun as it caresses his body. Claire, standing on Fae's other side looks around, smiling. It's her first time traveling collectively; she seems thrilled and excited to be included.

    I begin to wonder where we will find my mother. Arthur reaches out and searches for her door, but cannot see it. Fae and Claire begin to play in the flowers, ignoring the purpose of our visit to simply have a moment of joy together. I extend my mind to touch my mother's, and suddenly we are standing in a grove of tall neatly manicured bushes. The hedge runs along either side of us, and appears in front and behind us as well. Arthur looks around and utters, "I think we are in a hedge maze of some sort. We may need to explore until we find her." He turns and walks towards the rear, and then turns again, disappearing as he steps to his left. We follow, but it seems like the blind leading the blind. I, once again, reach out to feel where she could be. I see a dim light shining up ahead. I walk on, this time everyone following me. The hedge grows thick and coarse on both sides, with no way to see through to the other side. I keep my eye on the light dimly beaming on the pathway ahead of us, like the sun as it stretches across the lawn just before disappearing for the night. We round the corner, and there, crouched in a ball on the ground, is my mother. She hides her face in her drawn-up knees. I motion for everyone to stop, while I take a few steps forward. "Mom? Mom, it's me, Hannah. I am here now, you're safe." She raises her head and squints, as if the air itself hurts her eyes. "Hannah? I'm so confused. Where am I? I'm so scared." And then she begins to weep. I kneel down and embrace her, immediately feeling her terror and confusion as it oozes out of her splintered Spirit. Arthur remains where he is, but Fae comes forward and places her hand on my mother's brow. The look of horror that passes across her face is quickly replaced by tranquility. She unclenches her body, and soon, she is able to stand. Fae keeps her hand on her at all times, moving it from her head to her back, to her arm, repositioning her healing Talent throughout the terrified body.

Claire comes over and hugs her grandmother. "Grams, it's me Claire. Do you remember me?" Her voice, young and pure, sings around the hedges, like music. She looks up and smiles at her grandmother, sending more healing energy into my mother's broken Light. Soon we surround her with healing energy, and then Arthur steps forward to touch her arm. We are no longer in the hedge, but standing in a long white hallway. My mother screams. I look at Arthur and shake my head. He immediately touches her arm again, and we are suddenly in the backyard at our old house.

I look around and see the wonderful old tree. Pots of colourful annuals line the walkway by the back porch. Lawn chairs sit empty near the tree; but then I see the image of my mother fill one chair, and then the image of an infant sitting on a big blanket laid out on the grass, appears. Arthur whispers to me, "This is your mother's reference for a happy time in her life. It is a safe memory; one she holds close to her Spirit. It's what brings her peace, when she can find it."

My mother looks around, confused. Then she starts crying. The tears spill over and touch the ground, where flowers begin to grow. I look at Fae and she smiles. We loosen our hold on the frail body, allowing her to turn and gather in her surroundings. "I am *here*? How... how... I don't understand." Arthur takes her hand as a white linen-covered table appears. A large ornate tray, holding dozens of tea cups appears on the tabletop before her. "All your memoires are here, Caroline, here, in each of these pretty teacups. You need only touch the rim, and you can visit any memory you like. Would you like to try?" She looks at him, as if seeing him for the first time. Her eyes are still wide and rimmed with uncertainty, but as both Claire and Fae are still touching her, her overall anxiety level remains subdued. I take her hand and say, "Mom, I know this is so confusing for you, but let's pretend you are having a wonderful dream, where you can be free of worry and fear. Let's just find your joy again. Which cup looks good to you?" She turns her eyes from my face to the cups. She and I both lean forward slightly to view the cups. Inside each of them is a clear liquid, and in each reflection shines a picture, captured for all time. One reflection is of her holding me, the day I was born. Another reflection is her in a white wedding dress, with two older people, which I recognize as her parents, smiling at her. Each cup has an image of bliss or joy. I notice that there are no cups with sad or traumatic pictures, like the day my father died. I assume that Arthur has done a bit of work to edit those out. There is no need to view those. She needs serenity to mend her damaged Light.

She reaches forward and touches the rim of a cup that holds an image of the day I got married. Butterflies burst from the cup, followed by the sound of laughter. I can hear Ella Fitzgerald singing in the background, *Night and Day, you are the one...* as we watch the image of me dancing with Owen. I catch my breath. I was not expecting her to choose this one, so I'm not prepared for the emotion it brings up in me. I notice Fae bring her hand over and place it on *my* arm. I feel tears roll down my cheeks, and yet they are each filled with a drop of love and gratitude. I look at my mother and see that, she too, is crying. It is a lovely moment, caught forever between the two of us.

We spend a while longer at the table as my mother touches a few other cups, mostly from her childhood, and we share in her joy at reliving a memory that infuses her Light and gives her peace. Arthur finally motions to me that it is time to leave. I turn to my mother and gently whisper, "Mom, we will visit here again, very soon. Your Light is brighter now, which might help you cope better with, uh, things. We will come again, I promise." My mother, visibly disappointed that we can't stay, lowers her head. "Alright, but do I have to go back to those bushes?" Her voice is edged with fear. Fae touches her arm and says, "Caroline, I have a beautiful garden I'd like you to visit. You can stay there, and then we will know where to find you when we visit again." My mother smiles at the mention of a garden. She nods, taking Fae's hand as she leads her away. She glances back at the table as Fae guides her a few steps forward. Arthur smiles but does not move. Claire comes to stand beside me and, once again, takes my hand. Fae turns and waves goodbye, as the three of us fade into nothing.

My mother sits in the garden, which resembles our backyard, sipping a cup of coffee. She smiles as the sun warms her face, and a nearby Chickadee sings to her.

Six

As often as time will allow, over the course of about eight weeks, we take my mother on trips to look at her tea cups, and leave her placidly drinking coffee in the garden. In the waking world, she is now more lucid, and much calmer. Angela noticed right away, and credited the change to the extra time the family is taking to keep her connected to her world. Little does she know to what lengths we are going to achieve this.

I have decided to take a few extra-long days at the bookstore to help with inventory and other mundane tasks that my overworked brain does not mind sinking into. Since Nouri and Angela left, good part-time help seems harder to find, and although Janice and Cindy carry the brunt of the load, I know I need to step in and relieve some of their burden. When Janice and I finally found another set of hands to help out, I decided that I should train Jason, and let Janice have a few much-deserved days off. Jason is a quick study, and although the job itself is not difficult, it's the subtle things that he is clever enough to grasp right away. He has a wonderful sense of humour, and works well with customers. After a few days, I decided to allow him to run things out front, while Cindy and I deal with some stock-ordering issues. I suggest that Cindy go down to the basement, where the bargain books are, and start to do a count of stock. That leaves me sitting in the small office, going over other logistics. Staring at the computer screen is the last thing I remember.

I stand alone, with nothing but darkness lining the vision. All is black, with no sound, no smell, no light, and yet I can feel the texture of the darkness that surrounds me, like a heavy drape cloaking me from the Light. Then I see white and tan wings fluttering above me, and the figure of the Owl comes to rest on... nothing. No tree limb is evident, but he appears to be sitting upon one. His large amber eyes rimmed with black lashes stare at me, unblinking. I feel like a mouse, hiding under the bush, hoping not to be seen. He is All, and I feel humbled in his presence. After a moment the Owl speaks, his voice low, resounding of ages past, present and future, echoing through the dark; "Your gift allows you to see beyond Sight. Yet you cannot know beyond Time. What will come you cannot see, or alter, for this is the way of All; you may only learn from what Time offers to teach and continue to move forward to your final destination beyond the Now. I am One With All; I am the One who sees beyond Sight, knows beyond Time and Writer of the messages that Death dictates. Death, unlike Time, does not teach passively; it is brutal and unflinching. This you have learned and will learn again, until Death dictates to me that your final destination is in sight."

I feel a hand on my shoulder, and turn to see Jason, staring at me with a concerned look. "Your phone was ringing, but you looked, well, kinda spaced out, so I answered it. It was someone named Angela. She said you should get to the hospital. It's your mom."

I text Owen, and Arthur, before I take a few deep breaths and start the car. I am not going to panic. I tried to call Angela, but it went straight to voicemail. I already have a feeling that my mother is dead, but I won't allow myself to really feel it until I know for certain.

As I arrive at the hospital, I receive a brief text from Angela, saying to come to emergency and tell them who I am. The nurse will then get me to where they are. I shove my phone in my pocket and race to the entrance. As I enter, I realize that I should tell Arthur and Owen where to find me, so I dash off a quick text to both. Then, taking another deep breath, I make my way over to the emergency room nurse's desk.

After about five minutes, I'm taken to a curtained off area, where several beds are arranged in rows, with curtain partitions the only privacy to offer. I can hear people talking, some crying, in pain or sadness, and some beds sit empty. The nurse leads me to a bed towards the back of the ward, pulling the curtain open to allow me to enter. She walks around the bed to check on some electrical devices that are connected to my mother. My mother, who is still breathing, still alive. Angela stands in the far corner; her face streaked with tears. When she sees me, she bursts out crying and rushes over to hug me. "I'm so sorry Hannah. I'm sorry, I couldn't do anything. I called the ambulance, but I couldn't do anything." She sobs as I hold on to the poor young woman, who is rattled by the experience. I turn my eyes to my mother, lying on the bed, with a sheet covering her up to her waist, and several wires attached to various parts of her body. She looks peaceful, almost like she's sleeping.

Then she opens her eyes, and the fear quickly erases all calm in her expression. I drop my arms from around Angela, and immediately move over to my mother. The nurse, seeing the panic, attempts to calm her. "Mrs. Casey, Mrs. Casey, do you know where you are? Can you tell me what hurts?". I quietly say to the nurse, "My mother has dementia. She may not understand the situation." The nurse begins to fuss with the wires again. I turn to Angela, who is wiping her eyes with a tissue. "Angela, can you tell me what happened?" Angela takes a ragged breath and begins; "We were having lunch, just the usual. She talked about the garden she likes to live in, and that you were there as well as Claire, and then she said something weird about a little green girl. So, I just thought she's having one of her *moments*, you know," she smiles weakly. I nod as she continues. "I began clearing away the dishes, when I watched her get up from the table, she lost her balance and fell. Then I saw that her face, on the left side, had gone droopy. I told her not to move, and asked if she could smile. The right side of her mouth lifted, but not the left, and her eyelid was drooping down too. That's when I knew she must have had another stroke. I called nine-one-one right away. Then she wanted to try to get up, so I had to lie on the floor with her to keep her from moving..." she begins to choke up, and I know she is getting more upset, reliving that terrifying moment in her mind. I reach over and take her hand. "You did great Angela! I couldn't have handled the situation any better, really. You handled it better than I would have." She smiles gratefully and glances over to my mother. The nurse concludes her checks, and mentions that the doctor will be with us in a few minutes.

I stand beside the bed and take my mother's hand. Her left hand is dead weight, with no response to me squeezing her hand. I reach over and take hold of her right hand. It responds feebly to my touch. She holds fear in her eyes and it wrecks me to see her this way. I reach out with my mind and try to pry open the door to allow her back into the garden, but without Arthur and Fae, I cannot do it. I feel the tears sting my eyes as I look into her face, and know that she is falling, possibly not to return from that darkness. I lower my head so she can hear me as I whisper, "Mom, I am here with you. Don't be afraid. I know it's painful and scary, but we are all here to help you. Arthur and Claire and Fae, and Owen and Hannah One, we all love you so much and will help you through this. Just rest, I'm here..." I cannot say anymore, as my throat closes off the wretched moan I feel building up from the pit of my stomach.

She looks at me and tries to open her mouth to speak. She slurs out one single word: "Aaarrrdennn." I know she is trying to say garden. I smile at her, "Yes Mom, we will take you to the garden again. You can have all the coffee you want, and plant flowers, and watch the birds. We will visit you every day and Claire and Fae will dance for you. I know how much you love to watch them dance." I notice my mother's eyes slowly close, and her grip loosen. Even before the machine alarm begins its high-pitched peal, I know she is slipping into the darkness. I quickly get pushed out of the way as the nursing staff attempt to revive her lifeless body. Her body, that no longer houses her Light. Her Spirit moved on, waiting in the garden, waiting for her granddaughter to come and dance for her.

I look out across the cemetery grounds. Many headstones, sitting like rigid guardians of the dead, show decades of wear. The Maples tower over the green, well-kept lawns; silent watchers to the passage of never-ending mourners. My mother's ashes are placed beside those of her parents, Rose and Frank Whelan. An addition to the large headstone will read, *Caroline Rose Whelan Casey, Loving Daughter, Loving Mother.*

I smile softly, recalling the time she had to take me to a funeral when I was about ten years old. She had to admonish me for giggling at the display of the dead body. Thinking it a silly ritual, I had no human conception of the intricacies that are wrapped up in the process of grief. Now I understand more clearly, and feel a certain reverence for the customs that help humans cope with loss. It is not glorifying the body, but paying tribute to the memory of the person no longer here. It is one final time to gaze upon a loved one's features, and be able to say goodbye. The burial symbolizes the closure of life; The final seal of earth over our remains, returning to the true molecular form of being, before we were made human, and where our physical housing goes when it is no longer a viable entity in which to reside.

Claire clutches Owen's hand, her face a mask of grief. At the age of eleven, she is still too young to fully comprehend the situation. Owen is strong, strong enough for both of us, as I struggle to make my way through the days after her death. Hannah One has not come to the burial. She cannot stand for long periods of time, and the uneven lawn may cause a stumble. She said she would sit in the garden and think of all the wonderful memories she has of Caroline, and pay tribute to her in that fashion. I think that sounds like a place I want to be as well, rather than at this graveside.

Arthur and Grace have come along to provide support. I appreciate their presence, especially Grace, who has a calming effect on all of us, and is able to keep Arthur, who is now having some issues with his knees, from tripping over his big feet. Since my mother's dementia, her friends have drifted away, unable or unwilling to retain a friendship that would inevitably be one-sided. So, it is a small band here to say good bye, but it is those who are closest to her, and that's all that matters.

Seven

A yip-yipping sound, followed by a chorus of high-pitched howls, breaks into my dreamless sleep. I sit up in bed, and think about waking Owen, but decide to check out the origin of the sounds myself, and let him rest. I descend the stairs and head out to the back garden. The predawn light casts dim shadows, making everything grey and undefined, barring my ability to see clearly. What I can see are two forms, crouching by our old Maple tree. As I approach slowly, they move into a sitting position. From where I stand, they appear to be dogs. I take a few steps closer and see the angular shape of the muzzle and eyes, tall pointed ears, and a roughed grey-tan coloured coat. Coyotes. What are Coyotes doing in my backyard? How did they get here? The taller of the two Coyotes blinks his liquid tawny eyes and says, "You carry the weighty woes on your frame, and in your heart. You must yip at the moon, chase your tail, and find bliss in your pack. Let go of the woe; your fur coat will shine, your eyes will see clearly the miles ahead, and your nose will sniff new adventure. It is time to play, to lift off the yoke of sadness, and smile at your world again."

I look down at my arm, and see Claire's hand resting on it. I glance at her face, a portrait of compassion, as her entire body radiates healing Light. "Fae said you were out here. Are you dreamwalking?" I look back to the Coyotes, but they have vanished, just as the first rays of sun spill out of the horizon unto the Earth. I turn and take Claire's hand, and together we make our way back into the house.

When raising a teenager, it's like being drawn into a tornado. Every aspect of life revolves around that tornado. School recitals, projects, report cards, after-school clubs and gatherings with friends, all seemed to usurp each day of our lives over the following few years. I can hardly wait until summer arrives, if for no other reason than to have a break from the flurry. Claire loves school, evidenced by her stunningly good report cards, and the comments made by teachers and friends alike. When, finally the last school day of June arrives, we all breathe a collective sigh. Claire brings home bags full of papers, pens and other paraphernalia from her locker. She wants to go through and keep some of her work, and I agree that this would be a good idea. She is a brilliant creative writer, and has received top marks for her imaginative story-telling. Little did the English teacher know that these aren't necessarily works of fiction. She and Fae have times together that don't include anyone else, as Fae is able to pull her into different realms of life that she would never know to explore as a human. I almost envy her this time, wishing I had had a friend like that when I was young.

Arthur still visits often. Now well into his seventies, his hair white, but his eyes still gleam with the same mischief. Although he uses a cane, as arthritis has attacked both his knees, he remains active, and still offers life journeys to anyone who wants to explore their past. He most enjoys sitting with Hannah One, who, is by now almost ninety-five, and together they talk about a whole host of topics. She particularly enjoys talking about the trips she took when she was much younger, often with her husband, my grandfather, before they had my father in the picture. She loves that Arthur seems genuinely interested in what she has to say, but often apologizes for monopolizing the conversation. Arthur scoffs and says, "Just because you're *ancient* doesn't mean you don't have anything valuable to add to the conversation!" and he laughs. Hannah One knows his ribbing is all in fun, and simply laughs along with him. They sit in the garden, admiring the new perennials that Owen has planted along the back wall. Two old friends soak in the warm air, both feeling grateful for the day. Arthur turns his head as Claire appears through the side garden gate. She holds her hands together, close to her chest, sheltering something within her grasp. She has a pensive look on her face. "Is Mom around?" she asks, glancing towards the house. Arthur shakes his head and says, "She went into the store to help Jason with a delivery." Claire visibly relaxes as she approaches. "I just don't know what to do..." she trails off as she reveals a small kitten sheltering in her hands. Its fur is dark chocolate, with orange-mocha flecks running up from its nose, and along its body. The small eyes that blink at them are dark glossy pools of black with a sliver of green in the centre. It cowers inside her hands, fear making its body rigid. "I wish I knew what to do, I found him in the field, by the school, all by himself." Arthur stands up and takes a step as Claire approaches. He stretches out his hand and attempts to pat the kitten, but it hunkers against Claire's body. Arthur's face goes soft and his voice gentle, "Poor soul. Not a great start to things." The kitten looks up at Arthur, some sort of understanding registering on its face. Claire lays her hand on top of the kitten's back and lightly pats it, asking Fae to reach out and try to alleviate the kitten's fear.

Owen approaches from the back of the garden, intent on filling a watering can from the hose to water his new plantings, when he spies Claire. He squints, trying to see what Claire is holding, and when he recognizes it's a kitten, his expression is tender. He comes over and looks at the tiny ball of fur nestled in his daughters' arms. "Ooh, who do we have here?" Claire holds the little frame close to her chest, as she tilts her head, listening. A moment later she says, "Fae says the little one, who is male, goes by the name *OnanOff*. That is what his mother called him. She would say, you're *on and off* me all day, make a choice little one, and find a spot to curl up." And she smiles, bending to kiss the top of the little kitten's head. He blinks, still holding a look of confusion in his eyes. "Fae says he is very frightened. His mother had told him humans are not good, and not to go near them. Fae is trying to tell him we are safe." She goes silent, as if listening to the internal dialogue. Owen scratches his chin. "Well, this is a predicament. What should we do with OnanOff? Would you like him to stay with us?" She grins and nods eagerly.

Arthur laughs. "Good luck with your mother. You know how she feels about pets." Hannah One speaks up from her chair, about five feet away. "She had a dog, Fred, as a child. It was very difficult for her, and for my son," and she pauses to draw a breath at the mention of Hannah's father. "She had to walk him through losing the dog, as is the way of pets. She just wants to avoid having to relive that sort of heartache again. You know very well she loves *all* animals." She looks at Arthur, who was about to joke about something else, but decides to keep it to himself. Claire holds the little kitten close to her face and whispers, "we will love you and make a good home for you, I promise." She hugs the kitten gently, as Owen comes to rest his hand on the back of the little creature, who is beginning to purr. Claire says, "Fae says he seems okay with this arrangement. So, Dad," and she looks at her father with a sweet expression, "Can *you* be the one who tells Mom about OnanOff?" He groans, but nods in agreement.

OnanOff has proven to be a feisty little kitten. His timid demeanor has been replaced by a confident, cheeky manner that he makes no apologies for. He decided to share his story with me when he discovered he and I can communicate directly. He had lost his way by venturing out of the den his mother had created for him and his siblings. Some small humans found him and picked him up. They played with him, until a large human came along and told them to put him down and go home. Then he was completely alone, with no way to find his mother. That's when Claire found him.

His tortoiseshell markings are distinctive, and his eyes, now empty of fear, shine like green gems with flecks of yellow-gold. He sits on the front window sill, meowing at the small birds that tease him from their perches in the Birch tree outside. More than once I have had to explain to OnanOff the importance of leaving wildlife alone. It's a hard concept for him to learn, as he witnessed his mother hunt for food. Fae also explains to him that, as *wild* animals, it is Nature's intent that some eat others, but *domesticated* cats are not wild; and now that he's a housecat he has the complete care he needs, provided by his human companions, so there's no need to hunt. OnanOff half-heartedly agrees.

As Claire's sixteenth birthday approaches on December twelfth, I fret about what sort of party one organizes for a teenager. Fortunately, she herself has come up with the idea of combining the annual bookstore Christmas party with a celebration of her turning sixteen. Claire has made it very clear she does not want any gifts, but made the suggestion that if people feel like giving, she would be happy to see donations made to the local wildlife rehab centre. The annual Christmas event has been a staple of our family ever since that first party, years ago, when I bought the bookstore. All employees, past and present, make an effort to attend, along with many close friends of our family. Claire considers all of these people her extended family, so she is happy to celebrate with them.

I spend the morning decorating the living room with Christmas ornaments, and a banner that reads *Happy Birthday!* When the living room and dining room look sufficiently festive, I go to the sideboard to pull out the traditional Casey family Christmas tablecloth. The white cloth is looking a bit dingy now, but the red and green garlands are cheerful. Since it's part of our family history, I am not about to ditch it just because it's looking a bit old. I search for the large bundle of cloth napkins we'll need for the crowd, when my hand comes to rest upon the beautiful, hand-stitched tablecloth Shelagh made as a wedding gift for Owen and me, over sixteen years ago. I catch myself choking up, looking at the beautiful care that had been used in stitching the various small animals and flowers that adorn the hem and in the centre. A brief moment of guilt passes through my mind; I feel badly for not having kept in touch with Shelagh, after Dad died. He was the only connection between us, not having had time to develop much of a relationship ourselves, and so when he died, I found no desire to hold on to her. At the time, I believed that part of me wanted to let go of her as she served only to remind me of a life that my father would no longer be able to enjoy. I pull the tablecloth out of the drawer and decide it should be used, not hidden away. The painful emotion once attached to it is now replaced by gratitude for the gift she had so lovingly crafted for us. I spread it over the card table that serves as the dessert table. The small animals and butterflies, bright and jolly looking, make me smile.

Claire and Owen are in the kitchen busily making a few hot dishes, as well as finger-foods for people to munch on as they arrive. The house smells delicious, and I can feel my stomach growl in anticipation.

The first to arrive are Jamie, Mark and his husband Brian. Jamie, who has been separated from Neville for over a month now, is living with Mark and Brian while she sorts things out. She looks very thin, with dark circles under her eyes. She smiles, but the energy I once saw in her face is diminished. I assume her separation is the cause for her unhealthy appearance. Her son Aidan, now over seventeen years old, decided to live with Neville, so Jamie said she left them at their house, and is now staying with Mark and Brian for a while. She and Mark have forged a special bond over the years, remaining staunch supporters of each other's antics, for which I am so happy. I have been a fair-weather friend, at best, to Mark. Jamie and I both agree that life seems to be constantly pulling us in different directions, so our friendship is stretched and challenged much of the time. Yet we never totally give up on each other, and I count that a true gift.

Cindy and Jason arrive together, obviously now a couple. Janice and her partner Amelia also arrive, carrying a large tray of sweets donated by Jon and Cristina from the Sit N Sip, who, unfortunately cannot attend. Then Nouri walks through the front door, carefully guiding his aging mother inside. His dear grandmother, Nasrin, had passed away three years ago, which Hannah One found particularly hard, as the two of them had become good friends. Nouri is a busy professional now, but still keeps his family as a priority. After settling his mother in a chair, he goes back out to his car to retrieve his contribution to the pot luck, a spicy vegetable dish with rice. As he is exiting the front door, Angela Barry steps inside, a teary smile on her face. I have not seen Angela for quite some time, since she moved out of my mother's condo. She went on to find another job in a long-term-care home. She waves as Janice calls to her. I walk over and embrace her, tears touching both our eyes. I rub her back gently, and offer her some hot apple cider to chase those sad thoughts away. She smiles and nods, then follows me into the kitchen to greet other friends.

Arthur and Grace are the last to arrive. Arthur slowly makes his way to the living room to greet Hannah One. She has saved a seat beside her, just for him. After he makes himself comfortable he takes hold of her hand, like a pair of lovesick teenagers. Arthur leans in to whisper, "Can you believe our Claire is sixteen?" He smiles at her. "It can't be true, as you and I are still such spring chickens!" Hannah One laughs, "More like chickens with our heads almost off!". The pair cackles. Grace emerges from the kitchen with a cup of cider for him. "HO, can I get you some cider too?" Grace uses the same affectionate nickname as Arthur does. HO replies, "I think, my dear, I would actually like a wee glass of sherry. I think this is a special celebration, which means kicking our heels up a bit!" Grace smiles and returns to the kitchen to ask Owen where the sherry is hiding.

The house hums with life. I can feel myself fill with the energy of those around me, and I know everyone else feels the same. I glance over at Owen, who has just pulled the sherry bottle out of a cupboard near the refrigerator. He catches me looking at him, and smiles. It is the same smile I remember the first time we met, when Hannah One dragged us across the street to have coffee together at the Sit N Sip. The same eyes that looked lovingly at me, as butterflies danced around my head in the conservatory. I want to reach across the room and touch his face, feel his skin, kiss his lips. I love this man, more than I thought possible. His *being* is etched into my soul. His Light beams into my heart, warming and infusing it with his love. I never expected myself to be so emotional, so fraught with silly sentimental feelings; but then again, I chide myself, isn't this part of being human?

Eight

I look at the sky to find the Sun, but she is nowhere to be found. It begins to rain, not water droplets but, feathers. Tiny black, white, tan and grey feathers. They are small, delicate, like eyelashes of an elephant. They swirl like snowflakes in the wind. As I watch the feathery droplets descend I spy a magnificent Hawk sitting on a tree branch. His breast feathers shine tawny and white, while long tail feathers show ribbons of gold, black and brown. His eyes afire, blazing amber under long dark brows. He holds within his massively sharp talons, a Mourning Dove. Its eyes blank with death, its feathers pouring down from its lifeless body, like leaves falling from an autumn tree. I gasp in surprise, to see Death in such a primeval way. I feel my pulse race. The Hawk perches, holding its prey, endlessly decanting its life, to fall away to nothing. His sharp beak opens and words flow from it, as water from a faucet. "We are all in the Circle. One feeds upon another, who has fed upon another. Nourishing our bodies, yes, but also our Light, as we feed on each other's energy. I am Nature's Tool; one which she utilizes to keep Balance in Life, to help maintain the equilibrium. Where one passes into the Light, another can live. Balance. Human ego displaces Nature's Tools, creating a world in which imbalance and illness thrive. Pollution, disease, chaos; all human Tools that upset equilibrium of both the Spirit and the physical body. One has only to look closer to find that an imbalance festers in one dear to you."

I wake up and stare at the white painted bedroom ceiling, wondering what hard lesson is about to become my next mountain to overcome.

When I arise in the morning, the first thing I do is check on Hannah One. Now, approaching ninety-nine, it is a daily blessing to have her still with us. Although sharp as a tack, her mobility is becoming an issue. We decided that she should take over the sunroom as her bedroom, thus eliminating the need for the stairs. We dedicated the main floor bathroom as hers alone, and Owen bought a large wooden wardrobe that he placed in the corner of the dining room, to house what clothing she needs most regularly. Hannah One was very upset at first. She hated to think of the disruption this would cause within the house, but it was Owen who took her aside and said quite plainly; "I'd rather deal with a bit of disruption, than to have you tumble down the stairs. So that's enough of that." He hugged her gently and continued to rearrange the sunroom to accommodate the bed. Hannah One is stubborn, but not stupid. Once the furniture was all in place, she announced that she likes having her bed in a room with lots of windows overlooking the garden.

I turn my attention to Claire and Fae. Telling them about my vision of the Hawk, Claire looks troubled, saying that maybe it's not that I need to look at other people, but to myself. She frets that there is some health issue I am ignoring. The only way to appease her concern is to make an appointment with the family doctor for a physical. Fae mulls it over and concludes that there is something to be said about keeping an eye on those we love, and that it is possible that someone is in need of our help. That comment leaves me worrying anew.

Tonight, as I curl up with Owen under the covers, staring up at the same blank ceiling I gazed upon this morning, I slip my arm across his chest, and gently pull myself closer to him. His breathing is regular and even, as when you are relaxed, but I really have no way to detect if he has an ailment. Deciding to be honest, I tell him about my vision from the night before, and ask if he is feeling alright. He reaches across my body with his strong arm and caresses my shoulder as he responds, "I'm fine. Fine. Maybe a bit sore from lugging the wardrobe around, but otherwise I feel good. I know men over the age of fifty start to get *stuff*, so if it makes you and Claire feel better, I'll call the doc tomorrow and get a checkup too." He hesitates before saying, "You don't think it has something to do with Hannah One, do you?" I feel him swallow. I'm not sure what to think, but it doesn't help to have both of us worrying, so I reply, "I don't think so. For some reason it just doesn't seem like I'd get a vision about something we are *already* aware of and watching. No, I think it's someone else." Owen does not reply, and his breathing leads me to believe he has already started to drift off to sleep, leaving me alone to chew on my worry.

After Owen and I both receive a clean bill of health, I am left wondering if I have misunderstood the message. And as life starts to carry us along on the roller coaster once again, I keep telling myself I will look into this more closely, when I have some time. Claire, now a high school graduate, has decided to take a year off, to study, of all things, natural healing, with Grace. Arthur has suggested that Claire and Fae might learn more by observing and interacting with Grace, since she herself is a healer. The idea does not go over well with Owen, and even Hannah One has her reservations. "My dear, how do you plan to make money, support yourself? Will there be job opportunities for you after this training?" Always thinking of the practical side of issues, Hannah One makes a good point. Claire's response, using the affectionate nickname Arthur coined, "HO, I have my whole life to make money, earn a living. Right now, I'm eighteen. While I still live at home, with few expenses, I want to explore my options, and maybe make better use of *our* healing talent." She refers to Fae's ability to heal combined with her empathic Talent. She continues, "If we can help one person, then that's great. But if we help hundreds of people, that's even greater! Do you remember being my age? Did you know what you wanted to do for the rest of *your* life?". Claire smiles, and Hannah One nods, "Yes, I suppose you've got a point. Eighteen is young. When I was eighteen, I thought about getting married, having children, learning to cook for my family and keeping a clean house. Many women had professional careers, and I was envious of that. My parents just wanted me to find a good man and settle down. I was lucky I did find a wonderful man, your great grandfather. But I often wonder what it would have been like if I'd had a career of my own." Hannah One had taken on a job at a local flower shop, when my dad was a teenager, and she needed to find something to fill her days, but a *career*, for instance, as a doctor, or an architect, was never in the cards for her. She looks wistful, something I have not often seen in her. It makes me sad. To reach this age, looking back and wondering *what if*, knowing there is no way to turn the clock back, seize the opportunity missed the first-time round, right the wrong, make different choices. I don't think Hannah One has any regrets, but that may be wishful thinking, as all humans carry regret, whether they are aware of it, or not.

Owen is off for the summer break, and begins to wonder if he wants to continue teaching. He has been attempting to write a memoir about his time in Africa, but it has been a slow process. Between the teaching curriculum, marking tests and projects, and the rest of the family, it leaves him little energy to devote to writing. He also said the memoir would not be complete without another trip to Africa to follow up on the projects, and see how they have withstood the test of time. He would not even consider a trip right now, as he hates the thought of something happening to Hannah One, with him half a world away, unable to be there for his family. He would not leave the one person in the world that makes him believe he's a good *son*.

Today Claire begins her apprenticeship, so I offer to drive her to the Centre for her first day. By mid-morning it's hot, the air heavy with humidity. It's the kind of day that makes you want to forget about life, and simply sit under a shady tree, or in front of a fan. I plan to go to the bookstore to get organized for an upcoming sidewalk sale event, but first I can dovetail driving Claire to the Centre and delivering a book Grace had ordered. I also just happen to like catching the energy that circulates within the Centre and storing it inside me as I face the day. As we enter the front door, I find the air suitably cool, though not that hyper air-conditioned, *I need a sweater,* type of cold air conditioning. Claire makes her way to Arthur's room first, as Fae wants to ask him something about past life regressions. Grace appears to be busy with a client, so I sit down in the alcove, thankful for the respite from the outside heat. When I hear a familiar voice, it startles me and I look up to see Jamie following Grace out of the treatment room. Her face is pale, thin, and her body looks frail and delicate. I have not seen her for a few months, only having time to call or text. I had assumed that once the school year was over, we might have more time to get together, as Jamie would have the summer free. She sees me sitting there and a frown crosses her face. Then it's quickly replaced by a small smile. Grace quietly says to Jamie, "I'll go book the next session, while you talk with Hannah." She disappears, leaving us looking at one another, neither certain of what to do or say next. Jamie blinks and places a weak-looking arm across her torso, pain swimming across her face. It shocks me to see her like this. She slowly comes over and sits down in the large chair across from me, leaning her head back and closing her eyes for a moment. I am so shocked by her appearance I have no words.

Still with her eyes closed, Jamie whispers, "Guess you're wondering why I look like death warmed over? Well, turns out I haven't been too good lately. It's cancer." She opens her eyes to look at me. I see a small grey feather drift down from nowhere, to vanish as quickly as it appeared. Jamie, not having seen any vision of a feather, continues to look straight at me.

"What? How... I mean Jamie, why didn't you tell me? I can help..." I stumble over my words, still finding my way around my emotions. She sighs, "Han, it's been a long road. Started just after your mom died. I found a lump in my breast. Been trying to do chemo and radiation; it's been a tough climb back. I just couldn't add to your plate, telling you about it, after losing your mom and all. I just wanted to get this looked after, and get on with life. It was going okay, but I still need a few more chemo sessions, and it's wicked hard on my old body." My eyes fill with tears, but I fight them back. This isn't about how horrible I feel, it's about my dearest friend and her struggle. She continues before I can comment; "When I got the news about it being stage two, I left Aidan and Neville. I know it's crazy, but I didn't want my son to play nurse maid if I slid downhill. Neville needs to be there for him, help him through this, so that's what he will focus on. Neither of them are happy about it, but it's the way I want it. I can't see their faces full of sadness every time they look at me. I do see them every week or so, and Aidan texts almost daily, but I can't cope with *their* emotional reactions day after day and remain optimistic myself. I've got Mark and Brian, who are filling me full of good vibes every day." It surprises me to think of Mark stepping up and supporting his friend, but then I still retain this image of him as an immature free spirit, who just wanted to have fun. Obviously, I have greatly underestimated my friend. "He and Brian, who you know is a nurse, keep me eating, get me to treatments, and just plug me full of laughs to keep me afloat. It was just getting so hard to face the reality of it all, let alone tell you, my oldest friend in the world, that I might be, you know, on the way out." Now, as I see the tears streaming down her face, I stand up and rush over to hug her.

"Jamie, I'm sorry. I am so sorry. What can I say, there are no words... I just can't..." and then I feel myself cry. We hug for a few minutes before Jamie releases her arms and drops them back into her lap, her exhaustion ending our hug. I remain crouched down in front of her and take her hands in mine. Looking into her face I see the resolution there, but I also see the fear. She wants to be strong for her family and friends, but the uncertainty of her future must be agonizing to manage. "Are you getting help from Grace?", I look towards the office door, which remains closed. "Well, Grace is giving me some relief, especially those first few days after treatment, when she comes to Mark's house and does her number on me there. We are doing a lot of positive visualization and affirmations, Reiki, and some herbal supplements to hold down the nausea." She looks away, and sighs, "Never thought it would be like this. I figured we would be sitting in some old folks' home, bitching at each other about shit, you know..." she wipes her eyes with the back of her hand. I stand up and take the chair next to her. "Jamie, we can sit and bitch now, why wait..." and I try to smile as she grins back at me. I do not try to assuage her fears by quoting survival rates. I want to respect her feelings and not dismiss her fear of dying by prattling off statistics, as that will not alleviate the trepidation she feels about her *own* journey. My heart breaks into a million pieces as I look at her. Realizing she doesn't need my emotions on her plate as well as her own, I take her hand and squeeze it, saying "You know you have another optimistic friend here to help with anything; you know I am your number one fan!" She grins and some of her pallor fades.

Claire walks into the alcove and when she sees my face and then sees Jamie, she bursts into tears. She comes over and hugs Jamie, no words needed for her to sense what is going on. Jamie hugs her back. I look up to the ceiling, trying to clear my eyes, and see the expression of the Hawk, unblinking, benevolently staring down at me.

Week after week I go to visit Jamie at Mark's house. Although I try to visit during the week, Saturday afternoon is always a good day for me to have a longer visit with her. We sit out in the garden, or just curl up on the couch, drinking tea and talking about things, or watch a movie. I am delayed today, as I have to stop in at the store to check on how the two new employees, Azeer and Brenna, are getting along. Jason and Cindy are now managing things on the weekends, which allows Janice more time off.

When I arrive at the house, I find Brian and Mark in the kitchen, busily preparing some sort of healthy lunch for all of us. Mark indicates that Jamie is in the garden. Surprisingly, as I walk out the back door, I see Claire sitting beside her. I knew that Claire had been joining Grace while doing sessions with Jamie at the healing centre, but I didn't know she was helping Jamie on her own. They are not talking, or even moving. As I approach, I see that they both have their eyes closed. I take a seat in a lawn chair near Jamie. She lies on the lounger, a wool blanket covering her body. Although looking better, with a slight weight gain, she still looks thin. Her face has a slightly healthier glow to it. She has always been slender and athletic, having taught physical education during her teaching career. I realize that those intense athletic days are forever past her now. She could return to teaching, but her vibrant energetic *physical* style will be compromised by this disease.

I close my eyes and attempt to add my energy to the session of healing. My energy is not nearly as powerful as Claire and Fae, but it will count for something when added to the whole. I feel myself drift, and when I open my eyes to the scene before me, I see Claire and Fae sitting on the green grass beside two Coyotes, who, while growling and yipping, roll on to their backs and playfully nudge at them. Laughter rings throughout the garden, like a chorus of wind chimes caught by a teasing breeze. Then I see Jamie, come crawling out from behind a lawn chair, mock growling and howling at everyone. She raises her hand and swipes at the air with a pretend paw. She growls as she looks around for pretend prey to pounce on, and seeing me, calls out, "Hannah! Awesome! Come join my dream! This is such a wild trip! I can't believe this…" and she waves her arms around at the scene. She wears a smile that reminds me of when we were young and life seemed to hold so much promise, even in the face of challenge. She was always the one who looked at the positive, found the silver lining in the cloud and kept the optimism from leaking out of our youthful balloons. Then I hear music. It's a tune I am very familiar with; Jamie's favourite Beatle song that describes our relationship: *Two of Us*.

Two of us riding nowhere, spending someone's hard-earned pay, you and me Sunday driving, not arriving... On our way home, we're on our way home... you and I have memories, longer than the road that stretches out ahead...

I feel the tears in my eyes as Jamie stands up and comes over to me, giving me a hug as she sings, "You and me, we're on our way home..." She laughs and dances her way over to the Coyotes, who are lying on their sides, panting from play. Claire and Fae sit holding hands, energy radiating out of them like a furnace. Jamie sits down and begins to pat one of the Coyotes. He looks at me as his voice playfully tickles my mind; *Time to let go, Hannah. Time to play.*

When the session concludes, the three of us, still sitting in the lawn chairs and the lounger, open our eyes. Jamie smiles, looking like she's just eaten the best dinner of her life. Claire stands up, walks over to her and touches her face. It is maternal gesture, like one you would expect to see a mother give her child. But Jamie accepts the tender caress without hesitation. Then she closes her eyes, and slowly falls asleep. Claire motions for me to follow her into the house, leaving Jamie alone to rest. Just before we reach the back door, I gently ask, "Does Jamie *know* about, you, or us?" Claire just smiles, saying, "Mom, she is a very open Light, as I'm sure you know. She is accepting of you more than you realize. She's happy to know that *Fae and I* exist, out of Time, and Space. She would be okay with you sharing your truth, too." She looks back at the sleeping figure. "It's up to you, but as life throws us in so many directions without prior warning, you should not miss any opportunity to be honest with her. You may be sad in the end that you walked past this chance." She turns and enters the house. I can hear Brian's voice announcing that lunch is ready and waiting. Claire's exact comment is not audible, but her tone is appreciative for the spread laid out.

I glance back at my dear friend, now resting comfortably under a large Poplar tree, as it leans over to protect her from the sun's hot waves. The birds chime a song that weaves their visions of life and travel into rhythmic refrains. The flowers seem to glow more colourfully, and I wonder if Fae has helped them blossom so vibrantly. Feeling like I ought to heed Claire's advice, I promise to open my true self to Jamie at the first opportune moment.

NINE

I enter the front door to the sound of David Bowie playing on the record player. *The Rise and Fall of Ziggy Stardust* blares out of the speakers. Hannah One is giving another one of her lessons to Claire on *classic* music. She has quite an eclectic collection of records, which includes several of Bowie's albums. Claire is familiar with many of the artists who are the cornerstone of rock in the 1960's, including The Rolling Stones and The Who, but Hannah One wants her to hear about *all* the pillars that made a generation tune in and turn on to such incredible music. I drop my bag at the door and settle in the big arm chair to listen to *Suffragette City*. Claire is moving her body as she sits and listens to the songs. Hannah One rocks her shoulders to the beat, as she soaks in the music, feeling the rhythm right inside her Light. Seeing the two of them sharing a love for music, and other arts, is a gift, and reminds me of those treasured days my dear grandmother and I spent together when I was young.

As the record player clicks off after the final song, I rise and walk over and give each of them a hug. "This is a great way to come home. Seeing my two favourite people enjoying Bowie. Doesn't get much better than that!" I laugh. It feels like humour is harder to produce within my body these days. It's harder for me to spontaneously find humour in things, as Arthur does. I need to revisit the image of the Coyotes, telling me I need to play more.

The Human Experience

As Claire selects the next album, discussing with Hannah One whether it should be Tony Bennett or Pink Floyd, I shake my head at such diverse choices, then walk over to the dining room table with the intention of clearing off Hannah One's sketch pads and pencils, so we can get ready for dinner. All of a sudden, I have the urge to sit down and sketch. It's been years since I turned my attention to drawing or painting, always finding life's towline dragging me along with no respite. I open the large sketch pad and leaf through page after page of Hannah One's sketches. Flowers, birds, and little whimsical-faced animals like chipmunks and squirrels, adorn each page and make me smile. I come to a blank page and find myself picking up a number six pencil and moving it around the paper. The lead of the pencil slides over the slightly coarse paper, giving the image substance and depth. The image in my head is that of a bird, a Chickadee. Then I add a branch for her to perch on, and then the branch becomes a tree. It seems like I am being pulled into the drawing, the act itself blocking out the world, and there is only me, the pencil and the paper. The Chickadee wears a cheery expression and I can almost hear her singing.

Claire comes over and stands behind me. When the pencil finally stops moving, she leans in slightly to get a better look. "Oh Mom, that's wonderful! You need to do more drawings." I laugh, and turn my head to reply to her compliment; "When I retire and have time to burn, I will draw, and maybe write and paint. All things that take focus and energy. Right now, I should see if dinner is anywhere near ready. I'm starving!" I stand up and leave the pad open on the table, feeling reluctant to close it as I walk away.

Jamie is so much better after another two months of recovery time, that she's decided to move back home with Neville and Aidan. Her husband is relieved and happy to have her back, and Aidan is glad that his mother is on her way to feeling healthier. He plans to attend university in the fall, after having taken a few years off to "chill". They will have a few weeks together, before he packs up and moves to Ottawa. Claire has continued to visit with her twice a week. I was all set to have a heart-to-heart with her, but the timing never seemed to work. It was either that Brian or Mark was within earshot, or she was too tired, or had another doctor's appointment. It always seemed like there were road blocks between us.

Jamie called Claire this evening after dinner, and asked if she could borrow some of the creative writing she had produced when she was younger. Claire had told her about the stories she had written, and Jamie thought she could incorporate some of her stories into classroom lessons, as she felt they might inspire other would-be authors to try their hand at writing their own stories. Jamie has been offered a part-time assignment, teaching English to grade nine students. Part-time teaching is not necessarily a common opportunity, so Jamie is happy to be offered the chance to get back into it slowly.

It isn't long, maybe three weeks, before Jamie calls Claire once again. The tone of the conversation is enthusiastic and I'm curious to know what they are discussing. Claire is wandering around upstairs as she talks, so I only catch every other word before she disappears into her room again. It isn't until after the end of the conversation, when I hear Claire thunderously run down the stairs, that the holes in the conversation get filled in. "Mom! Mom, you won't believe this! I'm so excited, I can't breathe!" She stands for a moment as she turns a bit green, not from nausea, but from Fae stepping in to help calm her down. She takes a deep breath, as I wait eagerly to hear her news.

"Mom, oh crap, this is just so exciting!" She paces into the living room and finally I grasp her hands to get her to stand still. "Claire, tell me before you faint or I die of curiosity!" She laughs, taking a seat on the couch. "Okay, so, you know Jamie has been reading my stories, and she loves them! So, she has a friend, I can't remember the guy's name, but this friend works in publishing. She reached out to him to tell him about the stories, and he might be interested!" Her voice is becoming so loud, Hannah One enters the room from her sunroom-bedroom to see what all the noise is about. I need more information before I can reach the level of hysteria Claire is at. "So, you're telling me he wants to publish your stories?" She shakes her head, "No, no, it's that he's *interested* to see them, to read them, which means a foot in the door. Isn't that exciting?" She looks from me to Hannah One, who sits down with a puzzled expression on her face. "Dear, can you start at the beginning, I'm still trying to catch up to the exciting part." Claire groans, but after a quick rebuffing look from me, she sits down beside Hannah One and says, "Well, Jamie took some of my stories, you know the ones I wrote about Fae and me, well... she told her friend, um, Larry something, or Gary something... about the stories, and well, anyway, he works in the publishing business. I guess he's interested in reading them!" She stands up again, and jumps up and down a few times. As she is jumping, OnanOff enters the room and gets his tail stomped on as he passes by her. A loud caterwaul brings Claire up short, and she kneels down to comfort the irritated cat. She scoops him up and attempts to cuddle him, but he is still so annoyed he squirms, and succeeds in freeing himself from her grip. He leaps down and runs out of the room.

Claire sits down again, a bit of her steam escaping as she looks in the direction of where OnanOff had disappeared. Then she turns and looks at me, "Oh, and Jamie had a brilliant idea! She thought it should be illustrated. So, when we were talking about that, I told her about your drawing, and she said she recalled you used to draw and paint a lot when you were, well, you know, *young*." She said the last word as if saying it was going to hurt my feelings. At fifty years of age, I still *feel* young, even though the streaks of grey that ribbon my hair might beg to differ. She continues on, "I think it would be amazing, incredible and so, so, so great to do this together!" Her energy is once again at full throttle and she stands up, but does not attempt to jump around again.

Hannah One has a huge grin on her face. "What a marvelous idea Claire! I love it!" She smiles at her great-granddaughter, a gleam in her eye. The thought crosses my mind that *she* should do the illustrations, but after seeing how unstable her drawn images have become, more impressionistic than anything, I wonder if it might be too big a project for her to do. Then the proverbial light came on over my head. "It has been a long time since I've drawn animals, or people. I'm very rusty. I would consider it, *if* I have a Creative Director helping me. What do you say, Hannah One?" I smile at her, a memory of the two of us, as a young girl and her grandmother, sitting at the kitchen table drawing or creating art projects, blinks across my eyeline and then fades back into the past. She smiles; a smile full of appreciation for being included, for being reminded that she is still needed, valued, and loved, after ninety-nine years on this earth.

Ten

With Owen choreographing things, we form a creative outline for the logistics of the book. We decide to focus on a series of three books Claire has titled, "Fanny and Fae: Nature Detectives." When she was younger, Claire had written stories about Fanny and her "imaginary" woodland friend, Fae, and their quest to solve some of Nature's most interesting mysteries. With the help of another friend, Oggie, who sounds an awful lot like her father Owen, they uncover many fun and fascinating facts, while having a wonderful time using their imagination to its fullest. The two main characters in the story delve into a pond and become tadpoles, or take to the sky as birds. They climb the highest trees as squirrels and curl up in a rabbit's burrow to nap. These stories are particularly dear to me, as they remind me of the many times we ventured into the woods to explore and appreciate the beauty we found there. Owen volunteers for the role of Technical Director, providing the facts that will be sewn into each story, which will add an educational element to it. Hannah One and I discuss the illustrations at great length. We need to plot out the story panel by panel, and circle the key words that inspire the illustrations for each page. We leave it at the point where Claire starts to work on the actual storyline details, with advice or input from us when asked for.

Friendships are one of the most inconsistent things in human existence. We go through life, meeting other humans and connect with some, but not all. These connections, on average, can last a few months, years, or decades. We fit together at junctions of our lives, then move on when we are no longer attuned to each other. What once seemed like a thread that held a friendship together, is now too thin and breaks, or is untied, as the individuals grow in differing directions. It is rare and most treasured, to find the thread of a friendship that withstands the pull of Time. I am so grateful that my relationship with Jamie is strong enough to have withstood Time, and thrives, as we mature. I watch Claire go through a similar process. She was popular during her school years, but most of those friendships never stretched past the end of high school. I don't worry about Claire having friends, as she knows herself well enough to see when a relationship is worth the effort to maintain it or not. Then she met Lilah.

After meeting at one of Grace's meditation groups, Lilah has become a true friend. Her blond hair, green eyes and slender figure made me base my assumption that she is very popular, with many friends, but I was wrong. Lilah possesses a quiet self-assurance, and a quick-wit. She is very perceptive, and discerning in the friendships she cultivates. She and Claire seem to fit well together.

When Claire mentions that she is going to Lilah's house to sleep over with a few other girls, I think nothing of it. It wouldn't have been my choice, at her age, to stay over at a friend's house, but then I had ignored the idea that this can be a fun part of growing up as a human. Saturday afternoon rolls around and she leaves the house with a small overnight bag. "See you tomorrow!" She chimes as she heads out the door. Owen waves, not lifting his head from the mountain of assignments he's grading on the dining room table. I cheerily wave from the kitchen doorway, and call out, "Any trouble, just call us; we're here!" Claire groans as she shuts the door behind her.

I enter the dining room and stand behind Owen, who still has his focus on the essays. I lean over and wrap my arms around him, planting a playful kiss on his earlobe. "Hey you... wanna get lucky?" I laugh. He drops his pen and grabs my arms, pulling me around to end up sitting in his lap. He kisses me on the mouth, soft at first, but then with more fervor. He breaks the kiss long enough to ask, "What about Hannah One?" I glance back to the kitchen, knowing she is reading in the sunroom with a cup of tea, and a slice of home-made banana bread. "She's busy with her book right now." Owen stands up, takes my hand, and together we quietly race upstairs to our bedroom.

The house seems oddly empty without Claire and Fae's energy around. I know I need to get used to a shift in the vibration of our home as Claire gets older and will, at some point, want a place of her own. The three of us have a nice quiet dinner, and then Owen goes back to his papers, Hannah One settles in to watch some television, and I clean up the kitchen.

Feeling somewhat tired, I decide to head to bed earlier than I usually do. Owen kisses me goodnight as I once again, lean over his frame. After all these years he is becoming very weary of the extra work involved in teaching, and repeatedly talks about the idea of retirement. Part of me would love to see him retire, yet I wonder what he would do to fill his days, when connections to a youthful world are no longer integrated into his daily life. I lay on my back, trying not to think anymore; allowing my muscles to relax, my breathing to slow down, and my thoughts to unwind themselves, and become silent for the night.

I feel a cold nose nudge my hand. I look down and see a Fox sitting at my bedside, looking at me. His oval yellow eyes blink. "Hello. Are you here to deliver a message?" I ask, without surprise. After years of animal spirits coming to me, nothing surprises me anymore. Or should I say, very little surprises me.

"I am Fox. I am the Guide to enter the Fae Realm. My Spirit is one that walks *between places*, so I know the pathway to the Fae. I come to call you on, as one who needs to comfort another." I sit up in bed. "What do you mean? I need to comfort someone?" I feel confused. He blinks again, patiently answering; "You need only walk with me, and it will become clear, as I guide you forth. The In-Between beckons us onward." He turns and lopes out of the room. I get out of bed and follow.

As I leave the bedroom, a giant door appears before me. It's like a curtain, made of Ivy and Grapevine, laced with Morning Glory, red and white Clover, and yellow Cinquefoil, among other wildflowers. It is a work of art in itself. The vines move very slowly, almost like snakes, and the flowers lift their heads as I come closer. The Ivy begins to change colours, from glossy variegated green to autumn gold, to iridescent silver-gold. It is mesmerizing. Then the door fades; it does not actually open for the way to be clear. Fox gambols through the entranceway. I cautiously take a few steps, trailing behind the red-furred creature. He turns and says, "We enter the Fae Realm, where one resides who needs you. I will show you the way." He continues up a dark trail. All around us, tiny specks of light float and dart as we pass. I look around and see a feast of colour, with Black Eyed Susan flashing brilliant yellow petals; several Amaranthus draping their long furry pink fingers down in graceful waterfalls; Coleus borders the pathway, and gently touches at my senses. The scent of Lilac, Hyacinth and Lavender tickle my nose; and the path itself is cushioned by soft mossy patches that feel like tiny little pillows holding my bare feet aloft as I tread lightly along. The Elder trees seem to lean as we near them, but only in a curious manner. I feel no fear, for this is but another layer of existence, another province of the living, that dwells within Space and Time.

Fox stops and looks into a small glade. It is shaded, with Alder, Birch and Hawthorn trees ringing the border. In one corner, curled up in a ball on the ground, lies Fae. Encircling her is a bed of flowers, Gardenias, Hyacinth, Marigolds and Chrysanthemums. All the flowers have small fragments of speckled light pouring out from their colourful petals. Fox whispers, "Flower Sprites are trying to console and heal her distressed Light." I rush over and kneel down, careful not to damage any of the flowers. I can feel her fear. She looks up, yellow-green eyes flashing panic, as I reach across the bed of flowers to touch her. "Hannah, you have come. I sent Fox to bring you here. I cannot move, I cannot breathe, I cannot see, *her*." When she says "her," I immediately feel the panic grip my throat. "Has something happened to Claire? Why can't you see her?" Fae lies in a pool of her tears, the wetness soaking through her leafy skin. Tiny fairies begin to circle her head, emitting a strong healing energy as they alight on her arms and legs. "She has closed the door. I cannot see her. I cannot talk to her. I am once again behind the curtain that was open, but cannot pull it apart to find her. But I think you can…" I swallow. Is she asking me to dream-walk into Claire's mind? I vowed never to intrude into anyone's thoughts after having accidentally drifted into Owen's memory, and almost ruining my relationship because of it. I never want to invade someone's private memories or thoughts again. Fae, sensing my hesitation, says, "Hannah, you can do it without her ever being the wiser. Fox is the Master of Camouflage. He knows the artistry of shapeshifting. You will not be breaking your word of dream-walking by entering her mind and knowing her private thoughts, if you simply *hitch a ride* with shapeshifting Fox to view the scene. She needs help. *You* must help her." Fox is still sitting by the edge of the glade, watching with eyes that glow like small gold orbs.

I cannot think straight. My daughter seems to be in trouble, and Fae cannot get to her. Yet I wonder if this is the best course of action. I turn to Fox, who stalks closer, his bushy tail swaying horizontally as his hind quarters move. Fae glances at Fox and whispers, "You can trust in my guide; he will not fail you." Fae reaches out with her hand and places it over mine. I gulp, deciding that, despite my reluctance, if I can *check* on Claire without intruding directly into her mind, I must find out what is going on. I stand up, and turn to Fox. He nods, saying, "Good. You know what must be done. Your senses must reach out and touch your aura. The energy field around you is what gives you away. By adjusting your frequency and intensity, you will harmonize with the scene around you. This is a different type of walk than what you have done before. This walk merely allows one to be *witness* to events in the *Now*; it is not a memory, not an image on a door to visit; And most importantly, it is not an invitation to explore the private thoughts of those in the scene we witness. We are but shadows as we blend into the fabric of the landscape around us. I *am* the Master of Camouflage. I will help you cover your tracks. As you enter the scene, place yourself against the background, and focus on becoming one with it. Just as I fade into the brown-green of the forest, so too will you fade into the woodwork of a room. Pour your energy into the shape and colour of what will hide you, and you will become that. Do not worry, I will guide you if needed."

    I take a deep breath and open my mind to find Claire. A long dark tunnel becomes my focus. Then I find myself stepping through into a room. It's dimly lit. The sound of music blasts around me. I quickly find a wall, and, as Fox sits down beside me, we begin to blend into the beige paint. I slow my breathing, and focus on becoming the paint. I look down and see my hands disappear. I feel like I am here, but not here.

    I look around the room, and see Lilah. She is sitting on the floor, laughing, with a bottle of beer in one hand. A young man sits across from her, taking a hit from a joint and then passing it to Lilah. The music is so loud it's hard to concentrate on being camouflaged. Then I see three other people enter the room, all weaving and stumbling around, obviously drunk, or high. They are laughing about some unheard joke. Lilah yells at one girl to sit down and shut up, which seems to cause more laughter. Then Claire enters the room, holding a vodka bottle. She takes a swig directly from the bottle, spilling drops on her shirt and the floor. She stumbles across the room to sink down on the edge of the couch. She starts to talk, addressing no one in particular; "Shit, this is good! Should've done this long ago. Too much *being good*, isn't good!" and she laughs. Lilah tries to grab the bottle from her, but Claire holds on to it, "Nope, nope, mine, bitch! All mine, no *sharsies*! I'm so tired of sharing! I want my own stuff, my own mind, my *own* mind..." she trails off as she takes another gulp from the bottle, and then leans back into the couch until she is lying horizontally. A scruffy-looking boy staggers over and sits down on the couch, placing his hand on Claire's leg. He runs his fingers up and down her leg. She laughs, but then swats him away. "Fuck off Jared! Just get off! This is my time, for me, myself and me!" Then she laughs again, dropping the bottle off the side of the couch to spill on to the floor. "Shit! What a waste!" she shouts. She glances over in my direction, and squints her eyes. "Oh fuck, is that you? Why are *you* here? You furry little beggar!" I look down and see Fox grin, showing all his canine teeth. His voice in my head whispering, "You are the wall, you are the paint, but she is allowed to see me, so she can be reminded of who she *truly* is." Fox prances up and down beside me. Claire laughs, all the while her friends glance around, wondering who she's talking to. "Fox, why don't you tell Fae to go have her own party tonight! I wanna be left alone!" She tries to stand up and stamp her foot in an attempt to chase Fox away. He simply sits down and continues to look at her. It's Lilah, who, seeing her friend getting angry, says, "Geez, Claire, have another blast! Just relax, you're getting a bit weird." Claire looks at Lilah, and once again laughs. "Weird? You don't know weird... get in my head, it's always weird. Fuck am I drunk. *That* Fox needs to leave." And she points to the spot on the floor by the wall, where the invisible fox sits. Everyone laughs, thinking their friend is baked, or drunk and is now seeing things.

I'm not sure what to do. I cannot step in and reveal myself, as that would clearly be a violation of her privacy. She is, after all, almost twenty, and it's her body, her life. But, as her mother, I find her reckless behaviour both heart wrenching and infuriating.

Why did I come here, if I can't do anything? As I watch, she tries to sit down, but then suddenly leaps up and races to the kitchen. The sound of her vomiting in the kitchen sink is barely audible over the music. I realize that it's not my place to do anything *here*. I hope she will reconnect with Fae when this is over, and then, together, we can talk about how she is feeling. I don't need to tell her I witnessed this display tonight; I can merely explain that Fae was worried and reached out to me.

As if Fox can hear my thoughts, he utters, "Remember that it is better for you to remain in the background, and exert your influence without direct interference. She will not be receptive to directives. *You* are the Fox and must use stealth and camouflage to hit your mark, or you will be defeated by your hasty movement. Her struggle is not yours, but you can relate; and it is through this link that you will stand upon common ground, and go from there." I drink in every word Fox says, and know that if I'm hasty and say something too "motherly" it will only serve to make matters worse. He's right. By opening up about my own struggle for balance between my Alternate and human selves to her, I may be able to show her the support she needs, without trying to manage it *for* her.

Most teenagers go through a rebellious stage. I just assumed that Claire had avoided that. She has been so mature, so well balanced all these years, I had no idea she is struggling. As much as I dislike seeing her this way tonight, it's the wake-up call I need to see her in a more realistic light; not as the perfect daughter who has it all under control. I wonder if my mother ever had this revelation as I went through my own teenage years. A brief flash of memory arises as I feel my head fill with drunken fuzziness, in a darkened bedroom, making a bad decision with a boy I didn't even know, that almost cost me a piece of myself. The memory makes me feel vaguely nauseous. My focus wavers slightly, and I know I have to leave this scene or be discovered. I look down at Fox and he nods.

I am back at the vine-and-flower curtained door, but I want to see if Fae is alright. Fox whispers, "Fae is with her kind, and will find respite and love to heal her hurt feelings. She is young, and needs to learn the depth and complexity of human emotions, and how to bend like the flower, to the winds of her human's emotional state. This is but one more step on her journey. Nonetheless, she has hands to hold that will guide her along." The vines begin to move, and I feel myself being pulled out of the doorframe, to be left standing in the upstairs hallway of my own house.

The morning light awakens me from a dreamless sleep. It is still very early, but I feel like getting up. I make my way to the kitchen to make a pot of coffee, and meet Hannah One as she enters from her sunroom bedroom. We smile at one another, both happy to have a quiet Sunday morning to ourselves. Owen, sleeping soundly, will not likely rise for another hour or so. Hannah One sits down at the kitchen table, waiting for the coffee to brew. "I hope Claire had fun last night with Lilah. She needs to have fun; she is so focused on the book these days." I weigh the idea of telling her about my time with Fox, and decide to tell her the whole thing. She will have a good idea about how I can broach this subject to Claire, without causing World War Three. "Well, as it happens, I know exactly how much fun she had last night." Hannah One's eyebrows rise. "Oh no, Hannah, you didn't spy on her, did you?" I nod, but before she can scold me, I continue, "It wasn't like that. It was at the behest of Fae. Okay, it's a bit of a long story, so let me pour our coffee and then I can fill you in."

After a long discussion with Hannah One, we both agree on one thing; keeping Owen in the dark about his daughter's reckless behaviour is the best way to proceed. He has a tendency to overreact, and I could see him storming over to Lilah's house to confront her parents, who, I would later learn, were away for the weekend. He might also tell Claire she has to stop being friends with her. He may judge her for being a *bad influence*, whereas I don't really blame Lilah. It's a familiar scene for teenagers to experience overindulgence of alcohol, as I remember all too well. I don't condone this behaviour, but I also know that using heavy-handed tactics to stop this, doesn't stop it. It only forces it underground and possibly into riskier scenarios. I decide to heed Fox's advice and approach Claire from an angle that will not appear to be interfering or nosy.

When she finally drags herself through the front door, it's after noon. She looks pale and her eyes are half lidded. Recalling the one and only time I was hungover, I have a bit of sympathy for her body and its ailment, but not for Claire herself and her stupidity. She leaves her bag on the floor inside the door and puts her hand on the railing to help her up the stairs. She has not bothered to say hello, or even acknowledge that she is in fact, home. I call out from the dining room, "Claire? That you? Good, glad you're here. I have a question for you and Fae." She sighs heavily, and takes a few steps backward, but only enough to stick her head through the doorway. I know she is longing for her bed and what comfort it may provide her abused body, but I'm not going to let her go before seeing if she has reconnected with Fae. "Just wondered if you and Fae could look at these new drawings, see what you think of the expressions. Am I getting them right?" I hold up my large sketch pad, a series of rabbits in pencil filling the page. She swallows, and I wonder if she might vomit right then and there. Instead, she merely blinks her swollen eyes and replies, "They look fine. I'm sure they're good. Gonna go lie down now, not feeling well." I stand up and try to approach her, but she starts heading to the stairs. "Oh dear, that's too bad. Does Fae think you're coming down with a cold or something?" Playing dumb is not my favourite thing to do, but if I want to keep my spying expedition a secret, I have to follow this line of deceit. "Oh, for god's sake, Mom! Just leave it be! I don't know what Fae thinks, I don't want to know right now. I just wanna go to bed!", she says angrily and stomps up the stairs. Her raised voice makes Owen appear from the kitchen. He and Hannah One had been making lunch. "She okay?" he asks. I shrug my shoulders and causally reply, "Hard to say, but maybe it's *that time of the month.*" Owen nods, unwilling to ask any further questions. He turns and goes back to talking with Hannah One about their sandwiches. I return to the dining room table to look over my sketches. I will let her rest, for now, but later I know I need to talk to her more directly. I fear she has severed her connection to Fae forever, and the thought of our dear little sprite being cut off from us is more than I can bear.

I glance at the clock and it reads three fifteen. The afternoon sun shoots long, pale yellow rays across the floor. I feel like having a cup of ginger tea, and wonder if Claire might benefit from one as well. I take a hot mug upstairs to her bedroom. I knock, but receive no reply. I gently open the door, and find the room fairly dark with the curtains drawn. She is lying on her bed, curled up on her side, hidden under her comforter. I see my little girl again, as a young leafling, nursing her cold, wanting Mommy to make it better. I feel sad that the little girl is no longer here, that my days of being *the mother who made things all better* is no longer one of my roles. I swallow the lump in my throat as I enter the room. "Hey, Claire bear. How are you feeling? I brought some ginger tea that might help you if you're still feeling a bit sick to your stomach." I approach the bed as she slowly rolls on to her back. She looks tired, and the paleness of her skin leads me to believe she still feels miserable. I place the mug on her bedside table and sit down on the edge of her bed. She does not protest the intrusion; she just squirms around until she is sitting up. She reaches over to grasp the hot mug. She takes a tentative sip, and finding it too hot, begins to gently blow on it. "Is Fae helping heal you? I wish I could help you feel better, too." I place my hand on her leg, which is still warmly entombed in her comforter. She looks at me, but doesn't smile. "Fae is busy right now. I can handle this." I reach out with my energy and sense such a void in Claire's Light, it makes me sad. She looks down at her cup, "I just want to be alone for now. I'm fine, I think I just ate something that didn't agree with me, or something." She utters unconvincingly. I look away, pretending to be casual as I reply, "Well, maybe you should see the doctor. Food poisoning can be pretty bad. I don't want it to get any worse." She finally sips some tea, and then sighs. "Mom, I'm okay. I just want to sleep. Can I just sleep some more?" She places the mug back on her bedside table and wiggles down so she is fully enveloped in her comforter again. I reach out and pat her shoulder before standing up. Knowing I'm not going to get anywhere when she feels so awful, I decide to leave it for now. Fox said that Fae is being cared for, so I have to assume she is safe in the Fae Realm. I just need to find a way to make Claire okay in *this* realm.

Owen asked about Claire again at supper time, when the three of us sat around the kitchen table. Hannah One knows the reason why Claire feels so horrible, but she says nothing. I nonchalantly reply, "I checked on her a while ago. I think she has some pretty bad cramps. I took her some ginger tea, so now she's having a sleep." He seems content enough to hear that it isn't anything serious, and lets the matter drop.

As I distractedly eat my meal, only half-listening to Hannah One and Owen talk about gardening or something, I keep trying to formulate another way in which I can get through to Claire. My mind seems unable to create the subterfuge necessary to draw her out, and then Arthur's mischievous face pops into my thoughts.

After helping with the dishes and getting Hannah One settled with an evening tea and her favourite television show, I text Arthur to fill him in on the situation. I stress the fact that this is a secret, not to be talked about with Owen or Claire directly. He often misses the subtle cues about discretion, and blurts out news before thinking it through. This is one time I need his mouth to remain shut. He texts back that this is not something he can give a text answer to. It's too complicated for his fat fingers to type out, so he will drop by in the morning for a visit. I'm not happy about this answer, but since Claire will likely sleep through the night, there is no point worrying about a possible plan of action until tomorrow. I text Arthur to drop by after breakfast, as Owen is heading out to school early to prepare for a new class, and I don't have to go into the bookstore until lunch time. He sends a big smiley-winking face emoji as his only response. I sigh and hope he will provide me with more help than that.

The old clock in the hall chimes nine as Arthur arrives, cane in one hand, a large box of doughnuts in the other. "I knew you'd have the coffee pot on, and since I've had a hankering for these darn doughnuts lately, I thought I'd give *all* of us an early morning sugar rush!" He hands the box over to me as he unfastens his jacket.

I didn't realize that Claire was going to be home, as normally she would be at the Centre with Grace. She must have called in sick. She hasn't put in an appearance yet this morning. "Claire is still asleep upstairs, so we will have to keep our voices down. Let's sit in the kitchen so we won't be overheard, hopefully." Arthur grins, and places a finger to his lips and says, "Shhh…" I am not amused.

Hannah One already has a seat at the table, and a cup of coffee in hand. When she sees the box of doughnuts, she laughs. "You've been saying how much you wanted a maple dip doughnut lately! So, you gave in to your hankering." I place the box on the table and as Arthur takes a seat next to Hannah One, I pour coffee for him. With my back to him, I sarcastically comment, "You should probably skip the sugar in your coffee, just dip your doughnut in there, and you'll get all the sugar you need." Arthur frowns. He was told to watch his sugar and salt intake, which he tries to do, most of the time. "Just wait till you're old, Hannah, and someone tells you not to eat something. It's all you want to eat after hearing that!" He flips open the lid of the box and, after proffering the box to Hannah One, which she declines, he reaches in and picks up one maple dip doughnut and takes a large bite. Hannah One laughs, saying, "Remember to savor it, Arthur! It will be in your stomach soon enough, and you'll be sorry you didn't appreciate it in your mouth longer!" He frowns. He takes smaller bites after that, and then reaches in to try another flavour of doughnut that nestles in the cardboard box.

As we drink coffee, and watch Arthur scarf down the doughnuts, we quietly discuss the situation regarding Claire. I feel like the best solution is to come clean and tell her the truth. Arthur finally speaks up after his final mouthful of doughnut is swallowed. "Claire and Fae are like sisters living in the same bedroom. It was all well and good when they were little, and think it's fun, but as Claire grows and becomes an adult, it's not so much fun. Siblings will argue and fight, especially when they are in close quarters. I think Claire is deciding she needs her own space, like her own bedroom. We need to help her find her own space, without cutting Fae out of her life altogether. There must be a compromise for them. But I agree that truth is always the best route to resolving things, even if it means hurt or angry feelings."

Hannah One nods. "I think Arthur is right, but I worry about how Claire will react to hearing about you seeing her with her friends." At that moment, I hear a voice in the hallway. Forgetting that Claire has footfalls as quiet as a ghost, I didn't realize she had descended the stairs to stand in the hall and listen to our conversation. "You did *what!?*" her angry voice bounces off the walls.

She enters the kitchen dressed in jeans and a sweater. She looks directly at me, avoiding Hannah One and Arthur, who are both attempting to say something to calm her down. "I can't believe you spied on me! How could you do that? You said you'd never spy on anyone in the family! So, you meant everyone *but me*? It's none of your business what I do with my friends, with or without Fae!"

She stands there staring at me, and the expression *'if looks could kill'*, finally becomes very clear to me. Her fists are balled up, and I wonder if she's going to hit the wall, or maybe even me. I am so shocked. I have a hard time formulating a response. Arthur stands up and speaks in a soothing tone; "Claire, we can see how angry you are, and rightly so. You must be so mad that your privacy has been violated. If you let us explain, then maybe there is a way to mend this breach, so it never happens again. You need to know that what your mother did was out of love and concern for Fae, but also, for you. You are her Light, and she would do everything in her power to help and protect you. If you will just give her a chance to explain..." He seats himself again at the table, and glances at the box of doughnuts.

Claire, still standing like a rigid metal pole, loosens her fists. She glances at Hannah One, who smiles encouragingly at her, but remains silent. She looks again at Arthur, who wears a kind smile, and tilts his head towards the box on the table, indicating she can help herself to a doughnut. She glances at the coffee pot. Without a word, she pours herself a coffee, and leans over the table to pick out one of the remaining treats. She stands, leaning against the kitchen counter and says, in between mouthfuls of doughnut, "Well? I'm listening."

I know this is my cue to start explaining myself, but I am dumbstruck. Never having my daughter so angry at me before, it takes me a minute to get past the venom that I still feel clinging to my face. Arthur reaches across the table to pat my arm. Taking a deep breath, I start to explain, beginning with the arrival of Fox.

As I conclude, I add, "I'd never, *ever* want to violate your trust by dream-walking in your life. Fae was very worried that you weren't *safe*. I just wanted to make sure you were okay. When I was your age, I went to a party and got drunk, and things went *very* badly for me. My naiveté was my downfall." I gulp as a brief image of a dark room, and the pain I experienced, flashes through my mind. "Once I saw the situation you were in, I was afraid the same thing might to happen to you. I only stayed a moment, just to make sure you were able to take care of yourself. Fae was so distraught; I began to imagine the worst scenario." My eyes well up, and I feel the tears flow down my cheeks. The final sting of humiliation from that trauma rears its ugly head, as I lay myself bare to my daughter, so she hopefully, can understand my perspective.

Claire's expression softens the minute she sees my tears. She takes a few steps to lean over me slightly, placing a hand on my shoulder. "Mom, I'm sorry *you* had a bad experience. But you aren't me. I wouldn't get into that sort of situation; I just know it." I look at her and flatly say, "I was certain I'd never get into *that sort* of situation either, but I did." My tone makes her stop short; her youthful self-confidence shaken somewhat. She straightens up and returns to the counter to drink her coffee.

"Well, it still doesn't change the fact that I need privacy. I love Fae, but she's in my back pocket all the time, day and night. I don't think I can even have a dream without her watching me." Her voice has an edge to it. "I just want something of my own. I always have to share it with the voice in my head." Arthur nods in agreement. "I get what you mean, Claire. Your mom and I have spent our entire lives trying to balance our human aspect with our Alternate side. Constantly hearing the opinion of one side versus the other can be so tiring. There are things we can do to help you and Fae get a better balance, without shutting her out completely. I'm sure, when you search your heart, that there are times you're glad she is there with you." Clare hesitates to agree, firm in her stance on the issue at hand. "I need privacy so I can do things, you know, you know, have friends and like, go on dates, that sort of thing, without her talking at me or watching as I want to, maybe, kiss someone, stuff like that." Her cheeks flush slightly. I am beginning to wonder if the catalyst for this change is, in fact, a new relationship.

The Human Experience

"I think Arthur is right. There is a way to keep her connected, while allowing you time to have, uh, well, friendships, or whatever it is you want." I had less trouble talking to her about human reproduction when she was a child than I am now, as an adult, with the reality of her engaging in sex crossing my mind. Arthur stands up and excuses himself. Hannah One decides to rise as well, feeling like this might be a conversation best completed between mother and daughter. She heads off to her room to read. I sit there, gripping my coffee mug and thinking I'd like to put a whole doughnut in my mouth so I could avoid talking any further.

Claire sits down where Arthur had been sitting. She places her half empty mug on the table and looks at me. "Mom, come on. You must know I'm like, old enough to do *things*. I don't fool around though, not like some of the other girls I knew in high school. I've met someone, and he's special to me. I know it's right; it just feels right. But Fae is worried, and I think she feels left out. She keeps an eye on me when I really just wanna be alone with David."

David, so the unknown love interest has a name. It's the first time she's ever told me about someone she has feelings for. I watched her through high school, and wondered, at times, why she wasn't being all silly and lovestruck, as her friends were. I assumed she was rising above the adolescent infatuations, and with Fae's help, was simply learning more about who *she* herself is as she grows up.

"Fae is my best friend, and I love her. I'm just mad at her right now, because she doesn't like David. She needs to stop interfering and let me have my own life." Her tone makes me recall what Arthur had said about siblings arguing. I take Claire's hand in mine, and chose my words carefully. "Claire, I think Fae might have just been trying to look out for you, like all siblings should. She doesn't understand why she can't be a part of this aspect of your life, because she doesn't know any better. She has always had you there with her, and so she's hurt by this sudden banishment from your life. Isn't there some way we can compromise, and still have her in all our lives, but allow you times for uh, private stuff too?"

Arthur re-enters the kitchen and peers into the doughnut box. "Honestly, Arthur how could you even think of eating another one?" I scold him. He grins, as he picks up a chocolate covered pastry, "Easy, I'm not thinking about it at all!" Claire stands up, taking her empty mug over to the sink, and then turns to address us both; "Okay. If you two can figure out a way that Fae can stay with me, but leaves when I ask her to, then I will agree to try it. But one of you has to tell her to stop referring to David as 'that guy'! He has a name, and she needs to respect my choices in life." She spins around and leaves the kitchen, racing back up the stairs to her bedroom.

Arthur and I look at one another. "Well, okay, now what?" I ask. Arthur scratches his chin, concentration causing a deep crease across his forehead. "Well, since Claire has not opened herself up to Fae again, we have no way to talk with her about this whole mess. We need to see *if* Fae is willing to go along with this new arrangement. She may very well decide she prefers to be with her Fae brethren, and not bother with us at all." I feel saddened to think of life without Fae, even in the background. She is like a daughter to me, like another child I love deeply and want to continue to include in our family circle. Arthur traces a finger on the tabletop, while he squints, as if looking for something just out of his focal range. I still have no ideas, so I simply sit and wait for Arthur to percolate more of his thoughts. He suddenly taps the table with his outstretched finger, and exclaims; "That's it! Yes of course, it's so obvious, why didn't I see it sooner?!" I lean over and ask, "What? What's so obvious?" He smiles. "I have been trying to think of a way to reach out to Fae. She is in a realm I know nothing about. I have my ideas, but I have never actually traveled to the Fae realm. But *you* have. It will be imprinted on your door. We need only visit your door, and you can touch the memory to allow us to connect with their world. Simple!" He claps his hands together.

"Simple? I guess so, I just don't know if it will work. And how does that get Fae back to Claire?". Arthur stands up and stretches. "Oh no, this won't re-link the pair of them. That will be up to Claire. She will have to open that door, in her mind. But this will get *us* to Fae; to be able to talk with her, and see the lay of the land, so to speak, from her perspective. No point in presenting anything to Claire until we know Fae will agree to abide by her wishes." That makes sense, so I nod. Arthur continues, "Okay then. Shall we begin?" I blink. "What? Now? Um, I guess so." I glance out into the hall at the old clock. It reads ten-thirty. I had planned on getting to the bookstore around noon. By now, Janice is so accustomed to me floating in and out, I think she'd scarcely notice if I never came in. I stand up and look towards the living room. "Fine, but I'm tired of sitting at the table. I want to relax in a more comfortable chair. But first, I'll tell Hannah One what we're doing, so she won't freak out if she sees us comatose in the living room!" Arthur laughs and turns to head into the living room, where he takes a seat in the large arm chair in the corner.

I poke my head through the sunroom door and announce, "Arthur and I are going to see if we can connect with Fae. We'll be in the living room, so don't worry if you see us looking like a pair of space cadets." Hannah One laughs. She has her latest novel in her hands, and appears engrossed in her reading.

I walk into the living room and take a seat on the couch. A sudden exhaustion makes me lie down. My body is so fraught with the tension of the morning, I could lie down and not wake up until it's time for bed. I close my eyes and take some deep breaths. I start to descend into the place I like to float in where I'm not touched by trouble or care. I see Light around me, and feel the immense energy that is Arthur, swirl around my own Light. We float upwards, in search of my door.

I blink, and find myself, and Arthur, in the hallway, with my door in front of us. "Does this ever get boring for you? Taking others to their doors?" Arthur shakes his head. "Each time is unique. No two doors are alike, just as no two human experiences are alike. It's like viewing an ever-evolving work of art; every time you go, you expect to view the same painting, but the artist has changed or added some element that makes you gasp anew at the beauty that is *a life*."

I turn to look at my door, now over half full with images. The final image on the door is rimmed with dark light, as my face holds the pain of hurt caused by my daughter's anger. I shift my gaze away, preferring instead to focus on the image next to it, where Fox's pert little face is captured. I reach out and touch the picture, and then Arthur and I find ourselves in front of the vine door.

There is no Fox this time. A large rose appears in the centre of the door, and looks at us. She blinks a few times, smiles and the door fades, revealing the trail I walked on my first visit. Arthur wants to say something, but I hush him. This is not the time for levity, and any questions he has I know I cannot answer, so he needs to be patient. We walk carefully along the mossy trail, while small Finches and Swallows fly around us, their whispering wings fluttering tales of the forest we do not understand. I glance around and see dragonflies as they hover over the flowers, their stain-glass wings capturing the light and breaking it into colourful prisms that dance all over the grove. Brilliant butterflies sit on branches of the Alder trees, tending to the many chrysalises that hang down from each branch, their fragile antennae waving their energy to each of the cocoons.

We come to the glade where I had found Fae on my first visit. The spot where she had been lying is empty now, but I sense she is not far away. I look into the Birch trees, but they are empty. Then I spy a large Lilac bush, the fragrant flowers dark purple and shimmering with Light. Under the bush sits Fae, along with two other smaller Fairies who, upon seeing us, stand up and fly away. Fae looks over and seeing us, stands up and races over, her arms open wide.

"You have come again! I am so happy now! Can I go to Claire? Did she not come along with you?" She looks around, as if Claire is hiding behind one of us. I take one of Fae's delicate petal-like hands and we sit down upon a blanket of olive-coloured grasses, with little tiny yellow flowers that blossom throughout. Arthur sits down beside Fae, his old body agile and free of pain in this realm. He has an awed expression on his face as he says, "Fae, my darling Fae. We are happy to see you too. As you can see, Claire isn't here. Hannah and I came to visit you, and see how you are feeling." A cloudy expression crosses Fae's iridescent face. "I was sad, and now the hurt grows in my heart, where I would weed it out, but I have no tool to do so. Claire was so angry; I don't understand how to feel like that. I do not embrace feelings in the negative, for it serves no purpose. Conflict cannot be resolved by negative emotion. Only Love and Light help heal the gash created." She is sounding a bit more like an Alternate now, and I wonder if she has been mentored by the Fairies.

Arthur takes hold of her other hand as he replies; "Fae, human emotion is complicated. When a human is mad, this anger clouds the Light, and makes it difficult for them to see their way forward. They think the anger fuels their motivation towards resolution, but in reality, it does the opposite, and takes them further away from the answer." She nods, but says nothing, looking slightly confused. I look at Arthur who has been trying to explain things so carefully, yet I sense Fae is not grasping the meaning of his words. I look into her beautiful eyes and say, "Claire is growing up, as are you. She is starting to feel the need to be independent. She wants a connection with you, but she also wants her freedom, to have a life of her own, without sharing it all the time, with you." Fae's face wilts, and Arthur squeezes her hand as she glances at him. I continue, "This is not to say she never wants to be with you. She loves you and misses you now, as a matter of fact. But a change has to happen, so she can have her life with a bit privacy, when she asks for it." Arthur sighs. "Fae, what Hannah is trying to say is, Claire wants you back, but she wants to be able to ask you to *skedaddle* when she wants some privacy, you know, with David." Arthur winks, expecting Fae to read between the lines. She frowns. "Oh, *that guy*! He is always there, wanting to touch her, or talk to her, and she ignores me. She never ignores me when Lilah's around, or any of her other friends. We have been together *all* the time, but now she wants me to leave." She drops her hands in her lap and starts to cry, and her tears, as they drop on to the ground, make the tiny yellow flowers close up, protecting themselves from the sour drops.

Arthur reaches over and hugs her. "Oh, my, Fae. Now we can't have you crying, that won't do. You are frightening the flowers." She blinks her yellow-green eyes, and looks down at the flowers who begin to peek upwards, hoping the sad flow of drops is now contained. I raise my hand to Fae's cheek to wipe some of the tears away and gently say, "*You* are a beautiful Fae creature with your *own* Light. You only need to recognize this, and you will find your existence more rich and joyful. You are fortunate in that you have a home *Here,* with other Fae creatures in this beautiful realm, and you may also reside with Claire, when the time is right. It's up to you and Clarie to find a compromise. You just need to understand the balance she is asking for. It will be much better for both of you, believe me."

Fae looks around her, a small smile on her face. "I do love it *Here*. My friends are familiars, so we connect perfectly. I miss Claire, but I would also miss my Fae family if I couldn't spend much time *Here*. A balance between the two would be nice. I could do that. Be *Here*, when Claire wants to be with *that guy*," and she smirks. "I mean, *David*. I can fly with the birds, swim with the nymphs, grow with the flowers, and still be with Claire and my human family, all of whom I love so very much!" She reaches out and hugs me tightly. I never imagined such a lithe little creature to have such a strong grip.

Eleven

Two of the most vital parts of my marriage to Owen is trust and honesty. We have been through so much pain and uncertainty, that these have become unspoken essential elements that keep us together, so I know it's impossible to keep the situation between Fae and Claire a secret from him. I decide however, to present an edited version of the truth. He doesn't need to know about my dream-walk and that Claire had been drunk with her friends. He will simply learn the truth about Claire and Fae needing to make space for each other.

Upon hearing the news about Claire's declaration for independence, he reacts pretty much as I expected he would. He's pleased. Although he has tried, over the years, to like Fae, and understand the relationship between his daughter and this creature from a super nova, part of him has always held on to a sense of uncertainty about Fae's motives or intentions. He out and out refuses to actually meet Fae, ever. Arthur said he could arrange it through a mutual memory shared by the three of us, of when Fae arrived. Owen declined, stating that he does not need to meet her. It just doesn't feel *right* to him.

Arthur confided to me that he believes Owen is reluctant because he is embarrassed to meet her. He said the male ego is fragile, and Fae having "entered" his Light through his sacral area may have something to do with it. I laughed at the absurdity of that suggestion, but Arthur continued by saying, "Picture yourself accidentally walking in on your father in the bathroom. It's awkward, and embarrassing, for both of you. Then the awkward stuff continues, when next you see each other. Social norms dictate that there are certain things we keep private, like going to the bathroom, undressing, having sex, that sort of thing. Now, mind you, I know humans who leave the bathroom door open, don't care who sees them naked, and get a kick out of having sex in front of others, but that's not the norm. Owen is, primarily, a shy, prim kinda guy. He may feel like Fae has not only seen the insides of his private parts, but then passed through them when you guys had sex! That is enough to freak anyone out, but especially Owen!" I wanted to dispute his expression that Fae had been inside his penis, because, strictly speaking that's not accurate, but I know the point he was making. After twenty years, I find it hard to believe Owen is still feeling self-conscious about the fact that Fae was attracted to his splintered Light, and found a way in to help him. So I don't push the idea, nor does Claire. If it's meant to happen it will happen.

Once Claire hears that Fae is willing to work with her to give her more space, she opens her mind back to Fae. I knew the minute Fae returned, as Claire's sallow appearance disappeared, and was replaced by her usual rosy glow. Fae told Claire all about the new realm she lives in, and said that she will be happy to sequester herself there when needed.

The world seems to right itself once again, and is turning on an axis that makes everyone happy. Almost everyone.

I hear my phone chime as I get a text from Janice, asking if we can set up a meeting to discuss the bookstore. I am planning on going in today, so I text that I'll be there shortly, and we can have a meeting right away. The Christmas season is a very busy time, but when I enter the store, there is only one customer browsing through the children's section. Janice and Cindy are at the front counter talking, but, seeing me come through the door, Janice quietly says, "Can you keep an eye on things, Cindy? I'm just going to talk with Hannah for a bit, in the back-room." Cindy nods, and smiles at me as I pass by. The store, so well-manicured and bright with Christmas decorations, seems warm and inviting. I'm a bit surprised there aren't more customers in the store, but then sometimes they come in waves. You are super busy for an hour, and then nothing. I assume this is a *nothing* phase.

Janice and I sit down at the small desk in the tiny back room. She taps the laptop to bring up a display on the screen. It's a chart. I glance at it, but don't really understand its significance. Janice points to the screen and says, "It's not good Hannah. I've been looking over the numbers, and we're losing business, and it's not changing. I've been keeping track of this for a few months now, and I see a downward trend in sales. We have to make some changes, or we can't stay afloat." She frowns.

I am shocked by her statement, but then I have not been paying enough attention over the past year to really notice the decline. Janice has been running things so well, I just assumed it was all on track. She continues, "Lay-offs are inevitable I'm afraid. We just don't need six people to run this store anymore. We can't afford it. We can't even afford to bump up the inventory. I think we should just sell what's on hand, and then see how the year-end totals look. Hannah, I'm sorry, I tried. I think that between the big box stores and on-line shopping, we are becoming obsolete." Her chin trembles, and for the first time I realize how much I have left Janice to manage all this, without enough support from me.

"Oh, Janice! I should be the one to apologize. I should've been more involved, given you more support a long time ago. You just seemed to have it all in hand. I kinda left it to you. That was awful. Poor you, trying to figure out everything on your own." I feel the tears come to my eyes. Janice takes a breath, unwilling to give in to her own emotions, "I saw how you were dealing with your mom's passing, and then Jamie's illness, and having to care for Hannah One. I just thought I could somehow turn it around, but it's come to a point where, as the owner, you have decisions to make that as the manager, I cannot."

I glance at the screen, and see red lines spiraling downwards in the chart, and my heart spirals down as well. I can't think of what to do. I am not prepared for the idea of closing the bookstore. Janice stands up and squeezes her way by me, "I'm going to leave this with you to look over. I want to make sure Cindy is doing okay. She's feeling a bit of a cold coming on, so I may just send her home and take over the counter now." She closes the door, and I feel the walls of the tiny office close in on me. I close my eyes to keep the room from swallowing me up. I try to take a deep breath, but it feels like someone has a large hand wrapped around my lungs and is squeezing the air out of me. Panic covers my mind and blocks all entrance ways that reason could enter. I have never had a panic attack before, and if this is what it feels like, I hope never to experience one again. I take a long slow breath in and keep my eyes closed. Once I feel my heartrate go down, I open my eyes and reach over to open the email browser on the laptop and send the charts, and other information Janice has collected, to my personal email. I need a quiet place to study these documents before I can make any decisions about the way to move forward. After making sure the email has been sent successfully, I close the laptop and stand up. I feel dizzy and light-headed, and once again try to take in some air. I gulp what I can, still feeling like I am being suffocated. Keeping one hand on the back of the chair, I take a few more steadying breaths, and try to envision somewhere calm and pleasant. I see the Fae Realm. The colours and creatures blur before my closed eyes, but I don't need distinct images to feel the vast peace and equilibrium I experience when I am there. I attune my inner ear to my heart and feel a slight decrease in rate. I slowly breathe in, and for the first time feel my lungs fill. I hold my breath, and then slowly exhale.

After a few minutes, I pick up my coat and handbag and open the door. The cooler, fresh air of the store area helps revive me.

Cindy is still at the front counter, trying to convince Janice she should stay. I can't blame her; she probably needs the hours to help pay her bills. I can't think about Janice's comment regarding lay-offs as I stand there looking at them, so I walk towards the door, pausing long enough to make sure they have things in hand, and then say quietly, "Janice, I'm going to go over all the info you collected. I'll call you later, or more likely tomorrow, and we can talk some more." She nods, but says nothing, as she doesn't want to talk about the issue in front of Cindy. I step out into the cold December day, and take a sharp breath of frigid air. It feels like knives stabbing my lungs, but I hardly notice the bracing cold, as I walk along the street to my car, lost in thought.

I sit at the dining room table with the entire family, as we discuss the future of the store. I looked over Janice's income/expense statements, and other financial statements I had not paid enough attention to over the past six months or so. It's like a dam with a hole in it. You know that if you plug the hole in one spot, it may just rupture in another. Is it worth pouring more money into the business, if it is ready to burst and drown us in the long run?

A frown carves Owen's face, as he reads through the documents I had printed out. He is no financial expert, but he knows enough to give his opinion. Claire sits there, somewhat concerned, but a bit distracted as she looks at her phone while the discussion is going on around her. Hannah One sits with her hands folded in front of her, waiting for her chance to look over the papers. Once Owen places the papers back on the table, Hannah One reaches out, motioning for him to pass them to her. He leans across the table, handing her the six or seven printout sheets. She looks at them briefly, mainly focusing on the bottom lines, which are all printed out in red ink. I look back at Owen, but he seems deep in thought, and not about to voice his opinion. I can't contain myself any longer, so I speak up. "Well? What's the consensus? What should I do?" At this very moment I realize how much I miss my dad, and his calm rational business logic. He would have had ideas or solutions to this. I try to hear his voice in my head, but as each year passes his voice fades like a distant echo in a tunnel.

Hannah One is the first to reply; "Well, Hannah, I believe it is up to *you* what the next step should be. We can say close the business, or we can say sink more money in, but the bottom line is, it's your decision. *You* need to do what is right for you." I frown at her, "That isn't much help. I don't *know* what's right." She shakes her head, "Yes, you do, you just don't see it. You are letting a lot of emotional barriers hinder your actual view. Take away the emotion, and you might see it better." I continue to frown at her. I see the emotional obstructions very clearly. I have been connected to this bookstore for over thirty years; first as an employee and then for the past twenty years as the owner. I poured my heart into this store. It holds so many memories. It's the place I first met Owen. It's the place that my father and I jointly invested in, and he was so proud to see it continue to be successful under my care. There are a lot of barriers that I have to navigate in order to see a way out of this, one way or the other.

Owen finally speaks up; "It's a matter of finances at this point. It would involve either extending our line of credit, or taking out a business loan. Or it means dipping into our savings. I know there's money from the sale of your mom's condo, but you had that earmarked for retirement, and to help Claire, if she wanted to go to university. I think it comes down to this: how much are you willing to gamble, in order to keep things going?" Claire looks up at the mention of her name, but realizing it isn't a comment directed at her, returns her attention to her phone.

As Owen speaks, I begin to see the whole picture, from a slightly more objective viewpoint. He is right. It is a matter of deciding whether or not I would be willing to take money away from *our* future to save *my* present. Owen has no financial stake in the store, but he has money saved up in our retirement fund. It would not be fair to claw any of that money out and compromise his future security, let alone my own. A bank loan is not an option, nor would extending the line of credit. It's like the bank throwing a pair of water wings to me, the drowning person. Sure, it might keep me afloat for a while, but sooner or later the wings will lose their buoyancy, and then I'm back to drowning, and be in debt to the bank. I know I cannot bring emotion into this picture. It would certainly pull me under the water, and I'd lose all objectivity. "I don't think there is a viable option for keeping the store open." I feel the lump in my throat creep slowly up to my eyes, but I take a deep breath to keep from crying. "I'm not willing to sacrifice our future security for the store, when I truly believe it's on life support, and will not regain the life it once had." I stand up and leave the room, unable to say any more.

Janice's voice, as she answers her phone, is cautious. I say I want to meet with her again, but she says she would rather I "tear the bandage off quickly", meaning that she wants to know, without delay, what my decision is. "Janice, I'm so sorry. I've decided to close the store." I take a breath before continuing, so I don't choke up as the words come out. "I think we'll have a large closing sale to clear the inventory, and then the building itself will be sold, empty, as is." A picture flashes across my mind, of bare walls, a cold empty space where once there was so much love, so much community spirit. But I can't allow it to sink in. I find myself wanting to cry again, but I can't do that to Janice. She deserves more. *She* needs support now. "I wish I could tell you better news, but I think you know that this is the only option." Janice sighs in the heavy silence on the other end of the phone. Then, after I hear her blow her nose, she says quietly, "I thought I had prepared myself for this news, but the reality of it is still hard to take. You and I have been together at the store for so many years. I just don't know what's next for me, and that's a bit scary." Janice is also fifty-one, and the thought of her having to job-hunt makes me feel tremendously guilty. She coughs and sniffs a few times before continuing. "I am lucky though. Amelia has been promoted to regional manager, so she's pretty set, and can carry things, while I figure out my shit." I nod, then respond verbally. "I'm relieved you have support. You know of course that I will write you a glowing letter of recommendation, and if I hear of anything… maybe Owen knows of something, I'll let you know." We conclude our conversation talking about the staff, and a few other logistics about the close-out sale. I feel horrible, putting all these wonderful people out of work, but there is no other way out of this situation. I know the young people will roll with it and find other employment; it's Janice who has me worried. She is one of my dearest friends, and I want to help her along as best I can.

After announcing the news to the staff, Cindy and Jason offer to stay on and help with the final month-long inventory sale, but Brenna and Azeer opt to leave, so they can start new jobs as soon as possible. I know that between the four of us, plus Owen and Claire, we can manage the final leg of this heart-breaking race.

TWELVE

"*So, you think your life is complete confusion... because your neighbour's got it made... just remember that, it's a grand illusion... deep inside we're all the same...*"

    I wake from my coma-like nap, to hear the band *Styx* playing on the record player in the living room. Owen loves the song, *Grand Illusion*, as if it's an anthem to his life. The message is about societal brain-washing to buy more and to be more, with success based on material wealth, when the truth is, we are all the same. It strikes a chord with both of us. I sit up and stretch, feeling no less tired than when I lay down. I swing my legs over the side of the bed and stand up, feeling aches in my knees and lower back. I have not been taking care to exercise enough lately, and I'm feeling it now.

    Descending the stairs, I hear the rhythmic strains of *The Best of Times*, and peek around the corner to see Owen quietly singing the words as he sits and stares at his laptop screen on the dining room table. "The best of times, are when I'm alone with you..." Owen's baritone voice croons sweetly, and I feel myself melt a bit. He is not a great singer, but the emotion I hear in his voice is laced with his love for me. It makes me love him all the more. He has been trying to write his memoir for years now, and his mental process of: *play Styx and stare at the blank page until the words appear*, seems to be his go-to when he gets writer's block.

I quietly make my way to the kitchen to find Hannah One sitting at the table, a hot cup of tea in her hands. She has the newspaper spread out on the table in front of her. She glances up and smiles as I enter to turn on the kettle. "I hope Owen's music didn't wake you up," she says, as she glances towards the living room, a slight frown creasing her forehead. I take a mug out of the cupboard and measure out some loose tea into the strainer, leaving it perched on the mug rim, before coming to sit down at the table. I sigh and comment; "I don't think it matters. I didn't get much rest either way. I feel like I'm one hundred years old today." My grandmother chuckles, and when I realize what I said, I laugh too. "Join the club, kid!" she cajoles. When the kettle whistles I shut it off and pour the steaming hot water over the tea leaves. I reach into the cupboard for the cookie tin and place it on the table. It seems like all I do lately is nap and snack. Since the store closed, I find myself very lost, and exhausted from the emotional strain.

When the last day of the sale arrived, there wasn't much stock left, but what remained got packed up and sent to the local library, and the Voyager Class at the school Claire had attended, many years ago. When the place was cleared out, we decided to have one last party. Folding tables and chairs were brought in, pot-luck foods arrived with all those invited, and someone brought a large portable CD player to fill the empty space with music to lighten the mood. I was not in favour of this party, wanting only to be done with it all, shut the door, and cry. It was the staff and Owen who thought this would be a nice way to *celebrate* the store, rather than mourn it like a funeral.

All the staff, past and present, were in attendance. Arthur and Grace also joined the party, along with Jon and Cristina, who had the Sit N Sip across the street before retiring five years earlier. Their old shop is now a trendy clothing store. I felt great sadness the day I watched their sign being taken down, and watching all the chairs, tables and display cases being hauled away. I saw the place where hundreds of times I sat and had coffee, first with

Gwen, my parents, Hannah One, and then that fateful day when Hannah One invited Owen for coffee with us. I saw the day when I first began taking Claire to the shop for a treat after visiting the store. All those memories seem to float away with the sign being dismantled. Ironically, it's Hannah One who reminded me that my memories are not affixed to material objects here, but live in me, where I can view them whenever I want to. As much I as I know that material things are not what make a journey through life complete, I still feel the sense of loss as past landmarks that symbolize key points along my way are disappearing from my present.

It was a pleasant party, although a bit subdued. I could feel Claire and Fae sending me healing energy throughout the event, as I needed it. I appreciated the effort, because I believe it was the only thing that got me through that day. I am allowing myself time to grieve my loss, but I know I have to look for something new to focus on.

Owen enters the kitchen to pour himself a glass of water. "Oh, you're up! Good! Thought maybe we'd take a walk at the conservation area. I need to clear my head, and the walk would do us *both* good, I think." He has been so supportive all this time, never outwardly saying I need to pull myself together, but his false cheeriness grates on me. "If I want to walk, I'll walk. I don't need to be reminded of what's *good for me*," I snap. Hannah One draws her breath. "Now Hannah, Owen is just suggesting an outing. He wasn't saying anything else. If *I* got the offer to walk in the woods once more, I would not hesitate to go." Quickly I realize how selfish my statement was, and how thoughtless I'm being to everyone around me. I stand up, tea untouched, the tin lid still unopened. I turn to Owen and say, "Sorry. I'm just, well, tired, you know. I'll go put on my sweater, and we can go for that walk." I leave the room, but not before catching the triumphant look shared between Hannah One and Owen.

We don our boots, as early April can be very wet and mucky in the woods. The air is cool, and feels fresh in my lungs. There is no sun, only a blanket of grey, puffy clouds overhead, which seems to suit my mood. I watch my feet as we walk along, looking at the worn earthy trail, rutted from other hikers' footprints imprinted in the muddy soil. Owen, on my left side, walks silently beside me. I assume that he too, is caught up in his own thoughts. I know he is struggling with his writing, and now that he has decided to retire from teaching at the end of this school year, he feels more pressure to complete his memoir and do something with it. I know Claire has completed the writing portion of her book, and has been hounding me to complete the illustrations, so it can be passed along to a prospective publisher. We all have creative challenges ahead, but seem to be stuck.

Owen stops suddenly and I glance at him. He is looking over to the right side of the trail, so I follow his gaze and see a Doe. She is standing in a small clearing about fifty feet away. I smile to see her lovely gentle face. Owen leans closer to me and whispers, "Are you getting a message of some sort?" The peace I had found while looking upon the graceful creature is interrupted by his intrusive question. "Sometimes seeing an animal is just *seeing an animal*. You see her, I see her, she's just here, looking for food, most likely." My annoyed voice carries across the quiet glade and makes the Doe start. She moves back and blends into the woods behind her. Owen frowns and places his hands on his hips. "Okay, well, sorry I asked. You know, at some point you are going to have to stop being mad at everyone, and get on with your life. I'm getting a bit tired of being your punching bag." He drops his hands and begins walking again. I take a deep breath and close my eyes. Why can't I just stop being so emotional, so depressed, so angry? I immediately regret snapping at Owen. He is always looking out for me, and Claire, and Hannah One. He was my rock when my parents died. I need to crawl out of this hole I have dug myself into, and turn my sights on what comes next.

I quickly jog the space that has been created between us when he walked away, and take his arm. He stops and looks at me. There is no anger in his eyes, only hurt. Those beautiful blue eyes that hold love and light now hold the hurt I caused. I drop my hand but stand there, looking at him: His hair, dusty brown fringed with grey around the temples, his face still handsome and rugged, carrying lines from years of laughter and worry; and his mouth, a sad smile set upon the lips that have spoken lovingly to me through the years. I step closer and kiss him. It is a simple kiss, one that an old married couple might share as they walk out the door, or to greet each other in the morning. The familiarity of this act is not the important aspect. It is the unspoken communication of love that resides in their hearts for each other, come what may. Owen has a surprised look on his face when I step back. He smiles and reaches over to take my hand. We continue to walk the trail until we come to the small bridge that spans the tiny creek. The bridge where he declared his love, and produced a ring to show his commitment to that love, over twenty-one years ago. We stop and look around. The snow is still clinging to the far banks of the stream where the sun cannot reach, and patches of ice crystals still remain, like small frozen islands, on the slow-moving water. Dried brown and sand-coloured grasses and cat tails cling to the stream's edges, waiting to awaken again when Nature gives the signal. A few Juncos and Chickadees fly around and land in the Spruce trees on the far side of the icy stream.

I wonder if the descendants of Ol' Toad are sleeping in the mud, nestled deep below the stream's frozen surface, also awaiting fair weather. I can see Claire, perched on her favourite look-out rock, peering into the stream in search of water nymphs and tadpoles, her father by her side, equally as curious. I feel a tear in my eye, wishing for those simple, wonderful days to be here again. Owen stands close beside me and leans in. I feel his arms embrace me, and his voice close to my ear. "It feels like yesterday we were here with Claire, and now she's all grown up, and doing her own thing. I think we need to find *our* own thing now, the two of us. We're still young enough to enjoy this early retirement, so, we should make some plans. Maybe go on a trip or something." I lean back so I can see his face, while still maintaining our embrace. "You know we can't travel; I would never leave Hannah One, not now." Owen nods. "Of course, I didn't really mean *now*. I just think we could start thinking about things we might like to do, down the road, together." His expression indicates that he himself wouldn't want to leave my one-hundred-year-old grandmother for any length of time. I smile. "Yes, we could start thinking about things. I know you need to go to Africa. Maybe I can go with you, although I'd prefer to see more of Canada, like the Yukon." Owen frowns, and seems to pause a moment before speaking. "Yes, well, Africa would not be that great for you, as far as a holiday goes. I'd be working every day. To be honest, I'd prefer to concentrate on the work at hand, and not feel like I'd need to entertain you as well." I know he doesn't mean to sound harsh, but his words are pretty direct. "Oh, okay, no Africa. Fine, maybe I'll do my own trip when you're off saving the world." I try to sound glib, but my hurt is laced into the comment and does not slip past him. He takes my shoulders so I have to look at him and he says, "Han, we can have our own interests, and still be together. Just because I'd prefer to go to Africa by myself, doesn't mean that I wouldn't want to explore the Yukon with you. Or if you decided to go there without me, then I'd just have to revel in the experience through the re-telling of your adventures when you return. I don't want this marriage to always be about *us*, or *nothing*. We're still two individual people, with our own *journey*, as you put it, and sometimes that means going off on our own to explore that path. I want us to have things we experience together, but also things we do apart. That will strengthen us both when we come together again."

I look at him, and wonder what self-help books he's been reading. But what he says does make sense. If I tried going to

Africa, it would hinder Owen's experience, because he'd have to divide his attention between the projects he wants to focus on, and me. When I look at it from that perspective, it's not a trip I'd enjoy very much. I would not want to end up resenting all the things that pull Owen away from the two of us experiencing the trip together. That isn't fair to Africa, or Owen.

"Owen, you're right. I think that planning things that we can share together is a great idea, and planning things we do independently is good too. The more I think about it, the more I like it. It has been a tough time for me lately; I still find it hard to see my way ahead, but this plan gives me hope that I can see a few steps ahead, and that's all I need for now." I lean in again and kiss him, this time taking a moment to feel his mouth on mine, and let a little spark of our latent passion ignite. Owen responds, pulling me into his arms even closer. I can hear the Song Sparrows chirping delicately, and a Robin, making its neighing singsong somewhere in the distance. Nature's music plays in my ears as I open my heart to Owen's kiss.

Having packed away my pity-party attitude, I begin to focus on Claire's book. We start by doing a layout of the pages, and earmark ones that need an edit, to make the story run more smoothly. It's a long arduous process to create a good story, in a way that flows easily, page after page. Once I completed the final tweaks on the illustrations, thanks in large part to Hannah One's input on various aspects, we scan and print the coloured drawings and then match them page for page with the dialogue. Seeing it printed out makes it become real, gives it life. I can see where I wish I had added a few brush strokes to the fur of one character, or maybe made the eyes a bit bigger on another, but Claire is extremely happy with my work and said I'm just being overly critical of my drawings. Hannah One agrees, so I let it go.

The day finally arrives when the printed version is ready to be sent to the publisher. Jamie gave me the name of her friend, John

Stockton, who works for *One Two Three Publishing*. It seems a bit unprofessional to send the book printed out on eight by eleven computer printer paper, but Jamie assures me that John will be satisfied with this format. I address the large manila envelope and hand it to Claire to take to the post office. She takes a *selfie* holding up the envelope, her face full of anticipation and hope, and posts it to her social media page. After mailing the envelope it will simply be a matter of waiting for a response. I believe Claire is going to go crazy with impatience, so I suggest she begin to work on the second book in the series, to get a head start, when, although I silently say *if*, the publisher wants more books from her. She races up to her room and begins drawing up some new ideas.

Owen, meanwhile, calls from school, and says, "Hey cutie! How 'bout a date? I hear you're looking for something fun to do, and well, I'm in the market for something fun too!" I laugh, thinking Owen has gone a bit crazy himself. "I'm sorry sir, I think you have the wrong number. Who is it you're trying to reach?" I say in a mock old-time telephone-operator type voice. Owen laughs, replying, "Oh, I thought there was a beautiful woman at the other end of this line who needs a night out and I wanted to oblige!" I laugh, feeling my stomach tweak at his comment about being beautiful. Even after twenty some odd years he still makes me feel beautiful and desirable. "I suppose I could clear my schedule. Let's see, tonight, I have dinner with family, television and bed. Well, that sounds like something I can't miss. Tomorrow night, dinner with family, television and bed. Hmm, I'm sensing a pattern here. Well, you tell me what works and I'll see if I can fit you in." Owen coughs and says in a serious voice, "I hate to think of you missing your favourite television shows, but I think I can make it worth your while. How about tonight? Dinner at *The Cardinal*, with maybe a bit of dancing or listening to live music after that?" I smile, recalling the fact that I mentioned this place to Owen just last week. "I think I can fit that into my schedule, sir. Yes, that works. Okay, so I guess I'll just see you later." Owen chuckles. "I will meet you in the front hallway at seven. I love you." I feel my heart racing. It feels silly to react to my husband in such a pubescent way, but it's been so long since we really focused on *us*, it almost feels like a new beginning.

A wonderful dinner, followed by an evening of dancing with Owen, is the cure-all I need to finally push myself out of the doldrums. I have been so focused on what I had lost when the bookstore closed, that I failed to see all the wonderful things I still have in front of me.

I pull into the driveway, heaving a sigh as I turn off the ignition. I can see that the lid of the mailbox is propped up, and a manilla envelope is sticking out the top. It's been four weeks since Claire mailed her book to the publisher, and after the initial impatience, she seemed resigned to wait until she got an answer. Seeing the large envelope in the mailbox seems to indicate that the book is being returned. If Mr. Stockton had been interested, he would likely have kept it and called us in for a meeting. I swallow. This is not the news any of us wants to hear. I suspect Claire will be terribly disappointed, and I hate to think of her creative spirit having to cope with this rejection. I step out of the car, and walking up the steps to the house I reach in to pull the large envelope out of the mailbox. It's addressed to Claire, with a return address of *One Two Three Publishing*. My heart sinks. I open the front door, while carrying my gym bag in the other hand, the envelope tucked under my arm.

I hear the television in the living room. I take a few steps and peer into the room. Stretched out on the couch is David, Claire's boyfriend. He regularly hangs out at our house, so I'm not surprised to see him. He has his head propped up on two small pillows, his long, lean body filling the length of the couch. He has a crop of reddish-brown hair that looks, regardless of how often it is combed, unkempt. His bright, warm green eyes are glued to the television, as he and Claire watch a movie. Claire lies next to him, wedged in between his body and the back of the couch, her arms folded up and snuggled against him, reminding me of when Claire was a child, nestled up to Owen or me as we watched something fun on television. OnanOff has taken advantage and burrowed into a comfortable spot in the small of her back, a large tortoiseshell-coloured ball of fur. Over the years he has become slightly overweight, mostly due to all the spoiling he receives from Claire. He is very demanding and she gives in to him more often than not. Owen and I are not happy with his weight, and attempt to restrict his food intake, but OnanOff complains to Fae, who watches over the feline like a mother over her child. We are always found out and scolded by Claire for *depriving* the poor cat. He hardly looks deprived.

Based on the volume, the movie is one that contains a fair bit of violence and swearing. I glance over to see Hannah One, sitting at the dining room table, working on a jigsaw puzzle. Her eyes are not very good, so I bought her large piece puzzles, so she could work on completing it without getting frustrated, or strain her eyes. She looks up as she sees me, and smiles. She is also very hard of hearing now, so it's unlikely she is bothered by the language or gun fire coming from the television. Both young sets of eyes shift to me as I stand there, but make no attempt to rise. I wave at the pair on the couch as I turn and head towards the kitchen.

I decide to hold on to the envelope for now. As I walk down the hallway, the old wood floors creak, a sign of wear and age. I know the feeling. I have to keep reminding myself that, although I often feel my age, I have nothing to complain about when standing next to my one-hundred-year-old grandmother.

I place the envelope on the kitchen table and go to the counter to turn the kettle on. As I begin to search for a tea flavour I'm craving, I hear Hannah One enter the kitchen behind me. Without turning to her, I ask, "Tea?" I forget she can't hear, so I turn and repeat my question, this time making sure she hears me. She nods. Her eyes fall upon the envelope sitting on the table. She places her hands on the back of the chair and frowns. I follow her eyes and stare at the envelope for a moment, before turning back to the cupboard. Nothing more can be done about the envelope until we face the music and open it.

From the living room I hear music that indicates the end of the movie. A few words exchanged between the pair huddled on the couch, and then I hear Claire asking OnanOff to get off her. A large thump sounds as the big cat jumps down and stalks off, a bit grumpy. The couch groans as the two bodies sit up. Claire stands up and stretches. "That was pretty good, but not as good as I thought it would be." David says something I can't hear, and then the sound of floor boards creaking indicates someone is walking to the kitchen. Claire enters and is about to say something, when she spies the envelope.

"Oh my god! Mom! Why didn't you say this was here?" She reaches over and grabs the large envelope, carefully tearing the seal. I don't know what to say, so simply brace myself for her disappointment. Hannah One has taken a seat at the table, and she too appears to be preparing for Claire's reaction. She pulls out the contents, which is the original manuscript we had sent, plus a single white sheet of paper on top. It has the company logo and address across the top. From where I stand, it appears to be only about one paragraph long. Claire starts reading the letter aloud, an excited tone in her voice.

"Dear Miss Ross: I was very glad to receive your work and must commend you on the effort you and your family made to create such a wonderful book. You show a talent for writing, and present the subject in a clear and understandable fashion that children would enjoy. The illustrations are wonderful and help support the story. At this time, however, I am sorry to say that we are unable to take on your project. We are inundated with submissions of childrens' books, and find ourselves with more than we can publish. We are looking for a certain type of book, and unfortunately this doesn't fit our criteria at the moment.

Please feel free to resubmit your work in a year, or two, and we can see if the market trends have changed. Sincerely, John Stockton."

She drops the letter on to the table and looks at me. The shock on her face slowly dissolves into a mask of misery, as the realization seeps in. I see her beautiful blue eyes well up, as David appears behind her. He places his hands on her shoulders, but says nothing. She turns and buries her head in his chest, a soft muffled sob soaking into him. Her hair, tied in a long pony tail at the back of her head, flows down her back like a narrow chocolate stream, and sways slightly as she cries. I turn away, my own eyes filling with tears. It's one thing to have my own disappointments in life, but to see my daughter facing one of her own is very difficult. As a parent, you want your child's life to be filled with potential and positive experiences, and hope that these downfalls are few and far between. I can only hope that she will learn from this experience, and move on.

I turn back to the pair standing by the door, David consoling Claire with soft words and a hand rubbing her back gently. I wipe away my tears and clear my throat, "Well, okay, so now we know. Claire, this is only one company. We can submit it to others. Just because this guy says he's not interested doesn't mean it's all over. We just need to continue on and try again." Claire turns her head, still nestled in David's arms. "Mom, I don't think anyone will want this. You heard him say something about trends or criteria, or whatever the hell it is. What if all the companies follow the same trend thing…?" she trails off, sniffing.

Finally, almost on cue, Hannah One speaks up. "Claire, my dear. This is very disappointing, but you need to see the good things he wrote about the book. I think that he would not have written all those positives if he didn't think the book had potential. We need to take the positives out of this letter and use that to promote it to others. This is just one bump in the road, it's not a sinkhole." She smiles, looking satisfied that she had presented an apt analogy. I smile at her. Leave it to Hannah One to try to make lemonade out of lemons. Claire looks at her great grandmother and nods, wiping her nose with her sleeve.

"I suppose, well, we could get more copies made, and mail them out to a bunch of publishers. I suppose that would be okay." David smiles, and, gently hugging her again, comments; "I think that's a good idea. Why don't we look online to see what publishers you want to send it to, and we can make a list." David is an elementary school teacher, and being four years older than Claire, he has a manner, not unlike her father, of directing a situation into something productive, rather than see it all fall apart. I like David; he is growing on me. He stands over six feet in height, and with Claire at five foot four they look a bit lopsided at times, but his long lanky body seems to mold itself to fit them when they stand together. When I finally had an opportunity to sit and talk with him, I found him to be an intelligent and sensitive young man.

The pair leave the kitchen and go upstairs to Claire's room, presumably to work on her laptop. I'm not one of those parents who doesn't allow a child's boyfriend, or girlfriend, to be in their bedroom. If they are going to be intimate, they are going to be intimate wherever they can find a place. I just want her safe, and happy. She appears to have the birth control aspect of the relationship under control, so I try to curb my concern over that issue.

I turn off the kettle and make tea. Hannah One re-reads the letter. "It is so unfortunate. I do wonder how successful she will be in securing a publisher if, in fact, this business about trends in the market right now, is true of them *all*." She sighs. "I think this is going to challenging, and may or may not work out in the long run, but I'm glad she's trying." I place a steaming cup of tea in front of her. Sitting down, I take the letter from her and read it over quickly. The tone seems to imply that the market isn't interested in this type of story right now. I wonder how they decide what is "in" right now? Wouldn't you think a book that teaches children about nature and environmental issues would be a hot topic right now? I feel a bit of doubt nibble at the corner of my mind. As Hannah One said, would this rejection be widespread?

Thirteen

Ten large envelopes sent and ten returned. Some had form letters simply indicating the company had enough submissions and were not accepting more at this time. Some were a bit more personal, indicated by the fact that they referenced the material directly, but that it was not the type of subject matter they were currently interested in. It was ten stabs in Claire's heart. Each time an envelope appeared in the mailbox I felt my hopes sink a bit lower. By the time the last envelope arrives, which is about two months after she had sent it off, she barely acknowledges its presence as it lays on the kitchen table like a flat, manilla-coloured killer-of-dreams. She is unwilling to open it, so I take it upon myself to rip it open and view the last rejection letter. A fuse of anger burns in my stomach. How obtuse can these publishers be? Can they not see the value and quality of this story? A beautiful and funny story meant to educate, but also create a dialogue between parents and children, to open their eyes to the world around them, and how much we all need to step in and take an active role in taking care of our planet?

Claire sits at the dining room table, helping Hannah One with a new jigsaw puzzle. Two hundred pieces is proving to be a bit harder than she will admit, but with Claire's nonchalant help, they make headway with all the outside pieces. Owen walks through the front door, dropping his gym bag in the corner. Saturdays are very relaxed, with Claire home from the Centre, and now that

Owen is retired, we take this day as an unspoken day for family. Claire is still antsy to see her friends, and receives non-stop texts from Lilah, her partner in crime, but she also knows that this is an important time to cherish, with Hannah One's advancing age, as Fae reminds her often enough.

Owen enters the kitchen and announces, "Hannah One and I want to have a family meeting after lunch, so everyone be sure to stay put after we eat." He grins, but says nothing more. Even when I shoot him a quizzical look, he simply shakes his head and smiles. It would appear that the two of them have been scheming, and have some secret they now want to reveal to the rest of us. Claire sighs; I know she is secretly wishing to hang out with David today. Since school is over for the summer, the time they have together is more open, without constraints of his class-work tying him up. They spend a lot of time together. I have a brief memory of when I was her age and Julian was the one I wanted to be with night and day. I occasionally wonder what happened to him. I had heard, several years ago, through the university grapevine, that he had dropped out of school and taken over his father's land development business, even though he had seemed bound and determined to distance himself from it. I shake my head, dropping all thoughts of the past out of my mind like raindrops rolling off an umbrella. It was a lifetime ago, and I can now see that I was meant to go through that relationship to get to where I am now.

After lunch we gather in the living room to await Owen's announcement. He helps Hannah One into her special chair. We bought her a chair that, with the push of a button, will move and help her to stand or sit. When Hannah One is settled, Owen sits down in the large armchair and says; "Oh, um, Hannah One, I think you should start this conversation, after all it was your idea." He warmly smiles at her. Hannah One clears her throat and begins. "Well, yes, okay. Claire," she looks at her, a bright light of excitement in her eyes. "I know these past few months have been very disappointing for you. I myself cannot see the reasoning for all these publishers to say no to your wonderful book. So, I got to thinking, and with your father's help, you know, with all that computer stuff I can't figure out, we have created a plan for you." Claire frowns, not liking the sound of someone else making a *plan* for her, but remains silent, willing to listen. Hannah One continues, ignoring her great granddaughter's expression. "I was thinking, and your mother will back me up on this after all her experience with the bookstore, that we need to find a different avenue for publishing it. I remember seeing some books in the store that your mom had agreed to sell, that had been *self-published*. There was a display of soft-covered books on a shelf near the centre aisle, you remember Hannah?" I nod, recalling the day a very motivated young man came in with ten books in a box, and pleaded with me to find a space for them. His novel was actually quite good, having bought a copy myself. His novels sat for a while, and feeling sorry for him, I made a better display, and a sign that read, "Bentley's Choice - Read of the Month". All the books sold after that.

I turn my attention back as Hannah One continues. "I asked your dad to investigate how this process works, and how much a venture like this would cost." Owen stands up and produces a large folder, handing it over to Claire, who sits beside me on the couch. She opens the folder slowly, seeing page after page of information. Owen says, as he seats himself again; "There are a few options we can go over and see which way you'd like to proceed. I mean, *if* you want to proceed. This is simply a plan, not something you *must* do."

Hannah One claps her hands in excitement. "I saw all the options, and I'm most excited to see the book in print form. I know there are cheaper ways to have it on the internet as a digital book, but I think children need to *hold* books. They need to feel the pages, run their hands over the glossy cover, sink their eyes into the colourful illustrations. You can't have that tactile experience on the computer." Claire's expression remains neutral, as she closes the folder jacket. "But that would be pretty expensive. I don't have the money to try that, and how would I sell it? How do I promote it? It's probably not going to work at all, when I can't even afford to print out a single copy." She looks down at the folder sitting in her lap, looking dejected. Hannah One, trying to get Claire to look at her, speaks a bit more loudly; "Claire, dear. Don't you think I thought of that too? Why would I propose such a venture, if *I* wasn't going to back you up? I *myself* will pay for all the publishing costs." She places her hands in her lap, looking as if she is done with her presentation and now she is just waiting for the audience reaction.

I look between Hannah One, Claire and Owen, trying to gauge the opinion of each. Owen sits, looking receptive to this idea, and of course Hannah One is excited with her proposal. It's Claire who looks pensive.

"You don't have that kind of money. Don't you need it to, like, *live* and stuff?" Hannah One laughs, but then begins coughing. I rise to fetch her a glass of water, but she waves me off. "Claire, you are a dear for thinking about me, but I am *so* old. I should really be dead by now," and she chuckles to see everyone's shocked expression. "I've been around so long I've had plenty of time to save money. Now I want to spend it on this. I want to see it to fruition. I want to see you succeed where I know you can, with just a bit of help. You have all sorts of talent, and energy and ideas. I want to support you as you get a good footing in the world. It would do me a world of good to do this, Claire." She continues to smile, but carries a serious tone in her voice.

Claire looks at her tenderly, tears in her eyes. She opens the folder again, and begins to leaf through page after page. When she finally speaks, her voice is breaking with emotion, "Well, then I guess we have more work to do. I hope my team is ready, willing and able?" We all cheer soundly.

Seven weeks later, I'm sitting at the kitchen table, holding a copy of Claire's book. Hannah One was right about the tactile adventure you experience when holding a book in your hands. My eyes scan the glossy, brightly coloured cover, with large block lettering that reads, "Fanny and Fae - Nature Detectives", and in smaller type, under the illustration, I read the words, "By Claire D. Ross". I feel tears come to my eyes. It is so beautiful.

Four heavy boxes filled with books sit in the front hallway waiting to be carried upstairs to be temporarily stowed in the spare room. Although the book will be available to purchase on-line, we decided that having an inventory of hard copies would be useful. Owen reached out to the newspaper he once wrote for, and asked if any reporter would be interested in writing a piece about a young upcoming author. We have yet to get a confirmation on an interview. There are other ways to get the word out, including through social media, which Claire and David are handling.

I walk into the sunroom where Hannah One sits in bed, reading. She has been feeling a little off lately, so she spends more and more time propped up in her bed, listening to podcasts, audio books, or reading, if she feels like it. I look at her frail form and try not to think of the future. She looks up when I enter and smiles, her eyes coming to rest on the book in my hands.

"Oh, my. This is so exciting! I can't wait to see it!" She reaches out her wizened hand and takes hold of the book as I pass it to her. She lays it in her lap, and runs her fingers over the smooth cover. She lifts it up, and thoroughly examines the front and back cover. Then she carefully opens it to gaze upon the first page. She gasps as she reads the dedication. "To Hannah One - the Greatest of Great Grandmothers". She looks at me with tears in her eyes. I quickly come over to perch beside her on the bed. I take the book from her and gingerly squeeze her delicate hands. "She wanted you to know just how much you mean to her." I myself feel a catch in my throat, but swallow it down. The strength of our bond is no less today than fifty-one years ago, but the intensity with which

I feel it now overwhelms me. I need to cling to every minute I have with her, and imprint every little detail of her in my mind, knowing that someday it will be all I have to rely on to keep her near me. She pats my hand, taking her other hand and pulling out a hanky from her sleeve. "My goodness, that was a shock to the heart. But it touches me beyond words! What a wonderful girl Claire is, and how lucky have I been to know her, and love her. You have done well with her, my dear, you should be proud." I smile back. "I don't know about that; I think it was a community effort. We *all* brought some quality to her, and she developed her own self through all these elements, including Fae."

Hannah One blinks at the mention of Fae. She glances out the window to the garden, now in full August bloom, with Asters, Marigolds and Cosmos brightening every corner. Wistfully she says, "I wish I had been able to have Fae's influence on me as a youngster. It would have been so wonderful to be connected to her, and have that bond. I also wish that I could have gone to visit Fae's realm. Oh, to see those things, as Arthur describes it, the flowers, the fairies, the talking trees. It would have been astonishing to behold." She continues to look out the window, a melancholy expression making her wrinkled face seem older and more worn. I wonder why she has never mentioned this before. I also wonder why I had not thought to include her when we went Fae's realm. Arthur had been, as well as Claire, so why couldn't Hannah One? "I'll ask Fae if you can visit. We can all go, and have a wonderful experience together." I stand up, intent on texting Claire, and asking her to talk to Fae about this.

Hannah One's face brightens and the spark of Light that has, of late, been dimming in her eyes, is alight again. "Oh, oh, I don't know what to think. Aren't I too old to be venturing out in the woods? How does one get around *there*?" I laugh and sit back on the bed, jostling the book that sits by her side, "It's not that you go there *physically*; it's only your Light, your Spirit, that enters the realm. Physically, as you have seen, we just hang around here, on this plane, in a relaxed state of being. There you will be able to walk around, sit on the ground or climb a tree if you wish, without any impediments." She laughs, and claps her hands together. "I miss my young body, when I could walk the woods, and garden without the pain of age reminding me to slow down. How wonderful! I hope Fae will allow me to enter her world. It will be so marvelous!"

A few days later, on a quiet Sunday morning, I invite Arthur to come over. He loves visiting the Fae realm, and I thought it would be nice to include him. Now approaching eighty, he is slow moving, but still light-hearted in spirit. Claire is present, as is Fae. Owen announces that he will be gatekeeper, watching over all of us to make sure nothing interrupts the session. He is still unwilling to venture out of his own world, no matter the occasion.

Arthur talks us into the deep meditative state, whereby we reach a place together, standing in front of a large ancient gnarly-looking Oak tree. Arthur speaks to the tree, and then waits for a response. Before we had descended, he told us that he had discovered that the trees, in our world, act as doorways to the Fae Realm. If approached with the proper respect and intent, they will allow access. The key is to be patient, as the ancient trees feel no sense of Time or Space, and only respond when the wisdom of the Now deems it so. We stand waiting silently, until the tree dissolves into an open doorway, leading into the realm. A bright light shines on the path in front of us, and we follow it, walking softly on the mossy trail. Hannah One takes my hand, as is habitual now for us when we are walking in the human world. I glance down and wonder why she needs the assist, but then quickly realize she is nervous. I squeeze her hand and smile, and, reaching out, my other hand brushes against one of the tall Irises that line the side of the trail. To Hannah One's astounded eyes, tiny sprites pop out of the purple-hued flower, and float up and around us, like Dandelion-strands blown by a breath. She laughs, and it carries throughout the woods. Arthur stops and turns around to look at what Hannah One is laughing at. When he sees the tiny faeries, he grins. Claire does not stop walking; she simply glances back at the three of us. She's so familiar with this realm that hardly anything surprises her now. It's unfortunate that she does not revel in each visit, as she did in the first. Arthur comes to stand beside Hannah One, and whispers as he takes her other hand, "If you think that's amazing, wait and see!". He pulls her hand to lead her onward.

The light seems to be leading us into a large circular glade, ringed by several Birch trees. The tiny green grasses move like underwater weeds being pushed by a current; it is like a hypnotic dance. The mossy patches around the other grasses sprout tiny white and yellow flowers, no bigger than the head of a pin, bursting into light as they ascend. The sound of singing makes us all look into the trees. Small wood nymphs perch, like tiny Sparrows, on the tree limbs; their woody colouring a stark contrast to the white peeling skin-like bark of the tree. They appear to have the same elvish features as Fae; pointed ears poking through a veil of green vine-like hair, and their eyes shine with a yellow glow like small candles inside a lantern. Their skin is the colour of Maplewood, on their backs a set of wings, which when folded, look like green leaves, until they open and show gossamer, earth toned petal-like appendages. There are too many to count. Their song is symphonic; a harmonious entwining of voices that blend so richly, it almost makes you weep from hearing such a beautiful melody.

A yellow orb of light in the centre of the glade makes us shield our eyes as it grows brighter in intensity. I close my eyes, but can still see the glow through my shut eyelids. Then suddenly, the light fades. There, in front of us stands a magnificent, tall, slender woman. She wears a gossamer gown of forest green, richly woven with specks of light. The fabric is translucent, like morning mist drifting across a meadow. Her hair aqua green, with streaks of yellow, and tiny blossoms that open and close throughout her long flowing curls. The flowers, when opening, emit tiny specks of Light that float up into the air and take shape as miniature Fae or elf-like creatures. They float away into the trees, or settle to the earth and connect with a flower or plant. Her skin is earth-toned, a rich mahogany hue, with striated markings like wood, but with a glossy sheen like satin fabric. She spreads her arms wide and long tendrils of green ivy gently cascade down and take root. Small variegated leaves open, and upon each leaf rests a small wood-coloured faerie creature, which takes wing and flies off to the nearby trees. Several wood nymphs sing their bird-like songs to welcome the new arrivals.

Claire stops, and for the first time, looks surprised. This exquisite being is new to her, making her pause in her indifference. The being looks upon Claire and smiles. Then, she looks at each of us in turn, until her eyes come to rest upon Fae, who has silently entered the glade to stand behind us. Hannah One drops her hands away from Arthur and me, and takes a step forward. She looks upon this benevolent woman, and with awe in her voice says; "I am so grateful to be *Here*, in your Realm. My heart is full of joy and appreciation for being allowed to enter such a magical place." She steps back. The woman smiles and for the first time, she opens her mouth and says quietly; "You are all welcome. I am the Mistress of the Woods. I plant the seeds of the Fae and nurture these children, allowing them to be free to grow in the manner that suits them. Our realm is woven with peace, respect, and above all else, Love. The Fae are kindhearted and curious about humans. They love and care for your world, residing in the shadows, yet under your very noses. You need only look and listen, with your Light. My children enter your world through the flowers, the trees, the very moss under your feet. They are the keepers of secrets, the healers, the guardians of wisdom and knowledge. We understand that it is in the very fabric of *being* that we are connected to Spirit, to Gaia, to One who is All. The Spirits of the woods, the glade, the sandy beach, the frozen tundra, are all part of the Light. They are the source of Life's lessons and Life's answers. You need only look and listen with your Light to understand the lessons they offer."

The Mistress of the Woods turns her body, but her feet, under her long gown, seemed rooted to the spot. She points to the far-off trees. "These *Elder* trees house many elves, and are symbolic of Birth and Death, beginning and ending. They are the oldest of old, and provide protection and healing, as a mother protects and cares for her young." An old smooth-barked Elder tree seems to bend its leafy canopy towards us at the mention of it. She continues, pointing to a small grove of bushes off to one side. "The *Lilac* and *Hawthorn* are magic unto themselves, and are home to many Sprites and Fae. Their strong connection to the magic of the realm helps with creativity and growth. Plant one of these bushes in your own garden and feel its presence help shape your creative Light." She turns to face us and continues; "So you see, every plant, tree, and flower, houses a Fae that provides insight to the lessons and knowledge Nature wants to impart. *Here*, we are as One; our combined energy creates the Whole. This is a challenge for many humans. They cannot access the Whole when they look towards the material world to complete themselves. True completeness can be achieved simply by keeping your Light fed as you journey along through life. Nature's Lessons are free-flowing and feed your Light. Plant the seeds, watch the flowers bloom, touch the tree bark and listen to it hum, wait for the caterpillar to transform and see her fly. Remember, it is within you to connect to the Fae; you need only reach out with your Light, and open your heart to their messages."

She lifts her arms above her head, and her leaf-like tendrils extend into the sky, resembling tall sheaths of grain swaying in the breeze high above us. The tendrils open, and a massive shower of tiny multicoloured flowers slowly fall upon us, feeling like feathers tickling our faces. The sound of giggling erupts, as hundreds of sparkly points of light fuse outward from the tiny flowers, suspended in the air, reminding me of the stars in the sky. The

Mistress herself laughs, and the wind whispers around our bodies, gently swaying us back and forth. She ends with: "It is our way, to be All with One; we only wish humans would open themselves to the same. Go forth now, explore my realm, revel in the beauty; learn from each flower, tree and Fae creature, the ways that can bring you balance and joy for your own journey on the path." She lowers her arms, and, looking at Claire, she slowly brings her hands together in front of her, forming a cup. Fae, who has been standing at the back of the group, comes forward to stand in front of the Mistress, silently taking hold of what lies nestled in the palms of her hand. Fae turns and walks back to stand beside Claire. The light in the glade becomes very bright, as it did before, and we have to shield our eyes. When we open them, the figure of the woman has vanished, leaving only a small rosebush, with a single tiny butterfly perched upon a silky red petal.

We all gather around Fae to see what she holds in her hands. She opens them slowly to reveal a very tiny Fae creature, who looks identical to Fae herself. The little body moves slightly, opening its yellow green eyes and gazing up at Fae with curiosity. "Mother?" whispers the tiny voice. Fae lifts the tiny body to her breast and gently hugs her. "We are *All* One." she whispers, and smiles at Claire.

We spend a long time in the Fae realm. Hannah One is enthralled by all the creatures, and the flowers and fauna around her. She is enjoying the mobility of body that she lacks in her current human form. She plays with Claire, as if they are both ten years old again. We all feel such joy as Fae coddles and croons over her new offspring. We never question why this happened, as if there would be some logical explanation for anything *Here*. We simply accept the new being into the fold, and feel her own love and joy radiate back to us.

As we are heading back to the Oak tree doorway, Hannah One stops and glances back, as if trying to memorize all of what she has experienced. I feel regret for not bringing her here sooner.

She takes my hand and smiles, whispering, "This has been the most magical day of my life. It will certainly be hard to top this!"

Once we are back in our bodies and feel able to rise, Owen heads into the kitchen to make a pot of tea for everyone. Hannah One sits in her chair, a big smile on her face. "I can't thank you enough, everyone, for such a wonderful time! How amazing to think this realm is right *there*," and she reaches out with her hand, like she can touch it in the empty air. She drops her arm, a sudden tiredness showing on her face. "Hannah, my dear. I am awfully done in. Would you mind helping me to bed; think I'll have a wee nap. Later on, I'll have a sherry to toast this day! What a wonderful day…" she trails off, exhaustion pouring over her. I help her out of her chair and taking her arm, lead her to her sunroom bed. As we pass by Owen busily preparing the tea, she reaches out and touches him on the back. "Son, I really believe you are missing out if you don't open up to Fae. You will find yourself full of joy when you see her. It will lighten your soul, my dear boy." Owen turns and smiles at her, taking her hand and kissing it. "I will certainly think about it. Since you've jumped into the water, I can see it isn't that deep and scary after all." She smiles at him, and turns to me; "Yes, I think a nap will do me good."

I decide to follow Hannah One's example and have a small nap myself. Arthur wants to stay and talk with Owen, so I excuse myself and head up to my bed. Claire is already in her room, texting David, I assume.

It seems like I only just closed my eyes, when I feel a hand on my shoulder. I roll over to see Claire standing there, her face as white as a sheet. She bends over and says quietly, "Mom, Mom. You need to get up. Fae says you need to get up." I frown, feeling slightly disoriented. I glance over to see the clock face read three. I have been napping for an hour. I swing my legs over the side of the bed and stand up. I feel a wave of dizziness overtake me, and grab on to Claire to steady myself. I assume I just lost my balance. I look at Claire and see fright in her eyes. She whispers, "Mom, Fae says you need to go to Hannah One. Now." I try to swallow, but my throat feels suddenly parched. I try to take a breath, but my lungs will not work. I feel Claire take my hand and pull me towards the door, but my feet do not want to move, as if they are caught in concrete. "Mom, now." Claire's insistent tone makes me blink, and I realize that I have to get past this mummifying fright to go help my grandmother.

We quickly descend the stairs, and make our way through the kitchen. Arthur is nowhere to be seen, so I assume he has gone home. Owen, hearing our footsteps, makes his way to the kitchen as well, but stops short when he sees the expression on our faces. I cannot speak. I can only focus on moving one foot in front of the other, my only sensation being Claire's outstretched hand, pulling me along. We come to stand in the doorway of the sunroom.

I look over to the bed, and see Hannah One lying there, looking like she is peacefully asleep. I let go of Claire's hand and take a few steps towards her. I reach out with my Light to touch hers, but find it is not there. I stand frozen, and try once again. I can't feel anything coming from her. I come to stand beside the bed, and reach out my hand to hers. It feels cold. It feels empty.

I sit down and place both hands on her arm, willing the Light to return. Begging for her Light to return. I don't notice Claire and Owen come to stand beside the bed. Claire lets out a small sob, Owen taking her in his arms. I do not notice OnanOff jump on to the bed and let out a low mournful meow, his napping buddy no longer there for him.

I sit, unwilling to let the obvious thought into my mind; unable to do anything but sit there and wait. Wait for her to return to me; wait for this nightmare to be over, to awaken and find it not true, not real. I would wait forever, if need be.

Claire, still enclosed in her father's embrace, whispers, "Fae says she is with her, in the Fae Realm. She wanted to go back and be *there*. Her Light shines brightly in the garden." She begins crying again. Owen, his own face streaked with tears, holds her closely. I look at Hannah One's hair, now white as snow, loose strands lying upon her pillow; her hands in repose, soft and weathered, yet always full of loving touches; her face, slack with death, but holding a quiet dignity; her eyes closed to me, now, and always. The black pit I fall into muffles my uncontrollable sobs, and everything else disappears.

Fourteen

The days blend into one another as my mind has shut itself away from reality, pulling me deep inside its dark folds. I lie on the bed in the sunroom, clutching Hannah One's sweater, inhaling her scent, trying to capture it in my memory, attempting to hold on to the last vestige of her energy that lies within the fabric.

Sleeping seems to be the only release from the pain. And pain is all I feel. I find no joy in seeing the sales of Claire's book soar. I find no joy in Claire talking about Fae's new offspring. I find no joy in food, in nature, in anything. I lie upon *her* bed, day after day, unable to let go of my sorrow. When Owen suggested we remove the bed, I cried and said he was not to remove *anything*; anything that imprinted her on to me. Her clothes still hang in the wardrobe in the corner of the dining room. Her favourite mug still sits in the kitchen cupboard. Her books are still piled on the nightstand. Her paintings still hang upon the walls; sad reminders that the maker's hand is no longer on this Earth.

I force myself to eat, as my body's functions overrule my mind's desire to fade away to nothing. Nothing has taste; nothing sweet brings me energy; nothing hot stops the chill from residing in my bones. Owen's kindness goes unnoticed. My own family's grief ignored by my own. I can't help Claire through this. I can't help myself. Owen stands in as both father and mother to our daughter, but it makes little difference to me.

In search of Hannah One's favourite mug, I come across her bottle of sherry. Running my fingers over the embossed label, I take note of the gold lettering and the cold, dark glass bottle. I unscrew the cap and take a sniff. It's sweet, almost sickeningly so. I find myself reaching for the small, delicate sherry glass that always sits beside the bottle in the cupboard. I pour a small amount of the amber liquid into the glass. I sniff again, wondering what the attraction is to such a drink. I bring the glass to my lips and take a tiny sip. It burns, but not a hot burn; it's a sweet burn. I swallow, grimacing at the after-taste. It flows down my throat like a small rivulet of lava. I feel the ache in my chest diminish ever so slightly. I take another sip, and then another. I look at the glass, and find it empty. I refill it. This time as I sip, I find it goes down more smoothly, and makes the gloom-filled knot in my mind loosen up a bit more.

I take the glass and the bottle and return to the sunroom bed. I sit, propped up, looking out the window, as the autumn leaves wave hello from some low-hanging branches. Their colour brings me no joy. They only serve to remind me that Hannah One is not here to see their colourful display. I pour another glass, and this time I drink it quite easily. The room sways, as my head swims in an unfocused way. I pour another drink, and this time I raise the glass in a toast to my grandmother. I giggle, thinking of her drinking this stuff all the time. How did she not swim around the room too? My thoughts are groggy. I can hear my Alternate mind say, *"most likely because she did not drink half a bottle at once."* I frown. "Just shut up! Even better, just fuck off!" I tell the voice. I like the way I feel, or more to the point, don't feel. The pain is now locked outside of me, where I can't hear it banging at the door to get in. I empty the glass and as carefully as I can, place it on the nightstand, before laying my head down and closing my eyes.

Claire finds me on the bed, the sherry bottle precariously perched on the nightstand next to the glass. She shakes me awake. I blink, confused and lightheaded. "Mom, what the hell?

Why are you drinking *that?*" as she points to the sherry bottle. I raise my head and look at the bottle. I look at Claire and see her disapproving expression. Anger fuels my response, "Why don't you just stop bugging me? Let me be. I'm a grown woman, I can do what I want. Now, go away." I don't see the hurt in Claire's eyes as I roll on to my side, turning away from her.

The next thing I feel is a hand on my hip. I lay on my side facing away from the doorway, but I assume it is Owen. He gently rubs his hand along my side. I roll on to my back, and slowly open my eyes. "Claire went out with David, so it's just us for dinner. Are you hungry? I can make you something." The thought of food makes me nauseous, and my head hurts. I roll back on to my side, and croak, "Nothing. I'm not hungry. Just going to sleep." I close my eyes again and drift off.

The early morning sun tears at my eyelids. My mouth is dry, my throat cannot swallow and my head feels heavy. I shift my stiff body slightly so I can roll on to my back and slowly pry my eyelids open. The sun blasts all over the room, and part of me wonders how Hannah One ever slept with all this light. Then I remembered that she was an early riser, often before sunrise. Now I know why. Thinking of her, puttering in the kitchen in the early morning, makes me ache once again. I long to be rid of the pain. I can't continue to replay these memories in my head, or I fear I will go mad from the grief. Aside from my body rebelling against the invasion of the alcohol, my mind longs for the solace that the numbing drink offers. If it helps the mind, I can manage the body, I reason. I sit up slowly, and shift my legs to swing over the edge of the bed.

As I stand up, I pick up the bottle and gingerly take hold of the glass on the nightstand. The house is empty, with Claire at the Centre and Owen most likely at the gym, or visiting his friend Colin. He spends a lot of time these days with Colin, or other friends. I know it's because he can't stand to be around the house, watching me die a little bit more every day. I'm glad he's not around as I wallow in my misery.

I head upstairs to get dressed. Finding my shoes and purse I head out the door, to the liquor store.

The great thing about the medium of television is that it captures your mind and chains it to a hamster wheel, spinning you around and around on a non-stop loop of mind-numbing scenes, played out by humans pretending to be someone else. I want to be someone else, to escape the daily ache I feel when not imbibing, so I watch them, endlessly pulled into the world of make-believe. I stretch out on the couch, and focus my eyes on the screen. A movie I have seen several times already plays monotonously in front of me, as I sip sherry from Hannah One's favourite tea cup. I know I'm not fooling anyone by secreting my alcohol in a cup; but no one has confronted me, or called me out for drinking in the middle of the day.

The house is once again empty. The living energy that once warmed the very foundation seems to have evaporated when Hannah One died. It's as if the house itself has given up. I know the feeling. As the movie ends, I stand up and stretch, feeling the strain in my back from lying on the couch too long. Looking around the room I can't decide what to do next; have a nap, have another drink, or watch another movie. The general malaise I feel indicates a nap, so I head to my sunroom bed.

The room is cooled by winter's wind pushing at the windows. A light rain makes the windows appear as if they themselves are crying. I pull the comforter close as I sit glancing out the window. I turn my eyes away from the rainy view and catch sight of a very tiny movement on the rim of a potted plant that sits on a side table. The leaves of the plant droop slightly, needing a bit of warm sun and water. I have not tended to my house plants in a while, leaving their care to Claire.

The tiny speck moves along the edge of the pot and then stops. When I focus my fuzzy sights on it, I can just make out the shape of a black ant. Unusual to see an ant in winter, but then, it's possible it found its way into the house earlier in the season, and has taken up residence in the plant. I blink my eyes, ready to burrow down into my blanket of woe, when the minuscule voice of the ant resonates in my head. *"I am an ant. I am of little consequence to humans, but all in all, I signify strength. I am stronger than most humans can ever imagine. My strength comes from my own form, but also from the combined energy of All around me. My kin, my community, we all work collectively to pool our strength, so when hard times arrive, we are strong, together. We find comfort and support when we carry each other, as our combined strength supports all of us. You need to open yourself to your kin, to your community, and find the support and strength in each other, and then you will find the strength, together, to carry on."*

I roll over and grab a small book off the nightstand and toss it at the plant, missing it. After that, I hear no more advice from the ant.

Owen and Claire sit at the dining room table discussing logistics of the book, and the idea of a second book production. I lie on the couch, attempting to watch the television, annoyed by the distraction of their voices. "Is there any way you two can go somewhere else to talk? I can't hear the tv." I snap. Owen frowns, but says nothing. Claire, on the other hand, stands up, crosses into the living room and angrily turns the power button off. I'm about to object when she sternly says; "I'm having a business meeting. That outflanks any stupid tv show you're watching. If you would join us, I'd like your input on the illustrations for the second book." She points towards the papers on the table. I glance over at Owen and he meekly smiles. It would seem he has abandoned the hope that I will ever be the wonderful caring wife he has loved all these years, and I can't blame him for believing I don't care anymore. I do care, just not enough to stop drinking and rejoin the world once more. I stand up, and as Claire begins to move back to her chair at the table, assuming I am going to join them, she turns. Her shoulders sag, as I simply walk out of the living room and return to the sunroom.

A few hours later I hear a loud knock at the door, and then I hear Arthur's voice. Annoyance runs up my spine like hair bristling on a dog. I'm in no mood to put up with Arthur's interference. Then I hear Grace's voice as well. I can only make out a few words of the conversation, but it appears that Arthur is not able to drive anymore, as arthritis in his legs makes it too painful to work the brakes and gas pedal. A small voice deep down inside me whispers, *what a shame, poor Arthur, who loves to drive.* I pull the covers over my head, hoping he will leave me alone.

The next thing I feel is the heavy weight of someone sitting on the edge of my bed, and not entirely missing my body when they sit down. I manage to wriggle over to the centre of the bed, thus relieving my legs of Arthur's substantial weight. "Ah yes! It's alive! It moves under the murky waters of the swamp. Will we see if it comes out on to dry land? Only time will tell!", and he chuckles. I make no attempt to sit up, or even acknowledge his presence. I regret not pulling the sherry bottle under the covers before I hid. Arthur places a hand on my hip, and I can feel the energy penetrate the layers of blanket over me. It feels soothing, warm, almost like a ray of sun striking your back and heating your body through your clothes. I am tempted to be more accepting of his energy, but I feel the wall of heartache around me, sheltering me, imprisoning me.

"Hannah, my dear girl. I love you so much. It's very painful to see you like this. I wish I could talk to you as one Alternate to another, but I know *that* part of you isn't *plugged in* right now. I can say that you know this is the way of All, but you won't hear me. Please, please try to touch your Light so you'll remember that Death is but a doorway all humans pass through to set their energy free to re-form anew. I can only imagine how devastating this is for you, as I know my own sorrow is hard to bear when I think of HO, and how much I miss her Light. She resides with the Fae. We can take comfort in that she still shines brightly; we just can't see it here, on this plane."

His words crack open a door inside me. I feel tears streaming down my face, and it surprises me, as I thought I had no more tears left, my body having dried up and withered over the past few months. I can't bring myself to pull the covers off and look at Arthur, for fear the dam will burst, and I will never regain the control over the emotional flood that pushes at the gates of my mind. I simply muffle from under the comforter, "Thank you Arthur. Now, please leave me alone."

Fifteen

Owen enters the front door calling out for Claire. His excited tone leads me to believe it's good news. Claire bounces down the stairs, having spent the morning in her room, avoiding me. Owen stands at the foot of the stairs and announces in a loud voice; "We got it!" Claire squeals and lunges forward to embrace her father in a huge hug. I sit in the living room, curiosity nudging its way into my mind. Before I can ask, Owen enters the room and plunks himself down in his favourite chair. "Han, you're gonna be so happy! Our daughter is going to be interviewed on television! Colin actually got to talk to the producer of the *Morning's Here Show*, and she is going to be interviewed next week!" Claire screams and I cover my ears with the palms of my hands. It's been so quiet around the house, with no music playing as there once was, and no laughter like there used to be, that my ears ring from the unaccustomed noise. They begin discussing the details. I sit there, looking at my daughter, and part of me feels such pride at her success, yet part of me feels angry that she seems to be getting on with her life. Owen, noticing me staring at Claire, says, "Hannah, how about we do this as a family. All three of us go, and that way, Claire has lots of love and support through this amazing adventure!" I look at him with empty eyes. How can I feel happy, how can I support her, when I can hardly stand up, when my own sense of happiness is as elusive as the Loch Ness Monster? I shake my head and reply, "I don't feel well enough. I think you two should go, have fun.

Don't worry about including me; I know you two will be fine." I stand up and walk out of the room.

The live interview airs at seven-thirty in the morning. I set my alarm and when the bell sounds, I feel like I have been awakened from death. Owen and Claire's early morning movements never made a dent in my sleep. I look around the sunroom. The weak winter sun, itself only just up in the sky, tries to penetrate the cold grey clouds surrounding it. I sit up and decide to make a large pot of coffee to keep me awake long enough to watch the interview.

I switch on the television and make sure I have the right station. The cheerful host is doing some kitchen segment involving eggs, which I don't bother paying attention to as I make a pot of coffee. Then her chirpy voice announces that, after the commercial break, they will be talking with a new and upcoming author, whose book is creating quite a stir. I sit down with the hot mug, blowing on the contents as I stare at the screen. After some insipid commercials, the jovial music plays to indicate the return of the show. The host, Jenny Lang, sits in a fashionably uncomfortable-looking chair opposite my daughter. She makes the introduction. "Our next guest is an enterprising young author whose new book is a big hit with both children and adults. Please welcome Claire Ross." General applause sounds through the television speakers. A small voice in my head is also cheering.

The interview follows a standard format: how she got interested in writing, asking where she got her ideas from, and how challenging is it to find a publisher, among other questions. Claire takes her time, looking very relaxed as she answers. It helps that she and Owen had rehearsed all possible questions for days before the interview. When Jenny asked about the illustrations, I hold my breath. Claire smiles, and replies, "This project is a family affair. It was not only a creative effort on my part, but a multi-generational effort. My mother," and she waves at the camera, "was the inspiration and creative hand behind the illustrations.

She and my great grandmother worked endlessly on perfecting just the right images to convey the story. I could not have produced the book at all without my great grandmother; she financed the production of the book, oversaw the layout and helped with many more ideas. She was so amazing." The interviewer zeroed in on the past tense that Claire used; "Was?" Claire blanches, and swallows. "Yes, my wonderful amazing great gran, Hannah One, passed away in the summer, at the age of one-hundred. We all miss her so very much." She swallows again and takes a breath. Jenny, being a decent human being, utters her condolences before switching topics. She mentions the fact that many of the schools have received free copies of the book, and that a portion of the proceeds from every sale has been earmarked for local conservation efforts. She wonders how Claire makes any money off her book? Claire looks at her and says, a serious expression replacing the smile she has tried to wear throughout the whole interview, "Jenny, there is more to life than making money. My focus is on contributing to the community spirit, supporting children's education, and enlightening readers to ways they can be better stewards of this Earth. Providing a resource that creates a better understanding of our place in Nature makes me rich by my standards, and that's all that really matters to me."

Jenny smiles, her expression remaining neutral as she listens to this young, confident woman sitting opposite her. I suppose a lot of entrepreneurs are largely focused on making a profit, so her question was a valid one. Claire's answer was spot-on and reflected her true dedication to this project. Some invisible signal catches Jenny's attention, so she gracefully ends the interview by thanking Claire for being on the show, and remarks on how wonderful the book is, and that if anyone is interested in a copy, the information for purchasing a copy will be available on the show's website. The screen blanks for a quarter of a second, then a man appears, yelling about car prices and beating everyone else in town with his low rates. I aim the remote at the television and shut it off. I place the remote back on the coffee table, and for the first time, notice the tears streaming down my cheeks.

The sound of Owen and Claire entering the house startles me. I try to stay in the living room long enough to congratulate her, but the happy energy emanating from her is hard for me to bear. I comment, "You looked great. I like your outfit choice, and you said all the right things. It was wonderful. I know Hannah One would have loved to see you on television." Thinking I'd be able to make that remark without becoming emotional was my mistake. I feel a sob in my chest that wants to be released, but I swallow it before it escapes. My tear-filled eyes blur as Claire replies; "Thanks, Mom. I know she would have loved it. I'm glad you watched it on tv; I just wish you could have been there with us." She turns and heads up the stairs to her room.

Jamie appears unannounced on the doorstep on this dull Saturday morning. She has a tray full of coffees from a local shop, plus a box full of doughnuts. The doughnuts remind me of Arthur, and I feel a bit guilty at having been so dismissive of him when he last came to see me. Claire and Owen are busy with the book layouts, so they thank Jamie for the coffees, beg off the doughnuts and disappear into the dining room to work. I pull a coffee out of the cardboard tray and make my way back into the sunroom. Jamie picks up the last coffee and the box of doughnuts and follows me.
The snow had fallen the previous evening, layering everything in white, which perks up the drab colourless garden. I sit down on the bed, expecting Jamie to take the chair opposite me, but she also plunks herself down on the bed and lays the box between us, flipping the lid open to expose six multi-flavoured doughnuts. Chocolate, sprinkles, sugar glazed, and one plain one, all stare banally up at me. I reach in and take the plain one. "I knew you'd take that one! It's the worst one! Tastes like wallpaper to

me, and don't ask how I know what wallpaper tastes like!" she laughs, reaching in to pick up the chocolate one. "You always take the chocolate, so I avoid an argument and take one I know you wouldn't eat. Plain and simple, like this." and I hold up the unadorned piece of cooked dough. She smiles, "You always did look out for me. I wish I could do the same for you, now." She glances at me, and then towards the sherry bottle sitting on the nightstand, a pensive look crossing her face. She wants to help, but doesn't want to push it too far and be alienated, as Arthur has been. I take a moment before responding. "Jamie, I'm okay, really. There is nothing anyone can do. I just like having a small glass of sherry. It helps me sleep, keeps me from, well, thinking too much." Jamie takes a small bite of her doughnut, and then shifts her weight to sit a bit more comfortably on the bed. We are not teenagers anymore, and we both feel it when we sit in the wrong position. She takes a sip of her coffee and replies, "You know you can talk to me Han, if you ever want to. It must be hard to figure things out. I know you think the booze helps, but it really doesn't. In the long run it only pushes the pain along; it never erases it." She takes another bite and then drinks more coffee, allowing the silence to sit between us.

I'm not sure what to say. I just feel so hollow. I look at Jamie. "Well, I really don't remember how to feel, without this pain taking up so much room." I want to cry, but my eyes are dry and tired. Jamie simply nods, responding, "Sorrow can close you off to the living. It can lock you in a room, and close the curtains, shutting out everything. It can make connecting to *yourself* impossible, when all you recognize in yourself is the pain. But you're so much more than the pain. You need to allow the pain to reside in you, but not *become* you," and she waves her hand around in a circle, sprinkling doughnut crumbs all over the comforter. "You just need to remember that you are made up of more than your sorrow, so don't let the grief strip away *all* that is you, Hannah." She stuffs the remainder of the doughnut in her mouth, having said all she would say on the subject.

At first, I believe it's the morning sunlight that pokes at my eyes and makes me squint. But the Light is so much brighter, so pure and clean, without filter of clouds or windows. I stand alone in a Space without Time, without parameters of human conception. The Light dances and converges as other Lights funnel into the Space, and join with each other, rainbowing their energy across the void. I feel less burdened as my own Light vaguely responds to the touch of the energy that surrounds me. The Light coalesces into a ball of crystals, like a giant icy snowball, glowing and sparkling like gems in the sun. I reach out to touch the ball and find myself being pulled into it, like the embrace of someone who dearly loves me. I recognize this touch, and my heart stops.

"Dad? Is that you?" I know it's his Light. His pure love and energy flows over me and I feel filled with warmth, drinking it in and allowing it to fill my very core. Now I cry from joy, not sorrow.

"Hannah, you and I are part of One. I am the Light, as you are, as your mother is, as is Hannah One. Search your Light to see the truth; let go the human constraints of sorrow, for they do you a disservice. By wasting away as you are, you dishonour the Life Lesson that Death offers you; You belittle its significance, and you mar your grandmother's memory. Hannah One would not want to see you grieve in a way that holds you back from living. She would want you to continue on your journey. Hold her in your heart, knowing your Lights will shine again, possibly together. But even apart, you can still shine. You need to live again, for you. From these wounds comes wisdom, if you only open yourself up to learn the lesson. Hannah, this is what makes the human experience so full; it is not merely a straight path you follow to the end; it is a hike through climbs that are frightening, sad, and at times, rewarding and uplifting. It is the way humans learn, as they progress through their journey to the Light."

The Light shines a white glow, breathing and pulsating energy. I yearn to melt into it, stay there and be wrapped in the certainty of this place, but I also want to be with Hannah One. "Fae said she has gone to the Fae Realm. I want to go and see her there, but no doors will open to me." My father's voice gently strokes my mind; "She is there, but resides as a mere breath of air, a ripple upon the water, a streak of sunlight passing through a glade. She has yet to transition her Light, as she needs time to fully comprehend the passage from corporeal matter to the ether. And she needs the freedom to choose her way, without the chains of human emotions keeping her anchored to a spot that satisfies your need to slacken your sorrow. You know this well, from experience. You believe that your grandmother is the last thread in the cloth that connects your past life to your present life. You feel that the severing of the thread, by her death, has caused the entire fabric of your life to fail, to weaken beyond mending. The thread is still there, it is all around you, in the legacy of love she implanted in you, and in Owen and Claire. It is simply a matter of stitching your fabric to theirs, then you will see the cloth is not frayed and torn, but whole and sturdy. Let them in, and you will find the way back to life again."

The crystal globe shimmers and spins as shards of white Light shoot out and dance around me, the warmth and compassion of All imprinting my soul with a rich, nurturing love. The hollowness I felt is refilled now, like a dry well whose hidden underground spring opens and releases the water. I feel my father's loving touch one last time, as the Light moves and sways, and then lifts into the void.

I sit looking around the sunroom, and my eyes come to rest upon the dark-coloured glass bottle on the table. I feel a wisp of shame cross my mind, but dismiss it quickly, not wanting to dwell on what was, and cannot be changed. I stand up, grabbing the bottle by the neck and enter the kitchen. Owen is at the stove cooking some pasta for dinner. Claire is by the counter at the other end, cutting and gently lifting salad vegetables into a large ceramic bowl. Neither one acknowledges my presence, having become accustomed to my skulking manner. I stand in front of the sink and turn on the cold water. I unscrew the cap of the sherry bottle and begin to pour the contents into the sink, watching it converge with the water, turning the rich amber-coloured liquid to a watery brown, as it disappears down the drain. Owen turns, and his eyebrows shoot up. Claire stops cutting and stares at me, disbelief framing her face. Neither one of them speaks. I place the bottle in the recycle bin in the far corner and walk out of the kitchen, smiling.

Claire's book is very popular, thanks to word of mouth, an article in the newspaper, and her appearance on *Morning's Here*. Now, two weeks before Christmas, Claire sits at her laptop in the dining room, working on a new story layout, when her phone rings. The screen displays, *One Two Three Publishing*. She calls out to her father, who's in the kitchen washing the lunch dishes. He comes to stand in the doorway, a look of confusion on his face. Even though I'm close by in the living room, I stand up and come over to her, latching on to her unexplained excitement. Claire's hand trembles as she pushes the button and says, "Hello?" The voice on the other end speaks for a few minutes, with Claire replying in one or two-word answers. "Yes, okay. Yes, that works for me. Great. I'll be there, thanks." She presses the *end call* button, and then screams. I nearly jump out of my skin. Owen stands back a few feet as she whirls around. "Claire! What did he say?" Claire gulps air as she tries to calm down, but then starts to vibrate in place like a firecracker before it explodes. She looks at Owen and then her eyes dart to my face, a wild light in her eyes. She starts to jump up and down as she shouts, "They want my book!"

The meeting with the publisher went well. Claire, Owen and I attend as a family unit. They offered her a contract and stipulated certain conditions, and then laid out the royalties she would receive from the sales of the book. I touched Owen's hand when they discussed the payments, as we had done a bit of research ourselves, and made some comparisons of cost between us producing the book and selling it, versus the publisher. Mr. Stockton said this is a pretty standard contract that all new authors receive, with the exception that they overlooked the clause about *never* self-publishing the work before submitting it to them. I wanted to argue that we had, in fact, offered it to them, and their rejection left us free to go the self-publishing route, but Owen squeezed my hand and shook his head. He knows me too well. Claire said she would have her lawyer look over the contract before she signed anything. She said she would also have her accountant look over the figures and see if this is, in fact, a fair commission. Mr. Stockton looked somewhat surprised, but only by the widening of his eyes did he exhibit any emotion. He smiled, replying quietly, "Of course, that's an excellent idea. When you are ready just call, and we can set up an appointment to finalize things." Claire reached out and shook his hand. "Yes, I will let you know my answer, soon."

The December snow gently cascades from a cloudy sky as I walk the familiar trail in the woods. Claire has asked me to join her, to which I happily agreed. We wear warm woolen hats and mittens, as well as large chunky snow boots, for the snow is quite deep in places, and parts of the trail are not groomed. I stop to catch my breath, feeling very out of shape after months of lying around. I silently apologize to my body for having abused it so badly. I feel Fae's healing energy reaching out to me, as Claire stands beside me. She smiles without saying anything. We turn our gaze to the woods, now fully encapsulated in white layers, like frosting on a cake. The tall, bushy mint-green conifers hold mittfuls of snow, as if they are waiting for us to come near enough so they can drop their load on to our unsuspecting heads.

Claire puts her hand on my arm and asks, "Are you okay? Do you want to go back? I don't want you to get too tired." Fae's continued flow of energy gently swirls around the two of us. "No, no I'm fine. Just taking in some air. It's so fresh, and cold!" I shiver. We continue to plod through the snow until we come to the bridge. This place holds many memories for me, with Owen, Claire, and Hannah One. It's my dear grandmother who introduced me to these woods in the very beginning. As we walked these trails, she guided me, but she also showed me the way to navigate through the labyrinth of experiences that the human life offers. She never *told* me which path to take; she always knew I would find the way.

I look across the frozen stream and recall Ol' Toad, the water nymphs and dragonflies, the varied flowers that smiled in our presence and provided beauty nothing else could match. I feel alive again. It's a good feeling to connect with the Light, and the energy of *Here*. Claire takes a deep breath, and quietly says, "This has to be my favourite place in the world. I know it's yours, and it was Hannah One's as well. I have an idea, and I want to share it with you, but I don't want it to upset you." She looks at me, concerned. I nod, wondering what her idea could be, as she continues, "Well, in the spring, when the forest wakes up again, and the stream is running, and we feel like it's the right time, I thought maybe we should spread Hannah One's ashes *here*."

I feel a catch in my throat. I have not let myself think about actually parting with her only human remains left on this plane. I swallow the lump in my throat, and turn to look at Claire. She has tears in her eyes. I truly realize, in this moment, that I am not alone in my grief. She has been carrying her own sorrow, all by herself, without her mother to help her bear the weight of it. I reach out and hug her tightly.

Our soft sobs echo through the empty forest and drift up to the sky. A lone Blue Jay caws from a distance. I finally release her from my bear-like grip, and gaze into her beautiful blue eyes. "Claire, I think that is the most wonderful idea. She would love that." We turn and begin our trek back to the car.

I have resolved that the sunroom bed is no longer the place I should lay my head, avoiding the world. It's time I return to the bed I have been sharing with the man I have loved for so many years. Feeling the need for a nap I lay down on the familiar bed in our room, but find sleep evading me. My mind is happy to simply wander as my body rests. A slight rap at the bedroom door makes me roll over and sit up. The door creaks open, and Claire sticks her head in. "I'm sorry, I hope I'm not waking you up." I shift slightly as she crawls onto the bed to curl up beside me, something she has not done in years. I see the form of my daughter, a small girl, loving the time she could cuddle up with her mom, or dad, in their big bed. She would lie there and talk about what she and Fae were doing, or what she saw in the woods or garden, or some other beautiful trivial thing. I see her long brown hair, tangled and unkempt, as she wakes up between Owen and me, after sleeping in our bed when she needed reassuring. She is all grown up and her own woman now, but I will always see these images, as if they are real and tangible, as if only yesterday.

She reaches her hand across to touch my arm, running her fingers up and down my soft wooly sweater. I pull my other arm out to encircle her as I did when she was small. She fills my embrace with her adult form, but I still see my tiny daughter, her whole life in front of her feet, just waiting for her to take a step. This intimate time we share reminds me of the many times Hannah One and I curled up on her bed and I would tell her my troubles, or we would simply share our secrets. That memory, although framed with sadness, also fills me with comfort, as I continue the tradition with my own daughter.

"I called John, Mr. Stockton. We have a meeting set for day after tomorrow, just before their office shuts for the holidays. Oh, Mom," and she pauses, her voice taking on an anxious tone, "I can't believe this whole thing is happening. So much of my life all at once, I can't deal with it all. So much at once." I feel her grip on my arm tighten slightly, and I try to hold her a bit closer. I reply quietly, "I know it seems like a lot right now, but once we get this meeting over and done with, it will be in their hands. We can sit back and watch, as they promote and distribute the book. You need only focus on the next two in the series. And I have almost completed those drawings you need." I smile, feeling a bit like my old self; happy to be a part of something wonderful.

Claire sits up, looking hesitant. "It's not just the book, there's something more." She turns her head to look away, seemingly reluctant to tell me. "I should have told you before now, but well, you weren't, um, feeling well. You know…" she shrugs, and as I only blink in response she adds, "I haven't even told Dad, yet." Now it's my turn to sit up, feeling concern erase the calm that had settled over us moments before. "Claire, whatever it is, you can tell me. I can help, I'm here for you, now." She looks at me, her large blue eyes shining, a small smile spreading across her face.

"Mom, I guess there is no easy way to say this, so I'll just say it. Fae isn't the only one who's having a new life to care for. I am going to have a baby, too."

Book Four

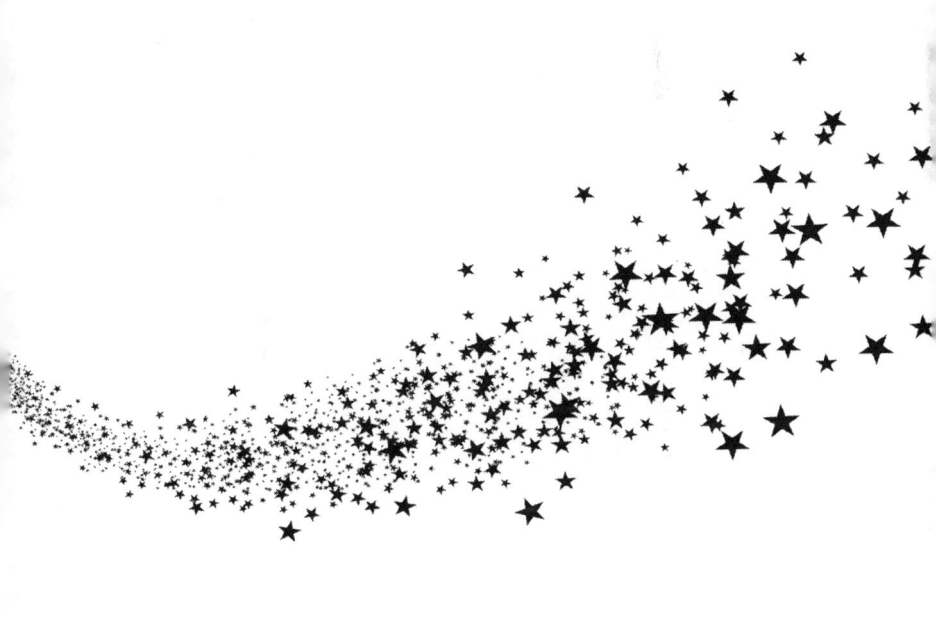

One

I walk the snow-covered path, noticing that all the grasses and bushes along the way are coated with frost, and glisten as the sun shines upon each crystal formation. I see a single set of Coyote tracks that beckon me to follow, leading me on. Eventually, the Coyote's soft pawmarks vanish, to be replaced by the hoof-prints of a Deer. The large condensed V formations sink deep into the snow, and leave the underlying grasses flattened. The single set of tracks lead me on for some distance, but in due course, the Deer's imprints disappear, only to be replaced by the four-set of a Rabbit. Two large flat impressions to show the back paws, with two smaller prints for the front paws; the Rabbit track hops along in a zig zag formation, onward moving. The tiny paws make shallow marks in the snow, compared to the deeper set of the Deer. As they diminish, I can't see any more tracks, except a long rope-like trail bulging up from under the top layer of snow. The winding trail looks like an unearthed tunnel, and I quickly realize a Vole left this unusual corridor in the snow. I follow its meandering route until I come to a widening of the path. A large empty field, unremarkable to view, stands to my left, and a tangled messy snow-laden path, flanked by two large Hawthorn at the entrance, stands to my right. No other markings in the snow indicate which way I should turn. Then I notice a white Dove nestled upon a snowy branch in one of the Hawthorns, invisible to all except for her eyes, which are black pearls in a sea of white feathers. She blinks and bobs her head once, whispering, "A time of new cycles has arrived. New worlds are being born. It is your choice now; you can follow the easy, humdrum route, staying closed off to the newness," her eyes glance towards the flat empty field, "or you can choose to learn from and release all that has passed. In turn, you will awaken the promise of a new, challenging, yet fulfilling future. You need only chose, and your path will set itself for you to journey." I glance at the empty field, appearing dull and predictable. I look at the shambolic path that passes under the branch the Dove perches on, and wonder how I will ever maneuver through it. I take a step towards the chaos, and seek to find my footing.

I awake to see tiny feather-like snowflakes float down from the ceiling, only to vanish as they touch my pillow. I lie quietly, pondering my vision, knowing full well there is no other direction to go, but the chaotic, challenging way. Six months ago, I may have chosen the flat predictable field to walk. But not now.

I stretch out my hand to feel my husband's body next to me, except he is not there. Oh yes, once again he has left me for his mistress, the African adventure. I roll on to my side and take hold of his pillow, wanting to smell some remnant of him there, but it only smells of laundry soap. Cradling the pillow, I drift back over the past five months, mixed with joy, and some trepidation.

Thinking of the day Claire announced her pregnancy, I recall my initial reaction to her news. Lying together on this very bed, my thoughts of her as my sweet young daughter were quickly pushed aside, as she announced her pregnancy to me. I found words escaping my brain, evading my tongue. My first thought was, how could this happen? My second thought was, she's way too young. I was able to contain my thoughts, realizing whatever I was about to say could make or break our relationship. I saw the joy in her face, and it was hard not to join her in her elation. I wondered if Fae was pulsating her joy outward, and that was part of the vibration I sensed. "This is certainly a surprise." It was all I could manage to say. I had so many questions, and so much worry, yet, at the age of twenty-one, she is her own person, in charge of her own body, and in the long run my opinion does not matter.

Claire smiled, placing her hand on her stomach. "I'm excited, and scared. Oh Mom, I know it's not the best time, and maybe you think I'm not old enough or something, but it is what it is, so we will have to figure things out from here." Her attitude led me to believe that she expected the news to be received with concern, rather than joy. I gently rubbed her back. "Claire, I will support *whatever* you want to do. I just need a moment to catch up to all of this. Did you say you haven't told Dad yet?" She nodded. I could only envision how well that conversation is going to go. I swallowed. "So, well, are you and David getting married, then?" Claire laughed as she swung her legs over the side of the bed and stood up. "He asked me, but I said no. I don't want to get married right now. Mom, I'm only twenty-one. How do I know if I want to tie myself to this man for the rest of my life? I love him so much, but I feel like I'm just getting started, and there is more out there I need to discover. I'm not referring to finding a better partner, I just mean *life* in general. We will always be tied together by our child, but that doesn't mean we have to be tied to each other." She looked down at her feet. "He was very disappointed when I said no. But we decided that, no matter what, we will raise this baby together. I just don't believe in marriage, at least not right now." She took two steps towards the door, and turned. "Um, I could use a hand with telling Dad about this. I doubt he will be as calm as you are, but maybe you can help him understand my side of it."

My mind jumps to the moment Owen learned of his impending grandfather-hood. His shock was quickly replaced by a peppering of questions, especially about the subject of marriage. He wasn't happy with her decision, preferring her to have the financial security of marriage. Claire firmly declared that she and David have a mutual understanding that he will be supporting his child, *no matter what*. Owen was not convinced, but Claire stood her ground.

I sit up and look around the empty bedroom. A large box of Hannah One's most precious belongings still sit in the corner. I avoid leaving my eyes on it for too long. What would she think of this situation? I smile, knowing her initial reaction would be delight. She loved babies, and loved Claire, so her heart would be with her, regardless of the logistics of her being a very young single parent. Standing up, I reach over to the bottom of the bed where I had tossed my robe the previous night, and slowly put it on. With the smell of fresh-brewed coffee in my nostrils, I make my way downstairs to the kitchen. Claire is sitting at the kitchen table with a cup of herbal tea in her hand, her nose deep in the pages of her pregnancy book. She reads everything about what to expect every month, what to eat and not eat, good exercises to try, and the list goes on. I have little recollection of what I did, or didn't do, when I was pregnant, so I offer little advice. She seems to have the matter well in hand, and revels in the process. Now, at seven months along, she is heavy, but feeling well. We shopped for a crib and stroller the week before, and Lilah, her best friend, hosted a baby shower for her two days ago, so she is well stocked with the essentials. She glances up when I enter the kitchen, and smiles as I say good morning.

I pour a cup of coffee and take the seat opposite her at the table. "I remember *your* grandmother was so excited when I was having you. She wanted to help out, and loved shopping for baby clothes. She was so happy." Thinking of the support and love my mother had shown me through those difficult months, especially when I began to hemorrhage right in this kitchen, makes my eyes tear up. Claire, without looking up from her book, says, "She was awesome. I miss her, just as much as Hannah One. They would have made amazing great, great, great, greats!" and she laughs. "I lost track of how many greats they'd be, but they would've been *so* great!" I smile to think of the excitement they would have felt for Claire and the baby.

As the months have passed, I find that, when I think or speak of Hannah One, gentle loving memories now buffer my heart from the pain. I'm able to speak of her with humour, and love, albeit tinged with sadness. The difference in my grief now is that I share it with Claire, and Owen, and Arthur, and whoever else loved her. That shared sense of love for her makes the grief manageable, like several ants carrying a large crumb, and not one ant struggling to do it all alone.

I sip my coffee, pulling over one of the large books to read the cover. The bold type lettering reads, *It's all about the Baby, a Guide to Pregnancy and Beyond*. I flip the book open to view glossy pages full of photos showing an actual birth. I feel my stomach clench, and quickly flip to another section. As beautiful as birth is, with the ushering in of a new life, it's also extremely gross. I smile, as a vision crosses my mind, of Claire's newborn face, glowing, as she was handed into a nurse's waiting arms, having just been extricated from my body. She was covered in bodily fluids, but all I could only see was her shining face beaming out at her new world.

Claire closes her book and drains her mug of the last of the tea. She rises, slowly, paces over and places her mug on the counter. She yawns. "I know it's only like, nine in the morning, but I am so tired. I think I'll stretch out before I go to the Centre at noon." She plods into the living room and unceremoniously lowers herself on to the couch, gradually shifting her legs up on to the cushions to lie down. "Oh crap," she mutters. She swings her legs back down and sits up, hoisting herself to the edge of the couch and then using her muscular legs, lifts herself up again. She stands up and frowns. "Are you okay?" I ask. She trudges back into the kitchen, heading towards the main floor bathroom. "Never fails; I get myself lying down and then I gotta pee!" I smile sympathetically as she closes the door behind her.

At nearly nine o'clock, as I sit in the living room reading, I look up from my book to see my very tanned, tired-looking husband come through the front door, returning after two months in Africa. He has one large suitcase that he nosily drops to the floor by the stairs, as I rise and come over to greet him. His bronze face is lined with smile creases, and his striking blue eyes, the colour of the Mediterranean Sea, shine at me from out of his copper-coloured face. We reach out to hug each other. As much as I secretly resented his need to leave me, to search out his fulfillment, there is something to be said about our reunions.

We kiss, and I hear my inner voice heave a sigh. After our lingering kiss, we break apart and he comes to sit down on the old couch in the living room. His frame seems to sag as he sits down, the weight of the end of his journey finally resting upon him. I sit beside him, and take hold of his hand. "You made good time. Obviously, your flight wasn't delayed, as you suspected it might be." He nods, looking at our fingers entwined. He places his other hand on top of our clasped hands, and says, "I'm very glad to be home. I'm exhausted. I guess I'm not as young as I used to be." He laughs. I make no comment, or ask if I can get him a drink, or something to eat. I simply want to sit beside him and bask in the moment. Stillness encircle us, like a cocoon. I know we will not have many more moments of quiet, once Claire's baby arrives. He shifts his hand to his face and rubs his eyes. Fatigue wears on his expression. Seeing how tired he is, I suggest he go to bed and sleep as much as he can, to rid himself of the jet lag. He slowly stands up, pulling me up with him. He gives me a hug, and then makes his way upstairs.

I return to the couch and pick up my book. Claire is already in bed, as she too has good reason to get as much sleep as she can. I look at the cover of my book, but the desire to read has left me. I'm feeling antsy for some reason, like I want to clean the house, or something equally silly for this time of night. The relief I feel now that Owen is home must have triggered some physiological response that is giving me energy, rather than slowing my processes down in preparation for sleep. Even after fifty-two years, my

Alternate is still in awe of the unique functions of the human body. Lately, I have even more questions about what seems to be going on within my own structure, with unusual mood swings, and these energy bursts followed by extreme fatigue.

I stand up and go to the kitchen. It's clean, all the dinner dishes having been washed and put away. I glance around, unable to land on some mindless physical project that will help purge me of this ill-timed liveliness. I walk through to the sunroom. I click on a standing lamp in the corner, illuminating the room, which spills incandescent light out into the garden. I sit down in one of the cushioned wicker chairs that faces the garden window. It was one of Hannah One's favourite chairs to sit in, before the room was taken over by her bed.

My eyes come to rest on a large box nestled in the corner of the room. It's the same box I had kept in my bedroom, full of Hannah One's treasures. I had moved it so that Owen will have room to unpack his gear. I just keep moving the box around, from room to room, unwilling to store it out of sight or open it and deal with the contents, for fear the pain will overtake me again.

I stare at the box for another minute, and then stand up. I take a few steps towards it, and then bend down to lift it over closer to the chair. I pull the folded lid open and look inside. The things Claire and I had wrapped carefully in bubble wrap stare up at me neutrally. My Alternate side is stating that, these are not *Her*, they are merely reminders of *Her*. The most important things are the memories and emotions I hold, not the old tea cup, or her favourite books. My human side still finds it challenging to reconcile my emotional responses with the logical reasoning of my Alternate. It's something I am learning to balance; Alternates may be wise, but when encased in a human frame, with hormones, and brains that react to emotional stimuli, the calm voice of the Alternate is not always going to be heard. I know opening this box is inevitable, so I might as well deal with it now, as difficult as it is.

I reach in and pull out a wrapped object. Laying it in my lap and unpeeling the wrap, I see her jewelry box. I open the lid, and bright shiny costume jewelry sparkles a greeting. There is one ring, sitting in its cushioned ring-ledge. It's her wedding ring - a simple gold band. It is slightly worn, having been on her finger for over seventy-seven years. She continued to wear it, even though fifty years had passed since her husband's death. I remember asking her why she still wore it, and she smiled, saying that the ring kept her company, as it kept her loving James close to her. I pick up the ring and slide it on my right index finger. It fits perfectly. I touch the ring and feel a bit of energy from it - a happy energy; happy to be worn again, happy to keep me company, as it brings Hannah One closer to me. I place the jewelry box beside me, intending to have it sit on the dresser in my bedroom, beside my own jewelry box.

I reach into the cardboard box again and find her tea cups, some framed photos of all of us, plus one of her parents, and a black and white photo of my father as a young adult. I trace the outline of his face in the slightly faded photo. His eyes are bright and full of mischief, and his smile is wide and honest. I place that photo beside the jewelry box.

Towards the bottom of the box are five books. These were her favourite books, ones that she would read over and over, and never tire of their stories. I know these books, often seeing her with one in hand, as she headed to the lounger in the garden for an afternoon read. My hand rests on one of my favourite books, Roald Dahl's *Charlie and the Chocolate Factory*. An image of the two of us, sitting together, reading this book, comes to mind. I was very young when we first read it together, but over the years she would pull it out and we would read chapters to each other and giggle at the imaginative writing. It was so funny, and so ridiculous, the manner in which the author "did away" with the horrible characters. I run my hand over the cover, taking in the unusual illustration on it, the bright red lettering, and the frayed edges and spine. It is a book well loved. I raise it to my chest and hug it like a long-lost friend. When I lay it in my lap, I notice the edge of a small piece of white paper sticking out from the top. I open the book to the page, and find a small envelope.

The envelope, hand written, is addressed to me. It is in Hannah One's hand-writing. I swallow. I carefully pull the envelope out of the book and gently place the book down beside the jewelry box and my father's photo. The envelope is not sealed, so I simply lift the back flap and withdraw the paper inside. Unfolding it, I draw a breath. It is a letter, to me, from Hannah One. I blink, as the tears begin to flood my eyes and blind me. I look away. Do I read it, or do I put it away, to face another time, maybe when I'm stronger? The thought of not knowing the contents outweighs my fear of touching the pain again. I look down at the page, and begin to read:

"*My Dearest Hannah; I am very happy you've located my letter. I knew you would come across it, when you are ready to read it. I am sitting here, in the garden, enjoying the sunshine, and the birdsong, and thinking of how much I will miss all of this. But my sadness is lessened simply by knowing you. Your presence in my life has reduced my fear of 'shuffling off this mortal coil', as Shakespeare put it, knowing there will be more for me after my earthly form ceases to be. I am ready now, at one hundred, to send my Light off to new adventures. Loving you, and Daniel, my darling son, and Claire and Owen, has been my life's joy. I could not have been blessed more than by having such a wonderful family love me. And, in the end, that is all that matters. You know it's not the material things. It is the connections and the experiences we have as humans that make this ride more complete. I need not worry about how you will deal with my passing. You will grieve, but find your way again. I have faith that you will stand strong and help your family carry on. My only wish now is that wherever I end up going, there's a garden, maybe some lovely birds to sing with, and some good coffee to sip. My only other wish is that someday we will meet again, so we can continue our wonderful adventure together. I love you; I love Claire and Owen. Give them my love. Yours, with infinite love, Hannah One."*

I cry quietly as I re-read her letter. I suck in my breath, all the while careful not to get any tears on the letter. I blink to clear my eyes so I can carefully fold the letter back up and slide it gently into the envelope. I place it back in the book and close it softly. Clutching the book once again, I hear her words in my mind, *you will find your way again.* I hold on to that phrase, as, with each tear, I let go of my sadness.

Suddenly feeling weary, I decide it's time for bed. I stand up and retrieve the jewelry box, my father's photo and the book, leaving the open box sitting by the chair. I reach out with my free hand to turn off the light. When the room is dark, a flood of moonlight washes in through the windows. A full moon shines like a pale white sun, illuminating a shadowy, mysterious garden outside. I close my eyes and wish for simpler times, when I was a girl, and all I had to cope with was growing up. Some small part of me misses the days when the heavy decisions of life were left to the adults in the room. But that is wishful thinking, and the experiences and love that life has presented to me make me content to be in the *Now.* I sit down in the chair and look up at the pure moon, shining in all its glory. I close my eyes and feel myself being drawn inward. I see the Light, and feel the compassion of beings as they wrap their energy around me, lifting me up. I step out of their embrace as I see my door. Many images reveal themselves as I scan it. My eyes come to rest on one picture. I was ten years old. Hannah One and I were in the woods having a picnic.

I touch the image and find myself standing in the clearing.

The sunshine warms my shoulders. My youthful self is sitting on a blanket, drawing, as Hannah One sits nearby, watching the Sparrows and Juncos flit from tree to tree. She stretches out her hand, palm raised and cupped, full of seeds. Seeing her makes my heart stop. I want to rush over and hug her. I turn away, feeling the intense pressure ease somewhat as I look upon myself. My long brown hair is tied back in a pony tail, to keep from falling into my face, as my bowed head concentrates on the sketch pad in my lap. Although my youthful self is wholly engrossed in moving the pencil over the sketch paper, she glances up and sees me standing there. She has a confused look on her face, as if she is trying to remember where she has seen me before. I glance back to Hannah One, who, sitting as silently as she can, wears a giant grin on her face as two little Chickadees perch on her hand and peck at the seeds. Her eyes are filled with happiness. I turn back to look at myself, and then sit down on the blanket. I discreetly peer at the drawing that sits on the paper. It's Hannah One and the birds. I lift my face to the sun, feeling it penetrate every pore in my skin, filling me with Light. I feel gratitude wash over me; feeling so fortunate to have had this experience, and to be able to revisit it whenever I want to. I look at the girl, sitting still beside me, watching me carefully. I speak quietly, wanting to preserve the beautiful tranquility as much as possible, "Hannah, this is a special moment in time. Cherish it, and cherish her. And try to remember to go with the flow. Allow yourself to experience life as the river flows. Fight the current, and you spend your life in a constant struggle. Let your boat float through the storms, and you will find it much better downstream. It is important that you take each moment you share with each person you love, as a piece of gold, to hold in your heart and cherish." I smile, and turn my eyes to Hannah One as I stand up. I briefly glance back at my young form, and, right before her eyes, I vanish.

A touch on my arm makes me start, and I look up to see Owen standing there. His smile is warm, but full of concern. I blink, feeling slightly disoriented, then, looking down, I see the book, still clasped between my hands. I smile at him and whisper, "I found a piece of gold; I want to share it with you." I stand up and head to bed, gently carrying the jewelry box, the photo and the book. Owen follows me, a perplexed look on his face.

Two

Noah Oran Ross came into the world on July seventh, at noon. Weighing in at just over seven pounds, his bright shining face and loud wail announced himself to us all. Claire's experience, unlike mine, went as smoothly as one could hope for when giving birth. I was privileged to be present, holding her hand, encouraging her to push, fetching ice chips when needed, and sending out as much of my own healing energy as I could. Fae's healing Light was present throughout the entire process. At times, Claire would talk, out loud, to Fae, which confused the nurse, as she thought Claire was speaking to her.

Claire and David decided to name the baby Noah, after David's grandfather. Oran was an unusual choice. It's an Irish name, meaning Light. Fae had named her little one *Orna*, so the pair would be linked by name, and possibly one day get to meet each other. Since David is in the dark about Fae's existence, he simply thought it was an interesting name, and assumed that, because of Owen's Irish ancestry, Claire had wanted to use this name.

Noah's sweet countenance is a ray of sunshine. Owen is an especially proud grandfather, hardly ever leaving Noah alone. Claire is happy, but exhausted. I tried to get up with her during the night to help with whatever I could, but found that she, who is breastfeeding, really didn't need much assistance. I got up nonetheless, just to show my support. I find myself, quite often, simply staring into his face, feeling the love wash over me to the point where I feel tears in my eyes. Not only am I blessed with having Claire in my life, but now this little entity, gracing my Light with his own. His bright tuft of auburn hair often standing up on end, and his beautiful hazel eyes that twinkle when he looks at his mother, make me smile and fill me with so much gratitude for this experience.

Soon enough, friends begin to visit to meet the newest member of the Ross family. Arthur is the first to arrive, with Grace by his side. There has been discussion between Claire and Grace regarding the Centre, as Grace is thinking of retirement, but is reluctant to leave her clients behind. She is waiting to see what Claire wants to do, whether she would take over the business herself, or just close up shop. The pregnancy threw a curve-ball in the dialogue, so nothing has been firmly decided yet. So Grace continues on, but I can tell she is ready to step back and let Claire sail ahead; it's just a matter of *when*. Claire knows she can count on our support if she decides to go ahead with this venture.

Arthur himself is doing much better since his doctor prescribed a new arthritis medication. His mobility has improved, which means he is chomping at the bit to get back into the world again. "I think you know it already," he whispers to me, after having a cuddle with the newborn; "he has no Alternate in him." I smile and whisper a reply, "Would you like to tell Owen? I think he will find this to be good news." Arthur smirks.

With the fine summer weather gracing us day by day, I find us heading to the woods for a picnic by the pond. As we walk along, Claire holds Noah carefully and points out all the flowers and fauna, or the dragonflies and other insects that float by. Owen and I smile at each other, knowing that our shared memory of bringing Claire here as a baby is jointly playing in our minds' eye.

When the days are hot and lazy we just sit in the garden, Noah laid out on a comfortable blanket with Claire beside him on the ground. She talks and sings to him, and at times Fae comes in and touches his Light and he giggles and coos. OnanOff lies beside the pair; our old, furry sentry, ever on watch for stray critters that might pass by and cause trouble, according to him. Now on the cusp of his senior citizen years, he has slowed down considerably, but still has a spark of mischief in him. So finely attuned to Claire, it was OnanOff who alerted me to the fact that she was starting her labour. He always slept with her, so when I found him jumping up on my bed, early in the morning, and nudging my hand, I knew something was amiss. *"Claire's energy has shifted. I can feel it. I think you need to go to her."* He jumped off the bed and stalked out of the room, his soft paws hardly making a sound on the floor. He knew before Claire did that *things* were in motion.

The summer seems to sprint by us as we create lasting memories of Claire and Noah experiencing many firsts as mother and son. I keep taking mental snapshots to fill my door with each treasured moment.

The autumn brings news that Claire's second book is heading to store outlets within two weeks, in time for early Christmas shopping. *Fanny and Fae - Nature Detectives* is also being suggested as an addition to the city's elementary school curriculum by the city school-board. We talk about the third book, conceptualizing the content and illustrations. Claire is playing with the idea of chapter books for older readers, and the publisher said that if she produces a few chapters they could read, they would consider adding these books to the series.

I wonder how Claire will find the time, and energy, to commit to writing a book. Between Noah, and working three days at the Centre, she seems to have a full plate. Her drive and enthusiasm for her characters, plus Fae's contributions to story ideas, is what is keeping her going. She exudes a confidence in her venture that makes me admire her determination.

The afternoon is bright and warm, one of the last truly summer-like days that late autumn offers. I always feel melancholy when the last leaf falls from the tree, signaling the end of dancing in the garden barefoot, picnics under the giant Oak, wearing short sleeves and sandals, and the greenness of each day. Today, however, the sun beams through the remaining golden leaves, the squirrels make busy-work of stocking up food and extra dried leaves to line their nests for winter, and the birds sing of summer past, and travels ahead through winter's woes. I lie on the lounger in the garden, half reading, half dozing, when I hear the back door open. I glance up to see Arthur, carefully making his way down the steps. I sit up, blinking away the lethargy I feel behind my eyes. Arthur makes his way over and sits down in the large garden chair opposite me. He sighs heavily. "My god, these old bones are hard to carry. I'm beginning to think that I should just visit you as my Alternate - nice easy Light that I don't have to lug around!", he chuckles. I see Claire come out of the house, Noah on one hip, and a tray of mugs balanced in her free hand. I'm about to say something, but decide to let it go. I stand up and rush over to take the tray from her. She laughs, saying, "Don't worry, if something was slipping, I'd just drop Noah and save the tea!" Arthur laughs. She walks over to the far chair in the circle, and lowers Noah to a sitting position in her lap. Arthur smiles at Noah, his eyes full of love. I sometimes wonder if Arthur feels regret that he never had children of his own. Being such a personal topic, I never asked him about it. I know his life is full and he carries few regrets. I think that is all that matters in the long run.

Noah coos as he gnaws on his fist and looks up at the Oak tree. Arthur, following his gaze says, "Yes Noah, this is Oak. He houses many Fae, who are keeping watch over you, and your mommy. You are one lucky boy to have so many fairies taking care of you." Noah looks at Arthur and blinks. Arthur laughs again, "Ah yes, the simple enjoyment of being a baby. No worries, other than food and love. It would appear, as one creeps upon old age, it's the same story. I just want food, and lots of love." He looks over at me and I chuckle.

The talk turns to Claire's writing and the newest book being published. Arthur is excited to hear the news, and encourages Claire to pursue her idea of chapter books. "I wonder how Owen is getting along with his work? I saw him eyeball-deep in his laptop as I passed by him to come out here. How is his memoir going?" I sigh. It seems like everyone is immersed in some interesting project, except me. I do have Claire's third book illustrations to consider, but in truth, that is a task to complete solely to help Claire with her venture. I have no project to call my own.

Claire speaks up before I can comment. "He's doing okay. He's frustrated that he can't remember some of the details from his first trip, but that was over *twenty-two* years ago, so come on!" she laughs. Again, her young age prevents her from seeing how, as one ages, the concept of the passage of time can become less clear. I sometimes think I was thirty-two only a *few* years ago, not twenty years ago. Arthur nods, likely having the same thought as I have. Now reaching eighty, he often said he wished he had written down more things. He sighs, commenting, "I can appreciate his frustration. There are times I can't remember what I did last week, let alone twenty years ago." He chortles before continuing, "I think the human brain is like a sponge. It soaks in life as we progress, but at some point, it becomes waterlogged, and we need to squeeze it out into a glass for safe keeping. Then we have more room to soak up more as we go along." He grins, as he often does, thinking he's so witty. I shake my head. "Knowing you Arthur, you'd miss the glass, and spill it all over the place." Claire laughs, making Noah jiggle on her lap. He frowns, looking up at his mother.

We sit quietly, drinking tea, and watch for the fairies in the tree. Noah gurgles and squeals, as a stray leaf descends and lands in Claire's lap. She picks it up and shows the reddish-brown leaf to him, twirling the stem between her fingers, so it wiggles back and forth. Noah giggles again, smiling that beautiful smile he owns. His little hand reaches out and grabs the leaf, quickly stuffing it in his mouth as Claire tries to fish it out. I laugh. It reminds me of Claire eating the dirt in the front garden.

Finally, Noah seems to be getting restless, or hungry, or a little of both, so Claire lifts him up into her arms, and, after Arthur plants a soft kiss on his forehead, she whisks him off to the house to be fed, changed, and put down for a nap.

Arthur and I sit in silence. The birds have found their own perches to rest the afternoon away, so their cheerful songs are absent. The tree stands, anciently reserved, not interested in communing with any humans. The old Oak misses Hannah One, and although it understands the process of life and death, it is nevertheless diminished by her absence. Its energy throbs within at a minimal pace. I feel sad for it, but I know that, being eternal in Light, the tree will go on, then pass away, and its energy, when the time comes, will feed other life forces.

Arthur shifts slightly in his chair. "Are you comfortable? Would you like the lounger instead?" I ask. He smiles, shaking his head. "I'm fine. Just moving the old frame around so I don't sit on my bony ass for too long." He scrutinizes my face. "So, how are *you* doing?" I know he still holds concern for my emotional well-being, after the past year or so. "I'm okay. Just feeling a bit unfocused. Even with Noah, and Claire's book, and helping Owen here and there, I just feel like I have nothing to sink my teeth into, to call my own." Arthur nods. "Yes, um, how old are you again?" I mention I am fifty-two. He nods again. "You have the financial ability to pick and choose what's next on your plate. You certainly still have the plate; you just need to figure out what you want to put on it." He pauses, deep in thought. "This sounds a bit redundant, considering what everyone around you is involved in, but what about writing your *own* memoir?" I look at him skeptically. "*Who* would want to read that? I doubt *I'd* even want to read it!" He shakes his head. "No, no, you're wrong. I mean *really* write it, including your Alternate perspective. Give truth to the words, infuse them with your Light. Tell your story as authentically as you can bear to. It will give you clarity, and if nothing else, it will give Claire a wonderful keepsake to have when you're gone." He pauses, and turns to look directly at me; "The other idea that crossed my mind is that maybe you and Claire could take over the Centre, *together*. You will bring your experience as a business owner to it for day-to-day operations; but I also see you in the role of facilitator. There is no greater personal reward than sharing your knowledge, and opening others to their potential. I think you'd be good at that." I don't respond, but allow his words to soak into my mind, take them at face value, rather than dismissing them out of hand. I simply don't see myself as a teacher. Jamie is the teacher, Owen is the teacher, David is the teacher. I am just... me.

Arthur surveys the fading autumn flowers near him as he speaks. "I know you think you're not suitable for such a role. I can almost hear the wheels turning, steering you out of this conversation. I will say this; sharing my knowledge of the Light has been one of the most rewarding *human* exchanges of my life. I want to quote a wonderful Canadian author, Matshona Dhliwayo, if you will indulge me; '*Your mind shines brightest when you enlighten others; your heart, when you encourage others; your soul, when you elevate others; and your life, when you empower others.*'"

He looks up into the tree and smiles as he catches sight of a small woodland sprite, her tiny face peeking around the trunk. He points and says, "I see you! Peek-a-boo!" The laughter of the sprite sounds like tiny wind chimes being tickled by a breeze. Arthur loves to play with the Fae, as they bring out the beautiful child within him. I smile, searching the tree for another sighting of the magical guardians who watch over us, and share their loving energy.

Three

Seven women congregate in a haphazard circle under a large Maple tree in the woods. Even with differing ages and backgrounds, they all have one thing in common: an interest in communing with their animal guides. Five of the women, myself included, sit in folding chairs, while the other two sit on a blanket on the ground. One woman, Matilda, or Tila, as she prefers to be called, sits on the earth, her bare feet connecting directly to the energy source. I really like Tila. She has a free spirit and knows her own mind. She, like me, is in her mid-fifties, and has been on her journey long enough to understand the inconsistency of life's lessons, and therefore looks at every opportunity as a way to learn.

I watch as the women write in their gratitude journals. I am happy to see that Janice has joined the group. Ever since I met her at summer camp, all those decades ago, she has been a steadfast friend. She's had a challenging time since the bookstore closed. She spent a lot of time trying to cope with a new job, and caring for her partner Amelia, who was diagnosed with chronic fatigue syndrome, which can be debilitating. I persuaded Janice to take a break and come out to the woods with us, to refresh her energy and get a little respite from the demands of her challenging life.

The group formed through the Centre, which has been jointly owned and operated by Claire and me for almost two years now. It has been a smooth transition after Grace retired, for Claire was already in the loop as far as logistics were concerned. Grace now happily spends her days with Arthur. They take little day trips here and there, or just enjoy a day of drinking in the world around them. Arthur loves having her by his side as he sashays into his eighties. Still spry and quick witted, he is a force of nature himself. I know Fae is sending her healing energy to him, as she did with Hannah One, but Arthur himself possesses a strong pure Light, and that keeps his home fires burning brightly. Arthur was right. Helping others discover their Light is one of most satisfying things I have ever done. We started our session with a beautiful meditation, and in that time, I was able to reach out and touch their energy, and aid them in opening themselves up to the Universe.

Tila smiles at me as our eyes meet. She and I have become good friends, and it's inspiring to have her in my life. I continue to treasure my friendship with Jamie, one that has stood the test of time over forty years. The framework of our friendship was built when we were young girls, so over the years we have had to adjust the structure many times. However, Tila relates to me as the person I am *now*. The relationships are equally rich and loving, just different. It's another reason why I find human relationships so complex and fascinating, and why I doubt I'll ever learn all there is to know.

The sun filters through the Maple, and I feel the warm breeze on my back. It's the perfect place to drift away and open your soul to Nature. I find myself closing my eyes and allowing the energy from the trees, the flowers, the nearby pond, and all the living beings around me, to fill me up. I see the Light sway before me, bright yellows and greens, entwining blues and indigos, all choreographed in an exquisite dance. The sound of three Grey Squirrels chasing each other pulls me back to the Now. Everyone in the group has their heads turned to watch these silly squirrels dash about in the tree branches, chittering at one another as they play. I speak gently to them with my mind; "Silly souls. What are you three up to?" They stop and lean over the branch they are all perched on, their black-pearl eyes taking in each member of the group, but finally coming to rest upon me. I smile, and wave to them. One squirrel is indignant in his reply. *You humans come to our forest and just sit there, upon our ground, making our grass all flat, and you call us silly? We know you want to learn from us, but first you must remove your judgement!*

The other squirrels remain silent, but inch their way off the branch to hug the trunk of the tree. One by one they make their way high up into the canopy, only to continue their game out of view. I chuckle. The women turn towards me, a surprised look on a few of their faces. I explain my amusement; "I told the squirrels they were being silly. They told me we looked equally dumb, sitting here, on the ground, doing nothing. Squirrel's message to me is, things aren't always what they appear to be. Silly play is actually a learning tool for them, and a way to communicate and show potential as a future mate. Before we are to learn from our animal brothers and sisters, we need to remove our judgment of them. It disconnects us from the true message they offer." A few of the women nod, understanding the depth of my lesson. Others simply look confused, still stuck on the idea that I might have actually spoken to the squirrels.

I stand up, feeling the need to stretch. The women, especially those who have been sitting on the ground, mimic my stretching. It appears that our session is drawing to a close, as quiet chatting begins, and one woman starts to fold up the blanket. I put no time-limit on our gatherings. They will conclude when they are supposed to. "Okay, we can meet back at the Centre, for anyone who wants to have coffee or tea. I'd like you to continue journaling, wherever you find a quiet place. It doesn't have to be the middle of the woods; it can be anywhere you feel the connection to your energy. If you want to write down the names of a few animals you feel a special connection to, and what draws you to them, next week we can explore their symbolism and its significance for you." A few *oohs* and *aahs* resound through the group.

We slowly make our way back to the parking lot, and four of the women climb into one car, obviously having car pooled. Tila and Janice get into my car and we head back to the Centre.

The Centre is not far from our meeting spot in the woods, and I soon find that everyone has returned for more socializing after our session. Claire is in the kitchen area, busily preparing pots of tea, and laying out some sweets on a large tray for those who need a sugar fix. Tila is busy buzzing from one woman to the next, handing out small paper flyers that announce her upcoming art exhibit at a local gallery. She is an amazing painter, but unlike traditional painters who place their love on canvas, Tila paints on *everything*. She paints murals on walls, cupboards, tiles, bookends, tables, chairs, toilet seat lids, and the list goes on. She uses bright vibrant colours and patterns, often of large faces or animals, African motifs, or simple geometrics. Her art reflects her energy, which is wild and uncapped. She herself is a free spirit, not worrying what others think of her, only that with each person she encounters she will take away some life lesson from them, if she can. She has her bad days, like everyone does, but she embraces them and takes from them what she can and moves on. Her energy is infectious, and I feel like I have a case of Tila-flu. My life took a turn to the happy side when I met her.

I feel very contented now, as a human female in her fifties. I try to find a sense of purpose with each day, and a calm amidst the storm of life that swirls around me. Claire is her own whirlwind, just like she always is, only now she is larger than life and has Noah along for the ride. Her partner David continues to be generously involved with them, both emotionally and financially. That soothes Owen's troubled mind. He constantly worries about her wellbeing.

Owen, now having completed his memoir about his time in Africa, is awaiting judgment from the publisher. It certainly helps that Claire has a good working relationship with *One Two Three*

Publishing, but the manuscript is being evaluated by a different department than the one Claire works with, so the book's future is not guaranteed. I only hope it is accepted, as Owen has poured so much of himself into writing it.

With all my ducks in a row, for the first time in long while, I relax and carry a forward-looking view of my life. It's only when I begin to wake up in the night, drenched in sweat, that I wonder why this is happening. It's Tila who reminds me that it's likely the menopausal monster rearing its head. And sure enough, once I think about it, all the signs are evident. A slight weight gain I hadn't noticed, until I tried on a pair of jeans I hadn't worn in a while, and found it tough to zip them up; those horrible sweats that make you feel like you just bathed in hot oil; to be quickly replaced by the need to throw three blankets on top of you when the shivering begins. And then there's the moodiness, which I hadn't attributed to anything except being over-tired from not sleeping well. Tila is a great resource for natural solutions to some of my issues. The idea of sharing our struggle as a community of women led me to form a new group, devoted to supporting each other through this phase of our journey. Tila is really the one who leads the brigade, as she has done a lot of research and is enthusiastic to share her findings. Twelve women join us bi-weekly at the Centre, for support, a few laughs, a few tears, and then we share a meal together. Potlucks have always been one of my favourite things to participate in, ever since Gwen held the annual bookstore Christmas potlucks at her house. That seems like another lifetime now, the span of years pulling the memories farther backwards, as I proceed onward.

At these gatherings, one thing that seems to be a hot topic of conversation is the general lack of sex drive affecting most of the women in the group. When I really look at my relationship with Owen, I have to be honest; it is lacking in the intimacy department. I see our relationship has grown into a comfortable, familiar, dull pattern. Owen is always the one to initiate things, but with me, at times, discouraging him with excuses. I feel somewhat guilty that I have little interest in sex, but when I hear that others feel the same, my guilt is lessened. The next step is to be honest and open with our partners, about the physical changes we are experiencing, and find alternative ways to show love and intimacy with them. These meetings are a true life-line for we women going through this time of our lives.

Claire sits down beside me on the couch, an air of serenity colouring her aura softly. She leans in, just as she did as a child, and I place my arm around her, drawing her close to me. Claire touches my free hand with hers and the energy exchange is palpable. "Mom, I have something to share with you." She pauses, and then says softly, "Fae thinks it is time to let you in." I continue to hug her as confusion races through my mind. I'm at a loss for words. It has been so long I thought that realm was lost to me, forever.

She gently strokes my hand, as a mother would her child's when offering comfort. "Fae wants you to know that the way to the Fae realm has been veiled to you, but now it is clear. She says, and I'm quoting here; 'it has been lost to you as you struggled to find the path on this human plane. You can transcend to Fae only when your intention is clear. Your frequency, your vibration, was fractured after Hannah One died, and it prevented you from accessing your true energy. Had the way been open, your intention would have been to seek out her energy and attach your fracture to her, in hopes she could heal you, or lift your sorrow away. It's not her responsibility to clear your void, to lift you up once again. She is on her own journey, and remains in the Light'." Claire sits up and turns to look directly at me. "Now, Mom, now is the time of change for you. Fae has seen it in your vibration; your intent is once again on the right path. This change has allowed the energy to flow, and so you can find the passage once again."

I sit still, slightly stunned. How many times have I tried to access the Fae realm after Hannah One died, and never found my way? The desolation I felt being locked out of that world was devastating. I assumed that I simply could not find the path. I never told Arthur or Claire that I was struggling, but it would appear that Fae has been aware all along. I take a breath and ask, "Why didn't Fae *tell me* I couldn't go there, when I was trying so hard, and failing? It felt so hurtful to be left out, like a cat at the door that no one would let in." I feel myself tearing up. Claire pauses, listening to Fae's response before repeating it. "She says it was a process you needed to go through to find your way. It was guided by your *own* Light, and should not be directed by others. You needed to take each step, as painful as it was," and she pauses as a frown crosses her face, "so you could arrive at this point in time. The lessons learned, and gratitude replacing the anguish, are all steps that led you *here*. The Fae will not help you cut the line to get to the end, as so much of the journey is in the steps that teach and guide you, as you travel." She takes a deep breath and again, gently pats my hand. "Mom, it's okay to be a bit mad at Fae, but really, she is right. You need to let that go, and listen more closely to your Alternate voice, as you have started to do more often now. You know how to lead *yourself* on, without compromising your experience as a human being. You're finally finding the balance you always wanted." She smiles at me, and for the first time I really see my daughter as an accomplished, mature, fully enlightened human, no more the immature teenager who wanted less to do with other realms, and more to do with teenage inanities. I reach out and hug her, thanking the Light for her presence in this adventure.

I glance around. There is nothing but black space everywhere. As my eyes adjust to the dark, I can see miniscule stars twinkling, far off in the distance. A thin moon shows its pale slivered body in the far-off sky. My own Light is dark and glimmering, like moonlight on water. I drift, with no purpose, no sense of direction, or means to maneuver myself, even if I knew which way to go. I focus my energy, and create a slender beam of light, upon which I perch and wait. I know not what I am waiting for, but I know I have nothing to do but wait. The light beam gently commences a downward slope, and I start to descend. The sun begins to shine and I can see below me a vast ocean. The water is calm, but dark and depthless. With no land in sight, I believe I will merely sink into the abyss and be lost to Time. It is then that a giant shell rises up from the water. Mottled green, yellow and red, it is the back of a giant Sea Turtle. A voice resounds within me, inviting me to find respite upon her shell. Turtle floats in the water, unmoving. I gently slide down and come to rest upon the massive back, her surface knobby, but surprisingly warm. I sit there, staring out at the boundless horizon. The sky is blue, but no birds fly within its frame. The water is like glass, upon which Turtle and I are suspended in Space and Time. I begin to wonder how, or if, I will see land, but the concern is erased as I simply sit, and know that when I am meant to find purchase on the Earth it will find me. When the surface of the water breaks, and the face of a Beaver appears, I know I am receiving the invitation to seek out far shores. "Will you help me find the shore?" I ask. Beaver says nothing, but turns and indicates I should take the small mound of soil that he balances on his flat, plate-like tail. I gently lift the earth off his tail and place it upon Turtle's back. Then Loon appears at the edge of Turtle's shell, holding a treasure of soil within her beak. I scoop the soil out and gently add it to the mound on the shell. When Otter comes to the surface with a scoop of soil nestled within his wet furry paws, I sense I am ready to begin. I thank Beaver, Loon and Otter for their gifts. I spread the soil over Turtle's back, and it expands to cover the entire shell. Taking a soft breath in, and infusing my Light and Love into the breath, I gently exhale over the soil. The soil forms a small island, upon which life begins to grow. Small flowers and grasses emerge and spread out, creating a larger island. Small animals and birds bring more seeds to plant, and as the island grows, immense trees sprout, taking root in the rich earth. Turtle moves slightly, dislodging the colossal island, with me on it, from her back. The island spreads its roots deep down, tenderly securing itself to the world in which it has been born into. I smile, and thank Turtle for her unwavering support. As she speaks, the animals of the water and land listen. "From which I came, I will return; but know that you can find aid in the most unlikely of places. You need only reach out with your Light, and you will be answered." She sinks into the water, disappearing into the dark blue-green profoundness from which she came.

I rise up, and, spying a path laid out at my feet, I walk along. Soon I come to a shady, wooded glen. Climbing down into the ravine, I see the rivulets that run out of rocky outcroppings, and many ferns that grow randomly, large leafy fingers waving as I pass. Looking up, the tree canopy is towering high above, their tops invisible to those below. A cool air sits in the glen, refreshing and clean. I am not certain of my way, so I call out for guidance. The Great White Bear materializes in front of me. The mammoth body is covered in thick, pristine-white fur, with only ebony eyes and nose to delineate her face. She stands on her hind legs and emits a loud earth-shaking roar. Then she leans forward, as her enormous paws land on the earth, each sharp claw cleaving the soil, leaving a gaping trench as she pulls her massive paw backward. She speaks with a low growl in her voice. "I am the Great Awakening of Power within. It is fierce and mighty, but tempered by Humility and Gratitude. You have been asleep, as your Light ebbs and flows. Now is the time of spring when hibernation ceases. You have emerged from your cave, and it is time to seek that which is now open to you. You need only step into the Light with this newfound Power and Gratitude, and the path will become clear." She lifts a giant paw and points to a large Elm tree. I turn to see a face upon the bark, its wooden eyes open and staring at me. I approach and reach out to touch the gnarly bark. It is cool, rough to the touch, and, as I look more closely, I see many ants and other insects busily traveling up and down the trunk. I look up and see Woodpecker and Jay sitting amongst the branches. Woodpecker blinks and makes a tapping motion with his beak. I bring my hand up to the bark and with one index finger extended, gently tap on the woody surface. The tree's eyes close, and it vanishes.

Before me is an open pathway, one which I am familiar with. I step on to the path and find myself face to face with the Mistress of the Woods. Her long yellow-green tresses coil and snake over her frame, as tiny flowers open their blossoms and specks of light pop out and float into the ether. Her dark skin glistens with dew drops, her gown, a Mediterranean-green colour, moves like waves upon the beach, slow and rhythmic. She bows her head in greeting, and gently utters, "You have once again graced us with your Light." I smile, happy to be in the place I have, for so long, thought out of reach. I look into her depthless eyes and reply, "I am so grateful to be given the opportunity to gaze upon your wondrous woods and dance with the Fae in the Light once more." I glance around, slightly nervous about asking her my question, but I need to know the answer. "Why was it so arduous for me to find the way again? The first time I sought out the Fae, it was Fox who guided me. This time, it seemed like a test, to see if I could find my own way?" She smiles and the songbirds take flight, singing a melodious chorus. They swoon around my head, and then land on her shoulders and the tendrils of her sunlit-streaked hair. "Hannah, you are of the Light. You know the way is the way, and when the time is right, it is open to you to find. You trusted your Light and allowed things to open before you as you sat on Turtle's back. You asked for aid, and even when the most implausible of guides came to assist, you did not question their ability to help. You accepted their gifts without judgement. You called upon your Power and met it in Great White Bear. She roared and awakened the forest to the newly birthed strength within you. You need only harmonize with your Light, as this will help you find the joy in each step of what is left of your human journey. As you walk the path Here, remember your intention; remember that, the human elements of emotion hold no sway here, as All is as it will be. You cannot redirect the Light of others to suit your desire. You know this, and understand this now, and wear this in your Light, as I can see. Go forward, seek your answers, find your *joy, and know that, as long as you listen to your Light, you will never lose yourself in the dark."* Her long arms reach up above her head, and she twirls, sending our shards of light that turn into tiny feathers that flutter through the air, transforming into miniscule Fae. They giggle as they waft along on a gentle breeze. The Mistress of the Woods slowly fades from my eyes, only to morph into a large Indigo-blue butterfly that sets herself aloft, and then disappears.

I turn and continue to stroll the path, taking in the flowers and fauna, the Fae that perch in the trees and hide behind the flower stems. I approach the glade and see Fae sitting under the Birch, a small child-like sprite by her side. She looks up as I draw near, and smiles. She stands and comes over to hug me. Her skin is slightly leaf-like in colour and texture; her eyes radiant pools of yellow, red and green, with sparks of blue. But most striking is her aura. She exudes compassion. I sit down and a tiny sprite climbs into my lap. Fae laughs, introducing Orna. *"She is not one to shy away from anyone who visits us."* I look closely at her face, her curved eyes that are sky blue, like Owen's, and long tendrils of brown silken hair, like Claire's, and an expectant expression I know I have seen myself wear at times. She is an amalgam of every human that Fae has come to know, and love. When she opens her mouth she speaks in a whisper. *"I have been waiting a long time to see you. I wish it didn't take so long for you to feel better."* I chuckle. She has Arthur's sense of decorum.

I listen as Fae talks about the activities they have been doing together, like growing butterfly wings and soaring over the glade, or planting Cowslips, Foxgloves and Bluebells and watching them blossom into tiny sprites. Orna tells me her favourite thing is to hear stories of Fae's star life, the tales of her time in the astral plane, as One with All. Orna's face shines from her own interstellar glow. Fae nods her head and smiles at me, whispering, *"I grow as a flower every day, with Orna as my sunshine and rain."* She opens her arms and Orna leaps up and falls into them. The sight reminds me of Claire, and I feel a slight ache, wishing to see my daughter right then. Fae points over to the far side of the glade and my eyes follow her finger.

"I think what you seek awaits you, there." I glance over and, under a big Willow tree, sits a figure. My heart catches in my throat. I know the Light right away. I feel the energy, and it is all I can do to contain myself. I stand up, take a deep breath to steady myself, and walk over.

Although the frame is slightly different, less aged, the face and expression reflect the spirit of her human form, and the energy she exudes leaves me no doubt Hannah One is sitting under that tree. I come closer, and she looks up at me. Her eyes beam as she stands up to open her arms to me. I run the last few steps and fall into her embrace. The circle of Love and Light locks us together. Our energy blends until she is me, and I her. There is only one Light and it casts a bright beam that lights the sky and touches the Universe. I never want to leave this embrace. Hannah One whispers softly in my ear, "I am not really Here, but you know that. I am in the Light, so this image is only pretend, but that you know as well. We are here, but then again, we are not. I am only grateful to share this moment in Time with you, in the Now." She pulls away to look at me. I swallow, and finding my voice, it all comes out. "I struggled when you left. I lost connection to my Light, as my human spirit, with all its complex emotions, pulled me into the dark. It was only when I found my Light again that I was able to make my way back. I am forever grateful to have felt your love and light in my life as a human. I love you with all my heart." She reaches out and strokes my hair. I gaze upon her face, once again trying to memorize each feature; the colour of her eyes, the tilt of her mouth, the tiny hairs that gently dance on her forehead as the breeze catches them. The sadness I felt at losing this woman, my grandmother, is now replaced by the understanding that what I truly connect with has not been lost to the Universe forever, only transformed into its purest form. A wave of relief washes over me, and I sink to the ground, still keeping my eyes affixed on her face. Hannah One smiles and looks off into the indistinct distance. "Know that my love is always joyful, and at hand, when you need it. I am Here, but then I am everywhere. We will be one when your energy deems it so, but until then, feel me in your Light, and know I am cheering you *on." With that she slowly fades, until all I can see is a shaft of sunlight peeking through the tree branches.*

I awake to find Owen cradling me in his arms. My face is wet from tears. His arms encircle me with strength, kindness and love. I tilt my head to see his face. He smiles gently. "I think you were having a bad dream, or something." I smile, as the vision slowly fades from my eyes, to be placed upon my door, along with all my other Life images. "No, it wasn't a bad dream, it was the *best* dream." And I stretch up to give him a long, slow kiss.

Four

As I get out of my car in the driveway, music greets my ears. The unmistakable disco rhythm makes me sway as I walk up to the door. The song that resonates out the window is a familiar one, a great classic disco tune *Love Train* by *The O'Jays*. Every day I thank Hannah One for her extensive collection of albums, in all manner of music styles. I walk through the door to see Claire and Noah dancing around the living room. My almost five-year-old grandson is fascinated by trains. He looked at the album cover and found the word *train*, so he had to hear it. The pair mime several of the phrases, signaling, *people get on board, join hands, on the love train, love train...* and prance around the room, pretending to stop and get more invisible people to *climb on board*.

When Claire sees me, she calls out for me to join them, so I drop my bag and *hustle* my way into their circle. I dance around the pair, showing off some *disco moves* that Hannah One had taught me, in this very room, many years ago. Noah becomes annoyed that I am disrupting the train movement. I laugh, and join in the conga-line, waving to the world to get on board. As the song ends, I collapse on the couch, winded. Noah laughs and jumps into the seat next to me. "Oh Grannah, you need to exercise! You are *so* out of shape!" I look sharply at Claire as she chuckles at the forthright comment from her son. I frown, hating to admit he's right. I look at him and, smiling, I say, "When you get to be as old as I am, you're allowed to be out of breath now and again!" I stand up, making my way to the kitchen. I hear Claire admonish her child for his comment, and the next thing I hear is his voice behind me, "Grannah, I love you anyway, even if you got *so* big you couldn't fit in the house!" I giggle and turn to wink at him as he disappears back into the living room.

The atmosphere in the house is very lively as we count down the days to the big family holiday we have planned for the end of June. To celebrate Noah's fifth birthday, Owen and I decided to rent a large cottage on Lake Jackson, near the old cabin we used to visit, when Claire was young. This cottage has four bedrooms, and the use of a nice waterfront, with canoes, a rowboat, and a small hot tub on the deck. We are definitely not roughing it.

I invited Tila and Jamie to join us halfway through our ten-day vacation. David will also be there to enjoy the holiday with Claire and Noah. They are building so many wonderful memories together as a family. It's lovely to view their journey as they travel together through this part of their lives.

Jamie has had some bad news lately. It's actually a double blow as her husband, Neville, has decided to move back to Jamaica to help out his ailing elderly mother. The pair have been slowly drifting apart over the years, and with Aidan grown and living a life of his own, there is nothing holding them together any longer. She is not dismayed at this ending, only resigned to its inevitability. Her main concern is that her cancer has returned. Another mass was biopsied and found to be malignant. Her attitude is strong, yet she acknowledges the truth as it stands before her. She needs to begin treatment again. My heart breaks afresh for her struggle. She has gained many friends and supports through her first battle, so she has a network of people, including Mark and Brian. I invited them to join us for an overnight stay, but they have obligations that will keep them in the city.

Owen is excited to celebrate his beloved grandson's fifth birthday, but also the fact that his African memoir is going into its third printing. It was picked up by the publisher and then, with

Owen's connections in the journalistic world, heavily promoted by the media. Critics loved it, and it reached the top ten on the New York Times bestseller list. I read his book and cried through many parts. He laid out his soul in those pages, and the brutal honesty of his own struggle grips the reader throughout, to see the revelation of Light at the end. It is a beautiful work of art, in words. I'm so proud of him, and by reading his words it draws me closer to Owen's true spirit, which I love beyond words.

Sitting in my softly cushioned Adirondack chair by the lake's shoreline, I look out across the expanse of tranquil water, it's deep indigo surface undisturbed by morning's breath upon it. I see the far-off, dark-emerald, wooded shoreline on the north side of Jackson Lake, with small peaks and valleys defining the tree line, like a curvaceous woman in repose. It's around six in the morning, the time when the veil between *Here* and *There* is thin, and one can almost see the energy vibrate across Space. This is my favourite time of day, as you see the day stretch out in front of you, a blank canvas yet to be filled.

I hold a mug in my hand, slowly sipping my coffee as I take in the sun rise. I sit facing east, watching as it sends out its tiny streams of pale light. The tree-tops to my left begin to change from dusky-green to pinkish-yellow as the light touches the canopy. Orange hues are added by Nature's hand, lending a warm glow to the stream of light that caresses the landscape. What once was grey and shadowy now becomes a pale, but warmer version of itself. Another hour and the richest colours of the day will be on display.

I glance down at my journal and pen cradled in my lap. There is something so tactile about writing on paper, as opposed to typing on a keyboard. It's like the words seep out through your hand into the ink, and then they are brought to life on the paper by the movement of the pen. I prefer to write when everyone is still asleep. My thoughts are then unbounded by distractions of family activity. Once Noah rises, there is little else that fills the day except his energy. His curiosity and insatiable energy are a blessing, and yet also challenging. Fortunately, he has two very energetic parents who are willing to dive into the water with him and keep his inquisitive nature and boundless spirit afloat.

I drain my mug of the last drops of coffee and place it on the small wooden table beside me. I unclip the pen from the cover of my journal, and opening it, find a blank page. The beauty of a blank page is that it is open to anything and everything.

Having spent the morning being busy with Noah, Claire and David decide to take a quiet drive around the surrounding countryside after lunch, and so they can steal a few moments of alone time. I don't blame them. She announces, before piling into the car, that she has left Noah in charge of taking care of his Grandad and Grannah. After all the swimming and exploring, he too, looks done in. I suggest he find his favourite book so the three of us can read it together. Owen takes a seat in one of the large deck chairs, while I take the other, and Noah climbs into his grandad's lap, book in hand. Before he passes the book to Owen, he pauses and looks at both of us, a questioning expression on his sweet face. "Grannah? Mommie told me about Fae, and all about you and Arthur too. You guys are special, with super powers, and see stuff I can't see. How come I don't have super powers?" I smile, but feel at a loss for the words that he would comprehend at this age.

It's Owen who speaks up first. "Noah, I'm just like you. We don't have *their* kinda super powers, but that doesn't mean we don't have our *own* type of super powers. Our super power is being super smart, and super amazing at stuff like, uh, swimming and drawing and liking nature and, well, being a *super* person to our family!" He winks at me, and I chuckle. Noah is still miffed, exclaiming, "But I want to have their powers too. I don't want to be *just* super smart and stuff." He turns his eyes down to the book in his hands. It's my turn to help him understand. "Sweetie,

Arthur and I don't actually have *super powers*. We can't leap tall buildings in a single bound…" I trial off as I see the reference is lost on this five-year-old. "Noah, what makes a person be that way, with what you call super powers, is how they, well, become friends with the energy inside them. You have this energy too, or *Light,* as I call it. As you get older, I can tell you more about it, and show you ways to be able to find the secret door to it. And once you open that door! Wow! You will not only be super smart and nice but you'll be able to soar with the Hawk, or swim with the Turtle, or anything you can imagine!" Noah frowns, and looks at Owen, "but what about Grandad? I don't want to find my secret door, if he can't find his. I want him to find his super powers too, so he's not all by himself." Owen's face crumbles. I see a tear in his eye, which he quickly wipes away. He brings his strong arms up to encircle his grandson and draw him in to an embrace. His voice, when he speaks, is soft; "Noah, don't ever worry about me. I *know* where my secret door is. Your Grannah showed it to me a long time ago. I just want to see how things go, before I decide to open the door and see what's behind it. Maybe sometime all three of us can go find these doors together. In the meantime, you just be you, and remember you are already awesome and amazing!" Noah smiles and pulls his arms up to hug Owen around his neck. I swallow, feeling the sting of tears behind my eyes. He looks over at me and smiles gently before pulling the book out of Noah's lap and saying, "Okay, young man, time to read! What book are we exploring this afternoon?" The book cover has dinosaurs on it. Owen smiles and opens to the first page.

Tila and Jamie arrived around noon today. Claire, David and Noah have taken out the canoe, after a morning filled with playing on the small beach, walking in the woods, and curling up with train books when they were finally tired. Owen spends some time drawing, a new hobby he has decided to pursue; but once Noah has recharged his battery, it's Grandad-Noah time as they head out

The Human Experience

to explore the world. Seeing Owen crouching down, showing him some insect or flower, and talking about how we are guardians of the environment, brings back vivid images of him with his daughter, sharing his love and knowledge, and instilling in her the same sense of wonder about the natural world that he holds dear. He is a wonderful grandfather. He strives to be the father and grandfather he never had. He has broken the cycle of abuse, and started his own cycle of love and compassion. He has left behind the man who needs validation to see his self-worth, and simply lives to be his best self, warts and all. Noah adores him, and it fills me with joy to see such a loving bond between the two of them.

The rest of the day is filled with canoeing, chilly dips in the lake, and a sumptuous dinner made by Tila and Claire. In the evening we gather around a large outdoor fire-pit, the bonfire sending small sparks into the sky, reminding me of the fairy sparkles the Mistress of the Woods would birth from her Light, the flames dancing yellow and orange, the coals glowing like tiger's eyes. I thank the tree for the sacrifice of its body, and hope the ashes provide nutrients for new life to grow. OnanOff lies curled up in Jamie's lap. Having become an elderly feline now, he is content to be included with the family holiday, although the car ride to the cottage was something he was not very happy about. We had to use two cars, as Noah has a lot of toys, books and other gear that, along with food, suitcases, and other incidentals, easily filled one vehicle and then some. OnanOff sat, disgruntled, in his crate in David's car for part of the trip, but complained, meowing plaintively, the entire time. Fae had tried to send the cat some healing calm love, but he wanted nothing to do with it. We pulled over, and Claire, with a huge sigh of relief, handed the poor old cat over to me. I took him out of the crate and placed him on my lap, where he curled up and slept the remainder of the trip. It wasn't the safest way to transport him, but I took the chance that he would be alright, and knew he'd be much happier with me quietly sending reassuring messages to him as we traveled. We can't be certain but, guesstimates are that OnanOff is approaching seventeen years old. His coat is less glossy and his movement slower as he ages, but his spirit remains bright.

    Slowly, the group begins to make their way back into the cottage. Noah is sound asleep in David's arms; the day's adventures having stripped him of any remaining energy. His small head, covered in thick curly auburn hair, lolls against David's shoulder as he lifts him up and gently whisks him away to bed. Claire follows beside him, looking much the same as her son, her frame sagging against David's other shoulder as the trio make their way up the steps to the cottage. Owen pokes the fire slowly, dislodging a piece of wood that sends more sparkling embers up. Tila, looking over at Jamie, notices that she too looks weary, so she offers an arm to help her to bed.

    Tila and Jamie have become good friends through our menopause group. Tila likes to call it the *Meno-Power Group*. The two of them are very similar in character, and outlook. Often throughout the day, I hear one or both of them laughing uproariously at something. It does my heart good to hear Jamie laugh. She needs to laugh, and be joyful, as much as she can. Tila is very sensitive to the situation, having lost a sister to cancer about five years ago. I watch as Tila gets up and approaches Jamie, to gently remove OnanOff from her lap. He's not pleased by the interruption of what had to be his twentieth hour of sleep today, and turns his raggedy old furry body in the direction of the cottage. I know I will likely find him curled up in the middle of our bed when we retire for the night. Tila gently nudges Jamie, who stands up, a little unsteady on her feet. She puts an arm around Jamie's shoulders, whispering her good night to Owen and me, before guiding her exhausted friend to the cottage.

    Owen and I sit on opposite sides of the fire pit, in silence, with only the crackle of the wood and the sizzle of the flames to break the silence of the night. I look into the night sky. I can see millions of stars spread out across the midnight blue sky. Some twinkle almost cheekily at me, while others are so distant they are almost invisible, but for the tiniest speck of light. The half-moon shines clearly in the south-eastern sky, a bright seacraft weighted down by its purpose, in an ocean of stars that move gently with their celestial tide. I never tire of looking at the sky, its infinite open face so readable; A happy blue Sky holds a sun full of love; a not-so-happy Sky is grey and shrouded, as clouds roll over its face; and the angry Sky, with dark clouds that cover its countenance, showering down its cold rainy tears. Earth looks up and is thankful for all the moods of Sky, as it provides sun and rain for growth, snow for sleep, and the dark starry canopy, with the moon watching, for guidance and tidal movement.

Owen pokes at the fire again, knocking down the larger log into the ashes, and looks over to me questioningly. "Are we heading to bed soon?". I nod, feeling the day in my bones; but knowing everyone had such a marvelous time, I smile to myself, thinking of all the wonderful pictures that have been added to each person's door. Owen stands up and stretches, and, glancing towards the cottage, says quietly, "I'm really glad Tila and Jamie are here. I've always admired Jamie for her strength, especially now. It will be good for her to have a few days of fun. And I'm getting to know Tila so much better now. She really is quite a character." He quietly chuckles. I have to agree. "Yes, Tila has her own style. I think that's what I really like about her. She has found her voice, her rhythm, and she's going to use that voice and walk the way she wants to walk through her journey. She inspires me to step out of my comfort zone, and permit my true energy to shine more." Owen nods, replying, "Yes, I've noticed you are, well, more content, or maybe it's more grounded, since you began hanging around with her. You seem happier, and for that, I'll always be thankful for Tila." I stand up and carefully make my way over to Owen to kiss him. He encircles me with his strong, loving arms. I break the kiss long enough to whisper, "It's not just Tila. You've been there for me when I needed it, even though you had your own shit to deal with. *You* are my port in the storm. I love you so much." He smiles, kissing me again, and then whispers, "I think we are each other's port in the storm. I can't imagine my life without you." He hugs me closely, almost as if he's afraid I'll fade into the dark if he lets go.

After a few minutes, when the fire makes more popping sounds, he slowly releases his arms and reaches over for the poker and begins the process of patting down the fire, enough to douse it effectively with a bucket of water. When the water is poured over the fire, it creates a shaft of steam that billows upwards, into the shadowy abyss, the wood hissing as the water attacks the heated surface. Then Owen lifts a bucket of sand and carefully pours it over the ashes to extinguish any heat or remaining ember. The dark of the night rushes into the space made by the evaporating fire light. But for the small stream of light flooding out a window from the cottage, darkness surrounds us.

When Owen is satisfied that the fire is sufficiently doused, he takes my hand, and together we carefully make our way to the cottage. Holding his hand, there is a sense of familiarity and trust in the touch, but I also feel the history of our passion, as his skin feels warm, rough and firm. I want his hand on more than just my hand. I giggle and he squeezes my hand, silently knowing my thoughts without the need to say anything.

I lie in bed, after a *very* quiet, but sensual session of love-making with my husband. I feel awake and attuned to the energy. There is a vibration in the air that hums and pulsates in my core. Suddenly I feel a hand on my arm. In the dimness of the room, I can only make out a figure standing beside the bed. The hand gently pats my arm, and I hear someone whisper, "Hannah, can you come with me? I need your help." It's Tila. I slowly rise and, realizing I am still naked, reach for my robe. I glance over to see the shadow of Owen's form, deep in sleep. I creep out of the bedroom to stand in the hallway with Tila. She has a slightly worried expression on her face, which contradicts the excitement in her voice. "There is someone outside calling me. I'm too nervous to go out alone, so, will you come with me?"

Astonished, I can hardly keep my voice to a whisper, "What? Who? *What?* Who would be outside, everyone is in bed? Do you know who it is?" I'm so confused; my questions are a jumbled mess in my head. She shakes her head, pulling me further down the hallway, away from the other bedroom doors. "I just know I must go outside. Will you come with me?" I look at her, and remembering her determination I know I can't talk her out of this, so I nod. She takes my hand and we make our way through the dimly lit hallway to the back door of the cottage.

The night air is chill and damp, making me regret I had not put on more than just my robe. Our bare feet gingerly walk across the slick deck. The night dew is heavy, and quickly my feet are cold and the damp. I search the dark, but can't see anyone. Tila leads me down the steps to the grassy area between the cottage and the forest. I can hear the water gently moving, touching the shore with a wet whispery kiss before pulling away again. The moon now sits in the western sky, and the stars have ebbed and flowed along their route as the earth revolves. I feel Tila's hand in mine, pulling me behind her. A stark contrast to Owen's rough, firm grip, Tila's is gentle, and soft. When she stops, I almost walk into her.

There, silhouetted against the half-moon, stands a figure. It appears to be a woman. She does not speak or move towards us. I reach out with my energy and find her energy reaching out to me. I know now that this being is not to be feared, but welcomed. Tila drops my hand, almost as if she knows this as well.

I speak gently, my voice penetrating the shadows. "Hello. Are you here with a message?" The space in front of the figure begins to glow, and soon her face becomes visible. She is beautiful, with bronzed skin, long black hair, braided and adorned with beads and feathers, eyes shining like black embers, and her body wrapped in a colourfully woven blanket. She steps forward, her hand outstretched, holding the glowing orb that lights the space between us. When she speaks, there is an ancient quality to her voice, yet the tenor is young. "I am Dawn; I am One that comes from *There,* who rides the Beams of Sun and Moon, and searches for souls who request guidance. I seek that which is Light, and find myself *two* souls possessing the energy of Mother Earth and the Universe." She smiles as she directs her gaze to me. "You walk with the dreams, and dance with the Fae. You are Light, and Infinity resides within you. I need not guide you, but bless your Light to shine upon others in their search for connection to the Universe and Creation." She turns her eyes to Tila. "I listen, as you whisper words of gratitude for each gift that comes to you. I am found in you, the desire to be guided to Light. I am *Here* now, to act as one of your guides as you journey onward. You are most fortunate in receiving *earthly* guidance from her," and she points to me. "She knows the way of Things, and can counsel you as well. Now travel onward with your dreams in hand, and you will find me beside you, carrying your dreams as well. Look for me upon the wind that whispers through the trees, in Grandmother Moon that waxes and wanes, and in Mother Earth who deems all creatures living upon her worthy of love and dignity. They will come to you to share my messages. You need only listen with your Light, and the words will resonate in your heart. Then you will know I am with you." She turns, but the orb of light remains suspended in front of us. She phases from a beautiful woman to a giant Raven, whose feathers shine like black diamonds. Her giant, sharp beak opens, to emit a resonating caw. She spreads her massive wings and launches into the curtain of trees that encircle us. The mammoth bird fades into the night, becoming one with the shadows.

 The orb glows more intensely. I keep my eyes closed against the blinding white light, when suddenly, I find myself in the dark. Lying in my bed, I place my hand upon my naked body. Disoriented, I sit up, and glance around the silent bedroom, and begin to question my dream. Owen still lies asleep beside me, and my robe is still draped across the end of the bed. Did I walk in Tila's dream? Or did Tila walk in mine? Questions stomp around the attic of my mind, yet an utter fatigue suddenly washes over me, forcing me to lie back on my pillow and close my eyes. My final thought, before I drift off, is that the answers will come when they are meant to, so I need only sleep, and be as patient as possible.

My internal clock tells me it's time to rise, even though the sun has not yet made an appearance. I don some sweatpants and a sweater so I can sit outside if I feel like it, and then creep out of the bedroom. The dull morning light penetrates the windows just enough to light the interior of the cottage and make it easier to find my way to the kitchen. As I have already prepared the coffee pot for a morning brew, I simply flick the switch on and await my caffeine fix. Then I hear a shuffling noise behind me, and turning, I see Tila enter the kitchen. She looks tired, as if she has not slept well. I feel surprisingly rested, having fallen into a dreamless slumber after our encounter with Dawn.

She smiles and whispers a greeting, taking a chair at the kitchen table. She glances longingly at the coffee pot. I say nothing, but disappear back down the hall to use the bathroom. When I return, the kitchen holds the aroma of brewed coffee. Tila stands at the counter, two mugs in front of her. She pours the coffee, then gingerly lifts the hot mugs over to the table and places a mug in front of me. As much as I want to chat, I am more focused on that cup of coffee, something I find my human body deems necessary to get my engine started in the morning. Tila takes the seat opposite me and quietly sips her coffee. She too, appears to need to jump-start her engine this morning. When our eyes finally meet across the table, I signal that we should take our hot drinks into the living room, where we won't disturb the sleeping household. I glance at the old clock on the wall, which reads six fifteen.

We sit closely on the overstuffed couch, and Tila pulls a large, multicoloured throw off the back of the it to cover our laps. As much as summer has arrived, her mornings are still chilly and somewhat damp. We nestle in together, like peas in a pod. We sip our coffee, both uncertain as to how to start the conversation. I know she is at a loss as to what happened in the woods last night, so I begin our dialogue. "Well, you must have questions about what happened last night?" She looks surprised as she speaks, "What? How do you know…Do you mean that wasn't some crazy dream I had? It was real?" She turns her body to face me. I smile, and say reassuringly, "Nothing crazy about it. We had a dream-walk together. I'm not sure if it was my dream and you entered, or if it was your dream and I entered. Either way, it was so amazing! You are truly blessed with Dawn as one of your guides." Tila wipes away some tears as she responds, "This is not the first time I have had, well, *visitors*, for lack of a better word, come to me while I sleep. This time I just assumed it was due to the fact that I have been reading a lot of Indigenous lore, and somehow it got into my subconscious, and made me dream it." She takes a few sips of coffee, glancing at me, but saying nothing more. I take another gulp of coffee and look at the painting on the wall, a generic landscape in the autumn. I want to choose my words carefully before I speak, but realize Tila is looking at me, waiting for my response to her comment. "Yes, well, I can't answer why Dawn finally made contact with you last night, but she obviously knows your intention and wants to support you. I believe you understand that there are many other planes of existence, not only the one that humans inhabit. Alternate realities, and dimensions that coexist in harmony, as Space and Time energy wills it. Some of the energy from these Alternate realms makes its way from plane to plane, in search of others who feel the Light, or in search of a deeper understanding of the meaning of their existence. The beings transcend the planes, and can appear before us, when they are either seeking to guide or seeking an experience. Dawn is wise

The Human Experience

and All-knowing, since her energy has existed before the making of humans. She comes to guide. She sees in you potential to travel the Light, and adds her own energy to help you find the way." She nods, still looking a bit confused, as she replies, "that is truly amazing. But I have to wonder, how is it that she seems to know *you*? She said you don't need to be guided, that you walk in dreams and dance with the Fae?"

I swallow, knowing she would ask this. I look her in the eye as I respond. "Tila, this may sound crazy but, I am actually an Alternate as well. I chose this human form to learn more about the human experience, so I can better appreciate this realm of existence. I have the ability to dream-walk, and communicate directly with all of Nature's wonderful creations." I see several expressions cross her face, from skepticism to amazement. She looks at me, her eyes searching my face for some clue, some hint that might show an alien inhabitation. I smile. "No, I *am* human. I have all the human attributes, physical, and mental. I just carry my Alternate energy with me, in what we refer to as, an *awake* form. When an Alternate decides to have a human event, we enter the body of an unborn baby, and our memory of our Alternate existence is placed away from us, so it does not interfere with our experience. We are meant to live a *human* life, free from the influence of the Alternate's perspective. However, some Alternates retain their memory, and must work to find the balance between the Alternate and their human counterpart. Do you understand me so far?" Tila swallows, and replies, "So, let me get this straight. You came here with the intention of having the experience of being human, with the understanding that you won't remember who you *really* are. But something backfired, so you remember that you came from somewhere else? Am I getting it?" I nod, knowing there are more questions coming my way. She pauses, as if trying to figure out which one to ask first. Instead she exclaims, "Holy mother of pearl! I knew there was something different about you!" she laughs, which she quickly muffles, so no one in the house hears. I smile at her as she turns back in her seat to face the room and pull the throw blanket closer to her. "I have so many questions. I don't know where to start. I hope you don't mind me asking them?". I nod, replying, "You heard what Dawn said. I am here to guide others to their Light. Who am I to hold back the knowledge that should be free to all who seek it? Let this all sink in for a while, and then the questions will come to you as they are meant to be answered." She nods, understandingly, but asks one question, "Does your family know who you are?", and it's my turn to stifle a laugh. "That, Tila, is a long story!"

A humid curtain descends upon the day, creating a lull in activities. No one feels very energetic, so some of us find comfortable chairs and lounge in the shade. Noah, Claire and David have been playing in the lake after lunch, but now all of them are having a nap. Owen, sitting up on the deck, has stuck his nose in his book, happy to retreat into a crime mystery. Jamie, Tila and I sit under the shade of several tall Maples, with our glasses of herbal iced tea, the glasses sweating from the ice cubes feeling the heat.

Somehow our conversation comes around to nicknames. Tila explains that she never cared for her full name, Matilda, as many people have tried to call her Matty, which she abhors. When her cousin had a baby, the child had a difficult time pronouncing Aunt Matilda, so ended up calling her Tila. She liked the moniker, so she kept it. Jamie talks about the fact that she never had a nickname, but recalls that I had one, back when I spent the summer at camp. She squints her eyes, trying to remember it. "It was such a weird name, and didn't really make sense to me." I think back, so many years ago, and briefly recall that the campers wondered about how I knew so much about the wild animals we saw around camp, and what they were communicating to us. Then the name comes back to me. "*Whispie*! They called me *Whispie*." Tila laughs and says, "There must be a story behind that one!" I want to tell the truth, about the campers who, one day, happened to catch me conversing with a Garter snake on the trail. I was concerned about his safety and suggested he find a more secluded place to rest. As I stood there staring at the snake, the campers approached and asked what I was doing. Without pause, I answered: "Asking him to move along so he doesn't get stepped on!" After that I was known as the animal whisperer, or *Whispie*. I pause before replying, knowing I can't be truthful in front of Jamie. Although she knows there is something *different* about me, I haven't told her about being an Alternate. I decide to reply with the first thing that comes to mind; "it's nothing really, just a hair style. I got a short haircut for the summer and some of the hairs would stand out, like wisps, I guess…" I trail off, knowing full well no one believes that lame lie. Tila smiles, replying, "You should be called, *Dances with Fae*!" and she giggles. I smile awkwardly, glancing at Jamie, who, for obvious reasons, would not get the reference. Tila cuts off her giggle when she realizes she has let something slip that she shouldn't have. Jamie sits still, with a look of confusion on her face, feeling left out of some joke.

It's in this moment I realize I have been avoiding telling Jamie the truth for so long because of my fear she would think I'm crazy, or look at me differently after that. How was I so easily able to tell Tila my truth, but not Jamie? I shake my head, wondering why I would wait so long, when obviously my dear friend would neither judge me nor dismiss our friendship. I shift in my chair so I face Jamie, and say, "You know, Jamie, there's something I've been wanting to tell you for so long now, but I guess I just never found the right moment. No, that's not true. I never found the courage to tell you. I have always valued our beautiful friendship, and I guess I've been afraid to talk about it for fear of rejection. I can't bear to damage our relationship." Jamie frowns, but reaches over to take my hand. "There is nothing you can tell me that will ever change my love for you, and you will always have my friendship. Unless you've eaten the last of the ice cream, then all bets are off!"

We all laugh, as her joke breaks the tension. I clear my throat and begin, similarly to the discussion I had with Tila the night before. "Remember when Claire spent time with you, when you first started having treatment? You would both do *visualization*?" She nods. "Well, this is going to sound crazy, but that wasn't actually a visualization; it was a form of dream-walking." I pause to gauge her response. She simply sits in her chair, smiling and nodding. With no other clue as to her reception of this news, I continue, "Well, um, I am actually from an Alternate plane. I have transcended to human form to learn more about the human experience, so I can better appreciate this realm of existence. I am human, but have a heightened vibration, or energy, which is my Alternate form residing in me." I scan her face for her reaction, but she just continues to smile, replying, "Hannah, it's okay. I kinda figured something was different, no, *special*, about you. And when Claire revealed Fae to me, I knew that her gift had to be connected to you in some way. As they say, the apple doesn't fall far from the tree." Relief and confusion wash over me as I was not expecting such a calm response. Tila sits in silence, although I feel like she wants to say something, but knows this is an important moment not to interrupt.

I stand up and step closer to Jamie, who also rises from her chair. We embrace, silently, for words no longer seem a necessity. I feel the tears breach my eyelids. The revelation of my true being is liberating, and I feel such relief, and joy. With every person I have spoken my truth too, from Hannah One to Jamie, I have felt within me a growing sense of self-empowerment.

The next thing I feel is Tila's arms encircling us both. She whispers, "I know this is *your* moment, but I can't help myself. The love emanating from you both is a magnet for me." We all giggle, not yet releasing our hold on each other, simply feeling the weight of the moment, and allowing the lovely Light to lift us up. Jamie finally sits down again, a look of fatigue showing on her face and throughout her body. She smiles weakly saying, "This is too much excitement for me. I think I'll retire to the lovely air-conditioned cottage for a nap." I help her to stand, but, shooing away the need for assistance, she makes her own way back into the cottage.

    I sit down and pick up my iced tea, drinking the now tepidly-cold beverage. I can feel the walls around me crumble as I come to understand that the mask I have worn all these years is no more a necessity around my dearest, oldest friend. My energy now released, I want to sing, or dance. The oppressive heat keeps its heavy hand upon my physical self, so, glancing at the lake, I simply stand up and head down to the shore. Tila remains in her chair, watching, as I make my way into the water, still dressed in shorts and a tee shirt, and dive into the chilly waters. I resurface with a loud cry, "Whoopee!" The water, stinging my blood, slapping my skin with its frigidity, and sending shock waves up my spine to my brain, feels so good after the insufferable heat. It's invigorating and cleansing. I can feel my old self gasping for air as the new one steps in, and takes a huge breath.

FIVE

Sitting in my garden at home, I watch dawn's first light peel back the night, exposing a new day full of promise. My mind wanders back to the cottage, and the utter stillness of the lake and forest at this time of morning. I close my eyes and recall Nature's soundtrack playing a gentle tune; when flowers opened up to the new light; the grass snapped and pinged as the dew dried off each petal; the songbirds alerted the other creatures of the world that a fresh day is set upon the earth and they must arise to it. The lake's surface would hum a low vibration, in preparation for the wind and currents that would soon arrive, and blur its glass-like reflection, creating the movement needed to keep it alive and re-energized.

    I open my eyes and glance around the garden, with all its colours and calmness, and feel lucky to have this small oasis of peace right outside my door. In my peripheral vision I see the tiny wood nymphs move about in the tree, but when I look directly at them, they are not there. This is a game we often play, and makes me smile at their mischievous nature. OnanOff naps in the lounge chair beside me, his front paws neatly tucked up under his old frame. He opens his eyes to try to catch the nymphs unawares, but they are too clever for him. He sighs in resignation and closes his eyes, returning to his slumbers. Now too old to chase, and wise enough to know better, he simply enjoys being outside.

The back door opening makes me turn to see who else is joining me in the morning revelry. Owen, a cup of coffee and his cell phone balanced in one hand, quietly closes the door, and descends the steps to join me. I smile as he takes a seat. He doesn't smile back, but wears a frown. After he places his cup on the small table between us, he places his cell phone in his lap. It's unusual for him to be so attached to this device, so I ask, "Are you expecting a call?" He looks directly at me and I see he has been crying. His eyes are slightly red and puffy. "Owen, what's happened? What's wrong?" He looks at his phone. "It's Aunt Regina. She died." Owen's aunt, who lives in Calgary, was not the easiest person to get along with, having strong and unmovable opinions about most things, but Owen was determined to keep his only relative in his circle, as much as he could. Over the years, since our wedding, he made an effort to visit her about twice a year. I went with him occasionally, but the abrasive woman rebuffed my attempts to be friendly. She preferred to focus on Owen, and I was fine with that. Eventually she was unable to take care of herself, so Owen arranged for her to move into an assisted-living residence. She grumbled and made life difficult for everyone around her, but he never turned away from her.

Owen wipes his eyes and continues, "She passed in her sleep. It was peaceful; probably the only peaceful thing she did in her whole life." He attempts to laugh, but fails. I reach out and touch his arm, "What can I do to help you?" He weakly smiles and places his hand over mine. "The facility called, and they will start making the arrangements. I'm just waiting to get confirmation of my flight details. There isn't much you can do, except maybe help me pack." He takes his hand off mine and picks up his cup, taking a few gulps. I look at his face as the morning sun starts to peek through the eastern sky, and I see the love and devotion he has for his aunt displayed there, raw and exposed by Death's proclamation. It's all I can do to stop myself from taking him in my arms and cradling him, until the sadness disappears. But I know I cannot erase the pain, only help him carry it. "I'll come with you. I want to be there, to help you through this. Why don't you rebook the flight for both of us?" Owen hesitates, but nods in agreement. He stands up and paces back into the house, to use his laptop to amend the booking.

I stand up, and, taking one more deep breath, start to head back into the house to pack our bags. One final glance into the garden, shows OnanOff staring at the tree again, intent on seeing a nymph. I quietly whisper to him, "Good luck old chum. I'll leave the back door open for you."

Over the course of two weeks, Owen was able to administer to most of his aunt's estate. Since she was in a nursing home there was little that needed to be done with her belongings. There were only a few family photos of Owen's mother, and Regina's parents, Owen's grandparents, that he wanted to keep, so we packed them into his suitcase to be brought home. The financial logistics were more time-consuming, but after having dealt with both of my parents' and Hannah One's estates, I was able to advise Owen, to save him extra work. It was when we were going through her will that we discovered the insurance policy she had maintained all these years, with Owen as the sole beneficiary. It seems that the woman with the sharp tongue and judgmental attitude, had a very soft spot for her one and only nephew. A bequeathment of two hundred and fifty thousand dollars awaits him.

The internment of her ashes in the cemetery took place in the second week into our stay. Owen, myself and the minister from the church who maintains the cemetery grounds, stood by the hole in the ground, and after a prayer and a few words spoken by Owen, he knelt down and placed her urn into the ground. That was it. He had cried his tears long before this day, so the sorrow he felt that day was tempered by acceptance of the inevitable.

Now one full week after we returned from Calgary, Owen has not yet mentioned the inheritance to Claire. He still feels the sting of guilt at not having moved his aunt from Calgary to Toronto, where she would have been close by for him to visit more often. She was against making the move, and would not listen to any suggestions Owen offered. He said, on the last evening before our flight home, that she should not have wasted her money on a life insurance policy, that she could have spent it on something for herself. Knowing the woman as I did, I was actually surprised she didn't do *just that*, but then I immediately chastised myself for such an unkind thought. After a moment to reflect, I said, "She wanted you to know how much you meant to her. Since she was unable to say it in words, she expressed her appreciation with this gift. If you don't accept it, it will diminish her intention." He nodded in agreement, although whether he took my words to heart was unclear. It will take a few months before the money actually arrives in the bank account, so I am hopeful he will have a better perspective by then.

After dinner, Claire and I sit, as Noah plays with some Lego blocks on the living room floor. He has drawn a plan, in pencil crayon, of what he wants to build. It makes me wonder if he has an engineering or architectural interest that may steer his career course in the future, or if he's simply so creative he just likes drawing out his ideas. I raise my eyes from studying Noah's construction to look at Claire, as she sighs and slowly looks around the room. Before I can ask her anything, she says quietly, "I really love this house. I have such wonderful memories that we've made over the years." She glances at a photo of Hannah One on the shelf nearby. "You know that David stayed here, with Noah and me, when you and Dad were in Calgary. It was funny, but we began to get a glimpse of what it might be like if we were *together*, all the time, you know, just the three of us. Those two weeks were great! And Noah really loved having his dad around so much." Noah glances at his mother at the mention of his name, then returns to his drawing. "So, we started to think, maybe we *should* move in together." Her announcement takes me by surprise, although it should not have. One cannot assume that one's adult child, regardless of the circumstance, wants to remain living with their parents, other than out of necessity. Now that Noah is five, and began school last year, the dependency that Claire had on us has lessened to some degree. Claire, looking hesitant, waits for my response. "Well, yes, I can see how this is an option worth exploring. I suppose you can split the cost of rent and other bills, so it may be quite do-able." She smiles, happy by my reaction. Part of me longs to hold on to her, and Noah, keeping them safe under my wing, away from the harsh realities of adulthood. But I look at my daughter, and see a competent woman, raising an amazing child, running her business, being creative and glowing with self-confidence. She does not need to hide under my wing.

She stands up, walks over to the table and picks up some loose papers. "I've been looking at places. David and I want to rent a small house, so Noah has a yard to play in. The prices are a bit steep, that's for sure. But we did see a house, actually about three blocks from here, with a rent-to-own option. It would be a great way to go, but neither of us has enough for the down payment, so we would just be renters, for the time being." I hear the bells sounding in my head. She doesn't know about the money her father is about to receive. That is the answer to her dilemma, but I dare not say anything until I talk with Owen. I smile and reply, "Well, that would be convenient if you're close by. Why not show the ad to your dad when he gets home, and then we can talk about it?" Claire excitedly clutches the papers, then lays them on the table to smooth out the creases she just created. "Oh Mom! I'm so excited!"

The day of the move is fast approaching, and after some discussion with him, it was decided that OnanOff won't relocate to the new house with Claire, Noah and David. The elderly cat doesn't want to cope with the change. As much as he loves Claire, he is happiest here, in his familiar home, with his garden, where he can live out his life with as little stress as can be afforded a house cat. He secretly admitted to me that he has never been keen on Noah, and the amount of noise that one five-year-old can emit. Claire is disappointed, but also a bit relieved, when she really considered the prospect of helping him adjust to a new house, which could be difficult for the old boy. She already has her hands full with packing, organizing a mover, and the various paperwork involved in buying a house. Owen stepped up to the plate, as I knew he would, and offered the full two hundred and fifty thousand dollars to Claire, as a substantial down payment on her first home. She refused, at first, but then, after some reflection, and discussion with Fae, not David, she reconsidered the offer. Fae wants to see Claire advance on her journey, and told her that ego, or pride, only play a part in hindering that journey. She also echoed the sentiment about receiving a gift with love, and not refusing it, for it diminishes the intention. Claire proposed a counter-offer; she insisted that Owen keep some of the money, for *his old age*, a phrase I wish she had considered more carefully before uttering it. Fortunately, Owen merely laughed at her indiscretion, and told her we both had enough money to live comfortably for as long as needed. His book sales, along with some wise investments on both our parts, have helped us create a nest egg that will sustain us. It doesn't hurt that the house we own has no mortgage, as Hannah One had paid that off years ago, just after I moved in with her. She too, had invested wisely.

As I enter Claire's bedroom to see if she needs additional boxes brought up from the front hallway, I see her sitting on the desk chair, staring blankly into space. I sense she is in communication with Fae. Claire's visits to the Fae realm seem to be happening more frequently, and I begin to wonder if the stress of the move is pushing her to escape the chaos. Sitting on the edge of her bed, I quietly sort through some of Noah's clothes. She had made a pile of clothing that no longer fits him, and wants to donate it to the local women's shelter. I pick up a small tee shirt, the design on the front triggering a memory of my grandson wearing it on several occasions. As he grows, he creates his own door, and it sits next to his mother's. Some of the images on the door hold this tee shirt, as he wore it on his first day of school, or played in the sand at the cottage. I neatly fold the tee shirt and place it into the box on the floor, thanking the inanimate cloth for providing the connecting thread to several poignant memories I hold dear.

Claire blinks, realizing I'm sitting near her. "Oh sorry, Mom. Just wanted to see Fae for a few minutes. You know, take a breather." She stands, crosses over to the dresser and pulls open a drawer. I continue to fold clothes and lay them into the box, and, trying to seem casual, ask, "Is everything alright with you? Are you having a hard time with this move?" She pauses in her sorting, and, turning to me, I can see she wears a conflicted look on her face. "Mom, I guess it's been a bit up and down. You know, it's just the stress of moving, the worry about paying the bills, all that stuff." She comes to sit down beside me, and I drop the little pair of pants I was folding, to place my arm around her shoulders. She leans into me, for a much-needed hug. "Claire, it's a big step, and I don't blame you for being scared, or worried. You're taking another huge dive into life, as you often have with everything you take on; with Noah, the Centre, and your books. But, as scared as you have been, you've always taken the plunge with confidence, and a sense of knowing your potential. I could not be prouder of the woman you are today." I hug her closely to me, still wanting to take her under my wing, shelter her from the stress of the situation, but knowing this stress will make her stronger in the long run. She pulls back to wipe a tear from her cheek and replies, "Thanks, Mom. I guess I just want to make sure I'm really doing the right thing, with David. I love him, and we are *all* so happy as a family.

I suppose I keep thinking that it might not last. Where will I be then?"

I pause, wondering if she is having doubts about David. It's not my place to interfere, but if she is going through with this plan because it's what is expected of her, I need her to know she doesn't have to do it. "Sweetie, life is full of uncertainty. There are no guarantees that you and David are meant to be together forever. Try to remember that *you* are the driver of your own destiny, not David, not me, or Dad. What sits most comfortably in your gut is most often a sign that you're doing the right thing. And you know that, come what may, you always have a home to come back to." She reaches out to hug me again, her voice muffled in my shoulder, "Mom, I'm pretty certain I'm doing the right thing, but in case I'm not, it means everything to me to know you and Dad will catch me if I fall." I hold her close, whispering, "Always Claire bear, always."

The house hums as voices reverberate around the rooms. A burst of laughter comes from the living room as a large group of women listen to a humorous story, likely told by Tila. It was Lilah's idea to throw a pot-luck house-warming party for Claire and David *before* the move, and I was happy to have the gathering at our house, as it seems like an appropriate place as a send-off for the trio. Claire sits on the couch, with Noah by her side. He keeps thinking one of the presents is for him, and so, unfortunately, his demeanor grows darker with each gift unwrapped. Pots and pans, blenders and utensils, but no toys. Claire reminds him that these gifts are for all of them to enjoy, but Noah will not listen. He sits sullenly, until I take him aside and whisper, "Go check out the garden." He disappears through the kitchen, and then I hear a loud "Oh ya!" from the sunroom, as Noah sees Owen standing beside a new bicycle out in the yard. I hear the back door slam and the muffled exclamations of an excited six-year-old out in the garden.

The women of the Meno-Power group have organized the food, and brought all the utensils and other items necessary to enjoy the party, even though I had offered to provide any and all items needed. It was a communal effort, to show support for our family at this happy, yet chaotic time. Lilah buzzes around, making sure everything is set, before she announces, "Please help yourselves to all the wonderful food! There's cold drinks and tea and coffee in the kitchen!" A few of the women make their way over to the table and begin to fill their plates with items. I watch as Tila enters the kitchen to retrieve a cold drink for Jamie, who sits in the large armchair, looking frail and worn. My heart stops as I look at her. As broken as her body has become, her resolve no less shines through. I hold my optimism for her recovery very carefully in my mind, not wanting to allow any negative thoughts to diminish what hope I hold onto.

Owen and Noah enter from the garden and make their way to the table to help themselves to the delicious fare. Noah takes his plate into the kitchen to avoid listening to all the boring grownup conversations, while Owen talks jovially with the women surrounding him. He has such charm when he wants to turn it on. I smile, as he tells a story that makes the women laugh. Unfortunately David had made a previous commitment to help a friend move today, and felt that he couldn't re-neg on his promise. I know he would have enjoyed the party, but insisted we go ahead and that Claire would tell him all about it later. He is a truly generous, open spirit, so it's no surprise he and Claire found each other.

The bathroom smells of lavender as I towel off from my bath. The aroma infiltrates my lungs and calms my senses. My robe, hanging on the back of the door, is clean from the laundry, and as I slip it on, it feels soft, fresh and comforting. I open the door and feel the rush of cold air against my legs. Standing in the hallway, I glance towards Claire's bedroom, now empty, except for her bed. Every time I see it, I keep thinking I should put some bedspread or comforter on it, make it less *naked*, making a less obvious statement of her absence. I still haven't made any changes to her room, to transform it into a guest room. Noah's room, also empty now, is in need of a paint job. As much as I love the animal stencils on the walls, which were perfect for my grandson as he grew from infant to toddler, the room is now outdated and in need of a new occupation. Owen and I talked about converting it to an office, but nothing has been done about that yet.

I clutch my robe front, thinking I should get dressed, but feel contented to allow the lazy day to spill out in front of me. When Claire and Noah lived here, lazy days did not exist. Every day had a direction, a chaotic dance of *to-ing* and *fro-ing*, and the house buzzed with that energy. Now the house, and both Owen and I, breathe a collective sigh, and roll ourselves into the quiet, more leisurely cloud that floats around us. I descend the stairs to hear the record player in the living room playing one of Owen's favourite Styx tunes, *The Best of Times*. Until I actually listened to the lyrics, I didn't understand his fondness for this particular song. The chorus plays, *the best of times, are when I'm alone with you... some rain some shine, we'll make this a world for two... our memories of yesterday will last a lifetime... we'll take the best, forget the rest and someday we'll find, these are the best of times...*

Owen sings to me as I stand in the doorway watching him. His eyes are alight with his energy, and there's something about his body language, his hands emoting with the words as he sings, his expression, sincere and open, that makes me so desperately want to hold him and feel him close. I take the few steps separating us, and open my arms to him. He reaches out and takes me in his arms, not to kiss or hug, but to dance. The floor disappears beneath my bare feet, as we dance on air, as we did on our wedding day. The world folds in on itself, where it becomes only us, standing there, swaying to the music. *But I know, if the world turns upside-down, Baby I know, you'd always be around...* his soft voice croons next to my ear.

His hands slide up my back and then down to rest on my hips. I can feel my robe-tie loosen with the dancing motion, and soon it falls open. I feel my naked body press against his frame. As the song fades, he turns his head to kiss me, while our feet land back on the floor. His hand reaches around to stroke the skin on my neck, and trace a path down to my breast. He leans in and kisses me on the neck and soon, I feel his hands caress my body. We collapse on the floor, passion carrying us along, uninhibited by the presence of anyone else close by. From years of sharing a house with Hannah One, and then Claire, and Noah, we learned how to conduct a discreet sexual life. Now, nothing holds us to account, and our freedom erupts right there, on the living room floor.

The scent of lavender wafts between us as our bodies merge, laughter ringing out as I bump my head on the hardwood, and discover the floor isn't as comfortable as it was for lovemaking thirty years ago. Nevertheless, neither of us is willing to break the spell and suggest a comfortable retreat to the bedroom. Owen reaches out and grabs a pillow off the couch, placing it carefully under my head.

The familiar curve of his back, the feel of his skin, warm and slightly rough, the look in his beautiful blue eyes, all sink into my spirit, and I soak up every atom of him, his love and passion illuminating my soul. We have a new chapter open to us now, and if this is one way of finding our way back to *us*, I can't wait to see what happens next.

Six

I watch as Fae and Orna play with two butterflies that teasingly land upon their heads, and dash away just before they can be caught. Claire sits under the Willow by the edge of a large pond, quietly talking with a wood nymph, as they watch the Mallards and Mute Swans coast along the water's clear surface. One Swan has eight signets in her care, their brilliant white down looking as soft as a cloud. My ears are treated to a chorus of songs from the Tree Swallows, Warblers, and Vireos. A few cheerfully bright Goldfinches flit from tree to tree, creating vivid yellow streaks as they weave back and forth across the glade. The trees sigh in the breeze, amplifying the wind's voice through their leaves. The light filters down through the branches from above, producing mosaics of green patchwork on the mossy ground. Deer quietly nibble on strands of grass on the far side of the meadow. There is a sense of serenity *Here*, which is something all of us visitors sorely need. Claire is taking advantage of a quiet afternoon to visit Fae and Orna in this realm, as Owen and Noah visit the natural history museum.

I turn my head to see Jamie sitting beside me, her bare feet touching the mossy ground, her hands reaching up to touch the diamond sparkles that float above her head. Her face mirrors the sparkles, enrapt in a pain-free vision. I wrestle with my own sense of peace. As much as I want to open myself up and join in the tranquility, part of me still holds in reserve the pain that sits in my gut.

Jamie has come to live with us, no longer able to manage on her own. She is in the late stages of her illness now. Mark and Brian have been coming over regularly to visit, bringing food and flowers almost every time. I know Mark feels guilty that they are unable to house their closest friend at their home, but they're renovating, so between the noise and the dust, it's not a good place for respite.

I feel the cold nose of a dog press against my hand and, looking down, I see Fred. A small gasp of surprise escapes my mouth. I chide myself, thinking, *of course he would come to see me; why should I be surprised?* This realm is open to all energies who are pure in their intent, and Fred, my beloved Beagle friend, is one of the purest energies there is. He snuggles down beside me, much the same as he did when I was a girl. I place my hand on his back and gently stroke his soft fur. From inside my head, I hear him speak. "You know the way of Life. We are *Here*, then we are *Elsewhere*. Never gone, only released into the Universe, shedding our physical nature to become One with our energy. I can sense you holding your sadness; it sits in your craw, like a dog with a bone." He softly chuckles. "You know the way, and you can lead Jamie into the Light, when it is time. Make it about her journey, not your sadness. Remember that holding on only serves to hinder those who wish to move forward." He looks up at me with his liquid brown eyes, and I nod. There is something about the human spirit that, although I know what he says to be true, nevertheless makes it near impossible to remain whole after the departure of someone you love. It's like repairing a broken vase - it may look almost the same on the outside, but the cracks have compromised its integrity, and it can't hold the water the same after.

I glance at Jamie again. Her expression is one that I file away, to be remembered over the years. I will not remember the pain, the frailness of her physical form, the sadness she feels at having her life cut short, nor her anguish at leaving her son sooner than she thought she would. Fred sighs, enjoying the rub. I smile, remembering the wonderful conversations we had as I lay upon the floor as an immobile infant, sharing my blanket with him; right up to the time I was old enough to walk with him, alone, around the neighbourhood. "Fred, you are a true Guardian of Spirit. You have helped me, and others, like my dad, throughout this journey. I'm happy to see you today, and thank you for your guidance. I feel your wise words sink in, and I shall try to heed them. I know you are always close by, and it's a comfort." He wags his tail, but says nothing.

Jamie looks over at me, and seeing Fred, she grins. "Are we getting a dog?" she asks, almost child-like in her enthusiasm at the prospect. I shake my head, "No, Jamie, this is Fred. He and I go way back. I've known him just a bit longer than you. I guess you are both my oldest friends, meeting for the first time." Jamie smiles and reaches out to touch Fred's head, giving him a light pat. He turns to look at her, wagging his tail. This time he speaks so she can hear him. "I have watched as you helped Hannah along the way, all these years, and I want to thank you for being a true friend to her. There is only so much a dog in another dimension can do!" He jumps up, emitting a laughing howl and runs around the pair of us. His antics draw Claire's attention, who cheerily laughs. Fae, Orna and some of the nearby nymphs and sprites all gather and begin to chase Fred, his barking laughter shattering the stillness, and peals of laughter ring throughout the glade. I drink in this moment, seeing Jamie so animated and free, and feel gratitude to everyone here for putting that smile on her face.

I sit in the sunroom and look out at the garden, tucked in for winter with a white blanket of snow helping the Earth hibernate until spring. Snowflakes gently cascade down, almost in slow motion, then catch a small gust to bustle into mini-snowy cyclones that dance around the yard. The sun is weak, barely smiling upon us, not enough to warm, only enough to shed light on the day.

I pull my eyes from the garden and look towards the makeshift bed, set up in the sunroom. We had originally planned on setting her up in the guest room, but Jamie felt too isolated upstairs and wanted to be able to view the garden and be a part of the house's activity, as much as possible. So we set up the bed, as we did before, in the sunroom. As I view the bed, memories of Hannah One attempt to etch themselves into the frame, but I quickly push them away. Jamie lies still, her eyes closed, her breathing calm in sleep. She is being prescribed pain relief now. It's the only relief that medicine can offer at this point. I look at her sleeping form, and cannot compare her frail, cancer-filled body to the vibrant, lively youth I knew all those years ago. Looking back, I dare not count how many years it has been. It's hard to imagine those two girls growing into the women we have become. I cannot place myself into the image of that girl, full of self-doubt and worry. Jamie was the Light that kept me guided throughout, with her spirited words of support. And, although she did not know it at the time, she was, along with Hannah One, a lifeline for my human side. She kept me grounded, and yet she helped me fly, in a different way than my grandmother did. Now it will be my turn to help her to fly. She will need to fly up and away from the pain she faces every day, and the sorrow she feels at having her life cut short.

Fae has relayed to me, through Claire, that she is near her end; her Light fades. Her son, Aidan, has been coming every day to visit. He just sits by her side, holding her hand, talking quietly about inanities. She responds as best she can, or simply closes her eyes and sleeps. His façade is a neutral mask, until he turns to leave, and then the gut-wrenching grief shows itself all over on his face. My heart breaks for him. Neville is arriving back in Toronto from Jamaica in two days, but I fear it will not be in time to say good bye to his first love. Jamie, while still able, wrote both of them letters, which she gave to me for safekeeping, until the time is right. She recalled me telling her about the letter I found from

Hannah One, and what comfort it gave me, so she thought she would follow her lead.

A small groan disturbs the quiet room as Jamie stirs in her sleep. OnanOff lies next to her, his purring a balm to my ears, as it breaks the silence that weighs upon the room. He looks up and blinks his aged eyes, but says nothing. He knows he can be present only to witness her passing, no longer providing the comfort he has over the past few months. I come over to sit by her side, fixing her covers to make sure she isn't cold. I think back to the day we sat in the glade, the Light shining through the trees, the peaceful scene providing a stage for an open conversation about her situation. She said she does not fear her death, but that she is more angry than fearful. Her anger centers around the fact that she does not get to see her son mature and possibly start his own family, and be part of that experience, along with other plans she made and can never see to fruition. Her only fear is not being confident of her Light, and its ability to continue on after her physical self has ended. As much as she loved spending time with Fae in her realm, her mind still wrestles with the human concepts of heaven and hell, and the immortal soul. Although she's never been religious, she still wants to believe in God, and in heaven. She fears she has not met the standard for heaven's entry. Has she been a good, kind, giving person? I tried to explain that her *Light* is all that matters. It is energy and it is infinite. It doesn't judge for *goodness*, nor punish the *bad*. It simply *is*. When human constructs are torn away with the flesh, the energy is all that remains, and it is a form without ego, without prejudice, or malice of intent. It may need guidance, it may need community to help direct its path, but that support is always abundant, as the Light steers the way. I know that she found some comfort in my explanation, but I believe she will truly find her peace once she allows her Light to pass along to the plane where she will experience it for herself.

I feel her life force waning, as her Light prepares to move along. I lean over and kiss her forehead, whispering, "I love you, and will miss your smile. I will tell Aidan that you loved him with all your heart. He and Neville will have all my love and support as they grieve. If you need to go, go with all of our love. It's okay to go Jamie, it's okay." The tears fill my eyes, spilling down my cheeks, a sorrowful waterfall. My hand on her back feels her body struggle for one last breath. She gasps one final time, and then it is done.

People have congregated to celebrate the amazing Jamie Beaumont LaTour. The April air is fresh, crisp and cool. Although the garden has chairs set up for visitors, the air is a bit too chilly, so all the guests remain in the house. This day has been set aside to rejoice in her life, and find solace with one another and their love for her. I turn from staring out at the garden, taking a moment to compose myself, and see some of Jamie's friends from her teaching days, in the kitchen, holding cups of coffee, quietly exchanging stories about their time spent with a wonderful teacher, and friend. Mark and Brian stand off to one side, chatting with one of the teachers whom they know well. I look at Mark's face, stoic in his resolve, but I know he is still torn up inside at the passing of his dearest friend, three months ago.

This small gathering of those who know and love Jamie fills the house with her energy. I look around the sunroom, now devoid of the bed we had set up for her. It is once more simply the sunroom; a hospice room no longer. I saunter through the kitchen, smiling at people as they acknowledge me. I turn to view the living room, where Tila and some of the women from our Meno Power group stand gathered around the table, trying some of the sweets laid out. They talk about a trip they have booked for next month, as a group, to England. I look over and see Neville sitting on the couch, nursing a beer. Even though Jamie passed in February his pain is nonetheless fresh and raw, and this day of "celebration", meant as a salve to heal those who are grieving, seems to provide little comfort for him. The letters Jamie had written to Neville and Aidan, I delivered yesterday, knowing today was going to be difficult for them. My hope is that they will find strength and peace from her words, which will help them move forward.

In the far corner of the room, Aidan talks quietly to Claire, while they look over the album collection. He pulls out *Rubber Soul*, by the Beatles, and places the vinyl disc on the turntable. He lowers the needle so it starts somewhere in the middle of the record. My ears pick up the simple guitar riff, and then the song starts; *'There are places I remember, all my life, though some have changed…some forever not for better, some have gone, and some remain… all these places have their moments, for lovers and friends I still can recall, some are dead and some are living… in my life, I've loved them all…'*

Aidan starts to cry, comforted by Claire placing her arms around him, feeding him healing energy from both Fae and herself. Neville stands up and goes to the window, staring out to the front yard. I walk over to him. He nods his head as I approach, and then glances in the direction of the record player. "One of her favourite songs. I never was a fan of the Beatles, but now it will hold a special place in my heart." He takes a swig of his beer. I stand close and place my hand on his back. I allow some healing energy to quietly infiltrate his body. There is nothing I can say to alleviate his grief. Sometimes what you need is just the presence of someone who understands your sorrow, but does not try to lift you out and away from it, when you need to walk *through* it to get to the other side. I just want to walk through it beside him.

Neville is a man who likes to move to his own beat, but moves with compassion, grace and an eye for finding the humanity in those most would find unworthy of the effort. Even with their differences that pulled their marriage apart, it never erased their love. Jamie never remarried or even bothered to date again. Her heart always belonged to Neville. He felt the same. The love was always there, but it was Life that made it difficult for them to always feel it. Now, the love remains, and it will have to fill the void each of these men feel, now that their anchoring bright Light has moved on.

I smile, knowing how much Jamie loved The Beatles. "Yes, Jamie and The Beatles. The lyrics of so many songs truly spoke to her. She had a song for almost everyone she loved. We have all been so lucky to have known her love." He wraps his arms around my shoulders and we hug.

Seven

A face stares back at me from the bathroom mirror. The cheeks, the forehead, the chin, all an aging landscape. The eyes, still green and deep set, hold the wisdom of realms, yet still seek the answers in this one. I smile, and see the lines around my mouth. A few new creases appear around my eyes. My face is like an evolving road map. You think you are familiar with the scenery, but Time plays her hand and changes the panorama as she moves onward. I take the brush and begin running it through my hair. Unlike many women, I'm not going to dye my hair as it greys. Like Hannah One said, grey hair is a sign of having lived. It's like a Crown of Age, to be proud of, and when you look upon it, you appreciate that you've come this far.

I am on the precipice of "the senior years", now having reached the age of sixty-two. From my viewpoint, looking out at life in general, I don't see myself in the senior category. I still envision this young woman, out in the world, trying to make her way. Placing the brush back on the counter, I take one last look in the mirror. Yes, I see her in there. The young woman who took on a bookstore and made it a success; wore a champagne-coloured lacey wedding dress, while butterflies frolicked around her head, and danced in the arms of a man who loves her beyond Time; the woman who bravely lived through a terrible childbirth, to raise an amazing daughter and see that child succeed on her own; the older woman who ventured into a new business helping create connections for people wanting to learn more about their energy; and most importantly, expanding her own Light with each experience, helping her become a fuller human. This woman, now playing with a strand of silvery grey that teasingly hangs down on her forehead, is finally walking in the shoes that fit her, taking the path that she is meant to follow, without regret for exploring other paths that only led to dead-ends. It is in the dead-ends that we learn more about ourselves, and our resilience to turn around and find the right trail that leads on. I sigh, feeling that, although there is more Time behind me than in front, I still want to make each step forward count.

As I descend the stairs and enter the kitchen, I am struck by the utter stillness within the house. Owen is out, volunteering at the local wildlife rehabilitation centre. He facilitated a fundraiser, in which he raised enough money to build three new specialized outdoor enclosures for recovering wildlife. He is now overseeing the construction, and enjoying every minute of it. He says it reminds him of his days in Africa, soaking in the satisfaction of helping the community.

I feel at a loss. Claire is busy with Noah and his classroom trip to the museum, and Tila is away on the trip to England with some of the group. I am left to my own devices, and wonder what they are, exactly. Standing at the entrance to the sunroom, I spy my book on a side table and sit down, picking up the weighty novel. I can't decide if I want to read, or maybe go for a walk.

Suddenly, in my peripheral vision, something appears on my shoulder. It's a small spider. Her tiny legs hold her minute yet sturdy body in place, as I attempt to shift my head to see her more clearly. Once the initial surprise at having a spider appear on my shoulder wanes, I ask her, "Are you okay? Do you need assistance to find a better perch?" The spider's outstretched forelegs wave like she is conducting an orchestra. A whispery voice enters my mind, *"I am the Guardian of Ancient Words and Creative Energy. I sense in you the desire to create, but the energy has not found its path as yet."* I blink, confused by Spider's comment, *"You* are the Guardian of Words? Does that make you a *muse*? Am I to derive some creative energy from you, so I can channel it into writing, or something?" Spider picks at a small thread on my shirt, replying, *"In ancient human realms, the Chinese sought to learn from Ts'ang Chien, the dragon-faced god who created their alphabet from his visions of the stars, and from the birds who graced the eternal shores, leaving their marks in the sand for all to view. The Norse humans looked upon Odin to find the written word, which he derived from living in the Tree of Life for several days, watching how the twigs fell to the ground and created patterns and words. Yet they are young, compared to Spider. She spun her web across the Universe, and those who gazed upon it saw the words in the geometric patterns and angles she produced. A primordial creation, to be guarded by her descendants since Time began Her. I am one such guardian, not a muse, but one who can awaken creative life already existing within you. For you to weave creative webs in the dark recesses of your mind, but not convey them to the Light of day, is a disservice to the Talent you have been bestowed. You yourself are Spider in Spirit. You walk the thread between waking and sleeping, the physical and spiritual, between Life and Death. You cannot see it, but you are a creative force that propels others to their potentials, yet neglecting your own desire to weave your own path. Look upon your daughter, your husband, and see their creative energies stem from your support. It is time you focus the support within yourself, to create that which is already set inside you, just waiting for creative birth."*

Spider lifts one leg and an invisible thread seems to appear stretching upward, fastened to a point I cannot see above me. I whisper my thanks to the Guardian of Creative Energy for her advice as she spirals up and out of sight.

After my conversation with Spider, I am feeling a nugget of inspiration in my gut. Abandoning my thoughts of reading or taking a walk, I go back upstairs and stand outside the doorway to Noah's old bedroom. We have converted Claire's room to a guest room, but never seemed to pinpoint what we would do with the other empty bedroom. Now, as I stand looking around, I see my easel, and a large table for working on other art projects, and a small desk in the corner for writing. I feel almost giddy as I look around. My hand aches for a paintbrush, so I go back down the stairs to the basement, where my supplies have been patiently waiting for me. I haul out the easel and drag it up the two flights to the room, and place it opposite the window, so the light will shine more naturally on the canvas that will eventually sit there. I retrace my steps and carry two boxes of paints and brushes to the new art room, forgetting I have no table to place them on. One more trip to the basement, which includes a fair bit of panting and sweating, to lug the card table we use for parties up and up and up. I wiggle the old legs into position, locking them into place and turning the table right side up. I place it against the far wall. Picking up the two boxes, I open their lids to peer inside. The smell of paint and pastels is a bit stale in my nostrils, and I wonder if I need to replace some of my materials.

After carrying a kitchen chair up to the room, I have a way to sit and go through my supplies. I see that most of the paints are still usable, with the exception of three that dried out from me not fastening the lids back on properly. My sketch paper is abundant. I have plenty of pencils for drawing. I am only in need of canvases and a few extra tubes of paint.

I hear the front door opening, so I call out, "I'm upstairs, come see what I've done!" After a moment or two, I hear his feet hit every creak in the wooden stairs as Owen ascends. He stands in the hallway for a moment, until I call out again, "In here, Noah's room." I stand up as I see him in the doorway. He's a bit grimy, but ever so handsome in his work clothes, so I take the steps between us and wrap my arms around him, planting a big kiss on his lips. His surprise is quickly replaced by his response to my kiss. I'm so excited to show him the room, I break the kiss, spreading my arms wide, announcing, "Welcome to my art room!" Owen smiles, with a hint of confusion crossing his expression. His eyes leave mine as he scans the room, taking in the makeshift table and chair, and the easel, standing naked on the far side of the room. His eyebrows rise slightly, and I can tell he's taking a moment to choose his words carefully. "Well, this is, uh, something. So, we've finally decided to use this room for your art projects? Hmm, let me think… yup, it's a great idea!" He smiles as I hug him tightly.

He breaks the embrace to walk around the room, rubbing his chin as he surveys it. "Now, this table and chair are not right at all, wouldn't you agree? You'll need an angled table for drawing, and a much better chair for support and comfort. What about lighting? How about I install some sort of system that will give you good, even lighting, so you won't have to worry about shadows." I laugh, seeing the organizer in him gleefully making mental notes about all the stuff he'll need to buy at the hardware store. I stand behind him, wrapping my arms around his frame and rubbing his chest. "I think you're the right man for this job! You're hired!" He laughs and pulls me round to stand in front of him, kissing me, slowly. Even after all these years, he makes my Light shine as bright, if not brighter, than ever before.

The paint slides across the canvas, taking on a life of its own, an energy flowing freely from my creative spirit. I see the colours blend and merge into the scene, and with subtle movements, I feel the canvas understand and respond. Stepping back to survey the entirety of the scene, I feel satisfied with the result. I dare not play with it any more, or I will ruin the flow within the image. I place my brush into the large water-filled jar on my worktable, with the intention of cleaning it later. I turn to look at the other canvases that line the walls of my art room. These past six months have been productive, and I'm very happy with the effort. Twelve canvases of varying sizes hang upon the walls, or sit on the floor leaning against the wall. The colours are bright, enthusiastic and playful. Some scenes are taken from Fae's realm, and include the Mistress of the Woods in her fine gown of shimmering green. Other scenes are derived from my years of walking the trails at the conservation area. Every scene has wildlife within it, sometimes obvious, sometimes not. The trees hold birds, the bushes hide rabbits, the sky lifts up the Hawk. In every scene I see myself; I can feel the wind on my face, the damp grass under my bare feet, and the sound of birdsong in my ear. Every picture is like a part of myself, open for the world to view.

Claire enters the art room with Noah in tow. They have been coming over to visit OnanOff, who has been feeling poorly of late. Now at around the age of twenty plus, every day with him is a gift. He has mentioned his aches and pains to me, and I have offered to help him pass on, but he seems reluctant to let go of this life at the moment. Fae sends healing energy through Claire with every visit, and that helps him feel more comfortable. He has said, in no uncertain terms, that he will tell me when the time is upon him.

She grins as she exclaims, "Oh Mom! These paintings are absolutely wonderful! I'm sad to see them hidden away here; they should be seen by everyone." I look around, feeling a bit of hesitation to share these highly personal works with people I don't know. "Claire, I doubt anyone would really want to see them. I like them, but that's because they have significance *to me*. Someone who isn't familiar with the places I've painted may not feel such a strong connection to the scenes." Claire shakes her head, watching as Noah takes a few more steps into the room and proceeds to look at each picture, slowly taking in the colours and the subject matter. Claire continues, "No, Mom, you're wrong. These would appeal to anyone who loves nature. The colours are amazing, the feeling pops right off the canvas to evoke a reaction from the viewer. I just love them! What do you think, Noah?" The young boy turns his head to address his mother. "Well, I like them. This is our woods, and here is Fae dancing with Orna. I like the squirrels in this tree!" His voice is full of excitement as he points to the things he likes most about each painting. My heart swells to hear his praise. It doesn't seem to matter what age you are; to hear a compliment from your child or grandchild means more than any comment from an art critic.

"Well, Mom, I think we should do an art show at the Centre. What do you think?" I feel myself take a step backwards, almost like I'm physically avoiding the question. "Oh no, no. That's not a good idea. I don't know. These paintings are so personal to me, it's hard to think of sharing them with the *public*." Claire gently replies, "Think of the enjoyment people would get from seeing your beautiful work. It may even bring some people comfort, or peace, to look upon the woods and see the tiny creatures at home. You know the people who visit the Centre would be thrilled to see your art. Come on, open yourself up, don't hide your creative energy under a rock." Her words ring in my ears, like Spider's comments from months ago, encouraging me to find my own creative path and follow it, which in turn encourages others to do the same. It would be hypocritical of me to turn away, using self-doubt as a motivator. I scan the room again, trying to imagine these paintings on the walls of the Centre; seeing people peer at them, and before I can inject their rejection into the scenario, I change it to view the same people looking upon the paintings and deriving some pleasure from them, just like Noah did a few moments ago. "Okay. You and your dad will have to figure out how to hang these things. I can never get that part right. You know Dad, always happiest with a work project to do!" Claire laughs as I reach out and pick up the jar full of brushes that need cleaning.

As luck would have it, Ginger, a client who regularly sees Claire for healing work, is the curator of a small art gallery downtown. Her gallery, *Up Front,* most often showcases new and aspiring artists. She feels that giving them a venue, when they are just starting out, encourages them to continue with their art. She said established artists often usurp the bigger galleries who are trying to sell, sell, sell, rather than provide the community with a new experience, and support a new artist. I really like Ginger. When she heard of our plans to hang some of my work at the Centre, she offered her gallery. She said that it would be perfect, with lots of exposure to the public, good lighting to highlight each painting, and even offered to have an open house, a sort of launch party to celebrate the exhibit. Claire was so excited to hear this news, she accepted the offer without so much as a consult with the artist herself. I knew she did that because she knew I would, once again, hesitate.

The one stipulation I make is that *none* of the paintings are for sale. Ginger blanches slightly, and Claire shakes her head. "Mom, Ginger needs to sell *something* to pay her bills." I look at Ginger and feel bad. "I am willing to pay any amount that would offset your expenses, or whatever it is you need to cover your costs for the showcase." I swallow, thinking of letting my paintings go, never to see them again, "It would be like selling my children," I try to explain without getting too emotional. Ginger smiles, nodding in empathy. "Hannah, these children are not meant to hide away in your house, never to have a life where others can enjoy them. You wouldn't want to keep your child at home, not to have the life they deserve?" It's such an odd analogy it takes me off guard. I once again hesitate, and then say, "I'll decide which paintings I may be willing to part with, but there are some I will not." Ginger nods again, and Claire groans.

The opening of the showcase is three weeks off, so I take the opportunity to enjoy the paintings nestled in my art room one last time, before they are set free upon the world. I see colours swirling on the canvas as if the wind blows them. My Light is infused in each canvas, in each brush stroke, but I know the best thing is to allow this energy to flow out and touch others. I have chosen to keep three canvases out of fifteen. They will be on display for the duration of the show, but not for sale. My favourite painting is of Claire, sitting by the edge of the pond, waiting for Ol' Toad to make an appearance. She would have been around eight years old. It is a treasured memory of mine; one I often call upon when I feel stressed.

As I sit quietly looking around the room, I can hear Claire slowly making her way up the stairs. She is heavily pregnant, and very uncomfortable. Unlike Noah, this baby was planned. Claire feels that Noah should have a sibling. Much like she has Fae as a confidante and ally, she wants Noah to have someone there for him as well. She heaves a heavy sigh as she stands in the doorway to the room. "Not long now, for you, and for me!" she chuckles, rubbing her back. I stand and offer my chair to her, but she shakes her head. "I only came upstairs to let you know I'm leaving now. Dad has Noah busy building birdhouses in the garden, so I'm off to the Centre. Tila and I are finishing up the last Tai Chi class today, and I don't want to be late. I guess I should say it's *my* last class today. Did I tell you, Tila wants to extend the class another ten weeks? That will really help our bottom line if she can keep that class and her yoga group going." She sighs again. "Mom, I am so tired. How am I going to have this baby, take care of Noah, and run the Centre? If I'm so exhausted now, I can't imagine me in a few months." She frowns, and once again rubs her back. Although she is not due for another five days, I wonder if her body is actually sending a signal to prepare. "Claire, sweetie, I can only imagine how tough all this is to carry. Remember that we are *all* here to help, so you don't have to carry it alone. David will be off in a month, once the school year ends, so he can help with Noah, and in the meantime Dad and I can help with our little man. Tila and I will be running the Centre, until you are up to coming in again. Your dad is here to help with *anything* you need, and you know how much he needs a project to keep him going!" She smiles, knowing my statement is made with love, and also knowing her father is not one who enjoys sitting around enjoying retirement.

Claire suddenly takes a sharp breath and holds her stomach. I come over to stand beside her in case she needs support. "Are you okay, Claire?". She smiles at the concern in my voice. "Mom, don't worry, Fae is monitoring the contractions. I think I'm in the early stages, so there's no rush." I blink, realizing she just said she is in labour. She's so calm and unperturbed by her situation. Once again, I am in admiration of my daughter's strength, both physically, and mentally. "Oh, well, okay, but I think I'll just tell Dad that we may be off to the hospital soon. Should I call David?" Claire inhales sharply and then tilts her head, listening. She is, of course, listening to Fae. She nods her head and says, in between breaths, "Yup, I do believe I've been given the green light from Fae. I think we should make our way. Oh damn!" I look at her, alarmed that she may be in pain. "What? What? Are you okay?" She laughs and takes my hand as I lead her out of the room, "I'm fine Mom, relax. I just realized I'm going to miss my last Tai Chi class!"

Alice Rose Heron Ross entered this world without any complications or fanfare. Weighing in at just over six pounds, she is tiny, and perfect, with a mop of auburn hair and blue eyes that twinkle. She looks so fairy-like, it's all I can do to keep from commenting on it when David is present. As much as Claire loves David, she has not shared the truth about Fae with him, yet. David is much like Owen: a firm believer in science and fact, and hesitant to believe in the world unseen. There is a way that he can have his foot in both camps, but it's not for me to show him how to do that.

Claire and David chose the name Alice for his grandmother; Rose for her grandmother; Heron, as Claire wants David's last name attached to his daughter, and Ross as her surname. She and David have no plans to marry as yet, although they would consider it now, for the additional tax breaks they would receive.

David and Owen take Noah out of the hospital room, leaving Claire and me alone with Alice. I pick up my granddaughter and look into her face. You hear these sappy expressions about looking at the face of an angel, but there seems to be no other way to describe the countenance of this baby. She bears a remarkable resemblance to Claire, aside from the hair colour, which is all David. It's more the expression; the eyes that look out and see her new life. I search for signs of an Alternate in her, but I am unable to tell. Arthur would know, but I hesitate to open that can of worms again. It will be up to Claire, if she wants to know or not. I feel a lump in my throat as I look at Alice. A swarm of emotional bees buzz around my head, recalling the day I first held Claire, and looked at her face, and felt that immediate bond. I know I felt the bond with Noah too, but this little girl has something that I can't put my finger on, a Light that shines so brightly, I can't look away.

Claire yawns, and shifts slightly on the bed. "Holy crap, I'm tired! You can stay with Alice if you'd like, but you'll have to excuse me while I lie here and die for a while." She chuckles and then grimaces at the slight pain her post-birth body feels. I place Alice back in the bassinet, and step over to help rearrange the covers on Claire. "Sweetie, I'll leave you both to rest. I know I would sleep better if I didn't have someone hovering over me. We're taking Noah out for dinner, so he doesn't feel too out of sorts with all the attention on Alice. You just rest. I think David said he was coming back a bit later. Then he can help with Alice, when needed." I lean over and gingerly kiss her forehead, sensing that Fae continues to send her healing love, causing Claire's aura to glow bright yellow and blue. It is a beautiful thing to see. Claire closes her eyes, feeling the energy cover her like a blanket of warmth and security. Before another breath she is asleep. I turn, and blowing a kiss to the sleeping infant, I quietly leave the room.

The full moon hovers above, its bright yellow craterous face starkly alone in the black sky. One can almost see each peak and valley upon the surface of the lunar giant. No stars are alight to show the path of angels and energy. Only a gemstone speck of Light appears in the dark canvas, and grows larger as it draws near. I cannot fathom its size until it looms large overhead, suspended in Time, by Space itself. His mouth is open, showing bright white glistening fangs. His scales, layered from his head to the tip of his tail, glow ruby, emerald and sapphire colours. His eyes are amber jewels that remind me of OnanOff's eyes. His long sinewy tail wraps around some invisible perch as his claws grasp at the air, finding purchase magically, out of nothing. I am not afraid of Dragon, only in awe. His fierce beauty and size fill the sky, blocking out the moon. He lowers his head, and utters through a steamy breath, "I am the Royal Ancient Light, come upon the dead of night, to seek the one who walks in dreams; she is human, but more, it seems. Hear and heed the words I share; A new phase is near, but just beware. Your soul for tempting others find, but you need to leave them far behind. Seek only Light, you will not fail, when darkness calls to no avail."

He raises his head and gives a thunderous roar, as he expels streaks of coloured Light from his open maw, like fire, without heat. The streaks sparkle and glow luminously in the dark, filling the black sky from one end to the other. He unfolds his massive wings and launches his immense form into the night, still covering the face of the moon as he takes flight. He disappears as quickly as he appeared, leaving nothing but streaks of colour across the vast sky, like the Aurora Borealis.

I can still see the colours across my eyelids, before I gently open them, only to gaze at the blank white bedroom ceiling above me. And, unlike the night sky, this view is unwavering in its dullness.

EIGHT

Standing in a room full of people who are viewing, and let's be honest, judging, your paintings, is more than a little overwhelming. I want nothing more than to hide away in the women's room for the remainder of the open-house, but I know I can't do that. Claire stands beside me, and I can feel the warmth of Fae's Light penetrating my core, giving me strength to smile and carry on. I had insisted that Claire stay home with Alice, but she would not hear of it, and, she admitted, she really wanted to get out of the house for an afternoon, without children.

I scan the room, to find Owen talking with Ginger, both smiling and laughing. He is a *people person*, and he has such Talent for making anyone he talks with feel like they are his number one focus, to the exclusion of all else. He asks good questions, and engages the person in meaningful dialogue. He was an excellent reporter and teacher, and he's an even better husband. I see Grace, as she watches Arthur entertain a small group of women from the Centre with some animated story he has pulled out of his hat. They break the dull murmur in the room with some loud guffaws. In this moment I realize how blessed I am to have so many dear friends here supporting me.

Claire touches my arm, and quietly utters; "Gotta find the ladies room. I'll be back soon. Why don't you mingle a bit. Everyone here is loving your work, and I think you need to hear that." She smiles, leaving me alone with my thoughts. I look around the gallery, estimating about thirty-five people in attendance. Most are friends or acquaintances, but there are a few strangers. Ginger said that some of her friends always come to open houses so they can meet the artist and form a connection, even a mentorship in some cases. Young artists who step into Ginger's sphere of influence certainly gain an advantage.

Suddenly I hear a voice at my ear, a familiar whisper that makes my skin prickle. "I always knew you were a great artist." I turn abruptly and come face to face with Julian Halliday. He grins as I stare at him, stunned to see him standing before me. His hair, now short and greying, makes his face much rounder than when he was young. His eyes, once full of humour, now seem dull and hard. I take a step backward, feeling the need to place as much distance between us as possible. "Julian? Wow, it's been years. What are you doing here?" He continues to smile, as he glances around the gallery. "I saw the ad for the show, and thought I recognized your photo, so I googled you. And there you were, with the art gallery's Instagram reference for the show. I knew it was you, even though you've changed your name." I frown, not happy to have him *googling* me. "Yes, I've been Hannah Ross for quite some time now. Um, how are you doing? Are *you* still painting?" His harsh laugh makes some people nearby glance over. It's almost a derisive bark. "No, no. Unfortunately I have no time for things *like that.* Happy to see you keeping up the good fight though. No, I'm working hard at the business still. In fact I just bought up a huge tract of land just north of the city, by the old airport strip. Maybe you know it? It's about twenty hectares of prime underused farmland. The city is spreading out, and north is the way many people are heading, so it's a great investment." I blink and take in his words, but have no way to figure out how to reply to his comment. Once upon a time he valued farmland, and cursed the developers who ravaged the land without due consideration for the impact as a whole. Now he seems to be in the same boat with them.

He stares at me, waiting for a reply. "Well, that's good. I guess that means you work for your father, still?" He shakes his head. "No, Dad passed away a long while back. I took over the business about twenty-five years ago. We had been partners ever since university." At the mention of school, I get an image of him, sitting at a desk, long wavy hair and crewneck sweater, paint staining his beautiful hands. Where did *that* man go? I want to pity him, believing he gave up on his own dreams, surrendering to the pressure of family obligation. But now I wonder if the young man I loved long ago was simply playing a role, and that his true self is in fact the one standing before me now.

Once again, I realize the conversation ball is in my court, but before I can say anything, Julian turns to view a painting that hangs to his right. He nods his head and comments, "Just love your work. It's so, um, imaginary. I don't remember you being into that fantasy-type of stuff. This looks like something out of Lord of the Rings." I look at the painting he is referring to. It's one of Claire and Fae sitting under a Birch tree. I frown. For some reason his labeling it *fantasy-type-stuff* leaves a bad taste in my mouth. He turns, and seeing my expression, adds, "Sorry, I didn't mean to sound condescending. It's been a while since I've looked upon, let alone commented on, someone's work. It's really a beautiful piece. I assume the little girl is your daughter?" I nod, but say nothing more. "How marvelous!" Almost on cue, Claire steps up to stand between Julian and me. She glances at him and smiles. "Hello. I'm Claire, Hannah's daughter." She extends her hand. Julian takes it and gives it a hearty shake, looking at me when he speaks. "Oh, my god! She looks just like you did when we were together!" Claire's eyes open wide and she looks at me. I lopsidedly smile, but still don't know what to say. Julian continues, "It's so nice to meet you! I'm Julian. I don't know if your mother has mentioned me, but we used to *paint* together, back in our university days." His wink makes me cringe.

Claire smiles, and says, "Oh, that's great! Imagine meeting up after all these years. That's amazing." I know she is grasping for something to say, as am I. Julian doesn't seem to notice how uncomfortable I am as he continues, "I was just about to ask your mom if she'd meet me for coffee soon, just so we can catch up, you know." He turns his gaze back to me, "I'd love to hear more about what you've been up to all these years." Claire glances at me as I blanche. She squeezes my arm and says, "Oh, what a great idea! You guys must have so much to talk about, what's it been, like, fifty years or something?" Julian bellows with laughter, making more of the visitors around him stop and stare. "Claire, you're hilarious! No, no, not quite fifty, but I sure don't wanna count. I dated your mom, let's see, I was about twenty-three or something..." he trails off, his eyes un-focusing as he tries to calculate. Now I feel the need to step in and steer this conversation away from the edge of the cliff. "Julian, I'm sorry, I really need to mingle with the other guests who've come today. I suppose we could meet for coffee, *sometime*, but I really need to find Owen now." Julian smiles, and pulls out his phone, "Great! Give me your number and I'll text you so we can meet up." I stare at his phone, knowing that I'm stuck between a rock and a hard place. Claire, not knowing the whole story, thinks this is a great idea, so if I give him the wrong number she may correct me. I feel sick thinking of him having my number. As I'm about to speak, Claire pipes up, "Oh Mom, I know you can't remember your number, I know how much she hates that thing." She turns to Julian and recites my number, as he enters it into his phone. She has sealed my fate now.

Julian reaches out and touches Claire's arm, to thank her. He turns to me and takes a step forward, as if to hug me. I take a step backwards and bump into the person behind me. I turn to apologize and find myself looking at Owen. A wave of relief washes over me. He smiles and wraps his arm around my waist, coming to stand beside me. I turn, a beaming smile now plastered on my face. "Julian, I'd like you to meet Owen, my husband." Julian's face clouds over, but only for a fraction of a second, then the smooth-façade reveals itself, as he extends his hand to shake Owen's. Claire leans in and says, "Julian and Mom went to university together. Isn't that crazy?" Owen frowns slightly as he looks at Julian.

Years ago, we had talked about previous relationships we had had over the years, before meeting one another. I recall the lengthy tale I related about Julian, and Owen's comment rings in my ears as their hands break apart. He said, if he ever met that guy, he'd have *a thing or two* to say to him. I look at his face, silently pleading for him to leave it alone. His frown softens as he catches my wary expression. He would never want to embarrass me by causing a scene. Julian mumbles something about it being *nice to meet you*, and places his phone back in his pocket. He turns to leave, but his departing remark makes my skin crawl; "Owen you are a *very* lucky man. Hannah, I'll be in touch!" I watch as he heads to the exit, and I feel Owen's grip on my waist tighten slightly.

The house feels like a security blanket, and I sink into its embrace like a long-lost child. The afternoon has been very successful, but more of an emotional strain than I realized. Before taking off my party dress, I walk into the living room and sit down on the couch. OnanOff, laying across the front window sill, opens one eye. His slumber only briefly interrupted by my entrance, he closes his eye and resumes napping. Owen hangs up his jacket and comes to sit in the large armchair opposite me. He lays his head against the back of the chair and closes his eyes. He too, feels the energy of the day drain from him. I lean down and pull off my shoes to massage my aching feet. Owen rubs his eyes and mutters, "Wow, I'm beat. Why don't we order in tonight? I don't think either one of us wants to cook." It isn't really a question, more of a statement. I nod, but don't bother with a verbal response. I feel disjointed from the room, from the day, as my mind reels back to Julian.

Something has been eating away at me ever since I laid eyes on him. My reaction, stunned at first, turned into something else as the encounter progressed. I could feel a small voice inside of me, possibly the younger version of me, saying, *you should have been nicer to him, and be happy to be invited out for coffee.* I realize it's all the emotions I packed up into that suitcase long ago, after he broke my heart. Each emotion - from self-doubt, as I questioned my possible over-reaction to his angry assault on my character and my wrist; to my anger towards him as he thought he had the power to *dictate* how the relationship should develop, I had all neatly packed in this suitcase in the lowest part of my mind. I believed, with the passage of Time, this suitcase would vanish; but Time did not make it disappear, merely moved it off to the side. Hannah One always said that when one avoids working through a trauma, you are merely stowing it in a suitcase. Eventually that suitcase will inch its way out of hiding, and before you know it, you trip over it. She was right, as here I am tripping over this mammoth box of emotions once again. The only difference is that I'm not the same person as I was when I was twenty-something, lacking the self-confidence to find my voice, and still very unsure of human relationships and their complex dynamics. Sitting up, I glance at Owen. He appears to have dozed off. I stand and quietly walk out of the room, heading upstairs to change out of my dress and wash the day off my face. As I put my hand on the railing to go up, I hear my cell phone chime in my purse, indicating a message. Assuming Claire is texting me, I reach in and pull it out. The number is unknown, but I know who it is. *I said I'd be in touch and here I am! How about coffee tomorrow?* My throat feels dry, and my eyes are sore, as if I had been looking at this screen for hours. I drop the phone back into my purse and head upstairs.

I lean around and kiss the cheek of the man with the wavy brown hair, as he sits at the kitchen table. He turns to look up at me. I smile and place my hand on his face. He stands up and pulls me into his arms and we kiss. It is a long passionate kiss, and I feel our bodies press against each other as desire mounts. For some reason I want to pull away, but I am caught in his powerful embrace and, finally giving up, I surrender to his control. We drop to the floor, as lust and power carry our bodies to feverous heights. The floor falls away, and suddenly we are sitting in large overstuffed armchairs, facing a fireplace, reading books, drinking wine, as a child plays at our feet. I look over at the man, his wavy hair now cut short. I do not recognize him. I look at the child, who has long wavy brown hair. He looks up at me and I see my face staring back. I try to take hold of the child's outstretched hand, but he falls away, and I am standing in a giant hallway, with white marble arches, and a round spiral staircase. A Christmas tree sits in the middle of the hall; it is white, with blood-red ornaments perched upon its branches. The man appears at my side and hands me a gift. I open the velvet box to find a diamond necklace. He takes it out of the box and places it around my neck. His voice in my ear, familiar and loving; 'Well now, Mrs. Halliday, I don't know what's more beautiful, the necklace, or the neck it sits upon. He leans in and kisses my neck. I feel myself lean back into his body, the heat once again rising from his touch. I open my eyes, and there, before me, stands a roomful of people, all holding cocktail glasses, raised in a toast. 'Here's to Mrs. Halliday, founding member of the Food for Thought campaign. Cheers!' The little boy races through the scene, but he is so peripheral, I cannot see him clearly. A hand reaches out and takes mine, the man leading me outside to stand in a field. It is decimated of life, as a large pyre of burning trees sends a huge black plume into the sky. 'We will do very well with this; it's a great investment.' The man squeezes my hand and I smile at him. The acrid smell of burning garbage fills my nostrils. I pull out an embroidered handkerchief and dab my nose. Turning, I am in a bedroom, lush carpeting under-foot, rich, dark fabric curtains hang against the wall, and a large oak-framed bed, covered with a silk duvet, occupies the centre of the room. The man, with redness in his eyes, grabs my arm with one large hand, and utters menacing words I cannot hear. I try to pull away, but he has me pinned against the heavy curtain. The sting of the slap as it lands on my cheek makes my eyes water. I try to cry out, but I have no voice. The diamond necklace comes off, dropping jagged pieces of glass all over the carpet, and as I try to run away, my feet are cut and bleeding. I hear the cry of the child, far away, fleeting, but I am unable to reach him. I cannot see anymore, I have closed my eyes, I have stopped thinking or caring, or living. I just am. Nothing more.

I wake up, feeling the sweat pouring down my spine. Owen is awake and sitting up next to me. His face, once again, full of concern. "Bad dream?" he asks hoarsely. I need a moment, as I sit up, to re-orient myself to where I am, before I reply: "Not sure really. It's almost like I saw what my life *might* have been like, had I stayed with Julian. It was horrible." Owen rubs my back softly. He leans over and kisses my cheek, which somehow still aches from the slap. He whispers in my ear; "I sure am glad you decided to ditch that guy." I smile and kiss him, trying to erase the stark images that haunt my mind.

Tila's white straw bonnet, with silk Daisies lining the brim, reminds me of Hannah One. I smile, thinking how much she would have loved that hat, and Tila herself. I try to focus on Tila's description of an outing she and the other women had while visiting some hamlet outside London. As much as I want to hear another tale from her trip, I have an ulterior motive to asking her for coffee today. I glance around at the other tables on the patio, with only one taken up by a couple enjoying some hot drinks and sweets. The Garden Café is usually fairly busy, so it's nice to find it quiet for once.

Tila pauses, aware of my distracted demeanor. "Okay, enough about the trip. I get the feeling there's something else on your mind besides hearing about how many scones I ate!" She laughs, picking up her tea cup and taking a large sip. I smile at her, knowing full well she would not be offended if I change the subject abruptly. "Well, Tila, now that you mention it, I am looking for some advice.

You're really the only person I can trust with this. There is no way I can to talk to Owen or Claire, so I'm afraid you got the short stick, my dear." Tila puts down her cup and leans forward. "Is it juicy? Scandalous? I'm always willing to pick the short stick, if the story is interesting." It's my turn to chuckle. "Sorry Tila, I doubt you will find this as titillating as you'd like. Let's see, where to begin?" I didn't want to spend a lot of time explaining my history with Julian, so I try to sum it up as briefly as I can. "Okay. Well, years ago, when I was in university, I met a man, a nice man, named Julian. We dated, and I really thought he was special, that he could be *the one*. Unfortunately, it didn't end well. I was hesitant to jump into having a sexual relationship… well, that's another story. Anyway, he was not the most patient or understanding person, and he believed I was just leading him on. It ended badly, and I was heartbroken." Tila nods, but says nothing, so I continue. "At the open-house, I know you didn't see him, but Julian was there." Tila's mouth opens, and then shuts. Her eyebrows shoot up, her surprise registering about the same level as when *I* saw him in the gallery. "Dear lord! Hannah! What the hell? Why was *he* there?" She looks around, and, realizing her voice carries, lowers her head and leans in. "Does Owen know about him? Holy cow! How did I not notice this going on? I was there all afternoon!" I pick up my mug and sip my coffee, taking a moment, trying to see the path of this conversation, before too many questions lead us astray. "Well, he said he saw the ad in the paper for the show, and wondered if it was me, so he *googled* me!" Tila laughs, and replies, "Only you could make that sound dirty! But please, go on, I'm dying here!" She leans in closer. "We had a sort-of nice conversation, I suppose. I felt weird and uncomfortable though, especially when he asked if we could meet for coffee sometime."

Again, the shock on Tila's face equals the way I felt when he asked me. "Oh my god! What the hell did you say to that? Tell me you told him to stuff it!" I shook my head, feeling like I let all of womankind down for not being more confident and decisive.

"Tila, there was something unauthentic about him. I'd like to believe that his life isn't what he truly wanted for himself. Maybe he got pulled into a life his parents *planned* for him, making lots of money and living high, foregoing his own dreams. I don't know; I just felt a bit sorry for him." I look down at the table, realizing I just expressed the conclusion my Alternate side came to, after the encounter. I was too caught up in the human emotions of fear and disdain to see the bigger, more compassionate picture. Tila reaches over and taps my arm. "Hannah, you of all people know that the choices we make, are the choices we make. It's how we learn from the consequences of our choices that matters. You can take a negative and find some ray of good in it, most of the time, if you look hard enough." I nod in agreement. "So, what *did* you say to him?" Tila asks, like a child, waiting to hear the end of the story, her eyes intent on my face. I swallow. "Well, before I could answer, Claire stepped in and thought it was a great idea for two old university friends to get together for coffee, so *she* gave him my number." Tila's hands slap the table, spilling her tea slightly. "Oops, sorry, I'm getting way too carried away here. It's not every day, especially at your age, that you get embroiled in a love tryst!" She laughs, taking a paper napkin and wiping away the spilled tea. I quickly reply, "Oh no, no, there's no love *anything* here. I was actually sick about her giving him my number, but what could I do? I thought, well, maybe I won't need to worry, he might not ever call or text. But," and as I hesitate, Tila jumps in, "Holy shit, he called?" I shake my head, "No, it was a text. But he texted me, like, three hours after we met at the gallery. I didn't tell Owen anything about it. He already knows the history, and I'm afraid he'll blow a gasket if he thinks I'd go meet him for coffee." I take a breath, feeling like I am running out of oxygen, despite being outside in the fresh air.

Tila scans my face, but her mind is elsewhere. She blinks and shakes her head, saying, "Well, I was just trying to see myself in your shoes, and what would I do? Doesn't matter though, does it?

My feet won't fit in your shoes any better than yours fitting into mine, right? All I know is, if I had an opportunity to come face to face with some of the men I've encountered throughout my life, I might have a few choice words to say before I was done. Give you closure, perhaps?" She looks at me questioningly.

"I think I should also tell you; I had a vision about him. It was quite unsettling, to say the least. It was, well, like I was seeing what my life would have been like, had I married him. There were some good times," and an image of our bodies, naked and thrashing across the floor in the throes of passion, crosses my mind. "But for the most part, I would have been miserable and terrified of his violent nature. I would have been untrue to my Light, wasting my life in a role I was never meant to play." Tila leans in again, "The good stuff, was it all about the sex?" I nod, feeling my face go a bit red. "It's always sex. We humans seem to think it will answer all the world's woes. But in fact, it just complicates them. If you take the hot sex out of the picture, what are you left with? Crap. A plate full of crap." She picks up her cup and drains the contents, and then gently places it back on the table.

"So, I still don't know what to do! If I meet him, then what? The only thing I can think of, is that I could help him realize that he can't pursue a friendship with me, that it just won't work. That way he will stop texting every day, and I can have some peace." Tila nods, and says, "Yes, I think facing him, and helping him see the truth of the matter will put an end to him harassing you. And as I say, it will give you a definitive conclusion to that chapter of your life. He may have a hard time hearing what you are saying. So be prepared for that scenario as well. I don't envy you my dear; it's a difficult situation. But I'm glad you shared it with me. You're right, there's no way Owen would see any other solution to this, other than to punch him in the nose. And Claire, dear girl, sees a world full of lovely people, with all sorts of potential. She hasn't had enough years on Earth to have her perspective become jaded, yet." I frown, hoping her lovely perspective never becomes cynical.

Claire walks in the front door, a baby carrier in both hands, diaper bag draped on her shoulder. Noah holds open the door as she struggles through. Now closing in on eight years old, Noah seems very conscientious about others around him. His kindness and empathy, especially towards animals, is very touching. I stand up and race to the door to lend a hand with all the supplies that she is lugging into the house. A get-away has been planned by Claire and David, and includes another couple, Lilah and George. Noah and Alice will be staying with Owen and me for the long weekend. Now that the weather has improved, we can all be outside in the garden, planting, weeding and occasionally looking for tree nymphs.

Claire places the carrier, with Alice resting inside, in a corner of the living room. Alice, a sound sleeper, doesn't blink an eye at all the noise and jostling. Noah retraces his steps out to the car to help his mother with another bag. His own bag sits in the hall, complete with toys, a chapter book and his clothes. His face is full of excitement, as there's nothing like a weekend with Grannah and Grandad.

The last two bags contain baby bottles, and some extra snacks and drinks for Noah. Claire hauls the heavy cloth bags into the kitchen, and unceremoniously dumps them on the counter. She turns, and spying the chair, takes a seat to catch her breath. "Holy moly Mom, what a lot of fuss, just for a weekend! I haven't even packed up my own stuff yet!" She takes the cold glass of water I offer her, and Noah accepts a glass of juice I pour for him. He takes it into the living room, pulls a book off the table that Owen had left out for him, and sits down on the floor beside his sister, who is still sound asleep.

The two couples are taking the train to Quebec City. They have reserved rooms at a bed and breakfast in the old part of the city, and plan on doing walking tours, and other touristy things. Owen and I are happy to have our grandchildren stay with us. Remembering, as a young mother, how much I enjoyed time away to re-energize, I am very supportive of their adventure. Claire drains the water in a few gulps and takes her empty glass over to the sink. She glances at the bags, but I assure her I can unpack them, with Noah supervising, of course. I sense a small bit of hesitation, knowing this is her first experience leaving Alice for any length of time. "I think you'll have great weather for walking, and I looked up the place you booked, and it looks lovely. I know you'll have a good time; you just need to go!" She smiles, knowing what I mean. "I have asked Fae to step back for the weekend, so I can be alone with David, you know…" she almost blushes. "I just want to reconnect with him. Lilah and George never got a honeymoon, so we invited them along, as our wedding gift, as a sort of delayed honeymoon for them." Her best friend, Lilah, had married George quite quickly and quietly, with only a handful of friends and family in attendance. I never voice an opinion about anyone's style in celebrating events like birthdays or weddings, but I was actually quite impressed by their practical view of the matter. Claire said they want to buy a house, so that is the priority; not a big, fancy wedding.

"I hope the kids behave for you. Alice is still waking up at night, but now it's only once, maybe twice. I have pumped enough milk for the weekend, and there is formula in the bag, if you need it." Claire fusses with the bags once last time before turning and entering the living room. In the other corner, near the table, I set up a bassinet for daytime napping. Claire quietly paces over to the car seat and lifts Alice out and gently places her in the bassinet. She wiggles slightly, but quickly calms down and remains asleep as she settles into the bed. Claire walks over to Noah, who is now sitting on the couch, still engulfed in reading the large book about animals. She sits beside him and her hand goes to his hair, rearranging a lock of auburn curls that seems to be getting away from him. He tilts his head slightly, not wanting her to bother with him, but then looks up and says, "You and Dad have fun! I'm going to build stuff with Grandad, and Grannah can play with

Alice. We're going to be busy!" Claire smiles and leans over to kiss his forehead. His arms reach up to give her a hug, and then picks up his book and slides off the couch, to go find his grandfather. "Noah, you'll find Grandad in the garden." He runs through the kitchen and out to the backyard through the sunroom door. Claire chuckles. "Guess I can go. No worries here!" She stands and gives me a quick hug before leaving.

My phone chimes, and I sigh. It can't be Claire, as she has literally just left the house. I pick up the phone and see the number. It's Julian, again. Pausing, I take a deep breath and reply, *Got the grandkids for the weekend but how about next week? Tuesday at The Garden Café at 1… okay?* I hit send and close my eyes, knowing full well I will get an immediate response. The floating bubbles show me he is typing. Then the whoosh sound brings his response to my screen. *Great!!! Can't wait!!! Have fun with the kids!* His enthusiastic, over-use of exclamation marks makes my eyes hurt, and the emojis he used does not help either. As I view a heart, two coffee cups, followed by another heart, I feel the knot in my stomach tighten.

I watch from the sunroom window as Noah and Owen sit under the tree, reading Charlie and the Chocolate Factory, Noah's newest favourite chapter book. My arms hold a bundle of love, as I glance down to see Alice's little hazel eyes open, blinking and staring straight at me. Her eyes, when she was born, were blue, but now they have changed into a colour that is a gemstone mixture of greens, browns and sand-coloured, like encapsulating the sun, the woods and the beach all in one colour. She squirms slightly, trying to free her arm. I move the blanket slightly so she can free herself, and out shoots a tiny hand. Fingers, small and delicate, stretch and point, almost emotive, like a dancer. I see an image of Alice, around the age of twelve, wearing ballet slippers, dancing to some melodious strain. Her long legs strong and graceful, her arms expressive, beautifully conveying the emotion of the dance, as her body moves like a small tree swaying in the wind. I blink, looking down at the infant in my arms, and wonder if I just saw her future, some sort of future dream-walk. She could be a dancer, or a mathematician, or anything she desires, as long as she is happy, healthy and loved. Owen's words about Claire echo in my mind. He had said those exact words when confronted with Claire's Alternate *situation*. The clarity of his words hit home, as now I truly understand what he meant. Nothing really matters, as long as they are healthy, happy and loved. My eyes search out Owen once again, and I look at his face, full of love for his grandson, and love for his life, as it evolves with every step. I see a sense of peace there, a resolution that began with Claire, and now completes itself with Noah and Alice.

    He glances up, sensing I am watching, and smiles. They are sitting on the ground, on a blanket. I open the door and step out on to the small deck off the sunroom. The air is warm, and smells of Lilacs. I carefully make my way down the steps to join them, sliding out of my house slippers, so my bare feet touch the cool, freshly growing grass. I hear their tiny grass voices as I pass, a mixture of annoyance and tolerance at being stepped on. I look up into the tree, and spy several nymphs, sitting on the branches, obviously listening to the story book being read. I make no comment about them so they will not dash away to hide. With some effort, I manage to lower myself, still cradling Alice in my arms, to sit next to Noah on the blanket. I place Alice on the blanket, and loosen her wrap, so she can move her legs and arms, if she so desires. I move my rear so I'm more comfortable, and nod that the reading should continue. No sooner has Owen commenced reading, when the moth-eaten shape of a very elderly cat appears from the house, making his way down the steps, to come and curl up on the blanket in front of Noah. OnanOff raises his head and looks at the baby, sniffs once, and then tucks his nose in his bushy tail, falling asleep almost immediately.

The Café is fairly busy as diners enjoy the sunny day on the patio. I make sure to arrive a few minutes early so I can pick the table for this meeting with Julian. I choose a patio table off to the side, and have my back against the outside wall, so I can see when he approaches. As I'm being seated, I mention to the waiter that I'm meeting someone, and that we'll order *as soon as* he arrives. I emphasize it will be two separate bills. Now it's just a matter of waiting, although not for long, as I see Julian make his way through the interior of the café, to the open door that leads to the patio. He is smiling. I take a deep breath.

He reaches the table, but I don't rise to greet him. I thought about it, but decided that giving him any opportunity to touch me, even giving me a hug, would be something best avoided. I smile back as he seats himself. The waiter walks over and we order coffee. Julian asks if I would like something to eat. I shake my head, no, but make no other reply. I smile at the waiter as he says he will be back momentarily with our coffees.

Julian scans my face, taking in every line and crease I have grown over the years. "I can't believe it; you haven't changed at all." I chortle as I respond; "You are so full of it! Or you need glasses!" He chuckles. I feel like it's appropriate to comment on his appearance, so I say, "I like the shorter haircut. It suits you." An awkward moment sits between us, as I try to figure out a way to begin what I came to say. Fortunately, the waiter arrives carrying a tray with two coffees and a tiny pitcher of cream and packets of sugar. After he places the order on the table, he leaves without further comment.

Julian pours cream into his coffee as he glances around, looking relaxed and casual. Finally, he leans forward slightly and asks, "So, tell me everything. How is your life going? How is the gang? Mark? Jamie? I think I heard that Neville and Jamie got married?". At the mention of her name, I feel my heart catch. I take a moment before I reply, "Well, yes, they did marry. But Jamie died a few years ago." Julian's smile vanishes, to be replaced by genuine grief. "Oh my god, that's so sad. I really liked her. She was a lot of fun, and I know she was a good friend of yours." He looks over, his head lowered so his glance is through his long dark lashes. I nod, but look down at my coffee, "Yes, she's the most wonderful friend I ever had. I miss her every day." I swallow the sadness and continue. "It's been hard on Neville, and their son, Aidan." I run my mind over topics to change the conversation to, feeling like I need to leave this one behind. "What about you? Did you marry? Children?" Julian's face clouds over slightly, "Oh yes, I took that trip to *marital world*, but it didn't work out. I have a son, Robert, but he's living in England now, with his wife and child. I don't see them much." He trails off, indicating that this isn't something he wants to go into detail about.

I lift my coffee mug up and take another sip, feeling the nervous tension between us. Julian runs his finger along the handle of his cup, and then says, "You know, I really miss the old days. Those were great times. Before you had to face the world, and do all this shit about running a business, or trying to be married and being a responsible adult. If only we knew then what we know now, as they say…" I look at his face and see regret and resignation on it. I sigh, "Well, Julian, it wasn't all wine and roses back then. I remember struggling through school, and, well, relationships. You may look back through rose-coloured glasses and see only the times you were happy, or had fun, and not look at the challenges you faced, or the heartaches you experienced. But there's no going back, no wishing it was *then* and not *now*. You can't un-write what is written on the page, only learn from it and move forward." Julian looks at me and smiles weakly, "I guess you're right. I do remember struggles with my parents, and school. I turned to drugs and alcohol to cope, then I just gave up, and got into the boat with their expectations and began rowing. I never wanted to leave the boat; I figured I didn't have the strength to swim on my own." He frowns. "Wow! We got serious way too fast! I think we should talk about something else, or you'll charge me for a therapy session here!" He laughs softly, and I smile back, feeling a sense of pity for him, my heart moving away from the anger I once carried for him, to be replaced by compassion. We have all made choices in life that, for one reason or another, either work out, or they don't. Looking back, you may say, *if only I had made a better decision, or made a different choice.* But there's no point in playing the *What-If* game, as that game only produces regret, which cannot always be resolved.

Before I realize it, I reach across the table and place my hand on his, and smile, "Your life is what it is, now. You need only look at where you came from to learn and grow; don't wallow in regretful thoughts. It won't change anything, and only serves to keep you from making the most of what is in front of you now." He places his other hand on top of mine, and I immediately wish I hadn't touched him. I hear the voice in my head saying, *don't give him the wrong impression, let go, now.* I gently pull my hand out from between his and pick up my mug. I lean back slightly and take a breath.

The waiter comes over and ask if we'd like any more coffee, to which Julian nods, but I decline. He drops two separate bills on the table after refilling Julian's mug. I place a ten-dollar bill and the receipt beside my near-empty mug. I want to cut this short, leave on a good note, send him on to his future without him clinging to his past, with me. He takes another sip and then asks some benign questions about Claire, avoiding any inquiries about Owen. I answer his questions as obliquely as I can, wanting to keep my life as closed off to him as possible. He pulls out his phone and shows me a picture of his grandson, Grayson. I smile and coo over the picture. I make no attempt to pull out pictures of my grandchildren.

I feel like I'm dragging this out much too long, so I take one final sip of cold coffee, and say, "Well, this has been nice, but I've got to be going now. I appreciate reconnecting with you, as it helps me get a sense of closure to our relationship. I know that sounds a bit rough to say, but I think you know it's true, that we are better off leaving things in an amicable way now, rather than how it played out all those years ago." I stand and turn to collect my handbag and sweater. Julian stands as well, trying to reach over to pull my chair out, but I'm already stepping away from the table. He places a twenty-dollar bill on the table and walks out with me. I make my way through the café, and out to the street. I feel the need to take a deep breath, as if I had been holding my breath for the past thirty minutes. Julian stands beside me. "I understand your feelings, and respect them. I don't agree, as I think we could still see each other, as friends, for now. I would like to try that. Can I at least walk you to your car?" I sigh, as I realize my blunt statement had no effect on him. He cannot see that I am not interested in fostering any type of relationship with him, his only focus being his desire to acquire something he cannot have: me. I don't say anything more, but simply turn and begin to walk towards my car, as he falls into step beside me. We walk in silence. I look straight ahead, trying to keep my pace steady, but unhurried. We round the corner and I spy my car. I begin pulling out my keys, walking slightly faster. Reaching the car, I push the fob to unlock the car, and turn to say good-bye.

    Julian's face, with the sunlight streaming on it, shows his age - the hard lines of sadness shadowed against the tan lines, as he smiles. I am about to say goodbye, when he steps forward and hugs me. I keep my arms sticking out, avoiding a reciprocal hug. He pulls away only slightly, his face inches from mine. "I can't believe how happy I am to see you again, and that you agreed to meet me. Over the years I always wondered about you, and so now I know." He leans in and kisses me. The foreignness of his lips against mine startles me. For a split second, I am so astonished by his brazen act I am unable to respond. I find myself dropping my bag and keys to push him away. He smiles, taking a step back, as he wipes his mouth. I bend over, with one hand, to pick up what I dropped, and, standing up straight again, I raise my other hand

and slap his face. His expression is one of shock, and surprise. How could he ever think that what he just did is acceptable? The amber-eyed Dragon echoes in my mind; *'Your soul for tempting others find, but you need to leave them far behind. Seek only Light, you will not fail, when darkness calls to no avail'*. My inner Dragon roars loudly in my mind.

"Okay, we are done here. Take out your phone. Let me see you delete my number and messages. Now!" He sheepishly pulls his phone out of his pocket and scrolls in his contacts until he finds my name. I watch as he pushes the delete button and then finds the text thread and deletes that as well. Without another word, I climb into my car, and slam the door. He stands off to the side and watches as I pull away. The last image of him stains my eyes: the sad, hardened face of a man so unhappy with his life, he has to burn it down entirely.

I open the front door, finding Owen in the living room reading a newspaper. He glances up when I enter and smiles. I drop my bag and walk quickly over to him, pulling him up and kissing him eagerly. He takes a breath, briefly looking at me questioningly. I merely smile and exclaim, "Just so happy to see you! I missed you so much this afternoon!" Owen grins and replies, "Well, you should go out for the afternoon more often!" He leans in and kisses me again, wiping away the smudge of Julian's face from my mind completely.

NINE

The date is set for Owen's new book tour. His African memoir has been so successful that the publishers prompted him to write another book. He chose the history of environmental activism as his subject. It has been three years in the making, and now they want to send him on a three-week junket to promote the new book. As much as I'd enjoy that fast paced adventure, my heart is not into traveling right now. Claire has been having some challenges with the Centre, and the children are so heavily involved in school activities, I feel like she needs my support now, more than ever. Owen's disappointment is muted when he takes a moment to look at her situation, and agrees Claire is a priority. Having gone to school plays, recitals, baseball games and rugby matches, I know my role as *Grannah* is still nothing near as strenuous as being *Mom*. As much as David wants to be there, his job makes it almost impossible to attend after-school events, so Owen and I have filled in as the cheering section for our grandchildren, and loving every minute of it.

In the meantime, I have started a new workshop at the Centre, aptly named *Mindful Life*. With the help of Tila, who teaches Yoga and Tai Chi; Janice, who now offers Reiki and energy healing; and Arthur, who joins in once in a while to help the group find their inner Light, we offer many opportunities to explore a new perspective on being. My goal is to help those yearning to stretch themselves out, to connect with the Universe. Once the connection happens, these people are not the same. There is no going back, no closing the mind to the realization that they are so much more than they thought they were.

I sit quietly and watch as the group collectively inhales and exhales, releasing the tension and stress from their bodies. I gently suggest that they envision a blue sky, clear and bright. "Focus on the sky, and if stray thoughts pass by, disguised as clouds, gently blow them away with an exhale, and allow yourself to be mindful in the present. The clouds are the things that happen in life: the experiences, the emotions you carry, and the distractions that keep you from being present in the *Now*. Don't focus on the clouds, just gently push them aside, and gaze at the beautiful sky." Many of the women look like they are concentrating too hard, while others wear placid, calm expressions. The compassion I feel for each person as they begin this journey, fills my heart to overflowing. I know now that this is the path I was always meant to travel. It's been a long road to find the way, and it was meant to be that way, as maturity and experience help to balance my viewpoint.

The group ends the meeting with affirmations, and many of the women rise out of their chairs to embrace each other. The collective energy spills out of the room, and I wonder if anyone nearby can feel it's warmth. Arthur, who sits in a chair off to the side, has his eyes closed. He often falls asleep, so I quietly approach and lean over to touch his arm. He opens his eyes and smiles. "Hannah, my dear. What a wonderful day. We certainly have great energy with this group. It really charged my battery!" He laughs. Two of the participants come over, and take up seats on either side of him, anxious to sit near the man who radiates such joy, love and light. Now, as he approaches ninety-two, he still carries himself as a young man, although his form is aged and bent. I don't try to picture my life without him, as it just doesn't seem right. He will pass into the Light, and I know I will still be able to interact with his Alternate self, but there is nothing like the *human* Arthur.

I help Janice and Tila with a tray of cups for coffee and tea, while some of the other women set out snacks. It's hungry work to mindfully travel, so I like to offer replenishment afterward. I take a cup of coffee over to Arthur, and he reaches out with a gnarled hand to accept the cup. The women, who seemed to have completed their discussion with him, move off to get their own refreshments. Sitting down next him, I feel Arthur mentally reach out, seeking through the group for Alternates, and Talents. "We do have a few here, although they don't know it. We will not be disrupting their journey, as they are not meant to be *awake*, if the Universe has not deemed it thus." He turns and focuses his eyes on me. "Now, tell me, how are the grandkids doing? I still find it difficult to think of you as *Grannah*. You are still that doe-eyed girl I met all those years ago, afraid of herself, afraid of how to proceed in life. Look at you now!". He touches my arm, and I can see a tear in his eye. "Oh Arthur, you're such a softy. It has been a long road, hasn't it? Yes, the grandkids are amazing! Noah is so compassionate, and smart. And Alice, well, she is just like her mother, full of purpose and drive. For one so young, she certainly seems to know where she wants to go. I'm not sad she has no Alternate in her, nor Noah. It is as it is. I think this fact also helps Owen feel less *left out* of the whole thing." I wave my hand around, trying to indicate the Universe. Arthur chuckles, "My girl, Owen was always going to have something to feel *less-than-worthy* about. Unfortunately, it is a byproduct of his upbringing. He has finally come into his own now, but it has little to do with learning that his grandchildren are not Alternates. It has to do with his own Light being lit, and staying lit, by his actions and experiences, with you, and with the world, as a whole. He now sees his value, as he writes his books, cares for Noah and Alice, and so on. Sometimes, as you know, it can take a lifetime before you see things the way you are meant to. Luckily, Owen still has plenty of time left to enjoy his Light, and life, with you and everyone he loves." He takes a sip of his coffee, "Oh, my goodness that's enough of that talk. I want to know when we can go visit Fae again *together*? It's always more fun when we travel together!" I smile, looking at his wrinkly old eyes, and still see the child peeking out from under his lashes. "Soon. I think we are long overdue, my friend!"

Grace's hands guide Arthur up the front steps and into the house. Ever the pilot of their adventures, she makes certain his mobility does not hinder him from getting the most out of his day. Arthur accepts the aid, without fuss or bluster. He knows he's old, and accepts that his body does not work as it once did. The love between Grace and Arthur buoys them up, and carries them through, and it warms my heart to know they have each other.

I usher them both into the kitchen, where, after choosing the tea they like to sample, I direct them to the garden. Grace, it turns out, has known about Arthur being an Alternate almost from the time they met. I never asked if she knew, thinking that the subject is between the two of them, and none of my business. Curiosity did rear its ugly head however, and I found myself asking Arthur once, years ago, about it. His nonchalant answer made me laugh. "Of course she knows! She's no dummy! She recognized the energy right away. She and I have had some amazing travels together, without even leaving our bedroom!" Arthur's double entendre made me cringe, but he just giggled.

As I walk over to the garden loungers set out under the tree, I see OnanOff lying on one of the cushions. In his usual curled up position, part of me feels badly for having to disturb him. He does, however, like Arthur quite a bit, so there may be consolation in a more comfortable curl-up on his lap for a while. Arthur and Grace follow behind, taking the grass slowly.

I lean over and place my hand gently on the old cat's back, to wake him. His form is cold. I place my hand on his head, but the energy has dissipated, into the ether and beyond. I sink down, and feel a small sob in my throat. Poor old fellow, alone as he departed this plane. I had repeatedly asked him if he wanted help moving on, and he had insisted he would say when the time was upon him. Poor OnanOff. Time does not always make itself known, until it is well upon you. I feel the tears streak my face, as Grace places her hands on my shoulders, radiating healing love to me. The ache, and I knew this would be inevitable, wells up from my gut into my heart. I can see Arthur take a seat across from me, his eyes also wet from tears. A moment passes, then two. I am stuck in position, helpless to move in my grief. Then I see Claire in my mind's eye. Her misery will be equal, if not more, for OnanOff was truly *her* cat. He lived with Owen and me, but his heart belonged to his savior, his best pal, his confidante, Claire. A new sorrow fills my throat, as another quiet sob erupts. Grace continues to rub and pat me on the shoulders, at a loss as to what else to do.

Finally, I feel my body respond to itself once again, and I rise up. Reaching over to the other chair, I pull a small blanket off the back and place it over and around his body. I can't think of what to do next, so I just lift the wrapped body, and place it on my lap, as I sit in his now empty seat. Grace takes a seat next to Arthur. He is blowing his nose and wiping his eyes. We know this is but one step for the wee cat, one of many on his journey, but our human aspects still grieve the loss of his Light on this plane, his energy shared with us daily, his time in *this* form at an end. Arthur coughs, trying to clear his throat, and I realize I have left our steeping tea in the kitchen. As I attempt to rise to retrieve the drinks, Grace, who, I swear is a mind reader, stands and heads up the steps to the back door, only to reappear moments later with a large tray of filled tea mugs. I nod, a sad, appreciative expression crossing on my face.

Arthur takes his cup and has a long satisfying sip. He inhales and exhales, fully expelling his sadness to the Universe for it to take on. He looks at me and says softly, "I feel the need to visit Fae. I believe we may find comfort there." As reluctant as I am to sit with a dead cat on my lap for too long, I agree to his request.

A few minutes later, Arthur, Grace and I stand in the glade, looking over at Fae and Orna, as they play in the pond, sending sparkles of splashing water into the air, where the droplets turn into the tiniest of Fae folk, almost like Damselflies, with wings like slivers of crystal-blue glass, and bodies like lithe dancers, long, slender and bending with movement. Fae turns to see us approach, and smiles. It is only when she nears us that she senses our unhappiness, and frowns. Her hands come up in a circular motion, causing waves of heat to emit and pulsate out towards us, coating us in what feels like the warm embrace of someone who loves you deeply. I cry out from the touch, and feel my melancholy shift within me. It will not take hold of me, it will simply sit there, while I come to realize OnanOff's energy has not been removed from my existence, merely moved along the web, to reside anew. Just like my father, my mother, Hannah One and Jamie.

As we stand there in the glow of Fae's healing Light, I see a flash of tortoiseshell fur, and the blinking amber eyes of a cat, staring at me from under a nearby fern. The cat's head appears, and he smiles. It is funny to see a cat smile, all toothy, with fangs protruding in the front, like a tiny vampire. He steps forward, as everyone turns to look at him. He sits back and licks a paw, in no hurry to present himself.

I kneel down and reach out my hand, but there is nothing there; it is but a wisp of smoke, a vision of Light and Air. The cat stops licking his paw and looks at each one of us, before speaking; "I am never here nor there, but everywhere. I am *in* the Light, but I *am* the Light. I am OnanOff, but I am a creature of Light now." He turns and grabs his tail, trying to lick it from one end to the other. I sit down on the ground and whisper softly, "I am sorry you left us, without guiding hands to help you travel forward. I was dismayed to find you alone, and left to your own devices. Now, I am alone and left to mine, as I hold your form close to me in my sorrow." I feel the tears spring to my eyes, picturing my still body cradling his lifeless form. He drops his tail and rises, doing a small stretch before moving closer, blinking his gemstone eyes at me, "Feed my body to the Earth, so I can scamper free in woodland realms yet unexplored; where I can find my kin and journey onward. Let my body feed the Earth, so new Life can grow where once there was only Death." He stands up and walks back towards the fern, slowly fading, like Light at dusk. He turns just before fading completely, and whispers, "Claire. Let her know she is with me, always."

Owen's face crumples as I tell him about OnanOff's passing. His book tour has wrapped up, and he has just arrived home and free to relax, until he finds a new project to occupy his time. He takes my hand in his and softly says, "He was such a great cat. I'm sorry I didn't get to say good bye to him. It seems like only yesterday Claire was standing in the garden, holding this little ball of fur in her hands. It seems like yesterday, and yet it also feels like a lifetime ago. Where is the time going?" I look at his hand holding mine, seeing the wear of age on his skin, the rough knuckles from working the soil in the garden, yet the tender way in which his fingers wrap around mine. I look into his bright blue eyes and see a tinge of regret there, possibly for the time that has escaped us, or for things left undone, that may never get completed. I smile and whisper, "Time has moved along as it should. We just need constant reminders to be mindful of it, and not squander it on things we can't control or change." Owen quietly chuckles, "Han, are you quoting me a line from your new workshop? It sure sounds like it!" We both chuckle, breaking through the shell of sadness we built while talking about OnanOff, and the prospect of growing older.

I sit staring at the computer screen. It is time to write my story. Claire has been hounding me for a long time now to write down my experiences. My intention is to give the story weight and meaning, as I draw the picture of my life in words. As I fill each page, I will avoid the tendency to dissect and reflect. It's important I record the experiences from the perspective that I carried then, not the way I see it now. To view the past with maturity and the *forget-the-bad-stuff-filter*, will distill the moment I am writing about. As much I desire to write that I was a very understanding youth, and gave the benefit of the doubt to my parents as often as I could, I know that my authentic experience was not that. I was difficult, opinionated and stubborn. I could not see the value in some of the interactions or events that seemed irrelevant to me, even as a young child. To record my *authentic* behaviour as I was growing gives truth to the story. Whoever reads it will then understand that, yes, I am an Alternate, with wonderful knowledge about *dimensional* life, but when residing in the body of a human, with complex systems that manipulate thoughts, emotions, and physiological reactions, all the Alternate knowledge in the Universe can't always win out over that.

I could write that I have been this all-benevolent being, blessing all who came within my sphere, and living a life full of peace and joy. But that is not the human experience, regardless of internal energies residing within. As humans, you need to experience the highs and lows, the good and the bad, to balance the journey. The whole of the experience is to find the balance, yet we may never find it exactly as we imagine it to be. Humans get to ride this roller coaster of Life, with its peaks and valleys; the screams, the nauseating sway as we round corners, the dropping of our gut as we descend, and the thrill of air rushing at us as we speed along. Every relationship, every experience is part of that ride, and be it good, bad or indifferent, it is what gets us to the point in which we recognize it *all* for what it is: The Human Experience.

Knowing now what I know, feeling all that I feel, seeing all that I see, understanding all that I understand, this is my *Now* story. It has taken over seventy years to reach this point, where I recognize that my inherent human nature has bonded with my Alternate to create a much better life experience for me. No more do I differentiate between my Alternate or my human reaction to the world. They are One; United.

As I imagine the pages filling with these stories, I find myself full of gratitude, amazement, and even slight regret for things not said, or experiences missed. And yet, there is a reason for these events or words to have been missed. I won't look back and second-guess myself. What has passed, has passed for a reason.

I sit at my desk and ponder how to begin my story as the sound of guitar chords resonates quietly up the stairs to my art room. Owen always wanted to learn to play the guitar, and said that when he's retired, and looking for a new challenge, he's going to take lessons. He strums and picks the strings, sounding melodious.

I pick up my phone and text Arthur. *'Having trouble writing can you help me to my door?'* A few minutes later my phone chimes, and I read his response. *'Hi Grace here. Arthur says get ready, he's tuning the world out as we speak… or something like that! Have fun!'* I close my eyes, and sink down to find my source, my grounding that helps me rise above. I don't hear the guitar anymore, I don't hear the slight whirr of the computer, I don't feel the warm summer breeze as it wafts in the window, tempting me to abandon my work and come play in the garden. I hear my heartbeat, I see the colours of my energy erupt and flutter, once again set free, and I feel myself being drawn to Arthur's Light. I open my eyes to find him standing in the long white hallway. Behind him is my door. It has several rows of images, hundreds, maybe thousands, all glowing with energy that I grew during the time the picture was created. Some images glow bright yellow, or blue, even neon pink, which I believe may be the more personal moments between Owen and me. Some pictures have a darker glow, almost muddy in tone. Glowing, but its frequency indicates a moment of trauma, or some other emotion that I found hard to carry.

Arthur smiles, a big Cheshire Cat grin. "I love meeting up like this!" He takes my hand in his and squeezes it. His image is of his current self, old, frail and worn. But the Light that shines throughout his form makes him look ageless, healthy, sound. I turn my attention to my door. I look at the first image. It's a view of my mother, from the vantage point of a newborn infant. I sink into that memory, recalling the sights, scents, and sounds, as I was being born, being held by the doctor, the nurses, and then my mother. Her expression, much clearer to me now, is of immense joy. Her tears fall freely as she gazes lovingly at me. Worn out, haggard and done-in from childbirth, I have never seen her so beautiful. I feel a lump in my throat, but Arthur places a hand on my back and moves the emotion from one of longing to see her again, to gratitude for having known her.

I glance along the row, and see images of my father, Fred the beagle, and Hannah One. Her face is young, vibrant and full of love. I see the pictures of the two of us, spending Saturdays together, exploring the world, whether it was at an art gallery or out in the woods. Again, my heart aches for these times past, but I quickly seize the feeling of gratitude for having had these experiences. I realize that this journey has been filled with moments and relationships that I can express gratitude for. My mind fills with memories, and all the emotions and reactions I felt when going through each experience, as if they happened yesterday. I close my eyes, silently allocating the door's images in my mind, so I can retrieve the pictures as I write. I feel Arthur pick up my hand again, and this time he raises it to his lips and kisses it. "You are remarkable, and full of resilience, strength, Light and Love, for all those around you. I am so much better for having known you. Thank you, Hannah." As I close my eyes, I feel him let go of my hand, and, after a moment, I find myself back at my desk. I place my fingers on the keyboard and begin to type:

I am born...

TEN

They say that Time is a friend to no one, but I disagree. If you make the most of it, Time can bend and shape itself to fit in all the experiences you are meant to have on your journey. It's when we sit and ponder the *what ifs* or the *I wish I had*, that we try Time's patience with us, and then we lose out. It's only natural to ponder a different course that might have taken us on another life journey, but to expend too much thought on that train, you will bypass many stations you are meant to see and experience. As I write, I look back and see the path laid out before my younger version, and how I walked along, sometimes with good intention, and at other times lost in human frailty or distress. But Time allotted me the days to work through each experience, seeming to know I would not look back with regret or disappointment for the choices I made. Time is my friend. It gives me a new day each day, to make of it what I can, or not, as is my choice. It's only when you don't pay attention that Time sneaks up behind you and yells in your ear. You spin around and see that your life has passed by. People are older, some are gone, children are grown and making lives of their own, and places you once thought of fondly disappear from the landscape, as if erased by Time itself.

 As I age now into my seventh decade on Earth, I realize the importance of keeping Time as my friend. Being present and mindful of it, as it walks along beside me. It has no ill will; it has no will at all. It has no intent, other than to keep moving, and one must keep pace with it, or be left behind. Age has been my friend, bringing new wisdom, and an outlook that can only be achieved through life experiences. Occasionally a young person can possess *an old soul* as part of their energy. They appear to be wise beyond their years, mature and grounded in their life's journey. I see Claire like this; an *old* young person. She had a few moments as a teenager when she rebelled, but overall, she has become a sentient wise woman.

Now, with Alice and Noah well into high school, she has blossomed even more. I glance at the photo in the frame that sits on my desk. It's a family portrait: David, Owen, the children, Claire and myself, smiling. The smiles are genuine and the love revolving around the group is evident. I pick up the photo and run my finger over Claire's face, stroking it. I whisper, "I love you so much, Claire bear." I place the photo back on the desk and look at the computer screen again. I have completed my memoir, and what I have chronicled makes me happy.

I close my eyes and feel the desire to visit Fae. I sink down and find my Light, and gather it around me. I go in search of Fox, my very first guide to the door of the Fae realm. I let go of expectations and ego. I simply sit and wait for Fox to arrive. Soon enough, I see his form appear in front of me, bright red fur and black nose, wet and investigating. He says nothing, but nods and turns to his right and trots off in that direction. I follow him, and with every step I take I see the path materializing at my feet. I glance from side to side and see colourful flowers blooming from the mossy earth. A ray of sunshine beams down, illuminating the trail, sending warm fingers across the flower's faces, making them smile. I know the way now, as Fox retreats into a wooded dell off to the left. I tread carefully, minding the mossy patches under my bare feet. I see the glade where most often I find Fae, and head there. As I round the corner and pass the Birch trees, I see Fae under the Willow tree. A tall figure stands over her, and it takes me a moment to realize it is Orna. It surprises me to see her transformation, as last I saw her, she was but a sprite, a child. Now she stands with the grace of a beautiful tree, with olive-green skin, flowing hair that resembles a cascade of emeralds, and long arms that wave like sheafs of wheat, a dance unto themselves. Orna is telling an animated story, and Fae sits, enraptured by the tale. I approach quietly, not wanting to interrupt.

Orna turns her head and spies me off to the side, and waves her hand for me to join them. I sit down beside Fae, taking her hand, feeling her skin, leaf-like, cool and soft. Once the story has reached its conclusion, Fae drops my hand to clap and cheer at Orna, who laughs and twirls, sending sparks of energy around the glade, igniting the nearby grass like tiny sparklers. Nothing burns. The Light merely twinkles, and gets absorbed by each blade of grass. Fae turns and looks at my face. "Hannah, you wear the human mask of age now. It must feel familiar, and yet foreign, when you look at yourself." I nod in agreement. I don't know how many times I've looked in the mirror and found myself surprised at the image. Through my eyes, sometimes it feels like I am still young, maybe only thirty, not seventy-three.

I look at Orna, who has walked over to the edge of the pond to talk with a nearby butterfly. "Orna has changed. She has grown up. How is it she has grown, but you still remain the same as when I first met you, when Claire was so very young?" Fae's eyes stray towards Orna, and she smiles. "Here, we can be whatever we wish. We can evolve, we can become Light, we can remain but a sparkle on the water's surface. You know we are all simply *Light*, and can express our energy in a form that suits us, or one that may help others to relate to us. You know I can dissipate and be nothing but a glow, an energy ball that moves from space to space. You are the same, outside of your human shape. Orna wishes to experience her energy in a variety of forms; she is a wild energy, one created from the joining of Super Nova and Fae Light. I enjoy her transformations, as it reminds me of a butterfly; moving through the caterpillar to emerge, after a time, to have wings and colours beyond sight."

When I look at Orna, I sense a common thread between her journey and mine. I began as a caterpillar, carefully inching along my Life line, only barely stretching out to see what was in front of me. Then, I found myself cocooning from life, existing but not living, hibernating, until my energy could realign with each new experience. Now I feel the butterfly wings sprout from my back, and the colours grow richer and deeper as I age. I take a breath, and feel I have found another answer to my many questions about the human experience. I turn to Fae and say, "It's funny how sometimes humans take so long to find the answers to Life's lessons. And yet I think there is a process to it, one that each of them must go through, to reach a point of understanding. It's like reading the ending of a book first. You see the answers, but you really don't even know what the questions are, until you've read the book from the start. I am seeing the final pages of my own book now, and I'm finding the answers, and they make sense to me, whereas before, they did not fit my Life, at that time. It brings me joy, and peace. I'm not afraid of what lies ahead. I can face it." Fae smiles, taking my hand and pulling me up. As she turns, a doorway materializes. It is a simple wooden door, with a brass doorknob. Fae looks at my puzzled expression and explains, "This door appears because you are ready for it to appear. It is but another gateway to find the answers you have yet to find, to add more pieces to complete your puzzle, called Life. If you are willing, I can lead you through this door, and we can see what awaits." I look from her face to the door. It has no markings, no indication of what lies beyond. I'm not afraid. I know that whatever I step into, it is but one more part of my journey. I know that Fae would not lead me astray, so I take her hand and together we walk towards it.

The door swings open and we step through it. The light is muted, but not dark. As we take a few steps inward, the light increases, reminding me of dawn's light, as it gently peels back the night, revealing a new day. Fae stands beside me, holding my hand. Slowly I begin to see figures appear out of the mist, indistinct yet visible. Fae quietly utters, "You know that humans have guides. As a human yourself, regardless of being an Alternate, you have guides too. This is where your guides reside, in your energy. There may be five, ten, or one hundred guides that come and go throughout your human existence. Humans are quick to call the messages from the guides *'a gut feeling,'* or their *'intuition'* or *'the voice inside their head,'* rather than acknowledging that it is, in fact, a message from a spirit guide. You yourself struggled throughout to hear the messages, until you began to tear down the wall you erected to block out your Alternate. As the two parts of your mind began to unite, you opened a channel for the messages to come through and be absorbed into your Light. You have gotten so many messages through animals, am I right?" I nod but say nothing, glancing around, as more forms appear out of the mist. "Well, guidance may appear in forms we are most comfortable with, or ready to accept. You have a strong connection to Nature, and so your guides began to connect to you through the use of images, like Hawk, or Raven."

A body steps forward, a stranger to me, yet his energy seems familiar. "I am Davian. I am your guide to Self. I aid in finding your voice, seeing your worth, learning to value your uniqueness. I come here with love and joy to touch your Light, and help you to grow, as you continue on." He steps close and hugs me. Normally I might repel a stranger trying to touch me, but this feels familiar, and very intimate. I feel his energy infuse me, and it makes me cry with a fullness of spirit. The intimacy is acceptable, as it is Self-Love that permeates my Light. He finally releases me and steps back, fading into the background. I glow with a sense of my own Self.

A woman approaches, and I gasp. It is Hannah One. I open my arms and we fall together. Our Light merges to become one, and our love is so overpowering, it almost makes me explode. She speaks without opening her mouth. "Hannah, I am in the Light, but I am *Here* for you. I am your feet, when you cannot find the way; your hands, when things are hard to hold; and your heart, when you feel your own begin to break. You are strong and wise now, as an old woman, but it doesn't mean you don't need your guides. Remember we are *Here*, supporting and co-piloting, so you don't have to do it alone." She steps back, while I try desperately to hold on to her. She smiles and sends a wave of compassion and love through her arms and into mine, helping me let go. I smile back, knowing she is with me, inside my energy, and beside me, as I traverse the last years of my journey.

Several other forms come forward, a chorus of compassion, and I feel a surge of love and kindness envelop me. Fae laughs and says, "So much love! So many guides who want to relate to you. We all think you are so deserving of every molecule of Light we can share." I laugh and cry at the same time, feeling overwhelmed by the number of beings that surround me. I look up and see Raven, Hawk, Dragon and other Spirit Animals I have encountered. All residing in the ether, but emitting their own form of benevolence towards me.

One last figure appears, and the others part as he steps forward. It is my father. His face is the one I remember, full of humour, and kindness. He walks up and hugs me. The power of his touch spans the eons of time we have been apart, and yet it feels like we just saw each other yesterday. He touches my hair and smiles. "You are the same child I cherished all my years on Earth. I reside in your Light, and help when I can. As much as I would like to say I've helped guide you, I think I am merely along for the ride. I want to see you succeed and grow; and you have never failed, even when things were at their worst. My love for you cannot be contained in my energy; it bursts out of me like a rocket." And he laughs, hugging me closer. I swallow and, finding my voice, reply; "Dad, I think I've always felt you are there, beside me. I guess I just always wanted you to move on, and find your way, and let go of me. But I am glad to feel you in my Light, being my best cheerleader." He laughs, takes a step back and whispers, "I am a part of you, as you are in your child and grandchildren. I will move on when I do. But in the meantime, I am content to stay close to your Light." He raises his hand and blows me a kiss as he fades into the background.

Fae reaches out and takes my hand. "You know this door is always open to you. You have opened yourself to the Light enough now that these things are more accessible to you. You need only open your heart to the sky, and it will rain down love and understanding." I see the light begin to dim, the figures still visible, but their forms are softened, subtler. I glance around, trying to memorize the door so I can find it again, as it sits in my energy. Fae notices and whispers, "Remember it's always there," and she points to my heart, "and now you have the key to open the door."

I enter the front door of the Centre and see Tila sitting in the lounge with a woman I don't recognize. It's not surprising that I don't know the woman, as the Centre has expanded and become a hub of the healing community since Tila became a partner in the business. Her connections to healing practitioners has led to an entirely new phase of the Centre opening up, with more services available to anyone who seeks holistic care and insight. She looks up as I enter, and smiles, giving me a small wave. I wave back as I make my way to the office. Claire is away on a holiday with David and the children, so I have offered to come in and manage things in her absence. Tila is wonderful at facilitating groups and workshops, but is highly unorganized. Claire's strength is her ability to keep all the day-to-day logistics organized. She and Tila make a good team. At this point however, with a new project on her horizon, and as Noah and Alice start to become more independent themselves, Claire feels the need for one more family trip together. Next month she will begin a new chapter in her life, wearing the hat of producer of a new children's animated series based on her *Fanny and Fae - Nature Detectives* series of books. She was approached by a Toronto-based company, who want to turn the beloved books into an animated television series. Claire is over-the-moon excited.

For now, I sit at her small desk in the office, and look at the stack of papers in front of me. Calls and emails need to be made to confirm attendance at a variety of upcoming events; bills have to paid; appointments with our various practitioners of holistic care need to be confirmed.

I hear the door open behind me as Tila enters the office. She sits down in the chair across the room and heaves a heavy sigh. "Oh, Hannah, I'm exhausted! It's been such a whirlwind lately! That was my final interview for a Naturopath. I've been trying to find someone whose energy fits our environment. I think I have the right person now, so I'll be reaching out to her this afternoon. I'll be glad to have that sorted out." We sit in silence for a moment, while I stare at the papers on the desk. Tila takes a large inhale and expresses it out slowly. "There, that's better. Now," and she looks at me, "how the hell are you? We haven't talked in a few weeks, so how are you doing?" I smile and turn my chair so I don't face the tasks that are bellowing at me from the desktop. "Oh, yes. It's all good, just been so wrapped up in finishing my memoir. It's now complete, but needs editing before I share it. It's been such a labour of love. Why is it that we deep-dive into these projects, but then forget to come up for air because we get so immersed in them?" Tila laughs. "Yes, you're right. I feel like I haven't come up for air since joining the team here. You and I are the type of people that, when we devote ourselves to something we believe in, we place our entire selves into it. Some people are able to piecemeal themselves out to tasks or causes, keeping enough for themselves at the end of the day. But we aren't built like that. It's exhausting to be *this* way, but my, it's so rewarding. I wouldn't want to have it any other way." She leans her head back and closes her eyes briefly.

I take a breath, and contemplate her words. "I think you're right. And I agree that putting your heart and soul into something you believe in is rewarding. I just think we need to find the balance between devoting ourselves to these ventures, and paying attention to cues that we need to maintain other aspects of life, like self-care. Otherwise, we will both burn out, and be of no use to anyone." Tila nods her head. "Yes, I agree. You'd think we'd know better at our age!" She stands up and heads to the door. "Making tea. Want a cup?" I shake my head, as I turn my chair back to the desk, "Best not, too many papers here. I might spill, knowing me!" Tila chuckles as she closes the door.

I turn my eyes to the papers and begin sorting through them. As I sit and try to figure out what the priorities are, I feel an odd sensation in my core. It starts out as a slight feeling of nausea in my gut. Then it rolls over itself to become a ball of what feels like energy that is slowly being released into the Universe, like air escaping a balloon. It isn't something I've felt before. I close my eyes and allow myself to sink down, to touch base with my body, and investigate the cause of the upset.

I open my eyes to see a giant web. It's the same web I saw many years ago with Arthur. The lines sparkle with vibrations of energy, making them gleam like spun silver. The lines are pulsating, causing me to quiver. I feel a commotion coming from below, as a giant orb of Light ascends, passing through the lines of the web without causing any to break. The light is bright, streaking blue, indigo, green and yellow. There is something familiar about the Light. Then I feel my heart stop. I recognize the Light. It is Arthur.

His voice peels inside my mind, like a chorus of birds singing. "Hannah, I am one with All, once again. We know our time as humans is fleeting, but this seems to have passed in a heartbeat. I am sad to leave Grace, and you and Claire, but we both know this is but a step forward. My old body was worn out, and deserves its peaceful slumber in the ethos now. Please help Grace find her way again. We have been each other's rock through the storms of life. She will need replanting in the soil to regain her roots, and carry on. I will miss my human adventure; it was truly enlightening. Hannah, enjoy every moment. As I said, it passes by too quickly." I reach out my hand and touch the orb. Cascades of yellow and blue run down my arm and dance around my body in wispy beams of light. I feel Arthur's energy touch mine one final time, before the orb ascends higher and higher, until it is but a gleaming star in the daytime sky.

I open my eyes, hearing my cell phone ring. It's Grace.

Grace holds the urn with Arthur's ashes in it. Claire stands beside her, radiating waves of healing energy to her. I know Fae is there, adding her love to the stream. Owen and I hold hands as we watch Grace open the urn and kneel down to place the ashes in our garden. He said it was one of his favourite places in the world, where he found joy, laughter, love, and companionship. The tiny wood nymphs sit on the tree branches and watch curiously. After lowering the ashes into the hole that Owen had prepared, she places a tiny Lilac bush into the hole and gently pushes the soil around the main stalk to get it securely planted. She takes the watering can I had left beside it and waters it, circling the base to make sure it gets evenly moistened. I hear her gently utter, "I plant you in the Earth to set you free, and water you, so you will flow into the Light to be carried forward. My love, My Arthur…" her voice breaks and she bows her head, muffling a quiet sob. Owen bends down and helps her to stand, keeping his arm wrapped around her shoulders, as we all come to stand next to her and place our arms around her. I wish I could take away her sorrow, but it is her journey, and this is part of it. I can honour Arthur's request though, and help her gain her footing again, so she can move forward, without discounting her need to grieve, and carry her sorrow as long as she needs to.

In my peripheral vision I catch a glimpse of a tall figure, standing off to the side, grinning mischievously while holding a cat in his arms. I turn to look, but no one is there.

Eleven

The Song Sparrow flits by over my head, expending a micro-joule of energy with each flap of her tiny, delicate wings. She lands on a branch of the tree near the front door of Claire's house, a singular welcoming committee, singing her beautiful tune. I send my thanks for such a welcome as I pass by and enter the house.

David sits at the kitchen table holding a cup of tea. He has grown a beard over the summer, and the look takes some getting used to. It's thick and a darker shade of brown than his reddish-brown mop of hair that sits on his head. He smiles and stands up, crossing the kitchen to give me a hug, as I place two bags of groceries on the counter. "Thanks so much, Hannah. You really didn't have to bother, but I appreciate it. It saves me the extra trip to *that* store." David is referring to a natural health-food store I shop at frequently, as they carry a wide array of organic products not found at the grocery store. I take the items out of the cloth bags, and David begins putting them into cupboards and the refrigerator. I walk over and place my hand on his shoulder. "I'm happy to help, any way I can. Are you enjoying the beard-growing experience? It must be freeing when you don't need to shave all the time." David chuckles as he replies, "Yes, it's a time-saver, although being home for the summer this year, I do have time to spare. I just felt like a change. Claire hasn't decided if she likes it or not. But Fae hates it!" He smiles, as he leans down to place some produce in the crisper drawer. I stop short at the mention of Fae. I'm not sure how to proceed with the conversation, not being aware that David knew about Fae. He glances at me and, noticing the look on my face, he continues, "Yes, I know about Fae. I have for a long time now. I think it was a tough thing for Claire to hide, and I did feel really privileged to be let into this aspect of her life. Fae has a great calming influence on Claire at times when she gets frustrated, like with the kids." I nod in agreement, and lean back against the counter, saying, "Fae has always been Claire's anchor. The two of them are really one, yet singular in their own personalities as well. I can't imagine Claire without Fae, although I think she would still be an amazing woman, regardless. Fae brings an added element to her life that has provided balance and support throughout. I think we are *all* lucky to have Fae around." David nods his head in agreement.

Heavy footfalls on the stairs indicates that Noah is about the house. His tall frame enters the kitchen, and seeing me, he crosses the kitchen in three strides to give me a short hug. No more the small boy always wanting to hold his Grandad's hand, Noah now stands as tall as his father, his own crop of wavy auburn hair looking like it hasn't been brushed in a week. He smiles as he reaches past me to grab an apple out of the basket on the counter. "Hi Grannah. Can't really talk now. I'm in the middle of a game!" He pulls open the refrigerator door and quickly pours a large glass of juice before retreating back upstairs to his room. Part of me mourns the days of the small child eager to sit with me and read books, or explore the garden, or build bird houses with Owen. I know, however, that this is part of the process, and you can hold on to memories; just don't try to use them to block Time as it pushes forward.

David shakes his head, and utters, "Sorry, Hannah. That was a bit rude of him. I wish we'd never agreed to let him buy that device. It's a challenge to get him off it, and interacting with the real world. Claire and I are going to set up some new boundaries for him, limiting his time on it, so he doesn't lose touch with life."

He turns and sits down at the kitchen table again, taking up his cup and draining the remainder of his tea in three gulps. I sit down opposite him, noticing the newspapers spread out across the table. David begins gathering up the stray papers, trying to make a clear spot for me at the table. "Don't worry David. I live with a teacher. I am used to papers being everywhere!" He chuckles, dropping the papers back down.

The front door opens and in walks a tall, auburn-haired, hazel-eyed girl, carrying some shopping bags. Alice, seeing me at the table, drops her bags and rushes over to hug me. Claire steps through the door, her own bags weighing her down. David steps in to take the bags and place them on the counter. She smiles as she sees me sit down at the table again, wanting to keep out of the kitchen chaos. "I didn't know you were coming over. I'm glad we decided to come home when we did. We almost stopped by the Garden Café for some cappuccinos, but for some reason I wanted to head straight home. Must have felt your presence here, even though I didn't know it!" She laughs. I watch as she takes items out of her bags, some for the kitchen, other sundries for the bathroom. Alice brings her bag over to me to show off her new sandals. "They were on sale, since it's already summer. I really love them!" She bends over and peels off her runners and socks, letting them drop to the floor, and slips on the sandals. Her feet, with slender toes and long delicate arches, reminds me of a dancer's feet, graceful and full of artful movement. She turns her ankles this way and that, trying to see how the sandals look. I smile and nod in agreement that they are just perfect for her. Her phone chimes in her pocket and she reaches in to pull it out. She turns and walks into the living room to answer the text from a friend.

I see myself in Alice. Her long hair, tied in a pony tail, her love for creative arts, and limited interest in things more academic in nature, all remind me of a younger version of myself. She wants to be an actor, and has found her joy in school plays, and an after-school drama club that encourages the students to look beyond the school walls to find additional creative outlets for the theatre arts. Claire heaves a sigh and comes to the table, pulling out a chair on the far side, plunking down as if she's made of lead. "Holy crap, I'm tired. It feels like I've been on a hamster wheel spinning around and not getting anywhere. Did I tell you the office called, and there's another hiccup in the production? I'm letting the guys handle it. They know better than me how to handle the situation. Anyway, how are you doing?" She pauses long enough to look at my face and provide me with a weary smile. I feel for her, and yet I know, as tired as she is, she wouldn't have it any other way. Her life is a flurry of creative impulses mixed with the vibration of her children, her partner and her career. I smile. "Oh, that sounds frustrating. I'm glad you have the team behind you to sort it out. I'm fine, the usual, you know. Oh! One thing; I've finished the memoir." Claire's eyes widen and she grins. "Oh my god, Mom! That's great! When can I read it?" I laugh, holding up my hands. "Wait, wait, wait. I said I finished it, but I still need to do a lot of editing. That will be a job in itself. But, maybe soon I can parcel out a bit, so you can read some." Claire stands up and comes over to hug me. "I am so happy you wrote it down. Now, I feel like I have a piece of you that I can always turn to, even when, well… whatever. It's exciting and I can't wait to read it!" She looks away, but not before I see a small tear in her eye. She sees me age; she knows the way of Life. She cannot face it, yet, but someday she will have to, so I'm glad that my written words may bring her some comfort.

She turns, walks over to the counter and plugs in the kettle. "David, did you make Mom a cup of tea?" David frowns. "Sorry, I guess I forgot to ask. Sorry, Hannah." He reaches across the table and places his large, kind-looking hand on my arm, giving it a pat. "David, it's no worry. I'm actually not staying long. I'm just happy to sit for a few minutes, and enjoy spending time with my family." Claire smiles as she busies herself in the kitchen.

The front door is open and music quietly wafts out. I hear Supertramp's, *"Even in the quietest moments",* as I walk up the steps. Owen, ever the die-hard classic rock fan, loves to listen to groups like Styx, Pink Floyd, and others. It no longer surprises me to hear what he chooses to play while doing a project, or cooking. The tune, *Lover boy* plays as I place my purse on the side table by the front door. Owen, in the kitchen peeling potatoes, moves his body to the easy beat, unaware I have come into the room. His body moves rhythmically, and his head nods back and forth, as he sings. I see the movement of his shoulder muscles as he moves, still strong and firm, despite his age. His hips move and I find myself wanting to take hold of those hips and move along with them. My stomach flutters, realizing that, even after all these years of marriage, the sight of him dancing, *as if no one is watching,* still turns me on. I step over to the counter and stand behind him, placing my arms around his waist. He startles, but glancing over his shoulder, he sees it's me, holding on and moving my own body to the rhythm of the music. He drops the potato and peeler into the sink and twists around to grab me, his hands wet from the water.

The piano chords resound, and I hear the song, *Downstream,* begin. It's one of my favourites. I wrap my arms around Owen's neck and begin to slowly dance, laying my head on his chest. The lyrics flow into me, and I feel filled up by the words:

You are the reason I was born… be with you through all seasons, I'll always hear you when you call…. We'll keep the lovelight shining, through each night and day, a lonely life behind me, oh what a change you have made…

The song talks about taking a boat, and enjoying the ride on the quiet ocean, with someone you love. It reminds me of the struggle I had to *go with the flow,* before I let go of the paddle and allowed my boat to simply float along with the current of *Life,* and see where it takes me. When I gave up trying to steer my boat, back paddle, or find the shoreline when things got wavy, I found the balance within the craft that kept me gliding on the water. There were times I felt like sinking my boat, but it remained upright, and kept the course laid out by the ongoing river, ignoring my panicked rocking within the gunnels.

Feeling Owen's light next to mine, I am filled with gratitude for his love and presence in my life. I raise my face to his and kiss him. He kisses me back, softly at first, then with the rising passion I know only too well. We meld together, like an old familiar couple, yet still have the passion of a youthful pair, who find it hard to keep their hands off each other. He gently moves his hand to take mine, and as the song finds its way to the conclusion, we make our way up the stairs to find our own conclusion, comfortably, in our lovely old bed.

Lying in his arms, I cannot imagine my life being any fuller, richer, or more complete. I listen to Owen's breathing, and memorize the sound, knowing one day one of us will have to move forward into the Light, and these small memories will become huge gems that will be treasured more than gold.

He slides his arms around me, and pulls me closer. I lay my hands on his chest, feeling it rise and fall with each breath. I feel his skin under my hands, warm, soft and slightly sweaty from our passionate efforts. I run my fingers across, feeling each muscle and curvature of his body, once again framing it in my mind, knowing it will be a treasure for me, later. Owen begins to play with a strand of my hair. He blinks, staring straight up at the ceiling, and quietly asks, "Hannah, do you have any regrets about the way your life has gone?" It's such a strange question; I tilt my head to try to see his face. "Owen, well, talk about out-of-the-blue type of question! Let me just say this; all humans have regrets, but I seem to be very fortunate, because mine are very few and far between. I don't regret the way my life has moved along. Actually, when I look back, I can see *why* my life followed the course it did, for the most part. Every experience I had, be it good or bad, has led me to this very moment in Time. And *this* very moment in Time is so precious to me. I wouldn't change one thing about my journey. I love you so much, and I love our family. I only hope you know how much *you* have made my life what it is." I feel the tears spring to my eyes. Owen pulls my chin up and kisses me, a soft tender kiss that conveys more than words ever could.

He shifts slightly so we can face each other. "I have to be honest with you. There is one thing I regret. It's something I've been thinking about a lot lately, I don't know why. Maybe it's been bugging me so much, because it's something I can actually *do*, before I really miss the chance to do it." I blink, unsure of what he's about to say, as a million things cross my mind at once. I wait for the millisecond to pass as he continues. "Well, I've been so reluctant to explore, well, you know, other realms. I guess that after my experience of you and Arthur taking me back to view my parents' car accident, I just felt like I never wanted to venture into that *stuff*, ever again. And when Fae said she had been *inside me*, before guiding herself to Claire, I felt, once again, like that was something that made me really uncomfortable. And, what if I went to her realm, and some other elf or creature tried to attach itself to me, again? I was just so full of, well, fear, I guess. I hear you and Claire, and Arthur, talk about Fae and her realm, and I almost wanted to go with you. I felt like I was missing out, but my pride, or insecurity, made me stand back. I think now I was foolish to fear it, but I can't change how I was in the past. I can only change how I move ahead." He chuckles, "See? And you thought I wasn't paying attention when you told me all about your mindful therapy workshops!". I try to figure out what to say, but before I can comment, he continues; "So, I was thinking, is there some way I can take a trip to see Fae, in her realm?"

My heart skips a beat. If there was anything I regretted in my life, it was that Owen had never wanted to be included in this aspect of it. I always assumed he didn't want to believe, that his silent judgement was dismissive. But that was *my* interpretation of his attitude. Now he says it was out of his own fear, or insecurity, that he lived in denial. I feel like the last piece of my puzzle has now been found on the floor, under my foot. I can pick it up, and place it carefully where it will complete the scene.

I take his hands and kiss them, trying to find the right words. "My darling man. What a wonderful, complicated person you are. I am forever thinking I may have you solved, then you throw me another fragment of you that makes me appreciate your depth of feeling even more. I would love to take you to Fae. She would love to have you visit her. It is but a heartbeat away, whenever you are ready." He looks down at our hands clasped together and whispers, "how about now?" I smile, squeezing his hands. "Yes. Wonderful. All you need to do is close your eyes, and feel yourself sink down, feel yourself let go of thought, expectation, and anything else you hold on to… just close your eyes and breathe slowly, and find yourself floating down, until you touch the ground…"

We stand at the leafy doorway to the Fae realm. It gently swings open to reveal the mossy path I know so well. I take Owen's hand and lead him onward. His face is full of joy; stunned into silence, he can only look around in amazement. I slowly lead him along the pathway, feeling the rays of the sun touch our skin, and stopping every so often so he can view the flowers and the tiny inhabitants that reside within each blossom. He leans over to look more closely, and then laughs as one tiny sprite floats up and, giggling, kicks him in the nose for being so nosy. He stands upright, rubbing his nose, as the sunbeams coalesce, slowly combining into the form of the Mistress of the Woods. Her beautiful statuesque figure is draped in silver-gold shimmering waves of mist, her long green-yellow hair filled with flower petals, and with each movement of her head, a tiny petal floats outward, transforming into a sprite or nymph. Her long arms reach up to the sky, and a cascade of gold leaves drop down, blanketing the mossy earth in luminous colour.

She turns her eyes to look upon Owen, who stands in awe of this magnificent being. "You have finally found the trust in your Light to follow your soul, and leave behind your doubt. You must never doubt your Light. You have it as much as any being around you. You have the energy, even though it has not manifested itself as an Alternate like Arthur, or Hannah. We are all from One, and form our Light as it is meant to be formed. Some are blades of grass, some are flowers; it does not make one less worthy than the other; All are unique and valid. You are *Here*, and we welcome you, as you open yourself to all the potential within the Universe. Never fear your Light; trust in it, and it will always illuminate your way."

She bows her head slightly, and a small glowing orb drops from her brow, floating in front of Owen to rest upon the ground. He reaches down and extends a single finger to touch it. His fear and insecurity vanish as the orb glimmers and expands, extending love and compassion towards him. The Mistress smiles, and quietly whispers, "This is an external piece of *my* Light, full of kindness, empathy and love. When we share our Light, it touches others, bringing them joy and peace. It makes our own Light glow and grow, as you can see. It never diminishes within us, unless we do not share it, and then it ebbs and fades, making room for distrust and fear to reside. Owen, you have the Light, and it is well lit within you. Allow yourself to open up and embrace what you learn while you are *Here*, as it will only serve to make your human experience much more fruitful." Her arms rise again, and this time a veil of green waves slowly descend, like a curtain lowering at the end of a play. It is sheer, and I can see the Mistress begin to fade as it descends, until she is but a glimmer of silver-gold in a sea of green waves.

Owen turns to me, tears in his eyes. I reach out and hug him. He still seems at a loss for words. "Owen, my love, find your voice. Ask questions, sing, laugh, whatever feels right. Your voice will not shatter the glade, or disturb the peace." Owen smiles, wiping his eyes. "Yes, well, I suppose I was worried that

I might scare someone away if I spoke." And he glances around, seeing small wood nymphs sitting in the trees, watching with eager inquisitiveness. I smile and wave at the small creatures in the branches. "The Fae are a curious folk, and those that are easily startled quickly become accustomed to new energy entering their realm. I'm actually surprised we haven't had more of them around, bugging us!" I giggle as I take his hand again.

Turning slightly to our left, I find the glade where Fae and Orna like to play. The Birch trees line the outer perimeter of the glade, making a white fence line. The grasses and flowers wave and dance as a tiny breeze catches them. Butterflies, bees and dragonflies flit about, touching each flower and blessing it with love as they proceed. Owen looks around, noting Daisies, Foxgloves, Cowslips, Bluebells, and a host of Coleus, all in blossom, creating a rainbow of colour throughout the clearing. A large Elder tree stands in one corner, flanked by Birches on either side; a silent sentry. In another corner, near the opening to the pond, stand Fae and Orna. They are waving to us. Owen stops short when he sees Fae's appearance. I imagine he expected her to look like Claire, or some human aspect of her. It takes him a moment to gather his thoughts before he takes a step forward.

Orna leaps into the air, a pair of dragonfly wings unfolding from her back as she takes flight, soaring overhead, emitting a high laugh, reminding me of Claire's laugh when she was a little girl. Owen glances up to watch the amazing sprite gently glide over and land on the far side, and then take off once again to return to Fae. I tug Owen's hand to nudge him forward. He glances at me, and I smile reassuringly.

Fae takes a few steps towards us as we approach. She is emanating a wave of compassion, directed mainly at Owen, and his reflexes visibly relax, making him take a breath and unclench my hand. She smiles and opens her arms to embrace the human that has, for so long, avoided contact with her. Owen opens his arms and welcomes the hug, tentatively at first, and then, as if a latch has released his arms, he takes Fae closer into his embrace. Once again, I see the tears stream down his face. He pulls away slightly to look upon her face, as she beams up at him, full of love and kind-heartedness. "It's like I'm hugging my long-lost daughter," he manages to say before he chokes up again. He lifts his hand and gently touches her face; a tender gesture, full of meaning, full of affection, as I have seen him touch Claire's face many times in a similar way.

Fae quietly utters; "I know you. I have seen your Light, fractured and small. Now it is full and beaming for All to see and feel. It makes me so happy to see you *Here*, and to feel your love boost my own energy." She leans in to hug him once more before releasing him. She keeps hold of his hand as she takes him over to meet Orna. Owen's eyes widen as he sees the beautiful creature standing there, her wings folded in behind her, like stain glass window panels. Her body is covered in narrow strips of glossy-looking reeds, woven together with coloured crystals embedded in the bodice, running down in sloped edges along her thighs. Her feet are bare, and slender, reminding me of Alice's feet. Owen smiles, feeling at ease. "My grandson's middle name is Oran, which, I suppose is no coincidence?" Fae giggles and replies, "Well, Claire and I had some idea about our children being joined in the Light, as she and I are. Noah, however, has other ideas right now, and is not ready to open himself up to commune with the Fae. He reminds me of his grandfather!" and she winks. Owen's eyebrows shoot up at the remark, but he says nothing. Fae continues to hold his hand, and I know she is circulating her calm, peaceful energy to help acclimatize him to everything. I suggest we all sit under the Willow tree on the other side of the glade.

Orna gracefully unfolds her wings to fly over to the giant Willow, and lands with as little effort as a feather landing on the ground. She closes her eyes, and her wings begin to diminish, until they have disappeared from sight. She sits down under the tree and folds her legs under her. Fae pulls Owen by the hand, pointing to this flower or that tree, introducing them to him as they walk over to Orna. She sounds like someone introducing one friend to her other friends. Owen begins to ask questions, and I feel myself breathe easier as he relaxes into his experience.

After some time, Orna decides she wants to play with the wood nymphs, so she says goodbye. As she stands, her wings reveal themselves once more, and she takes flight. Fae shakes her head, and turns to Owen, uttering, "Some Fae are very restless, finding it hard to sit, and be in the *Now*. It seems like they are often looking at the *what's to come,* and not being aware that *Now* is what matters most. They are curious and fickle, so this is the way of it. I have grown accustomed to her behaviour." She shrugs. I feel myself tire slightly, and Fae notices my dip in energy. "Hannah, I think we have had enough of a visit today. As much as I want you both to stay, I feel your physical body requires attention." Owen and I stand up, stretching our legs, and for some reason, my back is sore - a message from my physical self that I need to move in the *real* world.

Owen steps towards Fae and hugs her again. He kisses her forehead, and they exchange a few quiet words, which I am not privy to. My heart is full to bursting to see the union of these two, whom I love so dearly. Owen steps back, and I see a beautiful radiant smile on his face. His new sense of peace, and the release of fear, makes his Light shine so brightly, I can hardly look. I reach out and take his hand, and we turn to leave the glade.

Just as we reach the edge, we both turn and look back, to see Fae dancing with a sunbeam that has entwined itself around her. Owen whispers, "She is beautiful, and she's just like Claire. I wonder why I was ever afraid of her?" He turns to look upon my face, and asks, "Is this where you will want to come, when you die? Is this where I can come, when I go too? Do we even have a choice?" His voice sounds like a child, asking about the existence of Heaven.

I take a breath, glancing around the beautiful forest, taking in the array of colours, and sounds. I could be very happy to exist *Here*. "Owen, each of us has a journey, be we human, Alternate, Fae, or whatever else there is in the All. It's not for me say that you will come *Here*, or that I will, although it's a pleasant place to hang out, that's for sure." He smiles as I continue, "I know that whenever the time comes, you move on to what your Light feels is right. Many energies become ethereal guides, helping humans along their journey; others simply become Light, and live in the benevolent All, as where I came from. You may wish to have another human experience, and so you can do as I did, and transcend to the human realm and live out another human journey. I would like to reassure you and say we will always be together in the Light, and that our energies are intertwined for all Time, but it's not for me to say what will be. But, after today, I hope your uncertainty about Death, and what lies beyond, has lessened somewhat." He nods, but remains silent, as I continue; "There is one thing I have learned as a human; the human connection is as powerful an energy as anything in the Universe. It defies logic, but then, logic plays no role in it. It is love. Pure love. We mourn our dead because of the love lost. That immense power of *human* connection cannot be revisited in the *exact* same way, once the Light leaves the body. We can commune in the Light, as we are *Here*, with Fae. But the missing element is the substantive nature of the human body and mind, and its many-faceted functions that elicit emotions and physical responses. The *human* element just cannot be duplicated in other realms in the same way." Owen frowns and I realize I am losing him.

I pause, and then try to explain my point more clearly. "Being in the Alternate is like talking to someone on the computer. You see their Light, and you can sense their energy, but it lacks the *tactile* nature of the human touch or connection. In the Light we are but beams upon beams. We don't have body language or nuances of language and facial expression. Even when we walk the web of the Universe, we are Lights that touch the line, and then splinter, like rays hitting a prism. There is no true physicality to it, at least not like a human touching another human. I know what a flower is, but to sit in the woods and smell one, or touch it with my hand, is a completely unique human experience. To give birth, to bury someone, to paint, to dance, to hold hands, are all *unique* human experiences." I stop and take a deep breath, wondering if I have said too much. Owen looks contemplative. I raise his hand and kiss it. "I hope I haven't confused you." He smiles, and says, "I don't know how I feel about what happens after I die. All I know is that I want to make the most of the time I have left, with you, and our family. I don't think I'm worried about what comes after, although I'd like to think we will be together. That thought makes me less scared." I smile, and step closer to kiss him. "I like the thought of that too, so we shall do our best to make the most of our beautiful love, Now and Beyond Time."

I wake up in bed, Owen asleep by my side. Tears are streaming down my face. I look at his resting expression, and feel such a deep connection to him, to his energy, that I know, regardless of what I said to him just now, I will seek out his Light, after I leave this human realm, and I know he will do the same, across all realms in the Universe, until we are together.

My eyes stray upwards, and I see Hawk sitting in the invisible sky above me. He blinks, staring into my eyes, until we are one. I take flight, feeling the cool air beneath my wings, as I turn slightly and feel my muscles and strategically placed feathers respond to the change in direction; the Creative Spirit pumping through my veins, more powerful than blood. I see the world as shining and full of potential.

I cast my sharp eyes down to see my beautiful daughter Claire, and her family, enjoying a meal together, sharing quips and love equally, around the table; my friends, including Tila, who is leading a Light-energized Tai Chi class; my house, with rooms full of family history and love etched into every nook and cranny; my garden, a splendid refuge, where we all rest in the bosom of Mother Nature, until we feel refreshed. I see my body, lying beside the man I love with my entire being, and will love for as long as my Light shines. Seeing *All* that is before me, feeling *All* that is within my Light, the love and gratitude for a life full of tribulations and triumphs, I gather my energy to soar, higher and higher, feeling complete in my Human Experience.

ACKNOWLEDGEMENTS

My sincere appreciation to my dear friends, whose encouragement kept my fire lit throughout this amazing adventure.

A special thank you to Vicki Rostant for her critical eye and unwavering belief in me.

I would also like to express my gratitude to Creative Spirit and all my Guides, who continue to inspire me and send so much beautiful Light my way every day.

Manufactured by Amazon.ca
Bolton, ON